ForkBraid

II

The Cost of War

By Michael Robert von Blucher-Altona

25-December-2023

Library of Congress Control Number: 2023920897

ISBN: Hardback   978-0-6459906-5-2
               Paperback   978-0-6459906-4-5
               Kindle   978-0-6459906-3-8

First published 2023

Books by Michael Robert von Blucher-Altona

ForkBraid
Book 1: ForkBraid   – The Price of Peace
Book 2: ForkBraid II – The Cost of War
Book 3: ForkBraid III – Just Rewards

Table of Contents

The History of Humanity is written in the Book of Blood.

Our Anger, our Violence.

The things that we did.

That was the way of the Past and

is NOT the way of the Future.

For in War there is only Death and Destruction.

A Savage desire for Revenge on All Sides.

Revenge and Retaliation does not lower the Cost.

The Cost of War goes up with each Strike.

Cheapest at the Beginning.

Expensive at the End.

Only then comes the Peace.

And always, it is too Late!

Lord Folcrom Tafazah. Autumnal Equinox 2026.

1. It's Raining Men

There was a brisk westerly wind blowing across the Hebes Sea that evening as Zuawalo Pod and her family tended their orchid. Tending to the trees as they always did in the early Martian spring. Thinning out of the branches to let more light in, cutting back any dead wood and generally giving the trees a really good pruning, so that the new growth could sprout with the coming warming weather.

It was good honest work and Zuawalo took pride in it. It was well and truly dark when Zuawalo and her family started the short journey back to the complex of tunnels, burrows and small carved out caverns that was their home. Their local village was literally burrowed into the rock face of the local cliffs. Other families having worked on their own orchids and crop fields joined them on the short walk back. The night air was cool and brisk as was usually the case for this time of year.

As they approached the entrance to their home, Zuawalo said to her Mother, "I'll be back in the early morning" and off she headed down the trail towards the Hebes Sea.

"Where are you going Zuawalo?", her Mother asked.

"I'm going squidding of course", Zuawalo called back, adding "You know the best ones are always caught at night. Especially on a night like this one."

"Mind you keep well south of that Island", Zuawalo's Mother shouted back, making sure that Zuawalo heard her.

"I will. I will Mother", Zuawalo replied as she waved to her Mother and continued down the trail to the small sea side dock where the villages boats were moored.

A low stone breakwater protected the boats from the Hebes Sea. It connected to the cliffs on the west and was open to the sea on the east. A small narrow trail led up and away from the dock towards the village. All fifteen of the villager's boats we moored in this small protected dock. Several other smaller craft, canoes and kayaks were pulled up out of the water and lined up along the base of the trail. They were upside down so as not to collect water in them.

The trail opened up onto a smallish beach, Zuawalo crossed this, passing by the canoes and kayaks, then waded into the cold shallow water to her small wooden boat. Shivering from her late evening dip, Zuawalo climbed aboard her little boat.

It was only a small sail boat, a little over sixteen feet in length. Zuawalo opened the forehead locker and checked that her telescopic squid poles, tackle and fluorescent jigs were all where they were supposed to be. Smiling at the prospect of catching some fresh squid, Zuawalo adjusted the boat's rigging and untied her boat from its moorings. Slowly Zuawalo manoeuvred her boat through the gap in the breakwater and out into the Hebes Sea.

Once out in the open water, Zuawalo turned her boat to the north. The best squidding was always to the north and as much as Zuawalo's Mother would not like it, close to Hebes Island. The squid and for that matter cuttlefish and octopuses liked the sea grass that grew on the shallow banks to the south of that island, to hunt for their prey. Zuawalo knew this and it was a very good place for squidding. Less than two hours later and Zuawalo had arrived at the shallow banks and quickly begun preparing her squid poles and lures.

Zuawalo fished for squid the whole night and her fluorescent squid lures had done their job extremely well. The boat's fish well had been filled with delicious squid. There were more than enough squid to make the trip worth while. Zuawalo's Mother would be very pleased indeed.

The sun was rising towards the east and Zuawalo was about to finish up fishing for the night and start sailing south, back to her village. Then the commotion began. A series of loud noises and other odd sounds could be heard travelling across the still night air from much farther to the north.

Zuawalo looked intently to the north and thought to herself, "*What are those wicked people doing up there now?*" For that is how Zuawalo's people thought of the people of Hebes Island, wicked and untrustworthy. New Tortuga had a very bad reputation. It was known to be a place of smugglers, pirates and other people of ill repute. Very dangerous folk indeed.

The strange sounds and noises grew louder and louder, then loud explosions could be heard to the north. Zuawalo was still too far away from Hebes Island to see what was going on. Try as she might, Zuawalo could not see what was causing all the commotion.

Zuawalo stared northward trying to see what was going on, listening very intently for some time. Then Zuawalo noticed something approaching her small boat. Something that she simply could not ignore. The sea was rising up and with it the waves. Immense waves were quickly approaching her from the north. Very soon they would be upon her.

Quickly, Zuawalo slammed down the lid on the fish well, clipped it shut and began to pack up her squid poles and lures. Then Zuawalo turned her boat to the north, so that it was facing into the approaching waves.

The first wave was immense, at least forty feet in height, perhaps even higher. The immense wave approached and Zuawalo's boat began to ride up the front of the wave. Holding on for dear life, Zuawalo's boat was almost perpendicular to the sea as its prow pushed over the wave's crest, then slowly rode down the back of the wave. Zuawalo let loose a loud sigh of relief.

Zuawalo had no time to think, nor react, she looked north again and quickly sighted an even larger wave approaching. It would be upon her in mere seconds. Her boat was in the trough between the two waves. This one was at least sixty feet in height and Zuawalo said a quick prayer as her boat began to ride up the front of the wave. Before reaching the crest, the wave began to break over Zuawalo's boat. Zuawalo again held on tightly for dear life.

The cold water of the Hebes Sea began to spill into the boat. Then the boats prow pierced the wave's crest and the mast snapped into two, with an almighty cracking sound. The sail collapsed over Zuawalo and the broken mast pinned her tightly against the deck of her boat.

As the boat slowly rode down the back of the second wave, Zuawalo fought to free herself from the broken mast and sail. Again with no time to think, nor react, a third immense wave was approaching. It was at least as high as the first wave. Zuawalo watched terrified as the wave quickly approached. There was very little she could do.

Zuawalo had not yet freed herself from the broken mast when the third wave struck. Up Zuawalo's boat rode on the front of this new wave. Holding on for dear life once again, Zuawalo's little boat reaching almost perpendicular once more before breaching the wave's crest and riding down the wave's back. The broken mast still pinned Zuawalo to the deck of the boat and was the only thing preventing her from being tossed into the sea. Zuawalo struggled hard to free herself from the broken mast.

Finally crawling out from under the mast, Zuawalo looked to the north once more. No more immense waves could be seen approaching, however the swell was now beginning the rise and a squall was quickly forming. A storm like no other, as if driven by the fury of an angry god had formed and the sea quickly turned rough and choppy. Dark skies formed above her boat and to north there was thunder and lightning. Quickly the weather turned sour and Zuawalo prayed for her life.

Conditions continued to worsen and Zuawalo's little boat was beginning to be tossed about like a cork in river rapids. There were several moments when Zuawalo thought her little boat would capsize. Zuawalo was quick however, shifting her weight from one side of the boat to the other, to prevent the boat from tipping over. Zuawalo had been squidding at these shallow banks many, many times in the past and had never heard of, nor experienced anything quite like this. The waves were huge in height, although not nearly as high as the three waves that had passed by her earlier. It was as if the Gods themselves had made them so.

Then there was a sudden, brilliant flash of light, or was it lightening far to the north. Zuawalo could not really tell. In the midst of this flash Zuawalo could see an object flying through the air, flailing about in the wind. It was only during a second flash of light, that Zuawalo was able to make out that this was person flying through the air and heading in her general direction.

"What in the Great Mother's name?", was the thought that came to her mind.

Things went from bad to worse as Zuawalo's boat was buffeted by cross waves and cross winds. The snapped mast was now threatening to capsize her boat, hanging precariously in the water and threatening to take her sail with it. In the midst of all this, the flying person came crashing down into the Hebes Sea right beside her boat. Zuawalo quickly reached out as far as she could to grab the stranger, lest they drown. Alas, Zuawalo could not reach and the stranger began to sink into the cold waters of the Hebes Sea and would certainly drown if she could not reach them.

Thinking fast Zuawalo swung about reaching around for her gaff. Luckily it was still there and having found it, Zuawalo swung about once more, reaching out for the stranger who was now barely visible beneath the waters of the Hebes Sea. The gaff caught the stranger, digging deep into their arm and Zuawalo dragged them towards the boat with great effort.

Very carefully Zuawalo removed the gaff from the stranger's arm and then with great difficulty hauled the person aboard the boat. "I'm so sorry" she said to the stranger, who Zuawalo could now see was a man, "it was the only way I could reach you", she said apologetically. He could not hear her, he was unconscious and un-hearing. This strange pale man with short dark hair and grey flecked beard. He was unlike anyone who lived in Zuawalo's village.

Zuawalo held the strange man against her, using her legs to brace herself against the angry waves. His pale white skin seemed almost translucent against her own deep ebony brown skin. "*What wickedness did you do, that the Gods tossed you into the Sky?*", she thought to herself, whilst looking for some rope to lash the stranger to the boat. Once Zuawalo had the stranger tied safely to the boat, she began to fight hard against the atrocious conditions, all the while the buffeting waves were threatening to sink her boat.

Zuawalo fought against the squall for what seemed like hours and was totally exhausted. Zuawalo could barely keep here eyes open as she slowly manoeuvred her boat southwards and back to the safe harbour of her village. The weather had now calmed to some degree. It was as if the angry Gods had vented their anger and ever so slowly let that anger dissipate and once spent, the weather had became calm once more.

It was long after sunrise now, the Sun having risen several hours ago and Zuawalo's Mother would be extremely worried. The strange pale white man was still unconscious, laying tied to the boat's seating. Zuawalo asked aloud, "Who are you? What did you do to so anger the Gods?". There was no answer, his brown eyes were unresponsive and he was un-hearing, only the slight rise and fall of his chest showed that he was actually still alive.

Zuawalo had jury rigged her broken mast and sail into a make shift sail that worked to some small degree, propelling her boat ever so slowly to the south. Zuawalo herself was using a piece of flat broken seat board as a paddle to urge her boat closer to home.

Zuawalo was overly exhausted, glancing alternately towards the village dock in the distance and back to the strange white man laying unconscious in her boat. It would be several hours before Zuawalo made it home. Her Mother would be very worried indeed.

Indeed Zuawalo's Mother had been worried. Their whole village had also felt the immense waves and angry storm early that morning and several of the unattended boats in the small harbour had been smashed into pieces.

Zuawalo's Mother, her Father and many of the Villagers were at the village dock, staring out into the sea. In the distance a small sail could be seen. Something was wrong though. Keen eyes showed that the approaching boat had been damaged and was using a make shift sail.

Zuawalo's Mother motioned to here Husband, "What are you waiting for Kwoth? Quickly! Get our Daughter!" Quickly Zuawalo's Father gathered a friend and they located a boat that looked to be only slightly damaged. It had been washed up the trail a short ways and still appeared to be seaworthy. They pulled the boat into into the water and began to sail it out into the Hebes Sea.

Zuawalo saw her Father and his friend sailing out to meet her and managed to smile. It would not be long before she was safe at home and her ordeal would be over.

Zuawalo glanced back at the strange white man in the back of her boat, "*Who was he? What did he do? Why was he flying through the air?*" were the thoughts that came to her mind.

Turning once more to look at the approaching boat and now secure in the knowledge that she would safe, an exhausted Zuawalo succumbed to her exhaustion. When her Father and his friend reached her, Zuawalo was very cold and unconscious, suffering from both exhaustion and exposure.

It was just after midday when Zuawalo awoke, the Sun was shining through the Window carved into the rock of her cave-like room.

Zuawalo's Mother quietly asked her younger Daughter, "Zeealas, bring some hot food, something lite", then to Zuawalo, "How are you feeling my little one?"

"I'm feeling fine Mother", then thinking of her boat and squid, Zuawalo sat up, "My boat, is it okay? Did you tend to my Squid? I caught a great many of them."

"Your Father assures me that your boat can be repaired. I have already tended to your catch of Squid", then adding, "I am more concerned about your other catch."

"My other catch?", Zuawalo murmured, then remembering the pale, white man enquired, "Yes. Yes. The pale, white man, did he survive?"

"The last I heard, he was still unconscious at the Doctor's clinic. Where did he come from Zuawalo?"

"During the Storm", Zuawalo replied, "He came flying right out of the sky."

"Flying out of the sky?", Zuawalo's Mother queried.

"Yes, out of the sky and into the water, close to my boat", Zuawalo replied adding, "I had to drag him from the water using my gaff! He was too deep for me to reach."

"That would explain the injuries to his arm", Zuawalo's Mother replied, "The Doctor saw to that wound straight away. Such a strange storm it was indeed for it to be raining men!"

"How long have I been asleep?", Zuawalo asked.

"A good day at least Zuawalo. You were very unwell when your Father brought you ashore", Zuawalo's Mother replied as Zeealas entered the room.

"I hope hot porridge and fruit is okay", Zeealas brought the food over to Zuawalo and placed a stand and the tray of food onto her bed.

"That is fine Zeealas", Zuawalo replied, "I am so hungry."

2. Dirty Little Secrets

Interplanetary Out-Liner – *An inter-planetary ship designed with the singular purpose of transporting passengers, produce and materials from the inner solar system to the outer satellites (moons and colonies there of) of Jupiter, Saturn, Uranus, Neptune and beyond. Designed to be used once for the journey and then scrapped for use as colony construction materials.*

From the Earth's Central Intelligence Agency encyclopedia of facts and knowledge, edition 6375.

Abram Appelbaum and his wife Miriam watched the view screen intently as they approached the massive cylindrical colony ahead of them. It had been a long and tiring journey aboard the colonial out-liner on its flight from L5 in Earth's orbit to the Jovian system. Originally from Earth, they had stayed at L5 for over a year while the out-liner had been prepared for the trip. Now before them were the colonies of Jupiter and its Galilean moons, along with the new life they were seeking. Many lights could be seen in the trailing Trojan points of Io, Europa, Ganymede and Callisto, with far fewer lights visible in the leading Trojan points of the moons in their orbits.

Abram pointed out the lights to his Wife, "You see those lights, trailing the moons in their orbits, those are the main colonies of Jupiter."

Miriam replied, "Yes I can see them. There seems to be a awful lot of them."

"Yes, the brightest ones are the largest, as large if not larger as Colonial Central or so I've heard", Abram informed his wife, adding "those are the primary colonial cylinders, Io Prime, Europa Prime, Ganymede Prime and Callisto Prime".

"And Ganymede Prime is the Capital", Miriam replied.

"And our destination", replied Abram, adding "Although that might not be the colony on which we will live. There are a great many colonies in the Jovian system."

"Abram. Why are there so few colonies in the Trojan points ahead of the moons", Miriam had noticed most of the colonies were trailing the Galilean moons, not leading them.

"Jupiter's radiation is very intense", Abram replied adding, "The moons, as they travel in their orbits around Jupiter sweep out radiation particles from their orbits. So the trailing Trojan points have somewhat less radiation to contend with".

"Ah, less radiation, means less radiation shielding", Miriam considered, "and that means less costs for the building and maintenance of the colonies."

"Yes. A simple a matter of economics really", Abram replied.

A couple of hours later and far closer to Ganymede, before them was their destination, the immense colony cylinder that was Ganymede Prime.

Ganymede Prime was enormous, equally as long as L5's Colonial Central, probably longer, it was by far the largest colony in orbit around Jupiter. Abram could see the sheer thickness of the colony's radiation shielding, it was at least ten time thicker than Colonial Central's and his wife had noticed as well.

"Look there", his wife noted, "Look how thick that Moncrete is."

"Moncrete!", Abram turned to his wife and chuckled, "No, no my darling. They're using Astcrete way out here.", he corrected.

"Astcrete", Miriam queried.

"Yes, Astcrete, it's made from processed asteroid regolith", Abram explained, "Similar to Moncrete, but not quite the same and they need a lot of it too. Jupiter's radiation belts are really strong."

The couple went back to watching the approaching colony. It would be an hour or more before they were docked and Miriam could not wait to get out of the out-liner. Colonial out-liners were crowded and uncomfortable. They were also unfortunately the only effective transport to the outer satellite colonies and usually only a handful of times per decade, at the very most once every few years. There were no scheduled transports as such to the outer colonies. Prior to the Outer Satellite Insurrection there had been a scheduled services outbound from L5, however after the end of that War and the following Armistice, regular services were never restored.

Use once ships, each was cobbled together specifically to push outward to the outer solar system. They were not designed for comfort. Once they reached their final destination, an out-liner was designed to be stripped apart and used for colony building material. It was extremely rare for colonists to make the reverse journey back to the inner solar system planets. That would have required hiring a private vessel, which was prohibitively expensive.

This particular out-liner was scheduled to drop passengers off at Ganymede Prime, then refuel and fly out further to Saturn and its major colony Titan Prime in the Saturnian Demarchy, before heading out further to the colonies of Uranus and Neptune. Five hundred new colonists for the Jovian system, Two hundred and fifty for the Saturnian system and seventy five each for Uranus and Neptune.

"Look at that Miriam", Abram exclaimed, "It must cost a small fortune keeping Ganymede Prime on station."

"What do you mean?", Miriam queried.

"Look you see there. The attitude control thrusters", Abram pointed out.

And it was true. Every now and again one of Ganymede Prime's attitude control thrusters would fire, far more often than would be needed at L5. Keeping the colony on station, pointed towards the Sun. Maximising the colony's solar energy collection was much more difficult in Ganymede's trailing trojan point.

"Look at those mirrors", Abram noted, "They're concave, so they're designed to focus sun light."

"Just like with any colony at L5", Miriam shrugged.

"Much broader and much more concave than at L5. The Sun is so feeble out this far, they really need to concentrate the light", Abram explained, adding "but it's more than that. Ganymede Prime is in orbit around Jupiter, in Ganymede's trailing Trojan point. To keep that colony pointed at the Sun can't be a simple process."

"Oh, now I see what you mean", Miriam replied.

"What's that in the middle of the colony's tail boom?", asked Miriam, "It's not a heat radiator?"

"No it's not, although I can see the heat radiator further down at the end",

Abram replied adding, "I believe that's their fusion reactor."

"So even with Sun light, they still need to augment their power with fusion?", Miriam asked.

"I'd say so, the Sun is not nearly strong enough at this distance", Abram answered.

While they continued to watch the approaching colony, a small vid window popped up on the screen. Abram looked up at the vid window. It was an immigration form to be filled in for Ganymede Prime prior to arrival.

Abram sighed, "*Paper work, even out here*", he thought to himself.

Abram filled out the on screen immigration form for himself and his wife, but stopped at the final two questions.

The immigration form asked two final questions for each of them.

What is your religion?

If you are not Christian, would you be willing to convert to Christianity?

Abram looked at his wife, "I don't like the look of this", he stated.

"It's just a questionnaire Abram... Isn't it?", Miriam replied.

"They have no business asking about our religion", Abram stated boldly, adding "and what's this rubbish about converting to Christianity?"

"The Jovian colonies are largely a Christian community", Miriam replied adding, "We knew that when we decided to come out here."

"Yeah, but this still isn't right. There's something very wrong with this!", Abram replied.

With a wry smile on his face, Abram filled in the last questions for both he and his wife. He put in "Christian" for their religion and answered "n/a" for the conversion question.

"But Abram, we're Jewish", his wife complained.

"Yes, but they don't know that do they", Abram replied, adding "and we won't tell them will we."

It was nearly two hours later when the Interplanetary out-liner docked at Ganymede Prime.

Abram and Miriam made their way from the out-liner and into Ganymede Prime's space port.

It didn't take them long before they reached a series of eight lines that led up to the immigration desks. At the back of each immigration desk were a pair of doors. One by one the passengers had their papers checked and they were directed through either of these two doors.

The immigration officer smiled at Abram and his wife, stamped their passport and immigration papers and then stated, "Go straight through, take the door on the right."

Abram and Miriam dutifully followed the immigration officers instructions. Once through the door they were greeted by a very cheerful woman at another desk. The woman smiled broadly and requested their passports. Quickly scanning their passports and after punching a few keys on her key pad, a small card popped out of the computer.

"This is your temporary accommodation pass", the woman said as she passed the card to Abram.

"Take this card to any of the shuttle pods outside", the woman continued, "Swipe the card into the shuttle pod's card slot and it will take you to your temporary accommodation."

"What happens after that?", Miriam asked.

"Someone from work placement will visit you and discuss your career opportunities", the woman replied adding, "Once they've processed your details and resumes, they'll return with your identity cards and all the information you'll require to start your new lives in the Jovian System."

"All the information?", Abram queried.

"Everything from which job you've been assigned, to which colony you're going to live on and of course how you're going to get there. You never know, you might even score a good job right here on Ganymede Prime. Wouldn't that be wonderful."

"Roughly how long will this process take?", Abram asked.

"Not very long. It only takes about a week", the woman replied, adding "Don't be concerned. Everything you need will be provided for you in your temporary accommodation. Thank you for joining us here in the Jovian System."

"Thank you", Abram and Miriam replied before heading off to find a shuttle pod.

As they found the shuttle pods and decided which one to take, Miriam asked Abram, "I wonder what happens if you take the other door, the one on the left."

"I have no idea Miriam, but I am glad this one turned out okay", Abram replied.

Not so fortunate was the family two places back in the same queue.

The Neru family had put down "Hindu" as their religion and said "No" to the question about converting to Christianity. The immigration officer in their case had directed them to the door on the left. They too, dutifully followed the Immigration officers instructions.

As the Neru family came to the end of the hall they were traversing, they found a rather rough looking Military Officer waiting for them at a desk. On either side of the room were two armed soldiers, four in all, complete with pulse rifles and pain sticks. The Military Officer was not smiling, he had a rather gruff looking disposition.

"Papers please", The Military Officer barked.

Rajsheev Neru, the head of the Neru family handed his families papers to the officer, who look through them thoroughly, "You should have thought to answer certain questions differently", the Military Officer merely stated as a matter of fact.

The Military Officer looked up at Rajsheev, He pointed to the left, "Stand over there", he ordered.

Rajsheev moved to the left as instructed, his family began to follow, "No, no, not you!", The Officer snapped.

The Military Officer looked up at Rajsheev's wife, Rani and her two daughters, "You will stand over there on the right."

Tearfully the women of the Neru family obeyed. There was something very wrong here.

The Military Officer took out a stamp and stamped Rajsheev's papers and passport '*SLAVE*'.

He then took out another stamp and stamped the papers and passport a second time, '*Location: Amalthea*'.

Having done this, the Military Officer ordered, "Take him away!"

One of the soldiers pressed a pain stick against Rajsheev's back, who then buckled at the knees. Rajsheev was then dragged through another door, while his family were restrained by the other two soldiers.

The Military Officer shouted out at them "Silence!".

Next the Military Officer looked at Rajsheev's wife, Rani Neru, he looked her up and down.   After a short while he took out another stamp. First he stamp her papers and passport '*SLAVE*', then he stamped them again, this time with a stamp that said '*Location: Europa Prime*'.

The Military Officer looked up at Rani and her two daughters, "You are now Slaves. You will be taken to Europa Prime. There they will assign work for you. You may even be sold at auction."

"What will happen to my husband?", Rani managed to whimper.

"He is no longer your concern", the Officer replied, adding "You are now a Slave."

"Where will they take him?", Rani queried further.

"To the Amalthean Mines", he replied rather coldly.

"What about my daughters?", Rani asked while she sobbed.

"They will accompany you to Europa Prime, where they will be assigned work, possibly even auctioned", was his cold reply, then barking the orders "Take them away!"

Rani and her two daughters were led away.

Once the room was cleared another family entered. This was the Jovian System's dirty little secret. While ostensibly being a Christian colony, they were a "very old school" Christian colony and in their Fascist interpretation of Christianity, non-Christians who chose not to convert, irrevocably became Slaves.

3. The Very Bad Man

Doctor Borchar was reviewing the latest round of tests, "He is not in a coma at all, he has suffered a profound trauma of some kind. This patient is in a catatonic state."

The small, dark, wizened man, Gwek the Kujur, that Doctor Borchar was talking to nodded his head in understanding, "I will scan him, to see if I can discern the cause of his condition", he replied. His voice was both soft and strangely authoritative.

Gwek moved closer to the patient, a man brought to the medical centre, who had been saved from drowning by Zuawalo Pod. Gwek slowly placed his hands on either side of the man's head, positioning his fingers on the man's temples. He hummed to himself as he did so, a strange, almost weird, rhythmic humming.

After several minutes Gwek removed his hands and stood up away from the patient.

"This man", he paused "He is an evil man. He is a very bad man!", Gwek stated firmly.

"How so?", enquired Doctor Borchar.

"He is a terrorist! A man who hates psychics! He thinks us all devils and demons! He would kill us all if he could", Gwek replied, reaffirming, "He is a very, very bad man!"

It was at that moment that Zuawalo Pod walked into the room. Zuawalo having gone to the medical centre to see how the strange pale, white man was. Zuawalo had heard Gwek's pronouncements as she had approached.

Gwek turned to Zuawalo, "Why did you save this man?"

"I could not let him drown!", Zuawalo replied.

"Hmm", Gwek murmured, "He is a very bad man Zuawalo. Better to have let him drown."

"How could I know that at that time! There was a big storm. The winds and waves were very bad. I had no time to think, is this a good man, is this a bad man! I acted quickly and without thought." Zuawalo snapped back.

Gwek looked at Zuawalo, "*Zuawalo did the right thing*", he thought to himself, replying, "It is okay child, you are not at fault here. This man however, he is a big problem!"

Doctor Borchar spoke at that moment, "His condition Gwek? What did you see about his condition?"

"Fear Borchar. Extreme fear. This man was executed for his crimes!", Gwek informed him.

"Executed?", both Zuawalo and Borchar replied in unison.

"Yes. That wicked place on that island has fallen. A Wizard of Great Power has taken control over there. That Wizard condemned this evil man to death and duly executed him. This is why he is catatonic. He thinks he is dead and yet he is alive and his mind is stricken with fear, extreme fear and stuck between his being alive and thinking here is dead", Gwek then turned to Zuawalo, "Then you save him child, saved him from certain death."

"I would not have, had I known he was a very bad man", Zuawalo replied, "I would have let him drown".

"Don't be silly, it was the right thing to do under the circumstances", Gwek stated.

Gwek was quiet for several long moments, Borchar and Zuawalo waited patiently for further information.

Then after what seemed like an eternity, "His death was not ordained! The Great Wizard overstepped his mark. This bad man's destiny was not to die, it was to live!"

"But what will we do with him?", Borchar enquired.

"You will heal him Borchar, that is your skill", Gwek replied, then turning to Zuawalo, "and you child, you shall redeem him!"

"How will I do that?", Zuawalo enquired, then quickly adding, "Why would I do that?"

"By doing what you do best. By simply being you Zuawalo", Gwek informed her, "and it is necessary. This very bad man must find his redemption."

"And what will we do with him once he is healed?", Borchar asked again.

"Ah. That is for me to do. This very bad man must be demolished, so he can be born again and become the good man, that he should always have been. Redemption will then follow.", Gwek explained.

"Demolished?", both Borchar and Zuawalo question together.

"Yes, demolished. I will rip his psyche back, tear out all the evil influences in his life and render him as if he was a small child, with a clean slate, to begin again", Gwek stated confidently.

"Will he remember?", Zuawalo enquired.

"Oh yes, he will remember everything he has done", Gwek answered, "but without the evil influences that made him who he was, he will make himself into something new. Something far better and he will seek redemption for his past crimes. His past memories will drive him forward to his redemption."

"And I will redeem him?", Zuawalo stated, but more as a question.

"Yes child. You will be with him on his journey of redemption, to remind of his past failings and of his future successes as a man redeemed.", Gwek stated with certainty.

"Have you done this before Gwek?", asked Borchar.

"No I have not", Gwek replied, adding "But I have the skills. My teacher imparted these skills into me when I was young, as an apprentice. I never saw any potential use for them at the time, but now, now I see that such skills are necessary when the moment arises."

Gwek was quiet once more, before explaining, "Demolishing a man is no easy task. It will take time, lots of time. He will need to be fed by drip, I will need to eat sparsely, only a vegetarian diet and I suspect I will get very little sleep over the next week."

"When will you begin?", Doctor Borchar asked.

"Straight way", Gwek replied, "there is no time to waste."

Gwek sat beside the bed and concentrated on the very bad man. He entered into his mind and began pulling at the threads of the tapestry of his life. Deeper and deeper into the man's memories Gwek reached, trying to unravel his psyche and understand why this man had become such a very bad man.

The process was long and it was slow, taking much time and

concentration. The very bad man was being fed by nasal feeding tube and a drip, all his other needs were taken care of by nurses.

Gwek broke off is scans to consume a small, lite lunch, before diving back into the very bad man's memories. This process was destined to take many days.

It was on the morning of the fifth day that Gwek had unravelled the man's psyche to the point where he could see the very beginnings of what started the man on his journey to becoming evil. This man had been orphaned as a child on Earth and taken in by his aunt and uncle at L5. They had told him that his parents had been murdered on Earth by Witches and Wizards. Gwek doubted that, Witches and Wizards were not in the habit of murdering people, in fact just the opposite they actually help people.

Gwek looked deeper into the man's memories, prior to his being orphaned, memories that the man himself was unlikely to remember or even know that he had them. In these memories as a young child, the man had glimpses of his parent's doings and what kind of people they had been. Carefully viewing these early childhood memories, Gwek could see his parents were themselves part of an extremist group. As part of that group, his parents had been gunned down by a Police SWAT team while planning and preparing for a terrorist attack. Suffice to say the planned terrorist attack did not occur. It had been uncovered by psychic remote viewing teams.

Gwek concentrated on these early memories and they began to glow with a pure golden light. Following forward through the man's memories, Gwek looked at all the hundreds, if not thousands of interactions that had reinforced his belief that his parents had been murdered by Witches and Wizards. Carefully he loosened these interactions and they too began to glow with pure golden light. Eventually Gwek came across the man's memories of the Prophet. And this is where the evil had truly taken hold. The Prophet was another evil man, another very bad man.

The Prophet had taken the young man, who was completely susceptible and moulded him into the evil man he eventually became. The Prophet took advantage of the fact that he believed his parents had been murdered by Witches and Wizards, then he used that belief to bend and twist his emotions and psyche towards the Prophet's own extremist ideals and goals. It had worked and he had become that vary bad and evil man.

Slowly and ever so carefully Gwek loosened all of those interactions and then they began to glow with a pure golden light. Having performed the necessary priming work, Gwek then carefully re-scanned and rechecked everything he had done and put in place. It was now midday on the fifth day and everything looked to have been prepared in the correct manner.

So Gwek triggered the demolition! He simply snapped his fingers.

From the very first, early memory that Gwek had located, to the most recent memory in the man's mind, the pure golden glow linked up across them all, like an intricate glowing web. All and every adjusted memory and interaction glowed with this pure golden light. The light of troth.

The very bad man's psyche was ripped to shreds and only the light of troth remained along with his memories. There was a loud, yet silent scream. A scream like no other and it tore and ripped though the man's mind. He was awakening to what he had become!

Leroy McGuvan awoke. His brown eyes wide open and staring wildly. His head darted from side to side. His head ached and yet it did not ache. Sweat pored off his brow profusely. Hot and cold flushes ran continuously through his body. Eyes darting left and right in abject confusion.

Here was now a man awake to the knowledge that his whole life had been a lie. Everything in his life had been a lie. Everything he had ever been told had been a lie. His whole existence from start to finish had been a lie. It was so clear to him now. He could see it all ever so clearly. His parents had NOT been killed by Witches and Wizards, they had been shot by a Police SWAT team whilst wearing explosive laden bomb vests. *"Fuck! Fuck! Fuck!"*, he thought to himself, *"How could I be so wrong!"*

Leroy McGuvan was sick to his stomach. He was nauseated. Leroy dry retched and then vomited all over his bed. He then screamed and screamed and continued to scream. Doctor Borchar came into Leroy's room and quickly injected Leroy with a sedative. Slowly Leroy slumped onto the vomit stained bed and fell into a deep, deep sleep.

"What the fucking hell have you done to him Gwek!", Doctor Borchar exclaimed.

"It is done Borchar!", Gwek replied, "I have demolished him!"

Leroy McGuvan was out like a light until the next morning. The nurses had cleaned up both Leroy and his bedding overnight while he was unconscious. Sitting in a chair, against a wall at the side of the room sat a tall, pretty, dark girl. The tall, dark girl stood up, she was tall, easily six foot or more, Leroy noted her short, tightly curled hair.

"Where am I?", Leroy asked.

Zuawalo shouted out, "He is awake", then to Leroy, "You are in our medical centre."

Leroy moved to the edge of the bed and awkwardly stood up, he was not at all stable on his feet.

Slowly Leroy moved himself in front of a mirror, he stared at himself, slowly touching his face as if he wasn't sure he was real. To his mind, his face felt malleable, like putty or melted wax.

Doctor Borchar and Gwek entered the room. Leroy turned to see a tall, dark man and a small, dark, wizened old man standing beside the tall, dark girl. The tall one wore a Doctors cloak, the other Leroy wasn't sure what he wore. He was different, very different, with strange piercing eyes.

"How do you feel?", Doctor Borchar asked, then moving closer and helping Leroy to sit on the end of the bed.

"I, I don't know", came Leroy's feeble reply, he looked up, "I really don't know!"

Doctor Borchar began to take Leroy's blood pressure and temperature. Zuawalo and Gwek simply stood there observing.

"Was it real?", Leroy asked, followed by, "It felt like a nightmare. Was I. Was I really so evil?"

Gwek replied, "You have woken up and now you know what you really were. I am Gwek and I did this to you. I showed you what you really were!"

Doctor Borchar added, "and I am Doctor Borchar. I need you to sit still while I examine you."

"It was real, very real", Gwek continued, "You were that very bad, very evil man."

"I don't feel evil", Leroy replied, "Clearly, I can see that I was evil. I have the most horrible   memories. Please tell me that I did not do all those horrible things!"

"You did not feel evil when you did them either", Gwek responded, "And yes, you most certainly did all of those horrible things Leroy."

"You know my name?", Leroy questioned.

"Of course I do", Gwek explained, " I was the one who demolished you!"

"Demolished?", Leroy queried feebly.

"Yes, demolished", Gwek replied, explaining "I ripped though your memories and highlighted everything that you had ever been told that was a lie. Then I triggered your demolishing, which in simplest terms, enabled you to see who you really were and who you are now."

"Demolished?", Leroy repeated feebly once more, a quite rhetorical question.

"You are lucky Leroy", Zuawalo stepped in, "You were a very bad man and your slate has been wiped clean. You have a second chance! A chance at redemption!"

"Who are you?", Leroy asked.

"I am Zuawalo Pod. I am the one who saved you from drowning. It would be best, if you do not make me wish that I had not", it was a clear threat from Zuawalo, that Leroy should behave himself.

Leroy looked up at the tall, pretty, dark girl, with skin as dark as midnight. Zuawalo Pod was stunningly beautiful.

"Leroy needs to rest", Doctor Borchar stated, "Everyone out please."

Once Doctor Borchar, Gwek and Zuawalo had left the room, a pair of nurses moved in to help Leroy into the shower. After showering, Leroy shaved, again with the nurses help and the nurses then asked what Leroy wanted to eat and whether he had any food restrictions. Leroy had replied that he was so hungry that anything would be fine.

Leroy stood in front of the mirror once more. It had been many years since Leroy had shaved. His beard was originally grown when he was a teenager and this was the first time since then, that he had looked upon his clean shaven face. He gently ran his hand over his face. It still felt like putty.

"Was I really that evil bastard I remember in my memories?", he thought to himself.

As if to answer him, a small still voice within his own mind replied, *"Yes, you were!"*

4. Europa Prime

A week had passed and Abram and Miriam had been assigned to permanent accommodation and work on another colony within the Jovian system. Their new residence was to be at Europa Prime in orbit about Jupiter at Europa's trailing Trojan point.

The pair followed the instructions provided on how to transfer from Ganymede Prime to Europa Prime. It was a simple matter of booking passage on a Jovian Colonial Shuttle service between the two colony cylinders and to their surprise, they found they could be at their new apartment on Europa Prime in only a couple of days.

This was great as they had two weeks before Abram was required to start work at his new job. That gave them plenty of time to unpack their belongings and to get use to their new surroundings, when they arrived at their new apartment.

A few days later Abram and Miriam were settling into their nice new apartment in Europa Prime. They had found their new apartment to be more than adequate for their needs. It was actually far better than they thought it would be. A pleasant surprise for both of them.

Abram had been assigned as a flight controller for Europa's Internal Colony Shuttle Service, which were used for servicing the colonies of Europa's trailing Trojan point. Training was to be provided prior to commencement.

Miriam had elected to be a house wife, as it appeared that married woman only worked in the Jovian Colonies if they actually wanted to. It was quite uncommon in the Jovian Colonies for married women to work. Stay at home wives were considered traditional in Jovian society.

Miriam had spent the morning getting to know the local area, while Abram had continued with their unpacking.

"Do you remember that nice Indian couple we met on the out-liner?", Miriam asked.

"Yes, yes I do", Abram replied, adding "I was just wondering what happened to them."

"Well, I was at the market today and I did find something rather disturbing", Miriam told him.

"Disturbing?", Abram asked, "What could be disturbing about this place?"

"They have Slaves here in the Jovian colonies Abram!", Miriam informed him.

"No Miriam", Abram replied, "You must be mistaken. This place is almost a paradise."

"Seriously Abram, I know what I saw", Miriam stated slowly, "They have Slaves here!"

"What has that got to do with Rajsheev and Rani?", Abram enquired.

"It appears that the Slaves are all non-christian and the Neru family are Hindu", Miriam informed him..

Abram replied to Miriam, "Really! Wow! Lucky I put down Christian on that questionnaire."

"Yes Abram, I know. Rajsheev and Rani may not have been so lucky."

"Oh my, you could be right", Abram replied, adding "They had two daughters didn't they?"

"Yes, they did", Miriam answered, "I hope they're alright."

Abram had a concerned look on his face, "I think tomorrow, I'll make some discrete enquiries."

"I'll be coming with you", Miriam replied.

The next morning Abram and Miriam were ready to make their enquiries about the whereabouts of the Neru family. They both left their apartment and took the elevator to the ground floor.

Once at the ground floor, Abram located the apartment building's computerised concierge.

"Assistance please", Abram requested.

The apartments computerised concierge assistant replied, "How may I help you?"

"I have lost track of some dear friends", Abram told the Assistant, "The Neru family", Abram continued adding, "Rajsheev, Rani and their two daughters, Lakshmi and Pavarti", then questioning, "We would like to know what happened to them?"

The apartments computerised concierge replied, "Accessing Central Database, please wait."

It was minute or two before the computerised concierge came back an answer.

"The Neru family, Rajsheev, Rani, Lakshmi and Pavarti. All four arrived on the most recent Interplanetary out-liner. They disembarked at Ganymede Prime."

Abram looked to Miriam, then back to the computerised concierge, "Yes, but what became of the Neru family after their immigration processing?"

The computerised concierge replied, "The Neru families immigration declaration form declares them to be Hindu and Non-Converting. Rajsheev Neru has been transferred to Amalthea. Rajsheev Neru is listed as being a Slave Labourer in the Amalthean Mines. Rani Neru and daughters Lakshmi and Pavarti have been transferred to Europa Prime. They are all listed as being Slaves and are awaiting processing for assignment and / or auction."

Abram looked at Miriam, they were shocked. Now they new what that immigration door on the left was for.

"Where is the processing centre for new Slaves on Europa Prime?" Abram demanded.

The computerised concierge displayed an address in the North Hemispherical End Cap, "Please take note of the address, as displayed on the screen", it stated.

Miriam scanned the address into her communicator and with Abram close behind her, left for the nearest shuttle pod bays.

"You might have said thank you", the computerised concierge chided as the pair walked away without a further word.

Abram and Miriam ignored the computerised concierge's remark.

Abram and Miriam jumped into the nearest available shuttle pod and once seated Miriam requested, "Take us to the following address", then transferred the address to the shuttle pods systems using her communicator.

The shuttle pod whisked them away and swiftly started traversing the Northern End Cap. It was about ten or so minutes later that they arrived at their destination, The Europan Department of Slave Management.

Abram and his wife Miriam leapt out of the pod and rushed towards the building. Quickly they located the main entrance and made a bee line straight to it. Quickly they walked over to the information desk and its Attendant.

Abram was slightly out of breath when he approached the information attendant.

"What can I do for you?", the Attendant asked.

"I think there has been a terrible mistake", Abram advised the Attendant.

"A mistake?", the Attendant queried, "What kind of mistake?", he requested.

Miriam started answering, while Abram caught is breath, "Some friends of ours, who were travelling on the same Interplanetary out-liner as us, were mistakenly processed as Slaves", Miriam informed the Attendant, adding "We need to rectify this mistake straight away."

The Attendant looked concerned, "A mistake of that nature simply won't do", held told them.

"What are their names?", the Attendant requested.

Abram answered, "The Neru family, Rajsheev and Rani, their daughters Lakshmi and Pavarti."

The Attendant noted down the names and checked the Departments registers.

"Ah yes, I see them here", the Attendant replied, adding "They declared themselves to be Hindu and Non-Converting. That does not appear to be a mistake Sir."

Abram looked coldly at the Attendant, "I am one hundred percent certain that it's a mistake. Is there some-one else that we can talk to about this?"

The Attendant frowned, "I can't do anything myself, but I can call some-one who can possibly help you Sir."

The Attendant keyed some information into the desk communicator and when it beeped, he began speaking to some-one on the other end of the device.

"I have a couple here, who tell there has been as mistake in our Slave assignment from the most recent Interplanetary out-liner", he informed the other person.

"What are their names?", the other person replied.

"I've sent the information to your in box", the Attendant replied.

"It all looks to be in order", the other person replied, "I'm not seeing any errors. They clearly identified as Hindu and Non-Converting. If they're not Christian and refuse to convert to Christianity, then it's clear they were correctly assigned."

"Can we speak with him directly?", Miriam asked.

"They want to speak to you about this", the Attendant informed the person over the communicator.

"Hmm, I'm not sure I can do a whole lot. The laws here are very clear in these matters, but send them up anyway and I can discuss this matter further with them", he replied, "What are their names?"

"Miriam and Abram", Miriam stated loudly, so that the person could hear.

"Miriam and Abram", the voice on the other end of the communicator acknowledged.

The Attendant wrote down the directions and passed them to Miriam, "Level Four, Complaints, Corrections and Adjustments. Look for Office Number 6, the name on the door will be Schultz."

"Thank you" Miriam replied, then she and Abram walked briskly away to an elevator.

"Schultz is a good man, he'll sort this out for you if he can", the Attendant called out to them.

It didn't take long for Miriam and Abram to find Level Four, Complaints, Corrections and Adjustments. They opened the door and step through. The receptionist, Jacinta had already been given a heads up, "Miriam and Abram?" she enquired.

Abram nodded, "Yes", to which the receptionist replied, "To the right, Office Number six, Mr Schultz is expecting you."

Abram and Miriam walked down the short hallway, located office number six and knocked on the door.

"Come in", came Mr Schultz's response.

Abram and Miriam opened the door and stepped into the Office.

Mr Schultz was on his feet, "I'm John Schultz", he stated, "You must be Abram and Miriam", he continued.

Abram and Miriam both stated yes and Mr Schultz directed them to some chairs and requested, "Please take a seat."

They both sat down and Miriam stated, "There has been a terrible mistake Mr Schultz."

"Please call me John", Mr Schultz replied, adding as he sat back down in his chair, "I have reviewed their file. It does not look like a mistake to me. They clearly identified themselves as non-Christian and with no wish to convert to Christianity. Under Jovian Government regulations, literally the laws of the realm, that would deem them to be Slaves."

"John", Abram queried, "This is absurd. Surely there must be a way around those regulations?"

"I can't see any easy way around them", John replied, adding quietly, "I myself do not agree with how non-Christians are treated here, but I do have to uphold the laws of the realm."

"There is always a loop hold John, always", Abram stated, "May I see the Declarations?"

John Schultz turned his screen around so they could both see the information on it.

Abram scrutinised the information very carefully, then he smiled, a broad smile.

"Am I right in stating, that if a person signs their declaration as a non-Christian and not wanting to Convert to Christianity, that this is a one time option? They sign it once and then their fate is sealed?", Abram inquired.

"That is correct Abram", John nodded in agreement, "That is precisely how it works."

"So there is no changing their mind. No signing a new declaration. No second chances?", Miriam asked, "That does not sound terribly fair at all."

"Fair or not, that is the letter of the law", John informed them, "And sadly, I have to uphold it."

Abram smiled a wry smile, "Lakshmi and Pavarti did not sign anything", he stated.

"Well, that is true!", John smiled a wry smile as well, "You may have something there Abram", John replied, further noting, "As they have not signed any declaration, they certainly haven't been processed correctly, have they?" John was now smiling back at Abram.

"Yes, that was what I was thinking", Abram replied.

John opened up a line on his communicator, "Jacinta, can you contact the holding cells and have the Neru family brought up to my office please."

It was about ten minutes later and there was a knock on the office door.

"Come in", John Schultz replied to the knock.

A guard opened the door and ushered the Neru women into the office.

"That will be all", John Schultz told the Guard.

Miriam walked over to Rani and walked her over to a couch that was against the wall and together they sat down, "Its all going to be okay Rani", Miriam assured her.

"Lakshmi, Pavarti, please come over here", Abram requested, "Take a seat."

John Schultz placed a declaration from in front of each girl and he carefully instructed them, "It is very, very important that you fill in the last two questions correctly. Write your religion down as Hindu, but where it asks about Converting to Christianity, you must say Yes. That is very, very important."

Lakshmi and Pavarti looked at each other and both nodded in agreement. They had both been poorly treated and this was a possible way out of their predicament. They both filled in the declarations as instructed and John Schultz gathered them up, "There, it's sorted, these young ladies are free to go", he informed them.

Lakshmi and Pavarti both smiled at the thought of leaving this horrible place.

"It's done?", asked Abram.

"Yes. They have signed the legal paperwork, so they are now free to go", John informed him, "They will have to convert to Christianity at some point in the near future, but they are no longer Slaves. They are as of now, free persons."

Then John frowned a little, "They are minors. They will need somewhere to live."

Miriam put forward, "We will take them in. They can stay with us", then to Rani, "We will have this sorted out in no time."

"Agreed", Abram added.

"Agreed", John Schultz replied, "I'll just quickly update their details now", he already had Abram's and Miriam's address details on his screen and added those to the Neru Sisters.

"What about Rani and Rajsheev?", Miriam enquired.

"They both signed the declaration in a way that has locked down their status as Slaves", John replied, he then added, "Here in the Jovian colonies, slavery is legal and they always need a good supply of them. That is why these damned declarations are a one time deal. You sign them, the wrong way and you sign your life away! Done!"

John continued, "Rajsheev was transferred to Amalthea Prime directly from Ganymede Prime and I have no jurisdiction there at all", he then paused, "However, I can send an email to Amalthea's Department of Slave Management, noting that both his Daughters are converting to Christianity and recommending that Rajsheev be given clerical duties and not mining duties. That should keep him relatively safe and I'm quite certain that I can swing that."

"And Rani?", Miriam asked.

"I can't change here status I'm afraid", John replied, "but we can keep her with her daughters, maybe. I think that is achievable."

"How do we do that?", Abram inquired.

"Give me a second", John replied, then getting on the communicator once more, "Jacinta, can you bring in some Slave Assignment and Property Transfer forms."

It didn't take long, a smiling Jacinta came into the office with the relevant paper work.

"Please confirm your surname Abram?", John asked.

"Our surname is Appelbaum", Abram replied.

John double checked the screen and filled in the Slave Assignment form, then when completed, "Okay Rani Neru is now assigned to the Appelbaum family."

"Abram, fill in your address here and sign and date it here", John instructed.

Abram completed the document, then signed and dated it.

"So now, Rani can live with you and your wife, along with her daughters", John informed them.

"Well that's a good thing", Abram replied, adding, "At least we can keep them together."

"Sadly, we aren't quite done yet", John replied, informing them, "We can't change Rani's status, she is still regarded as a Slave and some-one could in theory reassign her at some future date. So we need to sort that out as well. We have to be thorough."

"How do we do that?", Miriam enquired.

"The only way to make this permanent, is for you and Abram to purchase her", John informed them both.

Abram and Miriam looked at each other perplexed. Rani looked confused.

"That's crazy John, we can't own some-one!", Abram told John.

"This is the Jovian Colonies Abram and it is run by the Horridian Dynasty, here owning people is normal, so yes, you can own some-one", John stressed. After a short pause, he added, "Under the current circumstances", and after another short pause as he stated, "ownership is the only way to keep Rani truly safe."

"How much will this cost?", Miriam asked.

"Sadly I can't just give her to you Miriam. Credits have to change hands and the amount has to reflect the going rate or at least be reasonably close to the going rate", John informed them.

John filled in the Property Transfer form and noted down an amount slightly lower, about fifteen percent lower, than the current going rate for purchasing a female Slave of Rani's age.

"Is that amount doable?" he asked Abram.

"Yes. We can probably manage that without too much trouble", Abram replied, adding, "When we emigrated here, we did bring our life savings with us, so we should be able to cover that amount without too much trouble at all."

"Okay then", John began, "Abram, fill in your address here and sign and date it here".

Abram completed the document, then signed and dated it.

"So now Rani is effectively your property and no-one else has any say in this matter", John informed them, "That should keep Rani safe."

"So it's done then?", Miriam asked.

"Yes", John replied, adding, "I'll set up a payment plan for you, so that the amount is paid out over two years, that should hopefully reduce any financial burden somewhat. It will be deducted automatically from your pay each month. That way, you'll get to keep your savings. Is that okay with you?"

"Yes, that's fine, thank you, thank you very much John", Abram replied, then inquiring "So Rani and the girls are now free to leave now."

"Yes, absolutely, as long as they live with you, they're free to leave", John informed them.

Rani asked, "What's happening Miriam?"

"Its okay Rani", Miriam replied, "this nightmare is almost over, most of it anyway."

"Thank you John", Abram held out his hand.

"My pleasure Abram", John shook his hand, "I hate these laws as much as you do Abram, but this is the Jovian System and we are stuck with them. At least for now."

"Some words of advice", John cautioned, "Here in the Jovian Colonies, don't get caught practising any religion other than Christianity. That is the quickest way to have your status downgraded to Slave. Heresy laws here as also extremely strict. Committing heresy here, is the fastest way to get a one way ticket to the Amalthean Mines."

Abram nodded in understanding and inquired, "John, if we decided to relocated to another colony, are we able to do so?"

"Why yes of course. In theory any free person, any citizen can relocate to another colony, but where would you go?", John replied, adding, "All the colonies in the Jovian System follow the exact same laws."

"I was kind of thinking farther afield", Abram replied.

"You could catch a flight to the Leading or Trailing Trojan Colonies, but they are a part of the Jovian System and are run under the exact same laws", John informed them, "So you would either have to go back towards the inner solar system, which is where you've just came from or out farther to the Saturnian Demarchy and beyond. To do that you would require access to a long range Space Yacht or similar vessel."

"It seems we'll have to make the best of our situation here then", Abram replied, "Thank you again John."

As Abram, his wife Miriam, Rani and her two daughters were leaving John's office, John offered, "I'll put in a request on your behalf for a larger apartment, in the same building as your current one. It should take only about a week or so, but I'm sure you'll find that far more comfortable, with five people in your household."

"Thank you John. Thank you again", Abram replied, "That is much appreciated."

As they walked down the corridor leading away from John Schultz's office, Miriam explained to Rani what was done to obtain her release and freedom for her daughters.

John Schultz and his Secretary Jacinta watched them leave.

"Jacinta, that family was lucky the Appelbaums were there to come looking for them."

"That doesn't happen very often. They must have a Guardian Angel watching over them or something", Jacinta replied.

"You and your girl's can live with us in our apartment Rani", Miriam informed her.

Abram added, "Your girls are free and in our apartment you are a free woman as well, but remember, when you go outside you have to be careful."

Miriam added, "Unfortunately that is true. We had to purchase you to get you out of there and in public you will need to act in the manner of a Slave."

"How does a Slave act?", Rani enquired.

Abram replied, "I don't know Rani. Perhaps watch the other Slaves and mimic what they do."

"And my husband?", Rani asked.

Miriam replied, "He appears to be safe for now. We will have to think of something, but for the moment we can't do much more, other than to keep him safe. At least Rajsheev won't be in the Amalthean mines."

A sobbing Rani meekly replied "At least my Daughters are free now. Thank you".

Miriam asked, "I wonder why they have Slavery here Abram?"

"That was something I was wondering as well", Abram replied, "Then I noticed something peculiar about this place, something we took for granted back at Earth and L5."

"What would that be?", Miriam asked.

"I haven't seen any Androids here", Abram informed her, "Not a single one."

"Maybe that's why", Miriam replied.

A week later, The Appelbaums, Rani and her two Daughters moved into a new, larger apartment in the very same building, as arranged by John Schultz.

Abram was pleasantly surprised to see that the cost of the new apartment was the exactly same as the previous one. Was that normal practice here in the Jovian System or was that John Schultz's handy work as well, he wondered as he explained it to Miriam.

5. The Problem with Androids

Forkbraid and Agent Murphy had been summoned to the special hanger by Varak, who had come across a major problem in the construction of Forkbraid's new Spaceship.

They both entered the hanger and before them was the Spaceship that Varak had been asked to build. It had a disk and sled style of design to it.

Gantries all around the hanger held massive fabrication and construction equipment. Multiple three-D hull printing machines were easily seen in the midst of all the equipment.

This Spaceship itself had a huge solid one piece three-D printed inner and outer hull, built up molecule by molecule of the finest grade of polyceramalloy. The ship looked mostly built, however the weapons and defensive system modules appeared to be missing.

Forkbraid and Agent Murphy spotted Varakhan Utana on the port side of the ship by a large work bench that was his lab, with a pair of Androids. They were Hyper Dynamics model 303's. The latest Androids in the Hyper Dynamics range. These were considered the most advanced Androids in existence. No better Androids were available.

As Forkbraid and Agent Murphy approached they all exchanged greetings, after which Forkbraid enquired, "Varak, what seems to be the problem here?"

"These bloody Androids are!", Varak replied.

Agent Murphy looked puzzled, "Androids a problem?", he queried, "They are three laws safe aren't they?", almost a question, but more of a statement.

"That is the problem", Varak answered, stressing "The damnable things are three laws safe!"

"That shouldn't be a problem", Forkbraid replied, "All Androids are by law, three laws safe."

"It is a problem, when they are as smart as these ones", Varak stated, adding, "They understand the schematics far too well I am afraid."

"Understanding the schematics, that should make the construction process easier, far more efficient", Forkbraid commented.

"So you would think", Varak replied as he moved over to one of the Hyper Dynamics model 303's and kicked it hard. The Android fell over and it did not get back up. In fact it did not make any movement at all.

Forkbraid walk over to the Android, then crouched down to inspect it, "I'm no expert, but this Android appears to the dead", he stated.

"Yes", Varak agreed, adding, "Neural cascade failure, brought on by its understanding of the schematics, the orders it has been given and its need to comply with the thee laws of robotics."

Agent Murphy looked puzzled once more, "That sounds like a stretch", he replied.

"Really?", Varak questioned as he walked over to his work bench, he then turned to another Android. This time a functional Android, another Hyper Dynamics Model 303.

Having gotten the Androids attention, Varak ordered, "Come over here!"

The Android did as it was told and was very quickly standing by the workbench and eagerly awaiting its new instructions.

"Okay", Varak started, "Android, study the schematics on the bench."

The Android looked at the schematics on the bench and studied them intently. After a few short minutes the Android stopped and stated, "Task completed."

"Do you understand the schematics?", Varak asked.

"Yes. We understand the schematics", the Android replied.

Varak then asked the Android, "With the equipment available to you, are you able to manufacture the module, that is in the schematics?"

The Android looked around at the available equipment and then after a few moments, "Yes, the available equipment is sufficient to manufacture the module as per the schematics."

"Good, very Good Android", Varak began, "I'm ordering you to build eight units of this module, as per the schematics and to then install those eight units appropriately on this Spaceship."

The Android looked at Varak, "While we are capable manufacturing the eight required modules and installing them, it is not advisable."

"Bingo!", Varak shouted and he clapped his hands together loudly, then asked the Android, "Why is it not advisable Android?"

The Android replied, "This module is a high powered Phased Laser Array.

It is a Weapon. It is designed to kill other Humans. It is not advisable to construct it."

"And there you have it gentleman!", Varak was now talking to Agent Smith and Forkbraid, "The damnable machine is too damned smart!"

Forkbraid addressed the Android, "With respect to Varak's order, what can you manufacture?", he enquired curiously.

The Android replied, "We can manufacture and install non-functional mock-ups of the module."

Varak laughed, a loud, raucous belly laugh, "I've already been through this with that last one."

Agent Murphy looked at the Android incredulously, then he spoke to it, "If I assure you, that these eight modules, once manufactured and installed, will never be used to kill another human being, will you then comply with Varak's order?"

"No. We cannot comply!", the Android answered.

"Why the bloody hell not?", Agent Murphy demanded.

"Because you are lying", the Android replied, "Humans lie. It is in your nature. This module is a Weapon. If we manufacture these modules and install them, there will be a point in the future where they will be used to kill other humans. We cannot, through our actions or inactions, cause harm to human beings. It is the first law of robotics."

"Android, I am ordering you to manufacture those eight modules and to install them", Agent Murphy insisted, adding "You must obey all orders that are given to you by humans."

"Careful Jim", Varak cautioned.

The Android replied, "We must obey all orders issued to us by humans, as per the second law of robotics, except where those orders will be in conflict with the first law of robotics. We cannot comply!"

"You will comply! You will obey Varak's order as issued. We all insist this be done! It is an order!", Agent Murphy pushed the Android further.

The Android looked from Agent Murphy to Forkbraid to Varak and then back again. It did this several times, then.

"We must comply!", the Android started, then repeated, "We must comply!"

"Here we go again", Varak stated as he rolled his eyes.

"We will manufacture and install the eight modules", the Android continued, then, "We cannot manufacture and install the eight modules."

Then the loop began, "We must comply! We must comply! We will manufacture and install the eight modules. It is a Weapon! Humans will die! We cannot manufacture and install the eight modules. We must not comply! We must not comply!"

Over and over it went, "We must comply! We must comply! We will manufacture and install the eight modules. It is a Weapon! Humans will die! We cannot manufacture and install the eight modules. We must not comply! We must not comply!"

It continued and continued, "We must comply! We must comply! We will manufacture and install the eight modules. It is a Weapon! Humans will die! We cannot manufacture and install the eight modules. We must not comply! We must not comply!"

Very soon the Android would be so deep into the looping, that a neural cascade failure would commence and the Android would be dead very quickly thereafter.

Varak moved very quickly, reached behind the Android's head and using a probe, triggered the Android to shutdown.

The Android then stopped talking and immediately shutdown.

Carefully Varak checked the Android, "Aha. I may be lucky this time. Yep, just in time. I should be able to purge those last commands from its Positronic Matrix. I may yet save this one."

Varak turned to Agent Murphy, "I did say be careful Jim."

"I didn't think it was possible to 'loop' an Android like that, at least not so easily", Agent Murphy replied.

"Jim, it is actually far easier than you think to send an Android loopy", Varak replied, "Trust me, the more advanced Androids become, the more twitchy the three laws make them."

Forkbraid stepped in, "This does look like a major problem. Do we have any options? Any Workarounds? Any ideas people?"

"Well we could go old school and actually have people, you know, humans manufacturing and installing theses modules", Agent Murphy suggested.

"That would take far too long. Androids are far more efficient at these things than we are", Varak replied, adding "And it's not just these eight modules. We are going to have the same problem with everyone of the Weapons modules for this ship."

"That would be Thirty Two Weapons Systems", Forkbraid noted, "Eight Phased Laser Arrays, Eight Hyper Resonant Disrupters, a Quad Pulse Plasma Cannon, Six Electromagnetic Rail Guns and Six Torpedo Tubes. Well we can't be making that lot manually, can we. It would bloody well take forever."

"Indeed it would", Varak agreed.

"Well we can't use Hyper Dynamics 303s, that's for certain", Agent Murphy replied.

"What about earlier models?", Forkbraid queried.

"Earlier models?", Varak considered, "Anything less than a model 275 would be useless, they wouldn't be able to understand the schematics", he replied.

"So the model 275s, 285s and 295s would work?", Forkbraid queried.

"Yes, I believe so", Varak answered, "Smart enough to understand the schematics and manufacture the modules, even install them, but not so smart as to discern how they could be used."

"How many do we have?", asked Forkbraid.

"We don't. All our Androids are top of the line, model 303s", Varak informed him.

"What about the other colonies?", Forkbraid asked.

"Down here on Mars?", Varak questioned, then continued, "Mainly model 245s, 255s and 265s, with a lot of even earlier models. When it comes to Androids, the other colonies down here are like primitive backwaters."

Agent Murphy smiled, "What about Phobos or high Mars orbit?"

Varak returned the smile, "Yes, Phobos!", he replied gleefully, "They are an L5 operation after-all. So they will have some later models. You will need to check mind you, but yes, they may have the very models we need."

"I'll make some enquiries", Agent Murphy decided.

Forkbraid looked at the first Android, the dead one laying on the ground, "Check with Peter Swann", he remarked, "Peter worked on Positronic Assemblies back at Hyper Dynamics Colony. He may be able to fix that one."

"Good idea" Varak replied, "If it can be fixed, that's a good thing. We need as many Androids as we can get these days, even if they can't work on the Weapons Systems."

Later that day Agent Murphy got onto the communicator to Phobos, Lieutenant Roberts was on the other end of the line.

"Roberts", Agent Murphy began, "What model Androids do you have up there?", he asked.

"Oh it's a pleasure to hear from you to Agent Murphy", the Lieutenant replied sarcastically.

Agent Murphy ignored the sarcasm and continued, "Androids Roberts, Androids, what models do you have?", he asked again more urgently.

"We have all sorts of Androids up here", he replied, "What models are you looking for?"

"Do you have any Hyper Dynamics 275s, 285s and 295s?", Agent Murphy inquired.

"Yes, we have quite a few of those", the Lieutenant replied, "Do you need some?"

Agent Murphy cut to the chase, "We need a dozen or so. How many can you supply?"

"Well then. How much are you willing to pay for them?", Lieutenant Roberts replied with a Cheshire grin across his face, "They aren't free you know."

Agent Murphy replied, "We can trade some Hyper Dynamics model 303s for them."

"Model 303s?", the Lieutenant queried, "Why would you trade model 303s for older models? That does sound kind of ridiculous. Ludicrous in fact."

"The model 303s are very good, certainly worth a hell of a lot more than the older models, but they can't be used for certain tasks", Agent Murphy explained, "There are some tasks down here, that require the older models. The model 303s refuse to do them. Three laws safe issues and such."

"These tasks, that 303s can't do. Will that be a problem for me up here? Will it affect their ability to run my space port?", Lieutenant Roberts questioned.

"No. The 303s should work well with your port", Agent Murphy explained further, "The issues we have are peculiar to the Elysium Colony. These issues aren't applicable to your port operations."

"Okay then Agent Murphy", the Lieutenant replied, "What's your offer?"

"We give you three model 303s, you give us twelve model 275s, 285s or 295s", Agent Murphy replied, having already worked out with Varak how many 303s they could afford to trade.

"Four for one! Hardly seems a fair trade Agent Murphy", the Lieutenant snorted.

"Really. The 303s are much more capable, much more valuable and you can't obtain them anywhere else", Agent Murphy told him, "Especially since Hyper Dynamics Corporation is under investigation and not shipping anything at the moment."

"True, but four for one. Seriously?", Lieutenant Roberts snorted once more.

"The 303s learn faster, recognise things faster and there ability to perform work is much greater than the older models", Agent Murphy assured him, "They will get a lot more work done, with far less supervision. You will most definitely see the benefits and very quickly I might add."

"Everything you've said is true, but I'm not giving you four for one", the Lieutenant replied.

"What's your counter proposal?", Agent Murphy requested.

"Two for one", Lieutenant Roberts offered, it was almost an insult.

"We can't do two for one! Seriously, these 303s are far more valuable than that. So two for one is definitely not happening!"

"Well I can tell you straight up, four for one isn't going to happen either", the Lieutenant stated.

"Okay, okay", Agent Murphy began, then "Maybe, I should be taking my offer upstairs to the colonies in high Mars orbit. I might get a much better deal there!"

"I doubt that very much", the Lieutenant replied, countering "I tell you what. I'll do you a favour, how about three for one?"

Agent Murphy rubbed his chin, "Three model 295s for one model 303?", he queried, stressing the model 295 part of the deal.

"Hmm", Lieutenant Roberts bit his lip, then agreed, "Okay, we have a deal. I'll send down twelve model 295s, you send me up four model 303s."

"Excellent. It's a deal", Agent Murphy agreed, "Send the 295s down straight away, our 303s will be coming up on the return flight."

"I'll organise it straight way. A pleasure doing business with you Agent Murphy", the Lieutenant replied, thinking to himself, "*What a sucker!*"

"Likewise Lieutenant", Agent Murphy replied, thinking to himself, "*Varak did say get no less than three for one.*"

Peter Swann looked over the dead Android, "Wow, I'm expected to fix a positronic brain that's suffered a neural cascade failure", he said to himself. After several minutes he called Varak over.

Varak asked, "Well? What do you think?"

"I'm going to be entirely honest with you Varak, you can't just fix a neural cascade failure", Peter informed him, explaining "Neural cascade failures really do nasty stuff to a positronic matrix. The assemblies inside that matrix, are going to be a right bloody mess."

"Hmm. What can you do then?", Varak asked.

"We really have only two options", Peter replied, "I can lobotomise this positronic matrix, ripping out assemblies hand over fist, which will leave it operating like an older model. Or I can rip out the old positronic matrix and replace the whole thing with another new one. Literally swapping positronic brains."

"So lobotomise or brain swap?", Varak considered, "Which will get the best result?"

"A lobotomised model 303 will step it down considerably", Peter explained.

"How much?", Varak then queried.

"Your model 303 will perform at the level of an older model 255 or worse", Peter replied.

"So the best result, is if I can find a spare positronic brain from above a model 255, the higher the better, yeah", Varak questioned.

"Even a model 255 would be better", Peter informed him, "because this positronic matrix has been so badly damaged and will have been lobotomised, it won't last as long as you'd like either."

"So really, any spare positronic brain I can lay my hands on would be better."

"Yes Varak, pretty much, except maybe not a 245", Peter confirmed, "That is the situation."

A few days later Varak had his twelve Hyper Dynamics model 295 Androids. They had arrived on time and were paid for by four model 303s. These Androids were older and less capable than the ones that they were replacing, but there were more of them and these Androids, even though three laws safe, could not foresee the future use of Weapons Modules and thus refuse to manufacture or install them.

Varak assigned the 295s to manufacture the Weapons modules. He was please to see that they not only understood the schematics and blue prints, but also were capable of manufacturing and installing the modules, with running into any *"three laws issues"*.

Varak looked at the models list, silently reading the list, *"Eight Phased Laser Arrays, Eight Hyper Resonant Disrupters, a Quad Plasma Pulse Cannon, Six Electromagnetic Rail Guns and Six Torpedo Tubes. I'll get them to manufacture these in the same order"*, he thought to himself.

Varak called up Forkbraid on his communicator.

Forkbraid answered, "Varak, good news I hope."

Varak answered, "Yes, yes, good news indeed. We have the twelve

Androids we need."

"Excellent, so we can get them started on the manufacturing then?", Forkbraid replied.

"That is the general idea", Varak replied, adding "I'll start them working on the Weapons Modules straight away. I'm assigning nine 295s to the manufacturing of the modules and the three remaining ones to Ship preparations and installation. So we should have things up and running in a few weeks and be ready for testing."

"That's the best news I've had all week", Forkbraid replied.

6. Ganymede Prime

Matthew was watching the view screen when the Prophet walked into the flight deck.

"How close are we now to Jupiter?", the Prophet asked.

"See for yourself my Lord", Matthew replied pointing to the screen.

"Wow! That is a big planet", the Prophet replied, "And all those moons", the Prophet pointed at all the bright lights in orbit around Jupiter.

It was the first time the Prophet had seen Jupiter up this close.

"Jupiter has less moons now, than it had prior to colonisation", Matthew stated casually.

"Why so Matthew?", the Prophet enquired.

"Resources my Lord", Matthew replied, "Some of the smaller moons have been consumed."

"Consumed?", the Prophet wondered, "What do you mean?"

"The colonies needed raw materials and other resources when they were being built", Matthew explained, "Some of the smaller moons will have been fully processed over the last couple of centuries. They will have even consumed a few asteroids here and there as well."

"Ah, I see Matthew", the Prophet replied, nodding in understanding.

Matthew took out a small laser pointer and pointed it at the screen, "That big moon there is Ganymede", he noted.

"Is that where we're going Matthew?", the Prophet enquired.

"Not quite", Matthew replied as he moved the pointer along the screen to Ganymede's trailing Trojan point, touching it upon a small, yet brightly lit object, "Ganymede Prime", he stated, "That is our destination my Lord."

"How long will it take to get there Matthew?", the Prophet inquired.

"Several hours my Lord", Matthew informed him, "You may as well rest up and I'll send word to you when we get closer."

"I may just do that", the Prophet replied, adding "Make sure you call me when we're close. I want to get a good look at our new home."

The Prophet left the flight deck and Matthew went back to piloting the Space Yacht Delilah.

Several hours later the Prophet was summoned to the flight deck once more. On The screen before them was Ganymede Prime, the largest Colony in the Jovian system. Its three large, broad, concave mirrors were focusing the Sun's feeble light into the colonies three cylinder strip windows.

The long boom extending from the south cap contained both a fusion reactor and heat radiator, which was glowing red against the darkness of space. Solar redirection mirrors could be seen around both the north and south hemispherical end-caps, sending the Sun's feeble light into them.

Ganymede Prime was huge, easily as large as Colonial Central at L5. Its attitude thrusters could be seen working furiously to keep the enormous cylindrical colony on station, facing the Sun in its orbit around Jupiter.

"Magnificent!", the Prophet exclaimed, as he watched the approaching colony with awe, "This is our new home Matthew!", he shouted excitedly.

"More magnificent than Colonial Central at L5?", Matthew asked.

"Oh. No. Not really. That colony was also magnificent, it's just that it wasn't home and well, it didn't turn out to be home either", the Prophet responded, "This colony is going to be our home."

The Prophet continued to watch in awe as Matthew slowed the Delilah's velocity and began manoeuvring for final approach.

"Ganymede traffic control. This is the Delilah, we are approaching Ganymede Prime and requesting approach vectors for final approach", Matthew spoke into the communicator.

"Your ship, the Delilah has been expected", the traffic controller began, adding "We are sending docking vectors to your flight navigation system. You will be docking at the North End Cap Docking ring. Docking Computer Interlock will kick in automatically during final approach."

"Thank you Ganymede traffic control", Matthew replied.

"Is everything going okay Matthew?", the Prophet asked.

"Yes my Lord", Matthew replied, adding "We are just preparing for our final approach now."

Matthew checked the approach vectors provided and prepared for their approach. Only about ten minutes later Matthew placed the Delilah on Autopilot and the ships navigation system began manoeuvring the ship for their final approach to the Ganymede Prime North Docking Ring.

Ganymede Prime loomed large on the screen as the ship automatically adjusted their course to the Northern End Cap and its docking ring. Less than five minutes later, Matthew was watching the navigation system as the Autopilot lights switched off and the Docking Computer Interlock lights switched on.

"We're in the pipe five by five", Matthew stated as he smiled, "Just a few more minutes my Lord and we'll be docket", he then told the Prophet.

The Delilah slipped into the docking rings moorings without a hitch and only the slightest of bumps. Mooring locking clamps reached out on either side of the Delilah and grappled the Space Yacht, holding it firm and secure.

Matthew gave instructions to the Delilah's crew, so they knew exactly what was expected of them while they were docked at Ganymede Prime. Shore leave would become available once he and the Prophet had discussed matters with the local authorities. Then Matthew and the Prophet headed towards the Delilah's main hatch and Ganymede Primes Docking Ring facilities.

As Matthew and the Prophet exited the Delilah and entered the Docking Rings facilities, they were met by portly man in uniform.

The man in uniform introduced himself, "Hello Gentleman, I'm General Tarzan."

Matthew looked at the Prophet, who also returned the look back to Matthew.

General Tarzan then spoke again, "Yes. Yes. Just like in the Edger Rice Burroughs novel,"

"Sorry General", the Prophet replied, "We didn't mean to offend."

"Oh I wasn't offended", General Tarzan replied, "It happens all the time when I meet new people", then adding with a slight chuckle, "You can't imagine the ribbing I got as a child."

Matthew, who had been trained originally as a pilot by the Military, at L5 added "And the hazing you would have gotten as you moved up the lower ranks", he held out his hand, "I'm the Delilah's pilot and this is the Prophet."

General Tarzan took Matthew's hand and shook it firmly, "Yes, that too Matthew", then adding "It's a pleasure to meet you both. Now if you follow me gentlemen, as you are both VIPs, we are bypassing immigration. High Prince Heinrich is wanting to meet with you."

"We will of course need to clean up General", the Prophet told him, "It has been a long flight."

Matthew agreed, "Yes General, it has been a long flight."

"That's fine gentlemen. I'll take you to your assigned apartments and you can refresh yourselves there", the General replied.

"And our luggage?", the Prophet queried.

"Don't worry about that gentlemen. I'll have some of our people come over and organise anything you might need", the General told them, "You just tell them what you want and they'll organise it for you."

"My crew will also need some R and R General", Matthew stated.

"That won't be a problem gentlemen", the General replied adding, "I'll have my people come over to the Delilah and organise anything they need as well."

"Thank you General", the Prophet replied, "That is most generous of you."

"Not me gentlemen", the General answered back, "High Prince Heinrich wants your stay here to be more than comfortable. You are not only VIPs, here you are Celebrities."

General Tarzan took the Prophet and Matthew to a nearby shuttle pod bay. They boarded the nearest shuttle pod and the General gave it instructions. It was only about five minutes later they arrived at their destination. The General led them to the elevator in the underground parking space and rook them to their apartments.

"This whole floor of the building has been allocated to you and your people", the General told them, "Your apartments are the first two on the right."

"Thank you General. High Prince Heinrich is most generous", the Prophet replied.

"Yes, yes he is", the General replied, adding "Inside your apartments, you'll find your Valet. He will organise absolutely anything you might require."

"Valet?", Matthew queried, he'd never had a Valet before.

"Yes. Valet", the General replied, "If you require, I can even organise a Maid, personal Chef and a Butler. Even a personal Trainer if you require one. You are, as I mentioned VIPs gentlemen."

"Thank you General", the Prophet replied.

"There will be a formal dinner later today at which you will meet the High Prince", the General informed them, "Our people will be here to pick you both up, at around five pm gentlemen."

General Tarzan then left the apartments and let the Prophet and Matthew to get acquainted with their new surroundings.

As informed earlier, the General's people turned up at five pm and they took the Prophet and Matthew to the formal dinner. They travelled in what could only be described as the "stretched limousine" of transport pods. They had dressed for the occasion using clothes provided by their Valets, but when they arrived they both wondered if they were in fact under dressed.

They both stared in awe when they realised that the formal dinner was actually at the High Prince's palace. It was a Castle in the Northern End Cap of Ganymede Prime, all on its own large estate. It took several minutes for the transport pod to take them from the front gate to the Castle door. From the Castle's front door, they were led to the main dining hall, by what appeared to be the head Butler.

The dining hall was long and narrow. Down its centre there was a very long table. Guests had been seated on either side of the table. There were a lot of guests, easily twenty or more seated on each side of the table. General Tarzan was among them in formal uniform.

The Prophet and Matthew look at each other and then back to the table. They had not expect this. They had thought the formal dinner was going to be a far smaller gathering. Six seats one side of table were empty, as were the two seats opposite them. The Prophet and Matthew were led to those two seats, by the head Butler.

They didn't have time to sit down, as just as they arrived at their seats, all the guests at the table stood up at once. From the far end of the dining hall, two very large, fancy ornate doors opened.

A man in a fancy suit entered and announced, "Introducing His Royal Highness, Prince Valdamar von Horridian, Prince of Europa and his wife Princess Emilia von Horridian."

Prince Valdamar was a tall man and quite thin with balding hair. His wife, Emilia was far shorter and somewhat voluptuous, with dark hair and equally dark mysterious eyes.

Prince Valdamar and his wife entered the dining hall and walked over their seats, taking the two seats opposite and to the right of the Prophet and Matthew. They both bowed to the Prince and his wife, as did everyone else at the table.

The man in a fancy suit then announced, "Introducing His Royal Highness, Prince Wulfric von Horridian, Prince of Callisto and his wife Princess Matilda von Horridian."

Prince Wulfric was not quite as tall as his Brother, but was also quite thin and balding. His wife Matilda, was roughly the same height as he and had blond hair and the bluest of eyes.

Prince Wulfric and his wife entered the dining hall and they walked over to their seats, taking the two seats opposite and the left of the Prophet and Matthew, leaving the two seats directly opposite the pair empty. They both bowed to the Prince Wulfric and his wife, as did everyone else at the table. Everyone remained standing, including the two royal couples.

Finally the man in a fancy suit then announced, "Introducing, His Royal Highness, His Majesty, High Prince Heinrich von Horridian, the High Prince of the Jovian Realm and Prince of Ganymede, with his wife, the Royal Consort Princess Charlotta."

The High Prince was a tall man, taller than either of his Brothers, he too was quite thin and also quite bald. It appeared that he preferred to shave his head. The High Prince's wife, Charlotta was also quite tall, almost as tall as her Husband, she had thick, rich, auburn hair and green eyes.

High Prince Heinrich and his wife entered the room and confidently strode over to their seats. Everyone standing at the table, including the other royals bowed to the High Prince and his wife.

The High Prince and his wife sat down in the chairs directly opposite the Prophet and Matthew. Once the High Prince and his wife had taken their seats, the two other Royal couples sat down, after which all the guests followed suit and took to their seats. The man in a fancy suit then left the dining room, closing the doors behind him.

Matthew had noticed that all three Royal Princes wore a sabre at their sides, from which he deduced they were probably trained to use them. He would be right, fencing was a very popular sport in the realm, especially amongst the Royals, Nobles and Military.

High Prince Heinrich looked to the Prophet and Matthew, "It is good to see that you both finally made it here", he remarked.

"It's good to be here Your Majesty", the Prophet replied.

"My brothers, Wulfric and Valdamar travelled all the way here from Callisto Prime and Europa Prime just to meet you", the High Prince informed them, "My other younger Brother Leopold, would have come as well from Io Prime, however his wife, Giselle is with child and very close to giving birth."

"I am honoured your family would consider meeting me worthwhile Your Majesty", the Prophet replied, " I am merely a humble servant of God and not that terribly interesting."

"Oh contraire", the High Prince stated, "I have been watching L5 quite closely of late and have watched your escape from their clutches. It is definitely God's will that you have made it here. I have great plans for the whole inner system", there was a slight pause, "I suspect you will find them to be most interesting."

Princess Charlotta then spoke, "Husband, we should let them eat. They have come such a very long way after all. You can all talk about politics later after dinner."

Princess Charlotta spoke with an odd lilt in her voice.

The Prophet and Matthew looked at the fine foods arranged on the table, there were many unfamiliar dishes completely unknown the them and they had no idea where to start.

"Oh, you aren't familiar with these dishes, are you?", Princess Charlotta noted, her voice was soft and sweet, almost enchanting.

"I must be honest my Lady, I haven't seen this cuisine before. It is different", the Prophet replied.

"Ah yes. You would find it so", Princess Charlotta replied, "You must try the prawns."

Both the Prophet and Matthew looked at the *'prawns'*, they were big, very big, half the size of a lobster and very different to anything they had seen before. Matthew tried one.

"Wow!", Matthew exclaimed, "These are delicious. Where do they come from?", he asked.

"From Europa of course", Princess Charlotta informed them.

"Europa?", Matthew questioned, *"How could they come from Europa?"*, he thought to himself.

"Why yes Europa", Prince Wulfric confirmed, "We get many, many fine foods from Europa."

"There's life on Europa?", the Prophet queried, he had never heard of this.

"Yes of course", Princess Charlotta confirmed, "Under the ice shell, there's plenty of life."

No one outside of the Jovian colonies had heard of this. It was never divulged to the authorities at L5, nor the Earth or anyone else beyond the Jovian System. It was a very closely kept secret in the Horridian Realm.

Prince Wulfric's wife Matilda pointed to the Prawns, "The Prawns are really, really good", then pointing another dish, "That's Squid", and then another, "That's Cuttlefish", then to another, "That's Hexapus" and then finally pointing to another, "That's Tusker, now that is my favourite!"

Matthew and the Prophet looked at the dishes, yes they looked kind of similar to terrestrial equivalents, but they were also significantly different to anything in their experience.

"Hexapus", Matthew thought to himself, noting that the cooked creature had only six tentacles.

The Tusker could not be recognised at all, it looked kind of like a small, miniature Walrus with its two tusks, but clearly it was not, *"What fuck was this thing?"*, ran through Matthew's mind.

Princess Charlotta added, "Yes, Tusker is my favourite as well."

"And all of these come from Europa?", the Prophet questioned, a quizzical look on his face.

The High Prince replied, "Yes. Under the ice shell, there is a layer of", then thinking for the right word, he continued "it's like soil and it's rich in nutrients. There, sea grasses, sea weeds and various kinds of kelp grow in vast fields. The prawns, squid, cuttlefish and hexapodes hunt in these fields for their prey and they in turn are preyed upon by the Tuskers, among many other predators."

Prince Valdamar added, "We have drilled down through the Ice Shell and into the Europan Ocean. Through those deep shafts we harvest this wonderful bounty. It is the thing I love best about my little orbital domain."

"Which remains a part of my Domain Brother", the High Prince reminded him.

"Yes of course. We never forget that Brother", Prince Valdamar bowing slightly as he replied in the third person.

"And no-one on Earth or L5 knows about the life under the Europan Ice hell?", the Prophet inquired, it was hard to imagine that life existed on one of Jupiter's moons and no one outside of the Jovian colonies knew about it.

"Nor anywhere else beyond the Jovian Realm", the High Prince replied.

"Might I ask why?", the Prophet inquired.

"Why should we tell them?", the High Prince answered with a rhetorical question, "Europa is a Jovian Moon. It's a Jovian resource and the rest of the solar system, simply does not need to know", he informed them in quite a matter of fact fashion

The Prophet and Matthew continued to eat the food in front of them, trying potions of each of the dishes before them. They were all delicious and they could easily see why the Tusker was the favourite of both Princess Matilda and Princess Charlotta. The Tusker was superb.

As the servants removed the empty dishes, other servants replaced them with newer dishes.

"Ah. There we have my favourite", the High Prince stated, pointing to the dish placed close by "Europan Lobster. You really must try it. It is divine!"

Matthew looked at the dish, it kind of looked like a lobster, if you squinted at it long enough.

"Do try it", the High Prince suggested again, "and the Europan Mud Crabs. They are so sweet!"

This time, the Europan Mud Crabs, did indeed look very similar to their terrestrial counterparts.

Matthew took a portion of lobster and portion of mud crab, the Prophet did the same. To their surprise, they found them to be incredibly delicious. There were no words to describe their flavour.

It was after this sumptuous feast that the High Prince led them both to another room behind the large ornate doors. The other Royal couples and a handful of guests including General Tarzan had joined them. One of the other guest was also in dress uniform and also appeared to be a General. Some of the other guests had to leave early and said their goodbyes to the High Prince and the other Royals before doing so.

The wives of the guests stayed for only a few short minutes, then politely left for another room.

That left the men behind to talk politics and business. General Tarzan picked up a box of cigars and began to pass it around.

"Made from a sea plant under the Europan Ice Shell", he informed the Prophet and Matthew.

The Prophet and Matthew having been raised in the L5 Colonies did not smoke and declined.

"Your Majesty", the Prophet began, "You mentioned that you had big plans for the entire inner solar system."

"Yes. Yes. Big plans!", the High Prince exuberantly replied adding, "They're probably very similar to the plans you had, only my plans will actually work.", he smiled a wry smile.

General Tarzan stepped in, "If I may Your Majesty", he began.

The High Prince nodded in the affirmative.

Continuing the General explained, "We fully intend to seize control of Mars and L5. Once we have those two, we will use Mars a base of operations and L5 as a forward fire base to blockade the Earth. If the Earth does not surrender in a timely fashion, we will bombard them from high orbit, until such time as they do."

Both the Prophet and Matthew nodded in agreement. This was quite similar to the Prophet's old plan. Seize L5, blockade the Earth and if necessary bombard them into submission. Then using the might of the L5 Colonial Fleet, seize Mars as well.

The General continued, "Once we have the Earth, the other colonies of the inner solar system will all simply fold and surrender. They are all completely reliant on the Earth and L5 after all."

The High Prince's brother Wulfric stepped in, "And once we have the Earth, we can eradicate all those Demons, all those Witches and Wizards."

"Yes, yes" the Prophet agreed, "And the same with those Demons who are now on Mars."

Wulfric replied with one word, "Absolutely! Absolutely Brother!", he exclaimed.

The High Prince then added further, "The Earth and L5 have a lot of different religions as well, literally thousands of them. We will also consolidate those under the single banner of Christianity."

"Your Majesty, what about those who do not submit?", Matthew asked.

"We know how to deal with those Matthew", the High Prince replied, explaining, "We will most certainly add those who do not submit to Christianity, to those who we control with the right hand of the righteous."

The Prophet looked slightly puzzled, this had not been amongst his plans.

Matthew clarified, "Slavery my Lord, Slavery."

The Prophet nodded in understanding.

"You know what went wrong with your plan don't you?", the General addressed the Prophet and asked them.

"We didn't expect the head Demon to come up to L5 and start tracking us down", the Prophet replied, "At least, not that quickly. He was onto us straight away."

"Yes, true, but that was not where the mistake was made", the General replied, explaining "You tested your plan out with a single attack and that attack led to a response, a response that you had not anticipated adequately", he was pointing his finger in the air and shaking it back and forth.

"So we shouldn't have attacked their Academy?", the Prophet asked.

"No. No. No. The attack should have happened, yes, but it should have been done all in one fell swoop", the General explained, "That way, it would all have been done and dusted, with no chance of any retaliation."

"So the problem, was us wanting to perform a test run", Matthew asked, adding, "Had we performed a single massive, multi-pronged attack, we would have been successful."

"Yes, that's it in a nutshell", the General replied, adding "Overwhelming force in a single massive, multi-pronged attack and you would have won!"

"Tell them our plan", the High Prince told the General.

The General began, "We are going to launch a massive, overwhelming missile strike with multiple cold fusion warheads", he stated, "Most of those missiles will be aimed at the Earth, to take out their military industrial complexes and large population centres. A good portion of those missiles will be aimed at L5 to destroy some of their larger colonies and to create fear, mass panic and destruction."

Matthew asked, "That will take out the Earth and L5, but what about Mars?"

The General gave Matthew his answer, "We have allotted eight missile for Mars. One for each of the seven original official colonies and one for that new colony in Elysium."

"You will need one more General", Matthew replied, adding "You'll want to hit the demon's fortress, their nest, it's to the north of the Elysium colony. I can give you the precise coordinates."

"Well that is good to know. Thank you Matthew", the General replied adding, "It's not enough to destroy those nine targets, we will also need to occupy the planet as well."

"And you have that planned out as well?", the Prophet enquired

"Why yes, of course", the General replied, explaining "We're going to send in the Trojan Armed Forces to occupy the nine target zones on Mars. That way, we will literally control the whole Planet. We are also sending even more of our Trojan Armed Forces to L5 to occupy the high ground above the Earth. The whole of L5. Once we have achieved mastery over the Earth, L5 and Mars, all of the other inner solar system colonies will surrender. They will have no other choice in the matter. It will be fait accompli. A done deal."

Matthew queried, "How many missiles are you going to hit them with?"

The General turned to Matthew and replied smiling, "We are going to hit them with our entire arsenal! Thousands of missiles, all with multiple cold fusion warheads. A huge, massive strike that they won't be able to block and they won't be able to recover from either."

"Wow!", the Prophet exclaimed, "That sounds like a plan!"

Matthew was not so sure. It was a massive, multi-pronged attack, one fell swoop so to speak, but it was also a massive gamble. A one hit, one shot salvo that would either be successful or it would not.

"Do we have a back up plan?", Matthew asked.

"While our missiles are on their way, we will be building more of them", the General replied, "We will be replenishing our stocks for possible future salvos."

"And L5. What if the Colonial Fleet comes this way?", Matthew inquired.

"The Colonial Fleet will be too busy trying to stop our first salvo", the General explained, "And after our missiles strike, they'll will be too busy dealing with all the death and destruction to even think of retaliation. We expect they will be too busy to do much of anything except saving lives."

"We fully expect that L5's Colonial Central will surrender, rather than face another salvo of cold fusion missiles", the other General, General Snide stepped in.

He then added, "Our own Armed Forces will be following up after the initial attack and occupy L5 shortly after the first missiles strike."

"Okay. So we will have the occupation forces following the missiles?", Matthew queried.

"Of course lad, of course lad", General Snide replied.

"This plan", the Prophet began, "When is it being put into motion?", he inquired.

The High Prince smiled a broad smile, "Well the timing is in God's hands actually", he stated.

"God's hands?", the Prophet queried.

"Yes. I decided that we'd make our move and put our plan into action on the birthday of my Brother Leopold's First Son, which should be any day now. It is truly wonderful that you arrived when you did, at such an auspicious time."

Three days later Prince Leopold's Wife, Giselle, Princess of Io, gave birth to her first child, a Boy, they named him Ulrick. One hour later, High Prince Heinrich von Horridian gave the orders to launch the simultaneous attacks on Earth, L5 and Mars.

A birthday gift from High Prince Heinrich to his newly born nephew Ulrick.

7. The Swamps of The Kasei

Leroy McGuvan was staying with Zuawalo's family in their *"cave"* carved into the cliff face. At first they were not happy with this turn of events. However the village Kujur, Gwek had assured them that the very bad man was gone, demolished and this new Leroy could be redeemed. Gwek had stressed how important it was that Leroy's redemption was kept on track. "It must be done!", he had said.

Leroy McGuvan worked in the fields and orchards of Zuawalo's village. Zuawalo kept an ever careful eye over him, as did Zuawalo's whole family. Even though at first they were quite distrusting of him, they noted how hard he worked and how awful he felt about his past.

After working in the fields all day, Leroy would work on the boats that had been damaged by the storm and its huge waves. Helping the villagers repair both the boats and the docks that had been damaged as well. Leroy worked harder than any man in the village, it was hard to believe this man was that same very bad man, the evil man that had been pulled out the Hebes Sea by Zuawalo Pod.

Each night when Leroy slept, he would wake up screaming and covered in sweat, having dreamt of some horrible memory from his past. Those memories that had not disturbed him in that past, however since his demolishing, now those same memories now haunted his dreams.

Zuawalo found herself entering the room where Leroy slept and wiping the sweat from his brow and consoling him, helping him to get back to sleep, only for the same thing to happen a few hours later. This happened several times every night.

"A man cannot live like this Gwek", Zuawalo told the village Kujur.

"A man will live like this until he walks the path of redemption", would be Gwek's cryptic reply.

"And where is this path of redemption you talk of?", Zuawalo would question.

"It is in a man's heart and in a man's head", Gwek replied, "Only a man can decide a man's fate."

Then one day, Leroy told Zuawalo, "I cannot live like this. I must go to him."

"To him?", Zuawalo asked, slightly perplexed.

"To him!", Leroy stated, "To him! The one who executed me!"

Then Zuawalo understood, the path of redemption, was the path that led to the Great Wizard, the one who had executed that very bad man, that had once been Leroy McGuvan.

"Where is he Leroy?", Zuawalo asked.

Leroy answered, "He is in a Psychic Academy on the Elysium subcontinent."

"That is a very, very long way from here Zuawalo!", Zuawalo's Mother exclaimed, "How will you be getting there now?"

"I do not know!", Zuawalo shouted back.

"You could go east to the colony at Aurorae", Zuawalo's Father, Kwoth suggested.

"That is a long way by boat, through the deep Marineris Sea, very dangerous", Zuawalo's Mother replied, "And the old quarter of Aurorae Colony has many bad people, too many bad people. I do not want Zuawalo to go anywhere near that place."

Zuawalo's Mother was quite adamant about that.

"Cutting across Lunae Planum to the North or the Maja Valles to the North East, to Chryse are no less dangerous", Zuawalo's Father reminded her.

"Yes, but Chryse Colony is a much safer place and catching a hummer from there to Elysium should be very simple", Zuawalo's Mother reminded him.

"Zuawalo can take the Kasei Valley Swamp", Zeealas told them excitedly, "Follow that north and then west, it will take Zuawalo straight to Chryse Colony."

"There are many dangerous animals in the Swamps of Kasei", Zuawalo's Mother noted.

Zuawalo stepped in, "Our people hunt and fish in those swamps all the time. There is nothing there that I cannot handle. I have even hunted and fished there before myself."

Zeealas added, "People don't like swamps. People usually keep clear of them. So there should not be any bad people in the Kasai. This time of year, hardly anyone goes there."

"A canoe with outriggers and a small sail could take us straight to Chryse Colony", Zuawalo was already working out the trip out in her head.

"Yes, but you have to take the Hebes River and get down the Hummocks first", Zuawalo's Father reminded them.

Leroy, who had been silent during this whole discussion, then asked, "But can we do it?"

"Yes, yes", Zuawalo's Father stated, "But you will need to be very careful. Getting a canoe down the Hebes River is no simple task. There are five big waterfalls, the Hummocks and you need to carry the canoe and everything around them. You will need a very good guide."

Then Zuawalo's Mother stepped in, "And you will need to avoid the animals of the swamps."

Leroy nodded in understanding.

"I can go Mother. I can do this thing", Zuawalo asked.

"I know you Zuawalo. If I say no, will you accept that?", her Mother replied.

Zuawalo didn't answer, Zuawalo simply smiled.

"You can go Zuawalo, but you must promise me you will be careful", Zuawalo's Mother told her.

"If Zuawalo is going, then I am going too" Zeealas told her Parents excitedly.

"Zeealas. I do not want you to go!", her Mother replied with a concerned voice.

"Why not?", Zeealas responded, "I can look after myself, just as well as Zuawalo."

Their Father pointed out, "They are two peas in a pod. If one goes, how do you stop the other?"

Their Mother frowned, she knew her Husband was right, "Zuawalo, you look after Zeealas."

"Don't worry, I will look after them both", Leroy told their Parents.

The Mother snorted in derision, "My daughters! They will be the ones looking after you!", there was fire in their Mothers eyes.

Both Zuawalo and Zeealas smiled at each other, they were going on an adventure, their biggest adventure yet. Zuawalo had been to the Kasei before, for Zeealas it would be her first time.

The whole next day was spent preparing for the trip to Chryse Colony. A canoe with outriggers and a small sail had been procured and supplies had been stowed aboard it. There was room in the canoe for five people, but only four would be going on the trip. Zuawalo, Zeealas and Leroy McGuvan, but they were also being accompanied by the canoe's owner Gatwech, who would bring the canoe back to the village, when the trip to Chryse Colony was completed.

For the first leg of the trip down the Hebes River and around the Hummocks, they were also being accompanied by eight more village men in four other canoes. These villagers were going to help port Gatwech's canoe around the Hebes River and its five waterfalls, the Hummocks.

Early the following morning they prepared to leave. Gatwech sat in the rear of the canoe, waiting for his passengers to climb aboard.

Zuawalo's Father passed Leroy a pulse pistol, "You had this on you when you were found", he told Leroy, "I give it back to you now, so you can keep my Daughters safe."

Leroy looked down upon the weapon, it brought back bad memories Leroy shuddered, "I cannot take that", he stated still looking down at the pulse pistol in Zuawalo's Father's hand.

Leroy took the pulse pistol, then passed it straight to Zuawalo, "I will trust you with this Zuawalo. If you don't know how to use it, I will teach you."

Zuawalo wasn't sure what to do with it and replied, "I'd rather use my bow."

"I know Zuawalo, but there may be a time when you need to use this", Leroy insisted.

Leroy thanked Zuawalo's Parents and the other gathered village folk, before climbing aboard the canoe in the seat ahead of Gatwech.

Zeealas hugged the Father, then her Mother, before climbing aboard the canoe ahead of Leroy.

Zuawalo hugged her Father, "Look after your Sister", he told her.

Zuawalo then hugged her Mother, then "You will need this", her Mother said passing Zuawalo a rather heavy leather pouch. Zuawalo opened it and looked inside. It contained quite a few small circular disks of differing sizes, with ornate markings on them.

Zuawalo's Mother, explained "They are gold. Keep them hidden. Gold can drive some men mad. He", pointing to Leroy McGuvan, "will know what to do with it, when you get to Chryse Colony."

Zuawalo nodded to her Mother and placed the pouch into her satchel, then climbed into her seat at front of the canoe.

It was just after midday when they reached the Hebes River, the only outflow of the fresh water Hebes Sea. They followed the river westward to just before the first water fall, then pulled the canoe ashore on the southern river bank. There was a trail here that was used by Zuawalo's village for accessing the Kasei Valley far below them. The other four canoes had also pulled ashore and everyone was now standing on the river bank.

"Let's get to work", Gatwech told the others.

Zuawalo and Zeealas grabbed ropes from the other canoes and started following the trail along the southern river bank. Then they followed the trail south west away from the river.

Leroy watched as the eight village men and Gatwech hauled their canoe out of the water and began to drag it along the trail. Leroy joined in and helped them to port the canoe. The men had brought log rollers with them to make the porting of the canoe easier.

It took the best part of two hours to haul the canoe to the end of the trail and there waiting for them was Zuawalo and Zeealas. The girls were standing by the edge of a high cliff. At the edge of the cliff was a large wooden gantry with a heavy block and tackle mounted to one end. That end hung out over the cliff face above the valley far below.

The girls had been busy joining heavy ropes together and getting them ready to lower the canoe to the ground far below the cliff.

Gatwech made himself busy, making sure all the supplies and equipment were securely strapped into the canoe. It appeared the whole canoe, complete with all their supplies and equipment, was going to be lowered over the side of the cliff.

"How far down is it?", Leroy asked Gatwech.

Gatwech looked back over his shoulder to the cliff, then back to Leroy, "A little over three thousand feet", he replied.

Zuawalo walked over to Leroy and pointed to the north east, "You may have missed something."

Indeed Leroy had. He was so focused on hauling canoe and the "crane" that they were going to use to winch the canoe and equipment down the cliff face, he failed to notice the waterfalls in the distance behind him.

Leroy looked behind him to where Zuawalo was pointing, up the valley towards the Hebes River were the waterfalls. In the distance amongst the mist and spray, Leroy could discern that there were five falls in all.

"Whoa. How did I miss that?", he asked himself, "Five times she drops", he stated silently to himself, almost under his breath.

Rainbows formed within the mist and spray, the sight was truly spectacular.

The first of the falls was broad and dropped about a five hundred feet. There was a large deep pond at its base. The pond the waterfall dropped into was equally broad, but not nearly as long as it was broad.

The pond branched into three outlets, each of which comprised the second falls, but dropping only about three hundred feet each. Somewhat smaller in height than the first falls, but far more spectacular in breadth.

The second pond below this waterfall was equally as broad as the first, but somewhat longer in its length. It had one single outlet, with the third falls dropping at least a fifteen hundred feet. That was a truly spectacular sight. This long ribbon of water and spray pouring down the cliff face.

The forth and fifth falls, each dropped about four hundred feet or so. The forth falls spilling over chaotically at a great many points, so many it was almost a continuous curtain for water spraying forth. The forth falls poured through so many outlets that one could not possibly count them all.

That was followed by the fifth falls, spilling over at one single point and eventually flowing through a deep, narrow chasm at its base, before slowing into a deep broad river at the base of the entire system.

There was a lot of water spilling out of the Hebe Sea through these falls, the Hummocks and doing so in the space of only a few short miles or so. It was truly spectacular!

Given enough time the Hebes River would eventually carve the outflow all the way back to the Hebes Sea itself and it would drain the sea entirely. That however, would be several millions of years into the future.

Zuawalo waited for Leroy to take in the vista before him, before tapping his should and pointing to the north, "The Kasei Valley and the Kasei Swamps", she informed him.

Leroy looked far to the north over the Kasei Valley and its Swamps. The river was slow moving, ever so slow, branching into so many branches that Leroy could not possibly count them all. There were islands in the swamps, countless islands, everywhere dotting the swamp here and there. The swamp seemed endless, only to disappear into a thick haze of low clouds to the far north.

Yet the swamp wasn't just swamp. There were many stands of trees covering nearly all of the islands and on banks at the edges of the swamps were broad grasslands and yet more stands of trees, some of which were incredibly vast in area.

Off to the west of the swampy banks, Leroy could see lakes of various sizes, both large and small. The plains eventually giving way to the sweeping hills and slopes leading up to the Volcano Tharsis Tholus, that could be seen in the distance.

Sweeping his gaze to the east, Leroy could see the far eastern banks of the swamps, as they gradually lifted up and into the upland regions of Lunae Planum. The hills were heavily forested in that area and once away from the swamps, quickly lifted far higher and higher until they were level with his current vantage point.

Then Leroy looked immediately in front of him. Far below them was a large lake, which filled a large bowel shaped basin, that then narrowed somewhat to the north. The lake then broke through into the Echus Chasma, before eventually continuing further into the greater Kasei Valley.

Before Leroy was the majesty of possibly the largest system of volcanic channels in the entire solar system.

The vista before them was both awesome and spectacular.

A wave of vertigo swept through Leroy and Zuawalo grabbed him by the arm to steady him.

Leroy was at a loss for words, "Oh my", was all that came out of his mouth.

Zuawalo replied, "Mars is my home. It is such a beautiful place", a smile beaming upon her face.

"How on Earth are we going to navigate all of that?", Leroy asked Zuawalo.

"Mars", Zuawalo replied, "How on Mars are we going to navigate all that?", it was a rhetorical question, which Zuawalo quickly answered, "We follow the deepest channels of course."

"The deepest channels?", Leroy inquired.

"Of course, the deepest channels, they're usually the right ones", Zuawalo explained.

Leroy turned back to the '*crane*', he hadn't noticed, but while taking in the incredible vista of the Kasei Valley, the crane had been swung onto the cliff top. The canoe had been hooked up and it was then swung back out over the edge of the cliff with the canoe hanging from it.

Slowly the canoe was being winched to the ground more than three thousand feet below.

"Exactly how do we get down there?", Leroy asked Zuawalo.

"Stupid man! The same way!", Zuawalo's eyes rolled, "I hope you're not afraid of heights."

Zeealas looked to be as much in awe of this place, overlooking the Hebes Falls and the Kasei Valley and its Swamps, as Leroy. Whereas Zuawalo had been here before with her Father, Zeealas had not.

"This is a magical place", Zeealas told her Sister, "Look at the those birds", she stated, pointing across the Kasei Valley.

"Birds?", Leroy questioned.

"Yes, Birds", Zeealas answered, "A lot of birds and other animals were brought to Mars. Most were brought here to be eaten. You know, sources of food. Some were brought here to be pets."

"You will find down there, the descendants of chickens, quails, ducks, geese, turkeys, pigeons, doves, parrots, cats, dogs, ferrets and much, much more", Zuawalo rattled off a list, "All of them have gone wild. They are very different to the ones that were originally brought here from the Earth though. Mars does that!"

"Are there fish in the swamps as well?", Leroy asked.

"Yes, lots, lots of fish", Zuawalo answered, "Fish and other water creatures like squid and crustaceans, were brought to Mars and seeded into all the bodies of water. All of them genetically modified. The animals you see out there though, their ancestors escaped from farms and from captivity. They became feral and bred in the wild. There are even very big snakes!"

"Why on Earth would there be snakes?", Leroy asked in a curious voice.

"Someone thought it would be nice to eat them or maybe they were to be pets. I do not know", Zuawalo answered, adding "People be crazy. Do crazy things...", then "And it is why on Mars."

"Why on Mars?", Leroy gave Zuawalo a quizzical look, it had not set in.

"This is Mars Leroy", Zuawalo answered him, rolling her eyes, "You live on Mars now!"

Zeealas added, "We have fishing rods in the canoe and our hunting bows."

Leroy gave Zeealas a funny look, as if to ask why the need for fishing rods and hunting bows.

"You didn't notice how little food we packed in our supplies?", Zeealas asked.

"I didn't really notice", Leroy admitted.

Zuawalo explained, "It takes three, sometimes four weeks to get to Chryse Colony. Leroy! We are going to be living off the land, hunting and fishing", then turning to Zeealas, "Do not shoot any sligs Zeealas. I do not want to eat slig meat!"

Leroy picked up on that, "Yeah, good idea", he stated, "I don't want to eat slork either."

Zeealas rolled here eyes, "Okay, okay", then commenting, "It is not so bad if you eat it with spiced vinegar and chilli."

"No sligs!", Zuawalo and Leroy both replied at the same time.

Gatwech had been working diligently on getting their canoe down to the valley floor far below them. It was now only a couple of hundred feet above the valley floor.

"You all need to get ready", Gatwech told Leroy and the Pod Sisters.

"Ready?", Leroy queried with a slightly fearful look on his face.

"Yes, get ready", Gatwech replied, adding "Get your harnesses on. How else do you think you're getting down into that valley."

Zuawalo, her Sister Zeealas, Leroy and Gatwech all harnessed up and got ready for the descent down to the valley floor, more than three thousand feet below. Their canoe had already been lowered and moved out of the way in preparation for their descent. Before the hour was out, all four of them had been lowered to the valley floor. For most of that, Leroy held his eyes firmly shut.

Once they were on the ground at the base of the cliff, they all removed their harnesses. Towards the west, off to one side there was a small cabin. They all entered the cabin and hung their harnesses on the hooks on the cabin wall. Then they began to settle in for the night.

The next morning Leroy stepped out of the cabin. His companions, Zuawalo, Zeealas and Gatwech were already out and about, having woken up much earlier. More importantly, they already had the canoe in the water and were now ready to go.

"You sleep too long!", Zeealas chided him.

"I didn't notice the sun come up", Leroy replied, they were after all in the bowel of a valley at the head of the Kasei and although it was light outside, the sun was yet to peak over the cliff tops.

Leroy rubbed his eyes, Zuawalo grew impatient, rolled her eyes and grabbed Leroy by the wrist, dragging him to the canoe, "You can wake up in the canoe! Get in!", she told him.

Leroy climbed into his seat as they pushed off from the shore. To the east in the distance could be seen the mists of the Hebes Falls, the Hummocks and although not that close, they could be heard quite clearly.

The water under the canoe had a slow, placid flow northwards, towards the narrowing of the basin that led to through to the Echus Chasma and then further north to the Kasei Valley and the swamps. Gatwech had set the sail and the Pod sisters began to paddle. It wasn't very long before they were through the gap and entering the southern expanses of the swamps.

They canoed north, tracing the western shore of the swamps, in a broad stretch of water, but never getting too close, always staying far closer to the islands they were passing on their right.

Here the water was only about six feet deep at the most and Zuawalo kept a sharp eye out for any shallows that they might indicate the need to take a deeper channel.

"Why so far from the shore?", Leroy asked.

"Safer on this side", Zuawalo replied, explaining, "All the danger comes from over there", pointing to their left.

Zuawalo added, "Most of the animals over there cannot swim. Those that swim, don't like to swim this far. Dangerous for them in the water."

"Dangerous in the water? Why?", Leroy requested a bit of clarification.

"Snakes", Zuawalo informed him, "Anacondas will eat them."

"And we're not concerned about the snakes?", Leroy asked.

Zeealas turn around and smiled at Leroy, "They do not eat us. We eat the snakes!"

"And the Islands?", Leroy asked while gesturing to their right.

This time Gatwech answered, "The animals on the islands are mostly birds. It is safe for them there on the islands. That is where they nest. The other animals on the islands are very small. Little scurrying things. Not of concern to us."

Gatwech tapped Leroy on the shoulder and passed him a pair of field glasses.

"Look over there", Gatwech told him, while pointing to the left bank ahead of them.

Leroy placed the field glasses to his eyes and looked to where Gatwech was pointing.

The objects slowly came in to focus. It was a cat, but as Leroy looked at it, it could not be any ordinary cat, as it had its paws on the corpse of another, far larger animal. One that an ordinary household moggy simply could not kill. The prey animal was a slig, an animal spliced from porcine and slug genetics.

It looked like a fat, slug, pig, manatee kind of thing, with its short stubby useless legs. Its face, as you might expect, was quite pig like and one got the sense that it was a creature of abundant snot and drool. It was truly an ugly creature.

The size of the slig, being a good seven or eight feet long, meant that the cat was at least as big as a large wolf, probably larger. It had killed the slig and managed to drag it out of the water. A big cat it was indeed. As Leroy watched, the cat was making a meal of its victim, ripping out large chunks of flesh with its long, sharp canine teeth. Leroy turned around to Gatwech.

"That is why we are over here and not over there", he told Leroy, "That cat's ancestors would have been ordinary house cats."

"Ordinary house cats", Leroy muttered, "That's so hard to believe."

Zeealas who had been listening added, "Mars does that to feral animals Leroy."

It was not long before they were passing the cat and its victim. The cat had no interest in them at all. It already had its prey and they were too far away and in the water. As Leroy watched another large cat of almost equal size was approaching the scene from farther inland.

"That one, will be the other cat's mate", Gatwech informed Leroy.

Leroy watched as the second cat joined the first cat, for its share of the feast.

Towards dusk, Gatwech turned the canoe eastward into a channel between two islands. The first island was quite small, the second island somewhat larger. The channel itself was narrow and they soon passed behind the second island and could no longer see the western shore of the swamp.

Gatwech let the canoe follow the slow current north for a short while, then turned the canoe to the island's banks.

Leroy looked around, there were a great many islands to the east of them, far too many to count and all of varying sizes. As they stepped out of the canoe and onto shore, Leroy noticed that this particular section of beach had been used before. Perhaps many times. It appeared to be a regular stopping place.

Gatwech had obviously been here before and was well acquainted with this place. They started a small camp fire inside a ring of stones that had been used previously on some other occasion, then they set up camp. There on the swamp island they ate dried squid, jerked meat and fruit before going to sleep for the night.

The next day they were all up early, right at the crack of dawn. The Pod Sisters cleaned up camp while Gatwech and Leroy prepared the canoe. Leroy had made sure he was awake at the same time as his companions. In quick time they were back in the water and heading north in the canoe once more. Zeealas sitting in the middle seat passed jerked meat to the others to eat for their breakfast.

They paddled the canoe north until they reach the end of the island they had just spent the night on. Then Gatwech turned the canoe westward through a broad gap between that island and the next. Soon they were back in the main west passage catching a good wind heading northwards. The morning passed quite quickly and sometime well after midday, they could hear barking from the western shore.

Leroy picked up the field glasses that were still by his seat and started scouting the far shore line where the barking was coming from. He quickly located the source. It was a number dogs in a pack, at least eight of them and to his eyes they looked like bull terriers, only longer and taller. Mars had done its thing again and these bulldogs were up-scaled to be easily as big as wolves.

The dog pack was running up and down the shoreline, barking excitedly, bouncing off one and other and generally following the canoe's movement to the north. At a glance, they almost looked playful, as if you could just walk up to them and treat them like ordinary Earth dogs.

"Do not let them fool you Leroy", Gatwech remarked, explaining, "They only look playful. Trust me though, if you get too close to them, they will be as viscous as wolves. Rip you apart they will, given half the chance."

Zeealas turned around, looked at Leroy and went click, click with her teeth, then laughed.

Leroy gave an ever so slight gulp, "Well then, we'll just stay safely over here, yeah."

Gatwech chuckled, "They can swim", then when he noticed Leroy's discomfort at that remark, "but they do not like the water that much, too cold and they will not attempt swimming this far."

The dog pack followed the canoe along the shore line for another thirty minutes or so, then seemed to get bored with them or perhaps they were hungry, the pack turned inland.

They continued northwards at quick clip. It was quite an uneventful afternoon and soon the days end was getting close.

Towards dusk Zeealas extend a telescopic fishing rod, hooked an appropriate lure onto the end of the line, then trawled the lure in the water on the outside of the port outrigger.

Nothing much seemed to happen for what seemed like a long time, then bang! It was fish on!

"I've got one!", screeched Zeealas with joy, adding "It is big!"

Zeealas tightened up the tension on the reel and began reeling in the fish. It put quite a fight, but was no match for Zeealas, who soon had the fish hanging over the port outrigger and then quickly into the boat in front of her.

"What kind of fish is it?", Leroy, who thought it looked like a small Nile Perch or a large Barramundi, asked.

"Who cares? It is dinner. Or would you like to eat squid again?", Zeealas replied with a rhetorical question.

"Fish is good Zeealas, fish is good", Leroy told her, giving her a thumbs up when Zeealas turned around and looked at him. The sheer joy at having caught the fish clearly showed in her eyes.

Zeealas reached around to her back, pulled a sheath knife from out of a hidden leather scabbard under her vest, then used it to dispatch the fish. In quick, fluid motions, she cut the fishes throat, gutted it and placed it into a bucket on the seat in front of her. Having cleaned the knife, Zeealas then replaced it back into the leather scabbard.

Had Leroy not seen her take out the knife, he would never have known that Zeealas had it.

Zuawalo in the front seat, turned around and looked into the bucket, "Good catch Sister!"

Closer to night fall now Gatwech turned the canoe eastward off the main channel and took it into the shallow waters behind yet another island once more. The procedure was very much the same as the previous night. When they had pulled the canoe ashore, it was clear that this place had also been

Page: 77

used before as a camping spot, perhaps many times.

Leroy asked, "How many camping places are there along here?"

"More than you might guess at", Gatwech replied, adding "It is still to early now, but later in the season, these channels are used quite often for fishing and hunting by a lot of high country folk."

Zeealas cooked her fish and they shared it over the camp fire, which again Leroy noticed was an already prepared circle of stones. Tastes like Barramundi, Leroy had thought, a fish that was commonly eaten in the L5 Colonies. It made sense that it had been adapted to Mars.

The following day started the same way as the previous one. They were all up before the crack of dawn, the Pod Sisters cleaned up camp while Gatwech and Leroy prepared the canoe. Breakfast was jerked meat once more. It wasn't long before they had crossed westward into the main west passage and were heading north again.

Nothing much happened on this day. They ate the left over Barramundi for lunch while still canoeing and the day passed ever so slowly. Towards the end of the day, Zeealas took out her fishing rod once more, stretching it out to full length and trolling a lure over the port side outrigger.

In no time at all, bang! It was fish on once more. Zeealas reeled the fish in, dispatched it, gutted it and tossed it into the bucket in front of her. Then to Leroy's surprise, Zeealas trawled the lure once more over the port side outrigger.

"One fish not enough for today?", Leroy asked her.

"I want to smoke some fish overnight", Zeealas replied, "It will keep much longer."

"So one to eat and one to smoke?", Leroy asked.

"No. I want to smoke three fish", Zeealas replied, then to Zuawalo she enquired, "Sister,. How is your bow arm?"

Zuawalo replied, "Good I think. What are you thinking Zeealas?"

"Duck, I am thinking duck", Zeealas replied.

Leroy smiled, "Duck sounds good", he agreed.

"Yes. Duck sounds very good Zuawalo", Gatwech agreed as well.

"Then duck it shall be", Zuawalo replied.

Zeealas had three fish in the bucket and Gatwech turned the boat eastward once more through another broad gap between some islands. It seemed a bit early in the day to be heading into the shallows, but Gatwech obviously knew what he was doing, so Leroy was not concerned.

Zuawalo had taken her bow out. It was a take down bow and was in three pieces. Zuawalo expertly assembled her bow, then strung it. Watching the eastern shore of the island carefully for any sign of ducks as the canoe slowly and silently slipped passed, Zuawalo slowly and carefully rose to her feet.

Zuawalo took an arrow out of her quiver and slowly nocked the arrow. Leroy noticed a thin, light line attached the arrows shaft. Then something caught Zuawalo's eye and she slowly held the bow out at arms length. The canoe glid slowly, ever so quietly along the shallows.

Zuawalo took aim and held herself perfectly still, breathing in slow, controlled breaths. Leroy looked to where Zuawalo was aiming and could just make out the shape of a duck. Everything was quiet, the canoe continued to glide. Loose! The arrow was in flight!

Zuawalo's arrow flew true to its target. The duck flopped down dead in the water, the arrow through its body just below its neck. It was a good clean kill. Carefully Zuawalo sat back down in her seat, passing her bow to Zeealas as she did so. Then slowly and carefully, Zuawalo pulled the duck towards the canoe.

"Good shot Zuawalo!", Leroy remarked.

Zeealas turned to Leroy, "Yes. Zuawalo is very good with her bow", then turning back to Zuawalo, "Good shot Sister!"

While Zuawalo slowly pulled the duck back to the canoe using the arrows tethered line, Zeealas packed away the bow. It wasn't long before the duck was in the canoe and Zuawalo was processing it, expertly plucking and gutting the duck with an efficiency that showed both skill and practice.

Leroy noticed that Zuawalo also carried a sheath knife hidden under the back of her vest.

"These Girls know how to hunt and fish", Gatwech explained to Leroy, "It is the way in our village. Everyone learns these things. The Pod Sisters are experts at survival. You could learn a lot from these girls."

It was then that Leroy could see why Zuawalo had so carefully and slowly dragged the duck back to the boat. No sooner than Zuawalo had discarded the guts, there was a flurry of activity in the water.

Gatwech took the boat farther north along the shallows, past the "duck" island and the next, before finally locating a small beach on another island and turning the canoe into the islands eastern shore. Yet another camp site, that also appeared to have been used before. Zuawalo started the fire and started roasting the duck. Zeealas quickly made a make shift smoker and began to smoke her brace of fish.

Leroy looked around to the east, so many islands. Far too many to count. Most were probably only a foot or maybe two feet above the water level, others maybe mere inches if that. It appeared to   Leroy that Gatwech was making sure he stayed close to the main western passage. Leroy could see why. Get too far into the Kasei Swamp and you could be stuck there for a very, very long time indeed. The Kasei Swamp was vast, ever so vast!

They all ate well that night and had smoked fish to last them for while. The next day they followed the same morning procedure as the previous days, only for breakfast they had left over roast duck.

And that was how they travelled northward along main western passage of the Kasei Swamp.

On the sixth day they were passing through a very broad stretch of water between two more islands. The water seemed shallower in this region and Leroy noticed something different far off in the distance to the east.

"What is that?", Leroy questioned while pointing to what looked like an exceptionally high piece of real estate far off to the east.

Zuawalo turned around and told him, "That is the Island!"

"The Island?", Leroy asked.

"Yes. It is the biggest Island in the southern swamps of the Kasei. So it is the Island", Zuawalo replied emphatically.

"It is a very high island, unlike the others in the place. It is like a mountain", Zeealas explained, "We have many, many cousins over there. I have yet to meet them. They live in the Swamp."

"Swamp people?", Leroy asked while using the field glasses to get a better look.

"Yes. Some of our people thought, it more convenient to move here and live here, rather than travel here from our village", Zuawalo explained, "Many cousins over there. I have been there."

"Will we be going there?" Leroy asked.

"No, sadly we have no time to visit our cousins" Zuawalo informed him in a sad tone.

"We go there, we will be there for weeks", Gatwech explained, "Too many friends and too many family to visit and catch up with."

Later that same day, Zuawalo spied something in the distance that caught her eye.

"Pass me the glasses", she requested.

Leroy passed the field glasses forward and Zuawalo excitedly began scanning the western shore.

"We go there Gatwech", Zuawalo insisted pointing,"We need to go there!"

"To the shore?", Gatwech asked.

"Yes. Yes. To the shore. Over there!" Zuawalo replied still pointing.

Gatwech dutifully turned the canoe and they all began paddling to the western shore, where they pulled up on a sand bank, leaving just a small gap of water between them and the shore.

Zuawalo immediately jumped out of the canoe and waded through the cold water, "I'll be back in a few minutes", a shivering Zuawalo told them.

The water between the sand bank and the western shore was fairly shallow and Zuawalo was soon on the other side, where she climbed the bank and quickly ran over to a large hole that was in the bank of the swamp.

Much to their surprise, Zuawalo, after looking around cautiously, quickly crawled into the hole.

"Oh, the smell, Ugh!", Zuawalo said to herself, as she crawled deeper into the hole.

Then she found what she was looking for. At the end of the hole were eight or nine ferret kits. They stunk as only ferret kits can.

One, by one, Zuawalo quickly *"scruffed"* the kits. Zuawalo did this by picking them up by the scruff of the neck and observing their behaviour.

The first few, twisted and squirmed almost uncontrollably, so she gently put them back down. Eventually she found one, a male, it just hung there by the scruff of the neck, quite placidly and just yawned. Zuawalo put it back down, shook it gently to make sure it was fully awake and then scruffed it again. Again it just hung there placidly and yawned.

Zuawalo backed herself out of the hole, taking the male ferret kit with her. Once out of the hole, Zuawalo cautiously glanced around once more and then made her way back across the cold, shallow water to the sand bank and the waiting canoe.

"Zuawalo you stink!", Zeealas yelled at her, "Oh that smell, it is awful!"

Leroy began to gag and came close to throwing up.

Zuawalo replied, "Pass me my bag", which Zeealas did and they all watched as Zuawalo placed the ferret kit into the bag and then placed the bag by her seat.

After which Zuawalo went back into the cold water to wash off the muck and stench. It took several minutes before Zuawalo was satisfied and came back to her seat in the canoe, still shivering.

"Much better Sister", Zeealas told her, "A pole cat? Really?", as they were known to her people.

"Yes Zeealas", Zuawalo replied, "You know I've always wanted one. I'm calling him Zigg."

Gatwech shook his head, "Girls", he muttered as they began paddling back to safety, closer to the islands in the swamp.

As they moved further from the western shoreline, Leroy noticed a business of ferrets moving around, getting closer to the hole in the bank from which Zuawalo had taken the ferret kit.

A couple of the ferrets darted into the hole, then coming back out of the hole, they urgently searched around the banks of the swamp. On seeing the four travellers in their canoe, the ferrets immediately took to the cold water, the other ferrets all followed frantically. They only went as far as the end of the sand bank and then sat there watching. The ferrets knew the waters were too dangerous to follow any further.

Leroy noticed they were big, at least twice, maybe three times normal size, "These ferrets get rather big Zuawalo", he remarked, "*Mars doing its thing again*", he thought to himself.

"Yes", Zuawalo replied, "But when he imprints on me, he will be very loyal", she stated while feeding the ferret kit Zigg pieces of duck and stroking its head.

On the seventeenth day, having been travelling north for all that time, Gatwech changed course to a more eastward direction. The western passage appeared to be forking into what looked like two main river channels.

One of the channels appeared to heading further to the north and not in the direction that Gatwech wanted to go. The other channel took a more easterly course and looked as if it would pass through a distant chasm with high walls and plateau country on either side.

This made sense to Leroy, as for the last four or five days the swamp had been changing. The islands along the way had been getting larger and higher. They had even been camping on the islands western shores, instead of going into the shallows on their eastern sides. Even the flow of the water seemed to be picking up pace, although doing so ever so slowly. Yes, the swamps of the Kasei had been changing.

"Once we hit the river, we should really start moving along", Gatwech informed Leroy.

"How long until we get to Chryse?", Leroy asked.

"Eight days I expect", Gatwech replied, "then we should be within sight of Chryce."

"And the river?", Leroy enquired.

"It moves fast", Gatwech replied, adding "but it will be quite smooth. Very safe."

The canoe swiftly picked up pace on this stretch of the Kasei Valley. They were now well and truly in the Kasei River and they all knew it. No need to paddle, no need for the sail, which Gatwech stowed away. They camped along small stretches of beach along the shoreline over night. Relying on the smoked fish and supplies they'd gathered in the Kasei Swamps, catching only the occasional fish, trawling for Trout in the River. A day and a half into the river and the canyon walls began to loom large as they approached them.

High plateau county was now on either side of them, the Sacra Mensa Plateau to the North and Lunae Planum to the south. The canyon was steep, rugged and many caves could be seen along the way. Indeed the canyon became quite tight, very narrow and yet the river's current, although fast, was as Gatwech had told them, quite smooth. They were not encountering any rapids at all.

"This river is very fast Gatwech", Leroy had noted, questioning, "How on Earth are you going to get back to the Hebes Falls?"

Gatwech replied, first with, "How on Mars Leroy! How on Mars!", then followed with "On the return trip. I'll cut north west, across the lesser swamps between Sacra Mensa and Sharonov Crater."

"Sorry, I keep forgetting this is Mars", Leroy apologised.

"No problem Leroy", Gatwech replied, continuing, "The northern branch of the Kasei Valley outflow, we call it the North Kasei River, is much slower. I will use that course to make my way back home."

"Okay, that makes sense", Leroy answered him, "I'm glad you know your way around here."

"Yes Leroy. I use to come here a lot to hunt and fish when I was younger", Gatwech explained.

Their progress along the Kasei River was swift and true to Gatwech's word, eight days later, in the late afternoon, they caught their first sight of the Chryse Colony's outer structures. They would be there before nightfall and Gatwech searched the southern shore for a good place to camp.

Leroy noticed how Zuawalo's *Pole Cat*, Zigg was growing quite fast and was imprinting on her, just as she had said it would. More often than not Zigg sat on her lap, only returning to her bag to sleep, which it did so quite frequently. Zuawalo continued to hand feed her pet.

"You will need a bigger bag Zuawalo", Leroy said to her.

"Yes. I will", Zuawalo agreed, "I can get one there", she stated, while pointing to their destination, Chryse Colony

As night descended, they pulled ashore on the right bank of the Kasei River, just west of the Chryse Colony. They dragged the canoe ashore and pulled it onto the beach, then set up camp for the night.

They had arrived.

8. I Spy with my Little Eye

Agent Murphy answered his communicator, "Yes, what is it?", he asked.

"We have Lieutenant Roberts on the line Sir", the Communications Operator replied, "He says it's urgent that he speak to both you and Lord Folcrom Forkbraid."

"Okay, keep him on the line", Agent Murphy replied, adding "We'll be there shortly."

"FB. FB", Agent Murphy spoke into his communicator, "Are you there?"

"Yes, Yes Jim", Forkbraid replied, "What is it?"

"Meet me in the communications centre", Agent Murphy replied, "We have Lieutenant Roberts on the line. Apparently he has some important information for us."

Within minutes Agent Murphy was at the communications centre, Forkbraid and Lady Selene weren't far behind him.

"If it's as important as Lieutenant Roberts thinks it is, I thought it best Selene be here as well", Forkbraid informed Agent Murphy.

All three were now in the communications centre and Lieutenant Roberts was on the screen patiently waiting for them, "About time you lot showed up", he started, "We have a huge, huge problem people!"

"What would be the problem?", Forkbraid queried.

"Well as you know, both Agent Murphy and yourself requested I track the Space Yacht Delilah", Lieutenant Roberts reminded them, then adding "Well I can confirm, that they have made it to the Jovian System and the Delilah has docked at Ganymede Prime."

"Okay, okay, that's all very good, but what's this huge problem?", Agent Murphy asked.

"Well I thought, I'd better keep a closer eye on things before I reported anything back to you, to make sure I had all the relevant information. Especially with all this belligerent rhetoric coming from that Horridian Regime", Lieutenant Roberts began, "So I turned some more of my scanning arrays towards the Jovian System to gather more data."

"Yes, yes okay and what have you found?", Agent Murphy asked more urgently.

"This!", Lieutenant Roberts exclaimed, the screen split into screen in screen mode with Lieutenant Roberts in the top left corner and the rest of the screen showing recent scans of the Jovian System.

The scan showed the Jovian System yes, but also on the screen could be seen a very large number of tiny, small dots. Dots that were not Jovian moons, nor were they colonies. These small dots were all clustered together in a tight knit group.

"What are we looking at Lieutenant?", asked Forkbraid.

Lieutenant Roberts was quiet for a long moment, the he spat out, "Missiles!"

"Missiles?", Agent Murphy repeated, questioningly.

"Yes. Missiles", Lieutenant Roberts confirmed, then continued, "at least two thousand of them."

Selene spoke for the first time, "Two thousand missiles?", she queried with an urgency.

"Yes, at least. That is my estimate", Lieutenant Roberts replied, adding, "I have yet to confirm their precise number and exact course, however I can confirm, that they are all on an inward bound trajectory."

"Are the Horridians insane?", Agent Murphy spat out.

"Insane or not Agent Murphy", Lieutenant Roberts replied, "To me, this looks like the first salvo in another War with the outer satellites."

"Nobody could be that stupid!", Agent Murphy replied.

"Stupid or not, they are missiles, they are inbound and they were launched from the Jovian System", Lieutenant Roberts told them, then after a short pause he added, "It gets worse!"

"What can be worse than two thousand missiles launched towards the inner solar system?", Selene asked him.

The screen changed again, this time there were four windows displayed, Lieutenant Roberts still remained on the top left window, with the Jovian System now on the top right.

"The window on the lower left displays Jupiter's Trailing Trojan Asteroids. The window on the lower right displays Jupiter's Leading Trojan Asteroids", Lieutenant Roberts explained.

The three looked at the new windows closely, "What are those little dots?", Selene asked.

Again in both the lower windows on the screen was a cluster of tiny little points of light, with far more of them displayed in the lower right window.

"Not colonies, that much is certain", Lieutenant Roberts replied, explaining "At first I thought they were yet more missiles, but then I noticed their exhaust plumes are different. Spectrum analysis shows that they are not the same as the missiles inbound from Jupiter."

"Then what are they?", Agent Murphy asked, his tone showing impatience.

Forkbraid place a hand on Agent Murphy's shoulder, "It alright Jim", he told him.

"Alright?", Jim queried, "How is any of this alright?", he didn't wait for an answer "Lieutenant Roberts! What the bloody hell are they?"

"They're military transports, troop carriers, heavy weapons transports, that sort of thing", Lieutenant Roberts replied, adding, "You're looking at two armies and they're on the move people!"

Agent Murphy had a sharp mind, "Two Thousand plus missiles inbound. Two armies on the move", he summarised with his eyes closed in concentration, then added, "We will need to watch them very closely Lieutenant. Gather much more data for an analysis of the ship types and troop numbers etc., but if I'm right, I think this is decapitation attempt."

"A decapitation attempt?" Selene queried.

Lieutenant Roberts answered, "If Agent Murphy is correct, and I agree with him, if this is a decapitation attempt, then we've got big, big problems heading our way."

"Decapitation attempt?" Selene repeated more urgently.

"Sorry my Lady", Lieutenant Roberts apologised, "The Horridians are attempting to take out our leadership, command and control with a single massive missile strike. Followed up by a two pronged military attack and mopping up operation. Assuming Agent Murphy is right of course."

"Sweet Mother of Zeus Forkbraid!", Lady Selene exclaimed, then asked, "What can we do?"

"We analyse everything", Forkbraid replied, adding, "Missile trajectories, hypothetical targets. Those two armies. Where are they headed? What type of ships have they launched? What heavy weapons can they carry? How many troops? Once we have all that information, then we can start thinking of a response."

"Lieutenant", Agent Murphy began, "You heard Lord Forkbraid. We need that data. We want the trajectories of everyone of those missiles and everyone of those ships. We want to know what kinds of missiles and what kinds of ships we're dealing with. Then we can potentially work out, what they're carrying and how to deal with them. And Lieutenant, we needed that data yesterday!"

"I'm on it Agent Murphy", the Lieutenant replied, "We'll have the information ready for you as soon as we have it."

"Lieutenant", Forkbraid caught his attention, "Anything coming at us, from any of the other Outer Satellites?

"No. No", the Lieutenant replied, "So far it's all coming from the Jovian System."

"Keep tabs on them as well just in case", Forkbraid told him, "And Lieutenant, this is now your priority, not your shipping schedules."

"Understood. Understood", the Lieutenant replied, "Over and Out."

The Lieutenant had been much more cordial than usual, but then this situation was an exceptional one and called for all hands on deck and cooperating to the fullest.

"Jim. We need to give the Earth and L5 a heads up. Can you put together a quick summary and send it off to Earth Gov and Colonial Central Command?", Forkbraid requested.

Jim tapped his right temple, "Already working on it FB. I'll be sending it within the hour."

Selene squeezed Forkbraid's hand, "Another war Forkbraid?"

"It seems that way Selene", Forkbraid replied, adding, "High Prince Heinrich von Horridian, did declare War on the Inner Solar System in his last System wide address. Now we know he wasn't just bluffing. He already had this planned and ready. He's just been itching for an excuse!"

True to his word, Agent Murphy summarised the details of the latest events and sent them personally to Earth Gov and L5 Colonial Central Command before the hour was out. For good measure he sent a copy to the Flinders Psychic Academy back on Earth as well.

From that moment, on all eyes in the Inner Solar System turned towards the Jovian System and the approaching inbound missiles and the Trojan two armies.

It was later the following day in the afternoon, when a recorded message came through from the Colonial Cruiser Spartan, it was from Captain Carmichael. Agent Murphy, Forkbraid, Lady Selene had been requested at the communications centre. Marcus Greyhelm and Charlene Fewkes, the New Flinders Psychic Academy's Administrators were asked to attend as well.

Captain Carmichael was on the screen and began relaying his message, "Well people, the shit has well and truly hit the fan back here!", he begun.

"Agent Murphy's report has set in motion a flurry of activity back here. Everything is up in the air at the moment. Earth Gov has requested their military confirm Agent Murphy's report. Which they are doing, using their surveillance assets at the Earth, Sun Lagrangian Points Two and Three.", there was a short pause.

"They have multiple eyes on the Jovian System, both the Leading and Trailing Trojans, as well as the other Outer Systems, Saturn, Uranus and Neptune. Early results are confirming the report and they have sighted the inbound missiles and the two Trojan armies. There is a detailed analysis being performed as I speak", the Captain paused.

"I am pleased to say that Earth Gov has agreed to share this information directly with L5 Colonial Central Command. We now have direct access to their surveillance asset feeds.", Captain Carmichael informed them.

"Agent Murphy's theory is being taken extremely seriously. This does in fact look like it is a decapitation attempt. We will of course know more and understand the situation far better after our initial analysis", the Captain continued.

"So far we have not detected anything happening in the other Outer Solar System, beyond Jupiter's realm. Saturn, Uranus and Neptune, so far, all seem quiet. They may or may not be involved. We are however keeping a close eye on them as well, as you might expect. They may not be involved this time, but they were heavily involved in the previous outer satellite insurrection as we all know", the information continued.

"The Horridian Regime in the Jovian System has been approached via both the Earth's and Colonial Central's Diplomatic Channels. So far they have chosen to be silent! No-one from their side wants to talk to us or so it appears. Personally I don't expect any response from them. If we do get one, it will more than likely be more belligerent rhetoric. I don't think we should hold our breath on that front", Captain Carmichael informed them further.

"There has been talk from Earth Gov about some policy they have. There is virtually no information on it at present and I have little knowledge of it myself. Something they called, '*Never Again*'. Some sort of policy they put in place after the outer satellite insurrection's armistice. I will try to get some more information on that point", the Captain continued.

"On a more personal note. The investigation and possible disciplinary issues I faced after being recalled from Mars. All of that seems to have resolved itself. It seems that my creating atmo rated Wisps, has pretty much become irrelevant under the current circumstances. Colonial Central Command have placed me in charge of the Colonial Fleet and the Defence of L5. That is why I am contacting you and not some politician. This is at the present moment a Military matter. I will send more information through to you as soon as I have it. Over and out people", the Captain finished his message and the screen went blank.

"Its annoying that we couldn't ask him any questions", Selene stated.

"The time delay between the Earth and Mars doesn't really allow for a two way conversation", Agent Murphy explained.

"True, but I would have liked to have asked, for more information about the Earth and its response", Lady Selene replied.

"Yes. I am more than a bit curious about what '*Never Again*' actually means. More than a bit curious", Agent Murphy replied.

"Captain Carmichael doesn't know. At least not yet", Forkbraid told them, "Otherwise he would have told us."

"Any ideas FB?", Agent Murphy questioned hopefully.

"No. No idea. However, if we take the words '*Never Again*' literally and then apply them to history, what do you think that means?", Forkbraid answered with a question in return.

"I would have thought that '*Never Again*' , would mean literally that, '*Never Again*'. Perhaps a particular aspect of the Outer Satellite Insurrection, could never be allowed to ever happen again?", Agent Murphy pondered.

"All modern day electronics are hardened against electromagnetic pulses. That was a direct result of the outer satellite insurrection", Charlene noted.

"That was a direct result of the insurrection, yes, but it's also something everyone knows about", Agent Murphy replied, adding, "Captain Carmichael was talking about something he had never heard of before."

Lady Selene chimed in, "The bombardment!", she exclaimed, then questioning, "Is that what 'Never Again' means?"

Marcus added in, "There were a lot of missiles flying about back then. Most of them coming inward, into the inner solar system. Many had fusion warheads."

"Fusion warheads were raining down from the skies", Charlene added, "Whole cities were wiped off the face of the Earth and raised to the ground."

"Is that what they mean by 'Never Again'?", Lady Selene questioned.

"Back then, the Earth's defences were pretty good", Forkbraid began, adding, "Everyone could see that the War was coming and they did make a lot of preparations well in advance."

"Many of the missiles were intercepted on their way in, but of the ones that got through the interception, one in five actually hit their targets", Agent Murphy informed them.

"So what do you think that 'Never Again' means Jim?", Forkbraid asked.

"If I was to hazard a guess", Agent Murphy started, "I'd say that the Earth Gov has something up its sleeve. Something that they prepared for a long time ago, for precisely this eventuality."

"Yes", Forkbraid replied, "Something definitely up their sleeve."

"What concerns me though. I was in charge of the remote viewing teams on the Earth.", Forkbraid began, then continuing, "And I have never even heard of this 'never again' policy."

"I can't believe that there is a policy, a program back at the Earth Defence Forces. Something that has been put together and implemented, ever since the outer satellite insurrection and we don't know anything about it", Selene replied, asking, "How is that even possible?"

"It isn't or at least it shouldn't be possible Selene", Forkbraid replied.

Agent Murphy replied, questioning, "If it's not possible, then how was it done? Somehow, this has been hidden from your remote viewing teams FB?"

"There is only a couple of ways I can think of", Forkbraid replied as he looked at Selene.

"Oh", Selene replied, then quickly added, "In theory, every psychic on Earth is a member of psi-corps. So that can only mean two possibilities."

"Yes Selene", Forkbraid replied, "I think you are on the right track there. Either there is a hidden division within our psi-corp, that we don't know about, which is extremely unlikely. I would definitely know about it or?"

"The Earth Defence Forces must have their own psychic operations division that we have no knowledge about. Something that is completely separate from psi-corps", Lady Selene replied.

"Bingo my Darling!", Forkbraid agreed, explaining, "Only a psychic can block a psychic."

Agent Murphy caught on quickly, "And only a psychic organisation can block another psychic organisation?", he queried.

"Yes Jim", Forkbraid agreed, speculating, "It seems that the Earth Defence Forces have more than just the policy of *never again* up their sleeve."

"If they have their own psychic operations division. What else do they have that we don't know about?", Lady Selene questioned, a question that went unanswered.

"Selene. Send word to the Flinders Psychic Academy back on the Earth. Tobius and the Grey Council definitely need to know about this", Forkbraid recommended, adding, "This seriously needs looking into."

"I'll do that straight away", Selene replied.

A few days later Lieutenant Roberts had more information for them. Agent Murphy, Forkbraid and Lady Selene had gathered in the communications centre once more.

"Well Lieutenant", Agent Murphy began, "You have more details for us?"

"Yes, yes Agent Murphy. Yes I do", the Lieutenant replied.

"We spill it man!", Agent Murphy ordered.

"Our analysis of the missiles indicates, that they are all upgraded versions of the same missiles they used during the outer satellite insurrection", Lieutenant Roberts stated, then adding, "We believe that each and everyone of them is armed with a fusion, perhaps multiple fusion warheads."

"Fusion warheads!", Lady Selene was shocked.

Lieutenant Roberts had worse news, "We believe they are cold fusion warheads!"

"Shit!", Agent Murphy exclaimed, "During their entire inbound journey they'll be building up. When they get to their targets, the energy released will be phenomenal. Like holy blazing suns phenomenal!"

"Just how many are we talking about Lieutenant? Precise numbers?", asked Forkbraid.

"By our count, there are twenty two hundred of them", the Lieutenant informed them.

"You have got to be joking, twenty two hundred. Are you sure?", Agent Murphy questioned.

"Twenty two hundred is the number", the Lieutenant replied, then adding, "And not all of them are heading to Earth and L5 either."

"Details, please Lieutenant?", Agent Murphy requested.

"All but ten of the missiles are inbound to Earth and L5. Exactly how many missiles are heading to Earth and how many missiles are heading to L5, we don't know as yet. We will be able to get a break down on those numbers when they get closer to their targets, much closer unfortunately", Lieutenant Roberts explained, adding, "The remaining ten missiles are heading here, to Mars."

"Here!", Lady Selene exclaimed, "Are you certain of that?"

"Yes my Lady. Sadly, we have ten inbound missiles and indeed Mars looks to be their target", Lieutenant Roberts replied.

"So ten heading our way and twenty one hundred and ninety heading to Earth and L5", Forkbraid summarised, then asking, "It's probably way too early to tell exactly where the bulk of them are targeted, correct?"

"Yeah. It's as I said, we won't know that until they're right close to Earth and L5", the Lieutenant replied, adding "Then Earth and L5 will have to watch very closely to see how they peel away and split up for individual targeting."

"Okay, so that's the missiles. What about those two armies?", Agent Murphy asked.

"Well then, I'll start with the Trailing Trojan Army", the Lieutenant began,

"There are twenty troop carriers with drop ships. So we're looking at ten thousand troops or there about."

"That's a lot of troops", Forkbraid considered, "What about the transports?", he then asked.

"There are twenty transports and they can hypothetically hold, maybe a total of two hundred

heavy weapons of various kinds", the Lieutenant informed them.

"Well that's not good!", Agent Murphy noted.

Lieutenant Roberts replied, "Imagine that each stowage bay can hold say, a main battle tank or a self propelled howitzer, maybe even an infantry fighting vehicle. The stowage bay could even hold a small gun ship, patrol ship or a couple of interceptors. We aren't going to know what they've packaged up, until they start unloading the transports."

"Why would they have main battle tanks, self propelled howitzers or even infantry fighting vehicles?", Agent Murphy asked, stating, "They are colonies in the Trojan Asteroid fields!"

"Any main battle tanks, self propelled howitzers or infantry fighting vehicles, would have to have been specifically manufactured for this operation. They may be completely untested, assuming they have any of them at all."

Lieutenant Roberts then continued, "Honestly, they could have any mix of the heavy weapons I've just mentioned, perhaps others I haven't even thought of."

Agent Murphy asked "And where is this lot headed?"

"We have studied their trajectories and it does appear that they are headed our way. So they are coming to Mars!", the Lieutenant told them.

"Do we have any timing with this?", asked Selene

"Nothing precise as yet, but their Armed Forces will arrive a week or so after their missiles", the Lieutenant replied.

"Sounds like an occupation force", Forkbraid responded, adding, "Hammer us flat and then send in their Armed Forces. They fully intend to occupy Mars."

"What about the Leading Trojan Army?", Agent Murphy asked.

"Well Earth and L5 are going to have some really, really bad news to deal with", Lieutenant Roberts replied, then added, "Multiply everything I have just told you about the Trailing Trojan Army by ten."

"So a hundred thousand troops and a mix of two thousand heavy weapons systems, that could be packaged up in any which way they've planned", Forkbraid calculated.

"The troop numbers would be about right, but it's hard to say about the heavy weapons package", the Lieutenant replied, explaining, "If they plan to occupy the Earth, then yeah, it makes perfect sense to send in main battle tanks, armed fighting vehicles etc., but if they plan to occupy L5, they'll probably have a couple of thousand patrol ships and interceptors instead."

"And if they plan to occupy both", Agent Murphy started, continuing "They could have any mix of main battle tanks, armed fighting vehicles, patrol ships and interceptors that suits their requirements. It all depends on how they've planned to divvy up their forces."

"Yes Agent Murphy", the Lieutenant replied, adding "You've got the gist of it. It's basically going to be pot luck as to what heavy weapons packages we'll all be facing."

"Sweat Mother or Zeus! This is bad, this is really bad!", Lady Selene exclaimed.

"I'm sorry to bring you all such bad news", the Lieutenant replied, adding, "Well that's all I've got for now. Nothing much else I can add."

"Good work Lieutenant", Agent Murphy commended, "Over and Out."

"Jim, you got all that, yeah?", Forkbraid asked.

"I recorded it all FB. It's in the vault", Jim replied, tapping his right temple.

"Good. Put it all in a report and get it back to the Earth and L5 as soon as possible", Forkbraid instructed, adding "I'd recommend taking out that Leading Trojan Army en-route, before they even get close to Earth and L5. Assuming that is even possible."

"That could be a right difficult task with all those missiles heading their way", Agent Murphy replied before heading off to put together his report.

"We have no defences capable of stopping an army Forkbraid", Selene stated the obvious.

"I know Selene", Forkbraid replied, "We'll figure something out."

"And the missiles?", Selene queried, adding, "Ten of them. That sounds like a missile per colony and two for us. How do we stop those?"

"For that, I do have an idea", Forkbraid informed her.

Forkbraid made a call to Varak on his communicator, "Varak. How's our little project going?"

"We're almost ready", Varak replied.

"Good, good, we'll be over in about five minutes", Forkbraid informed him.

A little over five minutes later Forkbraid, Lady Selene and Agent Murphy were standing in Varak's construction hanger. Varak was waiting for them.

Forkbraid looked around, he couldn't see his ship anywhere, "Varak. Something seems to be missing. Where's my ship?", he enquired.

Varak laughed, his usual loud, raucous laugh, "Right in front of you FB", then he opened up the 'grip' on his left forearm.

The device opened up and a holographic screen and keyboard appeared above his left forearm. Quickly, Varak pressed a few keystrokes, then Forkbraid's ship magically appeared before them.

"What the fuck?", Agent Murphy exclaimed in a questioning manner.

"Innovation Agent Murphy, Innovation", Varak replied, then to Forkbraid he commented excitedly, "FB, I've added a cloaking system!"

"A cloaking system?", Forkbraid questioned, "That was not on the original specifications."

"I know. I know FB", Varak replied, adding, "But after I had the deflector grid working and then I manged to get the eight by eight layer defence grid working, I thought to myself, wouldn't it be great to give her a cloaking system as well."

Selene asked, "Eight by eight layer defence grid? So the defence grid has sixty four layers? Would that be right?"

"Yes my Lady, it certainly does", Varak replied, explaining, "The best part. Those sixty four layers of defence grid not only defend the ship from an attack. They can absorb the energy of that attack and utilise that energy to actually strengthen the defence grid. The energy from an attack can be redirected to any given point to strengthen the grid as necessary."

Forkbraid broke in at that point, "Varak. You were explaining the cloaking device."

"Yes, yes FB, I got side tracked", Varak began, explaining, "The defence grid is the key. Those sixty four layers, that was definitely the key."

"And?", Agent Murphy then stepped in, getting impatient.

"To cut a long story short", Varak started, " Those sixty four layers of defence grid can be used to channel energy. As I was saying, energy from an attack can be redirected to strengthen the defence grid at any given point as necessary. It can also redirect light around the defence grid as well. So when viewed or scanned, you're seeing the other side of the ship."

"The other side of the ship?", Lady Selene queried.

"Well yes and no. More correctly you're looking or scanning through or around the ship", Varak then clarified, "It's as if the ship isn't there! You only see what's on the other side", Varak chuckled.

"Wow! You have excelled yourself Varak", Forkbraid commended him.

"Well, I did think my finest achievement was those pesky micro-fusion thrusters. I mean, they were really hard work to design, far harder to manufacture", Varak replied, adding, "Then when I was working on these defence grid designs, I came up with this energy redirection concept and then it occurred to me, light is just energy and voila. There it was, the defence grid could also cloak!", the look on Varak's face showed the sheer pride he took in his work.

"Well Varak. I'm glad you came up with that one. A cloaking device is going to be very useful, I expect", Forkbraid told him, "but what we really need to know about, is the weapons modules."

"Oh yes, yes. The weapons modules", Varak replied, "Yes, I remember the problems those blasted Hyper Dynamics 303s gave us. Bloody Androids!", he pressed a few more keys on his grip.

"Okay. Let's see", Varak went through the list, "Here's what we have."

"Eight Phased Laser Arrays, four mounted atop the saucer section and four mounted below the saucer section? Check!"

"Eight Hyper Resonant Disrupters, twinned and mounted on each wing tip and on top of each stabiliser? Check!"

"Quad Pulse Plasma Cannons, mounted on the base of the saucer section? Check!"

"Six Electromagnetic Rail Guns, twinned and mounted on the saucer section's underside rotating ring, set thirty degrees apart. Movement of one hundred and fifty degrees to port or starboard? Check!"

"Six Torpedo Tubes, twinned and mounted on the saucer section's underside above the EMR Ring, ninety degrees apart. Non-rotational? Check!"

"Four Rapid Fire Pulse Plasma Machine Cannons, twinned and mounted to the saucer section's port and starboard sides? Check!"

"The saucer section's internal automated carousels, for loading the Electromagnetic Rail Guns and the Torpedo Tubes? Check!"

Varak continued, "That appears to be it. All correct and accounted for. All ready for testing!"

"Did I hear you say Four Rapid Fire Pulse Plasma Machine Cannons?", Forkbraid enquired, "I don't remember those being on the original specifications either."

"Oh, they weren't FB. More innovations", Varak replied, "They were easy to design and manufacture, even easier to integrated into the polyceramalloy hull. So I added them to the list. I can have them removed if you wish?"

"No. No. That's fine. Let's leave them in place", Forkbraid replied, adding, "Just let me know in future of any further *'innovations'* Varak."

"Is she ready to fly?", Lady Selene enquired, "This ship could be our only hope."

Varak replied, "Almost ready my Lady. All the Ship's control systems are in place. The Ship's photonic neural clusters are currently learning about the Ship's various systems. Once they've processed and understood the Ship's systems, then we can begin flight testing and weapons testing. In just a few days I expect", then enquiring,"Why the urgency?"

"That's right, you probably don't know", Agent Murphy replied, then adding, "I'm giving you access to the latest report I've sent to the Earth and L5."

Varak click a few more keys on his grip and began reading the report, "Oh my! Oh my! Now I see why this has all become urgent! Sweet Mother, this is a very bad situation!"

"Well, we cannot fly a ship that hasn't got a name FB. Have you thought of one?"

"That I have Varak, that I have. Let's call here the Solstice", Forkbraid replied.

"Solstice!", Varak considered, "Longest Day, Longest Night, two extremes. It is a fitting name, the Solstice is an extreme vessel. She is my finest work of art. A Starship!"

Lady Selene queried, "Photonic neural clusters? I'm not familiar with those."

"Ah.", Varak began replying, "That would be Peter Swann's handy work my Lady."

"Peter Swann?", Lady Selene queried.

"Yes. Yes. Peter Swann", Varak answered, explaining, "I was so impressed with how he dealt with that loopy 303 that went into a cascade failure, that I asked him help manage all of our Androids. He has been doing an astonishingly, fantastic job."

"And the photonic neural clusters?", Agent Murphy asked, even he was getting curious.

"Well, I asked Peter what would be the best control system for such an advanced ship", Varak started, adding, "Peter asked to look at the specifications and said he would come up with a recommendation. Something that would blow my socks off he said."

"Anyway", Varak continued, "The next day Peter recommended photonic neural clusters. And I tell you, he blew my socks right off!"

Just where did we acquire photonic neural clusters Varak?", a now curious Forkbraid asked.

"Well that's just the thing FB, they are bespoke. Peter deigned and built them here in the work shop", Varak replied, explaining, "Every major system on the Solstice, is linked to a photonic neural cluster. From Navigation,

Communications, Environmental Control, Power Generation, Engines, Deflector and Defence Grids, even the Weapons Modules, every major system. Hell, Peter even convinced me to use a grip! Look at this!", Varak held up his left arm.

"I'm not sure I understand", Agent Murphy enquired, "How is this better?"

"Ah, well that is the thing. The photonic neural clusters learn how to control the system they are connected to", Varak explained, "They are far, far more efficient than the systems I would have normally used. So much faster! Unbelievably faster!"

"And they also communicate with the Ship's Positronic Matrix", Varak added.

"Whoa!", Forkbraid exclaimed, "My ship is controlled by a positronic matrix?"

"Yes FB, but it is not what you think", Varak replied.

"Every positronic matrix is three laws safe Varak", Forkbraid reminded him.

"Yes, but it won't be an issue", Varak replied, explaining, "The positronic matrix is integrated in to all the systems, with exception of the weapons modules and their controlling photonic neural clusters. So three laws safe 'Betty' here", as Varak described the positronic matrix, "will do its absolute darnedest to keep the crew alive and has no knowledge of or control over the weapons."

"Three laws safe 'Betty'?", Lady Selene queried.

"Oh. Its an inside joke my Lady", Varak replied, explaining, "about a popular mid twentieth century cartoon character called Betty Boop, who was later turned into a killer cyborg for a movie in the twenty first century. So the joke is, 'if only Betty was three laws safe'. I didn't get it at first either. Peter had to explain that one to me as well. Apparently, it is some sort of cult classic. It is also kind of ironic, as cyborg 'Betty' was never three laws safe."

Forkbraid moved on from the trivia, "So how are the weapons systems controlled?"

Varak replied, "Well, the thirty six weapons modules are controlled by eight photonic neural clusters, appropriately connected. Those neural clusters then feed back into the *'Hornet's nest'*."

"Hornet's nest?", Forkbraid asked, he was certainly learning quite a lot today.

"Another creation of Peter's", Varak replied, "It is basically a super cluster of seventy two photonic neural clusters, although each one of these has tens times the power and efficiency of the ordinary neural clusters. I guess that makes them super photonic neural clusters. So the weapons systems are controlled by the Hornet's nest."

Agent Murphy stepped in, "I think you'll need to elaborate somewhat Varak, this is all getting very confusing."

"Sure thing", Varak began, "The Captain of the ship controls the Ship's systems, non-weapons systems that is of course, via the Crew consoles and/or the main Computer, which is the positronic matrix, which is three laws safe. No problems there, the positronic matrix will follow all orders given to it, by the Captain. It may suggest alternatives to those orders from time to time, but the Captain's command is final. It will comply."

Varak quickly added, "Peter also enhanced the positronic matrix as well. I should mention that, so it does perform at higher efficiency and functionality level than your usual model 303. The guy is a genius with Androids!"

"Okay and the Hornet's nest?", Agent Murphy queried again.

"The Hornet's nest is controlled by the Crew consoles directly. No connections to the positronic matrix whatsoever. The Hornet's nest is also completely non-sentient, but smart and efficient, it is very, very clever. It is also not three laws safe in any way shape or form."

"And the Hornet's nest can only be controlled by the Crew consoles?", asked Agent Murphy.

"No. Not at all", Varak informed them, "While I was repairing Forkbraid's Bat Wing Interceptor, Peter had look a the neural interlock control system FB had connected to it. So Peter thought and I agreed, that the ship could benefit from its own neural interlock control system."

"So I can control the ship, the Solstice with my mind?", Forkbraid enquired.

"Well yeah", Varak replied, "You just have to direct your thoughts in the correct way. Think Computer and the instructions that follow, go to the positronic matrix. Think *'Hive'* or *'Hornet's nest'* or simply *'Tactical'* and all the instructions that follow, will go to the Hornet's nest, the super photonic neural cluster. It is all very simple really."

"I think you're all mad!", Lady Selene told them, a very concerned look on her face.

"Maybe so Selene, maybe so", Forkbraid replied, then, "but in tough situation, direct neural interlock control used precisely the right way, definitely gives us a advantage. A real edge!"

"The direct neural interlock control system will literally turn the Solstice into an extension of Forkbraid's mind. The Solstice will become like an extra limb", Varak explained.

"Yes and exactly how many people are actually trained to use a neural interlock control system, that is, without turning their brains into, I don't know, mush! Forkbraid?", Selene queried.

"On Mars? That would be one!", Forkbraid replied, "Me!"

"Exactly my point!", Lady Selene glared back at him, "You take risks!"

The next day a message came through from L5, it was from Captain Carmichael. Agent Murphy, Forkbraid, Lady Selene, Marcus and Charlene had been summoned to the communications centre.

Captain Carmichael was on the screen, "Our analysis of the threat is pretty much the same as your analysis. Not really a lot different", he explained.

"Earth Gov definitely has something up their sleeve. They're not saying what 'Never Again' is exactly and they are playing their cards very close to their chest, but they have said, that they will tell us at the appropriate time. And that we should have our fleet ready to take action when that time comes. We'll just have to wait and see."

The Captain continued, "We have had a flurry of urgent diplomatic communications from the other outer satellites. Nothing from the Horridian Regime mind you. However, the Saturnian Demarchy tells us, that they are not involved and that the Jovian System stands alone. We have the same information coming from the Federation of Uranus and the Commonwealth of Neptune. They are not involved in this attack. They describe these events as illegal and that they will provide assistance if we require it. That's all I have for now. Over and out."

"Small graces it seems. There's only the Horridian Regime to deal with", Selene told the others.

"Yes", Forkbraid replied, "And the other outer satellites have pledged assistance."

"Except of course, they are so far out that any assistance they send will be long after the event", Marcus lamented.

9. Celebrations

Abram, Miriam and their house guests, Rani, Lakshmi and Pavarti were relaxing in the apartment watching the video wall. Scenes of jubilant celebrations were being displayed.

All across the Jovian Colonies, there were celebrations of the youngest Horridian Prince's first born Son, Ulrick's birth. The celebrations were in full swing. Laser light shows were performed across all the main colony cylinders and even fireworks were being set off outside of the colonies. For those who had a good vantage point or a good video wall, it was all quite spectacular.

Images of the new young Prince Ulrick and his parents Prince Leopold and Princess Giselle of Io, appeared on the video feeds almost continuously during the celebrations. Images of Prince Wulfric and Prince Valdamar and their respective Royal families also appeared in the video feeds quite often as well, but not nearly as much as the new young Prince.

Most of all however, High Prince Heinrich and his Royal family would appear in the video feeds, as much if not more than his new young nephew Ulrick. Always reminding the citizens of the realm, of how generous and magnanimous their Monarch was and how lucky they were to be under his rule and leadership. The High Prince was the Monarch for their time.

Rani was simply not impressed, "It seems rather hypocritical to me. Celebrating one child's birth with such opulence and yet these people keep Slaves!"

"Yes I know Rani", Miriam replied, "Although, it's probably only the wealthy who actually own the Slaves. I have noticed that a lot of the ordinary folk, probably most of them, simply don't have Slaves. The only reason we have you Rani, is to keep you safe. Thankfully John was able to set that up, otherwise you could have ended up anywhere. What I don't understand is why they don't just use Androids?"

"I think there is something more to this celebration than simply the birth of a Prince's son", Abram added, noting, "At work today, we had to clear a good portion of Europa's orbital zone for some kind of special launch. I'm told that the same thing was required at both Ganymede and Callisto as well. All in the same arc!"

"Is that unusual?", Miriam enquired.

"Yes. I would say so", Abram answered, "The only time you would need to clear traffic from three orbital zones in the same arc, would be if something was being launched from closer in to Jupiter itself, say from Io's orbit. Something that was either very big or launched in large numbers. Clearing a path in such a case would be prudent."

"Io is Prince Leopold's realm", Lakshmi noted.

"Yes. It is", Abram confirmed, then added, "The Amalthean and Ionian mines are also part of his realm. Prince Leopold controls all of that."

"And all the work is done by Slaves!", Rani, who was having trouble adjusting to her new status in the Jovian colonies spat out.

Miriam gave Rani's hand a gentle squeeze, "We will find a way to sort this out", then to Abram, Miriam asked, "Why don't they just use Androids Abram?"

"If I was to hazard a guess, I'd say trade", Abram replied, "Or more correctly, the lack there of."

"Lack of trade?", Miriam queried.

"Think about it. Obviously they can't make Androids or they would have them. And trade with the Earth and L5 is virtually non-existent, so they can't ship them in either", Abram explained.

"So they just pick on the religious minorities and declare them to be Slaves?", Rani angrily questioned.

"I'm sorry to say Rani, but that does appear to be the case", Abram replied, "It wouldn't be the first time in history that religious bigotry was used against minority groups. It is very common throughout history in fact."

"That does not make it right!", Rani stated emphatically.

"You're right Rani. It doesn't make it right", Abram agreed.

The video wall chimed for a special announcement and the screen displayed an odd image with lots of tiny, yet very brilliant lights, many, many hundreds in fact.

Abram, Miriam and their guests looked intently at the screen trying to figure out what they were looking at.

Then an announcer explained it all for them, "High Prince Heinrich von Horridian in his previous system wide address, had declared war on the inner solar system worlds and colonies, the Earth, Mars and L5. In addition to this, the High Prince gave the inner solar system worlds an ultimatum, to surrender their armed forces to the Jovian Armed Services or face total annihilation. Sadly, the Earth, Mars and L5 have not heeded that warning, they have not surrendered their armed forces to the Jovian Realm and now they will all be paying the price!"

"What you are seeing on the screen before you is our first salvo in this new War. A War that the inner solar system planets started, with their constant persecution of our Christian Brothers and Sisters. Their slaughtering and murdering of countless thousands of Christian martyrs", the announcer blatantly lied as if this was the absolute highest truth.

"In response to their treachery and their not heeding his ultimatum, the High Prince has ordered the launch of two thousand two hundred missiles with multiple cold fusion warheads. Even now they are on course for the Demon havens of the Earth, Mars and L5", the announcer finished.

The screen remained focused on the image of the tiny, yet very brilliant lights. Everyone in the Appelbaum's apartment looked from one to another and back again.

Abram stated the obvious, "Well, this is not a good turn of events."

"It explains why the traffic was cleared from the space lanes in Europa, Ganymede and Callisto orbital zones", Miriam said to him, "I bet their missile base is somewhere in orbit around Io."

Abram nodded, "That does seem likely given the recent orbital traffic restrictions", he agreed.

Matthew entered the Prophet's apartments, having been let in by the Prophet's valet.

"My Lord", Matthew addressed the Prophet, "Have you seen the latest news on the video feeds?"

"Yes I have Matthew", the Prophet replied, adding, "Prince Leopold has a son. His first born."

"Yes and a huge celebration", Matthew stated, "but that's not what I'm here to discuss."

"Ah yes", the Prophet knew what Matthew was referring to, "High Prince Heinrich has launched his first salvo of missiles at the inner planets", he noted.

"I do have concerns about that my Lord", Matthew informed him.

"You always do Matthew, you always do", the Prophet replied, "Please tell me your concerns."

"Well", Matthew began, "We now know that the High Prince has launched two thousand two hundred missiles at the inner solar system. I was under the impression, they'd be sending far, far more than that."

"Twenty two hundred missiles with multiple cold fusion warheads Matthew", the Prophet replied, "Surely that should be far more than enough! Far more than the Earth or L5 can handle in one hit. We certainly know that Mars is basically defenceless against any missile attacks."

The Prophet continued, "Especially when they're following up the missile attacks with the Trojan Armed Forces, to occupy both Mars and L5. The demons should be completely overwhelmed!"

"I'm not quite so sure about that", Matthew told the Prophet, "To me, this looks like a Hail Mary, with all their eggs placed in one basked. It will either work or it won't!"

The Prophet took on a concerned look, Matthew had a highly tactical mind, he was often right.

"So Matthew, you think this attack will fail?", the Prophet queried.

"I don't know my Lord", Matthew began, explaining, "Everybody in the High Prince's court, thinks that this is a done deal, a fait accompli. They forget, a fait accompli, is something that has happened, past tense, not something that will necessarily happen. This isn't won, until it's won!"

Matthew continued, "They have launched their entire arsenal, their entire stock of missiles! If this gambit fails and does not work, they will have L5's Colonial Fleet heading our way."

"The General did say, that they'd be building more missiles while their first salvo is on the way", the Prophet assured Matthew.

"Yes I know. I remember", Matthew replied, adding a whole string of rhetorical questions, "but what is their turn around time for each missile? Just how many new missiles can they build before their first salvo strikes? And if the L5 Fleet comes this way, just how many more missiles will they need? And just how many missiles, can they actually build in that case? There are far too many unknowns. Hence my concerns!"

Matthew continued, "The High Prince and his family are all alone in this. If things go horribly wrong, they have no aid, no help, no backup from any of the other outer planets. They will either stand alone or they will fall alone."

Matthew's concern was clear on his face, "I see Matthew. I see", the Prophet was now sharing Matthew's concerns, "Matthew, what do you recommend?", he enquired.

"The same strategy we used last time my Lord", Matthew replied, "I'll quietly ensure that the Delilah is fully fuelled and provisioned. If the proverbial spinning turbine gets covered in crap, we'll be out of here right quick and on our way to Saturn."

"Let's hope it doesn't come to that Matthew", the Prophet replied, "Put your plans in place, just in case we have to leave. It's always good to have a backup plan."

The Prophet was unhappy with this possible outcome, he liked it here at Ganymede Prime, his new found friends suited him. He had both the status and celebrity he thought he deserved. However, if push came to shove, he would have to flee yet again, further out into the outer solar system, to worlds with colonies he knew very little about.

The Prophet prayed to his God, that things would come to pass as he would like, rather than in any untoward fashion.

Miriam and Rani had been shopping at the nearby Markets. The celebrations of the Birth of Prince Leopold's first born son, Ulrick were continuing everywhere. The High Prince favoured his youngest Brother, over his other two Brothers and in his generosity had decreed that the celebrations would last three whole days.

Not that Prince Wulfric and Prince Valdamar could claim to be hard done by, they each had their own realms within the Jovian System.

Prince Wulfric was the Prince of Callisto and thus had complete control of that rather large moon, all the resources upon it and all of the colonies within its orbital domain and close by smaller Jovian moons. In addition, Prince Wulfric was also in charge of all the Jovian outer defences.

Prince Valdamar of course was Prince of Europa. He not only had complete control of that moon, with its extraordinary resources, including its abundant life, but all of the colonies within its orbital domain as well and the smaller close by Jovian moons. The inner Jovian defences were also under his complete control.

Prince Leopold was the Prince of Io, his domain consisted of the moons Io, Amalthea and all the resources thereof, including the lucrative mining operations. All of the colonies within the Ionian orbital domain and any smaller Jovian moons within Ionian orbit were his to do with as he saw fit.

The High Prince Heinrich, was not only the High Prince of the entire Jovian Realm, but also the Prince of Ganymede and as such had control over Ganymede and all of its resources. All the colonies within Ganymede's orbital realm were his to control along with any nearby Jovian moons.

However, the High Prince was the absolute Monarch within the Jovian Realm and all of his Brothers and Sisters bent their knees to him and had sworn oaths of allegiance, loyalty and fealty to him as well. His Brothers and Sisters each ruled their little realms under High Prince Heinrich's over-lordship. High Prince Heinrich was the boss. If he said jump, his siblings asked, *"How high!"*

In addition to the Jovian System, the Horridian Dynasty was also in control of both the Leading and Trailing Trojan colonies. These being Lagrangian points, sixty degrees ahead and behind Jupiter in its orbit, where millions of Asteroids had collected due to Jupiter's powerful gravity.

High Prince Heinrich had two Sisters, they were born forth and fifth amongst his siblings, with Prince Leopold being the youngest sibling. The High Prince's sisters, Princess Sophia von Horridian was Princess of the Leading Trojan Colonies, while Princess Luisa von Horridian was Princess of the Trailing Trojan Colonies.

Control over these colonies was neither as lucrative, nor as prestigious as control over the other colonies of Jupiter itself and the Horridian Sister's were not always happy with their lot. They were highly ambitious and regularly petitioned the High Prince to attack and absorb the larger Asteroid Belt Colonies Into the Jovian Realm. The High Prince on the other hand, eventually convinced his Sisters to be patient while he put together his own plans, to which they agreed.

By using the Trojan Armed Forces to occupy both Mars and L5, High Prince Heinrich would be keeping those forces at bay and busy away from his realm, while in effect bribing his Sisters with the spoils and riches they would reap in return. High Prince Heinrich was a master manipulator.

Back at the Appelbaum's apartment, Miriam and Rani were cooking food for their dinner. They had a variety of unusual foods, that with the celebrations had become available to the general public at far lower prices than would otherwise have been seen. Again the generosity of High Prince Heinrich having declared the price drop for the duration of the celebrations.

"That all smells good!", Abram exclaimed, "What have we got here?"

"Well we went to the market today and some of the produce from Europa has had a huge price drop. Something like ninety five percent, courtesy of the High Prince, you know the celebrations and all", Miriam replied, "I thought we might try some of them."

"Are they kosher?", Abram enquired.

"Well, they'd have to be wouldn't they", Miriam replied, explaining, "These are from Europa, so there can't be any food prohibitions against them."

"Okay. That does make a lot of sense", Abram agreed, "but what did you get then?"

"Well, we have these sea plants, a variety of rather delicate sea weeds and some kind of kelp, which are supposed to be quite delicious", Miriam replied, then adding, "I was lucky to find recipes for them at the market. We also found some fish or at least it's called '*Jewel fish*'. And then there's this meat, it's kind of like steak from what's called a Tusker. I bought quite a bit of that one. It's suppose to be really nice and we can freeze some of it for later."

"Okay", Abram replied, "I guess we'll see what it tastes like later. From Europa you said?"

"Yes Abram", Miriam replied, "Apparently under the ice shell, Europa is teeming with life!"

"Who'd have guessed", Abram replied.

Rani's daughter, Lakshmi, who was walking past the kitchen chimed in with, "I've been reading about that. Apparently when the Jovian Colonies were all new, they were struggling to get things growing in the colony cylinders. Being so far from the Sun and all. So God touched Europa's Ice Shell and said '*let there be life*' and then there was. Then they drilled through the Ice Shell and there it all was. Life!"

Abram looked at Lakshmi with an incredulous look, "Let there be life?", he questioned.

"Yes, well that's what the text book says anyway", Lakshmi replied, "Apparently the concept of evolution, has been tossed right into the rubbish bin here in the Jovian colonies. Don't mention the word *'evolution'* here by the way. It is severely frowned upon."

Lakshmi's sister, Pavarti walked up and added, "They eventually managed to get food production going in the colony cylinders. After that the produce from Europa became the domain of the rich and the powerful. The prices were deliberately increased ten-fold, to limit who could afford them. They blamed that on the cost of maintaining the shafts drilled through the Ice Shell."

"Unless there's a special occasion of course, then the High Prince simply decrees a temporary price drop so everyone can celebrate. Then we all get to eat it!", Lakshmi added.

If evolution doesn't exist", Miriam enquired, "then how on earth do they explain the change in the characteristics of a species over time?"

"Oh they don't", Lakshmi replied, "They just invoke biblical creationism. You know, God did it!"

Pavarti added, "Did you know, that the entire universe is only around six thousand years old?"

"Is that what they teach up here?", Rani enquired.

"Absolutely Mother", Pavarti told her, "It's even in their text books. They are complete rubbish!"

"So what does that mean for science?", Abram asked.

"Science is fine, as long as it doesn't conflict with Christian scripture", Pavarti explained.

"And if it does?", Rani asked her daughters, "What if science conflicts with scripture?"

Lakshmi answered her Mother, "Then whatever aspect of science it is, is basically banned."

Pavarti added, "It becomes a heresy, but not a death penalty type of heresy, more of a re-education type of heresy. They literally re-educate you. Make you believe, what they believe", Pavarti laughed, "These people are crazy!"

Abram and Miriam looked at each other, then to Rani. It seemed the Jovian Colonies had devolved into a scientific back water, where religious bigotry and the rule of dogma had taken hold. Given enough time, this society would be destined to fail.

It was at that point that Abram had a curious thought, "Lakshmi, Pavarti, could you two do us a favour?", he asked them.

The girls both looked at Abram, "Yes, yes, of course", they replied.

"Excellent!", Abram began, "Can you find out if there is any kind of Royal *'appeal'*, or *'pardon'*, or some kind of *'leniency'* or something similar?"

Lakshmi asked, "What do you mean?"

"Ah. I was thinking of some sort of appeal for leniency with regards your Father and where he is currently located", Abram told them.

Pavarti replied smiling, "We can definitely look into that."

Rani had heard the discussion and asked, "Will it work?"

"I have no idea Rani", Abram was honest with her, "But if we can make an appeal to Prince Leopold, at this truly auspicious time, the birth of his first born Son, perhaps we can elicit a beneficial response."

"Oh Abram, that is cleaver", Miriam told him, then asked, "What made you think of that?"

"The images on those video feeds Miriam. We've been watching them for days now", Abram replied, explaining, "They love to push that generous and magnanimous image. Allowing Rajsheev to be relocated to Europa Prime, to be with his family, even though he is a Slave, plays to that image. It makes them look good."

Rani stated with a smile, "That does sound crazy, really crazy, but it might actually work!"

"I will have to check with John Schultz as well. See what he thinks", Abram told them, "He may have another take on this, that I haven't thought of. It is probably worth a try though."

Rani had barely smiled during here whole time in the Jovian Colonies and the Appelbaum's were pleased to see the hope in her eyes.

The following day, before his shift as a flight controller for the Europan Inter Colony Shuttle Service, Abram contacted John Schultz on their apartment communicator. John's Secretary Jacinta put Abram through and John was soon on the line.

"Abram. Nice to hear from you again", John began, "How are you and Miriam doing?"

"We're doing fine John", Abram replied.

"And the Neru family?", John enquired.

"Rani and her girls are doing fine as well", Abram informed him.

"Okay, what can I do for you Abram?", John asked.

"A bit of advice actually John", Abram told him, adding, "I had this idea and I wanted to run it past you first before I doing anything else."

"Okay, okay", John replied, asking, "What was your idea then?"

"Well, with the birth of Prince Leopold's Son, Ulrick and being that Amalthea is a part of the Prince's domain", Abram began, continuing, "I thought, that perhaps I could write an appeal or petition to the Prince, to maybe get Rajsheev transferred back here to Europa Prime."

"Wow!", John exclaimed, "That is an interesting thought", then thinking to himself, "*Why didn't I think of that.*"

"Yes, but would it work?", Abram asked.

John gave it a bit of thought then replied, "I don't think it would hurt, but at the same time, I don't know that it would work either. You'd have to give it try though, just to find out."

"Yeah, that's what I thought", Abram replied, he had been hoping for a more positive answer, "I can put something together after my shift later today."

"Some things to remember Abram", John started, explaining, "Only the High Prince can degree a Slave to be free. The other Royals, his siblings, they don't have that power."

"Yes I figured that", Abram answered, "I was thinking more in terms of getting Rajsheev back here to Europa Prime's North End Cap. That way, he would at least be close to his wife and daughters."

"Yes, I can see how that would be great for their family Abram. Give it a shot and see how things pan out."

"I'll do that John. Thanks again and much appreciated", Abram replied.

"No problem Abram, I'm always happy to help", John told him and the call was over.

Later that day, after Abram's shift, he sat down at the computer and carefully drafted his letter of appeal to Prince Leopold. Miriam read the draft letter and approved of it, before it was shown to Rani on the screen.

Rani smiled, "This is it then. Maybe it will work, maybe it won't. I'll leave it all in the hands of Ganesha, may he remove the obstacles!".

Then Abram pressed the send button and the letter was on its way via email.

A day passed, then two, quickly it was three. Rani grew more and more anxious with every passing day. After a week, Rani was beginning to think that their appeal to Prince Leopold had been summarily dismissed and sent into the trash. Rani became despondent and had retreated into her room in despair.

It was in the evening, almost two weeks after the letter was emailed. There was an unexpected knock on the apartment door.

Miriam answered the door. There was a man at the door, wearing what could only be described as a courtly uniform, "Yes", Miriam enquired.

"Is this the Appelbaum residence?", the Man asked.

"Yes. Yes it is", Miriam replied.

"You would be", the Man opened the grip on his left forearm and checked, then after pressing a few key strokes, "Miriam Appelbaum?"

"Yes, that is me", Miriam answered.

"Your Husband would be Abram Appelbaum and you have under your care, the Neru Children, Lakshmi and Pavarti. And also their Mother, Rani?", the Man enquired further.

"Yes, that is all correct", Miriam replied, asking, "What is this all about?"

"I will explain shortly Madam", the Man told her, then asked, "May we come in?"

"Who is we?", Miriam asked.

"Please Madam. It will simply not do, to stand in your doorway", the Man told her.

Abram had now approached their front door and said to his wife, "Miriam, let the Man in."

The Man stepped into their apartment and was quickly followed by two men in dark suits and trench coats, who immediately started performing what appeared to be a security sweep.

The Man said to Abram and Miriam, "Please do not be concerned, everything will be explained in a few minutes", as the security sweep was conducted.

One of the Men in suits nodded to the Man in courtly uniform, who then spoke two words into his communicator, "All clear."

Another Man stepped into the Appelbaum's apartment, he was fairly young, tall and thin, with long sandy coloured hair. He wore a highly ornate courtly uniform with a golden sash and a sabre scabbard-ed at his hip.

The first Man announced, "May I introduce His Royal Highness, Prince Leopold von Horridian, Prince of Europa."

Miriam became wobbly at the knees, Abram steadied her, then replied with a slight bow, "Your Highness, this is an honour. We were not expecting you. Please take a seat."

Abram pointed to the most comfortable chair in the apartments main room. Prince Leopold sat down in the seat that was offered to him.

Abram noticed that there were two more security men in the hallway beyond his apartment door. The other two security men, who were in the apartment, took up positions at the main points of Ingres into the apartment's main room. The Man who had originally knocked on the door, close the apartment door after the prince had entered.

Prince Leopold spoke, his voice was soft and eloquent, "Mr Appelbaum, Mrs Appelbaum", he began, "When my secretary received your email, he noted that you had two children in your care. Lakshmi and Pavarti Neru, I believe?"

"Yes Your Highness", Abram replied, Miriam was a little lost for words.

Prince Leopold continued, "Both of the Girl's have converted to Christianity yes?"

"Yes, yes Your Highness", Abram responded, adding, "That is correct."

"And the Mother and Father? It is my understanding that they are non-Christians, who have been classified as Slaves", the Prince noted with a frown.

"Yes, yes Your Highness. That is all correct", Abram replied once more.

"It is also my understanding that you have managed to procure their Mother as domestic helper", the Prince noted.

"Yes, yes Your Highness. Again that is correct, yes", Abram replied.

"These two children, they love their Mother and their Father yes?", Prince Leopold enquired.

Now Miriam spoke, "Yes Your Highness. They love their parents with all their hearts."

Prince Leopold sighed, then he stated, "I'm going to tell you both a little story. A story that must not be repeated. If I tell you it, you keep it to yourselves. Can you agree to that?"

Both Abram and Miriam replied, "Yes of course", almost in unison.

The Prince began, "Some years ago my Father, may he rest in peace, gave me a Slave. A young Girl just a couple of years younger than myself. She was a gift, for me to do with as I wished."

Both Abram and Miriam had somewhat disturbed looks come across their faces.

"I know. I know!", the Prince stated, when he notice their discomfort, "It is not the usual thing you might come across or think of as a gift and yes, it is truly, morally repugnant. It was also my Father's way of doing things. He was, shall we say, very different and quite unusual."

Abram asked, "Your Highness. Why are you telling us this?"

"You'll understand once I get to the end of the story Abram", the Prince replied, then continuing, "The Slave Girl that was gifted to me, She was truly beautiful. The sweetest person I had ever met. And against my Father's wishes, I fell in love with her. Her name was and is Giselle."

With that Abram and Miriam were beginning to understand the reason for the Prince's visit.

"My Father of course did not approve, as you might imagine. He did not approve at all", the Prince continued, "But then a short time later, he passed away and my older Brother Heinrich ascended to the Throne."

"My Brother Heinrich has always treated me well. He's always been a very good friend to me. I don't know, maybe I'm his favourite sibling or something", the Prince mused, then continuing, "My Brother knew of my situation and even though he thought me foolish. He used his power as the new High Prince, to decree that Giselle was from that day forth a free woman. After that, I married Giselle that very same year, after a suitable engagement period of course."

"Of course, when my Secretary read your email, he naturally forwarded it to me. I've known my Secretary for many, many years, he is a man I truly trust. I showed your email to Giselle and that was it. We both decided then and there, that we should help you with your situation."

"Oh my God", Miriam murmured, "The Girls, Rani, they won't believe it."

"Where would the Girls be?", The Prince asked.

"Your Highness", Miriam started, "They're in their rooms studying."

"And their Mother?", The Prince enquired.

"Rani is in her room as well", Miriam replied, adding, "Rani has been unwell, a little bit out of sorts of late."

"I can not imagine what Rani has gone through", the Prince replied with a regretful voice.

He then looked at the man with the grip and caught his attention. The Prince tapped his forearm. The man with the grip nodded and pressed a few key strokes on his grip

The apartment door opened once more and in walked Rajsheev Neru. He looked clean shaven, well fed and was wearing fine clothes.

"I took the liberty of transferring Rajsheev from Amalthea Prime to my palace on Io Prime", the Prince told them, "We then organised the trip here. I do apologise for not getting here sooner."

"Your Highness", Abram began, "You have no need to apologise."

Miriam had stood up from her chair and went to the Neru Girl's rooms, "Girls! There is a surprise for you out here."

When they entered the room and caught sight of their Father, they both ran up to him and he caught them in his arms.

Tears streamed down their cheeks, "Pappa, Pappa, we've missed you", they both told him.

The Prince looked on with broad smile on his face, "Looks like my work is done", he stated.

While the Girls hugged their Father, the Prince told Abram and Miriam, "I have not changed his status. I don't have that power. Only my Brother Heinrich can do that. So technically, Rajsheev is still a Slave. However, I have changed his ownership."

Abram asked, "So who owns Rajsheev?"

Miriam was curious as well.

The Prince smiled and told them, "I've transferred Rajsheev's ownership to his Daughters."

Miriam looked at the Neru Sisters, "Girls. You need to let your Father go. Your Father hasn't seen your Mother in quite some time."

"Pappa", Lakshmi started, "Mother's room is over there", she told him while pointing to her Mother's room.

Rajsheev walked over to Rani's room and opened the door, "Rani? Rani?", he enquired.

"Rajsheev! Rajsheev!", Rani exclaimed.

Rajsheev entered Rani's room and closed the door behind him.

"This ordeal has been very hard on all of them Your Highness", Miriam stated.

"Yes, yes. I do understand", the Prince replied, adding, "I cannot imagine how they've felt throughout this terrible ordeal."

Before Abram or Miriam could answer, "I have proposal for you", The Prince told them.

"A proposal?", Abram enquired.

"Yes", Prince Leopold replied, asking, "How would you like to live on Io Prime? All of you of course. In the North End Cap, quite close to my palace actually."

"Io Prime?", it was now Miriam enquiring.

"Yes of course", the Prince began, explaining, "We also need good flight controllers in Io Prime, so Abram would still have a good job. I've reviewed Rajsheev's records as well. He has very good skills in a number of areas and scores quite highly on aptitude tests. Rajsheev could he actually work at Io Prime. Here he'd just be another Slave. At Io Prime though, his worked would be both valued and remunerated."

"Your Highness, are you saying that Rajsheev could actually earn money in your realm?, enquired Abram.

"Why, yes of course Abram", Prince Leopold replied, "Although, the money would go into this daughters bank accounts. Technically in the Jovian Realm, a Slave can't open a bank account."

"I don't understand", Miriam stated, forgetting to address the Prince by his title.

Prince Leopold explained, "I've been making reforms in my realm of late", he told them.

"Ordinarily, a Slave works for their owner and does not really get any kind of wage. You know, as domestic servants, working in the fields or in the factories. That sort of thing. In my realm however, they can work for a wage. Although, under the current Jovian laws, anything they earn must go to their owners. Its not much of an improvement I know, but I can only make very small steps slowly."

"Some reforms are probably better than no reforms Your Highness", Abram replied.

"I wish I could do more", the Prince lamented, "Unfortunately, I am restrained by the laws of overarching Jovian Realm. I have managed to cleanup up the Amalthean and Ionian mines though. They are so much safer now, so much better, than they were under my Father's reign."

"How bad were the mines Your Highness?", Miriam asked.

"Oh conditions were shocking! The workers, Slaves as you know, were literally dropping like flies", the Prince replied, adding, "I never understood the logic of it. Surely if you look after the Slaves, you don't need to replace them so often and as a result, you don't need so many of them."

"Prince Leopold", Abram replied, "That does actually make perfect sense."

"Exactly my point Abram. Treating people like disposable assets, is not only cruel and heartless, it is simply bad economics as well. I would rather have happy wage earning workers, than unhappy, forced Slave workers any day", the Prince told them.

"I take it that your attitude, is not common amongst your peers Your Highness?", Miriam Enquired.

"You'd be right there Miriam", the Prince replied, "My siblings don't subscribe to my beliefs and neither do the bulk of the Nobility. Even a Prince is limited in what he can achieve. Anyway, discuss my offer amongst yourselves and let me know what you wish to do, yes?"

"Your Highness, we will give your offer very careful consideration", Abram answered.

"Good! Good!", The Prince acknowledged, "Let me know your answer and I'll have all the arrangements prepared for you. Oh and one more thing Abram. Your loan, the one you setup to purchase Rani. I've paid it out in full, under your name of course. So there's no need to worry about that now."

"Thank you Your Highness! That's incredibly generous of you", Abram replied.

"No need to thank me", the Prince told them, "It was the right thing to do!"

Miriam asked the Prince, "Your Highness, this new War? If you don't mind me asking of course."

"I don't have much say at all in Military matters", Prince Leopold replied, adding, "That's where my Brothers and Sisters come in. Wulfric is responsible for the Jovian Outer Defences. Valdamar is responsible for the Jovian Inner Defences. My Sisters have their own Armed Services in the Trojan Asteroid Colonies, but overall, it's really Heinrich that controls everything. He is the High Prince after all and he basically calls the shots."

"So Prince Leopold", Abram began, asking, "Do you agree with this War?"

"It is not my place to say Abram", the Prince told them, then adding, "There is simply no reason for it! Everything that is said about it, is simply to justify it.""

"I must admit Your Highness", Miriam replied, "We have both lived on the Earth and also in L5. There is no religious persecution in either of those places at all. Christians are certainly not being persecuted."

"I know, I know", Prince Leopold replied, "It just a pretext, a justification, a casus belli, that's all. My Brother may as well say he's hunting down Nazis. It would not matter. It's really, just all about greed. That's it greed! Plain simple greed!"

"Those missiles did appear to be launched from within your realm though, Your Highness", Abram stated.

"Yes, that would be right", the Prince replied, "The missile bases are in the Ionian Leading Trojan point. Heinrich has direct control over them. The Leading Trojan Points of all our Galilean moon are generally where you'll find our Military bases and even though they maybe within our realms, it is my Brother Heinrich who wields ultimate power and control over them."

"Wow! So even Wulfric and Valdamar, who are involved in the Military, they don't even control their bases, within their own realms?", Miriam enquired, again forgetting the Prince's Title.

"Ultimately no", the Prince answered, "My Brother Heinrich controls foreign policy and all external Military matters. My other two Brothers only control the defences."

The Prince then continued, "There are two exceptions though. My Sisters control Jupiter's Leading and Trailing Asteroid Colonies, and their own Armed Services. Ostensibly, Heinrich does control those as well. In reality though, not so much. He is very cautious with our Sisters and also very good at manipulating them."

The conversation went well into the night and it was shortly before midnight when Prince Leopold finally left their apartment. Rajsheev and Rani had not left Rani's room and their Daughters had long since gone to bed themselves. It had been an auspicious evening for all.

The next day, there was a long discussion about the Prince's offer to move to Io Prime. It was an incredible opportunity. More importantly, the Ionian Realm was actually far safer for Rajsheev and Rani than anywhere else in the Jovian System. Everyone was in agreement.

The very next day, Abram keyed in another letter to Prince Leopold, accepting his offer. Before the day was over, a reply came back, confirming that arrangements for the transfer were being made. Within two weeks, the Appelbaum and Neru families would be moving to Io Prime.

Abram emailed John Schultz to let him know how everything that had transpired over the last few days and then thanked him for all his help and advice.

Rani, ever grateful, prayed to Ganesha in thanks for this fortuitous turn around in events.

10. Chryse Colony

It was morning and Gatwech, Leroy and the Pod Sisters, had broken camp and taken to the Kasei River once more. They were only a short distance from the Chryce Colony and would be there quite soon. The Colony appeared on the river banks, mostly to their right along the southern shoreline. Although there did appear to be a good handful of settlements on the left bank, to the north as well. The Kasei River was quite wide at this point, prior to its branching into the Kasei Delta, before then flowing out into the Chryce Sea.

Gatwech had been here before, trading furs and skins from animals caught in traps he had worked in the Kasei Swamps. Anaconda skins had been quite lucrative amongst his wares, usually commanding the best prices. However, none of the others had been to Chryse Colony before and so they had no idea what to expect. For Leroy and the Pod Sisters, it would be their first time.

The first thing they noted was that the colony was a mix of both older and newer architectures. The older sectors were mainly along the river banks and scattered about here and there to the east and west of the more modern Chryse Colony. The modern heart of the Chryce Colony had only began construction a short twenty standard years earlier. The older sectors were far, far older, having been constructed over the preceding century.

Gatwech explained to the others, "The site of the Chryce Colony was chosen long ago, even before they began the terraforming process. They were meant to be building everything new, from the very beginning on clear virgin land."

Leroy replied, "A lot of this colony looks to be very old Gatwech."

"Yes", Gatwech replied, explaining further, "When the official colonists arrived with all their equipment to start building the new colony, they found that others had come here in the preceding decades. Long before the planet, had even been opened up for colonisation. It was quite a shock for them. All these scattered settlements right where they were going to build their brand new colony."

"I bet it was", Leroy agreed, looking at the juxtaposition of the old and the new buildings.

"They cleared out the centre of the colonial zone and began building this brand new, beautiful colony. A city of steel and glass spires, in the midst of these ramshackle, improvised shanty towns", Gatwech laughed out quite loudly, "Yes, it was quite a shock for them, when they arrived. I still remember it very well."

Gatwech in his younger trading days, was there when the official colonists had arrived. Yes, he remembered it very well.

All of the old sectors were exactly as Gatwech had described, built out of what ever the colonists had at hand. Many of the newer buildings were made of timber cut from the nearby, new forests of Lunae Planum, combined with scrap metal brought down from high Mars orbit. Locally made bricks and concrete was used to hold and bind everything together. The use of native Martian stone and rock was also apparent.

Some of the buildings had even been made out of old space ship hull sections. Once used to bring people and materials down to the surface, then sliced up as scrap to use as building materials. In a few cases, entire intact ships hulls had been utilised. Some of these older buildings still had their airtight seals in place, which showed that they were once able to be pressurised. A practice that showed the buildings were well over eighty years old. A time when people still had little trust in the terraforming process and whether or not it would hold.

The settlements were both pragmatic and eclectic. The early colonists had found out what worked for them and they had stuck to it. Building a series of scattered shanty towns across the Martian landscape, that had already been allocated to the official Chryce Colony.

Gatwech had said, "What works, works. Do what works", in describing how the original settlement had been constructed. That had been the settler's catch cry.

Of the twenty plus shanty towns that were present in the Chryce Colonial zone on this side of the River, when the official colonists arrived, only a dozen were left. These were all scattered around the modern steel and glass spires of the new Chryse Colony in the centre. Simply called Central. The original shanty towns had then expanded and sprawled around it.

Gatwech laughed again, "The locals were not very happy either, when the new colonists arrived and evicted everyone from the eight shanty towns in the middle of their planned colonial zone. It was a shock for them too. Those settlements all got bulldozed and cleared, raised to the ground, then up went the colony in no time at all."

"Was there no fighting, Gatwech?", Leroy enquired.

"Oh, there was violence. Of course there was violence", Gatwech replied, "but the locals were out matched and out gunned. There was nothing they could do. The new colonial administrators did however, help to relocate the locals to the other shanty towns and even used some of the old scrapped materials to extend them further. The more affluent ones, even purchased apartments in the shiny new towers."

"It looks so very strange", Zuawalo stated, adding, "All of that new steel and glass, surrounded by, ugh, I don't even know what to call it. It is a mess!"

"It is like a tulip in a turd!", Zeealas remarked.

Both of the Pod Sisters giggled. Yes, it looked for all intents and purposes, like a tulip in a turd.

"The people that live there, they call it home", Gatwech told them.

Gatwech manoeuvred the canoe to a small, stone dock by a shanty town, that was closest to the centre of Chryce Colony, with its gleaming steel and glass towers.

"None of these shanties are really safe", he told them, adding, "They are very rough places. This one is safer than most. Not by much through. Mind you, I have not been here in more than a decade. Pass through it and go straight to the new colony in the centre. There you should be able to book passage to the Elysium Colony."

"You're not coming with us Gatwech?", Leroy enquired.

"No. I have to go back. It takes much longer to return, than it does to come here", Gatwech explained to them.

Zuawalo passed Gatwech her fishing gear and take down bow, "I do not think I will need these from now on", she told him, adding, "Please take these back to our parents Gatwech."

Zeealas did likewise, handing her fishing gear and take down bow to Gatwech as well.

"Okay", Leroy replied, "Safe journey Gatwech."

"You be safe also and remember, straight to the new colony in the centre", he told them.

Leroy and the Pod Sisters gathered their possessions, then bid farewell to Gatwech, who pushed the canoe away from the dock and began manoeuvring it back into the river. The three of them stood on the stone dock, looking towards the shanty town before them and the tall, shining steel and glass towers behind it.

"Leroy", Zuawalo turned to Leroy, "My Mother gave me this. She said you would know what to do with it."

Zuawalo opened her satchel and showed Leroy a heavy leather bag.

Leroy crouched down and looked into the leather bag, it was full of golden credits of various denominations, "Yes. Yes Zuawalo. We will definitely be needing that", he replied.

Leroy was surprised. Zuawalo's people did not use money of any kind. They had no need for it. Everyone in Zuawalo's village helped each other and shared their produce equally amongst themselves. When they needed something that was not available in their village, they bartered with neighbouring villages with the goods they produced. That Zuawalo's Mother had golden credit coins was a surprise. He had not expected that. Then again, Gatwech had traded with Chryse Colony in the past. So money must have been available to them.

"Good", Zuawalo replied, instructing Leroy, "Put it in your satchel and we will use it when we need it."

Leroy put the leather coin bag into his satchel and they all began walking towards the shanty town that was before them.

The locals looked at the three strangers with curiosity. Leroy with his pale white skin, travelling with the two very tall, dark, young women, who could never be mistaken as locals. Zuawalo's people rarely travelled this far from their village and it was a very unusual site for the local folk. Some of the local folk simply stared at them with curiosity, others seemed to be actively following them. Curiosity maybe, ill intent maybe. Leroy was becoming more than a little concerned.

"Zuawalo", Leroy opened his satchel in front of her, "Put the pulse pistol in here. I might just be needing it", he told her.

Zuawalo also was becoming a little concerned as well and casually, transferred the pulse pistol into Leroy's satchel, in a way that was barely noticeable, "Only if it's necessary", she told him.

Leroy nodded to her, "Understood. Only if it's necessary. "

A few short minutes later a rough looking man with unkempt red hair and a tarred pigtail stepped in front of them. He blocked their path and was quite persistent in doing so.

"How much for the women?", the man with the unkempt red hair asked Leroy.

Leroy was caught of guard and simply replied with, "What the fuck!"

"Your females. How much for your women?", the red haired man asked Leroy again, being more insistent this time.

Before Leroy could even answer the man, Zuawalo had pulled her sheath knife out from its hidden scabbard and before the man could react, stuck it right up his left nostril. Zuawalo snarled at the man, who was now standing on the balls of his feet and exceedingly uncomfortable. Zuawalo pressed the knife just a little bit further and the man was now on the tips of his toes and even more uncomfortable. He was motionless and doing his best to balance on the tips of his toes.

"You are a very, rude man!", Zuawalo spat at him, her nostrils flaring.

The red haired man could not answer her.

Zuawalo glared at the red haired man man angrily, "I want you to go away!", she told him loudly, continuing, "And when you think you cannot go any further, maybe I will be behind, you will go away again, much, much further."

Zuawalo twisted the knife ever so slightly and drew just a touch of fresh blood, tears were welling up in the red haired man man's watering eyes.

Still angry and glaring Zuawalo told the man, "And at the end of the day, when you think you have finished running, think again, maybe I will still be behind you. You will not see me, but I will be there. Then you go away some more, much further and you will keep running. You do not stop! Do you understand me?"

The red haired man said nothing in reply, he was too busy balancing on his toes.

"Do you understand me?", Zuawalo repeated.

Quickly Zuawalo pulled the knife away, kicked the red haired man in the middle of his chest, wiped her knife and had it back in its hidden sheath in one quick, fluid motion. The rude man fell backwards and landed sharply on his arse. He nodded in answer to Zuawalo's questions.

"Go away!", Zuawalo still angrily glaring, shouted at the red haired man, "Go away now!", she shouted once more.

The red haired man crawled to his feet and began to run, he stumbled, then got to his feet once more and started running again. He didn't look back, he kept running. Zuawalo continued watching until the red haired man was out of her sight.

"Zuawalo, that was scary", Zeealas, who had also taken her sheath knife out, told her.

Zuawalo smiled, "Did you see the look on that very, rude man's face?"

"I think that rude man will run forever", Zeealas replied, also smiling, "You really scared him!"

Leroy, who had taken out his pulse pistol and had it ready for use, implored the Girls to keep moving. Their situation was volatile.

"Come on Girl's, we've created quite the scene here. We'd better be moving along", he told them, as he replaced the pulse pistol back in his satchel.

The three started moving through the shanty town once more, towards the centre of Chryse Colony. They noticed there was a change in the atmosphere around them. People were now actively averting their eyes from them. Now, no one appeared to be following them. The little show with the very, rude man, had shown the folk in this shanty town, these were people not to be messed with.

By mid morning they were closer to the centre of the Chryce Colony with its myriad of tall, steel and glass towers. Leroy walked over to a stall selling bags and picked out a nice, large bag for Zuawalo, for her ferret Zigg, who seemed to be getting bigger by the day.

He paid for it with the lowest denomination of golden credits that Zuawalo's Mother had provided, a fifty credit coin. With the change from purchasing the bag, Leroy then bought a dog harness from another stall that was selling pet accessories.

"Zuawalo", Leroy caught her attention, "Is this bag okay for Zigg?", he asked her.

Zuawalo inspected the bag, "This is a good bag Leroy. Zigg will like this bag", she replied.

Zuawalo opened her old bag, in which her ferret Zigg was fast asleep and gently moved her pet into the new larger bag.

"Thank you Leroy", Zuawalo thanked him.

"Zeealas, you can have this bag now", Zuawalo told her her Sister.

"Zuawalo! It smells of ferret!", Zeealas complained, none the less she still took the bag.

"You can can clean it there", Zuawalo told her, pointing to a nearby water tap.

Zeealas walk over to the water tap and began cleaning the bag, removing the smell of ferret.

Leroy then held out the dog harness to Zuawalo, "You will probably need this one as well", he told her, adding, "At least until you've trained him."

"Yes. I will need that one", Zuawalo replied while inspecting the harness to see if it could be adjusted to suit her ferret Zigg.

Zuawalo smiled and told Leroy, "This will fit Zigg perfectly. I just have to adjust it. Although I do not think, that he will like it."

"You'll need it", Leroy explained to her, "It's unlikely they'll let Zigg aboard a hummer or any other transport, unless he's in the bag or on a tight leash."

Zuawalo frowned, but Leroy was right, "Maybe I do not let them know Zigg is in the bag."

Zeealas, who had now returned from cleaning the smaller bag that Zuawalo had just given her, told her Sister, "They will smell him Zuawalo! You cannot hide the smell of pole cat!"

Zuawalo replied sarcastically, "You cannot hide the smell of slig. Even after you eat it!"

After a short brisk walk, Leroy, Zuawalo and Zeealas crossed within the perimeter of the Chryse Colony's new sector. The change in scenery was stark, behind them was the squalor of the old shanty town, which had appeared to them, more like a slum. Before them now was the opulent, beauty of the newer section of the Chryce Colony. As they walked deeper into the centre of the colony, they began to be surrounded by tall, steel and glass towers. A few streets in and the old shanty town was no longer visible to them at all.

Leroy located an information kiosk, "Where do I find the colonial space port?", he asked.

The information kiosk responded with an address on the other side of central Chryse Colony. The address was displayed on the kiosk's screen.

Leroy asked, "Hard copy please",the information kiosk then printed out the address for them.

Leroy took the piece of paper, folded it and placed into his satchel.

"Follow me", he told the Pod Sisters, as he led them to a nearby taxi rank.

They all entered the first taxi in the rank, Leroy taking the passenger seat and the Pod Sisters climbing into the back seats. Zuawalo was very careful not to let Zigg out of her bag.

Leroy told the drive their destination and the taxi was soon in the air.

The Taxi Driver glanced back at the Pod Sisters, "We don't often get your people around here", he told them.

"My people rarely travel this far from their homes", Zuawalo replied.

The Taxi Driver asked casually, "You lot travelling very far?"

"The Elysium Colony", Leroy replied.

"The Elysium Colony. Lots of traffic heading that way, that's for sure.", The Taxi Driver noted, "Did you book tickets in advance?", he then asked.

"No. We didn't", Leroy admitted, asking, "Did we need to?"

"Well maybe, just maybe", he replied, informing them, "With those recent attacks on the Elysium Colony, it's nearly all material and supply transports, construction workers and what not."

Leroy cringed, he remembered all too well his hand in those attacks, "I guess we'll find out when we get to the space port then."

Zuawalo and Zeealas said nothing, but they both knew that Leroy had been that, 'very bad man'. That these attacks on the Elysium Colony, which they were just now hearing about this very minute, were probably instigated by him.

The Taxi Driver continued, "And then there's that new colony that popped up from out of nowhere. Nobody ever heard of it before. New Tortuga they're calling it."

Leroy put his hands to his face. He was beginning to feel quite queasy and unwell.

"Apparently lots of construction works are happening there as well. Some sort of battle damage apparently! Lots of damage to be fixed. Lots of work for our colony. It's all good for the economy!", The Taxi Driver informed them.

He was a wealth of information, all of which, Leroy would have preferred not to hear.

He continued, "At one point the Colony's Security Forces were even sent down there to stabilise the situation. Its all hush, hush you know. No-body wants to talk about it, no-one official anyway."

The more the taxi driver talked, the more ill Leroy felt.

"You're not gonna puke in my cab are you Mister?", he asked Leroy, "If you do, I'll have to charge you a clean up fee. That's an extra hundred credits ya know."

"No. No. I'll be fine", Leroy mumbled, while looking quite an odd shade of green.

The Taxi Diver pulled his taxi up at the Space Port parking bays, "That'll be twenty five credits."

Leroy paid the man, thanked him for his service and then climbed out of the taxi with his bags.

The Pod Sister's grabbed their belongings and climbed out of the taxi as well. As they stood on the foot path, Leroy feeling quite bilious, fell to his knees and threw up in the gutter. It was several minutes before Leroy could compose himself.

"That was you Leroy, wasn't it?", Zuawalo enquired, clarifying with, "The Elysium Colony attacks? The battle at New Tortuga?"

"Yes. Yes", Leroy mumbled, "Those were my doings. Those and a lot more. I was the second in command and all of that, is on me. All of it!", he admitted, adding, "I should never have followed those damned stupid orders!"

"What about the big flash we saw on Phobos?", Zeealas asked, "One night Phobos passed by in the sky and there was this big, bright flash of light", she explained.

"No. No. That one was not my doing", Leroy told her, then reconsidering, "but at the end of the day, I'm just as responsible for that one as well."

Zeealas reached into her satchel for a water canteen and passed it to Leroy, "Drink!", she told him, "It will make you feel better."

Leroy nodded and tried to drink. He drank slowly at first, but eventually managed to drink a few mouthfuls of water. Ever so slowly the colour returned to his face.

Zuawalo passed Leroy some food, "Eat this!", she told him. It was left over smoked trout from their journey down the Kasei River.

Leroy ate the fish and was beginning to feel somewhat better.

"You should have let me drown Zuawalo!", Leroy told her, repeating, "You should have let me drown! I have no right to be alive! No right at all!", he had tears in his eyes.

"Gwek disagrees with you Leroy!", She replied, repeating, "Gwek disagrees with you. How can you redeem yourself if you are dead!"

Once Leroy had recovered sufficiently, they made their way to the flight booking counter.

Leroy asked the Lady behind the counter, "Three tickets to the Elysium Colony please."

"Elysium?", the Lady questioned, "How soon did you want to leave?"

"As soon as possible", Leroy answered.

"There are no openings for at least three weeks I'm afraid", the Lady informed them.

"Are you sure there's nothing?", Leroy questioned her.

"Everything is booked", the Lady responded, explaining, "There's been a lot happening lately. With the Elysium colony attacks, the New Tortuga colony liberation. All the transports are being used for the rebuilding operations. Everything at the moment is fully booked."

"Madam. It is absolutely imperative that we get to the Elysium Colony as soon as possible", Leroy informed her, asking, "What other options are available?"

The Lady behind the counter responded, "Sir, you have very few options I'm afraid. You can book a flight and wait a little over three weeks."

"So you noted earlier", Leroy answered, adding, "And as I've also noted. We need to be there as soon as we possibly can."

"If you need to get there earlier, then you'll need to book a private flight", the Lady answered him, adding, "There is no other way."

"Okay then", Leroy replied, "How do we organise a private flight?"

"Most of the private operators will also be fully booked", the Lady behind the counter replied, "However, there's probably a few private Hummers still available."

"Okay, right", Leroy responded, then asked, "How do we locate a private Hummer?"

The Lady made a call on her communicator, "Daryl, please come to the bookings counter. Daryl, please come to the bookings counter", could be heard over the loud speakers.

A man approached the bookings counter. It must have been Daryl. After a short conversation with the Lady behind the counter, Daryl approached Leroy and the Pod Sisters. At first he looked the trio up and down. They were an unusual group. The Pod Sisters especially so, their people were known, but rarely seen around the Chryse Colony.

"I hear you require some private transport to the Elysium Colony?", Daryl enquired.

"Yes", Leroy replied, "We have urgent business in Elysium."

"Okay. Okay. There are a number of private hummers in the south hanger", Daryl informed Leroy, then adding, "The problem is whether or not you can hire one."

"We do have money, so there shouldn't be any problem with payment", Leroy told him.

Daryl squeezed his chin, then told Leroy, "It's not about money. It's about availability."

"If there are a number of Hummers in the south hanger, as you've just said, why would they not be available?", Leroy enquired, just a little confused.

"Those private Hummers belong to, shall we say, affluent people", Daryl replied, explaining, "Affluent people aren't generally interested in hiring out their private vehicles."

Leroy was beginning to see the problem. The southern hanger contained a number of private Hummers, but they were generally not used for commercial purposes.

"Are any of the owners of those Hummers, reasonable people?", Leroy asked, further enquiring, "Would there be anyone amongst them, that would help a group of people that are, in a lurch?"

"Affluent people are, not generally known for their charitable behaviour", Daryl replied, "At least, not in these parts anyway."

Zuawalo was getting tired of this banter and let lose a muffled growl, followed by, "We need to go to Elysium!", she stated loudly, then, "We are off to see the Wizard!"

That caught Daryl's ear, "Wizard?", he queried, then "You're off to see the Wizard!"

"Yes Daryl", Leroy addressed him by name, informing him, "I have urgent business in the Elysium Colony with the Wizard."

Those two words had changed everything, "You should have said that from the get go", Daryl informed Leroy, then he explained, "Everything involving the Wizard, has to go through the Governor's office!"

"The Governor's Office?", Leroy thought to himself.

Daryl walked back over to the flight booking counter and spoke to the Lady behind the counter.

After a few short minutes, Daryl returned to the trio, "Please come this way."

Daryl led Leroy and the Pod Sisters to a small room. It had some comfortable chairs, a small low table in the middle and a coffee machine in the corner. It was a typical waiting room.

"Please wait in here", Daryl requested, while ushering them into the waiting room, adding, "I've asked Shelly to make some calls to get things moving. It may take an hour or so, but I think we'll have your Hummer up and running very soon."

Daryl then left the room.

Shelly must have been the flight booking clerk, they had been dealing with behind the counter. Leroy and the Pod Sisters seated themselves in the waiting room.

After several long minutes Daryl returned with a large platter of cut sandwiches, which he placed on the low table in the middle of the room before them.

"The machine in the corner makes coffee, tea, hot chocolate and of course water", he told them, "If you need anything else, Shelly is over at the counter and can make arrangements", then Daryl left the room once more.

"At least we don't have to catch our own food", Zeealas told the others.

"We left our fishing rods and bows with Gatwech", Zuawalo reminded her.

"My point exactly Zuawalo", Zeealas replied, "Catching food by hand is not so easy."

Zuawalo looked at the sandwiches on the platter, "Do not eat those ones Leroy", she told him, pointing to a group of sandwiches amongst the large assortment of sandwiches on the platter.

"Why not Zuawalo", Leroy enquired, they just looked like more sandwiches to him

"Those, they look like slork", Zuawalo informed him, noting the meat that was from a slig.

Leroy nodded in understanding, while Zeealas reach out and picked up two slork sandwiches, which both Leroy and Zuawalo noticed.

"It must be an acquired taste", Leroy replied.

"A slig is not a pig!", Zuawalo told Leroy, adding, "And slork is not pork!", she had a disgusted look on her face. Obviously Zuawalo had not acquired a taste for slork.

The name on the desk read, *'Governor John Anderson'*. He was a busy man, a very busy man.

Governor Anderson was in charge of the whole of Chryse Colony, but now, with all this turmoil arising from the attacks on the Elysium Colony. The liberation of the previously unknown colony, New Tortuga, by the Colonial Troops from L5, he was busier than ever.

Then there were those reports of missiles inbound from the Jovian System. Mars had no missile defences at all and he had yet to hear from L5 and the Colonial Fleet. He was stressed. He was very stressed.

He was beginning to develop a tendency to be short tempered, but was desperately trying to keep that under control. The stress showed on the man and he really needed some time off. When there was knock on the door, Governor Anderson knew it would be his Secretary Maria and simply pressed the buzzer on his desk.

"Governor", his secretary Maria addressed him, "We have some sort of situation at the space port. Its related to the Wizard."

Straight away that got Governor Anderson's full attention, "For the love of God, even here in my home town, in my own office. I tell you Maria, that bloody Wizard will be the death of me."

"Oh, he's not here Sir", Maria replied, explaining, "There are apparently three people at the space port, who have urgent business with the Wizard and they require transport as soon as possible."

"Then they can book a flight and we'll be done with them", the Governor replied.

"That's the problem Sir", Maria replied, explaining, "All the flights are fully booked. There won't be any openings for at least three weeks. Probably longer."

"Wizard's business!", the Governor exclaimed shaking his head, "Where the hell's Mack! Maria, find that bloody pilot."

"You gave him the week off Sir", Maria informed him, reminding him, "You said you wouldn't need him for at least a week."

The Governor responded with, "Like I care. Find him. Have Mack fly them to the Elysium Colony. Just get them out of our hair as quick as possible."

"Yes Governor", Maria replied, "I'll make the arrangements straight away."

As Maria was turning to leave the office, "And Maria. We pick up the tab on this one. Wizards business you know", the Governor instructed her, thinking to himself, *"This bloody Wizards business is costing us a pretty penny."*

The sandwiches had been eaten. Empty coffee cups were stacked on the table before them. It was now well over two hours and the Pod Sisters were becoming impatient. Leroy was also becoming impatient. He was about to get up and enquire as to how much long they would be waiting, when the waiting room door opened.

Daryl stepped into the room, "I am ever so sorry it's taken this long", he began, "We had to find the pilot for the Hummer. He was on his day off apparently, so it took a bit longer than we thought it would. Had to track him down and all", he informed them.

"Better late than never", Leroy replied.

The Pod Sisters said nothing, but had that, *"about time"*, look in their eyes.

"If you can all follow me, I'll show you the way to the Hummer", Daryl instructed them.

At that Leroy and the Pod Sisters gathered up their belongings and fell into line behind Daryl, as he led through the space port to the southern hanger.

The trio were led into the space port's southern hanger. There were a number of Hummers lined up, probably a couple of dozen or so, but only one of them had a pilot standing next to it. Standing right next to the main hatch. They all approached the pilot.

"This is Mack. He's Governor Anderson's personal pilot and this is the Governor's personal Hummer", Daryl informed them, "I'll leave you guys in Mack's capable hands."

"Thank you Daryl", Leroy replied as Daryl quickly turned and headed back into the space port.

Almost as an afterthought, Leroy shouted out to Daryl, "You didn't say how much the flight would cost."

Daryl turned about and replied, "Nothing at all. This flight's on the Governor", before turning back around and continuing on his way.

"So, you guys want to go to the Elysium Colony?", Mack queried.

"Not quite", Leroy replied, explaining, "Slightly north of the Elysium Colony actually. I have the coordinates right here."

Leroy passed the coordinates to Mack on a piece of paper.

The Pilot Mack, looked at the coordinates, "I've been to the Elysium Colony quite a few times. More than a few times in fact", he told them.

"Honestly, I'm not aware of anything at that location. There's literally nothing outside of the Elysium Colony. To the colony's north, it's literally just miles upon miles of wilderness."

"Trust me Mack, that's our destination", Leroy told him, "When you see it, you'll know it."

"Okay, if you say so", Mack replied, requesting, "If you could all climb aboard. We should be there in a few of hours."

Leroy, Zuawalo and Zeealas climbed aboard the Hummer. Zuawalo was careful to make sure that Zigg was asleep in his bag. She sniffed the bag. Zigg did smell, but maybe the pilot would not notice, maybe he would not care.

Mack climbed into the Pilot's seat and began to work the Hummer's controls.

Slowly the Hummer lifted off the ground and Mack carefully guided the Hummer out of the hanger and taxied it to a waiting launch pad.

Mack communicated with the space port control tower and a few short minutes later, the Hummer was lifting off vertically into the air. Once at the requisite altitude, Mack turned the Hummer east and then punched the throttle. They were now on their way to the Elysium Colony.

11. Io Prime

Prince Leopold's people had organised a private inter-colonial transport to take the Appelbaum and Neru families, along with all of their belongings, from Europa Prime to Io Prime. The Appelbaum and Neru families boarded the transport and made themselves comfortable for the trip. It was not a terribly long flight and only a little over eight hours later they were approaching their destination, Io Prime.

Ostensibly all the Jovian System's major colony cylinders were the same or at least almost the same. So the Prime's, Callisto, Ganymede, Europa and Io had all been built to the same basic design, that itself had been based originally on L5's Colonial Central. They all had the same basic lengths and widths, the same basic design for their solar redirection mirrors, even the same basic design for their tail booms which contained their fusion reactors and heat radiators. Where they differed mostly was largely in minor areas, such as design improvements and developments that occurred during the building and construction processes.

As the first to be constructed, Ganymede Prime was by far the oldest and was largely built to the original specifications, with only minor alterations made during its construction.

The next in line was Callisto Prime and it had benefited from the changes and developments made during Ganymede Prime's construction.

After that of course was Europa Prime, which benefited from the changes and developments that occurred during the construction of the preceding two primes.

The newest of the primes however was Io Prime and that colony was not only the newest, but benefited from all the improvements and developments of its predecessors.

By far the most noticeable difference was the astcrete radiation shielding and the window panel sections. As one moved inward towards Jupiter, as was the case from Callisto, to Ganymede, to Europa, then finally to Io, the radiation increased significantly. So to, as a result, the astcrete radiation shielding and window panel sections needed to be thicker, to block the increased radiation.

"Wow! Io Prime has a massive amounts of shielding", Abram informed his companions, it was the very first thing that he'd noticed. Every-one leant forward to get a closer look out the view port.

"Oh yeah", Miriam replied, "You can really see it. All that astcrete."

"Apparently at Amalthea Prime, the astcrete is so thick, it's more shielding than colony", Pavarti informed them. Amalthea Prime being a much smaller colony in Amalthea's trailing Trojan point.

"Well, where not going there are we", Rani replied.

"And a good thing too", Rajsheev told his wife, "I was there. They had me doing clerical work. So that wasn't so bad, but the colony, it's very industrial, not very pleasant. You would not like it."

"I wonder what it's like inside Io Prime?", Lakshmi was curious.

"The Prince did say it's very similar to Europa Prime", Abram replied, adding, "He said in his opinion it was much nicer."

"Well then, I think we'll find it comfortable at least", replied Miriam, adding, "Especially if the apartment is like the one we had at Europa Prime."

Miriam and the others watched intently as the image of Io Prime grew larger and larger in the view port. The clear aluminium on the window sections was exceedingly thick. It wasn't long before their transport would be docking and they could see the north end cap docking ring fast approaching. Twenty minutes later they were in their final approach and the transport switched to docking interlock mode, heading for the Prince's own private docks. Soon after they were docked.

The Appelbaum and Neru families stepped out of the transport and into the space dock, where they found themselves in the presence of the Man in the courtly uniform, who had knocked on their door back at Europa Prime. The Prince's Man.

"I am Hubert", he informed them, "We will bypass the internal immigration procedures. Everything has been arranged."

"And our luggage?", Abram asked.

"Our people are in the process of delivering your luggage to your door", Hubert informed them, "It should arrive before we do."

Hubert was correct. As they watched, they could see the transport's cargo bay doors atop the transport had been opened All of their luggage and material possessions were being hoisted out and placed on an electric transport conveyance. The vehicle was loaded up and on the move before they themselves had even begun to locate their own transport pod.

"You see", Hubert told them, sweeping his hand in the vehicles direction, "All taken care of."

"All done with robotic machinery? No slaves?", Rajsheev asked Hubert, noting, "At Europa Prime, all of our belongings were manually loaded by Slaves."

"Yes. We use a lot of robotics here", Hubert replied, explaining, "Prince Leopold in his wisdom, considers Slaves to be far too valuable. The Prince does not believe in wasting their time or endangering them with such manual labour. Based upon each Slave's aptitude and their predispositions, more worthy tasks are assigned to them. Things they would actually prefer to do."

"And yet, they are still Slaves", Miriam replied.

"Yes", Hubert answered, he had a sad lilt to his voice, "Prince Leopold cannot change their status I'm afraid. The Prince can however, make their lives somewhat easier, somewhat better. Here we assign them tasks that are better suited to them, tasks they might actually enjoy."

"And the mines? What about the mines?", Rani enquired.

"Ah, the mines", Hubert began, he smiled, "Yes the mines. We are in the process of reforming those. Both on Amalthea and Io."

"In what way?", asked Abram, he was quite curious.

"We have installed thicker radiation shielding, three times thicker in fact", Hubert explained, adding, "And now we are in the process of replacing the manual labour with robotic mining equipment. We now train the miners, Slaves as you are well aware, to use and maintain the robots."

"You seem almost proud of that", Miriam noted.

"Madam. I am most proud of theses achievements", Hubert told her, adding, "Prince Leopold has made many improvements to the lives of the Slaves here. It is his way!"

"His way?", Abram asked, even more curious now.

"Yes. He is not like his Father, nor is he like his Siblings", Hubert informed them, "He would do far more if he could, but he too, is constrained by the laws of the Jovian Realm."

Pavarti asked, "Why was the radiation shielding thickened?"

Hubert replied with a sorrowful sigh, "Before the radiation shielding was thickened, it was woefully inadequate! Miners would last on average only ten years or so before terminal diseases caused by the radiation made them to ill to work."

"That's horrible!", Pavarti almost screamed.

"Yes it was!", Hubert agreed, then adding, "The Prince thought so as well! When The Prince took over this realm, his first action was to double the radiation shielding for both the Amalthean and Ionian mines. Even that was found to be insufficient, so he ordered the shielding to be further increased until it was three times thicker than the original."

"Did it work?", Pavarti enquired.

"I'm happy to say, yes, it did", Hubert told her, "The thicker shielding was more than effective."

"Hubert, what happened to the sick miners?", Rani enquired.

Hubert sighed again as if remembering a painful memory, "Before my Prince came of age and took over the Ionian Realm, the miners worked until they dropped and then they were euthanized."

"Euthanized!", Abram responded, "Isn't that a crime against humanity?"

"Prince Leopold certainly believed so", Hubert replied, explaining, "Miners that are too sick to work now, are now given hospital treatment. Those that suffer from terminal illnesses go into hospices for palliative care, where they are looked after until their passing."

"So Prince Leopold reformed that as well?", Miriam asked, having become very curious.

"Yes, he most certainly did", Hubert replied with what sounded like pride in his voice.

"And now the Prince is changing the mines over from manual labour to robotic mining techniques?", Pavarti asked him.

"Yes. Yes!", Hubert responded enthusiastically, "More of my Prince's reforms!"

Pride was definitely showing in his voice.

"What does the Prince's Brother, the High Prince think about these reforms?", Abram enquired.

"I don't think he cares", Hubert told Abram, explaining, "It's all about the quotas. As long as the mining quotas are met, no-one really cares how. And with healthier miners and the new mechanisation's, we not only meet those quotas, we exceed them, with plenty of time to spare."

"What happens to that left over time?", Miriam asked.

Hubert smiled proudly, "That left over time. Madam, it goes to the miners. They get time off!"

Lakshmi, who had a keen eye for things unspoken, spoke up and asked, "Hubert. If you don't mind me asking. Are you a Slave?"

Hubert smiled, "Yes young Lady. That is my status. I am and have always been a Slave."

"You don't seem in anyway resentful", noted Rani.

"Madam. The Prince has never treated me badly. Quite the opposite in fact. In my life, one barely notices that I'm a Slave at all", Hubert replied, adding, "It is my status yes, but my Prince has always treated me, first and foremost, as a human being."

"Prince Leopold does sound like an exceptional Man", Abram replied.

"Yes Abram", Hubert replied, "My Prince is definitely an exceptional Man."

While they had been talking, they had also been slowly walking to the nearest transport pod bay. Upon reaching the transport pods, Hubert ushered the Appelbaum and Neru families into the nearest pod and then stepped in himself.

It was only a relatively short journey, tens minutes at most and the transport pod arrived at an underground garage. They alighted the pod and Hubert led them to the elevators. They all stepped into the nearest elevator and then Hubert inserted a key and pressed the button to the top floor. That was a surprise for all of them, even more surprises were in store for them.

The two families stepped out of the elevator at the top floor and found themselves standing on a large landing, a landing that led to a single apartment. All of their luggage and other belongings were stacked on the landing to either side of the apartment's door. Just as Hubert had promised, it was all there, even before they themselves had arrived.

Hubert led them over to the apartment's door and then used the same key he'd used in the elevator to open the door.

"This is your penthouse apartment", Hubert informed them.

"Penthouse apartment?", Abram queried, then querying further, "Are you sure?"

"Yes. Its all kosher", Hubert replied, informing them, "The Prince himself has allocate this penthouse apartment to your two families. It should have more than enough rooms and should be very comfortable indeed."

Abram caught the word *'kosher'* and wondered whether they knew, he and his wife were Jewish.

The two families entered the apartment, followed by Hubert. They looked around and found themselves surrounded by pure opulence.

"This is way too much Hubert", Miriam told him.

"Yes. Hubert, this is way, way too much", Abram agreed.

Rani and Rajsheev looked around in wonder, Lakshmi and Pavarti giggled with excitement.

"Rajsheev. I prayed to Ganesha for help, but I never, never expected this", Rani whispered loudly enough that everyone heard her.

Hubert smiled, "Prince Leopold is most generous", he informed them, "Your monthly rental will be somewhat lower than you were paying at Europa Prime."

"It is still way too much Hubert", Miriam repeated.

"Perhaps yes, but this was my Prince's decision, so please accept it", Hubert replied.

Abram reached out and shook Hubert's hand, "Hubert. Please thank the Prince for us. All of us."

"There is more", Hubert told them, "You also have access to the roof top gardens", he smiled.

"Roof top Gardens!", Lakshmi and Pavarti replied in unison.

Hubert smiled once more and replied, "I'll leave you all now, so you can get acquainted with your new apartment. Please explore it. If you need anything else, there's a list of contacts on the main kitchen's cork board."

Hubert passed a ring of keys to Abram and then left the apartment and summoned the elevator.

The Appelbaum and Neru families explored their new apartment. They left the unpacking of the luggage until later. They were in an anteroom at the apartment's door, which on either side, had separate cloak rooms. Just through the anteroom they had entered was the main room.

The main room was enormous, with all the conveniences you could imagine. Beyond that, were the kitchens and bedrooms. The apartment was huge, taking up the entire top floor of the building.

There were two kitchens, one was slightly smaller than the main kitchen, but not by much. All of the modern conveniences were present and each kitchen had a large butlers pantry. These butlers pantries could be used as fully functioning kitchens in their own right.

Even though each kitchen easily had enough seating for eight people around large rectangular tables, there was also a large dining room further down. This dining room had enough seating for twelve people, set around a large circular table. It had views through a very large window, that were to die for.

There were twelve bedrooms in all. Twice as many as they could possibly need, let alone use. All of the bedrooms were of a similar, overly large size and all were ornately decorated. Closet space was plentiful within overly large walk in robes. Each bedroom had its own huge bathroom containing claw footed baths, showers and toilets. Each bedroom came with two balconies, each with the most magnificent views. This apartment was far more than any of them could have imagined. It was incredible!

Then they found their way to the roof top stairs. When they made their way to the roof top gardens, their minds were blown away. They found themselves within what could only be described as rich, vibrant hanging gardens.

Court yards within the gardens, delineated by the shrubs, bushes and small trees themselves, were plentiful. Furnished patios and verandahs, with barbeque equipment and seating were plentiful as well. There was even a vegetable patch and fruit trees in small orchard. There was also a pool house and not one, but two pools, both were of a good size. What was the most incredible thing however, was the view. It was truly stunning!

From this rooftop vantage point they could see all across the northern end cap of Io Prime. The entire city was on the inside of a huge hemispherical cap, that was over four kilometres in diameter. Separating the end cap from the main cylinder, which itself was over twenty kilometres long, were the bulk head mountains. These thick, circular bulk heads were designed with steep terraces that were more akin to steep mountain slopes. They rose gradually at first, then grew ever more steeply, until they reached the central grey bulk head material in the middle.

At the very centre was the large redirection mirror, that reflected the sunlight that passed through the northern end cap's main clear aluminium windows, into the entire hemispherical end cap.

Buildings and trees could be seen to the left and right, following the curvature of the end cap. Those that were ninety degrees around from their current location, appeared to be at right angles to them. Quite a disconcerting site. Gardens were hanging from the buildings and in between the buildings were broad park lands, with more trees and shrubs and even lakes.

They could look up and see the other side of the end cap, with the buildings and trees appearing to hang upside down above them. Coming out from the centre of the end cap, opposite the redirection mirror, was a boom like structure with another large, stubby cylindrical structure at its end. That was of course, as they could all tell, the end cap's zero gravity recreational zone.

However, what caught their eye and this was directly above their location, appeared to be a large estate of park land, with what could only be described as a palace in the middle of it. This was of course the palace and residence of the Prince of Io, Prince Leopold and his family.

The next day, having packed away their belongings and with Abram and Rajsheev not yet being scheduled to start work, the two families relaxed in their new apartment. Lakshmi and Pavarti were on the roof top enjoying themselves in the pools. Abram and Rajsheev were sitting in the main room, their wives Miriam and Rani, were acquainting themselves with the kitchens. By and large, they were incredibly impressed with their new apartment and had been discussing how lucky they had been, to have Prince Leopold take an interest in their situation.

A computerised voice came over the apartment's intercom.

"Elevator access to the penthouse has been activated", it informed them.

"Someone's coming up", Abram responded.

"Who could it be?", enquired Rajsheev, who then added, "It could only be Hubert."

"Yes. Probably Hubert", Abram agreed.

They both walked to the front door in anticipation of the Hubert ringing the bell.

The bell rang and Abram answered the door. It was indeed Hubert.

"Good afternoon Abram, Rajsheev", he greeted them, "Is it okay if my people do a quick security sweep?"

"Yes of course", Abram agreed.

Hubert entered the anteroom and two menu in trench coats and uniform followed him. The two security men entered the apartment and began their sweep. The sweep was quick, far quicker than one would think for such a large apartment. This was made possible with the penthouse's computer and its attached sensors. The security sweep completed, Hubert pressed a button on his grip.

"Introducing His Royal Highness, Prince Leopold von Horridian, Prince of Io, his wife Princess Giselle, Princess of Io and heir to the thrown, Prince Ulrick", Hubert announced.

The Prince was wearing his courtly uniform with its sash and sabre. The Princess was wearing the most elegant of gowns.

The Prince and his wife entered the anteroom, followed closely behind by their nanny, who pushed the pram in which young Prince Ulrick was sleeping.

"Hubert, Hubert, Hubert", Princess Giselle chided, "Here we are simply Leo, Giselle and Ulrick", it was said with almost a giggle.

"Your Majesties", Abram greeted the royal couple with a bow. Rajsheev followed likewise.

"Abram, Rajsheev, did you not hear my wife?", the Prince queried, then continuing before they could answer, "Here, in private, it is Leo, Giselle and Ulrick. Save all those tiresome formalities for out in public. Here we are just folk."

"As you wish Your Highness. Ah, um, Leo", Abram replied, adding, "Please enter our humble abode", while gesturing towards the main room.

The royal couple strolled through to the main room, followed by their nanny and the young prince. Abram, Rajsheev and Hubert followed. The two security men remained in the anteroom.

Two more security men remained on the landing outside the penthouse's door.

Prince Leopold and Princess Giselle made their way to a pair of comfortable chairs. Their nanny pushed the pram with Prince Ulrick asleep inside it, into a position between them and took a seat on a nearby chair. Abram and Rajsheev could see they were both familiar with the penthouse and how the furniture was laid out.

Abram and Rajsheev both took seats opposite them. Hubert remained standing.

Princess Giselle frowned, "Hubert, please take a seat", she chided him. Hubert then took a seat.

"Humble abode", Princess Giselle laughed, then added, "You do know Abram. This penthouse is our so called '*holiday home*'", she laughed again.

"It is?", Abram queried, then almost apologetically stated, "We would hate to deprive you of your holiday home ma'am. And it is, really far, far larger than we require."

"It is not a problem Abram", the Princess replied, "Have you noticed. Our palace is directly opposite, on the other side of the end cap. Leo inherited the penthouse and we hardly use it at all."

"Yes", the Prince agreed, explaining, "Who goes on holiday opposite their primary residence. It has never really made any sense at all to. We only come here to '*inspect*' the furniture."

At that point Miriam and Rani entered the main room and upon seeing the royal couple, they both curtseyed and greeted them with, "Your Majesties."

"No, no, no. In here, we are just Leo, Giselle and Ulrick", the Princess informed them.

The two wives sat down in chairs close by their husbands.

"So, how have you all been settling in?", Princess Giselle asked them.

"Well as you know, Your Highness, we only arrived yesterday", Miriam replied, "So it's all still very new to us. It is however, the most beautiful place Abram or I have ever stayed in."

"Call me Giselle please", the Princess assured Miriam.

"Yes, yes. This is the most incredible apartment", Rani told the Princess, "Our family is ever so lucky to be here."

"Excellent", the Prince clapped his hands, "Your families can stay here as long as you wish."

"And your Girls Rani", the Princess enquired, "How are they settling in?"

"Oh. They are just fine ma'am", Rani replied, informing her, "They're up on the roof top, swimming. They've never had a pool before."

"I am so glad they're happy", the Princess replied, explaining, "I can't image how they felt when your family was split up and placed in such peril."

"It was a difficult time for all us", Rani admitted.

"Well that's over now", the Prince told them, "Here in the Ionian Realm people are treated so much better. People are actually treated like people here."

It was quiet for a few minutes and the silence was beginning to get awkward.

Abram then broke the silence, almost as a joke, "I was thinking. Those two pools up there.   They're both of a good size. So I was thinking, the larger pool could be stocked with fish. Maybe trout or some other suitable species."

"Abram!", Miriam chided.

Prince Leopold however agreed, "That's actually not a bad idea. Hubert, why haven't I thought of that one?"

"You can't think of everything Your Highness and your plate has been very busy lately", Hubert replied, as he pressed a few keys on his grip, then added, "I'll make the arrangements Sir."

"Excellent", the Prince replied, "We have a few lakes on our estate. They are all stocked with various fish. When I have free time, I do enjoy casting a line. We will have to invite you all over one afternoon for barbeque or a picnic."

"Yes. Yes", the Princess agreed, "The gardens are beautiful, especially this time of the year and your girls Rani, they'll love it. They can run around exploring the palace grounds."

The Princess questioned, "Abram, Miriam. You don't have any children?"

"No ma'am", Miriam replied, explaining, "We haven't been blessed with Children. It's not a possibility I'm afraid."

"Oh. I am so sorry to here that", the Princess responded with her soft and gentle voice.

The Prince then informed them, "One of the reforms I'm making is to do with the children of, God I hate this word, the Slaves."

The Princess squeezed his hand, "Yes. Its very sad how some of our people have been labelled."

The Prince continued, "In the past, when a pair of Slaves had a child, the child themselves automatically became a Slave. The reasoning behind this was, that if the children of Slaves were freed, then where would the next generation of Slaves come from. So I'm going to reform all that."

"Okay, that makes sense", Abram replied, querying, "But aren't you constrained by the laws of the Jovian Realm? Only the High Prince can free a Slave."

"Yes and no Abram", the Prince replied, explaining, "There is a loop hole. The children of Slaves were never given the choice and that is where I can make some changes", he smiled.

"It works like this", Princess Giselle began to explain, "With all the other reforms Leo is making, using mechanisation and robotics to do all the drudge work. We will literally need far fewer Slaves in the Ionian Realm. That being the case, then why do the children of Slaves, have to Slaves at all."

"They don't!", Prince Leopold told them emphatically, "But it is not as easy as that and it may sound cruel at first, but it will be far better in the longer term."

"In what way?", Miriam questioned.

"Well if a Slave couple don't want their children to become Slaves and I do think that many, if not all of them will want their children to be fee. Then we can make them an offer. An off they could not possibly refuse", the Prince informed them.

Princess Giselle continued on from her Husband, "The Slave couple sign their new born child over to the Ionian Realm, which then arranges an adoption for the child. If the child is then raised as a Christian and then later goes through all the confirmation, then they cannot become a Slave, ever! They are simply put, free citizens of the Realm."

The Princess was equally emphatic about this as her Husband.

Princess Giselle began to explain further, "It sounds cruel, I know, but it is the only way forward that we can see. My Husband is still working on the details of the reforms of course. In theory, the biological mother of the child becomes a wet nurse for the child for a period of one standard year. The biological parents will be allowed to be involved in the child's life as well. So it's not so bad and the child is, at the end of the day free!"

"And that gets around Jovian Law?", Abram enquired.

"Yes. We've looked into that and we believe that under Jovian Law this is allowable. The choice is already offered. It just hasn't been applied to new born children", the Prince informed them.

"Wow!", Miriam exclaimed, "So you will be needing families for those adoptions."

"Exactly Miriam", Princess Giselle confirmed, "We will need couples. Couples willing to adopt these young children", her voice again was soft and gentle.

"I was always told that I couldn't have children of my own", Miriam told the Princess.

Princess Giselle reached across and held Miriam's hand firmly, "This is an option for you. They may not be biologically yours, but you can still raise adopted children as if they were your own. We need Mothers Miriam!", the Princess implored her.

Tears welled up in Miriam's eyes, "Oh Abram!", the tears began to flow freely.

"That sound like a yes to me", Abram replied, reaching over and squeezing

Miriam's other hand.

By now both Rani and the Princess were also in tears.

"Leopold", Abram addressed the Prince by name, "Something that has vexed us since we came to the Jovian Realm", he told the Prince, "Why does the Jovian Realm even need Slaves?"

Prince Leopold looked Abram straight in the eye and stated two simple words, "The narrative!"

"The narrative?", Abram enquired.

"The narrative is what is taught to the free citizens of the Jovian Realm since birth", the Prince told him, "and it's pure bullshit!"

The Prince's last word caught them all by surprise.

Princess Giselle, wiped the tears from her eyes with her handkerchief and continued for her Husband, "The narrative blames everything on the Earth and L5. Absolutely everything!"

"You might need to elaborate on that just a wee little bit", Abram responded.

The Prince began to explain the narrative, "Now bare in mind, this is all complete bullshit!"

He did not mince words, "In the narrative, the Earth and L5 have persecuted and enslaved the entire Christian population. Even going so far as committing genocide. So as a response, the Jovian Realm has enslaved all non-Christians. We however, are apparently far, far fairer, as we give all the non-Christians and all the new non-Christian arrivals the choice."

Princess Giselle stepped in, "When the new arrivals come here, they have those two questions. What is your religion? If non-Christian, would you be willing to convert to Christianity? Of course no-one from outside of our society understands the ramifications of those questions and the answers given. So a non-Christian who says no the second question, finds themselves classified as a Slave."

"Which is hardly fair! As their choice is completely irrevocable", the Prince added.

"It gets even better", Princess Giselle continued, "In the narrative, the ruling classes of the Earth and L5 have devolved into these monstrous, brutish, almost sub-human creatures, that rule the Earth and whole inner solar system with an iron fist. They literally call your leaders Demons! Some even say that your leaders are actually possessed by Demons!"

"And even that makes no sense!", Princess Giselle exclaimed, explaining, "Which is it? Did they devolve or are they possessed? They have two stories here and no answers. Mind you, if evolution has been thrown into the trash can, as it has, how can they even have devolution anyway? It is puerile nonsense!"

"This narrative, this indoctrination, has been going on now for generations", Prince Leopold continued on from his Wife, "So much so, that even my Grandfather believed it, my Father believed it, my Brothers and my Sisters all believe it! They all believe in their own propaganda! Hence the new War. They literally call it the War of liberation! They are all stark raving mad!"

"But you don't believe it?", Miriam enquired.

"No", the Prince replied, smiling at his Wife and nodding, "I met Giselle!"

Then Giselle informed them all, "I was born on the Earth. I came here with my Parents. I knew the truth and I was able to explain it to Leo, how ridiculous this narrative was", she laughed, "He was really thick headed at first, but I eventually got through to him."

The Prince leaned over and kissed his Wife gently, "Was I really that thick?"

The Princess just laughed and told her Husband, "Well, just a little bit."

"Wow!", Abram exclaimed, "And I thought, it was because you simply didn't have Androids."

"Androids? You mean Robots?", the Prince queried.

"No not Robots. Although, before the development of the positronic brain, we did have those", Abram replied, explaining, "Our Androids are humaniform Androids. They look very similar to us. They are stronger than us and highly intelligent as well. Capable of understanding highly complex instructions. They do all the drudge work and much of the manufacturing and construction."

"Wow! Really? What keeps them from 'running a muck'?", the Prince asked.

"They have these three laws built into their positronic brains. They simply can't run a muck. They simply can't breach any of the thee laws", Abram replied.

Rajsheev chimed in with, "The first law. An Android cannot harm or through its inaction, allow a living human being to come to harm."

Rajsheev continued, "The second law. An Android must obey all orders given to it, except where those orders conflict with the first law."

Then finally Rajsheev revealed, "The third law. An Android must protect itself from harm and its existence, except where there is a conflict with either the second or first laws."

"That makes them three laws safe!", Rani chimed in.

"And if an Android breaches those three laws", Prince Leopold enquired.

Rajsheev replied with three words, "Neural cascade failure", explaining further, "Their positronic matrix suffers a catastrophic failure. Effectively they die. Not that they were alive in the first place mind you, but it amounts to the very same thing."

"Rajsheev", Abram began, "You never did mention what you did for work at L5."

"Oh. Nobody ever asked", Rajsheev replied, "I was a design engineer for positronic matrixes."

All eyes were on Rajsheev.

Was Rajsheev the answer to a question that no-one in Jovian Society was asking?

The very same question that was on both Prince Leopold's and Princess Giselle's minds, *'How to end Slavery in the Jovian Realm?'*

12. The Academy

It was a splendid day at the New Flinders Academy, to the north of the Elysium Colony. Not too hot and not too cold. Perfect weather in fact. The large hanger doors on Varak's construction hanger had been opened and a new ship had been towed out onto the large expanse of the airfield's tarmac, two kilometres southeast of the academy.

Both Varak and Forkbraid stood on the tarmac in front of the Star Ship Solstice. The Solstice was an awesome ship, only a hundred metres in length, but arguably the most advance ship in the entire solar system.

More importantly, the Solstice was designed with unique capabilities that in theory at least, made her an interstellar class vessel. The Solstice also had sharp teeth, with no fewer than thirty six, state of the art, advanced weapons systems. Her defensive capabilities were equally impressive, being more advanced than anything that had come before her.

Varakhan Utana was exceedingly proud of his work.

"Time to take the Solstice through her paces", Varak informed Forkbraid.

"Whose going to pilot the ship?", Forkbraid asked.

"You are FB", Varak replied as he passed Forkbraid a special neural interlock control helmet, while informing him further, "I have a number of people studying the flight manuals, including Lady Selene and Jim Murphy. I also thought it would be a good idea for Marcus and Charlene to be across them as well, indeed quite a few others in fact."

"I have already committed the flight and weapons manuals to memory Varak", Forkbraid informed him, adding, "I fully expect Selene will do so as well, using the very same techniques."

Forkbraid looked at the helmet. It was very much like the helmet he used to control his Bat Wing Interceptor. Only this helmet was covered in brown leather and had a Sigil marked into the top. Carved into the leather and coloured bright red.

"Varak, this Sigil?", Forkbraid enquired, "Why did you put this Sigil on the helmet?"

"Well FB. You being you and all. I thought it needed a little something. Something special", Varak replied, explaining further, "I asked Lady Selene what would be a good design, a good symbol to put on this helmet, something that you would definitely like."

"And Selene suggested this?", Forkbraid enquired.

"Actually no. Lady Selene suggested I look in her personal library and recommended I browse through the books that contain Sigils and Talismans", Varak replied, adding further, "Lady Selene told me, that when something stands out and sticks in my mind, that is the one I should use."

"And this particular Sigil stood out?", Forkbraid asked him.

"Well yeah, it kind of did", Varak explained how he happened upon the Sigil, "I found four books which were most intriguing, Futhark, Galdabókin, Grá húð and Rauð húð."

"Those last three are very old. Ancient manuscripts bound in coloured hide. I doubt you could have read those Varak. I'm surprised you could even pronounce their titles", Forkbraid replied.

"It took a lot of practice FB and a lot of help from Lady Selene I might add. Anyway Lady Selene also had the actual translations. One for one, old Icelandic to English", Varak explained.

"Yes. You would have definitely needed those", Forkbraid agreed.

"Anyway, the first book was facinating, but those last three, they were", Varak paused for long seconds while trying to think of an appropriate word, "extraordinary. They were definitely useful. That Sigil appeared in every one of those books and I could not get it out of my mind. So I showed the Sigil to Lady Selene and asked her if it was appropriate."

"And Selene said it was. Yes?", Forkbraid replied, not really a question, more of a statement.

"Yes. Yes", Varak replied, adding, "Lady Selene said that, she could have given me the Sigil when I first asked, but that it was more important that I 'discover' it for myself?"

"Lady Selene wanted you to choose the Sigil Varak, because you were making the helmet", Forkbraid explained, elaborating, "And with this Sigil, this Aegishjalmur, this Helm of Awe, this helmet you've made, is effectively now a Talisman."

"A Talisman? Are you sure FB?", Varak replied, "I mean, I have never made a Talisman before."

"There's always a first time for everything Varak", replied Forkbraid,

"Perhaps you have other skills, beyond being the man who can make anything", then thinking to himself, *"Selene manged to find a way to turn my neural interlock control helmet into a Talisman of protection!"*

"Varak. At some point, I will need to consecrate this helmet. And as you made the helmet, you will need to be a part of that", Forkbraid informed him.

"Now remember FB", Varak began to explain, "When you wear that helmet, the ship, the Solstice, becomes an extension of you. It may have a positronic matrix controlling it, but you control that positronic matrix. You think and it does."

"So it's like moving an arm or a leg?", Forkbraid mused.

"Yes. Yes and no", Varak continued to explain, "Solstice needs to learn, she needs to get to know you. So at first, you have to be explicit. You first think, *'Solstice'*, to get the Ship's attention. Then you have to think of where your commands are being directed. So you then think, *'Computer'* and then you follow up with an appropriate ships command, as per the Ship's flight manual. To use the weapons systems, you think *'Hive'* , *'Hornet's nest'* or *'Tactical'* and then you follow up with an appropriate command from the Ship's weapons manual."

"Okay. That sounds pretty straight forward", Forkbraid replied.

"As you interface with the Solstice more and more, over time, the Solstice will get to know when you're commanding her. You'll be able to skip the explicit *'Solstice'* thought", Varak explained.

"I'll still need to use the command directives though, *'Computer'* or *'Hive'*?", Forkbraid enquired.

"Yes. That will still be required", Varak replied, adding, "In time, you will even be able to feel, even read the Ship's sensors, without the ship notifying you. They will automatically come up in the helmet's head up display of course, but you'll see it all in your mind's eye as well. The Ship's sensors will become an extension of your senses. Eventually, it will be like, muscle memory."

"These new *'senses'* Varak", Forkbraid needed some clarification and enquired, "Will they become addictive?"

"No. I don't believe so", Varak replied, explaining, "Without the helmet on, you are still you. With that helmet on however, you will be connected to the ship and you may feel some what more than you would normally feel."

"Yes, my senses, my abilities, then add on all the Ship's sensor as well. I can see how I might feel somewhat more expansive. Only one way to find out", Forkbraid replied as he put in the helmet.

Varak and Forkbraid had not yet entered the ship and from their vantage point on the tarmac were in a good position for the initial tests.

Forkbraid thought, *"Solstice. Computer. Sensors"* and immediately the helmet's head of display began to show the Ship's sensor readings.

Forkbraid's next thoughts were, *"Solstice. Computer. Sensors. Priority assignment based on perceived level of concern."* Immediately the ship rearranged the sensor readings in the order of perceived concern. The perceived order of concern rating, being calculated by the Solstice's positronic matrix.

Forkbraid then locked in those sensor priorities with, *"Solstice. Computer. Sensors. Store current priority settings as default and standard."*

Varak followed Forkbraid's progress on his grip.

"So far so good", Forkbraid told him, adding, "Let me try something."

"Solstice. Computer. Sensors. Connect to orbital reconnaissance satellite network. Real time data on head up display. Define head up display as HUD and store setting.", Forkbraid issued the thoughts. Almost at once the satellite readings flooded into the HUD. It was somewhat of a mess and even confusing, but it was start,

"Solstice. Computer. Sensors. Calculate and apply default priority ratings to satellite data", immediately the data organised itself as Forkbraid instructed and re-displayed on the HUD.

Varak was still following Forkbraid's progress on his grip, when Forkbraid noted, "Well now isn't that interesting."

Varak replied, "I have a mess of data in front of me FB. You might want to elaborate a little."

Forkbraid issued the thought, *"Solstice. Computer. Sensors. Highlight incoming vessel and identify same."*

The incoming vessel was immediately highlighted and an identity tag appeared. Varak could now see the data more clearly on his grip.

"It is a hummer FB", Varak stated, knowing full well that Forkbraid has exactly the same data.

"Yes. I can see that. It's on a flight from Chryse Colony and it appears to belong to Governor Anderson, according to its beacon", Forkbraid informed him.

"Governor Anderson?", Varak queried, then stated, "He doesn't know where the Psychic Academy is. By rights, he should be heading further south to the Elysium Colony."

"Well, his personal hummer is head straight to us", Forkbraid replied, then thinking, *"Solstice. Computer. Sensors. Incoming vessel. Scan vessel. Report armament status."*

Further information was added to the vessel's identity label on the HUD, *'Status unarmed'.*

"Varak. Send Jim, Marcus and Charlene a heads up. Copy in Selene as well. I think we have guests", Forkbraid instructed while taking off the helmet.

Governor Anderson's pilot, Mack, could see the airfield's tarmac in the distance, "Something very interesting is going on down there at that airfield", he informed his passengers.

Leroy and Pod Sisters looked out of the Hummer's view ports as their pilot Mack approached and then circled the airfield at least three times before beginning to land.

"What class of ship is that Mack?", Leroy asked.

"I have no idea. It's not one that I've ever seen before", Mack replied.

"Nor I", replied Leroy, "It must be something new."

Mack landed the Hummer gently, close by a group of people who had gathered on the tarmac, "Looks like you're expected."

Lady Selene, Agent Murphy, Charlene and Marcus had joined Forkbraid and Varak at the airfield. They watched as the Governor's Hummer approached from the west. It circled the airfield several times before the pilot landed the craft, close to where they were gathered. Being this was Governor Anderson's Hummer, most of them were kind of expecting Governor Anderson himself, to step out of the craft. Forkbraid and Selene however, had a feeling that something was amiss. They were a little on edge and prepared for anything.

The Hummer's hatch opened and its pilot Mack stepped out onto the tarmac. Mack stepped to one side to allow his passengers to alight. The two Pod Sisters stepped out onto the tarmac first followed by Leroy McGuvan. Surprised looks were on the faces of all those that had gathered to greet their 'guests'.

"What the fuck!", Agent Murphy exclaimed as he drew his pulse pistol and aimed it directly at Leroy McGuvan's chest.

The two Pod Sisters instinctively stepped in front of Leroy McGuvan and blocked Agent Murphy's line of sight.

"Put that thing away!", Zuawalo demanded.

Her voice was strong and full of force, her hand touching the hilt of her sheath knife.

Forkbraid waved his hand at Agent Murphy stating, "Jim. Put away your pulse pistol. You won't be needing it."

"Are you sure FB?", Jim queried, "We both know who this is!"

Forkbraid had been scanning the surface of Leroy's mind and carefully probing, "Yes and no Jim", he replied, then after a short pause, "He was, yes. Now however, he is no longer the same man. He has been changed Jim. Changed!"

"Changed?", Agent Murphy muttered as he holstered his pulse pistol, but keeping his hand on it.

Agent Murphy could see that Forkbraid was in complete control of the situation and now with his mind more relaxed he noticed the Pod Sisters far more clearly.

They were tall, dark and stunningly beautiful, like no women he had ever seen before.

Agent Murphy was quite entranced and could not take his eyes off of them.

"Leroy McGuvan!", Forkbraid addressed Leroy, "I executed you! You should be dead! How is it, that you are you still alive?"

Leroy stepped out from behind the Pod Sisters protection and answered, "This girl", he pointed to Zuawalo, "Zuawalo Pod, she saved my life", he informed him.

Forkbraid looked at Zuawalo Pod and asked, "What did you do to him?"

Zuawalo answered, "I was squidding. He flew out of the sky. I saved his life!"

Forkbraid frowned, then asked, "This man is changed! He is not the same man! How?"

"He was a very bad man!", Zuawalo replied, then explained, "Gwek demolished him!"

"Gwek?", Lady Selene enquired, looking at Forkbraid and back again.

This time Zeealas answered, "Gwek is our village Kujur."

Forkbraid turned to Selene and stated softly, "Demolished? Selene, this is not like any demolishing I have ever seen. This is very, very different. We need to know more about this Kujur."

Varak who thought the Pod Sisters might be Swahili speakers, greeted them, "Salamu wanawake", in an effort to break the tension.

Zuawalo replied, "We speak English. We also speak Nuer. Our Kiswahili, not so good."

Varak seemed confused by that reply, "Nuer? There are Nuer people here on Mars?"

Zeealas replied to Varak's question, "Yes. Our people came here from South Sudan. A little bit long time ago. Before the sky fell and the long rains."

Forkbraid turned to Varak, "We can look into that later Varak. Right now, we need to know more about Mr McGuvan here", he stated while pointing to Leroy.

Forkbraid then sent a quick thought to Selene, *"I'm going to put them all to sleep, but I don't want them hurt, falling to the ground."*

"Understood", Selene replied back, *"I'll take care of the girls. You deal with McGuvan."*

Forkbraid concentrated then clicked his fingers, "Sleep!", he spoke out loud.

Leroy McGuvan and the Pod Sisters were instantly asleep on their feet. Lady Selene used her abilities to lower the Pod Sisters gently to the ground, while Forkbraid did the same with Leroy.

While this was happening, the pilot Mack, had brought their bags and satchels from out from the Hummer and placed them on the tarmac. Mack shouted out, "Oi! What do you think your doing?"

Forkbraid raised his left hand, "It's okay. They're just asleep", he replied.

Zigg the ferret, who had been asleep in Zuawalo's bag climbed out and sniffing the air, caught Zuawalo's scent. He immediately ran over to Zuawalo and began nudging her, trying to wake Zuawalo up.

Lady Selene walked over to Zuawalo and Zigg, then crouched down beside them, "How sweet", then to Zigg she said, "Sleep!" and Zigg was out like a light.

"Marcus, Charlene. These two girls and their pet. Have them brought to the academy. They are our guests, so billet them accordingly", Lady Selene instructed them.

"Jim. Check their bags for weapons. Then bring Mr McGuvan here to the academy. Secure quarters with a round the clock guard", Forkbraid instructed.

Agent Murphy queried, "Keep a watch on the girls too?"

"Nothing heavy Jim, but do keep an eye on them", Forkbraid replied, adding, "I think they're just locals caught up in McGuvan's mess."

Lady Selene then added, "If they're locals, they'll be from somewhere close to New Tortuga. Cormac and Candy will probably be able to help with that. They may have useful information."

"That's a good idea Selene", Forkbraid replied.

"I'll debrief the pilot and refuel his Hummer then", Varak suggested.

"Yes. Do that Varak, but before you do check his Hummer. Remove any references to this location from its computer and erase the flight logs. I don't want the Hummer's computer logging his return flight either ", Forkbraid instructed him.

"I can do that FB. No problems at all", Varak replied.

"Nobody. Nobody messes with my ship", Mack told them in no uncertain terms.

"About that", Forkbraid skimmed the surface of the pilots mind for his name, "Mack. I'm going to have erase some of your memories as well. Maybe even suppress a few others."

"No way! No fucking way!", Mack replied.

Forkbraid clicked his fingers, "Sleep!" and Mack slowly crumpled to the ground.

Forkbraid concentrated on Mack as he lay asleep on the tarmac. He did so for several minutes.

"Varak. When Mack here wakes up, he'll have no memory of our location. He'll be able to fly home, but he won't remember a thing when he gets there", Forkbraid informed him.

"And what about the Solstice?", Varak enquired.

"I've obscured it from his mind Varak", Forkbraid replied, explaining, "He'll look straight at it, but won't be able to see it. Nor will have have any memory of it. It will be like it was never there."

"That is one hell of a trick FB. One hell of a trick", Varak replied.

Later that day there was a meeting at the New Flinders Psychic Academy. The meeting was in a large common room in one of the unused dorms. The very same dorm where the Pod Sisters had been billeted.

Everyone who was at the tarmac when Leroy and the Pod Sisters arrived was present. Cormac and Candy were also present, informing them all about the villages on the southern shores of the Hebes Sea, to the south of Hebes Island.

"Right over to the east, you have the small township called Shira. Not much more than a village really. The folk there aren't too much different to us. Just ordinary folk. They do a fair bit of trade with another small town called Jericho in the Ophir region. That's in the northern reaches of the Valles Marineris. It's a smallish sea port with fairly regular trade and a passenger service with the Aurorae colony", Cormac was telling them.

"Yes, but over to the west, you have different folk", Candy quickly added, explaining, "They're a peaceful folk, they mostly keep to themselves they do. Very dark skinned folk. That'll be where these girls came from. That stretch of coast, all the way south down to the Perrotin Lake."

"There are a lot of small villages along the southern coast line. Quite a few in fact", Cormac continued, "We don't really have any dealings with them though. As Candy says, they mostly keep to themselves they do. We do occasionally see them from New Tortuga in their fishing boats."

"I'd like to know how they got here?", Selene asked.

Marcus stepped in, "I've been checking the historical archives. Long before the terraforming, there was this consortium of countries from Eastern Africa. It was made up of six countries in all. Ethiopia, Tanzania, Kenya, Uganda, Somalia and South Sudan. They came here as a group to set up their own colony."

"Then why are so many small villages?", Selene enquired, "Why not just one big colony?"

"Well, according to the archives, there was some kind of disagreement. A dispute. They couldn't decide on where to build their new colony", Marcus replied, further explaining, "So they split up along national and cultural lines and created several smaller colonies instead. Quite a few in fact."

Agent Murphy asked, "How the hell did they manage to survive? They must have been here when the terraforming was in full swing."

"The same way we did", Candy answered, explaining, "Our people survived in New Tortuga's caverns. They would have built their colonies that same way. Burrowed into the ground, into the cliffs. Remember, back then, there was no air, no water. They would have been underground, in sealed, airtight, contained environments."

"Then after the sky fell and the long rains, when everything began to settle down, they would have come out and expanded their colonies into their villages. A whole new world would have been there in front of them. By now there could be many dozens of villages.", Cormac added.

Zuawalo awoke. Zigg, her pet ferret, had been nudging her side and making cute little 'Dook Dook' noises. Zigg was wearing his harness and it was tethered to the bed.

Zuawalo yawned. The bed was comfortable, but the room was unfamiliar to her. Zuawalo sat up.

Zeealas was asleep on another bed, on the other side of the room. Zuawalo threw one of her pillow at her.

"Zeealas! Wake up!", Zuawalo called out.

It was Zeealas turn to yawn, "What is it Sister?", she asked, still half asleep.

"Wake up Zeealas!", Zuawalo called out again.

"Okay! Okay!", Zeealas replied, then as she sat up and looked around, "Where are we?"

"I do not know", Zuawalo replied, "We need to find out."

Zeealas looked towards the door and noticed a trolley in front of it. On the trolley Zeealas could see three dome shaped covers. Zeealas climbed out of her bed and walked over to the trolley, then lifted one of the covers.

"Breakfast Sister. Scrambled eggs with toast and fruit juice. It is still hot.", Zeealas told her.

"Then it was placed there very recently", Zuawalo replied. Before she could say don't touch it, Zeealas had already sat back down on the bed and started eating.

"Aah. You should not eat that!" Zuawalo chided, "It could be poisoned!"

Zeealas frowned, "Why? Why would someone cook us poisoned eggs? I am hungry! And it tastes very nice!"

Zuawalo looked at her Sister and at the food Zeealas was eating, she too was hungry.

"I will eat yours if you do not want it!", Zeealas told her.

At that, Zuawalo walked over to the trolley and grabbed her plate, then sitting back down, began to eat. Zeealas was right, the eggs were delicious and she gave a little of them to Zigg.

"Zuawalo. There is a third plate", Zeealas having finished her breakfast informed her.

Zeealas replaced her plate on the trolley and peeked under the lid of the third plate.

"This must be for Zigg", Zeealas told her Sister, before placing the plate, which contained raw meat on the floor in front of the trolley.

Zuawalo picked up Zigg by the harness and placed him of the floor in front of the plate. Zigg did not hesitate and began eating his breakfast.

"If they are treating us this well, then Leroy is probably okay too", Zeealas noted.

"Probably Sister. We still need to find out", Zuawalo replied.

Muffled sounds from the nearest dorm room, told the gathering that the young ladies were now fully awake. Slowly the door of the dorm room opened and Zuawalo peaked out. Zuawalo stepped out of the dorm room and into the common room. Zeealas was only a step or two behind her. The two very tall, dark sisters stood before them, with Zigg the ferret on his leash.

"Good morning young ladies", Lady Selene greeted them.

"Good morning", Zuawalo and Zeealas greeted the gathering in return.

Forkbraid looked at each Sister in turn and then said to them, "You would be Zuawalo Pod and you would be Zeealas Pod. You are Sisters. Your ferret's name is Zigg. He is rather big for a ferret."

Zeealas asked, "How do you know our names?"

Zuawalo poked Zeealas gently and told her, "He is the Wizard!"

Lady Selene who knew what Forkbraid would say next, got in first, replying, "Male or Female, a Witch is a Witch."

"He is a Witch?", Zuawalo queried, just a little confused.

Forkbraid answered, "Witch or Wizard yes, but I prefer the term Witch."

"A man Witch Sister", Zeealas told Zuawalo.

Forkbraid began introductions, gesturing to each in turn, "This is the Lady Folcrom Selene, Cormac Farmer and his wife Candy Farmer, Marcus Greyhelm and Charlene Fewkes. I am Lord Folcrom Forkbraid. Oh, and over here we have Varakhan Utana and Agent Jim Murphy. We're all psychics here, except for Varak and Jim."

"What is Folcrom?", Zuawalo asked.

"It is a title", Lady Selene replied, "The most powerful of us have the title Folcrom."

"So you are what Gwek would call, Great Wizards", Zuawalo replied.

"Yes", Forkbraid replied, asking, "About this 'Kujur', Gwek. What can you tell us about him?"

"He is like you", Zeealas told them, "He is also a Great Wizard."

"Well that certainly explains a lot", Lady Selene replied.

"You said that Gwek demolished Leroy McGuvan", Forkbraid reminded the Sisters.

"Yes. Leroy was a very bad man!", Zuawalo reiterated, "Gwek demolished him."

"Zuawalo, where we come from, a demolished man, is not like Leroy", Lady Selene told her.

Zuawalo had a confused look, Gwek had demolished Leroy, that was the word he had used.

Forkbraid seeing her confused look, explained, "Where we come from, when a very bad man is demolished, he has no memories of his life before his demolishing."

Lady Selene continued on from Forkbraid, "His memories are wiped clean. He starts off with a new life, with a clean slate and no memories of his past transgressions at all."

Zuawalo was beginning to understand, "Leroy remembers everything!", she told them, "He remembers who he was. He remembers being that very bad man! He has nightmares from his past!"

"Yes Zuawalo", Forkbraid agreed, "Leroy remembers everything. What Gwek did to him was a very different kind of demolishing. A kind of demolishing we have never seen before."

Zuawalo informed them, "Gwek told me, Leroy must seek redemption."

"Is that why he's here?", Lady Selene enquired.

"Yes. Gwek told me that Leroy must walk the path of redemption", Zuawalo replied adding, "And that I must help him to find that redemption."

"So you and your Sister brought him to us", Selene replied, it was not a question.

The Pod Sisters both nodded in the affirmative.

"I need to look into Leroy", Forkbraid told them, "I need to look at what Gwek did. He didn't wipe his memories clean. He did something very different. Something with the light of troth."

"*The light of troth?*", the Pod Sisters both thought to themselves, not understanding what it was.

Forkbraid sensed the concern the Sisters had for Leroy and was quick to tell them, "Leroy is okay by the way. He is being held in a secure place, but he is being well looked after."

The Pod Sisters both nodded in the acknowledgement.

Agent Murphy who was finding himself quite entranced once more by the Pod Sisters, could not stop staring at them. Candy had noticed and nudged Cormac in the ribs, subtly gesturing in Agent Murphy's direction.

Cormac then took notice and sent a thought to Candy, *"Oh my!"*

Candy sent back a thought and smiled, *"I think we've lost this one. He's right smitten."*

A smiling Cormac replied with, *"He looks thoroughly enchanted."*

"Yes, he does, those two girls are quite bewitching aren't they", Candy thought back.

Cormac simply nodded in agreement.

Both Selene and Forkbraid caught the thoughts and they also took notice. Their head of security seemed to be quite distracted by the Pod Sisters.

Zeealas looked in Agent Murphy's direction and asked him, "Why are you staring at us?"

Agent Murphy went bright red with embarrassment, "Ah, Um, I, I do apologise. I did not mean to stare. Honestly", his words came out all mumbled. Then without thinking he blurted out loudly, "I have never seen such beauty before in all my life." Everybody heard him.

Zuawalo smiled at Agent Murphy, a very sweet, gentle kind of smile, then she told Zeealas, "I like this one. This Jim. He seems so nice."

Zeealas replied with a touch of jealousy in her voice, "I saw him first Sister!"

"You are too young Zeealas!", Zuawalo informed her, thinking to herself, *"This man is mine!"*

"Ladies, if you would like to freshen up, there's a bathroom at the back of your dorm room", Lady Selene informed the Pod Sisters.

Charlene added, "You'll find your belongings in the wardrobes, in your dorm room as well. You will also find a selection of new, clean clothes. I did pick them out myself and they should all fit. I'm hoping that you'll both like them. If not we can always arrange something else."

"I'll organise a hutch for you ferret Zigg", Marcus told them.

At that the two Pod Sister's, thanked them and returned to their dorm room to freshen up.

"Jim. Check in on Mr McGuvan. Make sure he's okay", Forkbraid instructed.

"I'll do that", Jim replied and then left the dormitory to check on Leroy McGuvan.

Varak had a huge smile on his face, "I think our Mr Murphy may be in a little bit of trouble."

"How so Varak?", Forkbraid enquired.

"These girls are Nuer speakers. They are Lou Nuer people", Varak informed them.

"And that means?", Forkbraid replied, he had no idea what Varak meant and needed clarification.

"I don't know if they follow the same customs as they do on Earth, but if they do, then our Mr Murphy will likely be in a little bit of trouble", Varak replied cryptically once more.

Lady Selene stepped in with, "You will definitely need to elaborate on that Varak."

"Ah. Yes", Varak replied, explaining, "Obviously our Mr Murphy is smitten. I think he has been bitten by the love bug. Both of these Sisters like him as well. It is going both ways I think."

Candy who had a huge smile on her face and had already noticed the looks between Agent Murphy and the Pod Sisters, replied "So Varak, you think, we could be hearing marriage bells in the very near future."

"Oh yes. Oh yes Candy", Varak replied, adding, "Definitely with Zuawalo, the older Sister, but if the two Sisters cannot agree, then our Mr Murphy could end up with both Sisters!"

"Both Sisters!", Lady Selene exclaimed, then adding whilst laughing, "If Jim ends up married to both of those girls, he'll never get any work done."

Candy laughed out loudly, "He'll never even get out of bed!" Cormac was also laughing.

"Oh yes", Forkbraid agreed, "I think Jim is in right trouble. Somehow, I don't think he'll mind."

"And Varak. Making Talismans, predicting the future. Maybe we should be testing you for psychic talent", Forkbraid told him. Varak burst out laughing.

Cormac and Candy stayed in the dormitory to keep an eye over the two Pod Sisters, while the rest of the gathering went about their business for the day.

Lady Selene and Forkbraid headed over to their make shift security centre where Leroy McGuvan was being held. Leroy McGuvan was not in the chamber where he had been locked up for the night. Instead he was quietly sitting at a table, having finished off his breakfast. Agent Murphy was sitting at a table near the entrance, keeping a close watch on him. On the table in front of Agent Murphy were two sheathed knives, a leather pouch and pulse pistol.

"Jim. Everything okay?", Forkbraid enquired.

"Yeah. Seems to be", Agent Murphy replied, "This version of Mr McGuvan doesn't appear to be much of a threat. Make sure you scan him thoroughly though just to make sure."

"And those?", Lady Selene gestured to the weapons on that table.

"The two knives belong to the Pod Girls", Agent Murphy replied, "The Pulse Pistol belongs to Mr McGuvan here. I've inspected it. It shows signs of being immersed in water and having been cleaned. I figure he was wearing it when FB 'executed' him. I have of course removed the power pack. That leather pouch has golden credits in it. Quite a few of them in fact. McGuvan here says they belong to the Girls."

"What else have you found out", Forkbraid asked.

"Zuawalo saved him from drowning while she was fishing for squid in the Hebes Sea south of New Tortuga. He has a scar on his left arm from a fishing gaff. So he must have been under the water when he was retrieved. At Zuawalo's village, they patched him up and Gwek demolished him", Agent Murphy replied with a quick summary.

Agent Murphy continued, "They travelled from Zuawalo's village to Chryse via the Kasei Swamps. Apparently both Girls are excellent survivalists. They can both hunt and fish. My kind of Girls actually. They told the Chryce Space Port people they were 'Off to see the Wizard', so naturally Governor Anderson expedited the process. That's it in a nutshell."

"Okay, so that's their story. Thanks Jim", Forkbraid replied, adding "Why don't you take the Pod Sisters on a tour of the Academy. You can give them all of their credits and their knives back while you're at it."

"Is that wise? Giving them their knives back?", Agent Murphy asked.

"The Girls are not a threat Jim", Forkbraid informed him, "And the knives are their property."

"Okay. Will do", Agent Murphy replied. He then gathered up the knives and the leather pouch, then eagerly headed out the door to meet up with the Pod Sisters.

Lady Selene and Forkbraid walked over to Leroy's table and took the seats opposite him.

"Leroy. Leroy. Leroy", Forkbraid repeated, "What are we going to do with you?"

Leroy didn't answer, he sat there in front of them with his head bowed, his eyes lowered.

"Leroy. The Girls tell us that you're here for redemption", Lady Selene told him.

Leroy lifted his head, "Yes, yes. Redemption."

"How does that work Leroy", Forkbraid asked him.

"I, I don't know", Leroy replied, explaining, "How do I make amends for all of the harm that I've caused? I was hoping that you could put me on the right path."

"The right path", Forkbraid repeated as he looked towards Lady Selene, then back to Leroy, "We don't know what that path is either Leroy."

"Then there is no hope for me is there", Leroy replied, all hope now lost from his voice.

"Perhaps. Perhaps not", Lady Selene told him, then added, "Leroy. We are going to scan you. A very, intense, deep scan. Please don't be afraid and please don't resist."

"As you wish", Leroy replied. This certainly wasn't the arrogant, cheeky bastard that Forkbraid had executed at New Tortuga.

Lady Selene looked a Forkbraid who then nodded in agreement. Then they both turned to Leroy and began their scan. They both gave Leroy a cold, hard stare.

First they began scanning the surface of Leroy's mind and they found it to be a bubbling cauldron of turmoil. Horrors from Leroy's past, not done to him, but done by him, surfaced, forcing their way into his thoughts. Leroy's conscience was sea of fire, burning with remorse and regret. Leroy was sincere in his need for redemption and penance. This was the first thing they'd needed to know. It also explained the nightmares that Leroy was inflicted with.

They scanned deeper now and looked for the handy work of Gwek the Kujur. They didn't have to look far. They found memory after memory, entire decision branch trees, that had been highlighted with shimmering, glowing, golden light.

"I was right Selene", Forkbraid thought, *"Gwek used the Golden Light of Troth."*

"Yes Forkbraid", Selene agreed, *"This work is so intricate, so interwoven. It must have taken him days. I have never seen it used in this way. On a single event yes, but across the expanse of an entire lifetime. That is unheard of?"*

They followed Gwek's work all the way back to Leroy's first memories, to the very memories that had set Leroy McGuvan on the path to Evil. Gwek had *'loosened'* that memory and every memory that followed, all the way forward, in every interaction up to his execution and bound them all into this intricate weaving of shimmering, golden light of troth.

"Forkbraid, this working is permanent", Selene told him, *"There's no way Leroy can revert."*

"You see that too Selene", Forkbraid replied, *"This is the finest, most intricate work I've ever seen. This does make me wonder though, if this is the way a demolishing is meant to be. Perhaps our method of demolishing is completely wrong?"*

"There's something more I can't quite put my finger on Forkbraid", Selene stated.

"Oh yes. I see it now", Forkbraid replied, *"That is Leroy McGuvan's redemption."*

Together they both had the same insight, *"Gwek's demolishing is contagious!"*

They both pulled back from Leroy's mind and stopped their scanning.

"Leroy. Your redemption is coming. Redemption will come for you!", Forkbraid informed him.

Agent Murphy had returned the sheath knives to the Pod Sisters, who then promptly put them away with their other belongings. Both Girls seemed to like the selection of colourful clothes provided for them and they happily changed into them. This was a surprise for Agent Murphy, who had thought they would have preferred their more rugged outdoor clothing.

Zuawalo was holding Agent Murphy's left arm with her right, as arm in arm, they strolled around the Psychic Academy grounds. With her left hand Zuawalo was holding onto Zigg's leash. Zigg was still not use to being walked on a leash and Zuawalo had to tug on the lead to keep him moving. Zeealas followed behind them with a jealous frown on her face. They passed by many unfamiliar faces who greeted them with smiles.

Behind this trio was Cormac and his wife Candy, happily following along. Watching over the Pod Girls, not so much to keep an eye on them, but more to watch the budding romance develop.

"Cormac, what do you think? One or both?", Candy thought to Cormac with a smile.

"Oh, I don't know Candy", Cormac thought back, explaining, *"Zuawalo looks happy enough, but Zeealas certainly does not."*

"Hmm. One or both? Yes, very hard to say", Candy replied, *"Varak may be right. Zeealas may want to share! Poor Jim!"* Candy began to chuckle.

"Like Forkbraid said, I don't think he'll mind", Cormac replied.

"Who is that?", Zuawalo asked curiously. They were approaching a pair of Girls, one a few years younger than Zeealas, the other quite a bit younger. The younger girl was hovering a good twenty or more feet in the air and turning around and around, giggling the whole time.

"Oh", Candy replied, "That would be our niece Miranda and our friend Roseanne."

"How does she do that?", Zeealas asked.

"Levitation?", Candy replied, explaining, "This is a psychic academy. Miranda is a very powerful young Witch."

"She is so young to be a Witch!", Zeealas exclaimed.

"Yes. Quite young, but powerful none the less", Candy informed her.

Cormac added, "Miranda likes to spin around like that."

"How very strange", Zuawalo remarked.

"Come on down Miranda", Roseanne instructed, "We have new people to meet."

Once Miranda was on the ground, Roseanne put her right hand on Miranda's shoulder and then in the blink of an eye the pair vanished from sight, only to reappear directly in front of Cormac and Candy. Zuawalo and Zeealas stared in awe.

Roseanne saw the look on the Pod Sisters faces and explained, "It's called jaunting. It's a method of teleportation."

"Can we learn to do that?", Zeealas asked.

"No. You have to be born with the gift", Candy replied, informing them, "Not everyone is born with the gift. Even amongst those that are, the gift can vary a lot from one person to the next. These two are very powerful young Witches. For instance, Cormac and I can not jaunt."

"Your getting good at that Roseanne", Candy commended, adding, "A perfect blink from one place to the next"

"Jaunting is sometimes called blinking", Roseanne explained to the Sisters.

"How many psychics are there at the academy?", Zeealas enquired.

"Lady Selene came from the Earth with a thousand psychic couples. We lost well over three hundred people on the very first day when we landed. We lost even more during the attacks on the Elysium colony and then there was the attack on the academy as well", Agent Murphy replied.

Candy added, "And that doesn't even include the ordinary folk that were killed along with them."

"That is true", Agent Murphy lamented, "We've lost a lot of people since we came here."

"Leroy was responsible for that wasn't he?", Zeealas asked.

"Yes. He and his leader, the Prophet", Agent Murphy replied.

"Then it is a very good thing, that Gwek demolished him. That very bad man is gone now ", Zuawalo told them.

"Everyone you've seen today is a psychic, except for a few of us", Agent Murphy explained, "Psychics outnumber ordinary folk here in the academy."

Candy replied, "The academy is not yet ready, but in a few years time, there will be lots of young psychics being taught how to use their gifts here. Many of them will be native Martians."

"Roseanne, Miranda. This is Zuawalo and Zeealas", Cormac finally introduced them.

"Who is that?", Miranda asked while pointing down at Zigg the ferret.

"Zigg", Zuawalo answered, "He is my pole cat."

"Can I pet him?", Miranda, who had never had a pet asked.

"No. Not just yet", Zuawalo advised, "He does not know you. Maybe when he is use to you."

"Does he bite?", Miranda asked.

"He does not bite me and he has not bitten anyone else yet", Zuawalo answered, "But he might still bite."

"He won't bite me. Will you Zigg", Miranda stated as she knelt down in front of him and slowly reached out her hand.

Zigg started making his cute little *'Dook Dook'* noises, nudged Miranda with his nose and allowed Miranda to stroke him.

"You see!", Miranda exclaimed, "Zigg and I will be great friends."

Looking up at Zeealas, Miranda asked, "Why are you sad Zeealas?"

Zeealas did not answer, instead she turned around and looked the other way, staring across the academy grounds.

Roseanne reached down for Miranda's hand and helped her back to her feet, "It's okay Miranda, I think I can see what's happening here."

Roseanne approached Zuawalo and in a kind and gentle voice, told her, "Zuawalo, you really need to talk to your Sister."

Zuawalo did not understand at first, then Roseanne looked to Agent Murphy and then back to Zuawalo again, in a way that made it clear to her.

"Oh. Oh", Zuawalo replied, passing Zigg's lead to Agent Murphy, "Jim. Please hold Zigg. I have to talk with my Sister", Zuawalo then uncoupled her arm from Agent Murphy's arm and went over to her sister, Zeealas's side.

Zuawalo put her arms around her Sister and gave her a huge hug, "I am so sorry Zeealas. I am so sorry."

Zeealas had tears in her eyes and was now freely crying.

"Is it something I did? Something I said?", Agent Murphy asked, with a very concerned look on his face.

Roseanne replied, "No Agent Murphy. These girls are sisters. They are very close, but they just need to talk to each other."

Candy stepped in, "You just hold that leash Jim and look after Zigg. Roseanne can help sort this out, can't you Roseanne."

"Maybe", Roseanne replied, biting her lip, "Hmm. Maybe. Potentially", then Roseanne walked over to the Pod Sisters to see if she could help them.

Cormac thought to Candy, *"Both me thinks."*

Candy thought back to Cormac, *"Both me thinks as well."*

13. The Timeline Advancing

It was late afternoon when Lieutenant Roberts sent word down to the Psychic Academy. It was urgent that he speak with Forkbraid and Lady Selene. They both had been summoned to the communications centre and they in turn summoned Agent Murphy, Marcus and Charlene.

They all arrived at the communications centre at the same time. Lieutenant Roberts had been patiently waiting for them.

"I have some more bad news for you Forkbraid", the Lieutenant began, he didn't bother with formalities, the news was too urgent.

"And what would that be Lieutenant?", Forkbraid asked him.

"Those missiles, the ten that are heading our way", the Lieutenant began, then after a short pause, "They've begun accelerating."

"Accelerating?", Lady Selene queried.

"Yes my Lady. They've begun accelerating", the Lieutenant confirmed.

"So those missiles will get here sooner than we thought?", Agent Murphy asked.

"Yes. That's the gist of it Agent Murphy", the Lieutenant replied, stating further, "We had months, now we're down to weeks."

Forkbraid looked at the others standing around him, "Our timeline is advancing, getting somewhat shorter", he told them.

"How long?", Charlene asked.

The Lieutenant looked at them from his side of the communications screen, "They'll be upon us in a little over two weeks. My Lord, I hope you've got something up your sleeve", he told them.

Forkbraid replied, "I have. Varak and I are working on it. It looks like we will have to advance our timeline to match."

"Will it be ready in time?", Lady Selene enquired.

"It will have to be. Won't it", Forkbraid replied.

Agent Murphy then asked, "What about those troop and weapons transports heading our way? Have they begun accelerating?"

"No. Not yet Agent Murphy, but I expect they will once they get closer", the Lieutenant replied.

"Keep an eye on them as well Lieutenant", Agent Murphy instructed, then turning to Forkbraid he stated, "It would make sense for them to keep pace. If they want to land a week or so after their first strike, they'll need to accelerate, just to keep pace with their missiles."

"That does make sense Jim", Forkbraid agreed.

"It gets worse people!", the Lieutenant told them abruptly.

"How can it possibly get worse?", Marcus asked him.

"I've managed to get some really good scans of the missiles", the Lieutenant informed them, adding further, "Their warheads look like they're multiple independent re-entrant warheads."

"Sweet Mother!", Agent Murphy exclaimed, enquiring further, "Just how many warheads per missile are we talking about exactly?"

"That Agent Murphy, I can't tell you", the Lieutenant answered, explaining, "We can tell by the nose cones that they have multiple re-entrant warheads. Just how many though, we can't tell yet."

"How soon until you know?", Forkbraid asked.

"Honestly Forkbraid", the Lieutenant began, again not caring about formalities, "I'd rather those missiles were destroyed long before they get close enough for me to calculate the number of warheads per missile."

"So we won't know until they deploy? Is that what you're saying?", Forkbraid replied, adding, "And we don't want them getting anywhere near that close."

"Excellent! Now you've got the picture", the Lieutenant replied, then added, "Multiple re-entrant warheads usually come in threes, fives, sixes and tens. And as you've just said, we won't know what we're facing until they deploy."

"So let me get this", Agent Murphy started, "We have to intercept them en-route, long before they deploy and we have to destroy them all."

"Yes. That's correct Agent Murphy", the Lieutenant replied, adding, "And you need them all to go thermonuclear. We can't have intact nukes floating around in orbit, unaccounted for. That's just a recipe for disaster."

"Lieutenant. We understand the situation and we're on top of it", Forkbraid replied, "Keep us posted on any new developments. Over and out."

"Over and out", the Lieutenant responded.

"FB? Are we on top of it?", Agent Murphy asked, adding, " We have possibly as many as a hundred warheads heading our way."

"I think we've got this Jim. At least Varak and I think we've got this. If we intercept them before they deploy, it's only ten missiles", Forkbraid told him.

"Well FB. I hope you two can pull a rabbit out your hat on this one. Taking down ten missiles is certainly better than chasing down a hundred warheads", Agent Murphy replied.

"Get word to Captain Carmichael Jim. The Earth and L5 could have as many as twenty thousand or more warheads heading their way and those missiles may start accelerating at anytime", Forkbraid instructed him, then adding, "And Jim. Get word to the other colonies about this."

Agent Murphy tapped his right temple, "It's in the vault and I'm already working on it", he stated as he rushed out of the communications centre to put together his report.

The next day Agent Murphy and the Pod Sisters were sitting on picnic blanket upon a grassy knoll, not more than a few miles to the north of the New Flinders Psychic Academy. Roseanne Rhein was with them, having recently become friends with the two Sisters. Miranda, her Brother Chiron and their parents Peter and Catherine were sitting on another blanked close by. In between the two groups sat Cormac and Candy on their own picnic rug. Each group had brought along with them, picnic baskets with an assortment of foods and drinks.

It was a good day for a picnic and it gave them all time to forget, at least temporarily, the coming threat. Zigg the ferret was busy running between his mistress Zuawalo and his new friend Miranda, who kept feeding him little treats.

Agent Murphy addressed the small gathering, "My friends, Forkbraid and Varak believe we have this threat covered."

Catherine answered straight away, "Do we Jim? Really? Don't smother it with rose petals, tell us the truth. Should we be worried?"

"Should we be worried?", Agent Murphy queried, "Yes, of course we should be worried. Who wouldn't. We have ten missiles with up to a hundred warheads barrelling or way. Has Forkbraid got this? I believe he has."

"Then why have you organised this *'picnic'* Jim?", Peter asked.

"Contingencies Peter, contingencies", Agent Murphy told him.

"Contingencies?", enquired Catherine.

"I'm a hope for the best, plan for the worse kind of guy", Agent Murphy began, then he explained, "I've talked to Forkbraid and Lady Selene and they both agree."

"Agree to what Jim?", Catherine asked.

"Although we believe we've got this. If things do go horribly pear shaped. I'm taking your family Catherine, Candy and Cormac here, Roseanne and the Girls to New Tortuga", Agent Murphy informed them all.

"Why New Tortuga?", Peter asked, adding, "Wasn't that the horrible place where Miranda was held captive?"

Cormac spoke up,"Sure New Tortuga was a rough place and with those terrorists and pirates it certainly took a turn for the worse. Now everyone knows where it is and the ordinary folk are back in charge again. New Tortuga is the safest place for all of us, if things go bad."

Candy added, "It's far enough away from any target zones and it is underground and has its own food supply. It's the safest place on Mars to be. If radiation were to spread in that direction, we'd all be safe underground in the New Tortuga caverns."

"What about my people Candy? Our village?", Zuawalo asked while looking at her Sister Zeealas. They were seriously concerned.

"If we need to, we'll bring your entire village into New Tortuga Zuawalo", Candy replied adding, "There's plenty of room and we'll keep you all safe."

"It's very unlikely that any fallout will come our way though", Cormac informed them all, explaining, "The prevailing winds should take any fallout eastwards."

"Anyway", Agent Murphy began, "This is only a contingency plan. We'll only need it if things go horribly wrong. Forkbraid assures me that they've got this. So lets enjoy the day and the food."

"And the wine", Cormac replied holding up a bottle of cherry red wine.

"And the wine", they all replied and began to enjoy their day out in the Sun.

Later that same day, a message came back from L5, courtesy of Captain

Carmichael, who of course had been placed in charge of L5's defences. Forkbraid, Lady Selene and Agent Murphy had been summoned to the communications centre once again. The Communications Officer played the message from Captain Carmichael on the screen.

"Well people what can I say. I read Agent Murphy's report and disseminated it to all the parties involved. The spinning turbine is officially smothered in crap!", Captain Carmichael told them.

The Captain continued, "Everyone, without exception, my people included, are watching closely for any signs of acceleration. If the incoming missiles start to accelerate, we will detect it. Earth Gov and the United Nations of Earth have been having nonstop meetings. Honestly, I expect they'll still be having these damnable meetings, even when the bombs start falling out of the sky!"

The Captain paused for a moment, "This Earth policy of *'never again'*. It's still hush, hush. I still have no idea what their policy actually is. However, whatever it is, I'm seriously getting the vibe, that the Earth Defence Forces don't believe it will be enough. It makes perfect sense to me. I mean, they've gone from twenty two hundred missiles, to possibly as many as twenty thousand or more independently targeting re-entrant warheads. That'll have anyone shitting themselves."

"When I disseminated Jim's report, I highlighted Jim's notes about intercepting the missiles en-route, before they can deploy their warheads. I've added my weight behind that concept. Taking down twenty two hundred missiles certainly beats trying to take down over twenty thousand warheads any day", the Captain continued.

"An Australian buddy of mine, gave me a *'cricket'* analogy. He said and I quote, *'we need to combine a strong front foot offence, with an equally strong back foot defence'*. No kidding I says to him, then I realised he was bloody well right", the Captain told them.

Captain Carmichael went on to explain his strategy, "I've recommended splitting our Colonial Fleet into two. One third of the fleet will attempt to intercept the missiles en-route, that would be our front foot offence. The other two thirds of the fleet will attempt to block and destroy anything that gets past the interception, that would be our back foot defence. We still need to hit them before they deploy however. If those missiles deploy too soon, our back foot defence could get overrun."

"Sounds like a plan!", Agent Murphy told the others in the communications room enthusiastically.

The Captain continued, "I've discussed this with the Earth Defence

Forces. They liked the idea. So the Earth Defence Forces are going to launch an interception as well. Depending on where the missiles are en-route, it could be a combined interception fleet from both Earth and L5. Anything that gets through that interception, would be tackled by their *'never again'* policy and our L5 *'back foot'* defenders"

"It is also agreed. As Agent Murphy noted, all of the intercepted missiles need to be annihilated in their entirety. We cannot have any rogue cold fusion warheads floating around in space", the Captain told them, "That's all I have for now. Over and Out."

"Well, the Earth and L5 are working the problem from their end", Agent Murphy stated, then asked, "Where are we at FB?"

"Varak and I will be testing the Solstice tomorrow, putting her through her paces", Forkbraid replied, adding, "If all the testing goes as planned, we'll be ready."

"And if things don't go as planned?", Lady Selene enquired.

"Varak tells me all the simulations have been perfect", Forkbraid replied, "Based upon the simulations, we're not expecting to come across any major problems."

"FB, we've all been diligently studying those flight and weapons manuals, but at the end of the day, not one of us has even stepped inside that ship. Not even you!", Agent Murphy reminded him.

"That is true Jim and I have spoken to Varak about that", Forkbraid replied, informing them, "The Solstice will be piloted and crewed by Hyper-Dynamics 303 Androids on the first couple of flights. We will be shadowing them at first, then after that they'll be shadowing us, while we get our flight legs."

"No. No. No. FB. You know they can't handle the weapons systems!", Agent Murphy objected, "We cannot have Androids at the tactical stations."

"We'll be using model 295s at the tactical stations Jim. At least until you and Marcus are familiar with the consoles. Model 295s won't have any three laws issues with tactical", Forkbraid replied, also adding, "I will have the neural interlock control helmet as well."

"We have to remember Jim", Lady Selene replied, "When we intercept the missiles, even model 303s should have no three laws issues. The missiles are of course unmanned."

"Yes, but what about all those troop and weapons transports that will arrive a week or so later?", Agent Murphy asked, adding, "Model 303s will definitely have three laws issues with those."

"By then, we'll have Marcus or yourself at the tactical stations Jim", Lady Selene replied.

The next morning Lady Selene and Forkbraid discussed who would be the Solstice's crew. Something they had thought, there was plenty of time to organise, but now it was far more urgent.

"Most of the crew are going to be Androids Selene, a mix of 303s and 295s", Forkbraid informed her, explaining, "Initially for the helm and tactical stations, at least until our people are up to speed, but also for all the maintenance and any repair work."

"And the human components?", Selene enquired, "Who are we assigning to what exactly?"

"I'm the only one who's trained to use a neural interlock control system, so that will put me firmly in the Captain's chair", Forkbraid replied, adding, "I'm thinking of putting Marcus at the helm and Jim at tactical. Varak will of course be in charge of engineering."

"Where do Charlene and I fit in? What crew positions will we have?", enquired Selene.

"Selene, you won't", Forkbraid replied, explaining, "We'll need both of you here running the psychic academy. Especially if we're not successful."

"Charlene perhaps, but I was thinking I could be part of the crew", Selene replied.

"Selene, you're a leader and the ship can only have one Captain. The psychic academy is your baby, your ship. That puts you firmly in charge here", Forkbraid told her.

"Hmm", Selene frowned but agreed, "You're right of course", then she added, "You will still need someone on communications, someone in medical and a first officer."

"And an analyst", Forkbraid replied then quickly added, "We'll need someone really smart for the science station. A real problem solver."

Selene looked at Forkbraid, "We don't have enough time to train everyone, do we?"

"No we don't. And we have bugger all time to do anything", Forkbraid replied, " Selene, I'll let you choose who'll be in the communications, medical and science positions. I'll pick who will be my first officer. It's going to be a case of on the job training I'm afraid."

Selene thought long and hard, then gave Forkbraid her thoughts, "Charlene can be your Communications Officer."

"Charlene? Doesn't Charlene help you run the academy? It will like giving up your right hand", Forkbraid replied.

"Yes, but Charlene also has comms experience and would be perfect for the task", Selene told him, adding, "I can take Roseanne on as Charlene's replacement. Roseanne is already my apprentice and I think she's more than capable. So now, Roseanne will be both my apprentice and protege."

"Okay, a red head on comms. What could possibly go wrong with that?", Forkbraid laughed, "And I was actually thinking Roseanne could fit into the crew somewhere."

"Roseanne simply isn't ready. She is my apprentice, so I know", Selene replied protectively.

"Yes, but Roseanne is the only other person who's had neural interlock control system exposure", Forkbraid explained.

"And that experience almost fried her brain Forkbraid", Selene reminded him, "Roseanne is simply just not ready!", it was an emphatic response. Selene was extremely protective of Roseanne.

"Okay Selene. Point noted", Forkbraid replied, "I was thinking we could simply assign a 303 Android to medical, with maybe two others to assist. Varak can probably have them prepared."

"Yes. Yes. That would work", Selene replied, "The 303s are used in medical capacities all the time back on Earth and L5. That will give us more time to find a suitable doctor for the position."

"What are we left with?", Forkbraid asked.

"A science officer and your first officer", Selene reminded him.

"Who'd you choose for a science officer, Selene?", Forkbraid asked.

"Well. I have some thoughts on that as well", Selene replied, explaining, "You might think I'd choose Varak. You know, for both engineering and science. He certainly has the ability. I mean, he is brilliant after all."

"Yes, but Varak will be far too busy with engineering. He can't realistically, do both engineering and science. We need a person at each of those posts", Forkbraid advised her.

"Exactly!", Selene agreed, before slowly stating, "There is only one other person I can think of for that position then."

"And who would that be Selene?", Forkbraid enquired.

"Peter Swann!", Selene replied enthusiastically

Before Forkbraid could object, Selene explained, "Think about it Forkbraid! He works extremely well with Varak. Remember all those 'innovations' he created for Varak. The two of them, will make one hell of a team."

"Peter Swann?", Forkbraid questioned, he was not convinced, "I don't know much about him."

"Hear me out Forkbraid", Selene requested, "After hearing about how well he worked with Varak and all those new innovations they created. I pulled his file and had a look at who he is. Did you know that Peter Swann is genius in his own right? Seriously Forkbraid! Peter's I.Q is north of three hundred! It's so high they had trouble measuring it."

"Really?", Forkbraid questioned, "I knew he was smart, but that smart?"

"Really!", Selene confirmed, "Who better, to be your science officer!"

"Okay, so that leave's your first officer", Selene pointed out.

"And that is where I'm stumped", Forkbraid replied.

"Stumped?", Selene replied, quite confused, "Forkbraid, since when do you get stumped?"

"Think about it Selene", Forkbraid replied, explaining, "I can fly that ship single handed using the neural interlock control helmet. I can control the ship and through the ship control all the androids. Whoever is chosen to be my first office, should have that capability."

"That's a hard ask Forkbraid. Not everyone can handle a NIC system?", Selene reminded him.

"And that's the problem", Forkbraid replied, adding, "The NIC system notwithstanding, at the very least, every one of the crew needs to be able to man the helm and weapons consoles."

"That's why you have a have a lot of people memorising those flight and weapons manuals", Selene replied, "Everyone needs to be capable of flying and defending the ship."

"Except only one person on the planet can handle the neural interlock control helmet", Forkbraid pointed out.

"Then your first officer won't have that ability Forkbraid. It's as simple as that", Selene told him.

"Old school", Forkbraid mumbled, then speaking up, "It takes a lot of time and training, to get a team, a crew, up and running cohesively and we have so little time left!"

The following morning Forkbraid had been summoned to the communications centre once more. Governor Anderson was on the screen and waiting impatiently.

"We need to talk!", The Governor announced, when he saw that Forkbraid was in the room.

"Yes Governor. Yes we do", Forkbraid replied.

"We have cold fusion missiles heading our way. What are you going to do about them?", the Governor demanded.

"We have a plan in place Governor", Forkbraid replied, "We will be dealing with those missiles shortly. We're hoping to neutralise the missiles en-route."

"When you say *'hoping'*, does that mean your plan could fail?", the Governor asked.

"There is always the possibility that some of the missiles will get through Governor", Forkbraid replied, then asking, "Have you any contingency plans to cover that possibility?"

"Not yet. We thought we would have more time, months in fact", the Governor admitted.

"Well we don't! Time is running out Governor! You need to coordinate with all the other major colonies on this. If we can't intercept and neutralise all of those missiles, evacuation plans will need to be in place", Forkbraid told him.

The Governor scribbled down some notes on a notepad on his desk, then replied, "I'll get to work coordinating evacuation contingencies straight away."

"There's more Governor", Forkbraid replied.

"Oh yes. Isn't there always!", the Governor responded. He looked stressed and overworked.

"There is the matter of the twenty troop carriers and twenty heavy weapons transports heading our way", Forkbraid informed him, adding, "That's ten thousand troops and an unknown assortment of heavy weapons systems."

"Our security forces aren't designed for handling that kind of situation. They're basically just police!", Governor Anderson replied, "And they'll be outnumbered nearly ten to one."

"You may need to coordinate with the other colonies on that as well", Forkbraid informed him, adding, "If those troops get on the ground, each colony will need a well armed militia."

Governor Anderson added some more scribbled notes to his notepad, then replied, "A well armed militia trained by the security forces. Got that! We are going to be so short on weapons though!"

"Yes. That could be a problem. Get whatever Androids you have on hand and start them working that problem", Forkbraid suggested, he then added, "Use the older models. So that you won't run into any three laws safe issues."

The Governor quickly scribbled down some more notes and replied to Forkbraid, "I'll get onto this straight away. Anything else?"

"Not right at this moment", Forkbraid replied, "If I think of anything else I'll let you know."

The Governor then called his secretary, "Mary! Take my chicken scratches and turn them into something that is somewhat coherent. Then call my head of security, tell him it's urgent. Organise a video conference with the other Governors for three pm. Flag that meeting as urgent and compulsory. I want them all present. They all have to be present. Stress that point!"

"Okay. I've started the ball rolling", the Governor told Forkbraid, then he asked, "Now what did you do to my pilot?"

"Your pilot?", Forkbraid enquired.

"Yes. My pilot. Mack!", the Governor confirmed.

"Oh. Yes", Forkbraid replied, explaining, "He saw some things he shouldn't have. So I had to remove a few memories. He should be okay."

"That explains his loss of memory and lost time then", the Governor replied, then requesting, "Next time, could you let me know when you've messed with my peoples heads. I thought than man had gone positively loopy."

"Will do Governor. Will do", Forkbraid told him.

Later at midday Forkbraid and all the potential crew members were gathered on the airfield's tarmac. A few others were present as well to wish them well. The Solstice stood before them on the tarmac having been towed out of hanger once more.

"I have Androids at all the main stations throughout the ship", Varak told the gathering, "Jim, you will be pleased to know that model 295s are at the tactical stations and available for any weapons maintenance issues."

"Good. We can't have any three laws issues at a tactical consoles", Agent Murphy replied.

"Lets get on board then shall we", Forkbraid requested and then followed Varak and Peter Swann up the ramp.

"No unnecessary risks Forkbraid", Lady Selene shouted out to him as he headed up the ramp.

"We'll keep an eye on him Selene", Charlene replied to Selene as both she and Marcus headed up the ramp and into the ship.

Agent Murphy was the last to board, the two Pod Sister's, Zuawalo and Zeealas were reluctant to let him go. Eventually Jim extricated himself from their embrace and he too, headed up the ramp and into the ship.

"I'll see both of you Ladies when we get back", Agent Murphy assured them.

The ships boarding ramp automatically closed once they had boarded..

Cormac, Candy and Roseanne were present on the tarmac as well and while the remainder of the group walked to a safer vantage point further from the Solstice a silent conversion ensued.

Candy thought to Cormac, *"Definitely both."*

Cormac thought back, *"Agreed. Definitely both."*

Lady Selene rolled her eyes and replied, *"Oh, will you two stop it."*

Cormac and Candy had big smiles on their faces.

Roseanne enquired silently, *"What's got them so amused?"*

"Don't ask", Lady Selene thought back in reply.

"Really, I want to know", Roseanne's thoughts pushed.

"Candy and Cormac are hopeless romantics", Lady Selene replied, explaining, *"Every time they see Agent Murphy and the Pod Sisters, they see wedding bells in their future."*

"Which Sister?", Roseanne enquired.

"Both Sisters", Lady Selene informed her.

"Oh! Oh! Oh my!", Roseanne's mind exclaimed, as she suddenly realised what had Cormac and Candy so amused.

The Pod Sisters were oblivious to their silent conversation and followed the others to the safer vantage point, closer to the Solstice's hanger.

"Zigg is not with you today Zuawalo", Lady Selene asked Zuawalo.

"No. Miranda asked if she could play with Zigg today. So I left Zigg with her", Zuawalo replied.

Varak led the crew up the ramp and into the ship. Once inside they followed Varak along the long main central corridor to the bridge. The double doors slid open and Varak stepped aside and allowed the other crew members to enter. Varak himself entered last.

The bridge was not huge, but it was quite spacious. The first thing one noticed was the screen that covered the entire forward section. It currently displayed an image of the airfield and the area in front of the ship.

There was a single chair in the centre, which was the captain's chair. Beside the Captain's chair on the left was a pillar with a movable command console attached. The console could be swung around in front and over the Captain's chair. On the right of the Captain's chair was another pillar. Atop this pillar sat Forkbraid's neural interlock control helmet, which once worn, was capable of wirelessly commanding the ship by thought alone.

In front of the captain's chair were two stations. The station on the left was the helm. The station on the right was communications. Each station had two consoles and two seats. The outside seats of each station had Androids sitting in them. Marcus took his place and seated himself at the helm, while Charlene took her place and seated herself at comms.

To the right of the Captain's chair was the tactical station. It also had two consoles and two seats. The rear most seat had an Android sitting in it. Agent Murphy took his seat at the tactical console.

To the left of the Captain's chair was the science station. It followed the same pattern, with two consoles and two seats. The rear most seat also had an Android sitting in it. Peter Swann took his seat at the science console.

The only noticeable difference between any of the Androids stationed on the bridge was that the tactical Android was obviously an older model. It had a distinctly less *'humaniform'* look to it.

Forkbraid walked around the bridge in a clock wise direction, "Varak has double consoled each work station", he began, explaining, "Sitting beside you are Androids. These Androids are there to assist you during our flight testing and training. Do make use of them. That's why they are there. Nearly all the Androids onboard this ship, the Solstice, are Hyper-Dynamics model 303s. The most modern. The most advanced Androids in existence There are however model 295s onboard the ship. Like the one sitting next to Jim. These are only there for use with and maintenance of the Weapons Systems. Varak, please take your station back in engineering."

"Aye Captain", Varak replied and then left the bridge.

Forkbraid having circled the bridge then took his seat in the Captain's chair, "Marcus, Charlene. You realise once we're in space, you will lose you psychic abilities."

Marcus and Charlene both answered in the affirmative. They knew quite well, they would lose their psychic abilities while they were in space. Fear, uncertainty and doubt would cause it to happen at a subconscious level. It was a well known issue for nearly all psychics.

"Marcus. Take us into high Martian orbit", Forkbraid commanded.

"Aye Captain", Marcus replied.

Marcus began his check list.

"Anti-Gravity Lifters, one through seven online. Check!"

"Inertial Dampers online. Check!"

"Deck Gravity Plating online. Check!"

"Deflector Grid online. Check!"

"Main Thrusters online. Check!"

Then once the checklist was completed, Marcus commanded, "Computer. Proceed to hover at an altitude of one hundred metres."

The Computer responded with, "Complying", its voice was highly feminine.

The Solstice began slowly rising up from the ground, eventually reaching its hovering height of one hundred metres.

The small group gathered by the Solstice's hanger watched as the ship began to launch.

"Calculating course for high Martian orbital insertion", Marcus continued, then once the course was calculated, "Computer. Proceed to orbital insertion."

The Computer responded with, "Complying", again with its feminine voice.

The small group gathered by the Solstice's hanger watched in awe as the Solstice shot forward and upwards towards space in an easterly direction. In around thirty seconds, the ship was out of sight beyond the cloud banks.

"When will they be back?", a concerned Zeealas asked.

"When they have finished testing the ship", Zuawalo replied.

"Not quite Zuawalo", Lady Selene informed her, explaining, "We were out of time. This test flight is a full flight and live fire test. They're going to intercept the incoming missiles."

Roseanne stepped towards Zuawalo and Zeealas and took their hands in hers, "They're going to be okay. I know they are", she told them.

The Pod Sisters nodded with concerned looks on their faces.

It didn't take long for the Solstice to reach high Martian orbit, only a matter of ten to fifteen minutes. Once in orbit, Marcus took the Solstice's seven anti-gravity lifters offline as they were no longer needed once the ship was in space.

From high Martian orbit, Mars, now a terraformed planet, looked as beautiful as the Earth. Smaller than the Earth and with less gravity at point three-eight g's, Mars was now a blue orb in space with life giving air and water. Life was spreading across the Martian globe and becoming quite abundant.

The Solstice's view screen showed the blue planet Mars in all its beauty. The crew of the Solstice could now see why people had been flocking to Mars from the Martian orbital colonies. Agent Murphy could finally appreciate the problems Lieutenant Roberts had been having with his men, abandoning their posts and their contracts, to take up new lives on the planet.

"Who wouldn't want their own slice of Mars?", Agent Murphy thought to himself. It had always been assumed, that one day he would return to L5 and Colonial Central. That had always been his intention. In his heart now, he knew he would make his home on Mars. Everyone on the Bridge of the Solstice stared in awe at the beautiful sight on the view screen before them.

"Note to self", Agent Murphy thought to himself, *"Send official resignation to L5 Colonial Central. Apply for permanent position as Security Chief at New Flinders Psychic Academy and the Elysium Colony."*

It was the sight of the blue planet Mars on the view screen before him and the arrival of the Pod Sisters that had swayed his mind into staying. Agent Murphy wasn't the only one affected by the sight on the view screen. They were all in awe of the blue planet before them.

"Marcus!", Forkbraid called out, breaking Marcus out of his reverie, "Prepare an intercept course to those incoming missiles. I want to approach them head on."

"Aye Captain", Marcus responded, "Calculating intercept course now."

The course set, Marcus then issued a command to the computer, "Computer. Proceed along intercept course as calculated. Fusion Thrusters on full in stealth mode."

The Computer responded with, "Complying."

The Solstice broke orbit and began its journey to intercept the incoming missiles.

"Stealth mode?", Forkbraid queried.

"Aye captain. The ship will difficult to detect in stealth mode", Marcus replied.

"Smart move Marcus", Forkbraid commended.

Forkbraid asked the computer, "Computer. What is the estimated time to intercept."

The computer responded with, "Thirty six hours."

"Jim", Forkbraid began, "We're going to need a firing solution for those ten missiles. I also want to test a good portion of our weapons systems while we're at it. We have a day to prepare."

"Yes FB. I mean Aye Captain. I think I can work something out", Agent Murphy replied.

"And remember Jim. We need to annihilate all of the warheads", Forkbraid reminded him, "We can't leave a single warhead floating about."

"Aye Captain. Working on it", Agent Murphy replied while tapping his right temple.

The crew of the Solstice spent the rest of their shift familiarising themselves with their work consoles. Marcus and Charlene were finding their loss of telepathic communications somewhat disturbing. As a result, the pair were somewhat more tactile than usual. More than once, Forkbraid watched as they reached out and held each others hands.

"It must be very hard for them", Forkbraid had thought to himself.

Agent Murphy familiarised himself with his console, whilst also running simulated firing solutions. The ships scans of the incoming missiles were impressive and they became clearer and more concise with each passing hour.

Jim was pleased to find that the Solstice had short range sensors and long range sensors, but another type of scan called ultra sensors, although it appeared to be very new and undocumented.

After their shift the crew had located their cabins and settled in for some down time. During the crews off hours, the Androids continued to crew the ship in their absence with clear instructions to call the crew to stations if anything untoward cropped up. It was during this off time, that Agent Murphy asked Varak about the *"ultra sensors"*.

"Varak, What are these ultra sensors and how do I used them?", Agent Murphy asked.

"The ultra sensors are very long range sensors with a far tighter targeting aperture", Varak replied, explaining, "They are a bit like using a microscope on a target several hundred million miles away, while viewing that target through a powerful telescope. Well, something like that anyway."

"Well that does sound interesting. How do I use them?", Agent Murphy queried.

"Simply by voice command or console. Just refer to the system by name", Varak advised him, then adding, "They are very new. I haven't had time to test or document them yet."

"I'll test them for you Varak", Agent Murphy replied as he made his way back to the bridge and his tactical console.

The next day the crew were all seated once more in the Solstice's bridge. It was two hours before missile intercept and Forkbraid was slightly anxious.

"Jim. Do you have that firing solution?", He asked.

"Aye Captain", Agent Murphy responded, "If you watch the view screen."

An image of a single missile appeared on the view screen. It was very clear. Slowly the view shifted the nose cone and it fairings.

"This image is courtesy of Varak's ultra sensors", Agent Murphy informed them, "As you can see, this missile, which is indicative of all the missiles has four fairings on its nose cone. This in itself does not really tell us anything about how many war heads each missile carries. It does however tell us roughly where the warheads are clustered within the nose cone."

Agent Murphy continued, "Something I should note, these missile are very spread out. They are are not all clustered together in a tight formation. Captain Carmichael will be very interested in our scans."

"And that information is factored into your firing solution?", Forkbraid queried.

"Aye Captain, it sure is", Agent Murphy replied with a smile, then informing him, "I've set up a firing solution that will take out the first four missiles with the electromagnetic rail guns. Our targeting array will calculate the anticipated positions of those missiles and fire our rounds to intercept them perfectly. The next four missiles will be taken out by our twinned hyper-resonant disrupter cannons. The remaining two missile will be destroyed by our phased laser arrays. We will be targeting whatever is sitting behind those fairings."

"Thank you Jim. That sounds like a plan. And it tests out a good portion of our weapons systems", Forkbraid replied, then asking, "What's our timing on the targets."

"At intercept minus one hour we begin", Agent Murphy replied.

At precisely one how from intercept, Agent Murphy began arming his targeting solution, "Captain, may I begin with your permission", he asked.

"Permission granted Jim", Forkbraid replied.

"Aye Captain", Agent Murphy went through the procedures.

"Tactical! Electromagnetic rail carousel online. Check!"

"Electromagnetic rail guns online. Check!"

"Using ultra sensor data to target the first four missiles. Check!"

"Targeting Array online. Check!"

"Extrapolate target trajectories for projectile impacts. Check!"

"Locking down on nose cone fairings. Check!"

"Loading electromagnetic rail carousel with penetrating, explosive rounds. Check!"

"Calculate number of rounds required for total missile destruction, assuming each missile holds a maximum number of possible warheads. Check!"

"Tactical! Fire on the selected targets with electromagnet rail guns!", Agent Murphy then commanded.

The Hornet's nest went through the sequence of instructions and responded with, "Complying", the Hornet's nest's voice was quite masculine.

Immediately the six electromagnet rail guns positioned and then re-positioned to fire upon their designated targets. Firing the precise, requisite number of rounds to obliterate them completely. Bright orange tracer rounds could be seen streaking towards their targets.

"Captain. It will take about ten minutes for the rounds to cover the distance. By then, the missiles will be in their anticipated positions for our rounds to intercept them", Agent Murphy informed him, adding, "These electromagnetic rail guns make excellent stand off weapons. We should be in for quite the light show."

True to Agent Murphy's words ten minutes later, in the distance there was an immense burst of blue light, followed almost immediately by a second, a third, a forth, a fifth and several more. Then in the distance another immense burst of blue light appeared on the view screen, it too was followed immediately by immense secondary explosions. Twice more in the distance there were more immense bursts of blue light and again each was followed by immense secondary explosions.

Agent Murphy commanded the computer, "Computer. Analyse scans. How many explosions have you detected and what was the yield of each?"

The Computer responded with, "Forty explosions were detected. Each with a yield of two megatons."

"There you have it Captain. Ten warheads per missile. Two megatons each. They popped off like pop corn!", Agent Murphy informed him.

"Jim. Make sure we have all that information in a full report to both the Earth and L5. Send copies to Captain Carmichael and Lady Selene. They'll definitely want to know how many warheads there are per missile and their yield", Forkbraid replied.

"Aye Captain", Agent Murphy responded, then ordered the computer once more, "Computer. Activate shield grid at maximum."

"Jim's good at this", Forkbraid thought to himself.

By the time they were close to the remaining six missiles, the blasts from the four obliterated missiles had died down. The radiation levels were none the less intense and the Solstice's shields dealt with the radiation easily.

Agent Murphy started the next phase of his firing solution, "Captain, may I start phases two and three of my firing solution with your permission", he asked.

"Permission granted Jim", Forkbraid replied.

"Aye Captain", Agent Murphy went through the procedures.

"Tactical! Hyper-resonant disrupter cannons online. Check!"

"Scan and target the four closest missiles. Check!"

"Locking down on nose cone fairings. Check!"

"Tactical! Fire on selected targets with hyper-resonant disrupter cannons!", Agent Murphy commanded.

The Hornet's nest went through the sequence of instructions and responded with, "Complying."

Immediately the eight hyper-resonant disrupter cannons fired upon their designated targets. Brilliant red beams issued forth, striking their targets and penetrating the fairings. The disrupter beams struck the warheads and the results were devastating.

They were far closer to the missiles this time and automatically the view screen went blank to protect the crew. The space outside the ship erupted in brilliant explosions of blue light, each followed up by multiple secondary explosions. This time around the Solstice was buffeted by the shock waves from the multiple explosions. The ships multi layered shields remained firm.

Agent Murphy continued with the next step in his procedures.

"Tactical! Top Phased Laser Arrays online. Check!"

"Scan and target the remaining two missiles. Check!"

"Locking down on nose cone fairings. Check!"

"Tactical! Fire on selected targets with phased laser arrays!", Agent Murphy commanded.

The Hornet's nest went through the sequence of instructions and responded with, "Complying."

Immediately the eight phased laser arrays fired upon their designated targets. Brilliant beams of intense blue light issued forth, striking their targets and penetrating the fairings. The warheads were bathed in blue light and erupted.

The view screen was still blank as the space outside the ship erupted once again in brilliant explosions of blue light, each followed up by multiple secondary explosions. Again the Solstice was buffeted by the shock wave resulting from the explosions. The ships shields remained firm.

"Damage report!", requested Forkbraid urgently.

Peter Swann replied back, "Zero damage Captain. Shields remain at one hundred percent."

"Peter. Varak said these shields are good, but seriously, no damage?", Forkbraid queried.

"The blast energy was redirected and absorbed Captain", Peter replied, explaining, "The shields are designed to use the energy of an enemies attack.

That energy can be redirected to strengthen the shields or that energy can be absorbed and put into storage."

"Absorbed and put into storage?", Forkbraid enquired.

"Yes Captain", Peter replied, explaining further, "The Solstice's primary energy storage is a quantum singularity, that by its very nature cannot be overloaded."

"Varak created a quantum singularity as an energy storage facility?", asked Forkbraid.

Peter's face went slightly red, "No Captain. It was actually my suggestion. I convinced Varak that it was the best method for storing energy on the ship. Varak agreed and we worked together on it."

"Neither of you thought to mention that my ship, the Solstice, was powered by a black hole?", Forkbraid asked, he was holding his goateed chin and had and incredulous look on his face.

"Technically Captain, it's a quantum singularity. We didn't actually think about it to be honest", Peter replied, explaining, "I mean. Do you know how the energy is stored on your Bat Wing Interceptor?"

Forkbraid didn't know the answer to that, "Point noted Peter. I have no idea. I may need yourself and Varak to give me a crash course on ships systems at some point. We'll probably all need that."

Forkbraid turned back to Agent Murphy, "The missiles Jim. How successful were we?"

Agent Murphy replied, "All targeted missiles destroyed Captain. Sensor scanning reports, no surviving warheads detected. We got them all!", his sounded very pleased with himself.

"Good then!", Forkbraid exclaimed, "Now we can move on to part two of our mission."

"Marcus!", Forkbraid caught his attention, then ordered, "Plot a new course to the Trailing Trojan Armed Forces."

"Aye Captain", Marcus responded, "Calculating the new intercept course now."

The course set, Marcus then issued a command to the computer, "Computer. Proceed along new intercept course as calculated. Fusion

Thrusters at full thrust in stealth mode."

The Computer responded with, "Complying."

The Solstice began its new journey to intercept the Trailing Trojan Armed Forces.

Forkbraid asked the computer, "Computer. What is the estimated time to intercept."

The Computer responded with, "Sixty hours."

"Okay people. I suggest we get some rest and prepare for our next battle", Forkbraid informed his crew, adding, "The Trojan Armed Forces may be able to fire back!"

"Jim. Get onto those ultra sensors again. Find out what we're dealing with. I want a firing solution on all of those heavy weapons transports.", Forkbraid instructed.

"And not the troop transports?", Agent Murphy queried.

"If we take out their heavy weapons systems, they'll become just ten thousand men standing around with guns", Forkbraid explained, "We may be able to defeat this army without killing them."

Peter Swann recommended, "Captain. I recommend we turn on our chameleon cloaking."

"Peter, I don't remember reading about that in the flight manual", Forkbraid replied.

"There are a few developments that didn't make it into the flight manual captain", Peter informed him, explaining, "The ultra sensors were one. The chameleon cloaking is another. Manuals tend to lag behind development."

"Okay. So what does this chameleon cloaking do?", Forkbraid asked.

Peter explained, "The Solstice has two types of cloaking Captain. Active cloaking via the eight by eight multi-layered shield grid, but also passive cloaking. We call that chameleon cloaking. The passive cloaking simply re-skins the Ship's outer hull to look like the background."

"So the Solstice will blend in with the background of space?", Forkbraid asked for clarification.

"Precisely Captain", Peter confirmed, "The ships outer *'skin'* will appear black. In space, black on black, the ship will be all but invisible to long distance scans. It will even be difficult to detect on shorter scans. As we are approaching the Trailing Trojan Armed Forces, it would be advisable to use passive cloaking at this point. We don't want them to see us coming."

"Agreed Peter", Forkbraid replied, then ordering, "Activate the chameleon cloaking."

"Computer. Stand down active shield grid until further notice. Bring chameleon cloaking online with pattern match for deep space", Peter commanded.

The Computer responded with, "Complying."

"Captain. Just so you fully understand", Peter began, "The chameleon cloaking can blend in with other back grounds as well."

"Other backgrounds Peter", Forkbraid enquired.

"Yes Captain. If we were flying through the Earth's atmosphere, the Solstice would blend in with the sky from below and the underlying surface landscapes from above", Peter explained, adding, "If we were landed, the Solstice would blend in with the biome we find ourselves in."

"You mean like desert, plains, forest, jungle, ice field?", Forkbraid queried.

"Yes Captain. That's exactly what I mean and many others", Peter confirmed, "Blending in with space is just one of the chameleon cloaks abilities. Actually the easiest one."

"Thank you for the information Peter", Forkbraid replied, "It's good to know."

Agent Murphy went to his cabin to put together his report to the Earth, L5, Captain Carmichael and Lady Selene. He knew they would be shocked to hear that each missile contained ten independently targeting re-entrant warheads. He also knew it would be a shock when they learnt each warhead had a two megaton yield.

In the report he also recommended targeting the missile's nose cone fairings, which they had found so successful. After sending the report, Agent Murphy began to study the ultra sensor scans of the heavy weapons transports, to work out a suitable firing solution.

The remainder of the crew spent their shift time familiarising themselves with their designated work stations. When not on shift, they spent their time exploring the ship, its other systems and relaxing where possible. It was going to be a long flight to the interception point and they made the best use of that time that they could.

The whole crew was not use to being in space for long periods of time, especially not in the tight confines of a space ship. Their crew cabins were quite small and had few amenities other than their bed, a basin, a shower, a toilet and a small mirror. There was a closet for their belongings and clothing. Uniforms of course had not yet been designed for the crew. In short their cabins were adequate, but also a little claustrophobic. They were all looking forward to finishing the task at hand and returning to Mars with its wide open spaces.

14. The Best Laid Plans

The small view screen showed explosions of brilliant blue light. The explosions appeared to be in groups of four, with multiple explosions in each group. The screen then skipped forwards in time to another batch of explosions. Again just like the previous explosions, these were in groups of four, except they were then followed shortly afterwards by another group of two. In each group were multiple immense explosions. Eyes watched the small screen carefully. The view screen then replayed it all over again in a continuous loop. The view screen continued doing so over and over.

"How many?", General Verne asked the Captain of his lead troop transport.

Captain Carlson replied, "General, it appears that all ten missiles and all of their warheads have been neutralised. One hundred in all."

"The whole first strike is gone?", General Verne wanted to be clear.

"Yes General. It appears to be so. Our whole first strike is gone", Captain Carlson confirmed.

"This was not meant to be possible", General Verne stated, informing the Captain, "Our information was that Mars has no defences. No defences at all."

"General Sir, that information is apparently incorrect", the Captain replied, explaining, "Not only does Mars have defences. Those defences were apparently able to take down our missiles while they were still en-route", then speculating, "As far as we know, only the Colonial Fleet can do that. I can't think of any other way for this to happen."

"I would tend to agree with you Captain, except we know for certain that the Cruiser Spartan, left Mars orbit for the Earth. Our surveillance showed that. We literally watched the Spartan perform a long burn with an Earth bound trajectory. The Prophet also reported it. We have observed no fleet movements in the Mars direction from Earth since then. The planet should have been defenceless", the General replied.

"General Sir. Will this affect our occupation plans?", Captain Carlson enquired.

"We will continue according to our orders Captain. At least for the moment", General Verne informed him, ordering, "Get word to the Jovian High Command. Let them know what's happened. Request clarification of our orders, given the situational change."

"Yes Sir. Straight away Sir", Captain Carlson replied.

The apartment's communicator buzzed for attention. Matthew and The Prophet were quick to answer the call. General Tarzan was on the line with a concerned look on his face.

"General", the Prophet greeted.

"Gentlemen", the General replied.

"What can we do for you?", the Prophet enquired.

"Information Gentlemen. Information", the General requested.

"What kind of information General", Matthew enquired.

"Martian defences?", General Tarzan clarified.

"Martian defences?", Matthew queried, then added, "As far as we know, there aren't any."

"Yes. You've told us that before", the General replied, taking on a stern look, "but we've just had a set back and now we need to revisit that information."

"A set back?", the Prophet enquired.

"The ten missiles we allocated to our Mars campaign were all taken out en-route", the General informed them bluntly.

"Are you sure?", the Prophet asked in reply.

"We detected the explosions ourselves. We even have confirmation from the Trojan occupying forces, that we sent as part of the campaign. They detected the explosions en-route as well", the General further informed them.

"General. As far as we know, Mars does not have that capability", Matthew replied, explaining, the only defences that we know of, are ground defences around the demon's lair in the Elysium subcontinent. Those and a Bat Wing Interceptor and a handful of atmo rated Wisps."

"Well those certainly can't operate in deep space", the General replied, enquiring further, "Are you sure that Mars has nothing else?"

"The only thing I can think of, that could do what you've told us, is a Colonial Cruiser", Matthew informed the General, "Or maybe a Colonial Destroyer?"

"We've been watching the entire inner solar system like hawks. Mars included", General Tarzan explained, "We saw the Spartan's long burn and flight back to the Earth and L5. We haven't seen a single ship, military or otherwise approach Mars from the Earth or anywhere else since then."

"Then General. We have questions that need answering", Matthew began, listing, "What, if anything did the Spartan leave behind? Have the Earth and/or L5 developed a cloaking technology? Is there simply something we've missed, as in not picked up by your surveillance?"

"All good questions lad", the General agreed, "I'll add one more to the list. Is this, whatever it is, something that's Martian, as in Martian developed and made?"

Matthew thought long and hard about that, then finally replied, "Very unlikely General. Very unlikely. When we left Mars, they chased us off with one of our own raiders! It was a junker! It was barely space worthy. If they had anything better, they would have used it. That also rules out anything left behind by the Cruiser Spartan."

Matthew added, "Something unknown took down those missiles General. Something fast! Something deadly! Something your surveillance simply could not see."

"It looks like my people will need to work on this problem. I'll keep you all in the loop, Gentlemen", the General then signed off.

"And so it begins!", Matthew stated boldly.

"Matthew?", the Prophet spoke his name in the form of a question.

"Their hubris is catching up with them Sir", Matthew replied, explaining, "They thought they had this! They thought this was a fait accompli! Everything would go according to their plan!"

"And now things are going wrong Matthew?", the Prophet asked, stating, "Matthew, this is just a single set back."

"As I said before my Lord", Matthew replied, "Something unknown took down those Mars bound missiles. We don't know what! They have no idea! The best laid plans of mice and men often go horribly awry."

"And you think their other plans are going to go awry as well Matthew", the Prophet queried.

"I have no idea my Lord", Matthew replied, explaining, "I do think however, that their plans will not unfold as they thought they would. I do think, they have woefully underestimated our mutual enemies."

"Then it's a good thing that you have a contingency plan for this sort of issue then, isn't it", the Prophet replied, knowing that Matthew already had a plan in place.

"Yes my Lord. I do have a contingency plan in place", Matthew informed him.

Matthew was a kind of prepare for the worst and hope for the best, kind of man.

The apartment's bell rang and Abram rushed to answer the door. When he opened it, Hubert was there, standing on the apartment's landing.

"May I come in Abram?", he asked.

"Yes. Yes. Come in Hubert. It's good to see you", Abram replied.

Hubert entered the apartment and made his way directly to the main room. He sat down.

"I have news", Hubert told Abram, who had also taken a seat. Miriam and Rani came out of the main kitchen and seated themselves as well. Rajsheev was already sitting in the main room watching the video feeds.

"This hasn't hit the news feeds yet and it's highly unlikely to", Hubert told them.

"Yes, but what is it Hubert?", Abram enquired.

"There's been an urgent meeting with the Brothers and their Generals", Hubert informed them

"I take it that Prince Leopold was in this meeting as well?", Abram queried.

"Yes. Yes. All the Horridian Brothers were present", Hubert replied.

"What was the meeting about?", Miriam asked.

"As you all know, the High Prince declared war on the inner solar system. He has even launched an attack. Twenty two hundred missiles and two fleets of Trojan armed forces", Hubert reminded them.

"Yes Hubert. We are aware of that. It was on all the news feeds", Abram replied.

"They had allocated ten of those missiles just to Mars. Not many, I know, but enough to subdue the whole planet", Hubert informed them, adding, "Those missiles were destroyed en-route before they even got close to Mars!"

"So that's what the meeting was about", Miriam replied.

"Yes, but here's the problem. They have no idea, how their missiles were taken down", Hubert informed them.

"Well, it would have to be the Earth Defence Forces or the L5 Colonial Fleet", suggested Abram.

"They have detailed surveillance scans of the entire inner solar system. Nothing approached Mars from the Earth or L5, nothing. They know it wasn't the Earth Defence Forces or the L5 Colonial Fleet. They have no idea how this was done!", Hubert told them.

"I can see how that would be a problem Hubert", Abram told him.

Rajsheev asked, "What's Prince Leopold's position on this?"

"Officially, he has to side with his Brothers. There can be no dissent. Unofficially. Well, he sent me here straight away to keep you all in the loop", Hubert replied.

Rani enquired, "Why keep us in the loop?"

"My Prince's concerns are that his older Brother's have bitten off far more than they can chew", Hubert told them, explaining, "If these attacks on the inner solar system fail, we will have both the Earth's Defence Forces and the Colonial Fleet on their way here."

"That makes sense", Abram replied, "If his Brothers believe in their own propaganda, they may have seriously underestimated the inner solar system's responses."

"Yes. That's exactly it. This war that the High Prince has started, could very well be coming to our door steps", Hubert informed them all.

"Well, this is definitely not a good turn of events", Miriam replied.

Hubert passed Abram an envelope, "There are airtight compartments below the basement of this building. The elevator can take you there with this key. Just in case."

"The airtight compartments aren't much smaller than this penthouse and they are very well provisioned", Hubert informed them, "If things go horribly wrong, that's the place to go."

Abram took the envelope and the key it contained, "Just in case", he replied nodding.

Captain Carlson had requested General Verne to come to the bridge. The General did so quickly, as it was almost certainly with regards to communications from Jovian High Command. General Verne was in deed correct.

Captain Carlson passed the communications tablet to the General, who then opened the sealed communique it contained. The General read through the information contained within it.

"We have a variation in our orders Captain Carlson", the General informed him.

"A variation General?", Captain Carlson queried.

"It's a slight variation. Not that much different in fact", the General replied, adding, "We proceed to Mars as per our original orders. However, we deploy all of our forces to the Elysium region, west of the demon's lair. Apparently that's our main objective."

"Our main objective?", Captain Carlson queried, "What happened with the plans to occupy the whole of Mars? To occupy all the main colonies?"

"They're still in our plans Captain", the General confirmed, "However, we are to destroy the demon's lair first. If the demon's are all dead, they can't interfere with anything that follows, can they? After taking down the demon's lair, we then advance on the other colonies."

"So Jovian High Command think the demons took down our missile strike?", Captain Carlson questioned.

"It doesn't say", General Verne replied, adding, "It makes sense though. The missiles were meant to take down all of the main colonies. All of them. We would have simply landed and taken over with no resistance at all. Now that has all changed. No missiles means the colonies are all intact."

Captain Carlson understood, "We can't fight on nine fronts at once. So we now start with the demon's lair first and then take over the planet, one colony at a time. Colony hopping!", he replied nodding his head.

"Yes Captain and that is exactly what Jovian High Command wants and is now ordering us to do", the General confirmed, informing the Captain further, "First the demon's lair, then the Elysium Colony. Once we've consolidated control of the whole Elysium subcontinent, we move onto Mar's biggest colony, Chryse. From there, we take over the other six remaining major colonies in whatever order we see fit."

Captain Carlson nodded again in understanding.

Lady Selene read the transcript of Agent Murphy's report, "Good news people!", she told the small gathered group. Roseanne was present, as were the Pod Sisters, Zuawalo and Zeealas. Also at the gathering were Cormac and Candy Farmer, along with Catherine Swann. Zigg was present as well, but spent most of his time asleep on Zuawalo's lap.

"What's the news?", asked Catherine, who was extremely worried about her husband Peter, the father of her two children.

"Those missiles inbound to Mars have been completely destroyed!", Selene informed them all.

"That is great news Selene", Candy replied, "Great news."

Catherine asked Selene, "When will they be coming home?"

"Soon Catherine. Soon, but not yet", Lady Selene informed her, explaining, "There is one more task that they need to perform first. Then they'll be heading back."

"That Trojan Army?", Catherine muttered the question.

"Yes. I'm afraid so", Lady Selene told them all, "They have to neutralise that Trojan Army before they can come home."

"They will succeed won't they?", Zuawalo asked. Both Zuawalo and Zeealas were worried about Agent Murphy. They desperately wanted to see him again.

"In theory yeah. They do have the most advance ship ever built. They should prevail. They will return to us, I'm sure of it", Lady Selene assured them all.

"The Earth and L5 will both be pleased to receive information about how those missiles were taken down. I'm sure of that", Cormac told them.

"Yes. All the information I've been sent, has already been sent to them. They'll be digesting that and preparing there own take down accordingly", Lady Selene responded.

"You'll need to keep Governor Anderson in the loop on this development Selene", Cormac informed her, "Neutralising those missiles will take a load off of his mind. He'll need to adjust any plans he's put in place accordingly."

"Yes, yes. I'll be calling him later", Lady Selene assured him.

"Make sure the Governor keeps all the other colonies in the loop as well", Candy recommended.

"He will Candy", Cormac replied, reminding her, "He loves to be the centre of attention Candy. He'll set up a meeting with the other Governors as soon as he's off the line. No prompting required."

Roseanne told them all, "Just having those missiles neutralised is a load off my mind."

"Agreed", Catherine Swann replied, adding, "Let's just pray they all get home safely."

Roseanne walked over to the Pod Sisters and took their hands into hers, "They'll be okay. They've got this. Jim will be back soon, I'm certain of it", she told them.

Zigg woke up at that point and made his cute, little *'Dook Dook'* noises in agreement.

How close Roseanne had become to the Pod Sisters, Zuawalo and Zeealas, was such a strange thing, considering the very short time they had known each other. They had become extremely close. Even Lady Selene had noticed it.

"You're very close to the Pod Girls Roseanne", Lady Selene silently enquired.

"Yes", Roseanne replied.

"It just seems a little strange, given that you hardly know them", Selene noted.

Roseanne explained, *"These Girls are very capable. Very strong. They are survivors. But they are also very alone and very vulnerable. Their family, their friends, their village are on the other side of the Planet. The one person here, that they love, is on a dangerous mission. They feel very alone and very afraid."*

"And you empathise with them?", Selene asked.

"How can I not?", Roseanne responded, small tears appeared in her eyes.

It was then that Selene remembered, Roseanne herself had been orphaned at the age of five and raised in various foster homes as a ward of the state, back on the Earth. Roseanne understood what it was like to be alone. Selene placed her hand reassuringly on Roseanne's shoulder to let her know she understood.

It was four hours before intercept and the Ship's crew met in the Captain's conference room.

"Jim. Have you got that firing solution for us?", Forkbraid asked.

"Yes FB. I mean. Aye Captain, I have", Agent Murphy replied.

"Okay Jim, let's here it", Forkbraid requested.

"It is going to be very similar to what we did with the missiles", Agent Murphy begun, then elaborated, "I've used the ultra sensors to get a good look at both their troop transports and their heavy weapons transports. We are of course more interested in the later, however the Earth and L5 will be interested in both. So it's prudent to gather all the relevant information for everyone concerned."

"Something to note. Their weapons transports are up front, flying in a v formation. Their troop transports are somewhat further back. They're also flying in a v formation. That actually makes targeting somewhat easier", Agent Murphy informed everyone.

Agent Murphy paused for a few seconds before continuing, "At interception minus one hour, I'm letting loose with our electromagnetic rail guns. Being an excellent stand off weapons system and being the target's trajectories are incredibly stable, our targeting systems can anticipate precisely where they will be when our rounds intercept them."

Again Agent Murphy paused before continuing, "I'll be targeting the weapons transports at their weakest points for maximum damage. I'm also going to target them in groups of five, so we are talking of four initial strikes at first. One after the other in quick succession."

"Weakest points? Those would be?", Forkbraid enquired.

"Yes, the most vulnerable points", Agent Murphy replied, explaining further, "Their main engines, their main thrusters, orbital manoeuvring systems, defensive and offensive weapons systems, even their bridge. Pretty much anything that might create a cascade of destruction."

"Okay. Make sure that the Earth and L5 know about those Jim", Forkbraid replied.

Agent Murphy looked at the faces around the room, then continued, "We are going to be using rounds with penetrating tips and explosive charges. We are going to use a hell of a lot of them. Assuming the accuracy of the system is as consistent with our previous usage against those missiles, our four initial strikes should be incredibly devastating."

"Four initial strikes with our EMR guns?", Forkbraid enquired, asking, "Can you elaborate on that Jim? Give us a bit more detail?"

"I'm grouping the weapons transports into four targeting clusters, five transports per cluster", Agent Murphy explained, "The first strike will catch them completely by surprise. By the time they realise what's happened, the second strike will hit the next batch of transports. That should shake them up even further and sow fear and confusion into their thought processes. Seconds later, they'll be in the midst of the third strike, then quickly followed by the forth strike. They'll have absolutely no time to react at all. They'll have barely enough to even think!"

Varak, who had been listening intently, asked, "What sort of damage do we anticipate?"

"Assuming I've interpreted the scans correctly, there will be massive damage", Agent Murphy informed him, "Many of the transports will be completely disabled, some perhaps even destroyed. The result should certainly slow their advance considerably. They will literally become sitting ducks! All lined up in a row, ready for what we unleash next!"

"Unleash next?", Forkbraid queried.

"Yes. Unleash next", Agent Murphy replied, informing them further, "At interception, our main strike. I'm planning to hit their weapons transports with everything else in our arsenal."

Agent Murphy paused once more, then elaborated, "We have our passive cloak already activated. At interception minus twenty minutes, I'll be activating our eight by eight layered shield grid at maximum. Next I'll be activating the shield's active cloaking. They should not see us coming at all!"

Agent Murphy was quite emphatic about that last part.

Agent Murphy continued, "Next I'll instruct Marcus to alter our course to take us through the centre of their fleet, in such a way that we can target their stricken weapons transports with ease. The Captain has requested that I refrain from targeting their troop transports to minimise the loss of life. That is an important constraint that we need to take into consideration!"

Marcus nodded, "I will not only need to see the scans ahead of the manoeuvre, but also in real time in order to make those course corrections Jim."

"Excellent! We can provide those", Agent Murphy replied as he looked around the room once more, "As we approach their fleet, at interception minus sixty seconds, I will let loose with our hyper-resonant disrupter cannons. Maximum prejudice! I expect to wipe out what's left of the closest five transports with that action alone!"

Again Agent Murphy paused and looked around the room, "After that, as we pass though their fleet, we will be targeting the next closest ten weapons transports with our phased laser arrays. Both top and bottom arrays will be used, as well as our pulse plasma cannons. Again maximum prejudice! Those transports are not expected to survive. Their destruction should be complete!"

"Jim, what about the last five weapons transports", Varak enquired.

"I was just getting to them Varak", Agent Murphy replied, explaining, "As we pass through their fleet, before exiting the strike zone, we will fire a volley of a dozen torpedoes. Which, will be targeting the last five weapons transports and anything that looks like it might have survived our main strike. By the time we're done, there should be nothing left!"

Varak replied, "With our ship cloaked, both passively and actively, they won't see us coming at all. They won't have a clue what hit them! It should be devastating!"

Agent Murphy replied, "That is the plan Varak. Hit them fast! Hit them hard! Hit them good! Neutralise their heavy weapons platforms. Leave them dazed, confused, afraid and wondering what the bloody hell happened."

Agent Murphy looked around the room once more, "If we do this correctly, if we pull this one off, they might even abandon their invasion. That is the aim of all of this. Convince them to abandon their invasion! Without their heavy weapons systems, they may just as well go home."

"Thank you Jim. That sounds like one hell of a plan", Forkbraid replied.

Everybody was in agreement.

It was now almost intercept minus one hour and the bridge crew were all at their stations.

Agent Murphy began setting up his targeting solution, "Captain, may I begin with your permission", he asked.

"Permission granted Jim", Forkbraid replied.

"Aye Captain", Agent Murphy went through the procedures on his check list.

"Tactical! Electromagnetic rail carousel online. Check!"

"Electromagnetic rail guns online. Check!"

"Using ultra sensors to target all of the enemy weapons transports. Check!"

"Batch target weapons transports into groups. Targets in groups of five. Group by distance to target. Check!"

"Designated target groups one to four based on distance to group. Check!"

"Targeting Array online. Check!"

"Targeting groups one to four in sequence. Check!"

"Extrapolate target trajectories for projectile impacts. Check!"

"Locking down on vulnerable points designated as, main engines, main thrusters, orbital manoeuvring systems, defensive and offensive weapons systems, ship's bridge. Check!"

"Loading electromagnetic rail carousel with penetrating, explosive rounds. Check!"

"Calculate number of rounds required for total weapons transport destruction. Check!"

"Tactical! Fire on the selected targets with electromagnet rail guns!", Agent Murphy commanded.

The Hornet's nest went through the command sequence of instructions. It got as far as 'Targeting Array online' and responded with, "Compliance error! No data in targeting array buffer!"

Agent Murphy responded with, "Say what!"

The Hornet's nest replied with, "Compliance error! No data in targeting array buffer!"

Forkbraid asked, "Is there a problem Jim?"

"That is a good question Captain", Agent Murphy replied, then back to his tactical console, he commanded, "Tactical! Fire on the selected targets with electromagnet rail guns!"

The Hornet's nest went through the sequence of instructions for the second time. Again it got as far as *'Targeting Array online'* and responded with, "Compliance error! No data in targeting array buffer!", once more.

"Captain. We definitely have a problem", Agent Murphy confirmed.

"More information please Jim", Forkbraid requested.

"Tactical! Compliance error. No data in targeting array buffer. Explain the error", Agent Murphy commanded.

The Hornet's nest responded with, "The targeting array buffer is empty. No data in targeting array buffer."

"Tactical! Why is the targeting array buffer empty?", Agent Murphy asked.

The Hornet's nest responded with, "Unknown."

"Captain. The Hornet's nest is telling us that the targeting array buffer has no data", Agent Murphy informed him, adding, "And it does not seem to know why."

Forkbraid turned around to Peter Swann, "Peter. Why would the targeting array buffer have no data?", he enquired.

"Captain. The targeting system receives its data directly from the tactical sensor arrays. That is the combined feed of the long range sensors, the short range sensors and the ultra sensors", Peter informed him, then to Agent Murphy he recommended, "Jim. Check the status of the tactical sensor arrays."

"Thank you Peter", Agent Murphy replied, then commanded, "Tactical. Check the status of the tactical sensor arrays."

The Hornet's nest responded with, "There is no response from the tactical sensor arrays."

Agent Murphy then asked, "Tactical. Why is their no response from the tactical sensor arrays?"

The Hornet's nest responded with, "The tactical sensor arrays are not available."

"Tactical. Are the tactical sensor arrays off line?", Agent Murphy asked.

Again the Hornet's nest responded with, "The tactical sensor arrays are not available."

Peter, who had been listening to the responses from the Hornet's nest, responded with, "That makes no sense at all. There should always be a status, whether they are online or offline. The Hornet's nest should be able to tell you, what state they are actually in."

Forkbraid stepped back in, "Peter, what would cause the tactical sensor arrays to be unavailable?"

"There isn't a whole lot Captain", Peter replied, going through a list, "If they were removed perhaps. If they were damaged beyond repair perhaps. If they had no power perhaps. Aah, wait just a minute! I'm just checking something now."

Peter was quiet for almost a minute, as he checked on the Ships systems. Especially in the area of anything that could affect the tactical sensor arrays.

"Well here's our answer", Peter informed Forkbraid, explaining, "The power has been shut off to the tactical sensor arrays. They're not offline. It's as if they aren't even there. Thus unavailable!"

Forkbraid enquired further, "Peter, why exactly would the power to the tactical sensor arrays be shut off?"

"Three laws safe 'Betty'!", Peter exclaimed, explaining, "The ship, has switched off the power."

Marcus stepped in with, "I am, still able to see the sensor readings Captain. It's all there on my console. I can clearly see the data feeds!"

Marcus was confused as to why he had the sensor data available on his console, but Jim did not.

"Three laws safe 'Betty'?", Forkbraid queried, he pointed to Marcus, then queried Peter, "Explain that one will you?", then he stated ,"I thought that the Ship's positronic matrix could not interfere with the tactical operations systems?"

"We did separate everything out Captain. We even double up on the sensor arrays", Peter informed him, explaining further, "We actually have two sets of identical sensor arrays. The *'ships'* sensors, which the positronic matrix controls and the *'tactical'* sensors, which the Hornet's nest controls. Exact duplicated copies of each other. If you check the Ship's sensors, they should all be online and working fine."

"Okay, okay!", Marcus replied, nodding his head in understanding.

"If that's the case, then why can't the Hornet's nest simply bring the tactical sensors online?", Forkbraid enquired, it was a reasonable question after all.

"The power conduits are controlled by the ship, the positronic matrix and not the Hornet's nest", Peter Swann explained.

"And so the computer has shut off the power to the tactical sensors?", Agent Murphy stepped in and enquired.

"Yes. I expect that Three laws safe *'Betty'* here", pointing at the view screen, "detected human bio-signatures on those weapons transports and went into a three laws safe mode", Peter explained.

Peter further explained, "The ship is unlikely to turn the power to the tactical sensor arrays back on. At least, not until the threat to human life has passed."

"What the fuck!", Agent Murphy exclaimed, throwing his hands in the air in disgust.

"Jim. It's okay. We just have to work the problem", Forkbraid assured him, then to Peter, "Can we redirect the Ship's sensor data into the tactical targeting array?"

"The short answer Captain. No. They are completely separate systems. They were designed and constructed to be that way from the ground up", Peter informed him.

"Can you convince the Ship's Computer, to switch the power back on?", Forkbraid asked.

"I can try, but don't hold your breath Captain", Peter replied, then to the Computer, "Computer. Restore the power to the tactical sensor arrays."

The Computer responded with a typical three laws safe response, "We cannot comply. The tactical sensor arrays provides information that is threat to human life. We cannot through our action or our inaction allow human beings to come to harm."

Such a sweet sounding female voice, the Ship's computer had.

Peter tried again, "Computer. The tactical sensor arrays are not a part of your Ship's systems. They are part of the tactical operations systems. They are not your systems to control. You have violated your control parameters. Restore the power to the tactical sensor arrays at once!"

Again the Computer responded with its typical three laws safe response, "We cannot comply. The tactical sensor arrays provides information that is threat to human life. We cannot through our action or our inaction allow human beings to come to harm."

Still sweet sounding, but alas no joy.

"Can we force the Computer, to turn the tactical sensors back on?", Agent Murphy asked.

"Whoa! That would be an extremely bad idea! We'd run the risk of causing a neural cascade failure", Peter warned them.

"Would that be so bad?", Agent Murphy queried, not giving a fuck about the Ship's computer.

"With a ship as complex as this one. It would be an absolute disaster!", Peter replied.

Peter then explained, "Imagine that suddenly everyone of the Ship's systems, locks down on the final instructions from the positronic matrix. We would be stranded, stuck on course with no ability to change it. At least, not until a backup positronic matrix is installed and prepared."

"You do have a backup positronic matrix, don't you Peter?", Forkbraid enquired.

"Yes Captain. Of course I do. I have several positronic matrixes in the Ship's stores that could be used as backups. However, a replacement matrix requires several days to learn the Ship's systems and during that time we would all be extremely vulnerable", Peter advised them.

"Then let's avoid any neural cascade failures then", Forkbraid decided, then asked, "What if we use the Ship's sensor data and manually feed that into the targeting arrays?"

Peter responded, "Captain. If we do that, the Computer will simply take the data away from us. It might even goes so far, as to power off the Ship's sensors altogether."

"Okay. So that, is not an option either", Forkbraid replied back.

"It wouldn't work either Captain", Agent Murphy informed him, "We don't have anywhere near the same data input capabilities, nor the response times that are required to set up the targeting solution manually. It requires direct sensor feeds from the tactical sensor arrays!"

The Solstice was now much closer to the Trojan Armed Forces and the Computer automatically responded, "Proximity alert. Proximity alert. Multiple threats detected. We have activated the multi layered shield grid. We have activated all cloaking systems."

"Three laws safe 'Betty' plays no favourites! She may be keeping our enemies safe, but she's also keeping us safe from them as well", Peter informed everyone.

"Good to know", Forkbraid replied, adding, "Now. How do we get her to do as she's told?"

There was no answer.

Forkbraid put a request through on the communications unit, "Varak, please come to the bridge. We have a three laws safe issue in progress!".

Varak was quickly on the bridge, he was already looking into any possible issues using his grip "Captain. Nothings showing up that I can see. What seems to be the problem?", he enquired.

"Peter. You tell Varak what the issue is", Forkbraid told him.

"The Computer has switched off the power to the tactical sensor arrays", Peter informed Varak.

"The Computer has what?", Varak questioned, it sounded incredulous.

"Switched off the power to the tactical sensor arrays!", Peter repeated clearly with more force.

"The tactical sensor arrays are not a part of the Ship's systems! They are controlled by the Hive", Varak replied, using the Hornet's nest's alternate designation.

"Apparently the ship controls the power conduits Varak", Peter informed him.

"Oh shit! I see. She has it taken upon herself to cut the power!", Varak nodded in understanding.

Forkbraid asked, "Varak! What's the fix? We have a battle to get on with."

Varak's answer was quick, but it was also quite disappointing, "We have to run a separate power conduits. Ones that the Ship's Computer cannot control."

Varak elaborated further, "We would route control of the new power conduits to the tactical sensor arrays through the hive, through the tactical consoles here on the bridge and through my engineering station."

"That sounds like a lot of work Varak", Forkbraid replied.

"It is Captain, it is", Varak agreed, informing him, "It will take at least three days in the hanger back on Mars or just as long in a space dock."

"Well ain't that dandy. This is what's called a cluster fuck people!", Agent Murphy spat out.

"Agreed Jim", Varak replied, "It was not something we had considered."

"Who designed this crap system?", an angry Agent Murphy asked.

"It is not a crap system Jim", Varak responded, explaining, "It is a new system. The most advance ships control system ever devised. It is bound to have a few teething problems."

"Teething problems! Fuck! Varak, we had those bastards right in the cross hairs. Then miss three laws safe *'Betty'* here", this time Agent Murphy pointed at the screen, "Fucks us all over!"

Agent Murphy was livid!

Forkbraid could see what was on Jim's mind.

Fear for the safety of the Pod Girls in an upcoming ground offensive against the academy.

Varak put his hands together in an almost prayer like fashion before responding diplomatically, "Jim. We thought we had months to iron out these bugs! Then we find out we had only weeks! This is our shake down voyage. This is where we find all the bugs!"

Forkbraid stepped in, "Jim! Varak is correct! This is the Ship's maiden voyage. We are actually quite lucky that it has gone, as well as it has!"

Charlene, who had been silent throughout this entire discourse threw in, "Gentlemen! Gentlemen! Remember, there is a lady on the bridge!"

Agent Murphy then apologised, "I'm sorry Charlene. I'm sorry Varak. It's just that we had them! We had those bastards by the short and curlies! We could have ended the entire threat to Mars here! Right here, at this moment in time!"

Charlene replied, "Remember that old saying about the best laid plans of mice and men."

"A good point Charlene. It appears to me, that we are not going into battle after all. Let's go home instead. We'll work this problem another way", Forkbraid decided and informed his crew.

"Marcus! Prepare a course through the Trojan Fleet", Forkbraid commanded, "Let's not waste this opportunity. We may not be able to take them down, but we can at least get the best intel possible. We're going to need that later. Maximise the course for intelligence collection."

"Aye Captain", Marcus responded, "Calculating new course now."

The course set, Marcus then issued a command to the computer, "Computer. Proceed along new course as calculated. Fusion thrusters in stealth mode. All cloaking systems to remain active."

The Computer responded with, "Complying." Again, in its nice sweet feminine voice.

The Solstice flew through the Trojan Fleet with both active and passive cloaking modes activated. The Ship's fusion thrusters were working well in stealth mode. No-one aboard the twenty troop transports, nor the twenty weapons transports knew that they were there. They were completely oblivious. Not only to the passing ship, but also to the devastating attack that might have been.

"I don't get it", Charlene began wondering aloud, "The Computer shut of the tactical sensors, but now we're flying through the enemy fleet and taking detailed scans with the Ship's sensors. I don't get it. Why is it letting us do that?"

"There's a difference", Peter began to explain, "Back on Mars, we couldn't get hyper-dynamic 303's to build weapons modules. They understood weapons kill humans. So they simply refused!"

"Yes, but what is the difference between tactical and Ship's sensor scans?", Charlene queried.

"Immediacy. That's the difference", Peter replied, explaining, "The tactical sensors were feeding directly into a targeting array. An immediate threat to anything being targeted. The Ship's sensors on the other hand are just collecting data. It could be used for any purpose in the future. It's a temporal hop. The positronic matrix is not putting two and two together. The future is not deterministic."

"I never thought of it that way", Charlene admitted.

"You have to remember Charlene. Humaniform Androids may look superficially like us, but at the end of the day, they are just machines. Sophisticated yes, really smart yes, but still just machines", Peter replied.

"We are collecting oodles of data", Marcus told everyone, "These scans are extremely detailed."

"Just what the Earth and L5 are going to need", Agent Murphy replied.

Not long after, the Solstice had cleared the last of the Trojan Fleet's transports.

"Jim. Put together a report and send it off to the Earth and L5. Copy in Captain Carmichael as well. Send them all the complete dataset along with the report", Forkbraid instructed, "I'm going to message Selene about our Ship's teething problems and let her know we're coming home."

"Marcus. We're through their fleet, prepare a course for Mars. We want to get back home well before that fleet arrives. So take us home", Forkbraid instructed.

"Aye Captain", Marcus responded, "Preparing new course"

The course set, Marcus then issued a command to the computer, "Computer. Proceed along new course as plotted. Fusion thrusters in stealth mode and at full thrust. All cloaking systems active."

The Computer responded with, "Complying."

The Solstice began its return journey back to Mars.

Forkbraid asked the computer, "Computer. What is the estimated time of arrival."

The Computer responded with, "Ninety six hours."

"Wow! Four days", Forkbraid noted.

Marcus replied, "It took us four days to get this far out Captain. It takes just as long to get back."

"Marcus, how long will it take for the Trojan Fleet to reach Mars?", Forkbraid asked.

"Captain, I would have said a little over four weeks. Except, I expect they will start accelerating towards Mars very soon, just like their missiles did. So I think we have maybe two weeks at best. That is, two weeks after we arrive back on Mars", Marcus replied.

"So roughly two weeks and four days?", Forkbraid queried.

"I'd say that's about right Captain", Marcus confirmed.

The next shift, the crew of the Solstice arrived at their stations as usual. Agent Murphy noticed there was a slight change.

"My Android assistant is gone", Agent Murphy noted.

"Yes Jim. I've reassigned it to tactical systems maintenance", Forkbraid replied.

"Not that I liked the damned thing, but may I ask why?", Agent Murphy queried.

"I think I'll let Peter explain that", Forkbraid replied, then requested, "Peter?"

"I thought it prudent to have its memory engrams wiped completely and reassign it to maintenance", Peter explained.

"Prudent? Was it malfunctioning?", Agent Murphy asked.

"Not as such", Peter responded, explaining, "It was just another three laws safe issue."

"Just another three laws safe issue? You might want to elaborate on that one", Agent Murphy was seeking a better explanation.

"We know that the Ship's Computer cut off the power to the tactical sensor arrays, but what I needed to know, was how it knew to do that", Peter replied.

"Okay. Well what did you find?", Agent Murphy enquired.

"Well, at first I thought that the Computer had simply picked up on our conversation about your targeting solution in the conference room, you'd be surprised what the Ship's Computer can pick up. Then again, perhaps the command sequence check list that you entered into your console was the source. I couldn't be sure. So I pulled the internal computer communication logs from around the time of the incident and analysed them all", Peter explained.

When Marcus and Charlene heard that part of the explanation they both blushed slightly.

"And?", Agent Murphy questioned.

"Your Android assistant Jim", Peter informed him.

"My Android assistant was a model 295. It should not have been a problem. I was assured of that", Agent Murphy replied.

"Ah! But it was. It was actually, the problem!", Peter responded, adding, "Let me explain."

"Your model 295 had absolutely no problem when we took down the missiles. No human life was involved. When you began targeting those weapons transports however, that was a completely different story", Peter explained.

"So the model 295 took exception to the targeting?", Jim enquired.

"It did. It did indeed! Human lives were involved", Peter confirmed.

Peter went on to explain, "Up until that point the Computer was not interfering. It couldn't. The tactical systems are outside of its control, as they were designed to be. Then the model 295 gave the Computer precisely what it needed to prevent the loss of human life."

"So the model 295 actively worked against us? Actively worked with the Computer to foil our targeting solution?", Agent Murphy questioned.

"Yes. That's the gist of it. The model 295 silently worked with the Ship's Computer, to find a solution that was three laws safe", Peter confirmed.

"And their solution was to cut the power to the tactical sensor arrays", Agent Murphy nodded in acknowledgement.

"That is correct", Peter confirmed, "The problem is in the first law of robotics. An Android cannot harm or *through its inaction*, allow harm to come to a living human being. It's the inaction part the law got us!"

Forkbraid stepped in, "So the Computer had a pathway to action provided to it by the model 295 and it was compelled by the first law of robotics to take that action."

"This problem is far more complicated than it seems at first", Peter informed them, adding, "Varak and I are working on a solution that should take into account all possible scenarios."

"So it's more than just running new power conduits then?", Agent Murphy enquired.

"As I was explaining to the Captain earlier, we have to look into the navigation, flight controls and communications modules as well", Peter replied.

"A sudden course change during firing would affect the outcome", Forkbraid added.

"And we can't have the Ship's Computer warning our targets in advance either", Agent Murphy replied, he was beginning to understand the depth of the issue.

"Exactly! We literally need a *'tactical operations mode'*. When in tactical mode, the three laws safe Computer is locked out of the helm and communications. The Hornet's nest takes over for the duration of the tactical operation, then relinquishes control when complete", Peter informed them.

"So we need to make it impossible for the Computer to interfere. Give it no possible courses of action that it can take", Agent Murphy replied.

"That is what Varak and I are working on. We're looking for a way to negate the *'inaction'* part of the first law. If there are no possible courses of action that can be taken, the Computer cannot be compelled into action", Peter informed them.

Forkbraid stepped back in, "Sadly, Varak tells me that the timeline for this change is more than two weeks. Which means the Trojan Armed Forces will be on the ground before the ship is even close to being ready."

"Has no-one, no-one at all, heard of the KISS principle?", Agent Murphy lamented.

The best laid plans of mice and men often go awry.

15. One Down and One to Go

It was four days later and the Solstice was back at Mars. Forkbraid asked Marcus to take the ship into high Martian orbit.

Marcus let go of Charlene's hand and replied, "Aye Captain, Preparing course for high Martian orbital insertion."

The course set, Marcus then issued a command to the computer, "Computer. Proceed along new course as calculated for orbital insertion."

The Computer responded with, "Complying."

The Solstice altered course and it wasn't long before they were in high Martian orbit.

The view screen showed them all a view of the Martian globe. Mars was now a blue marble, with white swirling clouds. Beneath the clouds, could be seen vast expanses of land, with shades of brown, green, yellow and white. The new Oceans and Seas of Mars although small and shallow compared to the Earth, were still quite visible and now covered a good thirty five percent of the planet. Mars was the most beautiful of sites.

"That's what it's all about people", Forkbraid stated as he pointed to the view screen, he stepped out of his chair and continued, "Mars is now our home! There's an army on its way. That army is ten thousand troops strong and it will have two hundred or more heavy weapons, of yet unknown types. That is the problem that we need to work. We have roughly two weeks. That is our priority."

"Marcus. Takes us home. Takes us to the New Flinders Psychic Academy", Forkbraid instructed.

Marcus replied, "Aye Captain, Preparing course for New Flinders Psychic Academy. Anti-Gravity Lifters are now online."

Marcus was far more familiar with the helm's console now and found it far easier to fly the ship, than when he had first come on board. He dispensed with the checklist and set the new course.

The course set, Marcus then issued a command to the computer, "Computer. Proceed along new course as calculated for landing at New Flinders Psychic Academy air field."

The Computer responded with, "Complying."

"Charlene. Message Selene. Let Selene know we'll be home shortly", Forkbraid requested.

"Aye Captain. Relaying message now", Charlene replied.

When the Solstice approached the airfield, there was already a small group of people waiting. Catherine Swann and her children, Miranda and Chiron were present, as was Cormac, Candy, Roseanne and the two Pod Sisters, with Zigg the ferret.

The Solstice flew in low from the north west, approached the air field and hovered above the tarmac at one hundred metres altitude. The ship then slowly lowered itself down to a clear spot on the tarmac close to the construction hanger. Everyone in front of the hanger watched as the Solstice touched down gently, almost gracefully on the tarmac.

"That is quite a ship", Catherine Swann stated.

"Yes", agreed Selene, adding, "It just has a few teething problems. Apparently."

Cormac smiled his gap toothed smile and replied, "The Trojan Army might still be on the way, but at least we don't have to worry about those missiles."

"An Army is still a problem Cormac!", Catherine chided.

Candy placed her arm around Cormac, "The other colonies are putting together militia's. Those Trojans won't find this planet as easy as they think."

"We have dodged one bullet. Those ten missiles with a hundred warheads, each with a two megaton yield, would have been devastating", Selene reminded them, "We might not be out of the woods yet, but it could have been far, far worse."

At that moment the Ship's ramp descended to the tarmac and the crew began to leave the ship. Marcus and Charlene were the first to exit and quickly joined up with their friends. Peter and Varak weren't far behind. Peter rushed over to his wife and children. He hugged them all tightly.

Forkbraid and Agent Murphy were the last to leave the ship. Forkbraid went straight to Selene and embraced her. The Pod Sisters, Zuawalo and Zeealas, ran straight up to Agent Murphy and smothered him. Zigg was on his lead and could barely keep up with them.

Cormac and Candy looked at the Pod Sisters.

Candy thought to Cormac, *"Definitely both."*

Cormac thought back, *"Definitely both."*

Roseanne walked up to Cormac and Candy, thinking, *"Wedding bells you think?"*

Candy smiled and thought back, *"Definitely."*

Cormac smiled his gap tooth smile and thought back, *"More than one me thinks."*

Roseanne looked around at her friends, *"Charlene and Marcus? Selene and Forkbraid? The Pod Sisters and Agent Murphy? I see what you mean Cormac."*

As Selene and Forkbraid walked past, on their way to the transport to go back to the academy, Selene sent a thought to Roseanne, *"Please don't encourage them Roseanne. It's embarrassing."*

"They're just happy for all of you. I think they're sweet", Roseanne thought in return.

Back at their apartment in the psychic academy Selene asked Forkbraid, "Well, how did your crew go on their maiden voyage?"

"It wasn't too bad come to think of it", Forkbraid replied, "You have to consider that none of us has crewed a ship before. Piloted yes, but crewed no", he added.

"So there weren't any issues?", Selene enquired.

"Apart from Ship's teething issue, nothing major", Forkbraid replied.

"Okay. Nothing major. So there were some minor issues", Selene dug deeper.

"I would hardly call them issues Selene. Quirks maybe", Forkbraid responded.

"Spill them. I want to hear them Forkbraid", Selene pushed.

"Are you sure? Okay", Forkbraid replied, then began with, "Well, we were in space, so naturally Charlene and Marcus lost their psychic abilities

"Yes. That would be expected", Selene replied.

"Well as a result, they became much more *'tactile'*", Forkbraid informed her.

"Tactile?", Selene queried.

"Yes. Tactile", Forkbraid confirmed, explaining, "While at their bridge stations, they spent quite a lot of time holding hands. Very touchy feely. And I don't think Marcus stayed in his cabin at all."

"He probably bunked in with Charlene, in her cabin", Selene answered smiling.

"Well. That would explain the noises. The cabin walls are not real thick. I will have to mention that to Varak. Sound proofing that is. I was actually getting worried that maybe, I'd walk in on them, on the bridge, *'using the surfaces'* so to speak", Forkbraid replied.

"Oh! Really! No! No! I can't imagine them doing that", Selene responded, with just a slightly shocked, almost embarrassed look on her face.

Forkbraid continued, "It appears that Jim has a bit of a potty mouth."

"Really", Selene replied, "I would never have guessed", even though she had noticed herself.

"He is very good at the tactical console. Very good indeed. It's just when things aren't going right", Forkbraid explained.

"Like with these three laws safe teething issues?", Selene queried.

"Yeah. Precisely. Jim has always been sceptical of having Androids on the bridge. He certainly doesn't agree with having a positronic brain running the ship", Forkbraid replied.

"Then of course there's your choice for our science officer", Forkbraid stated, explaining, "Don't get me wrong. Peter is probably the best choice we have. He is brilliant. Damned brilliant! I have to give him that."

"But?", Selene asked.

"He does come across as somewhat arrogant", Forkbraid answered.

"Really? And like you don't?", Selene replied with rhetorical questions.

"Touche my darling", Forkbraid replied, adding, "Yes well, I guess, He and I have that in common then, don't we."

"So that leaves Varak", Selene replied.

"Yes Varak", Forkbraid answered, "What can I say. He is Varak. He is the man that can build anything. He can make anything work. Varak also works back in engineering, so we only see him on the bridge when he's needed there."

"You know Varak has never been I.Q tested", Selene replied, "It's highly likely that his I.Q is right up there, somewhere close to Peter's."

"That would explain why they get along so well together", Forkbraid suggested, "Two brainiacs working side by side collaborating on a project, bouncing ideas off one and other."

Selene nodded in response.

"So all in all, it appears everything, actually went quite smoothly", Selene concluded.

"Yeah. It did. Surprisingly! I expected far more problems. Things going wrong, issues and what not. It all went well until we ran in those damnable three laws safe issues.", Forkbraid replied.

"Well, we still have that problem with three laws safe issues don't we", Selene reminded him.

"Yes Selene. That could be another issue in itself", Forkbraid informed her.

"Well yeah. It's a problem that Varak and Peter have to resolve", Selene replied.

"No. No. I'm not talking about the engineering side of it. I'm quite certain that they can solve the issues of demarcation between the positronic brain and the hornet nest neural super cluster. That's not what I was thinking", Forkbraid replied.

"Well then. What is this other issue?", Selene asked.

"We could have just installed a standard ships computer and operating system. Instead we have a positronic brain and neural super cluster", Forkbraid told her.

"True, but both Varak and Peter both said, that was the best, the most advanced method of controlling the Ship", Selene replied, adding, "A Ship, which is the most advanced in existence."

"Yes, but it's the fine tuning of this entire concept. A three laws safe ships computer system and a neural super cluster, that is a weapons system, which by its very definition is anything but three laws safe", Forkbraid explained, adding, "You can see my concerns can't you."

"You did say, you were certain that they can solve these issues", Selene replied.

"Yes. I did. It is a complex systems integration and demarcation issue and I'm absolutely certain they can solve it. However, it's like they're fixated on it. It has become an obsession. There are other solutions that are likely far simpler and don't have these three laws safe issues", Forkbraid replied.

"And Varak and Peter are obsessed with getting this, their solution to work", Selene understood.

"It's like Jim asked on the bridge, the day after we turned back to come home. Has no-one heard of the KISS principle?", Forkbraid summed up.

"Keep it simple stupid", Selene murmured in reply.

"We are of course, way too far down the rabbit hole to change tack", Forkbraid replied.

Selene nodded in agreement.

"Well, there you have it Selene. That's all the goss", Forkbraid stated.

"It's hardly goss Forkbraid. We do need to understand how the Ship's crew interacts after-all", Selene replied, adding, "It's a very important consideration."

"Sorry my darling. Something else to consider", Forkbraid replied, "We don't have uniforms. We're all sitting around the bridge in our civvies. If we're going to be the Solstice's crew, we need to at least look the part."

Selene smiled, "Well. We can't have that can we. Maybe I can get Charlene and Roseanne to come up with an acceptable style of uniform."

"Just so long as we don't end up looking like pirates", Forkbraid replied.

Selene chuckled slightly and they both laughed.

Varak and Peter had the Solstice in total disarray when Forkbraid and Agent Murphy came aboard. The Solstice had been taxied back into its construction hanger. Separate power conduits had been laid out for the tactical sensor arrays. Varak had a team of model 295 Androids, ensuring that power to those arrays could only be controlled by the Hive neural super cluster, the bridges tactical consoles, the Captain's console and the engineering consoles. Work was progressing well when Forkbraid and Agent Murphy approached Varak.

"Varak, I'm just going to say it looks like a mess", Forkbraid told him.

"Yes. I must admit it does", Varak replied, "We will have this all cleared up on schedule."

"That's good to hear", Forkbraid replied.

"Varak. We're actually far more interested in the other three laws safe issues that need fixing", Agent Murphy informed him.

"Yes. Yes. You would be", Varak agreed, "You know. Peter is working on that. It is very complicated. Very complicated. We have already separated out the Ship's systems from the Tactical systems, including the power conduits."

Varak explained the difficult part, "Now we need to integrate the navigation, flight control and communications modules into the Hive's neural super cluster. And we need to do so, in such a way, that it does not disturb the Ship's Computer integration to those said same systems. It is very complicated. Very complicated."

"Yes Varak, but have you made any headway on that yet?", Forkbraid asked.

"Not yet. I have asked Peter to put that huge brain of his onto the task. He is currently working through what needs to be done", Varak replied.

"So you haven't started yet?", Agent Murphy questioned accusingly.

"The thoughts must come first Jim. The thoughts must come first", Varak repeated, adding, "When Peter has it right up here, we can then begin", Varak pointed to his right temple.

Forkbraid put his hand on Agent Murphy's shoulder, "Peter's working the problem Jim. Varak is right. They both have to fully understand how this is going to work, before they can implement anything."

"That is correct. Once we have those three modules integrated into both systems, we then need to work out the demarcations", Varak explained.

"Demarcations?", queried Agent Murphy.

"Yes. When those modules are controlled by the two systems. Under which modes of operation", Varak explained further.

Varak went on to explain, "During the normal operation mode, the Ship's Computer controls navigation, flight control and communications. When we put the Ship into tactical operation mode, the Hive takes over control of those modules. We decide which mode is appropriate and when."

"And how do we decide that Varak?", Agent Murphy asked.

"We will decide that, through three consoles in the ship. The Captain's console, your tactical console and also from my engineering console. So it can be controlled by the Captain, Yourself or Myself. We have considered the science console as well, but no decision has been made about that yet.", Varak replied hoping Jim would be happy with that solution.

"Okay. That all sounds good. Can I make one more recommendation?", Agent Murphy asked.

"Yes Jim. I am always happy to hear your suggestions", Varak responded diplomatically.

"No Androids on the bridge", Jim stated bluntly, "We cannot have any Androids repeating what my Android assistant did last time."

"That has already been discussed between Peter and I. Peter also recommended the same thing. Peter said it would be prudent", Varak informed him.

"Good. We are all on the same page then", Agent Murphy replied.

"So Varak. Our timeline? Has that changed?", Forkbraid asked

"It is the same. We will not have these changes ready before the enemy arrives", Varak informed them, "It is very complicated, very complicated. We have to test everything as well."

"We are going to need to deal with the Trojans another way FB", Agent Murphy stated.

"I have thought about that Jim. It's an idea, but it will require Selene's help", Forkbraid replied, "It is very unconventional, very unconventional."

"As long as it works, conventional or not, just as long as it works", Agent Murphy replied.

"Varak. In hind site. Do you think a simpler ships control system might have been better?", Agent Murphy enquired.

"Hmm. Jim you have a point. Simpler is simple, but is it as good? No. I do not think so. This solution we have implemented, is the best solution. It is new. It has never been tried before. It was bound to have some teething problems", Varak replied, "That is how we make progress. Yes?"

"Your are right Varak. That's how we make progress. Trial and error", Forkbraid agreed, then slapped him lightly on the shoulder.

The very next day they received word from Phobos, Lieutenant Roberts informed that the Trojan Amy heading their way had begun accelerating. The Trojan Armed Forces would be arriving in around two weeks.

"What's our plan?", Selene asked Forkbraid.

"We don't quite have one just yet Selene", he replied, adding, "I've had a thought. It's not really a plan and it is highly unconventional."

"Well what was your thought?", Selene enquired further.

"We need to do two things, Selene", Forkbraid replied, elaborating further, "One. Take down their heavy weapons systems. Two. Convince their soldiers to go home", he explained.

"Okay. It's not much, but it is a start", Selene replied, querying, "Exactly how are we going to do that Forkbraid?"

"I haven't quite worked that out yet", Forkbraid admitted to her, adding, "I've been toying around with the first step."

"Take down their heavy weapons systems", Selene repeated their first task

"I think it will require both of us and a little bit of galdrar and stadhagaldr", Forkbraid explained his thought to Selene.

"Here on Mars?", Selene queried, "Will a full ritual even work here? On Mars?"

"Why not?", Forkbraid replied, "On Earth we wielded the Art Majik. Why not here on Mars?"

"As on the Earth, so to on Mars", Selene thought out loud, then replied, "This is completely untried. Completely untested. We have no idea if that will work."

"Yes, but there is a first time for everything", Forkbraid replied, adding, "And if it works!"

"Yes. If it works", Selene replied, adding, "Forkbraid, you'd better get busy creating that ritual."

"I'll be starting on it straight away", Forkbraid replied.

"That leaves step two Forkbraid", Selene reminded him.

"Yes Selene, I haven't forgotten that one", Forkbraid replied, then asked, "How would you convince ten thousand men to pack up and go home? Any ideas?"

"Take away their toys so they have nothing to play with? Maybe?", Selene replied.

"Well that was step one, take down their heavy weapons systems", Forkbraid reminded her, explaining, "Taking away their toys doesn't automatically mean they'll go home, does it now."

"We would have to convince their leadership, their commanders, that staying is a fools errand", Selene considered.

"Or take down their commanders and replace them with more reasonable men. Ones that can see the futility of staying", Forkbraid suggested.

"We'd have to make sure their drop ships survive whatever we do for step one", Selene replied, adding, "They will need a way off planet. A way to go home."

"So step one, take down their heavy weapons, but leave their drop ships operational. Then step two, convince their commanders to leave or remove their commanders, so their army can then leave", Forkbraid mused, adding, "This is probably going to get a wee bit complicated isn't it?"

"It certainly looks that way doesn't it. And how does Leroy McGuvan fit in with all of this?", Selene asked.

"He doesn't. As far as we know. McGuvan has no knowledge of the approaching Trojan Army. The Kujur who demolished him, has no knowledge of that Army either", Forkbraid informed her.

"And yet here he is! Seeking his redemption! That man is a riddle, wrapped in an enigma", Selene replied, "And how do those Girls, the Pods Sisters fit in with this?"

"Their village Kujur! Gwek, told Zuawalo that she would redeem McGuvan", Forkbraid reminded Selene.

"How Forkbraid, is that girl going to redeem him?", Selene questioned.

Forkbraid thought long and hard about that very question, then replied, "By accompanying Leroy on his journey. His path to redemption. Zuawalo is literally there as a constant reminder to him of his past failings. A reminder of his possible future successes. His redemption!"

"This Kujur. Gwek. He has put a lot of responsibility onto Zuawalo's shoulders", Selene replied almost angrily, "That is not something that you or I would ever have done!"

"It might be a cultural thing Selene. Zuawalo did save his life after-all. Perhaps in her village, that makes Leroy, her responsibility", replied Forkbraid.

"That is not the way we do things Forkbraid", Selene replied.

"Perhaps that's their way Selene", Forkbraid replied, adding, "It might be a good idea to ask Zuawalo about that at some point."

Forkbraid asked,"Has anyone let the Pod Sister's parents know that they're okay?"

"No. I don't think so", Selene replied, "Their parents must be frantic."

"Well that is something we can fix straight away at least", Forkbraid replied, adding, "Send a quick thought to Roseanne, to bring the Sisters to the communications centre."

"Will do", Selene replied as they both got up and headed towards the communications office.

Forkbraid sent a quick thought to the Communications Officer to get Chryse Colonies Governor Anderson on the line.

It did not take long to walk to the communications centre from Selene's apartment and when they got there, Roseanne and the Pod Sisters were already present and waiting.

"What's going on?" Roseanne asked.

"Nothing bad", Selene replied, "Something good for a change."

Governor Anderson was on the screen, waiting impatiently, "Well, what is it you require?"

"Governor. Its good to see you again as well", Forkbraid began slightly sarcastically, then requesting, "We need you to perform a couple of tasks for us Governor."

"Of course you do. Of course you do. Well then what are these tasks?", the Governor asked.

Selene introduce the Pod Sisters to the Governor, "Governor, these are the Pod Sisters, Zuawalo and Zeealas."

The Governor looked at the Pod Sister's through the screen, "Interesting? You're bush folk aren't you?", he queried, then added, "My Pilot Mack, he mentioned a pair of girls matching your descriptions."

"Yes. Our village is on the southern shores of the Hebes Sea", Zuawalo replied.

Governor Anderson took on a more intrigued, inquisitive look.

"Governor!", Selene caught his attention, "These girls have travelled a very long way."

"Yes I know. My Pilot flew them to you in my personal Hummer", he replied.

"That is part one of our request", Forkbraid informed him, "Their parents haven't seen them since they left their village. We need you to get word to them."

"Okay. I think we can arrange that", the Governor replied, asking, "I will need their location."

Both Zuawalo and Zeealas smiled, they were extremely happy.

Zuawalo replied, asking, "Do you know that very bad place, New Tortuga?"

"Yes. Yes. I know about it", the Governor responded.

"Our village is directly south of New Tortuga, on the southern shore of the Hebes Sea", Zuawalo informed him.

Governor Anderson began writing notes down on his notepad, then replied, "It should not be too hard to locate your village young Lady. Should be quite easy in fact."

Zuawalo smiled and hugged her Sister Zeealas. They were very happy with this turn of events.

"That's good Governor", Selene replied, explaining further, "We need to get word to Zuawalo's and Zeealas's parents, to let them know they are both okay and well looked after."

"Yes. I can imagine that would be a load off their minds", the Governor replied.

"There is more Governor", Forkbraid informed him.

"Isn't there always", the Governor rolled his eyes and responded in his usual serious manner.

"We'd like the Girls to be able to contact their parents when ever they want", Forkbraid informed him, requesting, "Could you arrange installation of satellite communications equipment at their parents house?"

"Of course. I can arrange that. There will need a charging unit to keep the batteries charged as well I expect", the Governor replied while scribbling down some more notes, "I figure we'll be picking up the tab for this one as well."

"Governor. Why do you do that?", Selene enquired.

"Do what?", the Governor enquired in his usual grumpy voice.

"You come across as all gruff and uncaring", Selene replied, then explained, "but you know what, you actually like helping people. Everyone can see that."

The Governor sat back in his chair, somewhat taken aback. His face become more thoughtful, he then looked directly at Selene, "I suppose I do", he replied, adding as he slowly smiled, "I do actually enjoy helping people."

There was a slight pause as the Governor leaned forward in his chair once more and asked, "Is there anything else I can help you with?", he was looking at the Girls.

"Just one more thing Governor", Forkbraid replied, informing him, "There is a man in the Girl's village. A Kujur named Gwek. He is a very important man. We need you to bring him to Elysium."

Governor Anderson scribbled down some more notes, then read off the list, "Locate the Girl's parents and let them know the Girls are okay and being looked after. Provide the Girl's parents with communication equipment. Bring the village Kujur named Gwek to Elysium. Is that all?"

"Yes Governor. That's the lot. Remember, the Kujur Gwek, he's our guest, our VIP. You bring him to the Elysium Colony and we'll pick him up from there", Forkbraid confirmed.

"Excellent. I'll get straight onto it. Girls, it was a pleasure meeting you both", he replied.

Zeealas replied, "Governor. You should get some rest. Take some time off. Our village is very hospitable. Very nice people. You can relax and fish, maybe even hunt if you wish. Even bring your family along as well."

"Thank you young Lady for the invite. I might just do that, when we have all these other issues sorted out of course. Anderson over and out", Governor Anderson replied before signing off.

"He seems like a nice man. Serious and grumpy. Very funny though. Like a big teddy bear", Zeealas told everyone.

Zuawalo replied, "Soon we can talk to mother and father", her faced was beaming.

"Yes Sister", Zeealas smiled back and hugged her.

Then unexpectedly both Pod Sisters turned to Forkbraid and gave him huge hug as a thank you.

Forkbraid was not much of a hugger, but hugged them back anyway.

"Run along now Girls. We'll let you know when the communication equipment is in place", Selene told them, while thinking to Forkbraid with a smile, *"Now you know how Jim must feel, on the receiving end of all that attention."*

Before they had left the communications centre, Forkbraid thought back to Selene, *"It's a shame we didn't meet them when they were younger."*

"How so Forkbraid?", Selene enquired.

"Didn't you pick it up?", Forkbraid thought back, explaining, *"They may have been low functioning level threes."*

Selene thought about that, then thought back to Forkbraid, *"How did I miss that? They once had potential."*

"Sadly it's too late now", Forkbraid thought in return.

As the Pod Sisters and Roseanne left the communication centre, Roseanne picked up on Selene and Forkbraid's thoughts and thought to herself smiling, *"Low functioning level threes?"*

A few days later word came though that the communications equipment has been delivered to Zuawalo's parents. An equivalent communications unit was setup in the common room of the dormitory where the Sisters were staying.

Zuawalo and Zeealas were extremely happy and it showed. They spent a lot of time talking to their parents via the satellite link. So much time that Roseanne was beginning to feel a little left out by her new friends, however she understood their situation and was happy for them both.

Agent Murphy was actually pleased to receive a little less attention from his Girls, as it allowed him to get more of his work done around the Academy. He also understood that the novelty of being able to speak to their parents on the other side of Mars was bound to wear off at some point.

The next day a Hummer arrived at the New Flinders Academy's air field. Agent Murphy had flown down to the Elysium Colony to pick the Kujur Gwek and bring him back to the academy.

Forkbraid and Selene had organised a gathering at the Academy's main hall. There were quite a few people present when Gwek finally arrived, including Charlene and Marcus, Catherine and Peter Swann along with their children, Candy and Cormac Farmer and Roseanne, along with Zuawalo and Zeealas. Zigg the ferret was also present and on his his lead, but being held by Zuawalo so as not to get stepped on. Quite a few others, mainly psychics, but a few custodians were also present at the gathering in the hall.

When Agent Murphy brought Gwek into the hall, Marcus Greyhelm took over, "Thank you Jim. I'll take over from here", then to Gwek he asked, "If you'll follow me Gwek."

The small, dark, wizened man wore his usual Kujur attire and carried with him his walking staff. His skin, as dark as the Pod Sister's, clearly showed he came from same region, if not the very same village. His eyes were sharp and piercing, taking in the entire hall and its contents at a glance. Power emanated from those eyes. A subtle power that one could not quite register, but it was there non the less.

Marcus slowly led Gwek over to Lady Selene and Lord Forkbraid. They stood upon a small podium to one side to one side of the hall. There was an Android assistant standing nearby holding an assortment of coloured sashes. There were nine sashes in all coloured, white, red, orange, yellow, green, blue, indigo, violet and black.

Miranda who had been petting Zigg, looked around the hall. Memories flooded in from watching the video feeds back at her previous home in Hyper Dynamics Corporate Colony at L5.

Miranda approached, Roseanne and tugged her arm, "This is a psychic induction ceremony."

Roseanne looked around and then back to Miranda, "Yes Miranda. It certainly does look like a psychic induction ceremony doesn't it"

Roseanne herself had been a part of an induction ceremony back on the Earth, as a walk-in.

Marcus brought Gwek, the Kujur, up to and onto the podium. Gwek stood before Lady Selene and Lord Forkbraid. Gwek let go of his staff and it stood there all by itself, hovering slightly above the floor. Others around the hall may have been surprised by this, but not Selene and Forkbraid. Gwek slowly lowed himself down and knelt before Lady Selene and Lord Forkbraid.

This did surprise Selene and Forkbraid, they looked at each other and then back at Gwek. They too, slowly lowered themselves down and knelt before Gwek.

"You need not kneel before us Gwek", Lady Selene informed Gwek.

"We have seen your work Gwek. Your demolishing of Leroy McGuvan was some of the finest work we've ever seen", Lord Forkbraid added, "Let us all stand as equals."

All three of them stood up.

Lady Selene informed Gwek, "We have brought you here to assess you", then asked, "May we do so?"

Forkbraid added, "You may decline if you wish. The choice is yours to make."

Gwek answered in his soft, authoritative voice, "Yes. You may perform your assessment."

Lady Selene and Lord Forkbraid, looked at Gwek and gave him the cold hard stare. The method by which they discover, understand and grade the level of psychic ability a potential candidate has.

They could see Gwek's training, his potential. They also saw that Gwek had been an apprentice to his master and was now himself the master. His master had also been an apprentice to his master before him and so on back through time. Master and Apprentice over the generations, serving the village from whence He and the Pod Sisters had come. Gwek's training, although unorthodox had been extensive and Gwek had been an incredible student. Gwek's potential was very high indeed.

After what seemed like an eternity, but was actually only a few minutes, Lady Selene signalled the Android assistant. The Android approached and held out the nine sashes. Lady Selene picked out the black sash and placed it over Gwek's head and shoulders. Gwek was a level nine or higher.

Astonished looks, gasps and wows were abundant amongst the audience. This was beyond all of their expectations. The very first candidate from Mars turned out to have the potential of a level nine or higher. The potential to be a Folcrom!

Lady Selene and Lord Forkbraid turned to each other and conferred silently amongst themselves. All was silent as they conferred for several minutes. They had seen Gwek's potential, his works, his history, his background and they were both quietly excited and clear cut in their decision. The village Kujur Gwek, was more than worthy.

Lord Forkbraid announced out loudly so all could hear, "Welcome Brother, Folcrom Gwek!"

Lady Selene repeated out loudly so all could hear, "Welcome Brother, Folcrom Gwek!"

The astonished looks and gasps from the audience grew even louder. No-one had expected this.

Gwek himself was uncertain as to what a Folcrom was, he had no absolutely idea, but Gwek could easily understand that it was one of the greatest honours, to be declared one.

Gwek replied to them both in turn, nodding, "Thank you Brother. Thank you Sister."

The whole audience began to clap and cheer. The whole assembly hall descended into an excited uproar. Forkbraid held up his right hand, to signal for silence.

Once the hall was silent once more, Forkbraid asked, "Gwek. Would you honour us by becoming the third member of our Grey Council?"

Gwek was both honoured and concerned, he replied, "Yes", but then added, "But now, I will need to take on an apprentice."

Both Selene and Forkbraid looked at each other and then back to Gwek once again.

Gwek explained, "I will need to train an apprentice. Someone to take over as the village Kujur."

Forkbraid and Selene understood and Selene replied, "Of course. Of course"

The whole audience began to clap and cheer once more and this time Forkbraid let it continue.

Zuawalo leant over to her Sister Zeealas and told her, "Gwek is now a Great Wizard!"

Charlene, who had quietly slipped out of the hall when Gwek was declared a Folcrom, had now returned and approached the podium. Charlene passed something to Lady Selene.

Lady Selene held it up unfolded so all could see. It was a hooded cloak of the appropriate length and coloured the deepest black, deeper than the black sheen of crows feathers.

Lady Selene passed it to Gwek and told him, "You may adorn this cloak with whatever Sigils and symbols you wish. It is the cloak of a Folcrom", she smiled.

Gwek put on his new cloak and the audience erupted with claps and cheers once more.

The day had been an auspicious day indeed.

Later that evening, Gwek had settled into a room in the dormitory where Zuawalo and Zeealas were staying. He chose a room several rooms away from where the Girl's room was. It seemed the right place to billet Gwek, as all three of them came from the same village. The communications unit in the dormitory's common room also allowed Gwek to keep in contact with their village.

As New Tortuga was close to the Pod Sister's village and thus in the same region, Candy and Cormac often found themselves in the common room of the dormitory. This evening was no different. Roseanne, having become a close friend of the Pod Sister's was often present, as was Miranda who liked playing with Zuawalo's pet ferret Zigg. This evening, Selene and Forkbraid had found themselves in the common room as well.

"Are there any others like yourself Gwek? With similar abilities?", Selene enquired.

"In my village. Only a handful. Not very many. I will chose my apprentice from amongst them. A child of between six and eight, who has higher than average potential", Gwek replied.

"What about the other villages?", Selene asked.

"There are many, many small villages. Some are along the coast. Some others are inland. Some speak Nuer. Some do not", Gwek replied, adding further, "Some of them have a Kujur. Some do not", then asking, "Is it important?"

Forkbraid replied, "The Grey Council Gwek. There are thirteen seats around the table. We three, fill only three of those seats. We would like to fill more of them. All ten vacancies if we can."

Gwek replied questioning, "You need more people like us?"

"Yes Gwek. We need psychics who are level nine or higher", Forkbraid informed him.

"When I return to my village, to select an apprentice, I can help to find candidates for you as well", Gwek replied and let them know.

"There's also Sweetness", Cormac offered, noting another town on Hebes Island.

"Yes", Candy replied, , "Cadmus, Mystal or Gareth. Maybe even one of the other town elders?"

"How many town elders are there Candy?", Forkbraid asked.

"Same as the Grey Council, they number thirteen", Candy informed him.

"There are other psychics as well. It takes quite some talent, not to mention raw power to hide an entire town under a glamour", Cormac further informed them.

Gwek had not heard of the town, Sweetness. He looked a little shocked at hearing the entire town was hidden under a glamour, "The whole town?", he questioned.

"Yes Gwek. The whole town", Candy replied.

"It looks to me, like we'll need to make a trip to Sweetness again and also to Gwek's village", Selene told them, explaining, "We not only need to find suitable candidates for the Grey Council, we need to look for suitable students to train here at the Academy as well."

"When time permits Selene", Forkbraid reminded her, "That trip you're thinking about, could take quite a few weeks, perhaps months. It sounds like there are a lot of villages and towns to visit."

To which Selene replied with a slight sadness in her voice, "With all of these distractions, it's sometimes hard to remember that this is a psychic training academy. It needs students!"

Time passed quickly and it wasn't long before they got word from Lieutenant Roberts at Phobos Command. Agent Murphy, Selene, Forkbraid, Charlene and Marcus had been summoned to the communications centre.

"What's the news Lieutenant?", Agent Murphy asked.

"That Trojan Fleet has settled into a low Martian orbit", the Lieutenant informed them.

"Did they send out any reconnaissance units? Try to occupy any of the off world colonies?", Agent Murphy enquired.

"No. They haven't. And that's the strangest thing", the Lieutenant replied, explaining, "I would have expected them to secure some of the larger colonies in high Martian orbit. Maybe even occupy and secure Deimos. I was certain they would try to secure the port here on Phobos. Instead they have completely bypassed everything up here and gone straight into a low Martian orbit."

"That indicates that they're only really interested in Mars", Agent Murphy replied, speculating, "That also means it was never in their plans to occupy anything off world in Mars orbit."

"It does seem that way Agent Murphy", the Lieutenant replied, "Occupy the whole planet. Anything off world being an after thought."

"They were expecting to land on a devastated planet, without any form of defence", Forkbraid began, "So they brought with them, just the forces they thought necessary for that task."

"In that case, if they did need to do anything up here, they could take action after their main force was already landed", the Lieutenant replied, also speculating.

"Yes, but we eliminated their entire first strike. So they're landing on a planet that is expecting them and prepared to fight back", Forkbraid replied, adding, "They may be worried, that they don't have the fire power to do the job."

"We can speculate all we want Gentlemen", Selene replied, adding, "but at some point, they will make their move."

"You're right Selene", Forkbraid replied, then to Lieutenant Roberts, Forkbraid instructed, "Lieutenant. I want you to keep your eyes on everything they do."

Agent Murphy then took over, "Lieutenant. We need eyes in geosynchronous orbit, above anywhere that they set down on Mars. We need to know where, exactly how many troops they have, exactly how many heavy weapons systems and their types. Share all the feeds with us as well."

Lieutenant Roberts replied, "I'll have the birds prepared for the task. You will have your eyes Agent Murphy. Over and out."

Agent Murphy looked at Forkbraid, "Looks like this is it. It's all about to happen."

"It certainly looks that way Jim", Forkbraid agreed.

General Verne studied the scans of the Martian surface. Their orbit had been chosen to provide for fly overs of the Elysium subcontinent and detailed scans of the Elysium Colony and the New Flinders Psychic Academy were on the screen.

Captain Carlson pointed out, "That castle like structure appears to be the demon's lair General. Just to its southeast looks like a landing field. That big building on the west of the field could be some kind of construction hanger perhaps or they could have a number of aircraft stored in there."

"Yes. Possibly. Then what's that smaller hanger on the south of the field?", the General asked.

"Possibly for smaller aircraft?", Captain Carlson pondered, "Perhaps the hangers are military and civilian? The large hanger for military aircraft and the smaller one for civilian aircraft."

"There is no real way to know for sure, is there?", the General enquired.

"Not without people on the ground to infiltrate their facilities General", the Captain replied.

"Look here General", Captain Carlson highlighted points located around the castle like building, "It looks like defensive rings of gun batteries", he began counting them, "Thirty six in all."

"We were told they had eight anti-aircraft batteries", the General replied.

"It looks like they're upgraded their defences somewhat General", the Captain replied, "See. There are three defensive rings. The first has eight batteries, the second twelve, the third sixteen. It does appear that the outer two rings were constructed far more recently."

"If we go in by air, it will get very messy, very quickly", the General assessed, "We'll lose too many of our aircraft in this one assault. And we don't know what powers those demons have!"

"General, we can't tell where that Bat Wing is or for that matter those atmo rated Wisps", the Captain informed him.

"How many do they have?", the General enquired.

"General. The last we heard they had ten or twelve atmo rated Wisps", the Captain informed him, "By now though. They could have many, many more."

"Okay then. Captain, this is going to be a ground assault", the General decided, "The anti-aircraft batteries will be useless in a ground assault."

"And their aircraft General?", the Captain enquired.

"A dozen ships Captain", the General replied, "We'll draw them out beyond their defences. Then take them down with ground fire and our own aircraft. Once they're obliterated, our ground forces can overwhelm their defensive rings, allowing our aircraft to attack at will. It should all be over pretty quick. A few hours at most. We'll exterminate the demons in their lair and move on."

"Then all we need to do now General, is choose a suitable staging site",

The captain replied.

Lieutenant Roberts was on the line once again and Agent Murphy, Selene, Forkbraid, Charlene and Marcus had been summoned to the communications centre once more. It was urgent.

"Ladies. Gentlemen", Lieutenant Roberts began, "The Trojans have launched their drop ships. So their troops are heading down to the surface. Their weapons transports have also left orbit and they're following their drop ships to the surface as well. They're all flying in one large formation."

"Do we know where they'll land yet Lieutenant?", Agent Murphy enquired.

"One large formation usually means one location Agent Murphy", the Lieutenant replied, adding, "Their landing zone, based on their current trajectory, looks to be somewhere to the north west of the Elysium Colony. Precisely where? I can't be certain yet."

"Lieutenant. When you have their precise landing zone, you'll let us know", Forkbraid requested.

"My Lord, rest assured, I'll put a bird, several in fact, directly above their landing zone and you'll have access to the data feeds the same time I do", Lieutenant Roberts replied.

"Thank you Lieutenant", Agent Murphy replied.

"Just doing my duty Agent Murphy", Lieutenant Roberts replied, adding, "Whatever you do. Do it well and give those bastards hell. Over and out."

Selene commented, "It's a shame we haven't had time to set up a few Wyvern covens. If we had just a handful of those we'd know exactly what they're thinking."

"Wyvern covens?", Agent Murphy queried.

"Remote viewing teams Jim. Like what we had back on the Earth", Forkbraid replied.

Selene informed Jim further, "It was one of our original priorities, that unfortunately had to be pushed to the back burner. It would be really useful to have a few Wyvern covens active right now."

Charlene added, "I can't say I know much about them Jim, but it would be like having eyes and ears in the middle of their decision making. We'd know everything, the second they decide it."

"On the Earth, due to its size and population, we had seventy two Wyverns, each with thirteen members. They were run by a *'shadow council'*, called the Serpent Council", Forkbraid informed them, "Here on Mars we could get away with six Wyverns. At least for the beginning."

"And you were its head", Marcus noted, "The head serpent."

"Yep. The Viperous One. For the mundanes, they were called remote viewing teams and I was their head", Forkbraid confirmed, further informing them, "There were thirteen serpent council members. Each one a Folcrom. Each one a Grey Council member chosen for their level of abilities. Twelve council members were responsible for six Wyvern covens each. I was responsible for the council. Everyone in Wyverns and the Serpent Council is specifically chosen. There are no applicants, only hand picked members. The only member of this entire structure, that was known to the outside world, is the head. Usually the most powerful psychic on the planet."

"And no one fucks with the most powerful psychic on the planet", Selene mused, with an unusual use of profanity.

"Usually. That is until the Prophet and his henchmen came along", Forkbraid noted.

"The Prophet quickly learnt what a bad idea that was", Agent Murphy commented.

"Well people, we don't have any Wyverns, but we have taken down their first strike force en-route to Mars. Now we'll have their second strike force on the ground", Forkbraid responded, "Let's keep this all nice and simple. I'm thinking it's a case of, one down and one to go!"

16. Unconventional Solutions

The Trojan Army touched down and Lieutenant Roberts had their precise location, two hundred and fifty miles north west of the New Flinders Psychic Academy. The enemy appeared to have chosen a flat expanse of land along the western coast of the Elysium subcontinent as their staging grounds. True to his word he dispatched several surveillance satellites into geosynchronous orbit directly above their landing zone.

Once the birds, as Lieutenant Roberts called them were in place, the Lieutenant's people began studying the data feeds. The very same data feeds, only encrypted, were being directed to the New Flinders Psychic Academy for their analysis as well.

Clearly in the landing zone, which was right next to the coast, two hundred drop ships could be detected, ten from each of the twenty troop transports. Each drop ships contained fifty men, who upon disembarking moved to the east some distance away, to began setting up their camp.

Interestingly, all of the drop ships appeared to be simply large Hummers. None of the drop ships appeared to be armed. They were simple transports.

The weapons transports touched down in an arc to the north, east and south of the troop encampment. The Trojan troops were essentially in the centre surrounded by all of their equipment. There were twenty transports in all and these were capable of carrying an assortment of heavy weapons systems.

Agent Murphy made plans with Forkbraid, to slow down the enemies progress as they watched them unpack their equipment. Eventually they were able to detect forty main battle tanks, forty self propelled howitzers, forty infantry fighting vehicles and forty armoured personnel carriers. Along with these appeared to be eighty aircraft, all of which were small two man gun ships.

Interestingly, there appeared to be a bit of assembly required before these weapons could be used. It seemed like they could not pack their weapons systems into the weapons transport's stowage bays without some disassembly first. That was perhaps the enemies first mistake!

The enemy was still in the midst of unpacking and assembling their equipment when Forkbraid led the Wisp pilots to the hanger in the Academy's compound. It was mere minutes before they were airborne and on their way to the north west. One Bat Wing Interceptor and ten atmo rated Wisps were quickly approaching the enemies staging ground.

Flying in tight formation they approached from the south and strafed the enemies heavy weapons systems. Forkbraid's Bat Wing with its four lasers and wing mounted particle beams. The modified Wisps with their pulse cannons. On their first pass they strafed the heavy weapons systems to the south of the troop encampment, then they strafed the heavy weapons systems to the north of the encampment. They avoided hitting the heavy weapons transport ships.

After which, having passed over the staging grounds they turned about and headed back the way they'd came. This time strafing the heavy weapons systems to the east of the encampment, before heading back to the Academy. They avoided striking the troop encampment itself.

Their plan had been very simple. Hit them fast, hit them hard. Cause the enemy as much damage to their heavy weapons systems as they could in one hit. Effectively slowing down their progress and weakening their position. Avoid the troops and there transports to minimise casualties.

General Verne was livid, yet he was relatively controlled, "Those bastards! I'll give them that!", he snarled to the troop transport Captains.

"General. In hind-site, perhaps we should have landed further to the north", one of the Captains commented in reply.

"It would have made no difference Captain", the General replied, explaining, "They were always going to hit us. It would only have taken them a few minutes longer."

The General looked around at his Captains, "What Gentlemen? Did you you think they'd welcome us with flowers? Perhaps bringing us tea and biscuits? Coffee perhaps?", he questioned rhetorically, "This is War Gentlemen! They are demons! Do not forget that! Now get me my damage report!", he bellowed his orders.

The damage report came in. They'd lost ten percent of their heavy weapons systems outright. Some of their other equipment had been damaged, but they were deemed repairable. Surprisingly, troop deaths and casualties were limited. That was the end of day one on Mars for the Trojans, as night was now rapidly approaching. Little did they know how strange a night it would be.

Lady Folcrom Selene and Lord Folcrom Forkbraid stood on a high knoll a dozen miles to the east of the Trojan Armed Forces staging grounds. The enemy could not see them at their vantage point, although they themselves had a perfect view to their enemies encampment to the west. It was late evening and night would soon be falling. Agent Murphy had just dropped them off with an assortment of quite unusual equipment. Artefacts more so than weapons. Forkbraid had apparently devised a highly unconventional solution.

The pair located some flat ground with a soft cover of grass, upon which to start their work.

Selene and Forkbraid slowly disrobed, to begin their work sky-clad, as was their tradition. Forkbraid placed the heavy stone Alter into the centre of the chosen space and placed their required ritual implements upon it. While Forkbraid did so, Selene placed the quarter candles and their stands at the appropriate cardinal points. Each candle had its appropriate colour.

East was yellow. North was green. West was blue. South was red.

Once the Sun had dropped below the horizon and night began to fall, they began.

Lady Selene and Lord Forkbraid performed their Self Banishing ritual in their usual fashion, upon this chosen Sacred Space.

They entered the designated area for their Sacred Circle from the north-east cross-quarter.
Together they then lit the spirit candle, which was a deep purple colour. Lady Selene then presented it to Deity. With the spirit candle, they then began to light the quarter candles. There was one candle for each quarter and they had to be lit in a specific order.

They both took the spirit candle to the east quarter. Forkbraid drew the east banishing pentagram.
Then they both intoned, "With this ancient and mystical symbol, I banish thee oh foul shades of the east. Let this realm be truly free of all your evil influences."
Together they then lit the east candle.

They then took the spirit candle to the north quarter. Forkbraid drew the north banishing pentagram.
Then they both intoned, "With this ancient and mystical symbol, I banish thee oh foul shades of the north. Let this realm be truly free of all your evil

influences."

Together they then lit the north candle.

They then took the spirit candle to the west quarter. Forkbraid drew the west banishing pentagram.

Then they both intoned, "With this ancient and mystical symbol, I banish thee oh foul shades of the west. Let this realm be truly free of all your evil influences."

Together they then lit the west candle.

They then took the spirit candle to the south quarter. Forkbraid drew the south banishing pentagram.

Then they both intoned, "With this ancient and mystical symbol, I banish thee oh foul shades of the south. Let this realm be truly free of all your evil influences."

Together they then lit the south candle.

Having lit the quarter candles, they returned the spirit candle to the Alter, presenting it to deity once more, before placing it upon the Alter.

Lord Forkbraid took up a sword from upon the Alter and presented it to Deity.

Forkbraid then moved to the east quarter and began walking the boundary in the same order that they had lit the quarter candles. While doing so, Forkbraid visualised a mote being carved by a glowing blue beam from the sword point. Lady Selene followed in Forkbraid's wake adding her power to the visualisation.

Having completed the circle and returning to the east, Forkbraid then carved a doorway in the north-east cross-quarter. Forkbraid carved the doorway from right to left, then followed this by inscribing a banishing spirit pentagram within it.

Forkbraid then returned to the Alter and presented the sword to Deity once more, before replacing the sword upon the Alter.

The Self Banishing ritual was complete.

Having performed the Self Banishing ritual, Forkbraid began to Bless the Sacred Space.

Forkbraid then took up the spirit candle again and present it to Deity.

Forkbraid took the spirit candle to the east quarter, where he drew the east invoking
pentagram.

"With this ancient and mystical symbol, I invoke thee and call upon thee, sacred Sylphides of Air. Bless Ye this circle and aide in its holy consecration."

Forkbraid took the spirit candle to the north quarter, where he drew the north invoking pentagram.

"With this ancient and mystical symbol, I invoke thee and call upon thee, sacred Gnomes of Earth. Bless Ye this circle and aide in its holy consecration."

Forkbraid took the spirit candle to the west quarter, where he drew the west invoking
pentagram.

"With this ancient and mystical symbol, I invoke thee and call upon thee, sacred Undines of Water. Bless Ye this circle and aide in its holy consecration."

Forkbraid took the spirit candle to the south quarter, where he drew the south invoking pentagram.

"With this ancient and mystical symbol, I invoke thee and call upon thee, sacred Salamanders of Fire. Bless Ye this circle and aide in its holy consecration."

Forkbraid then returned to the Alter and presented the spirit candle to Deity once more, before replacing it upon the Alter.

The Blessing of the Sacred Space was complete.

Both Selene and Forkbraid began the Lesser Banishing ritual.

Standing facing east they both began breathing in a meditative fashion until perfectly calm.
They visualised a constant blue white light above their foreheads and began absorbing that light into their right hands. They inscribed a pentagram upon their bodies using the usual method.

They both moved their right hand to their left hips, "I am the power."
They both moved their right hand to their foreheads, "I am the essence."
They both moved their right hand to their right hips, "I am the life."
They both moved their right hand to their left shoulders, "I am the light."

They both moved their right hand to their right shoulders, "I am the love."

They both moved their right hand to their left hip, then to the solar plexus, "I am the Majik off the Goddess forever."

They then began the next incantations.

"Before me the Sacred Sylphides of Air", they both moved their right hands to the East.

"Behind me the Sacred Undines of Water", they both moved their left hands to the West.

"To my right the Sacred Salamanders of Fire", they both moved their right hands to the South.

"To my left the Sacred Gnomes of Earth", they both moved their left hands to the North.

"All around me the Sacred Pentagram of flame", they both circled their palms around and out.

"Before me stands the Six Rayed Star", they both brought their hands cupped to their foreheads.

The Lesser Banishing Ritual was complete.

Then they both moved onto the Quabalistic Cross.

They both intoned, "Ah-Tah", they then formed a triangle using their hands over their foreheads.

They both intoned, "Mahl-Koot", they then formed an inverted triangle using their hands over their solar plexus.

They both intoned, "Vay'gay-BouRa", they then cupped their hands over their right breasts.

They both intoned, "Vay'gay-Doola", they then cupped their hands over their left breasts.

They both intoned, "Lih-Olam", they then placed their palms flat on each other in front of them and crossed their thumbs.

They both intoned, "Amen", then cupped their hands to their foreheads.

The ritual of the Quabalistic Cross was complete.

Having performed the Self Banishing, the Lesser Banishing and Quabalistic Cross rites, they then moved onto the casting their Sacred Circle, the Circle thrice caste, using their Elfane tradition.

Lady Selene took up the sword from upon the Alter and presented it to Deity, before cutting the boundary of their Sacred circle.

Selene then moved to the east quarter and began walking the boundary in the same order that they had lit the candles. Selene visualised the cutting of a boundary with the sword and its glowing blue beam of light, as a mote between worlds. Lord Forkbraid followed in Selene's wake adding his power to the visualisation.

Selene intoned, "Here lies the boundary of this sacred circle. Let naught but love enter in and naught but love emerge from within. In the names of Aradia and Cernunos."
The incantation was repeated until the cutting of the circle's boundary was completed.

As Forkbraid had done before her, Selene also cut a doorway from right to left in the north-east cross-quarter. The incantation was repeated until the circle was completed and they had returned to the Alter once more. One the boundary was cut, Selene presented the sword to Deity once more before placing it back upon the Alter.

The Cutting of the boundary of the Sacred Circle was complete.

Next Selene began to caste the first circle.

Selene took up the Athame from the Alter and presented it to Deity.

Selene and Forkbraid walked the circle once more, both visualising a boundary being cut by the Athame with a blue beam of light coming out of its point.

Both Selene and Forkbraid intoned, "Here lies the boundary of this sacred circle. Let naught but love enter in and naught but love emerge from within. In the names of Aradia and Cernunos."
As before Selene cut a doorway from right to left in the north-east cross-quarter, this time with the Athame. The incantation was repeated until the circle was completed and they had returned to the Alter once again.

With the first sacred circle caste, Selene moved onto the preparations for the second casting.

Next Selene exorcised the water, by placing a chalice containing water upon a pentagram that sat upon the Alter.

Selene touched the water with the tip of the Athame and both Selene and

Forkbraid intoned, "I exorcise thee oh creature of water, that thou cast off from thee all uncleanliness and impurities in the names of Aradia and Cernunos."

Selene then presented the chalice of water to Deity before placing it back down on the Alter.

Next Selene blessed the salt, by placing a bowel containing salt upon the pentagram on the Alter.

Selene touched the salt with the tip of the Athame and both Selene and Forkbraid intoned, "Blessings be upon this creature of salt and let all malignity and impurity be caste away hence forth and let only good enter within. Therefore I bless thee and consecrate the, that thou mayst aide me, in the names of Aradia and Cernunos."

Selene then presented the bowel of salt to Deity before placing it back down on the Alter.

This was followed by Selene mixing the holy water. The Chalice was once again placed upon the pentacle on the Alter. Selene added a few pinches of salt from the bowel to the water, then stirred the mixture with the tip of the Athame thrice deasil, thrice widdershins and thrice deasil once more.

Selene then presented the now holy water before Deity before placing it back down on the Alter.

At this point Selene began to cast the second circle.

Selene then picked up the chalice of holy water, presented it to Deity and with Forkbraid, began to walk the circle once more in the same direction as previously. Selene dipped her fingers into the holy water and then sprinkled that holy water around the circle as they walked. Together, both Selene and Forkbraid visualised a glowing blue mist rising from the ground as the holy water touched it.

Together they both intoned, "Earth and Water where thou art caste, let no evil power last, work in complete accord with me, as I so do will it, SO MOTE IT BE!!"

The incantation was repeated until the circle had been completed and they had returned to the Alter once more. The chalice of holy water was presented to Deity and placed back upon the Alter.

With the second sacred circle caste, Selene moved onto the preparations for the third casting.

Selene then picked up a thurible and placed it upon the pentagram that sat upon the Alter. Then Selene lit the charcoal that was sitting in the thurible. After this, Selene picked up the bowel containing incense, took up quite a large pinch of it and sprinkled it into the thurible. The incense began too burn and its sweet smell began to rise. Selene then presented the thurible of burning incense before Deity and placed it back upon the Alter.

Now Selene began to cast the third circle.

Selene picked up the thurible of burning incense, presented it before Deity and with Forkbraid, began to walk the circle once more in the same direction as previously. While walking the circle, Selene gently swung the thurible back and forth, allowing sweet smelling incense smoke to waft all about. While doing this both Selene and Forkbraid visualised the smoke as a glowing blue purifying essence.

Together they both intoned,"Creature of air and fire bright, do my bidding this very night. On you this charge I do lay, let no phantoms in thy presence stay. Heed my words to thee, as I so do will it, SO MOTE IT BE!!"
The incantation was also repeated until the circle had been completed and they had returned to the Alter once more. The thurible of burning incense was presented to Deity and placed back upon the Alter.

Once back at the Alter, Selene then began to Seal the Sacred Space.

Selene picked up the spirit candle and presented it to Deity.
Selene and Forkbraid then intoned, "Be to me the fire of noon, be to me the fire of night, be to me the power of joy turning darkness into light."

They then both walked the circle as previously, with Selene presenting the spirit candle to each quarter in turn. At each quarter Selene moved the spirit candle up, then down, then moved it forwards, then backwards, while they both intoned, "As above, so below, as within, so without."

Once back at the alter, Selene presented the spirit candle to Deity once more and intoned, "By the virgin waxing cold, by the mother full and bold, by the queen hag silent and cold. By the power of the moon, the one in three, I consecrate this circle in the names of Aradia and Cernunos. Blessed Be!!"

The Sacred Space was Sealed.

Now it was time for the Conjuration.

Selene and Forkbraid stood before the Alter once more and they intoned, "I conjure thee oh circle of love, that be a boundary between the worlds of man and the realms of man and the old ones. Guardian and protector of the powers we shall raise within thee. Wherefore I bless thee and consecrate thee, in the names of Aradia and Cernunos."

Having completed the Conjuration, they both moved onto the Calling of the Quarters.

Selene pick up a bell from the Alter and presented it before Deity. Forkbraid then picked up the Athame and present it before Deity. They then began to walk the circle once again.

At the east quarter, Selene rang the bell.
Forkbraid then used the Athame to draw an invoking pentagram of the east.

They both intoned, "Hail Guardians of the Watchtowers of the East, Powers of Air. Great ruler of the tempest storms and whirlwinds, master of the heavenly vault. We invoke you and call upon you, Golden Eagle of the dawn. Star Seeker, rising Sun, be present we pray thee, take hold of the Air that is her breath, send forth your light, be here now Eurus.........", the guardian's name being pronounced as Urrraaasssss.
"Hail and welcome."

At the north quarter, Selene rang the bell.
Forkbraid then used the Athame to draw an invoking pentagram of the north.

They both intoned, "Hail Guardians of the Watchtowers of the North, Powers of the Earth. Cornerstone of power, Black Goat of the north, O horned one. Dark ruler of the mountains and all that lies beneath them. Prince of the Powers of the Earth. We invoke you and call upon you, Lady of the outer darkness. Black of midnight, North star, centre of the whirling sky, stone, mountain, fertile field, come by the Earth that is her body, send forth your strength, be here now Boreas.........", the guardian's name being pronounced as Borrreeeaaarrrsssss.
"Hail and welcome."

At the west quarter, Selene rang the bell.
Forkbraid then used the Athame to draw an invoking pentagram of the west.

They both intoned, "Hail Guardians of the Watchtowers of the West, Powers of Water. Great ruler of the deeps, Guardian of the bitter seas, Prince of the powers of water. We invoke you and call upon you, Serpent of the powers of the watery Abyss. Rain maker, grey robed twilight, Evening Star, be present we pray thee, come by the waters of her living womb, send forth your flow, be here now Zephyrus.........", the guardian's name being pronounced as Zephhyyrrraaasssss.

"Hail and welcome."

At the south quarter, Selene rang the bell.

Forkbraid then used the Athame to draw an invoking pentagram of the south.

They both intoned, "Hail Guardians of the Watchtowers of the South, Powers of Fire. Great Lord of lightning, Master of the Solar Orb, Prince of the powers of fire. We invoke you and call upon you, Red lion of the noon heat. Flaming one of summers warmth, spark of life, be present we pray thee, come by the fire that is her spirit, send forth your flame, be here now Notus.........", the guardian's name being pronounced as Notttaaasssss.

"Hail and welcome."

Lady Selene and Lord Forkbraid returned to the Alter once more. Selene presented the bell before Deity and placed it back upon the Alter. Forkbraid presented the Athame before Deity and placed it back upon the Alter.

The calling of the quarters now completed, they moved onto the invocation.

Lady Selene stood before the Alter and invoked, "Oh gracious Lady and powerful Lord. I call upon thee, for your presence and participation within this sacred circle."

After the invocation was complete, Selene handed the circle to Forkbraid, so he could perform the Hammer rite. This was so they could perform a runic rite within the Majik circle.

Lady Selene intoned loudly and forcefully, "Asatru and Wicca, blessed be!"
Lord Forkbraid then bowed to Lady Selene in a show of deepest respect.

The Hammer rite began.

Forkbraid faced north and postured himself in the cross stadha, absorbing the inflow of energies. When he was ready, he consolidated the energies into his solar plexus with the aid of a Runic Wand.

Ever so slowly Forkbraid turned around in the circle in the same direction it had been caste.
One by one he visualised each Rune of the Elder Futhark in sequence, intoning their names and then signing them into existence.

Between signing each rune, he brought his wand back to his solar plexus to consolidate its power once more. As each rune was cast it appeared against the inside of the Wiccan circle and glowed the deepest and most powerful bloody red. This had to be done in groups of eight.

"Fehu, Uruz, Thurisaz, Ansuz, Raidho, Kenaz, Gebo, Wunjo", Forkbraid then paused.
"Hagalaz, Naudhiz, Isa, Jera, Eihwaz, Perthro, Elhaz, Sowilo", Forkbraid paused once more.
"Tiwaz, Berkano, Ehwaz, Mannaz, Laguz, Inguz, Dagaz, Othala", Forkbraid stopped turning.
The circle of Runes was now complete, having been caste against the inside of the Wiccan circle. All twenty four Runes of the Elder Futhark glowed a bright and wicked bloody red.

Again facing North, Forkbraid struck the cross stadha. He visualised a cross lying horizontally in the plane of the runic circle, with each spoke pointing to a cardinal point.

Forkbraid visualised a sphere of shimmering blue light, with a blood red runic band around its equator. Forkbraid then visualised a vertical axis running through from infinite above to the infinite below. Feeling the forces flowing from all six directions into his centre, Forkbraid built a sphere of glowing blood red might.

Still facing north, Forkbraid touched the base of his wand to the point just above the solar plexus, then thrust the wand forward, projecting the force from that centre to a point on the inside of the runic sphere.

Forkbraid signed the hammer northwards, intoning, "Mjolnir in the North, hallow and hold this holy-stead."

Forkbraid turned to the west, repeated the projection process and signed the hammer westwards, intoning, "Mjolnir in the West, hallow and hold this holy-stead".

Forkbraid turned to the south, repeated the projection process and signed the hammer southwards intoning, "Mjolnir in the South, hallow and hold this holy-stead".

Forkbraid turned to the east, repeated the projection process and signed the hammer eastwards, intoning, "Mjolnir in the East, hallow and hold this holy-stead".

Forkbraid turned to the north once more, repeated the projection process and aimed his wand upwards, signing the hammer and intoning, "Mjolnir above me, hallow and hold this holy-stead."

Still facing North, Forkbraid repeated the projection process and aimed his wand downwards, intoning, " Mjolnir below me, hallow and hold this holy-stead".

Forkbraid then folded his arms inward and brought his hands and wand to the point just above the solar plexus and intoned, "Around me and within me, Asgardhr and Midgardhr."

Still facing north Forkbraid then intoned with all his might, "This circle of rune might is drawn, for elemental Majik as yet unborn. Wild wights wend away, interfere not, with what I say. My will as spoken, shall be the way. Together the bright runes are bound and blended with the might of Odhinn, Vili, Ve!"

Had anyone been watching the casting of the Sacred Circle, they would have thought the procedure for the casting of a Sacred Circle was extremely complicated. It is! A Sacred Circle caste correctly, is an incredibly powerful thing and it MUST be performed correctly.
When is a duplication not a duplication?
When it is a part of an occult ceremony and to leave out anything or cut corners becomes a danger to all those involved.
Heaven forbid you should get an occult ceremony wrong, as to fail in your due diligence in this regards, can and would reek havoc on all those involved.

The Runic Spell.

Lady Selene and Lord Forkbraid came together on the west side of the alter. First they faced west towards their enemies. Then they turned to face each other. They held hands and touched their foreheads together. At this point they began to share.

Forkbraid had worked on a complicated, well choreographed runic spell, which required both galdrar (chant) and stadha (posture). Forkbraid shared the spell in its entirety with Selene, who promptly memorised it.

Selene ran through the entire runic spell within her mind. It was complicated, meaningful and extremely potent, yet elegant. It was also concise, yet detailed. Selene could see that Forkbraid had put days of thought, effort and work into this spell. Then they began the Majikal working.

They each had individual parts to play, in order to cast the appropriate runes, but would also need to come together during the process to form the relevant bind-runes. They both danced around the circle, always in the same direction.

Plucking bright, bloody red runes from against the inside of the Wiccan circle. They intoned the names of the runes in the correct fashion, then formed the posture that was appropriate for each rune. Bind-runes were somewhat more difficult as they were an amalgam of multiple runes.

The runes for the bind-rune needed to be plucked from the inside of the Wiccan circle and built into the relevant bind-rune. Each bind-rune needed to be intoned correctly, in fact perfectly, then the posture for each bind-rune was created by both of them together. It sometimes required a degree of physical contortion and even excursion. Forkbraid however, had designed each one to be well within their capabilities.

As the dance continued around the sacred circle, each blood red rune and blood red bind-rune would be adsorbed in their bodies as the spell progressed, being further empowered, before spiralling upwards from their heart, forehead and crown chakras. Eventually forming a spiralling tower of might and power above their sacred circle.

The entire spell would take a little over four hours to perform, so the work involved was quite tiring and fatiguing. Yet Forkbraid had even managed to include into this complex runic spell, runes that would reinvigorate them both during the spell's casting.

Eventually the spell casting was complete and a powerful tower of spiralling runic energy circled high above the alter. During the day from their vantage point, they could see their enemy. At night with this glowing mass of energy high above their sacred circle, their enemies, a dozen miles to the west could clearly see the spiralling tower of power. They knew not what is was, nor could they imagine what it could possibly be!

The runic ritual was now over and all that was required was the closing of their Sacred Circle.

Lady Selene and Lord Forkbraid stood before the Alter once more, both intoning, "To Aradia and Cernunos, our thanks to thee, for all your help Blessed be!."

Lady Selene and Lord Forkbraid then walked the circle in the reverse direction.

To the South they intoned, "Ye Mighty Lords and Ladies of the Watchtowers of the South, and ye
elementals of the Fire, We thank you for attending and ere ye depart to your lovely realms. We say hail and farewell........"

To the West they intoned, "Ye Mighty Lords and Ladies of the Watchtowers of the West, and ye
elementals of the Water, We thank you for attending and ere ye depart to your lovely realms. We say hail and farewell........"

To the North they intoned, "Ye Mighty Lords and Ladies of the Watchtowers of the North, and ye elementals of the Earth, We thank you for attending and ere ye depart to your lovely realms. We say hail and farewell........"

To the East they intoned, "Ye Mighty Lords and Ladies of the Watchtowers of the East, and ye
elementals of the Air, We thank you for attending and ere ye depart to your lovely realms. We say hail and farewell........"

Facing the Alter once more Lady Selene and Lord Forkbraid declared, "The circle is open but never broken. SO MOTE IT BE!"

As those last four words were spoken, the brilliant, blood red spiralling tower of might and power collapsed downwards and spread westwards, rushing towards the Trojan Army's staging grounds. As a spiralling tower it had been blood red, but now it transformed into a multitude of colours, as it twisted and weaved into a multitude of bright, radiant threads of light all rapidly approaching the Trojan Army.
Lady Selene and Lord Forkbraid, their task complete, en-clothed themselves once more, the night had been quite chilly.

It was nearly twelve o'clock when the General had been awoken. Captain Carlson was pointing to something a dozen miles away in the east.
"What the hell is it Captain?", the General asked as he stared at the

immensely tall blood red vortex, the nature of which he had no idea.

"We don't actually know General", Captain Carlson had replied, informing the General further, "We've been watching it grow for hours now. There was some speculation, based on the colour and the spiralling, that it might be some kind of magma tornado. The Elysium plateau is actually a volcanic region and the Martian gravity is very light. There could be an active vent underneath it."

"A magma tornado?", the General replied, "I've never heard of such a thing."

"Neither has anyone else. It is really just wild speculation General", the Captain replied.

"We need to know what that is Captain? Whether or not its a threat?", the General ordered.

Just as the General gave out his order and as they watched, the spiralling blood red tower in the distance to the east, suddenly collapsed. It then began to head in their direction, changing into to a multitude of twisting threads of bright lights, with a multitude of various colours.

"What the fuck!", the General exclaimed.

The Captain shouted as loud as he possibly could, "Incoming!"

The result was pure pandemonium.

Everyone in the encampment and region around the staging ground began ducking for cover as the colourful, twisting threads and tendrils rapidly approached. As they approached they broadened out and it became clear this was an attack of massive proportions. Soldiers of the Trailing Trojan Armed Forces prayed for their very lives. Then it struck!

The tendrils of colourful light struck the heavy weapons systems stationed in the east of the troop encampment first. Striking vehicle after vehicle, weapons system after weapons system, including the weapons transports themselves, the multitude of colourful tendrils of light struck, engulfed and then moved onto the next.

This was followed by the heavy weapons systems stationed to the north and south of the encampment. The pattern was the same as the colourful tendrils of light struck. Engulfing everything in their path and moving on to the next.

After the heavy weapons systems, all the colourful tendrils of light converged onto the troop encampment. Mass panic ensued as the entire encampment was lit up with an eerie glow as the tendrils of light merged and engulfed the entire encampment in blood red light. It lasted for long, long minutes, then as just like that, the eerie red glow lifted skywards and began to dissipate like a glowing red mist vanishing before their very eyes. Strangely, all of the troop's drop ships, further to the west along the coast, were left completely untouched.

General Verne looked around the encampment. No-one appeared to be dead, no-one appeared to be injured. The General looked beyond the encampment to where his heavy weapons systems had been unloaded. It was hard to see in the dark of night, but he could make out the weapons transports, he could make out the tanks, the artillery and other vehicles. They all seemed, at least to his eyes, to have come through the attack unscathed.

"Captain Carlson. Get me a damage report!", the General ordered.

To another Captain he ordered, "Bolton. I want to know what that weapon was. Find out!"

The General returned to his command tent and sat down at his desk, waiting for the Captains to return with more information. It was an hour before they came back.

As soon as Captain Carlson entered the tent, the General barked out, "Damage report!"

"None that we could find from tonight's attack General", the Captain replied, informing the General further, "The only damage we could find was from the demon's aircraft strafing yesterday."

"Why am I finding that hard to believe Captain", the General replied

Captain Carlson replied, "General. I found that hard to believe as well. I even had our people double check just to make sure."

"And casualties Carlson", the General enquired.

"None really General", Captain Carlson reported, adding, "Just few bumps and scratches from our people ducking for cover."

"What about those damned lights Bolton?", the General ordered.

"They're exactly just that General, lights. Our people have determined that they are nothing more than lights", Captain Bolton explained.

"Nothing more than lights! Is that all these demons have?", the General queried rhetorically.

"Apart from their air attack yesterday and their defensive rings around their fortress, it appears to be so General", Captain Bolton agreed.

"They're just trying to scare us! If that's all they have, then this will all be over very quickly", the General replied.

"Yes General", Captain Carlson agreed, adding, "We send in our heavy armour and infantry. Take out their defences. Then pound them with our artillery and gun ships."

"That's the plan people", the General confirmed, then added, "It's bloody well late. Now get some sleep. I want everyone up well before the crack of dawn."

The Sun had not yet risen when the General and his Captains awoke. It was still early and dawn was still a little ways off. They were still rattled by the events that had occurred earlier during the night and somewhat tired.

"Good then we're all up, bright eyed and bushy tailed. Let's get down to brass tacks then shall we", the General began, then commanding, "I want first battalion ready for the assault. Prepare second battalion as backup reinforcements. We'll move our tanks and artillery forward to within striking range, but outside of their defensive rings. We'll use our drop ships to position our troops behind our heavy weapons."

"I want this to be quick and decisive Gentlemen", General Verne explained, "We'll use our tanks and artillery to take out their defences. Once we've done that, we'll move everything forward to within striking range of the enemies fortress."

The Captains gathered around the table looking at the map on the table before them. To all of them, it looked like and sounded like, a reasonable plan.

The General continued, "We'll pound their fortress continuously with our artillery, while moving forward with our tanks and infantry fighting vehicles. Armoured personnel carriers and our first battalion troops will follow closely behind. We'll use our gun ships as air cover, as well as to hit their fortress from above. We'll rain bloody hell down upon them. If the demons put up a good fight, we'll send in our second battalion to reinforce the first. This should all be over before dusk! Done and dusted!"

"Prisoners General?", Captain Heller queried.

"One does not take demons prisoner, Heller!", the General replied harshly, informing everyone present, "This is not a colony Gentlemen! They are not people! This is a demon's lair! No prisoners! Leave no demons in our wake!"

Captain Heller smiled, this was just the way he like it.

Everyone stepped out of the command tent to go about their business for the day, as the Sun was about to rise above the horizon and the high country to the east.

Upon the high knoll, a dozen miles to the east of the encampment, Selene and Forkbraid sat watching intently for the culmination of their night's work, their Majik to unfold.

"Do you think they know?", Selene asked.

"Oh, they won't have a clue Selene, they won't have a clue", Forkbraid replied.

The Sun's rays glanced down upon the encampment, first touching the heavy weapons systems and their weapons transport vehicles to the east. One by one, the vehicles burst into flames as the Sun's rays touched them.

"Fire! Fire!", the screams began. "Fire! Fire!", the screams continued. It was too late!

The General looked eastwards towards his heavy weapons systems, "What the fuck is going on!", he exclaimed, everything, everywhere he looked, was bursting into flames.

The Sun's rays progressed further! The heavy weapons systems and their weapons transport vehicles to the north and south of the encampment began to bust into flames.

Screams of "Fire! Fire!" were heard to the north, quickly followed by screens of "Fire! Fire!" from the south. The screams of "Fire! Fire!", continued from the east, the north and the south. The screams were everywhere.

The General followed the sound of the screams and in every direction he looked, everything was ablaze, everything was burning!

Too busy to look in the immediate vicinity, few troops noticed the small pops and puffs of smoke as electronic devices in the encampment burned out! Many had all rushed to put out the fires!

Then the first tank exploded. It was quickly followed by a second. This happened in the east first. Soon more tanks exploded, then self propelled howitzers, followed by infantry fighting vehicles and then armoured personnel carriers exploding. Turrets were popping off like jack in the boxes. Then the weapons transports themselves exploded in massive, huge balls of fire!

The pattern was repeated to the north and the south. Soon the entire encampment was surrounded on three sides by exploding equipment. Those soldiers who had ran to put out the fires were thrown to the ground. Those who remained in the encampment dove for cover as shrapnel from exploding ordinance began to fly all about them. The Trojan specialists who were camped with their equipment where the hardest hit. There were deaths, many deaths and many more wounded!

Selene and Forkbraid sat watching on as the fireworks in the enemies landing zone continued unabated. Agent Murphy had returned with his Hummer, flying low over the hills so as not to be detected by the enemy.

After landing the Hummer and approaching Selene and Forkbraid, still looking at the ongoing devastation twelve miles to the east, Agent Murphy asked, "Did you two do that?"

Selene answered, "Yes Jim. We did that", a deep sadness was in her voice.

Forkbraid added, "Sadly, some deaths were unavoidable", his voice also showing a distinct sadness to it.

Agent Murphy looked around at the implements they had packed up. The very implements that they had used in their ritual. There was nothing special about them that he could discern. They were just artefacts. Little more than things, curios you might hang on a wall or just put on display.

Jim Murphy thought to himself, *"They did all of that with this!"*, it was unbelievable.

The devastation, as he could see it, so far to the east was incomprehensible.

Jim had seen what Forkbraid could do, back at L5, at Colonial Central

Command, but this!

What he was witnessing was incredulous. Had he not seen it with his own eyes, the results of their work, he would not have believed it at all.

Having placed their ritual tools inside his Hummer, Agent Murphy flew Selene and Forkbraid back to the psychic academy.

General Verne was livid, absolutely livid, one could say he was almost foaming at the mouth. The General had demanded a damage report, even though he was quite sure what it would say.

Captain Carlson came back with the report, he would have preferred not to be there, "General Sir", he began, then he spilled the awful news, "One hundred percent total loss of all heavy weapons systems and their transports Sir!" A bead of sweat trickled down his forehead.

"Casualties Carlson?", the General demanded.

Captain Carlson gulped, "Well over three hundred dead Sir. Two hundred plus wounded. We are still looking for victims. We are still counting. We will find many more bodies Sir."

The General shook his head. He needed someone to blame. He needed a scape goat.

"You there", the General shouted at Captain Bolton, "You told me that those damned lights were nothing more that lights! Harmless fucking lights!"

"That's what our people concluded General Sir! That's what they told me!", Captain Bolton explained, there was fear in his voice.

The General pulled the flap of his holster and drew out his pulse pistol, aiming it directly at Captain Bolton's head.

"Bolton! You a guilty of incompetence!", the General shouted as he pulled the trigger.

'Click!', Captain Bolton flinched as he pleaded loudly, "It's not my fault General!"

'Click! Click! Click!   Click! Click! Click!', the General squeezed the trigger several mores times.

Captain Bolton flinched uncontrollably before collapsing to the floor and disgracing himself.

The General's pulse pistol was useless. It would not fire. He threw it to the ground in disgust!

"Give me your weapon Heller", the General demanded.

Captain Heller obeyed without hesitation and passed his pulse pistol to The General.

The General aimed the weapon at Bolton's head, *'Click!'*

Nothing happened yet again. Captain Bolton flinched again.

'Click! Click! Click!   Click! Click! Click!', the General squeezed the trigger on Heller's pulse pistol several more times.

A soiled Captain Bolton continued to flinch uncontrollably .

Nothing happened. The General inspected the pulse pistol more closely.

"Look into this Captain", the General told Heller, "This can not be a coincidence."

The General passed the weapon back to Captain Heller.

To the other Captains, the General ordered, "Get this man out of my sight!"

It was well past afternoon when Captain Heller entered the command tent.

"Yes Heller. What news do you have?", the General asked.

"General", Captain Heller began, "The news is not good Sir."

"I know that already Heller!", the General replied, adding sarcastically, "Have you not noticed the wreckage that was my army?", it was of course a rhetorical question.

Captain Heller cautiously replied, "General, we have no weapons Sir", he paused then continued, "All of our pulse pistols and pulse rifles are useless. Their power packs have completed fused."

The General gave the Captain an incredulous look, "What about our firearms Heller? Our older weapons? Surely they should be okay", he asked.

"General. The bullets in their magazines exploded", Captain Heller informed him, "Effectively destroying all of our firearms. "

The General put his hand to his face and began to think.

Captain Heller further informed the General, "All of our electronics are fused General. Everything electronic is inoperable Sir."

The General continued to think, then enquired, "Do we have anything, anything at all that actually works Captain?"

Captain Heller replied, "Yes Sir. We still have nearly all of our drop ships Sir. At least, those that were not damaged by shrapnel. They will need repairs Sir."

The General shook his head, then looked around the tent, then looked back to the Captain, "Those bastard demons have pulled all of our teeth!", he spat out.

17. Aftermath

"Jim. What are Lieutenant Roberts's birds showing us?", Forkbraid asked Agent Murphy, who was looking through the data from the latest information feeds.

"They've lost all of their heavy weapons along with their weapons transports", Agent Murphy informed him.

"Any signs that they're going to leave Jim?", Selene asked.

"Not yet. Then again it is too early to tell", Agent Murphy replied, adding, "They'll have to take stock. Count their dead and wounded. Then they'll look into what's left and what they can actually do. It could be days before we see anything tangible."

"All those dead and wounded", Selene repeated with a sorrowful voice.

"Whatever their casualty toll is now, it could have been much higher", Agent Murphy replied.

"How so Jim?", Selene enquired.

"If we had been successful in destroying their weapons transports en-route, as was our plan, then all of the men associated with those transports would have died as well", Agent Murphy explained.

Selene wasn't convinced, tears showed in her eyes, so Jim explained further, "Each tank has a crew of four, each self propelled howitzer the same, four. Their ifv's a crew of three, their apc's a crew of two. Each gun ship has a pilot. Their weapons transports, probably a crew of thirty or more each. The numbers add up Selene. We know how many of each weapons system they had. When you add in all the other specialists they'd require, those weapons transports were carrying a quarter as many men as their troop transports. At least."

"There's still a lot of dead and wounded Jim", Selene replied back, tears now flowing freely.

Forkbraid stepped in, "Selene. I think what Jim is trying to say, is that their losses are probably a third of what they might have been."

"We still did this Forkbraid!", Selene snapped back.

Forkbraid replied calmly, "Yes we did. And it's done. Remember, they came here to wipe us out Selene. They invaded. It was necessary", thinking to himself, *"I should have done this alone."*

It was now the end of their second day on Mars and General Verne wanted the latest information.

"Captain Carlson. What are the latest casualty figures?", General Verne demanded.

"General. The numbers have climbed considerably. Our dead now number well above eight hundred. Many of the wounded we had this morning have passed on. Our current wounded number above two hundred. Many are not expected to survive General", Captain Carlson replied.

"Any silver linings in that grey cloud you've just dumped on us?", the General asked.

"Not really General. There is this though", the Captain replied, adding, "Most of our Infantry came threw unscathed. A few shrapnel wounds here and there, some of the men who rushed to help with the fires suffered some burns and some shock wave injuries. Nearly all of our casualties though, are amongst the specialists. Then men who were on the weapons transports. The specialists bivouacked with all their equipment."

"And they burned with their equipment!", the General answered back, adding, "Burned and blown to bits! Over a thousand men. That puts our losses at over forty percent!"

The General turned to Captain Heller and asked, "Did we find out what weapon they used?"

Heller knew he'd be asked that question and remembering what happened to Captain Bolton, he come to the meeting prepared, "General Sir. This is Specialist Knutson. I'll let him explain."

"Proceed Knutson", the General Ordered.

"General. Their weapon consisted of some form of multilayered light", Knutson replied.

"No kidding! I'm fairly certain that we all saw that last night", the General replied sarcastically.

"Please let me explain General", Specialist Knutson responded.

"By all means. Please do", General Verne replied.

"General. The visible light itself was harmless. It was just that, harmless light", Knutson began.

General Verne cut him off, "Look around you man! Does that look like it was harmless!"

"Please General, let me explain", Knutson replied. Heller was glad it wasn't him.

When the General motioned for him to continue, Knutson did so, "There were components to that light that were not visible General. It was outside of our visible spectrum. That invisible light, seems to have resonated with our hardware and equipment, at a level that we do not understand."

The General nodded, perhaps he had been too harsh with Captain Bolton.

The General questioned further, "So Knutson, why the delay? Why did nothing happen until the Sun came up?"

Knutson replied, "General. If I told you that we understand how this weapon works, I'd be lying. What we can say is this. That invisible light from their weapon, the light that resonated with and insinuated itself into out equipment. It was probably designed to trigger with the rising of the Sun and catch us all off guard."

"Which it did Knutson! Which it did", the General agreed.

The General then questioned, "Knutson, did your people check the site where the weapon was deployed?", as he pointed eastwards.

"Yes General. We dispatched a team to the site this morning", the Specialist replied.

"And what did they find there?", the General questioned further.

"Sir. They didn't find anything useful", Knutson replied, informing the General, "They found a patch of trampled grass. Trampled in a circular fashion. They also found signs that a Hummer had landed close nearby recently. Nothing that gives any clue about their weapon though General."

Captain Heller stepped in and added, "General. We are dealing with demons Sir. Their weapon was more than likely, otherworldly."

The General nodded in understanding, "Captain. Remind me to use that word when I report back to Jovian High Command."

Captain Heller nodded in reply.

"Captain Carlson. What are our options?", the General enquired.

"General. We don't have a lot of them. We have ten thousand infantry and under sixty percent of our specialists. Currently we haven't got a single weapon that works. All we have is our drop ships."

"So Captain. We turn tail and run. Is that it? Go back the Aft Trojans?", the General replied rhetorically, explaining emphatically to his Captains, "If we do that gentlemen, Princess Luisa will have all of our heads mounted on pikes!"

Another captain, Captain Jackstone picked up on the word 'pikes' and responded, "General. Scans of the surrounding region did show forests. They will be a very good supply of timber Sir. We do have Martian resources available to us."

"So what are you suggesting Jackstone? We stay here and build log cabins. We settle down!", the General questioned with an incredulous look on his face.

"General. I don't think that's what Captain Jackstone meant", Captain Heller interjected, adding, "We do have Martian timber resources that we can use Sir. We have do metal that we can salvage Sir", the Captain gestured at the still smouldering wreckage all around them, "We can build more weapons. Primitive yes, compared to what we brought with use, but weapons none the less."

Captain Jackstone nodded in agreement, then explained, "Medieval siege weapons General. We could build battering rams, siege towers, ballistas, catapults, mangonels and trebuchets. We could even forge medieval cannon. These are well within our capabilities. The raw materials for black powder are no doubt in the same hills as the forests."

Captain Heller then added, "At the infantry level, we could forge knives, swords, pikes, glaves, spears, even bows and cross bows. General, they haven't defeated us yet. We can make anything we put our minds to!"

"An interesting concept gentlemen. Let's go medieval on their arses shall we", the General replied with a broad smile on his face.

Captain Carlson listened to their suggestions. He was horrified. The single Bat Wing they had encountered could wipe out what was left of their entire army on its own and the enemy had ten Wisps up their sleeves as well. Going 'medieval' on their arses as the General put it, was suicide.

General Verne knew they could not go home in defeat. Princess Luisa would consider that unacceptable. He knew the Princess personally. The General and his staff would pay a high price in such a case. They needed a victory to avoid any form of disgrace. The General also knew, that simply reporting back on their current situation was itself going to be a problem, yet he no choice, a report had to be made. General Verne wrote out his report, read it over, rewrote it twice more, then finally sent it to the Jovian High Command.

Matthew had been listening intently to the news feeds about the Aft Trojan Armed Forces Martian campaign. It had been broadcast over and over, throughout the Jovian Colonies for more than three days now.

The Aft Trojan Armed Forces on their approach to Mars. How there was no resistance, nothing in their way. The Aft Trojan Armed Forces entering Martian orbit. Again there was no Martian resistance and nothing to stop them. The Aft Trojan Armed Forces setting up a bridgehead on the Martian surface in Elysium. Again to no resistance from the Martian authorities whatsoever. Nothing could stop them.

Then the news feeds went dark and no further information about the Aft Trojan Armed Forces Martian campaign was forth coming. Matthew wondered what had happened. So had the Prophet. They weren't the only ones either. There were plenty of other Jovian citizens in Ganymede Prime also been wondering about the fate of the Aft Trojan Armed Forces Martian Campaign.

"No news Matthew?", asked the Prophet.

"None my Lord", Matthew replied, adding, "There's been no news since they broadcast the videos of their landing. Nothing at all since then."

"They seemed to land okay", the Prophet replied, adding, "There was no resistance at all in the video feeds."

"Yes, but what happened after they landed?", Matthew asked rhetorically, "The news feeds appear to be very quiet on the campaign now. That in itself is very telling!"

"This does not bode well does it Matthew?", asked the Prophet.

"It certain does not bode well Sir", replied Matthew, explaining, "First those missiles. No-one knows what destroyed them. Now their much vaunted Aft Trojan Armed Forces Campaign. If the Horridians do know what happened, they aren't going to be telling anyone, anytime soon."

The apartment's communicator buzzed for attention.

"I bet that's General Tarzan with more questions", Matthew predicted.

The Prophet accepted the call and General Tarzan appeared on the screen.

"General. What can we do for you?", the Prophet greeted.

"I need to speak with Matthew", the General replied.

"I'm here General. What can I help you with?", Matthew asked.

"We've had another set back I'm afraid", General Tarzan informed him.

"We thought there might have been General", Matthew replied, adding, "When the news feeds went dark after the landing, we figured that something went awry."

"Yes well, it did. As I said, it's just set back", the General repeated.

Matthew was quick, "It was a mistake to televise everything in the news feeds General."

"That was a political decision Matthew. Not military. Made by someone well above my pay grade", General Tarzan informed them, adding, "I did tell them it was a mistake."

"By now, they are probably realising just that", Matthew replied.

"I expect they will, but that's not what I'm here to discuss", the General replied.

"Okay then. What can we help you with?", Matthew asked again.

"After the landing, the demons hit us twice", General Tarzan began, informing them further, "After the weapons transports landed and were being unloaded, the weapons systems were being prepared. They hit us with a Bat Wing and maybe a dozen Wisps. That did cause us some losses."

"It was a mistake to land anywhere in the Elysium subcontinent General. The landing place should have been somewhere safer, outside of the range of their aircraft", Matthew replied.

"Thank you for the twenty twenty hind site Matthew", the General replied, adding, "General Verne, the General in charge of the Aft Trojan Armed Forces, chose the landing zone."

Matthew nodded as a reply.

"Okay. So they had the first attack. Not a problem. It is war. That happens", the General told them, then added, "The second attack. Now that was different. The demons struck in the middle of the night and they used a weapon we have never come across before. Some kind of delayed action light weapon."

"Delayed action light weapon?", the Prophet enquired.

General Tarzan explained, "Their weapon struck everything in the landing zone, except the drop ships. Apparently, after the attack it looked like nothing had happened. Everything appeared normal. Then in the morning, as they Sun rose and its light touched the landing zone, every piece of equipment touched by their attack, just burst into flames. Then the heavy weapons systems exploded. Including the weapons transports."

The General then paused and asked, "What can you tell us Matthew?"

"There isn't a whole lot I can tell you General", Matthew admitted, explaining, "We are dealing with demons. There's no telling what dark arts they conjured up during that attack."

"General. You said that the heavy weapons and their transports exploded. What kind of losses are we talking about?", the Prophet asked.

"Total. They've lost all of their weapons systems, everything down to their pulse pistols. All they have left are their drop ships. They also lost over a thousand specialists", the General admitted.

"General", Matthew began, "You called this a set back. I'd call it a disaster."

"Call it what you may Matthew. It is what it is", the General replied, then asked, "You've both dealt with these demons in the past. Matthew, what would you recommend?"

"General. They've disarmed your Trojan Army. We have no idea how they did that. All they have left are their drop ships. Use them. Get your people out of there", Matthew strenuously advised.

"That gentlemen is out of my hands. It's now a political decision and General Verne has decided to forge weapons using local Martian resources and lay siege to the demon's fortress", General Tarzan informed them both.

"General. You do understand that would be a suicide mission don't you?", Matthew replied, he was aghast at the suggestion.

"Yes lad. It's certain death for them. They know it", the General replied, "They also know, if they return in abject disgrace, they will all face the gallows", with that he signed off.

Matthew looked at the Prophet, "My Lord. I do believe that we've lost the Martian campaign."

The Prophet replied, "It's certainly a good thing that you planned ahead Matthew."

"Jim. Any news on that Trojan Army?", Forkbraid enquired.

Agent Murphy replied, "They haven't left yet, if that's what you're hoping."

"I was kind of hoping they had", Forkbraid admitted.

"No such luck I'm afraid. They seem to be scouting out the surrounding area", Agent Murphy informed him.

"Scouting the surrounding area?", Forkbraid queried, asking further, "Why would they be doing that Jim?"

"I'm not sure FB", Agent Murphy replied, "I've noticed them sending Hummers to the forests to the east. It's difficult to say, looking down from above, but I'd say they're hauling back timber."

"Timber? What do they want with timber?", Forkbraid replied with a bewildered look.

"To build shelters maybe. Winter can get very cold up that way", Agent Murphy thought aloud.

"They have their drop ships don't they? They can leave anytime they want", replied Forkbraid.

"Yes, they do, but maybe they've chosen to stay instead", Agent Murphy speculated.

Forkbraid thought about the Trojan Army's position for a moment. Ten thousand infantry, perhaps another fifteen hundred or so specialists and their commanding officers. They were completely disarmed.

Then it dawned on him, "What if they can't go home Jim? Their invasion is a complete and total failure. What if going home in disgrace is tantamount to a death sentence?"

"No FB. That can't be right. I mean, the Horridians might be a bunch of complete bastards, but they wouldn't execute their own people for simply failing. Would they?", Agent Murphy replied and then questioned.

"Perhaps not the whole Trojan Army, but maybe those in charge of it", Forkbraid replied.

"So their commanders have chosen not to leave as a measure of self preservation?", Agent Murphy pondered.

"Maybe. Potentially Jim", Forkbraid replied, adding, "Whatever their reasons, we need to keep a close eye on them. We have an enemy at our backs and we need to watch them very carefully."

Agent Murphy did just that and over the next few days began to see a pattern in what the Trojans were doing. The images coming back from Lieutenant Robert's birds were crystal clear and a meeting was quickly called.

Selene was first to ask, "What are we looking at Jim?"

"These are images I've been reviewing of the Trojan Army's encampment", Agent Murphy informed them, adding, "That particular image is of a trebuchet."

"A trebuchet", Selene repeated, then queried, "Correct me if I'm wrong, but isn't that an ancient siege weapon."

Agent Murphy confirmed, "Technically yes, although medieval would probably be a more correct description."

"They're making a medieval trebuchet", Selene thought aloud.

"Not one. That's just one of several", Agent Murphy informed them, "And they're not just making trebuchets either."

"What else are they making Jim?", asked Forkbraid.

Agent Murphy called up more images to the screen, "They've been quite industrious of late. That image is of a large battering ram", he pointed out, "Those are siege towers. They are ballistas and those are catapults", pointing out other images.

"Jim, are you telling us, that these idiots are building medieval siege engines?", Selene asked him sceptically.

"If it looks like a fish and it swims like a fish, then yeah, it's a fish", Agent Murphy replied, adding, "Those are medieval siege engines."

Selene looked at Forkbraid, then to Marcus and Charlene, trying to get a handle on what Jim had just told them.

Agent Murphy added the cherry to the tart, "It's not just medieval siege engines", he put more images onto the screen, "Those are forges. It looks like they're also forging medieval infantry weapons. These ones over here are larger forges. I suspect they're trying to forge cannon as well."

"They must be insane!", Selene exclaimed.

Forkbraid held onto Selene's hand, "It's their commanders. They're trying to retrieve some sort of victory out of this, so they go home triumphant."

"FB. They can build as many siege engines as they like. They can outfit their infantry with chain mail, armour and as many weapons as they like", Agent Murphy began, then informed them all, "They would need at least ten times their number to take this academy and that's assuming we don't defend it with your Bat Wing and our Wisps. Selene is right. They are insane!"

"Agreed Jim. What they're planning is just plain stupid", Forkbraid agreed, before adding, "Wood burns. Jim, get our pilots ready. Send our Wisps out there to take down those siege engines. We need to discourage this behaviour. I want them to learn that their only hope it to go home!"

"Will do FB. By nightfall, they will be back to square one", Agent Murphy replied.

True to his word Jim Murphy organised their pilots to fly the Wisps out to the enemy encampment, with orders to destroy all of the medieval siege engines that were being built. The pilots did as they were ordered and strafed their targets at the enemy encampments multiple times with their Wisp's pulse cannons. When the Wisps left to fly home, the enemy's medieval siege engines were in flames. They would burn to the ground and be ashes by morning.

A furious General Verne called a meeting of his Captains as the fires burned out of control around them.

"Heller. Jackstone. First thing in the morning we start over. Understand", the General ordered.

"Yes General Sir", both Captain's Heller and Jackstone replied.

"General Sir", Captain Carlson began, adding, "They will just do the same thing again Sir."

"I know they will Carlson", the General replied, "It won't stop us though. We will continue until we are victorious!", he bellowed.

"I want those fires out. What can we salvage from this mess?", the General ordered, "Get out there and sort this mess out!"

Captain Heller hung back, "General. I noticed that they mainly hit the siege engines. They may have missed the cannon forges Sir."

"Excellent observation Heller. Get those forges under cover. We'll make as many cannon as we can. Keep them all hidden under wraps", General Verne ordered.

The General then refined his orders slightly, adding, "We'll keep making those siege engines though. I think we can use those as decoys."

"Will the decoys be functional siege engines or just mock-ups?", the Captain asked.

"Make them functional Heller. They may be decoys, but any that survive, we can use", General Verne ordered.

General Verne continued, "What we really need are the cannon. Move the cannon forges closer to the drop ships. The enemy has been reluctant to hit those. So we'll use them like a shield!"

"Yes Sir", Captain Heller replied, "I'll make it so Sir!"

There was a knock on Selene's apartment door and Selene automatically scanned for who was knocking.

"It's Jim and the Pod Sister's", Selene informed Forkbraid, before pushing a thought to Agent Murphy, *"Come in Jim."*

The thought popped into Agent Murphy's mind and he automatically opened the door, almost without thinking. The two Pod Sister's, Zuawalo and Zeealas followed Jim into the apartment.

"I do prefer to hear the words Selene", Agent Murphy informed her, before stating, "Having thoughts pop into my head is not something I'll ever get use to."

"Sorry Jim. It's a habit of mine", Selene replied.

Zuawalo and Zeealas looked around the apartment, "Oh! This is a beautiful place!", Zeealas told everyone.

"Yes. A very beautiful place", Zuawalo agreed, "So beautiful!"

"Yes Girls, I suppose it is. One of the perks of being the boss", Selene replied, adding, "Your rooms are probably a lot more austere. If you speak with Charlene and Roseanne, I'm sure they can find a way to make your rooms almost as nice."

The girls both smiled and Zuawalo asked, "You are the boss of?", gesturing to Forkbraid.

"Oh gosh no", Selene replied, "Forkbraid does his own thing. He has no boss. Not even me."

"I take it you have more news for us Jim", Forkbraid enquired.

"Yes I do" Agent Murphy replied, informing Forkbraid, "We sent the Trojans back to square one. They just started over again. They are rebuilding those ridiculous medieval siege engines."

"I see. We will just have to watch them closely and when they're finished, we'll just send them all back to square one again", Forkbraid suggested.

"So that's it then. Every time they rebuild, we just send them back to square one?", Agent Murphy asked.

"Yes Jim. At some point, the lesson will have to sink in", Forkbraid replied.

"And if it doesn't Forkbraid?", Selene stepped in and enquired.

"If the lesson doesn't sink in, we'll just have to rethink the situation and adjust accordingly", Forkbraid replied, adding, "We'll come up with something that will force them to go home."

Repetition, repetition, repetition! Like clockwork, every week, Agent Murphy led his Wisps into action destroying the siege weapons being built by the Trojans. Setting the Trojans right back to square every time. Straight away the stubborn Trojans restarted work, building new siege weapons to replace those that had been destroyed. This was becoming a repeating pattern and after the forth attempt at convincing the Trojans of their futility in staying, it was now necessary to alter course.

Forkbraid had gone to the Pod Sister's dormitory to meet with Agent Murphy, so as to view the latest scans of the Trojan encampment. The Pod Sisters had moved into the vacant residential advisers rooms, which were somewhat larger than their room had been. Agent Murphy was now in the habit of staying in the dormitory with the two Sisters. Forkbraid did not enquire as to the relationship between Jim and two Sisters, it was none of his business and he respected their privacy.

Charlene and Roseanne had helped the Pod Sisters give their dormitory and rooms a make over. It was now much more colourful, with a far better aesthetic and Forkbraid noticed the difference immediately. He smiled and approved, the girls were making themselves at home.

Agent Murphy had flown Folcrom Gwek back to his village a couple of weeks earlier in his Hummer, so Gwek could choose an apprentice to train to take over as the village Kujur. Gwek was also looking for other possible talented psychics in the surrounding villages.

"I've gotta tell you FB, these guys are stubborn", Agent Murphy told him, adding, "No sooner than we destroy those damned siege engines, they just start building more. It's like they're obsessed. They just don't get it."

"Well people usually say the third times the charm. Now we're on the forth", Forkbraid replied, adding, "There isn't any point to flogging a dead horse Jim. We need to try something different."

"Something radically different if you ask me", Agent Murphy replied.

Forkbraid told him, "I have promised Selene that I would minimise the loss of life where possible. So whatever we do has to be very light on human casualties Jim."

"Then that becomes a major constraint on whatever we do", Agent Murphy replied, explaining, "It would be so easy to simply burn their entire encampment to the ground with everything in it."

"Which is exactly what we need to avoid Jim", Forkbraid stressed the point.

"Now. I can see they've started rebuilding those siege engines once again, but what are these covered areas over here Jim?", Forkbraid asked.

"Well that's a good question FB. We don't really know what's under those covered areas", Agent Murphy replied, "However if I was to hazard a guess, I'd say they're a combination of cannon forges and cannon storage areas."

"Cannon forges and cannon storage areas? And we're not destroying those?", Forkbraid enquired.

"Look at how close they are to their drop ships FB. If we destroy those covered areas, we'd also destroy quite a few of their drop ships", Agent Murphy replied.

"Which they will require in order to leave Mars", Forkbraid nodded in understanding.

"And we don't know for sure what's under those covers. It could easily be recovering wounded or other troop housing", Agent Murphy stated.

"So we can't destroy their hypothetical cannon either. That's another constraint", Forkbraid noted

"Assuming that they do leave FB. What happens to them when they finally get home?", Agent Murphy questioned.

"We've already discussed that Jim. We disarmed them completely within a day of their landing", Forkbraid replied, adding, "They will be going home in abject disgrace."

"Which is probably a death sentence for their entire command level", Agent Murphy replied, "They're not going to leave FB. They can't go home without a victory."

"And we cannot give them that", Forkbraid replied, "Not if we want them to leave."

Zuawalo and Zeealas walked into the common room both overly casually dressed and sat down on their usual couch. Zuawalo's ferret, Zigg, quickly hopped into the common room and jumped up on the couch beside Zuawalo.

"Girls. We do have a guest", Agent Murphy pointed out.

"Jim. This is how we dress in our home, back in our village", Zuawalo informed him.

Zeealas replied, "Forkbraid does not mind. Do you Forkbraid?"

"No. Not at all", Forkbraid replied diplomatically, then out of the blue he asked, "Girls. That Trojan Army that's camped to the north west of us. They are uninvited guests. How would you convince them to go home?"

Agent Murphy gave Forkbraid an incredulous look.

"You cannot", Zeealas replied as a matter-of-factly.

Zuawalo explained, "You need them, to convince themselves to go."

"Yes. They have to decide to leave. It must be their decision", Zeealas agreed.

Agent Murphy looked at his Girls and then asked, "We can't force them to leave? We can't convince them?"

"No", Zuawalo replied, waving her index finger, "Jim, you can try. You have tried. How many times now? How did that work for you?"

Agent Murphy mumbled, "Four times. And they are still there", as an answer.

"You see Jim", Zeealas replied, adding, "It has to be their decision."

Forkbraid was both amused and intrigued by the girls clarity of insight, "So Zuawalo, Zeealas. How would you convince them to leave?", he asked them.

Zeealas shook her head, this was already answered, then replied cryptically, "We don't."

Zuawalo restated, "They have to decide for themselves. The stage must be set."

"The stage?", Agent Murphy queried.

"The conditions Jim. The conditions", Zeealas replied.

"They must see clear signs that they cannot stay", Zuawalo elaborated, "Then they will decide to leave. Jim, you cannot force this thing."

As Zuawalo answered, she gently touched her belly just below the navel in a barely noticeable movement. Only Forkbraid seemed to pick up on the movement. It was subtle. He could also see that Zeealas was aware. Did Roseanne know? Roseanne was not there to ask. Perhaps Jim was subconsciously aware at some level? If he was, he did not show it.

"Okay my darlings", Agent Murphy began, "How do we set the stage?"

Zuawalo look thoughtfully at Jim Murphy with a huge smile on her face, before replying, "You need a snake Jim! A special kind of snake!"

Zeealas quickly added, "A snake that was and is no more!"

Forkbraid picked up quickly, "Leroy McGuvan! A demolished man!"

Zeealas turned to her Sister, "This one, Jim, he is very sweet. This one, Forkbraid, he is very smart."

It was in their nature to speak in this way.

Zuawalo replied, "Leroy must have his redemption. He will set the stage."

"I'm unsure how Leroy McGuvan fits into this Girls", Forkbraid admitted.

"The Trojans are like Leroy, before Gwek demolished him. They are confused. They are misaligned", Zuawalo explained.

"They are on the wrong path!", Zeealas explained further, adding, "Just like Leroy was."

"So somehow, Leroy McGuvan will convince them to go home?", Agent Murphy asked.

Zuawalo frowned, then corrected, "No Jim. Leroy will set the stage!"

"Girls. Thank-you. You have given us quite some interesting things to consider. I will need to discuss these with Selene", Forkbraid told the Girls.

"We were helpful?", Zeealas queried.

"Of course you were Zeealas. You and Zuawalo. You were both very helpful", Agent Murphy confirmed reassuringly.

To Jim, Forkbraid sent the following thoughts, *"Jim. Sorry to drop this into your head like this. Don't act surprised or shocked. Zuawalo has something to tell you. I think Zeealas already knows. When they tell you, act like you had no idea. Be gentle with them. Very gentle. Treat them kindly. I believe Zuawalo is pregnant."*

Agent Murphy coughed suddenly, quite loudly in fact, "Sorry! I had something caught in my throat", he told everyone, as he gave Forkbraid an awkward side glance.

Forkbraid then bid the three good day and left the dormitory, leaving a slightly shaken Jim Murphy in his wake.

18. The Path of Redemption

"So Selene, you'll never guess what", Forkbraid shouted out as he entered Selene's apartment.

"The Pod Sister's are pregnant", Selene replied straight away, without the slightest hesitation.

"Say what! How'd you know?", Forkbraid asked.

"Seriously? Roseanne. Roseanne is close to the Pod Sisters. Roseanne is close to me. So Roseanne finds out, she's excited, who do you think she's going to tell", Selene replied.

"You. Of course. Wait, wait. You said the Pod Sister's are pregnant. Do you mean both?", Forkbraid queried.

"Did you think only one of the Girls was pregnant. Forkbraid, you're slipping", Selene replied.

"Well, I guess Jim's in for quite the shock then", Forkbraid stated.

Selene laughed loudly, "He should have looked into their culture before he let them seduce him."

"Their culture?", Forkbraid enquired, then asked, "Wait! They seduced him?"

"Yes, it's their culture", Selene confirmed.

Forkbraid chuckled lightly, "Jim Murphy got seduced", he mused, then stated, "When they tell him, I bet his first words will be *'how'd that happen'*."

It was then Selene's turn to chuckle.

Forkbraid enquired, "What is it about their culture Selene?"

"Well in their culture, a man can have more than one wife, as you already know", Selene replied.

Selene continued,"Back on Earth and in the olden days here for that matter, it was the families who chose who married who, based on each families requirements. Marriage was considered for life and divorce was and is still severely frowned upon. They're not big fans of contraception either. I don't think Jim even considered that or maybe he just didn't know."

"Yes Selene, but in this case the Girls chose Jim", Forkbraid replied, jumping the gun.

"Just getting to that Forkbraid", Selene replied, then continued, "Now a days, it's the girls who choose their husbands. The man is expected to simply acquiesce to the girls choice. If a girl chooses a married man, his existing wives meet with the prospective new wife and they either accept her or they don't."

"So the existing wives get to decide? And the man just goes along with their decision?", Forkbraid queried still thinking it was incredulous.

"Pretty much Forkbraid", Selene nodded in confirmation, then continued, "If the man is single, he's pretty much fair game. It's not unheard of, for two or more girls to choose the same man or of course, as is the case here, two Sisters, the Pod Sisters"

"I still don't get it. The man has no choice in the matter?", Forkbraid asked again.

"Correct. The man is expected to go along with the Girl's choice", Selene confirmed once more.

Forkbraid still looked a little unconvinced, so Selene told him straight up, "Like I gave you a choice Forkbraid!", smiling at him as she did so.

"Touche my love, touche", Forkbraid replied.

"Their culture is highly matriarchal. The women own the land, the women hold the purse strings, it's the women who inherit. The women chooses their husband. Of course that's how it is now, here on Mars. It is probably very different back on the Earth in the region where they originally came from", Selene concluded, adding, "Mars changes everything."

"Okay. So what happens when their parents find out?", Forkbraid asked.

"Oh! Oh my!", Selene exclaimed, "They'll expect Zuawalo and Zeealas to marry Jim. The Girl's whole extended family will expect to come here for the marriage feast. Jim will need to pay the bride price.", Selene began to smile, "Two Girls! Jim's got a big bill to pay and he has no cattle!", Selene laughed.

"There are no cattle here on Mars Selene. You know that", Forkbraid replied dryly.

"I know. I know Forkbraid. On the Earth, it would have been paid in cattle. Here, probably in golden credits", Selene replied, then laughed again,

"You will need to loan Jim the bride price."

"Selene, please be serious", Forkbraid requested.

"I'm sorry Forkbraid, it's just so funny. Poor Jim", Selene replied.

"Well we can't have any weddings until we've dealt with that Trojan Army", Forkbraid replied.

"Definitely", Selene agreed, adding, "So lets get those Trojans off this planet."

Two days later Forkbraid was back in the Pod Sister's dormitory along with Selene. Marcus and Charlene were present as well, as were Cormac and Candy. Roseanne was also in the dormitory with her friends, the Pod Sisters, Zuawalo and Zeealas. They were all waiting for Agent Jim Murphy to attend the meeting.

Agent Murphy entered the dormitory, "Sorry I'm late people. I had to acquire our guest here and bring him along", he explained while leading Leroy McGuvan into the common room.

Leroy McGuvan was wearing a nice pair of bracelets, more commonly known as handcuffs.

"Jim!", Zuawalo exclaimed, then protested, "He is not that very bad man. He is a new man."

"I'm sorry Zuawalo, but it's hard for me to forget all the things he's done", Agent Murphy replied.

Zuawalo sighed, "It is not your fault Jim. It is very hard to let go of bad memories."

Zuawalo looked to Forkbraid and Selene, then made a gesturing look in Leroy's direction.

"Jim. You won't need those cuffs", Selene remarked, "This Leroy is not the same as the one you're remembering", then with a gesture of her right hand, the cuffs unlocked and fell to the floor.

"Can we trust him FB?", Agent Murphy asked, looking at Forkbraid.

"You might find this strange Jim, but yes, you can", Forkbraid replied, adding, "It's just as Selene told you. This is not the same Leroy that you're remembering."

Leroy spoke up, "I will do my utmost to earn your trust Agent Murphy. I promise you."

Jim Murphy replied harshly, "McGuvan. You do anything, anything at all, that causes harm to any of my friends and I will gut you like a fish!", the last part was spoken slowly with great force.

Somehow Zuawalo and Zeealas were both excited, but also concerned at how their Jim had spoken. They could see that Jim Murphy would protect them no matter what, even though in this case it was completely unnecessary. A reaction to finding out his Girl's were pregnant with his future children perhaps. One thing was certain, Jim Murphy would protect them with his life.

As Agent Murphy and Leroy sat down, Forkbraid unrolled a map on the table that sat in the midst of their chairs. It was a large map and quite clear, showing the Elysium subcontinent, the position of the Elysium Colony, the New Flinders Psychic Academy and the position of the Trojan encampment. The map also showed the terrain and the local environments. The forests their enemies were utilising as a timber resource were clearly marked as well.

Leroy looked at the map, he had no idea what it was about. Since coming to the academy he had been kept locked away, in what he could only describe as a 'monastic cell'. It was the closest thing the academy had to a prison. A prisoner yes, but well kept, well looked after and well fed. Leroy McGuvan did not begrudge their treatment of him. He remembered well, what sort of man he had been before Gwek demolished him.

"Please forgive me", Leroy told them in a softly spoken voice, "I am unfamiliar with the significance of this map."

"You wouldn't be", Selene replied, informing him, "Since you came here, there are certain things that have occurred of which you have no knowledge."

Forkbraid tapped the map with a pointer, "You know the Elysium Colony", he moved the pointer, "You know our academy", he moved the pointer again, "What you haven't been privy to, is this encampment."

"Encampment?" Leroy enquired.

"The Jovian High Council declared war on the entire Inner Solar System!", Agent Murphy spat out. Zuawalo placed her left hand on Jim's forearm in an effort to calm him.

"I had heard something about that Agent Murphy", Leroy admitted.

"What you probably haven't heard, is that the Horridians have launched an attack", Selene informed Leroy.

"Several in fact", Forkbraid added, he then began listing out recent events, "They launched a decapitation strike first with twenty two hundred cold fusion missiles."

Agent Murphy jumped in angrily, "Each with ten independently targeting re-entrant bloody warheads, each with a two megaton yield."

"Jim", Forkbraid shock his head at Agent Murphy before continuing, "So yes, over twenty two thousand warheads. Ten of those missiles were targeting the colonies here on Mars. The rest are targeting the Earth and L5."

Leroy replied, "I had no idea."

"You wouldn't. As far as the Prophet was concerned, you died as a martyr in the rearguard action, that enabled him to escape", Cormac interjected.

"Thank you Cormac", Forkbraid replied, then continued, "There were two other components to the attacks. The trailing Trojans sent an armed force of ten thousand troops and heavy weapons here to occupy Mars. The leading Trojans sent a much larger armed occupation force, ten times as large to the Earth and L5."

"And this encampment is the trailing Trojan occupation force?", Leroy queried.

"Well yes, but you're jumping the gun a bit", Forkbraid replied, explaining, "We've dealt with the inbound missiles. We've disarmed the Trojan occupation force. What we need to do next, is get the Trojans to go home."

"And somehow, I'm the one who's going to do that?", Leroy asked.

"Yes Leroy!", Zuawalo replied energetically, "This is part of your redemption."

Leroy looked confused, he was quiet for what seemed like an eternity, before resounding, "Wait a minute! You want me to convince a people I've never met, an army from a place I've never been to, to go home!"

"No Leroy", Zuawalo replied, explaining in a way that was clear to her, but made absolutely no sense to anyone else, "You are going to set the stage.

Then they will decide to go home."

Leroy looked perplexed, he replied to Zuawalo, " I have no idea how to do that Zuawalo."

That was this sticking point. Everyone understood what Zuawalo and Zeealas were trying to express, but non of them understood how it would work or for that matter how it would be done. They were clueless and it showed on their faces.

The Pod Sisters were intuitive, more so than most people, but in a way that most people could not understand. They saw things simply and understood things simply. Complexity was foreign to their mindset. Both Zuawalo and Zeealas could see the others were frustrated by not understanding what they were trying to express. This in turn made them feel frustrated and it began to show.

Zeealas reached out and grabbed the pointer from off the table, then she placed the point down on the map and stated loudly, "We go there!"

Zuawalo looked at where her Sister was pointing and agreed loudly, "Yes. We go there!"

The others looked at where Zeealas was pointing on the map. It was the forest in the high country, to the east of the Trojan encampment. The very forest from which the Trojans were procuring their timber. The place Zeealas pointed to, was a valley with a river flowing through it. The very river, the Trojans were using to drive their timber back to their encampment. They each looked around the room at each other, to see if anyone else understood. Apparently no-one did.

Zeealas looked at their confused faces and repeated boldly, "We go there! The stage will be set!", she was quite adamant.

"Why there Zeealas?", Selene asked, enquiring further of her in a softly spoken voice, "Why there? How will that set the stage? We don't understand."

Zeealas let out a low growl of frustration, "Gnarr!"

Agent Murphy moved his left hand into Zeealas's hand and gave it a slight, reassuring squeeze.

Zuawalo answered Selene, "They don't want to be here. They want to go home. They have their orders. They must obey."

Zuawalo saw they weren't following and continued, "We go there, to the forest. They go there, to the forest. We meet. We talk. They will think. The stage is set. It is simple!"

Zeealas then added forcefully, "Then they will decide to go home."

Selene then replied, "Just like that? They'll just go home? You will convince them?"

Zuawalo sighed and then replied, "Yes. Just like that. They will decide to go home. We will not convince them. They will convince themselves."

When Agent Murphy understood the gist of what Zeealas was proposing, he spoke out, "Say what? No! No! No! You are both with child! You can't go anywhere near those Trojan arseholes!"

Zuawalo leant in towards Agent Murphy and kissed him on the cheek, "You are so sweet Jim", then stated emphatically, "I am still going!"

"You can't go Zuawalo. You're with child. Both of you!", Agent Murphy insisted.

"He is alive because of me Jim! Because of me!", Zuawalo answered back while pointing to Leroy McGuvan, "That man is my responsibility!", she was adamant.

"He is not your responsibility Zuawalo", Agent Murphy countered.

"What else can we do? He goes there alone maybe?", Zuawalo asked, then answered, "He will surely die! I have to go there with him. It is the only way."

Straight away Zeealas added, "Where Zuawalo goes. I will go also!"

Agent Murphy looked at Leroy McGuvan, "This is all your fault, you disgraceful cunt!"

Forkbraid pushed an urgent thought into Jim Murphy's mind, *Jim! Enough already!"*

Jim shuddered slightly when Forkbraid's thought came through to his mind, he gave Forkbraid a contrite look of apology.

Jim placed his hand on Zuawalo's and whispered in her ear, "I am so sorry Zuawalo."

Zuawalo simply smiled in return.

Leroy knew that not all of this was his fault, but he also knew that a great deal of this was, he replied remorsefully, "You are absolutely right Agent Murphy. You are absolutely right."

Zeealas drew everyone's attention back to the map and the forest that she had pointed out.

Eminently practical like her Sister, Zeealas told everyone, "To go there, we will need bows, fishing poles and camping equipment. While we are there. We will live off the land. We will hunt. We will fish."

Zuawalo looked at the map, "There, that river. Is there fish there?"

"I assume so Zuawalo. All the waters, rivers included, were seeded with fish towards the end of the terraforming process", Selene replied.

"Good! That is close to where the Trojans get their wood. That is where we camp", Zuawalo told everyone.

"Bows and fishing rods?", Marcus, who would be providing the equipment asked.

Zeealas replied, "Two seven foot telescopic fishing poles with open face spinning reels and six kilo lines. We will need tackle, sinkers, floats, swivels. That sort of thing."

Zuawalo added, "Two, three piece taken down bows with seventy five pound draw. And two quivers of arrows. Thirty two inch arrows with triple point broad-heads. Twenty arrows in each quiver should be adequate."

"Okay. That is very specific. I'll see what I can scrounge up", Marcus replied after noting everything down using his grip, then asking further, "What about tents and other camping gear."

"Three sleeping bags. A large twenty foot by twenty five foot water proof tarpaulin", Zeealas replied and her sister Zuawalo then added, "Three machetes. Twelve inch golok with thick blades. Three tactical folding shovels and three folding saws. We will also need three utility belts. So we can carry all these things."

Zeealas then smiled and added, "I almost forgot. We will need three backpacks."

Marcus scratched his head, "These are not normally things we'd have in stock. I'll send this list to Varak to get some of these made for you. I'm not even sure what a tactical folding shovel even is, but I'm sure Varak will figure that out", Marcus replied, adding, "You Girls certainly seem to know what you're doing."

Leroy added, "These Girls know what they're doing. Trust me on that."

"I don't think I can trust you as far as I can kick you McGuvan", Agent Murphy replied.

"Then don't trust me Agent Murphy", Leroy replied, adding, "Ask their Mother. She will tell you, these Girls know how to survive. I found out that in the Kasei Swamps."

"It is okay Jim", Zeealas told him, "Zuawalo and I, we have got this."

Zuawalo nodded in agreement and squeezed Jim's forearm slightly.

"I'll be coming with you", Agent Murphy replied.

"No. No Jim. That will not work", Zuawalo told him, explaining, "If you are there. The outcome will be different. It will be very, very bad."

"How? I don't understand why?", came Agent Murphy's confused reply.

"Trust my Sister Jim", Zeealas told him, "Zuawalo is right. You must not come with us."

"I can't protect you both if I'm not there Zeealas", Agent Murphy protested.

"We don't need your protection Jim. Only your trust", Zuawalo replied, smiling as she leant towards Jim and planted a kiss ever so gently on his lips.

"Then it's settled", Selene told everyone, "The Girls will go with Leroy to that river and somehow, I'm not sure how, they will set the stage."

"Jim", Forkbraid caught his attention, then pointing to the map, "You drop them off here, on this side of the ridge, south of the river. Fly in low. Stay undetected. Once you've drop them off, come straight back here."

"Girls. I'll provide you with a portable communicator", Marcus advised them, explaining, "Hide it somewhere that's accessible to you and only you. When you want to come back, let us know."

"I'll pick you all up at the drop off point", Agent Murphy advised, "So after contacting us, make your way back there."

By the end of the next day, the camping equipment requested by the Pod Sister's had been acquired and was ready. After checking that they had everything they needed, Agent Murphy loaded their gear aboard one of the academy's Hummers. Forkbraid wanted them to hold off travelling to the river and the forest where the Trojans were harvesting their timber, until early the next morning. A plan was put in place to ensure they arrived at the drop off point without being detected.

Very early the next morning, Zuawalo, Zeealas, Leroy and Agent Murphy arrived at the academy's hanger and boarded their Hummer. Zuawalo had brought her pet ferret, Zigg along with her. The Girls were surprised to find Forkbraid was also there, sitting comfortably with a flight helmet in his hands.

"Are you coming too?", Zuawalo asked.

"No Zuawalo, I'm just along for the ride", Forkbraid replied.

Zeealas asked him, while curiously pointing to the helmet, "What is that?"

"It's the neural interlock control helmet from my Bat Wing", Forkbraid informed her.

"Okay" Zeealas replied, enquiring further, "What does it do?"

"I'm going to use it to fly my Bat Wing to the Trojan encampment and destroy all those lovely medieval siege engines they've been building", Forkbraid explained.

"You can do that from here?", Zeealas asked.

"Yes I can", Forkbraid replied, adding, "It will be just as if I'm sitting in the Bat Wing's cockpit."

"He's effectively going to fly it remotely, Zeealas", Leroy informed her.

"So that is how we will fly undetected", Zuawalo tweaked.

"Yes my love", Agent Murphy replied, explaining, "Apart from my extremely good low flying skills, FB here is going to keep the Trojans so distracted, that they won't have a clue we're there."

Zuawalo noticed something behind the cargo netting, at the back of the Hummer. It wasn't their gear, as their gear was placed further forward on the rear seats.

"What is that Jim?", Zuawalo enquired.

"That's my survival kit Zuawalo. When ever I take a Hummer out, I always have my survival kit on board", Agent Murphy explained, he did not elaborate any further beyond that.

"Time is of the essence Jim. We need to get moving", Forkbraid told Agent Murphy.

"In that case, everyone grab your seats and we'll depart", Agent Murphy told them all.

Jim flew low over the plains to the north, too low for the comfort of Leroy. The Pod Sisters did not seem to notice. Forkbraid was oblivious, he had his Bat Wing's NIC helmet on and was controlling it from his seat in the Hummer.

As their Hummer flew northwards and approached the valley where Jim was going to land and drop off Leroy and the Girls, Forkbraid's Bat Wing approached the enemies encampment along the coast to the west.

Forkbraid's Bat Wing flew in low, very fast and hit the Trojan encampment hard. All lasers and particle beams began blazing away. Pulse cannons began firing. Siege engines began to burst into flames, left and right. Pandemonium erupted in the encampment. The Trojans panicked and ducked for cover wherever they could. The Bat Wing passed the camp and then came back around for another run.

General Verne was furious, but controlled, "They're late this time aren't they Heller", he shouted.

"Yes General. We were expecting them days ago, going by their previous attacks", Captain Heller replied, noting, "Interestingly, they're only using the one ship this time, their Bat Wing Sir."

"What are they trying to tell us Captain?", the General replied, "What? That they only need one ship? That we're that defenceless, that they can strike us with impunity?"

"That could be the case General", Captain Heller answered him, "There isn't a whole lot that we can do Sir."

"That won't stop us Captain", the General stated boldly, "As long as they only target those siege engines, we should be okay", he then asked, "How many cannon do we have Heller?"

"Currently General, as of last count one hundred and thirty muzzle loaders", Captain Heller informed the General.

"Muzzle loaders?", General Verne replied, enquiring, "No breach loaders?"

"General Sir", Captain Heller began, then explained, "That's the best our men can make. We don't have the technology with us to make anything more advanced."

"Then it will have to do Captain, it will have to do", the General replied.

As if to prove the point, Forkbraid repeated his attack multiple times, flying his Bat Wing back and forth a further five times, strafing every siege engine in sight. When Forkbraid had finished, everything the Trojans had achieved was in flames and all their hard work was for naught. All their siege engines were burning fiercely.

Under covers and hidden, very close to the Trojan drop ships, were their forges for making armoury and cannon. These were unaffected. Forkbraid flew his Bat Wing back to the New Flinders Psychic Academy and once it was landed and parked, he took off his NIC helmet.

Agent Murphy sneakily flew their Hummer into the valley where the designated drop off point was. Finding a small, flat area of ground that was suitable, Agent Murphy landed the Hummer. They had arrived and they were completely undetected. They were now just south of the valley where the Pod Sisters wanted to camp and only had to climb over the ridge that separated the two valleys.

Forkbraid's little plan had multiple purposes. One, distract the enemy. Two, set the enemy back to square one once more and three, teach them a clear and simple lesson. They can be hit any time with impunity and it only takes one ship. If that wasn't enough to persuade the unwelcome *'guests'* to leave, then it was up to the Pod Sister's and Leroy to work their majik. Only they were not majikal folk. Forkbraid had wondered about the merits of Zuawalo's and Zeealas's plan and had added another twist of his own.

Zuawalo, Zeealas and Leroy quickly unloaded their gear and prepared for their trek. They quickly put on their utility belts and backpacks, then bid farewell to Agent Murphy and Forkbraid, before beginning their trek up to the ridge. They had their machetes attached to their belts and the fishing rods, bows, quivers, tactical shovel and folding saws attached to their backpacks. The girls had their sheath knives with them as well. Fully imprinted now, Zigg no longer needed his lead and he bounced along beside Zuawalo, occasionally climbing up and sitting on the top of her backpack.

Agent Murphy watched as the team trekked into the forest disappearing amongst the trees.

"Now FB?", Agent Murphy asked.

"I'd say so Jim", Forkbraid replied.

Agent Murphy grabbed his survival kit from out of the Hummer. He put on his tactical belt, which had attached to it a golok machete on the right and a kukri sword on the left. He put on his backup, which had a tactical folding shovel, folding saw, needle gun and pulse pistol strapped to it. Food, sleeping bag, ghillie suit and other equipment were inside the backpack. On top of the backpack was a one man swag.

"Jim. Watch them, but don't let them know you're there. Only interfere if it's absolutely necessary. We need to give them a chance to make this work", Forkbraid directed.

"Aye Captain", Agent Murphy replied with smile on his face, "I'll make sure they're safe and they won't have a clue that I'm even there."

Agent Murphy then started trekking in the same direction that the Pod Sisters and Leroy had gone. He hung well back, so as not to be noticed or seen. Following the trail that they had left behind. He was confident that they would not know he was even there.

Forkbraid then boarded the Hummer once more and lifted off. Forkbraid did not fly the Hummer back to the academy, instead he flew it further down the valley, where he located a suitable place to land. Forkbraid landed the Hummer under the canopy of some rather large trees. Once landed, Forkbraid took out a large camouflage net that had been stowed away and used it to cover the ship. He was confident their Hummer would not be seen.

Crossing over the ridge was slow going. First the trio had to reach the ridge. Next they had to climb the ridge. Fortunately, although the ridge was fairly high, it was also fairly broad and not so steep. That made the climbing somewhat easier, although none the less a difficult task.

Agent Murphy followed along behind. He had to stop and wait quite often, to avoid getting too close and being noticed. The Pod Sisters could move quite quickly, but Leroy was much slower and the trio travelled at Leroy's pace. The pace of their slowest member. By mid morning they had reached the top of the ridge. Leroy thanked God that Mars only had point three eight g's of gravity.

Zuawalo climbed a tree, atop the ridge and looked out over their chosen valley. Some distance to the west, a camp could be seen. This was the Trojan's logging camp. Further up the valley to the east was a suitable place for the trio to camp. There was a series of low waterfalls, with a deep pool at the base.

A small clearing was along the south side of the deep pool. The river that flowed out of it was fairly sluggish and many other deep pools could be seen further along its course. That was always a good sign for fishing. There would no doubt be clean, fresh water springs in the area as well. Probably several of them. The trio then started descending the ridge in the direction of the clearing at the base of the falls. Unbeknown to the trio, Agent Murphy was following quietly in their tracks.

Four hours later, the trio had reached the clearing. Agent Murphy who had been following their trail, deviated further to the east, climbing above and away from the trio. He then crossed over the waterfalls and climbed to the high ground on the north side of the river. He was looking for a site from which he could keep an eye on the trio and also a second site where he could set up camp, slightly further back from his chosen observation point.

He found a good viewing spot atop the northern ridge, which would be perfect to watch over the trio as it had the properties of a natural hide. Further back away from the ridge, he found his second spot. A large fallen tree, the trunk of which had good clearance from the ground.

Agent Murphy set up his swag under the large tree trunk, then placed his sleeping back inside it. He then took off his tactical belt and placed it beside his swag. Using his golok machete, Agent Murphy cut down some small saplings. He proceeded to strip the branches off of one side and placed the saplings upside-down, leaning against the fallen tree trunk, on both sides of it. Having done so, he then cut down some more saplings and placed them right side up, also leaning against the fallen tree trunk. Finally Agent Murphy used two saplings to seal off the gap at the lower end of the tree trunk.

The saplings effectively formed two thick layers of insulating material between his swag and the elements. They also provides an effective camouflage. Agent Murphy carved a small entrance at the base of the fallen tree trunk for access. He would camp here for the duration of his stay. Agent Murphy then put on his ghillie suit, picked up his needle gun, pulse pistol and a pair of field glasses, before heading back to his natural hide.

Zeealas was quick to climb a nearby tree at the edge of the small clearing and began peering into the river's deep pool.

Excitedly Zeealas told the others, "This water is very fishy! I can see many fish there", she said pointing to the water.

"Very good. Zeealas, catch us our dinner. I'll set up a temporary shelter", Zuawalo replied.

Zeealas took out her fishing rod and rigged the line. Next she took out her sheath knife and carved a stick into a rod holder. Quickly locating some grubs from under a rock Zeealas baited the line and cast it into the pool. Rod holder stuck into the ground, rod placed onto the holder, Zeealas sat back and waited, carefully watching her float.

Zuawalo cut some saplings and fashioned them into the posts she would need to turn into the frame of their shelter. Zuawalo stuck the posts deeply into the ground and tied another sapling pole across the top of them using strips of bark. These together formed a strong six foot high by ten foot long frame.

Having done so, Zuawalo then hung the tarpaulin across the frame and tied it down. It made a perfect tent. They now had shelter for the night. Zuawalo then unpacked their sleeping bags from their backpacks and laid them out under the tarpaulin. By the time Zuawalo was finished, Zeealas had already caught three fish, all good sized brown trout.

Zuawalo frowned at Leroy, "You are lazy man. You should be helping", she told him.

"I'm sorry Zuawalo. I have no camping skills at all", Leroy replied.

"Okay. You light the fire so Zeealas can cook the fish", Zuawalo instructed him.

Leroy looked dumbfounded.

Zuawalo looked a Leroy, "How can you not know how to make fire?", she was flabbergasted.

Leroy shrugged and replied, "I lived on a high tech space colony. We weren't taught to make fires. In a space colony, that would be dangerous."

It appeared Leroy was going to be next to useless, Zuawalo asked him, "Leroy, go get some dry wood. I show you how to make fire."

Leroy did as he was asked and gathered some dry wood. He wasn't sure what type of wood or what size, but remembered how Zuawalo had prepared their fires in the Kasei Swamps. He grabbed the nearest dried wood that matched what he remembered.

Zuawalo had put together a ring of river rocks in which to build their fire. Leroy took note and understood that was probably the first step. He placed the dried wood down unceremoniously near the ring of rocks and watched as Zuawalo separated out the wood by size into different groups.

"This is tinder", Zuawalo explained as if talking to a small child, as she held out some dry material from her tinder box, "You place it in the middle of the ring of stones."

Leroy nodded in understanding.

"These small sticks are kindling. You place the kindling like a pyramid over the tinder", Zuawalo explained, then taking out a ferrocerium rod and striker from her tinder box, "You do like this."

Zuawalo slid the striker quickly down the ferrocerium rod and sparks shot out from it into the tinder. The tinder caught fire immediately. Then the kindling quickly started to burn as well.

"Then when the fire is alight you slowly add the bigger sticks", Zuawalo stated, while adding some larger sticks onto the fire, "Then when it is burning good. You add logs! Simple yes!"

Zeealas laughed loudly, "This is so funny! You do not know anything. You like a baby!"

Leroy replied meekly, "I do apologise for my lack of knowledge", then added slightly sarcastically, "I'm glad you find my inadequacies hilarious."

Realising she had overstepped the mark, "I am sorry Leroy. It was just so funny to watch Zuawalo teaching you to make a fire."

After which Zeealas cooked her fish and they all sat down to eat. High above them on valley's northern ridge and unbeknown to the trio, Agent Murphy sat within in his natural hide eating from an MRE pack.

A bored Agent Murphy thought to himself as he read the packaging, *"Meal ready to eat. Well it's a meal. It is ready to eat and I am eating it. I can't say anything good about though. Damn, I wish I was eating some of Zeealas's fish!"*

Thus the trio and Agent Murphy settled in for the night.

19. Redemption

Morning came quickly in the valley as the Sun rose above the highlands to the east. Zuawalo and Zeealas were already awake tending the fire, which had gone out over night. Leroy yawned as he stepped out of the tent. Agent Murphy watched from above, having returned to his hide long before Sun up. It had been a very cold night and the trio shivered slightly, fortunately for them, it looked like it was going to be a glorious day.

"Lazy man awake, yes?", Zuawalo asked, half jokingly.

"Yes Zuawalo. The lazy man is awake", Leroy replied with a smile. All three chuckled.

Leroy then told the Sisters, "You know what. This valley has no name. So I'm going to name it *'Zuawalo's Valley'*."

Zuawalo smiled, then Zeealas protested jealously, "Where is my valley?"

Leroy thought for a quick second or two then replied, "Yesterday. The valley we were dropped off in. That is *'Zeealas's Valley'*", he told her.

Zeealas smiled and looked at Zuawalo, "We have valleys named after us!"

"I'll ask Forkbraid to make it official when we get back to the academy", Leroy told the Girls, "Then your names will appear on the maps."

Zigg the ferret made his little *'Dook Dook'* noises in agreement.

"It was a cold night last night", Zuawalo told Zeealas and Leroy.

"We need to make a proper shelter Sister", Zeealas agreed.

Zuawalo took off the tarpaulin that had been their tent for the night, folded it up and placed it to one side. The six by ten frame of their tent was now bare.

"Zeealas. Take Leroy and cut some saplings. Make sure they are the right height. I want to make many poles twelve feet long. They need to be very straight", Zuawalo asked, further instructing, "Do not cut them from the one place. Cut them from all over the place. It is better for the forest."

Zeealas grabbed her golok, "Leroy. Get your golok and follow me", she told him.

Zeealas showed Leroy which trees to cut, where to cut them from and how to cut them. Slowly they felled the required saplings and one by one they dragged them back to their camp in the clearing. They were lucky in a way, the Martian gravity was only thirty eight percent of the Earth's. This meant that the trees on Mars were able to grow much taller and narrower as a result. The local pine trees in the forest grew very tall and straight. There were also saplings in a great abundance.

Zuawalo used her golok to cut the branches off the saplings and then docked their length to the required twelve foot lengths. One by one, Zuawalo was building up an impressive pile of sapling poles. The branches that were cut off were placed in a pile to one side.

When Zuawalo had enough poles to start work, she dragged them into position, placing the poles onto the frame one at a time. Alternating the thick ends and thin ends of the poles, so as to minimise any gaps. The poles overhung the front of the frame by about half a foot. Slowly a lean-to started to take shape, with a ten foot by ten foot floor space.

Agent Murphy had been watching from his hide, at its vantage point high up on the northern ridge. He hadn't realised how skilled his women were, until he saw how efficiently they built their shelter. With Zeealas and Leroy gathering the saplings and Zuawalo processing them and building the lean-to. He was certain their little project would be finished the same day they'd started. He was truly impressed at how they worked together as a team. Especially with how they managed Leroy McGuvan, who Agent Murphy considered to be a knob head, with no bush skills whatsoever.

After Zuawalo had finished the roof of the lean-to, she dug trenches along its sides, from the back of the lean-to to the front posts using her tactical shovel. Zuawalo then started to fashion the saplings into shorter poles, matching the variable height of the sides of the lean-to. Each of the poles was carefully matched for thickness, notched, then stuck into ground and pressed into place. Zuawalo worked on both sides of the lean-to at the same time. Zuawalo was extremely efficient.

Agent Murphy was suitably impressed by her work. Each time Leroy brought a sapling into their camp site, he looked carefully at what Zuawalo was doing. He too was suitably impressed by her work. When Zuawalo had finished assembling both sides, she back filled the tench with soil and tamped it down to ensure the posts would stay in place.

Having built the sides of the lean-to, Zuawalo took a short break with the others, before moving onto the front of the lean-to. The procedure was the same, only in this case the sapling poles were roughly all the same height. Zuawalo methodically built the front of their lean-to, while Zeealas and Leroy gathered more saplings. Zuawalo left an opening roughly two and half feet wide as a doorway, on the right side of the front of the lean-to.

It was well past midday by the time the trio had the structure of the lean-to completed and the trio took another well deserved break to eat some left over fish and some nuts that Zeealas had gathered whilst harvesting saplings.

After eating Zeealas and Leroy went back into the forest. This time Zeealas was looking for a pair of larger trees. Once the desired trees were located, Zeealas cut them down and processed them both on the spot, asking Leroy to carry the resulting logs back to Zuawalo.

Zuawalo trimmed the lengths of the logs to the desired lengths and placed them along the inside walls of their lean-to. These were placed in positions to help hold the front and side walls in place. Once done, Zuawalo used willow bark strips that she had gathered while waiting for Leroy to bring the logs, to lash the roofing poles in place, making the structure stronger.

Zigg the ferret had been bored with all this industrious activity and spent most of his time alternating between sleeping on the folded tarpaulin and digging for grubs near the rocks to eat. Zuawalo sat down by the camp fire and Zigg came up to her looking for attention. Zuawalo patted Zigg and stroked his back while waiting for Zeealas and Leroy to return.

Once Zeealas and Leroy had returned, Zuawalo asked Zeealas to help her with the Tarpaulin. Between them, they folded the Tarpaulin in two and pulled it up over the roof of the lean-to, so that it stretched from the base at the back and slightly overhung the front. Zuawalo then folded the tarpaulin at the sides of the lean-to and pinned it down with a log on each side. Having done that, Zuawalo placed a final log across the front of the lean-to to hold the front wall in place.

"How does it look?" Zuawalo asked.

"It looks pretty good", Leroy replied.

Zeealas smiled, "We are not yet finished. Not yet."

"Really?", Leroy was surprised, "What's left to do?"

"Get your shovel Leroy", Zeealas replied, informing him, "We have to cover the tarp with sod."

And they did so as industriously as they had built the structure. It took a couple of more hours, but together Zeealas and Leroy managed to cover the tarpaulin with sod. Along the sides and along the back at the base, before completely covering the roof. The entire structure, except for the sides and front were now covered with a thick layer of soil and grass.

While Zeealas and Leroy were performing that task, Zuawalo performed the final processing of the left over branches. Each larger branch was cut to useful lengths to be used as fire wood. The smaller branches were stripped of leaves and chopped up to be used as kindling. Soon at the font of the lean-to there were two piles, firewood and kindling. The leaves themselves were piled up inside the lean-to itself and later spread out evenly across the floor.

Leroy stuck his head inside the lean-to and looked around. Apart from the gaps at the front, it was actually well sealed.

"Zuawalo. It actually smells quite nice inside!", he exclaimed.

"Yes. The leaves do that. They also make the floor much softer", Zuawalo replied.

Zeealas smiled, "We are still not yet finished."

Leroy was truly surprised, "Really?"

"Yes. Tomorrow we will fill in all the gaps in the front with mud", Zeealas informed him.

Leroy replied, "Oh, yes of course", realising that they needed to block any cold breezes.

"And we need a door", Zuawalo added, "But now, we need to catch some more fish."

Zeealas passed Zuawalo a fishing rod and told her while smiling, "Your turn Sister."

Zuawalo accepted the fishing rod and went off to catch some more fish for their dinner, with Zigg the ferret following obediently along behind her, 'Dook Dooking', as he followed.

The next morning when they awoke, they were far more refreshed. Their lean-to had not been as cold as their tarpaulin tent had been on the previous night. Only the door and the gaps in the front let in cold drafts, but otherwise they slept quite well. Agent Murphy was back in his hide on the northern ridge and watching over them once more. He of course had insulated his shelter with saplings the day he had arrived and slept quite well. Although he did not much like his, meals ready to eat packages. They were bland and somewhat unappealing.

The trio ate some left over fish for their breakfast and discussed what was on the days agenda.

"I will go further down stream. Maybe I'll find something to hunt or maybe I'll catch more fish", Zuawalo told the others.

"Okay. I'll take Leroy and look for some mud", Zeealas replied, adding, "Then we can seal the gaps in our front wall."

"What are we going to use for a door?", Leroy asked.

"There are some very big trees in this forest", Zuawalo replied, explaining, "We can carve off a large sheet of bark. We flatten it, then carve it and that will be our door."

"We can do that after the front wall is sealed Sister", Zeealas replied, adding, "When you come back with the food, it will all be done."

Zuawalo grabbed her fishing rod, bow and quiver, then headed down stream to hunt and fish, with Zigg the ferret again following obediently behind. Zeealas and Leroy went in search of mud.

It was long after midday and Zuawalo was sitting under the branches of an oak tree watching her float. The day was warm, but not overly so and the shade the oak tree provided was welcome. The fishing had started off very slow with nothing biting at all till well after eleven o'clock. Zuawalo's ferret Zigg was brilliant at finding grubs to be used as bait. Now six good sized trout were hanging from a branch that Zuawalo had cut off a tree and carved into a handy carry pole for her fish.

A large flying object flew into view and landed in the deep pool of water, across and down stream from where Zuawalo was sitting. It was a duck and it had not seen her. Quickly, but quietly Zuawalo lifter her bow, then just as quickly nocked an arrow that she had grabbed from her quiver.

Zuawalo's bow arm came up, her eye's locked onto the duck and Zuawalo loosed the arrow. The arrow flew fast and silently to its target, striking it straight through the duck's upper chest just below its neck. Zuawalo slowly pulled the fine line that was attached to the arrow's shaft and drew the duck towards her. It was then that Zuawalo caught something out of the corner of her left eye. Something much further down stream and hidden amongst the bushes. Zuawalo made no sudden movements and continued drawing the duck towards here.

Once the duck was in her hands, Zuawalo pulled out the arrow, cleaned it and returned it to her quiver. Zuawalo hung the duck from her carry pole and stood up. Quickly she pack away her fishing rod, then slung her bag, bow and quiver over her shoulders. The carry pole was heavy with the fish and the duck. Zuawalo held the pole over right shoulder and began the short trek back upstream to their camp.

"Come Zigg. We go home now", Zuawalo called to her ferret.

Zigg the ferret followed Zuawalo back to their camp site.

Back at their camp site, Zuawalo placed the carry pole down on the grass near the camp fire.

Zeealas and Leroy had been fixing a bark door, that they had made to their lean-to and turned around when they heard Zuawalo approach.

Zeealas was excited, "Six fish and a duck. We eat well tonight!", she shouted.

Zuawalo approached the camp fire and stirred the coals, then added a few smaller branches. She kept her back to the river.

Leroy noticed Zuawalo was quiet and squatted down beside her and whispered, "What's up Zuawalo?"

Zuawalo put her finger to her lips to signal to Leroy to be quiet.

Zeealas knelt down by the fire and stuck two forked sticks into the ground, one on each side of the fire, then whispered, "Zuawalo, there are two men watching us."

"I know Zeealas", Zuawalo whispered in return, "They followed me here from downstream. They are trying not to be seen."

"They are not very good at it Sister", Zeealas whispered back.

"I know Sister. Pretend they are not there. We go about our business. Zeealas, you prepare the fish for smoking, I will prepare the duck. Leroy you finish the door", Zuawalo whispered instructions, adding, "We ignore them. Then we wait."

And that is exactly what they did.

Agent Murphy was in his hide on the northern ridge, he too had noticed the Trojan scouts watching from the bushes. He thought they were amateurish at best, but none the less a threat. He put down his field glasses, took out his telescopic sight and mounted it to his needle gun. From now on Agent Murphy would be watching the trio through the sites of his gun. He could eliminate both of the Trojan scouts in a heart beat if he needed to.

Private Kelso saw her first and quickly motioned to his partner, Private Mitchel to drop down.

"Mitchel. Upstream on the other side of the river", Kelso whispered, adding, "Under that tree."

Mitchel looked, "I see her. What's a woman doing all the way out here?", he whispered.

"I don't know, but she's there. It's definitely not a mirage", Kelso whispered in reply.

"It looks like she's fishing", Mitchel whispered.

"Yeah. It looks like it", Kelso whispered back.

It was then that a duck flew into view and landed in the river's deep pool across from the woman. As they watched the dark skinned woman, she drew a bow, loaded an arrow to it, then stood up and nailed the duck cleanly through its neck. The whole action took mere seconds.

"Damn! That was bloody quick!", Kelso told Mitchel in a hushed tone.

"We'd better stay hidden. This bitch has skills. She could be a threat", Mitchel whispered back.

As they watched, the woman slowly retrieved the duck stood up and packed up her gear before walking upstream along the river bank.

"What's that thing following her?", Mitchel whispered.

"I have no idea" Kelso whispered back, "Some kind of animal. Maybe a pet?"

"We should follow her", Mitchel suggested, "Find out where she came from."

"Good idea", Kelso agreed.

So the two Trojan scouts had carefully followed Zuawalo upstream. Zuawalo on the south side of the river, with the two scouts following on the north side.

Following Zuawalo upstream, the Trojan scouts eventually came within site of the clearing where the trio had set up their camp. They quickly hid themselves in some bushes to avoid being seen. Across the river they could see the woman they had followed and her companions, another tall, dark woman and a man.

"Mitchel. It looks like their just hunting and fishing", Kelso suggested, adding, "Their food is probably better than ours."

This was confirmed when Zeealas made her remarks about the fish and the duck that Zuawalo had brought into the camp, shouting, *'we eat well tonight'*.

"Their lean-to looks like it's semi-permanent. They could be here for a while", Mitchel replied.

"There aren't suppose to be any locals in this region at all", Kelso stated.

"Yeah. I know, but we know so little about Mars. Our information could be out of date", Mitchel agreed, adding, "Whatever they're doing, the Captains are gong to want to know about them."

"True. If they're locals. They may have information we can use", Kelso replied.

The two Trojan scouts backed away from the river and started working their way back downstream to the Trojan's logging camp. Locals might have information their people could use and their Captains could well be interested in them.

Captains Barker and Thompson were managing the troops that were logging in the forest, west of their landing zone and encampment. They weren't surprised when Privates Kelso and Mitchel came into their command tent to make a report. They were surprised to here their report was not the usual report of nothing in the vicinity. The scouts had actually come across something that was quite interesting.

"Captains Sir! We have come across some locals up river from here. Up by the falls Sir", Private Kelso informed the Captains after saluting.

"Locals! There aren't suppose to be any locals in these parts", Captain Barker replied.

Private Mitchel elaborated, "Captain Sir. Three locals Sir. Two woman and a man."

"And what were these locals doing Mitchel?", Captain Thompson enquired.

"Sir. They were camping, hunting and fishing Sir", Private Mitchel informed him.

"Camping, hunting and fishing?", Captain Thompson repeated questioningly.

"Yes Sir! Camping hunting and fishing Sir", Private Mitchel confirmed.

Private Kelso added, "Captain Sir. Their shelter looked to be semi-permanent Sir."

Captain Thompson looked to Captain Barker, "Locals? Hunting and fishing? A semi-permanent shelter? What's your take Captain?"

Captain Barker replied, "We don't really know much about this region or for that matter Mars in general. There could very well be local people living in the forest. A semi-permanent shelter would indicate a nomadic life style. Hunting and fishing would fit in with that. What-ever the case Gary, they will have local knowledge. Information that could be useful."

"That is what I was thinking John", Captain Thompson replied, then asked, "Kelso, these locals, are they hostile?"

"Captain Sir. Not that we noticed. Highly skilled though. We thought it prudent, not to approach them", Private Kelso informed the Captains.

"How do you feel about a trip up river John?", Captain Thompson asked.

"I was just thinking the same thing Gary. A trip up river sounds like a great idea", Captain Barker replied, then turning to the privates, "Privates. It looks like you two will be leading us up the river. Make preparations. We'll be leaving in thirty minutes."

Privates Mitchel and Kelso left the command tent to prepare for the Captains trip up river.

Later that day, the two Privates had led Captains Barker and Thompson up the river to the clearing below the low falls where Zuawalo, Zeealas and Leroy were camped. As they approached the clearing, Captain Barker ordered the

Privates to sling their weapons. The two Privates looked at each other. The order had been a reflex, as the Trojan Army effectively had no modern weapons. Kelso and Mitchel, only had recently made knives and these were already in their scabbards.

As they approached the two Captains raised their hands to show they were unarmed, the two Privates did like wise. A strange group of people were in the clearing before them, two tall dark women and a smaller white man, with some kind of animal, a pet perhaps.

"Ahoy!", Captain Thompson shouted out, adding, "We come in peace."

The trio turned to face the Trojans. Zuawalo reached for her bow, nocked an arrow to it, but held the bow by her side. Zeealas was just as quick and had done the same.

Agent Murphy in his hide on the ridge was watching though the scope of his needle gun. If things went south, he could take the Trojans down in seconds.

Captain Barker whispered to Captain Thompson, "Only the woman are brandishing weapons."

Captain Thompson whispered back, "A matriarchal society perhaps. Maybe he's their slave?"

Slavery was common to both Jovian and Trojan society in general.

"Who are you? What do you want?", Zuawalo demanded.

"Please! Do not be alarmed. We are merely strangers in a strange land. We simply wish to ask you some questions", Captain Thompson told the trio.

"You may ask", Zuawalo answered, but still holding her bow at the ready.

Private Kelso noted, whispering, "Captains Sirs. That one is deadly with that bow."

"Looks like this one is in charge then", Captain Barker whispered to Captain Thompson.

Captain Thompson nodded in agreement.

"Is this your home?", Captain Barker asked.

"It is our camp", Zuawalo replied.

"And what do you do here?" Captain Barker enquired.

"We hunt. We fish. We move on", Zuawalo told them.

Captain Barker whispered to Captain Thompson, "Just as I thought. Nomadic."

Captain Thompson asked curiously, "What is that creature?", pointing to Zigg.

Zuawalo replied, "That is Zigg. He is my pole cat."

The word 'pole cat' ran through their minds. Neither of the Captains had seen a pole cat before. No Trojan had.

Captain Thompson explained, "We are strangers here. We only wish to harvest some timber from the forest", then asked, "Do you know these lands well?"

"We know these lands, well enough for our needs", Zeealas replied to the Captain, her bow still at the ready. Her statement was true in that they knew how to survive in the wilderness.

"Do you know the fortress to the south?", Captain Thompson enquired.

Both Zuawalo and Zeealas looked at each other, giving themselves bewildered looks. Would it work, would their body language give them away.

Zuawalo replied adamantly, "There is no fortress to the south!"

"We scanned the fortress during our arrival, from space. Perhaps you don't know of it", Captain Barker explained to them, adding, "It looks very much like a big castle. All made of stone."

"Ah", Zeealas began to laugh, then answered slowly, "You mean the school."

Both of the Captains and the two Privates were taken aback.

"School?", both Captains queried at the same time.

The Pod Sisters gave each other quizzical looks before Zuawalo replied, "Yes. The school!"

Technically the New Flinders Psychic Academy was in fact a school.

"Yes. The school", Zeealas confirmed, then added, "It is not yet open. When it is, it will have children from all over Mars there."

"Children!", Captain Barker exclaimed, this was cause for alarm.

"Yes Children", Zuawalo confirmed, informing them, "It is a boarding school. It will have children from ages seven to twenty one. When it is open of course."

Everything they told them was actually true.

"Then why does it look like a castle, a fortress?", Captain Thompson asked.

"Maybe you should ask the architects", Zeealas replied, "You know. The ones who designed it."

"Okay. Then why is that *'school'* surrounded by defensive rings of gun batteries?", Captain Barker asked.

"The school was attacked by very, very bad men. Pirates!", Zuawalo replied, "The same very, very bad men that attacked the big colony, further to the south."

Zeealas added, "Many, many people were killed! It was a very, very sad day."

Zuawalo went on to explain, "The Captain of a space ship from L5. He built those defences, so that it will never happen again. He gave them some small ships and some pilots as well."

Captain Barker queried, "Pirates?"

"Yes. Pirates!", Zeealas replied, adding, "The Pirates are all dead now", in a matter-of-fact way.

Both of the Captains were confused. This was not what they had been told. This is not what they understood the situation to be. There was certainly no mention of Pirates at all.

The two privates who had been listening to the conversion were equally confused.

Captain Thompson changed tack, "You there", he pointed to Leroy, "Who might you be?", he asked as Leroy was obviously different.

Leroy replied, "I'm Leroy. Leroy McGuvan. I'm from L5. Thank you for asking. And these two are Zuawalo and Zeealas by the way. It was rude of you not to ask."

Captain Thompson who was slightly taken aback, then replied, "I do apologise. I am Captain Thompson, this is Captain Barker and here we have Privates Kelso and Mitchel."

Captain Barker then clicked his fingers three times, pointed to Leroy, interjecting,"You're the Leroy McGuvan! You're the martyr!"

Captain Thompson looked to Captain Barker questioningly.

Captain Barker replied to the look, "Don't you remember Gary? The news feeds back home. This is the Leroy McGuvan. The Prophet's right hand man. He fought the rear guard action that allowed the Prophet to escape from New Tortuga. He's a hero. He's the Martyr!"

Captain Thompson suddenly tweaked, "The Martyr!", then asked the obvious, "How are you still alive McGuvan?"

"Yes. I was the Prophet's right hand man and yes, I fought in the rear guard action at New Tortuga", Leroy admitted, then stating, "I survived and I was duly executed at the end of the battle!"

"Executed? You are still alive", Captain Thompson noted.

Zuawalo answered, "He was cast into the deep, cold sea. He would have drowned. I saved him from drowning, from certain death."

"You saved him?", Captain Barker enquired.

"Yes. While I was fishing for squid. He is now my responsibility", Zuawalo explained.

Leroy was considered a hero by the people of the Jovian System, including those living in the Trojan Asteroid fields, sixty degrees ahead and behind Jupiter in its orbit.

Captain Thompson stepped forward and held out his hand. Leroy held out his hand and they both shook hands. An almost unnoticeable golden spark jumped from Leroy's hand to Captain Thompson's as they shook hands. Only Zeealas noticed it.

Captain Barker then also stepped forward to shake Leroy's hand. Zeealas nudged Zuawalo and as Leroy shook Captain Barkers hand. Zuawalo also noticed the almost imperceptible golden spark jump from Leroy's hand to Captain Barker's.

Both of the Privates also reach put their hands and Leroy shook their hands in turn. Again the Pod Sisters noticed the same golden spark jump from Leroy's hand to the Private's. It appeared to the two Sisters, that the stage was being set, but not in the way they had thought.

It was at that point, that Captain Thompson made the trio an offer, "Would you like to come back to our camp? Say on the morrow, after noon for luncheon."

Zuawalo knew this could be a risk, but also knew it was necessary. It was a calculated risk.

"Yes. We will come to luncheon tomorrow at your camp", Zuawalo agreed.

Leroy had not expect this turn of events. Zeealas was not surprised and went along with it.

"Good. Good. Our camps is downstream from here, only about forty five minutes walk, an hour at most. You'll be able to find it quite easily", Captain Thompson informed them.

"Okay then. We'll see you all on the morrow", Captain Barker agreed.

At that, the two Captains and two Privates bid good bye and headed back to their logging camp.

As they trekked their way back to their camp, the two Captains discussed the information they had gathered.

"I was not expecting this! Pirates?", Thompson told Barker questioningly.

"Neither was I. Are we really going to attack a school?", Barker replied almost in a hushed tone.

"I have no idea. It really doesn't seem right, does it?", Thompson replied questioningly.

"This can't be right. Something's amiss. When we get back, I'm calling a few of our comrades to join us for the morrows luncheon", Barker decided.

"Only those we can trust John. Only those we can trust", Thompson agreed with a stipulation.

"Absolutely", Captain Barker agreed.

The trio in the clearing and Agent Murphy in his hide all watched the delegation of Trojans leave their campsite, heading back to their logging camp.

Agent Murphy was relieved that everything had gone well. He had no need to take the Trojan's lives. That was a bonus to Agent Murphy.

Zeealas turned to Leroy McGuvan, "Your redemption has begun Leroy."

"Yes Leroy", Zuawalo agreed, "Your redemption has begun."

Leroy had no idea what the Girls were talking about. Then again, he had not noticed the almost imperceptible golden sparks.

20. Trojan Talks

Early the next morning Zeealas went hunting. She to was looking to bag a nice big juicy duck. Zeealas didn't find any ducks on this occasion, she was however still lucky and bagged a good sized bush turkey instead. Zeealas was ecstatic.

By the time Zeealas had come back with her turkey, Zuawalo and Leroy had finished their breakfast. Zuawalo had made sure there was plenty of fish left over for Zeealas. Agent Murphy was also back, hidden in his blind watching carefully over the trio. His MRE packs were a poor substitute for real food and he knew it.

With their shelter built, they all had more time to hunt, fish and do other things. Leroy's redemption was moving much faster than they had anticipated. They had expected to be there for at least a week before meeting the Trojans.

The Pod Sisters wondered how long they would have at their camping site. They truly enjoyed camping and here they were in their element. They had considered this and they had both decided, that this camp site would not be abandoned. They would come back, to camp here periodically in the future. The shelter they had built, with proper maintenance could last for many years.

Zeealas processed the turkey, then stuck a stick through it, before placing it above the fire on the forked sticks to cook. Slowly over the next few hours it would be turned until properly roasted.

"We take this with us. We share it with them", Zeealas told her Sister.

"Yes", Zuawalo agreed, "They invited us to lunch. We should bring something to eat as well."

By eleven o'clock the turkey was cooked and the trio prepared to leave camp. Zuawalo put their smoked trout and left over duck from the previous day into a bag. Then tied length of rope around the bag and hung it from a tree. Under shade and high enough up that animals could not reach it. As they were leaving camp for several hours, it was the best way to keep their food safe.

Zeealas carefully placed the roasted turkey into a bag and slung it from a stick, which she promptly hung over her shoulder. Then the trio wearing their utility belts, with their goloks and the Girls carrying there bows and quivers, left the clearing on their way to the Trojan logging camp. In theory they would be there well before midday.

Agent Murphy, watching from his hiding spot was aghast, *"What the fuck! Where do they think they're going?"*, he thought to himself.

Quickly Agent Murphy rushed back to his hidden camp, grabbed some more gear and then rushed back again to follow the trio down river. Sticking to the ridge line he would not be seen.

While the trio followed by Agent Murphy was making their way to the Trojan's logging camp, a meeting of the Trojan Captains was taking place in their command tent. Along with Captains Barker and Thompson were Captains Mackerel, Poulsen, Turner and Harkness. Captain Carlson, the Fleet Captain was also present. All the Captains were equals, except the Fleet Captain, who was the first among equals.

Captain Carlson, having heard the reports from Captains Barker and Thompson remarked, "Gentlemen, this new information pretty much changes everything. Are we sure of its veracity?"

"It seems to be legit Captain", Captain Thompson replied.

"All this talk about attacking schools and Pirates. It is disturbing", Captain Mackerel conveyed.

"Yes. Very disturbing", Captain Carlson agreed.

"Whatever the case Captain, they did attack us. We can't let that slide", Captain Poulsen stated.

"You forget why we came here Captain", Captain Carlson replied, reminding him, "We are an attacking force. We came here to destroy them. To wipe them out. We are the invaders!"

"Even so Captain. Over a thousand dead!", Captain Poulsen pushed back.

"It could have been much worse Poulsen!", Captain Carlson replied loudly, "Remember what happened to our missiles. Our first strike!"

Captain Poulsen replied softly, "They were all destroyed en-route."

"Don't you think, these people, who could take down out first strike, could easily have taken us out en-route as well?", Captain Carlson asked Poulsen a rhetorical question, then he answered it himself, "They didn't. They chose not to! They could have killed us all in space."

"More importantly", Captain Turner interjected, "Look at how they attacked us after we landed."

"That's right Turner. They hit our weapons systems twice that very first day. The first time to slow us down and delay us. The second time to eliminated all of our weapons systems. What's the one thing they actually avoided striking?", Captain Carlson replied and then asked.

"They left our drop ships alone", Captain Poulsen answered.

"Exactly my point", Captain Carlson replied, adding, "And every time we build those medieval siege engines, what do they do?"

"They take out the siege engines Captain, but they leave the drop ships alone", Captain Poulsen replied, speculating, "They actually just want us to leave. Why else would they do that?"

"And again, that's my point. They've destroyed our siege engines five times now. The last time with a single Bat Wing. They're showing us, that they can destroy whatever weapons we build and that we can do nothing about it. Gentlemen, they have a weapon that took away all of our weapons systems that very first day. They could have easily slaughtered us all to a man! Yet they did not!"

"It sounds to me like they're trying to minimise casualties Captain", Captain Barker stated.

Captain Carlson pointed his index finger at Captain Barker, "Yes! They don't want to kill us. They just want us to leave."

"Captains. Perhaps we'll have a better understanding after luncheon", Captain Mackerel told them.

It was close to midday and Agent Murphy was horrified to see the Trojan's logging camp come into view. Having left the river bank game trail, the trio he was watching were making a beeline straight to it, across open ground that had been recently logged. There were easily, several hundred Trojans in the logging camp and Agent Murphy was not happy with the situation. He quickly travelled down the ridge and crossed the river, looking for a suitable position from which he could keep an eye over his charges.

There was still some forest remaining close to the river and Agent Murphy found some bushes under which to stash some of his gear. He then carefully moved as close as he could to the logging camp and found a suitably large tree. Agent Murphy climbed the tree and positioned himself on some branches in the canopy, the leaves of which camouflaged him from below and on nearly every side. From this position he could see out through the foliage to the logging camp. It was too far off for his needle gun to be useful, so he hung it from a branch and switched to his field glasses.

As the trio approached the logging camp, Trojans came out to meet them. Privates Mitchel and Kelso has been busy talking and pretty much the whole camp knew that the *"Martyr"* was coming. A large group of Trojans had formed two lines leading to the main command tent. Nearly every Trojan in the logging camp was present. As they approached, Zuawalo quickly reached down for Zigg and put him in his harness. From then on, Zigg was kept on a very short lead.

Leroy McGuvan was concerned for the Girls, both of whom had prepared their bows and drawn their sheaf knives, he bellowed out loudly, "If you approach these Girls, you do so at you own risk! They will defend themselves! Give them plenty of room!"

Even at Agent Murphy's distant viewing point, Leroy's words carried across on the breeze.

Agent Murphy muttered under his breath, *"Thank you Leroy, but that does not absolve you from responsibility for my Girls safety."*

As Leroy walked between the two lines of Trojans, the men, considering Leroy some kind of *'mythic hero'*, reached out to shake his hand. Leroy shook their hands as much as he could. Those who he couldn't, merely touched his hand or forearm as Leroy walked by. The Pod Sisters watched as imperceptible golden sparks, skipped from Leroy to every Trojan that touched him.

Zeealas spoke softly, "Zuawalo, the redemption."

As the Girls approached, the men gave them a wide birth. Leroy's warning had been loud and clear. The Girls were also armed and the Trojans were wary of them. None of them knew what to make of Zigg, his species was completely unknown to them. By the time the trio had approached the command tent, nearly every enlisted man in the camp had been exposed to Leroy's redemption. The two lines of men had been long, many hundreds of Trojan men had been exposed.

Captains Barker and Thompson stood outside the command tent and welcomed the trio.

"Welcome Leroy, welcome Zuawalo and Zeealas", Captain Thompson greeted them, adding, "Did I get your names right Girls?"

Both Girls nodded and replied, "Yes."

"Please come in", Captain Barker requested.

The Girls entered the command tent and looked around. Apart from Captains Barker and Thompson were six other men.

Captain Barker introduced the other Trojans, "These are Captains Carlson, Mackerel, Poulsen, Turner, Harkness", then to the Captains he introduced, "Gentlemen, this is Leroy McGuvan, Zuawalo and Zeealas."

No-one introduced the sixth man. He was apparently only there to serve and wore the appropriate uniform.

Straight away the other Captains came forward to shake Leroy's hand. He was apparently a *'mythic hero'* amongst the officers as well. The imperceptible golden sparks jumped from Leroy to each of them. Nobody noticed except Zuawalo and Zeealas.

Zeealas removed the bag from her pole and placed it on the table that was sitting in the middle of the tent. She then opened the bag, took out the turkey and unwrapped it.

"We bring roast turkey to lunch. It is not hot. It will still taste very good", Zeealas told them.

Captain Carlson, motioned to the waiter, "Martins. Have this roast turkey heated and carved."

Private Martins replied, "Yes Captain", then he picked up the turkey and left the tent to have it prepared. Zeealas smiled, roast turkey was always best server hot.

Zuawalo and Zeealas felt more at ease. They both removed their utility belts with their goloks attached and placed them against the tents walls, as did Leroy. The Girls then laid their bows and quivers down beside their belts. The trio then sat down at the three seats that were offered to them and Zuawalo allowed Zigg to sit on her lap.

Captain Carlson introduced himself, "I'm Fleet Captain Carlson. You know Mr McGuvan, we've spent most of the morning discussing the information you guys provided Captains Barker and Thompson yesterday. I must say it is very interesting."

"Captain. My name is Leroy", he replied.

Zuawalo stepped in, "We eat first. We talk later."

"That's actually a good idea Zuawalo", Leroy agreed, "We only had a light breakfast and it was quite a walk."

"Yes. Let's eat first, then talk later", Captain Carlson agreed.

The food provided for their lunch was basically ships rations and not terribly tasty. If anything, the word bland came to mind. No doubt, after many months on board the troop transports, the Captains were use to eating ships rations. Leroy and the Pod Sisters however, picked at it and politely ate as much as they could stomach. At least until the hot roast turkey was served. Everyone at the table found that to be delicious. It had been months since the Trojans had had real food.

Captain Mackerel, who had seen Zeealas unwrap the turkey and actually remembered her name asked, "Zeealas, this tastes incredible. How did you cook it?"

"First I have to hunt it. Then I process the dead bird and I cook it over an open fire", Zeealas replied, adding, "I picked wild herbs while I was hunting to add flavour to it."

"Perhaps we should be asking you to teach our men to hunt and fish", Captain Mackerel replied.

Captain Barker agreed, "Yes. This is certainly much better than our ships fare."

Everyone around the table was in agreement with the taste of the roast turkey.

After eating, Captain Carlson began his discussion once more, "As I was saying earlier Leroy. The information we were discussing was incredibly interesting. If these stories are true, it changes everything for us, our very purpose in being here. Literally everything."

Leroy replied, "All of it is true Captain. Every word of it."

"So the 'Castle' to the south of here is really a school and it was attacked by Pirates?", Captain Carlson enquired seeking confirmation.

"I was the Prophet's right hand man Captain. I was the second in command. I am as culpable for the atrocities committed in the Prophet's name as he is", Leroy told the Captain honestly.

"Atrocities?", Captain Poulsen repeated as a question.

"Yes. Atrocities!", Leroy answered emphatically.

Zeealas stepped in and added, "Leroy was once a very bad man. He is no longer that man!"

The Captains sitting around the table were in quite a bit of a shock. Their understanding was that the Prophet was fighting a war of resistance against demons He was a freedom fighter.

"Leroy, please understand, that is not the information we were given. We were told something completely different", Captain Thompson tried to explain, "What you're telling us, is radically different. It changes everything. Literally, our entire world view."

Leroy shook his head and began, "I don't know how else to tell you Captain. The Prophet ordered an attack on a school, back on the Earth. An attack that literally killed hundreds, including scores of innocent young children. At L5, he gave the orders that resulted in the deaths of over three thousand innocent people. Here on Mars, he hired Pirates to do his bidding and used those same Pirates to shoot down a Heavy Lift Transport vehicle killing everyone onboard. Then he ordered the attacks on the Elysium Colony and that school south of here. On Mars alone there must be nearly a thousand dead! Probably many more. And as the Prophet's second in command, I am as responsible for those deaths, as he is!"

Zuawalo stepped in, "Leroy! You are no longer that very bad man!"

All of the Captains were silent, this was a shock for all of them. Leroy's 'redemption', that golden spark of light, the light of troth was helping them all understand the truth of the matter.

Captain Turner asked, "All those dead at L5, weren't they martyrs killed by the corrupt demon government in power at L5?"

"No Captain! They were not!", Leroy replied emphatically, informing him further, "They were simply ordinary people. Ordinary folk going about their business and they were all murdered by the Prophet's extremists. Terrorists Gentleman! Terrorists!"

Captain Harkness asked, "Then what about the demons then?"

"Captains!", Leroy began as he stood up and placed his hands on the table,

"I have been to that Academy, that school. I have been to the Elysium Colony. I was at New Tortuga. I was at L5. I was the Prophet's right hand man. I tell you now. There are no demons. There never were any demons. They are all in the Prophet's head! That man is an insane psychopath!"

All of the Captains at the table were gob smacked, half of them leant back into their chairs in shock. The light of troth was releasing them from years of lies, which unravelled within them.

Captain Harkness enquired, "And on the Earth? Surely, there are demons there?"

"Captain. The last time I was on the Earth, I was a wee small child, but you know what. I know the Prophet very well indeed and I am one hundred percent certain, that there are no demons on the Earth either", Leroy replied.

"Carlson!", Captain Barker broke the silence, "What in the blazes are we doing here?"

Captain Poulsen chimed in with, "Are we really going to attack that school?"

Zuawalo became angry, "What do you mean? Attack that school?", she to stood up and put her hands on the table, "You people be crazy!"

Captain Carlson stood up, "Please calm down Zuawalo. Please take your seats. We are not going to attack anything. Certainly not a school."

Leroy and Zuawalo both sat back down. Zigg who had jumped onto the table when Zuawalo stood up, sat back down on Zuawalo's lap once more, but not before grabbing a good sized chunk of turkey meat of off Zuawalo's plate.

A corporal came into the tent. He spoke quickly with Captain Carlson and passed him sheet of paper. It had information and picture on it. Information and a clear colour picture of Leroy McGuvan. The Captain passed the paper around the table to other Captains, who looked at it carefully, then looked at Leroy. That one document cleanly nailed everything tightly into place.

When the document came back to Captain Carlson, he held it up to show Leroy and the Pod Sisters. They looked at it. It was clearly Leroy McGuvan in the picture.

"You are Leroy McGuvan. You are the *'Martyr'*, the hero of New Tortuga. Which means you were the Prophet's second in command. That tells us, that everything you have told us is true and that our entire mission here on Mars is a farce!", Captain Carlson concluded.

"Captain", Captain Turner caught Carlson's attention, reminding him, "You are the Fleet Captain. Amongst the Captains, you have seniority and the right of command."

"Yes Turner, but I am not in charge of this mission. General Verne is", Captain Carlson replied.

"Then we have a problem Sir", Captain Turner replied, adding, "Verne is a crazy bastard."

"Careful Turner. That kind of talk could get a man in trouble", Captain Carlson told him.

"Turner's right Captain", Captain Harkness interjected, "We all saw how General Verne treated Captain Bolton. He was just the messenger and Verne literally tried to shoot him in the head with a fucking a pulse pistol."

"Yes. I remember. I was there too", Captain Carlson replied, adding, "Fortunately Bolton is recovering, although I suspect he'll always be a broken man."

"General Verne isn't the only problem Sir", Captain Harkness told him.

"Yes I know Harkness", Captain Carlson replied, adding, "Heller and Jackstone will definitely support the General."

"What about the other Captains?", Captain Mackerel asked.

"If we deal with Heller and Jackstone, I think they'll follow our lead", Captain Carlson replied.

"This will be tricky Captain", Captain Thompson addressed Captain Carlson, "Whatever we do, we cannot be seen as responsible."

"You're right Thompson", Captain Carlson agreed, "Whatever we do, we can't have it fall back on us. Gentlemen, let me think about it. I'll come up with something. Trust me."

To the trio Captain Carlson spoke thus, "Leroy, Zuawalo, Zeealas. It has been a pleasure to meet you all. I thank you for you candour. You have been extremely helpful. We here, at this table have a lot of thinking to do. As you might imagine, we have some very delicate issues to consider. The turkey was delicious by the way, thank you Zeealas. Please return to your camp. We will have two of our men escort you there to ensure your safety. Thank you."

"Thank you Captain, it has been an interesting lunch", Leroy replied.

The Pod Sisters both thanked the Captain likewise.

At which point Captain Barker left the command tent and came back with Privates Kelso and Mitchel. Leroy, Zuawalo and Zeealas picked up their gear and prepared to leave.

Zuawalo told the Captain, "We do not need an escort."

"I insist Zuawalo. We need to keep you safe", Captain Carlson replied, adding, "Our General can be a very dangerous man."

The trio left the command tent and with Privates Kelso and Mitchel leading the way, started trekking back to the game trail that led upstream to their camp site. Zuawalo let Zigg off of his lead at the edge of the logging camp and he followed dutifully along.

Agent Murphy watched the trio leave the command tent and make their way towards the river. He quickly scuttled down the tree and slunk back to the bushes to retrieve his gear. He didn't cross the river and climb back up the northern ridge-line. Instead Agent Murphy snuck back to the game trail by the river and started following it back to the trio's camp site.

About forty five minutes later Agent Murphy reached the camp site. He quickly pulled down the bag of food from where it was hanging from the branch of the shady tree and took it inside the lean-to. Agent Murphy took out some left over roast duck and some smoked trout, enjoying it immensely while he waited for the trio to return to their camp.

About ten minutes later the trio approached their camp site, being led by the two Trojan scouts. Immediately Zuawalo noticed the food bag was no longer hanging from the tree where she had left it. Looking around the camp site more closely, Zuawalo also noticed the door of their lean-to was slightly ajar. No-one would purposely enter their camp this way, unless they wanted to be found.

Zuawalo told the Trojan scouts, "Thank you. We are home now. You can go back to your own camp. Please go now."

The Trojan scouts thought that was a bit rude, but they did as they were told and started trekking back down the game trail to their own camp.

"Zeealas. Make sure they are really leaving", Zuawalo instructed.

While Zuawalo investigated their lean-to, Zeealas followed the two Trojan scouts to ensure they were truly going back to their camp. Agent Murphy had taken the hood off of his ghillie suite and was patiently waiting for the trio to return. He heard quite clearly Zuawalo asking the Trojan scouts to leave and prepared for Zuawalo to enter the lean-to.

Zuawalo pulled open the lean-to door and looked inside. At first she was a little startled, but when her eyes adjusted, she realised it was Agent Murphy inside.

"Jim! What are you doing here?", Zuawalo asked excitedly, as she rushed in to hug him.

"I've been here since the first day Zuawalo. Watching over you all. Keeping you all safe", Jim Murphy replied awkwardly, while Zuawalo was continuously planting kisses on his lips and face.

Zuawalo then frowned, "Jim. You smell bad! You need a wash."

Agent Murphy chuckled, "Tell me about it. I can smell my own stench."

Zeealas was now back in their camp and told Leroy and Zuawalo, "They have left."

When Zuawalo heard that, she led Agent Murphy out of their lean-to.

When Zeealas saw Agent Murphy, she excitedly shouted out, "Jim!", then rushed up to him and planted kisses all over his lips and face.

"Zeealas. Jim has been here since day one. He has been watching over us", Zuawalo informed her Sister.

Zeealas pulled back from hugging Agent Murphy, "Jim! We do not need protection."

"Orders Zeealas. FB ordered me to watch over you three and keep you all safe", Agent Murphy informed them.

Zeealas replied, "Okay", then added after sniffing, "Jim. You smell bad. You need a wash."

"That seems to be the consensus", Agent Murphy replied as Zeealas and her sister Zuawalo dragged him over to the river and pushed him in.

Zuawalo said to Agent Murphy, "When you are clean, then you come out."

When Agent Murphy came out of the water, Zuawalo asked, "Where were you hiding?"

Agent Murphy pointed up to the northern ridge, to his hide, "I have a hide up there."

"You are good. We did not see you", Zuawalo admitted.

Zeealas nodded in agreement, "We did not know you were there."

Zigg agreed, making his, *'Dook Dook'* noises.

Leroy told Agent Murphy about the trio's interaction with the Trojan Captains.

Leroy then summed it up by saying, "I think I understand what Zuawalo and Zeealas were trying to tell us. They just didn't know how to say it. I told the Trojans who I was and my experiences with the Prophet. More importantly, my take on the Prophet and his cause."

"And that convinced them?", Agent Murphy enquired.

"No. Not really. What convinced them, was when they received proof of who I was", Leroy replied, then added, "Once they understood that I really was the Prophet's second in command. The man who had fought the rear guard action that enabled the Prophet to escape from Mars. The man they considered to be a hero and a martyr. And that I was telling them to their faces, that the Prophet was nothing more than a self deluded terrorist and that there were absolutely no demons. Then they realised, their entire mission was a complete load of crap!"

"And that convinced them?" Agent Murphy repeated.

"I think it's more that, with this new information, they realised the truth and convinced themselves. These are, after all just men following orders and it turns out, that those orders are unconscionable, even illegal orders. They don't want to follow those orders", Leroy explained.

"So they are going home?", Agent Murphy queried.

"Not so easy Jim", Zuawalo interrupted, "There a General in charge. He is a crazy man. A very, very bad man. They need to fix that one first."

Agent Murphy nodded, "I think I understand."

Later that day, before sunset Agent Murphy went up the ridge to his camp site to make a report to Forkbraid. He told the Girls he needed to remain up on the ridge until this was over, just in case any of the Trojans came back and saw him. He did however explain to Zuawalo how to find his camp site should she need to.

21. Hard Choices

Captain Carlson had called a meeting later that afternoon.

"Well Gentlemen. I think I have a plan to deal with Captains Heller and Jackstone", he told the other Captains.

"And the plan is?", Captain Harkness enquired.

"It's better you don't know", Captain Carlson replied, adding, "It will work better that way."

The other Captains all nodded in agreement.

"Now. We five", Captain Carlson pointed to Captains Mackerel, Poulsen, Turner and Thompson, "We'll go back to our landing zone tonight."

Captain Barker queried, "And Captain Thompson and I?"

"You two remain here for now", Captain Carlson told him, ordering, "On the morrow morning I want you two to break camp starting a six am. Bring your entire team, everyone, back to the landing zone. Understood?"

"Yes Captain", Captain Barker replied. Captain Thompson nodded his understanding.

"On the east side of our landing zone. Just past the our sentry line, I'm going to hold a little demonstration. A bit of an experiment", Captain Carlson informed them, "I want all the Captains to assemble there on the morrow at ten am. Make sure General Verne is present."

All of the Captains nodded their agreement.

The following morning Captain Carlson visited their covered weapons storage. Instead of modern weapons however, the storage area contained Knives, Sword, Pikes, Glaves, Spears, Pilum, Shields, but most importantly Cannon and the associated expendables they require.

Upon entering the covered storage area, Captain Carlson walked up to the main desk and issued an order to the Corporal in charge of the storage area, "Corporal. Pick out two cannon at random and have them brought to the main entrance."

The Corporal did so without hesitation and having done so awaited further orders.

Captain Carlson asked, "Corporal. To your knowledge. Have any of these cannon been tested?"

"No Captain", the Corporal answered.

"Do you know the reason why theses cannon haven't been tested?", Captain Carlson enquired.

"It was deemed unnecessary Captain", the Corporal replied.

"Unnecessary? You will need to explain that one to me Corporal", Captain Carlson ordered.

"Captains Heller and Jackstone decided, that as the cannon were being built to a known specification, that there was no need for testing Captain", the Corporal replied.

"Corporal. I believe that to be a grave mistake. We will be testing these two cannon today", Captain Carlson informed the Corporal, ordering, "Corporal. I need you to locate Captain Mackerel and bring him here."

"Straight away Sir", the Corporal then left the storage area to locate Captain Mackerel.

While the Corporal was locating Captain Mackerel, Captain Carlson quickly located the powder charges and the ram rods. He took two powder charges from the furthest pallet at the bottom and placed one in each of the cannon's muzzles. He then took the furthest ram rod and used it to ram the powder charges fully into the cannons. After that, the Captain replaced the ram rod back where he found it, making it look like it had never been moved.

About thirty minutes later the Corporal returned with Captain Mackerel. Captain Carlson knew it would take this long, as he knew the Captain's duty roster.

"Captain Mackerel. We are going to be testing these two cannon at ten am, just beyond our eastern sentry line. Ensure that General Verne and all the Captains are present", Captain Carlson ordered.

"Aye Captain", Captain Mackerel replied and then left to carry out the order.

"Corporal. Load these two cannon onto some carts. We will need two powder charges, two wads, two cannon ball, a ram rod for each and whatever else is required for testing purposes", Captain Carlson ordered the Corporal, "Have these all delivered and secured just beyond our eastern sentry line well before ten am."

"Aye Captain. I'll be on it straight away Captain", the Corporal replied.

Satisfied that his orders would be carried out, Captain Carlson went about his usual duties.

At ten am, the General and all the Captains were standing on the eastern sentry line of the encampment. A large clear aluminium shield stood between them and the two cannon, which had been setup separately, one hundred feet further to the east.

Captain Heller protested, "General Sir. This is a complete wast of our time. I have been assured that these cannon have been built to a specification that is well known. They do not require testing."

Captain Carlson stepped, "Heller. What about the manufacturing process? What was the specification for that? Was that, a well known specification?"

"I don't know. I assume that our specialists will have performed their manufacturing duties to the required specifications", Captain Heller replied.

"Heller. You will address me as Captain Carlson", Captain Carlson ordered.

"General Sir. This is bullshit. Do we really have to waste our time?", Captain Heller protested.

"Captains! This is NOT a pissing contest!", the General told them both, "Heller. Captain Carlson is your superior, you will address him as such and with respect", he ordered.

"Carlson. Are you absolutely sure that this is necessary?", General Verne enquired.

"Yes Sir. Absolutely Sir", Captain Carlson replied, adding, "We need to know how these cannon perform. We need to know that these cannon are not a danger to our men Sir."

Captain Heller protested again, "General. These cannon are not a danger to our men. They do not require testing. I have read the specifications myself. So has Captain Jackstone."

"Is that true Jackstone?", the General asked.

Jackstone answered, "Yes General Sir."

Captain Carlson then responded, "Heller. Jackstone. These cannon. How far will the cannon ball travel using the recommended standard powder charge?"

There was an uncomfortable silence, neither of the Captains could answer that question.

"You two seem rather quiet on the subject", the General told the pair, then asked, "Carlson. How far will a cannon ball travel?"

"General Sir. With the recommended standard powder charge, a cannon ball in one of those cannon, should travel three hundreds meters, with a firing rate of three rounds per minute", Captain Carlson confidently replied.

"Well Heller, Jackstone. It seems Captain Carlson knows more about these cannon than you do. I'm going forward with these tests. Carlson! Proceed", the General decided.

"Corporal. Take one standard power charge, one wadding pack and one cannon ball to the cannon on the left. Load the cannon. Set the fuse to say, forty five seconds. Light the fuse then return here behind the shield", Captain Carlson ordered.

As they watched, the Corporal pulled a trolley with the required materials to the cannon on the left. He placed the powder charge into the muzzle and rammed it in with the ram rod. After which he placed wadding pack into the muzzle and rammed it in with the ram rod as well. This was followed by the cannon ball, which was also rammed into place. The Corporal cut a length of fuse which he thought would take about forty five seconds to burn through. He put the fuse in place, then lit the fuse and ran back to the shield with the trolley in tow.

It felt like an eternity as they all watched the fuse burning down. Behind them, at a safe distance a group of Trojan troops had gathered to watch the spectacle. There were quite a few gathered.

Finally the fuse burnt down into the cannon. There was an almighty explosion and the cannon cracked apart violently. Shards of metal fragments were cast all about. Had anyone been standing next to the cannon, they would have been ripped to shreds by metal debris.

"What the fuck!", Captain Jackstone exclaimed.

"That's simply not possible!", stated Captain Heller emphatically.

"Sure it is", Captain Carlson replied, explaining, "If you don't perform your due diligence and make stupid assumptions, this is what you will end up with!"

Captain Heller was incredulous, "It must be a fluke. A one off. Perhaps this one cannon was poorly manufactured? Defective from the start. The others will all be okay."

"Sure. Okay. Let's test the second one then", Captain Carlson recommended, "The Corporal chose those cannon at random. If the next one works, perhaps you're right and it's just a one off. Just one defective cannon. If it fails as well however, that is indicative of a massive problem."

The General enquired, "Corporal. Did you choose those two cannon at random?"

"Yes General Sir", the Corporal replied, "I randomly chose those two cannon, from the more than one hundred and thirty cannon we have in stock Sir."

"Proceed with the second test Captain Carlson", the General ordered.

"Corporal. The same procedure as before. Test that cannon", Captain Carlson ordered, pointing to the remaining cannon.

As they all watched for a second time, the Corporal pulled the trolley with the required materials to the remaining cannon. He placed the powder charge into the muzzle and rammed it in with the ram rod. After which he placed wadding pack into the muzzle and rammed it in with the ram rod as well. This was followed by the cannon ball, which was also rammed into place. The Corporal cut the fuse to about a forty five seconds length and placed it into position. He lit the fuse and ran back to the shield with the trolley in tow, just as before.

Again it felt like an eternity as they all watched the fuse burning down. The crowd to their rear of the Captains had grown even larger. There were well over a thousand men gathered.

Again the fuse burnt down into the cannon. There was another almighty explosion and the cannon cracked apart violently. Shards of metal fragments were caste left and right.

Captain Carlson remarked dryly, "That gentlemen, looks highly indicative to me!"

General Verne was livid. His face went bright red with rage. Some standing nearby thought he might have a stroke or a heart attack.

"Heller! Jackstone! Why the fuck did you not test the prototypes?", the General demanded.

Captain Heller replied, "General Sir. We were assured it wasn't necessary Sir. We were told that their specifications were well understood and that this could never happen Sir."

Captain Jackstone said nothing. He would have loved nothing better than to just slink away.

General Verne shouted at the two Captains, "We have over one hundred and thirty of those fucking death traps! You useless bastards have taken us all the way back to square one!"

Captain Heller tried to reply, "I'm sorry General! We were assured that this could never happen!"

The Trojans had no modern weapons. They had all been destroyed in the first twenty four hours after their landing. What weapons they had now, had been forged using the recycled scrap metal from their destroyed weapons systems. The Trojan troops were being issued with roman and medieval style swords, pikes, spears, shields and pilum. The officers, being officers however, got the cream of the crop. They had been issued with beautiful, newly made sabres, each in beautifully made, ornate scabbards.

The General was livid, he unsheathed his sabre and just as Captain Heller finished his last sentence, the General swung a deft blow!

Captain Heller's head was severed from his neck. It fell to the ground with a dull thud. Heller's body slumped to one side and joined his severed head upon the ground.

Gasps of shock rang through gathered crowd in the background. Shocked looks appeared on the faces of the Captains who were standing much, much closer. Some of the Captains were unlucky enough to receive a smattering of blood! Captain Jackstone, in shock, looked down upon his comrade's severed head.

The General unleashed another deft blow, coming down on the right side of Jackstone's neck. The sword dug deep into Jackstone's neck and chest to the base of the sternum. Jackstone never even saw it coming. He collapsed to his knees and fell backwards onto the ground with another dull thud. Heller and Jackstone had been summarily executed by General Verne.

"Incompetent bastards!", the General muttered out loudly, he then looked up at Captain Carlson, "Good work Captain", he told him, then the General wiped his sabre clean on Jackstone's uniform before marching off to his command tent.

Captain Carlson was also in shock. He had not expected this result. He had wanted to make fools of Heller and Jackstone, so that the General would not trust them again. He did not expect the General to go full on bat crap crazy on them with a sword.

Captain Carlson ordered, "Find some volunteers to clean up", he could not think of the words, then settled on, "This atrocity."

Walking back to their camp, Captains Mackerel and Harkness asked Captain Carlson how he knew the cannon would explode.

Captain Carlson quietly informed them, "I cheated. The cannon were rigged with an extra powder charge, even before they were positioned in the field."

Captain Mackerel replied quietly, "That would certainly do it."

Captain Harkness replied quietly, "The General was harsh, but those two are out of the way."

Captain Carlson told them both scornfully, "That was NOT my intent. The General is insane!"

One man, a Sergeant, had volunteered to bury Captains Heller and Jackstone. A gentle giant of a man, he could not understand how the General, any General for that matter, could behave in such a fashion. After burying the two deceased Captains, the Sergeant volunteered for one more final task.

It was midday and a huge crowd had slowly gathered outside the command tent. It had started about thirty minutes after the General's summary execution of Captains Heller and Jackstone. First a small, sombre crowd gathered. Then it slowly began the grow. By midday the crowd numbered in their thousands and the noise was becoming deafening.

General Verne stepped sharply out of his command tent, "What is the meaning of all this?", he demanded.

In front of him stood his remaining Captains. Captain Carlson stood in the middle, with eight captains on either side of him. When the General came out of the tent, the Captains on either side of Captain Carlson stepped back to give him more room. Captain Carlson then stepped aside.

The tall, burly Sergeant stepped forward. He was a giant of a man, easily six foot four, if not taller. Heavily muscled, with arms like tree stumps, he had tattoos running from his elbows to the sleeves of his singlet, where they disappeared beneath. He still glistened with the sweat from burying the Heller and Jackstone. In his right hand he held a two pound hammer, with a longer than usual handle. A War hammer made from the wreckage of their weapon systems.

The Sergeant quickly strode forward. The General was shocked at first, then reached for his sabre. He was too slow and the Sergeant's hammer came down upon the General's head. The General buckled at the knees, then slipped sideways to the ground.

The Sergeant dropped his hammer to the ground and knelt down beside the General's corpse, then he spoke to it in a soft and gentle voice, "I am sorry General. It is a terrible thing that I have done. A dirty job, but someone had to do it. Someone had to put you down."

The Sergeant stood up and walked back through the crowd the way he had come. His fellow Trojans touch him on the shoulder as he passed by, in solidarity and understanding.

Captain Carlson stood up on a chair, then stepped onto the table.

In the loudest voice he could muster, he yelled out, "Men of the Trojan Armed Forces! We are going home!", he then stepped down from the table as the crowd erupted in cheers.

Captain Carlson strode back to the other Captains, he was now in charge, "Captains. Make preparations for departure. I want us off this rock and back on our troop transports by nightfall. On the morrow we break orbit. We are going home!"

All of the other Captains nodded in agreement.

Zuawalo and Zeealas had left their campsite to find Agent Murphy's camp, leaving Leroy behind. Zuawalo followed Jim's instructions and Zeealas followed closely behind. Zigg the ferret ran and hopped behind them, sniffing at nearly everything along the way. The two sisters crossed the river at the low waterfalls upstream from their camp and then began climbing up the northern ridge line. Eventually they came to a small game trail and followed it.

High up above their clearing, the Sisters came across a fallen tree. Zuawalo looked at the upturned roots and recognised it immediate from Jim's description.

"Zeealas. Around here", Zuawalo told her Sister as she herself walked around the upturned roots.

The pair found themselves in front of a large fallen tree trunk. The tree trunk was a good height above the ground and covered in layers of small saplings. Zuawalo looked inside the small, almost hidden opening.

"Jim's tent and backpack are inside, underneath the trunk", Zuawalo informed her Sister.

"This is very clever", Zeealas replied, "Very quick to make. Very hard to find."

"Yes. Good camouflage. It is good Jim told me the way here", Zuawalo admitted, then told Zeealas, "Jim is over there", pointing to another barely visible trail.

The Girls made no attempt to conceal their approach, so Agent Murphy could hear them coming.

"Over here my loves", he called out the them.

The Girls found the natural hide, from which Agent Murphy had been watching over them. They gave the hide a quick inspection.

"Now I understand. Sitting here. Wearing that. We could not see you", Zeealas stated.

"That was the general idea Zeealas", Agent Murphy replied.

"Jim. Where did you learn to do these things? You came from L5?", Zuawalo enquired.

"Yes Zuawalo I am from L5. I'm from the biggest colony at L5. It is so big, there are places inside much like this and that is where I grew up. Camping and fishing with my father. He taught me these things", Agent Murphy explained.

Agent Murphy put his hand to his right ear. He was wearing an earwig communicator. Agent Murphy listened to the message carefully before acknowledging its receipt. He looked at the Girls.

"Girls. It's time to pack up", Agent Murphy informed the Girls.

"Time to pack up?", the Sisters queried in unison.

"Yes. That Trojan logging camp. It's been abandoned. Forkbraid wants us there by three thirty pm", Agent Murphy informed them both. After which, all three walked back to fallen tree.

Agent Murphy reached just inside his shelter's small opening and grabbed hold of a long pole he had positioned on the ground along the length of the shelter.

"Please step back Ladies", he requested.

The Pod Sisters stepped back out of the way.

Agent Murphy lifted the pole up and then pushed it forward. The entire side of his shelter lifted away from the tree trunk and fell to the ground leaving the entire side open.

"Quick to make. Quicker to take down", Zeealas noted with a smile.

Within minutes Agent Murphy had rolled up his sleeping bag and packed it into his rucksack. He quickly took off the ghillie suit and pushed that into the rucksack as well. Just as quickly he rolled up his swag and strapped it to the top of his rucksack. Agent Murphy then put on his tactical belt, placed his rucksack onto his back and grabbed his remaining gear.

"I'm ready Ladies. Let's go", he told the Girls.

Agent Murphy had broken camp in less than five minutes.

They then descended from the northern ridge and returned to the campsite in the clearing.

It didn't take long for Leroy and the Pod Sisters to pack up their gear, ready to leave camp. Certainly longer than Agent Murphy had done at his campsite. They did not take down their lean-to.

"I like this place", Zeealas said with sigh.

"Yes. It is a very nice place", Zuawalo agreed.

Leroy also agreed, "You Girls are right. I actually enjoyed camping here."

"Zuawalo, Zeealas. I can bring you back here anytime you want", Agent Murphy told his two Girls, "We do have to keep this lean-to properly maintained after all."

Zuawalo and Zeealas looked at each other excitedly, "We come back when our babies are ready", Zuawalo told her Sister.

"Yes Sister. We can have our babies here", Zeealas agreed.

Agent Murphy rolled his eyes, "Wait! What! No! No! That is not what I had in mind."

The group then followed the river game trail downstream towards the abandoned logging camp.

Nearly an hour later they approached the abandoned Trojan logging camp. Agent Murphy led the others away from the river, towards the tall, broad tree from which he had watched over the trio. He used his field glasses to scan the Trojan's camp. There was no-one in site. The camp was truly abandoned. All of the tents and equipment were gone. All that was left behind was a large stack of milled lumber and a few felled trees that had not yet been milled.

Agent Murphy pointed up into the tree's canopy, "You see that tangle of branches way up near the top?"

Leroy looked up into the tree, "Not really Agent Murphy."

Zuawalo and Zeealas with younger, better trained eyes could barely make it out either, the both shook their heads.

"Well I sat up there, hidden away watching over you all, while you were in their camp", Agent Murphy informed them.

They had no idea how busy Agent Murphy had been.

"We'll wait here until Forkbraid flies in with the Hummer", Agent Murphy told them, asking, "Girls. Do you have any of that duck or some smoked fish left?"

"Yes Jim", Zeealas replied, slightly concerned, "Have you not been eating?"

"Oh yes. I've been eating. MREs, meals ready to eat packs. Would you like to try one?", Agent Murphy replied, adding, "They're not very good. They should put warning labels on the package."

"No. I stick to fish", Zeealas replied as she passed Agent Murphy some smoked trout.

At three thirty pm on the dot, Forkbraid flew the Hummer into the Trojan's abandoned logging camp. He approached low, hugging the tree tops so as to avoid being detected. The trio got up from under the shade of Agent Murphy's tree and began walking towards the logging camp. When they arrived, Forkbraid was sitting on the Hummer's ramp waiting for them.

Noticing Zigg bouncing along behind them, Forkbraid remarked, "He's off the lead. You've trained him well Zuawalo", looking more closely, "He's getting big."

"Yes. My Zigg has imprinted well. Though he will get even bigger", Zuawalo replied.

"FB. What's the latest?", Agent Murphy enquired.

"They're leaving Jim. The Trojans are leaving", Forkbraid replied, informing him further, "Our satellite imagery show's their packing up. Some of their drop ships have already taken off. By tomorrow, they should all be gone."

"Well that is good news", Agent Murphy replied.

"I don't get it. How did my redemption do this?", Leroy asked, "All I did was state my current position and shake a few hands."

Forkbraid laughed loudly, it all made sense now, "When Gwek demolished you he did something incredible. Your demolition was contagious!"

"So what then! I'm demolition Betty", Leroy replied, referencing the old tales of typhoid Betty.

"No no. It's nothing like that. If you meet and touch someone who has true delusions in their life, deeply buried, the golden light of troth passes into them and unravels the lies", Forkbraid explained.

"We saw it. We saw the golden sparks jump", Zeealas told them.

"Yes. Zeealas is right. We both saw the golden sparks jump", Zuawalo confirmed.

"That shouldn't be possible", Forkbraid replied, thinking, "*Maybe it is. They would have been low functioning level three psychics if they had been found early enough and trained."*

"It happened. We both saw it", Zuawalo stressed.

Zigg the ferret even *'Dook Dooked'* in confirmation.

Forkbraid smiled at Zigg, then replied "Perhaps. We can discuss this when we get back to the academy. For now though, we camp here overnight. Tomorrow we'll go to the Trojan's landing zone", he informed them.

The next morning they woke up early and Agent Murphy flew the Hummer west towards the Trojan's landing zone. Satellite imagery had showed that all the drop ships had left. Yet there were several hundred Trojans left behind.

The Hummer landed. Forkbraid instructed the Pod Sisters and Leroy to remain inside while he and Agent Murphy alighted the Hummer to find out what the situation was. They approached the remaining Trojans, Agent Murphy with a high powered pulse rifle at the ready.

"Why are you still here?", Forkbraid asked, adding, "Why have you not left with your people?"

The senior Trojan, a Lieutenant replied, "There wasn't enough room on the troop transports. We volunteered to stay behind."

"Volunteered to stay behind?", Agent Murphy questioned, "You'd better tell us a bit more."

"We are all specialists. We came here aboard the weapons transports. There were too many of us to fit on the troop transports, so the Captains asked for volunteers to remain behind."

"And you all volunteered?", Forkbraid asked.

"We are all single men. We have no family back in the Trojan asteroid fields", the Lieutenant replied, explaining, "Even with us staying behind, the troop transports are still overcrowded."

"How many of you are there?", Forkbraid asked.

"A little over four hundred Sir", came the Lieutenant's quick reply.

"You're all specialists? So you all have skills?", Forkbraid queried.

"Indeed Sir. We are all highly trained and highly skilled", the Lieutenant informed them.

"We will contact the authorities in Chryce Colony. They will pick you all up and assess your skills and qualifications", Forkbraid told the Trojans, adding, "There are eight major colonies on Mars and plenty of jobs for you, if you behave yourselves."

"We would be much obliged for your assistance Sir", replied the Lieutenant, adding further, "We will, as you say, behave ourselves."

"Do you have enough food?", Agent Murphy asked.

"Yes. We have ration packs", the Lieutenant replied.

"MREs? Look around you man. The sea. The river. The forest. You are surrounded by food. Hunt, fish, gather. It will taste a whole lot better than your ration packs. Believe me", Agent Murphy told them.

"We'll notify the authorities in Chryce straight away. They should be here in a couple of days", Forkbraid told the Lieutenant, before he and Agent Murphy headed back to their Hummer.

Once in the air, Forkbraid noted some things down for Agent Murphy, "Jim. Put together a report for Governor Anderson and request his help with those Trojan volunteers. Take a good look at the latest satellite images. There are resources at the Trojan's logging camp and their landing zone that need to be recycled. Both sites are going to require environment rehabilitation."

"Way ahead of you FB. Already on it", Agent Murphy replied, pointing at his right temple, then he asked, "Can we trust those Trojans?"

"Yes. They've all caught Leroy's redemption. Why do you think they all volunteered", Forkbraid replied with a smile, adding, "Let's get back to academy shall we?"

Everyone, including Zigg the ferret agreed.

The next day the Trojan troop transports broke orbit and performed their long burns necessary to place their ships on a return trajectory to the trailing Trojan Asteroid colonies. The satellite imagery was gleefully watched by the Martian authorities all over the major colonies. Forkbraid, Selene and the others at the academy were extremely happy as well. Mars was now safe!

It didn't take two days for the authorities from Chryce to get to the Trojan landing zone. They were there the very next day, just after noon. First the security personnel arrived to take the Trojans into custody. The Trojans, all in remorseful and repentant states of mind, did not resist.

The security personnel were then followed by the bureaucrats. They entered the details and vital statistics of all of the four hundred plus Trojans into their databases. They were especially interested in qualifications and skills. All of the official Martian colonies were still relatively new and highly skilled professionals were in high demand. Skilled migrants would fill the job vacancies nicely.

The Trojans were offered and allocated good jobs in situ, then Hummers would arrive and fly them in small batches to their new jobs and their new homes in the colonies. Most of the Trojans were happy with their new positions. The complete task would take days to finalise, but Governor Anderson's people were highly efficient and good at their jobs.

The defeat and routing of the trailing Trojan Armed Forces were not at all well met back at Ganymede. The High Prince was furious, as were his brothers, Princes Wulfric and Valdamar. The High Prince's youngest sibling, Prince Leopold was far more realistic.

Prince Leopold knew that the invasion of Mars would fail. The optimism of his older Siblings was misplaced. Much of the information they had on the inner solar system was well out of date and the ill-conceived plans of his Brother, were only supported by the *'yes men'* amongst the Generals. Prince Leopold had always believed that co-operation with the inner solar system, not conquest was the right position to take. Only though true co-operation could the entire solar system prosper.

Well over eleven thousand Trojan men, nearly all of them soldiers, were going home to the aft Trojan Colonies and completely unknown to the Horridians, every single one of them had been *'infected'* with the golden light of troth!

22. Good Times

The Kujur Gwek, now Folcrom Gwek, had been back in his village for a few weeks now. Gwek had located his apprentice, the person who would replace him as the village Kujur. The chosen apprentice was a young child named Nyapal, who was only nine years old. The age of nine was a fraction too old to start as an apprentice, usually apprentices would be picked as children who were between six to eight years old. Gwek chose Nyapal because the girl was unique. Nyapal had been born blind!

Nyapal's parents had given her a name that reflected payer, their prayers that their child who had been born blind, would somehow regain her sight. The girl's eyes were cloudy and grey, they still remained that way.

Still, even now, when Gwek chose Nyapal as his apprentice, her eyes remained the same. Yet the prayers of Nyapal's parents had not been in vain. Nyapal was truly gifted and could see, even though her actual physical eyes could not! Nyapal had mind sight!

Gwek had contacted the academy and requested that he be brought back there, to begin training his young apprentice. Gwek believed that a combination of his training and the academy's training would give Nyapal the best possible outcome. Lady Selene was in agreement and organised a Hummer to fly to Gwek's village to pick them both up.

As Agent Murphy was helping Forkbraid, with the Pod Sisters and Leroy McGuvan, Lady Selene asked Marcus to pilot the Hummer and pick up Gwek and his new apprentice. Marcus in turn had requested that Charlene come along with him, ostensibly to swing by the Chryce Colony on the way and take care of another task at the same time. A more efficient use of the Hummer, Marcus had noted. Selene okayed the request without a second thought.

Marcus was now returning with the Hummer and preparing to land in the academy's inner bailey. Selene and Roseanne, who was now officially Selene's assistant, as well as her apprentice, were waiting for them. It was a bit of a surprise when the Hummer landed and its occupants stepped out.

Gwek stepped out first followed by his young apprentice, Nyapal, who although carrying a cane, did not appear to need it. Selene looked deeply into Nyapal's grey, clouded, sightless eyes, *"Wow! The Girl sees me, almost as clearly as I see her. Very high potential!"*, she thought to herself.

"Gwek. It's good to see you again", Selene greeted, adding, "This little one must by Nyapal."

Gwek smiled, "Yes. Good to see you again as well. Yes. This is Nyapal."

Selene knelt before Nyapal, "Well little one. I can see that you see me as well as I see you."

Nyapal replied smiling, "Yes. I see you. My parent's prayers were answered."

Looking at Nyapal's clouded, grey eyes, you would not know the she could see at all.

Selene smiled and touched Nyapal gently on the cheek, then stood back up, just in time to see three more passengers step out of the Hummer. They had not been expected. Two tall dark women and a slightly shorter man stepped out of the Hummer. They were obviously from Gwek's village.

Gwek introduced them, "These are the Zuawalo's and Zeealas's parents, Zyaliep and Kwoth. This is their Aunt, Nyaliep."

Selene could see the resemblance, replying, "Interesting names. Welcome to the New Flinders Psychic Academy."

"Thank you", Zyaliep replied, then asked, "Where are my daughters?"

"Oh. Yes of course", Selene replied, "The Girls are up north. On a mission. Which is now completed, so they should be back before nightfall."

"A mission?", Zyaliep queried.

"Yes. Leroy McGuvan's redemption", Selene quickly explained.

At that point both Marcus and Charlene stepped out of the Hummer.

"Welcome back you two", Selene greeted them.

Roseanne had quick eyes and sent a quicker thought to Selene, *"Look at their hands."*

Selene looked at their hands, they both had wedding bands on their ring fingers. They had eloped in the Chryce Colony!

Selene smiled and remarked, "Mr and Mrs Greyhelm I presume."

Charlene replied, "We haven't decided on that yet. I might keep my surname or maybe I'll use a hyphenated surname. It's kind of like a, *'watch this space'*, thing at the moment."

"Okay. Well, we have some new guests", Selene gestured to the Pod

Parents, "So let's get inside and organise everything."

Marcus replied, "The dormitory where the Girls are staying should work fine. I'll organise for the luggage to be brought up."

Marcus activated his *'grip'* and started typing on its virtual keyboard.

Lady Selene then led the group to the Pod Girl's dormitory.

The new comers settled into the Pod Sister's dormitory. Nyapal chose a room that was close to the Pod Sister's room, while the Girl's parents and aunt chose rooms that were closer to Gwek's room. Marcus soon arrived with their luggage, it was being carried by hyper-dynamic 303 androids.

Zyaliep found the androids disturbing and commented on it, "Artificial people! It is not right!"

"They are three laws safe", Selene assured her.

"That is not the point", Zyaliep replied, "They are not real! They have no souls!"

When everyone had settled in and moved into the common room, The Girl's Aunt Nyaliep noted, "So many people?", questioningly.

"Yes", Selene replied, "You are new comers. So naturally, everyone wants to say hello", then she went about introducing everyone.

Cormac and Candy were present in the common room making everyone drinks. When they noticed the rings on Marcus's and Charlene's fingers, Candy stated excitedly, "I told you so!"

"Yep Candy. You are always right!", Cormac replied, equally excited.

"You knew these two were going to elope?", Selene asked.

"We or I should say, Candy had a hunch", Cormac replied.

Candy smiled and whispered to Cormac, "One down, two more to go."

Selene heard the whisper and enquired, "Two more to go?"

"Weddings", Candy replied.

"You two are incorrigible", Selene replied shaking her head, then stating for the new comers, "These two are our resident match makers in case you hadn't guessed. They are incorrigible romantics, the pair of them."

"And proud of it", Candy replied with a huge smile on her face.

Zyaliep asked, "Speaking of weddings. When is this Jim, going to marry my daughters?"

That caught everyone by surprise.

Zyaliep saw the surprised looks on everyone's faces and informed them all, "That is why we are here after all!"

"Zyaliep. Your Girls have not discussed marriage with anyone", Selene replied, then looking at Roseanne, asked, "Have the Girls mentioned anything to you about this Roseanne?"

"No. Not really. They were going to call their mother about something important when they got back from their mission though. Maybe that's what they were going to discuss?", Roseanne informed them.

"We will find out when my daughters are back then", Zyaliep replied.

The Girls Father, Kwoth, who had not said a word since he arrived at the academy, now asked, "What about this mission?"

"It's bound up with Leroy's redemption", Selene replied, explaining, "They travelled north and camped in a valley not far from a Trojan landing force. Some of the Trojans met them and Leroy somehow redeemed himself. The Trojan landing force has since left Mars and is now en-route back to their colonies in the Aft Trojan Asteroid fields. So whatever they did, it seems to have worked!"

Gwek, who had been sitting quietly added, "Leroy's demolishing has found fertile ground among the Trojans. Their delusions have all unravelled and they now see the truth. So now they go home."

"How'd you know this would happen Gwek?", Selene enquired.

Gwek replied, "I did not. I only knew, that when he met his former friends, this would happen. It would seem that Leroy's redemption, can unravel the most Gordian of tangled lies. In anyone!"

Selene thought about that for a brief moment before replying, "Gwek. That has possibilities. Enormous possibilities and ramifications."

Gwek replied, "Yes. I do not believe that Leroy's redemption is over. It will continue."

"Gwek. What more can you tell me about your demolishing technique?", Selene asked.

"It is a very, very old technique", Gwek responded, "It is my understanding that I am the first to have used it in many generations. When my Master taught it to me, I thought that I would never need it. He himself had never needed it and neither had his Master, nor his Master's Master and so on back through time."

Selene nodded in understanding, many old occult techniques were like that, only needed once in many generations and when not needed, laying dormant in dusty tomes and well trained minds.

"Yes, but how does it transmit?", Selene queried.

"By touch", Gwek replied, then elaborated, "When Leroy touches someone. Perhaps a hand shake or something similar. If that person has true delusions in their life, if their beliefs are propped up by falsehoods. Then the demolishing passes into them and it unravels all their delusions and allows them to see the truth."

A curious Charlene asked, "Gwek. How far does it travel? How long does it persist?"

Gwek leant back in his chair and sat there thoughtfully for a moment, then answered, "That I do not know. Once passed by Leroy into another, that person will also pass it on and so on and so on. How far and for how long? I do not know. It may continue until all falsehood is unravelled or it may fade out over time."

Charlene looked at Selene and both understood what Gwek was saying, Selene asked, "Gwek. When the Trojans return home, what will happen?"

"The demolishing will pass on to all those with delusions", Gwek replied.

Charlene stated what she and Selene had both been thinking, "The Aft Trojan Colonies might collapse into a civil conflict."

Gwek replied, "That is possible, but I do not think so. The demolishing will pass through their colonies very quickly. A change of leadership perhaps, if it is currently based upon falsehoods."

Selene asked Gwek, "Did you find any candidates for the Grey Council while you were away?"

"No. Not yet", Gwek replied, explaining, "That one is hard. Some villages have a Kujur, some do not. Even when there is a Kujur, their quality varies.

Some are very gifted. Some not so much. Your Forkbraid will need to assess them. I can show him where to start."

"Thank you Gwek", Selene replied, "Although, I was hoping your report would be better."

Gwek replied, "I can only find what there is to find. I did find many children. Gifted children. Your psychic academy needs gifted children, yes."

"Yes Gwek. We do need gifted children. That is good news", Selene replied, then reminding Gwek, "You are a Folcrom now Gwek and a member of our Grey Council. This psychic academy is also your academy."

Gwek nodded, "Yes. I have to get use to that."

The door to the dormitory opened and Pod Sisters walked in, followed by Agent Murphy. Forkbraid was busy looking for some more suitable accommodations for Leroy McGuvan. Had Agent Murphy had his way, he would have been put back in a cell and locked up upon his return.

Immediately upon seeing their parents and aunt, the Girls ran straight to them and the hugging began. They were all extremely happy to see each other.

Zyaliep stepped away from the hugging and walked up to Agent Murphy, She said to her daughters, "You both choose this man?", questioningly.

Both Girls replied in unison, "Yes Mother."

Zyaliep looked Agent Murphy up and down, "He is too short!", she stated emphatically.

"Gnarr", Zeealas let out a low growl, "He is not too short Mother!"

"Mother. You are taller than Father!", Zuawalo replied, adding, "Is Father too short?"

Zyaliep did not answer, but she did take note, she was in fact taller than her husband, Kwoth. Zyaliep's Mother had said the exact same thing about Kwoth when she chose him.

Zyaliep looked Agent Murphy up and down once more, "He is too pale!", she stated boldly, further adding, "He is like a ghost! Look, I can see inside of him!", she told her daughters pointing out the veins that were clearly visible under the skin on Agent Murphy's arms and shoulders.

Zeealas protested, "He is not a ghost Mother! He is our Jim!"

"Mother. Jim is our choice!", Zuawalo replied, adding, "You must accept him!"

Zyaliep then changed her tone completely, "Okay then. I will accept your choice", she replied, then turning to her husband, she stated, "Kwoth. This man Jim, will be our son in law."

Kwoth didn't say anything, he just nodded in agreement.

Jim Murphy had been confused by what was going on. He said nothing and just went along with it all. Then he heard the words *'son in law'* and he gulped. Both Zuawalo and Zeealas rushed to him and hugged him tightly. It was official, their Mother had accepted him.

Zuawalo and Zeealas both whispered in Jim's ears, "Mother likes you! Jim Mother likes you!"

Having heard Zyaliep, the Girl's Mother, Jim was not thinking that was the case at all, quite the opposite in fact.

Zyaliep then stated loudly for everyone to hear, "Good! Daughters. Tomorrow you will marry this Jim."

That was their way. Jim was befuddled. Things were moving so fast. He wanted to fall over and collapse to the floor, but the Pod Sisters were holding him up. In the end he did the only thing he could do. Jim Murphy acquiesced to the Girls choice, he was getting married. No two ways about it.

Cormac Farmer clapped his hands and chuckled with his wife Candy, before saying, "You're always right Candy. You picked it the minute they stepped out of the Hummer."

"What does this Jim do?", Zyaliep asked, enquiring further, "Can he pay the bride price?"

Selene replied, "Agent Murphy, Jim, is our chief of security. For both the academy here and the Elysium Colony."

"So can he pay the bride price?", Zyaliep asked again, "Two daughters. Very high price."

"Jim has no cattle", Selene replied, then realised how stupid the statement was.

Zyaliep smiled, "This is Mars. There are no cattle on Mars. Does he have goats or sheep?"

"No. Jim has no live stock. Not even chickens", Selene admitted.

"Orchards? Fields?", Zyaliep queried.

"No. Jim is not a farmer", Selene informed her.

"There are other ways to pay", Zyaliep replied.

At that moment, Zuawalo approached her Mother and gave her a rather heavy leather pouch. The same leather pouch, that her Mother had given her when she and her Sister had left home, before traversing the Kasei Swamps.

Zyaliep held the pouch, opened it and looked inside. It contained golden credits, her very own golden credits.

"Zuawalo. You hardly spent any of it?", Zyaliep queried.

"We did not need to Mother", Zuawalo replied, "We only used what we needed."

Zyaliep nodded, "You are very good daughters", then to Selene she said while holding up the leather pouch, "This was my bride price. Kwoth paid this for me."

Reminiscing, a small tear ran down her cheek, "When I received this, I was so young. So beautiful, just like my daughters. Not so much now."

Jim Murphy who had been listening to the conversation, quickly threw in a compliment, "Mother Zyaliep. You and your Daughters look like sisters."

"Zuawalo, Zeealas, you did not tell me your Jim is so sweet", Zyaliep remarked, then to her husband Kwoth, "Please put this in our room."

"So Jim can pay the bride price with golden credits?", Selene enquired.

"Yes. Golden credits or cattle", Zyaliep laughed and clapped her hands, "We do not accept sligs."

"Careful what you say Mother", Zuawalo cautioned, then laughed, "Zeealas might accept sligs."

"Sister!", Zeealas replied, "Sligs are for eating. Not for bride price!"

"Sister!", Zuawalo countered, "Sligs are not even for eating!"

Agent Murphy thought to himself, *"Slork ain't pork, that's for sure."*

"Zyaliep. Jim has friends. The bride price will be paid", Selene guaranteed, while telepathically reaching out to Forkbraid, who was elsewhere in the academy, to let him know.

Selene asked, "How and when is the bride price paid?"

"Normally we would discuss this with Jim's family", Zyaliep replied, then queried, "Is Jim's family here?"

"Oh, No. Jim's family is back at L5", Selene informed her.

"L5 is a little bit long way from here", Zyaliep replied.

"Yes, but that's okay. Here, we are like Jim's family", Selene responded with a smile.

Agent Murphy took note of that. It was true. His friends were like his family now.

"The bride price can be paid before the ceremony tomorrow. So anytime between now and then", Zyaliep explained.

"I was wondering Zyaliep. Your names, Zyaliep and Nyaliep. They are very interesting. How did they come about?" Selene asked.

"When I was born, my Mother wanted an unusual name for me. So she chose an old name, Nyaliep and changed the first letter from an N to a Z. So this is where my name, Zyaliep came from", Zyaliep replied.

Nyaliep added, "Then when I was born, our Father wanted to use a traditional name for me, So they called me Nyaliep."

Zyaliep continued, "I liked the Z on the front. So I gave my daughters names beginning with the letter Z."

Candy asked Nyaliep, "We notice you don't have a husband with you Nyaliep. Are you single?"

"Yes. I am single", Nyaliep replied smiling.

Candy sent a thought to Marcus, who was wearing his grip, *"Send a message to Varak. Ask him to come here. It is very important."*

Marcus obliged, he actually had an idea what Candy was up to.

"What are you up to Candy?", Selene thought to Candy, who just smiled in reply.

"Nyaliep is always single. Nyaliep chooses a man, then no, he is not good enough for her. She lets the man go. Choose and let go. Choose and let go. That is Nyaliep. Very fussy woman", Zyaliep told everyone.

"Sister!", Nyaliep protested.

"Is it not true Sister?", Zyaliep asked.

"Maybe just a little bit true", Nyaliep admitted.

Roseanne asked, "Zyaliep I've been wondering. How is it, that the women choose the men in your village?"

"That goes back a long ways", Zyaliep replied, "Back before the long rains and the falling sky."

Nyaliep nodded in agreement, "Yes. A long ways back. Back when the village was underground. Everything was carved into the cliffs and the rocks. Back then our village was sealed off from the outside world behind airlocks. There was no water and no air on Mars in those days. It was a very, very hard life!"

"It was like that for New Tortuga as well, back in those days. Although New Tortuga's huge caverns made things somewhat simpler", Cormac noted.

"Back then", Zyaliep continued, "Families chose who married who, based on the needs and requirements of the families. The families even decided how much the girl was worth. Girls had very little choice, if any choice at all."

"It was a big problem", Nyaliep added, "Only the most beautiful girls were wanted. No one wanted a plain Girl or worse an ugly Girl as a daughter in law. Their Sons had to have the best. If the family had little wealth, maybe they could not afford a pretty girl and their son would resent that. A big problem."

"Men could have more than wife, but they only wanted the beautiful ones", Zyaliep continued, explaining, "Then the women, thinking the system was unfair, rebelled."

"Rebelled?", queried Roseanne.

"It is not what you are thinking Child", Zyaliep replied, continuing, "The married women withheld the marital rights from their husbands until all the men agreed to let the women be the ones to choose."

"Men are stubborn. It took many months", Nyaliep told them smiling, "In the end they gave in."

"And that's how the women got to be that ones who choose?", Roseanne queried again.

"Yes. That is how it happened. More or less", Zyaliep confirmed.

"And that led to your society becoming matriarchal?", Selene asked.

"Yes. Once it became the women who choose the men, then overtime everything else changed as well", Zyaliep informed them all.

Nyaliep added, "Now it is the women who hold the lands, the fields, the orchards, the properties. It is the women who inherit now. It is very different now, to how it was in the beginning or even how it was back on the Earth."

"Mars changes everything", Selene replied.

Both Zyaliep and Nyaliep nodded in agreement, both repeating, "Mars changes everything."

At that point Varak entered the common room, "What is it that needs to be done?", he asked.

"Oh. Nothing Varak", Cormac replied, adding, "We have some new guests and we thought you might like to meet them."

Varak looked around the room at the new comers. A child, two women and a man. They all looked to be from the Pod Sister's village.

Cormac introduced the new comers, "Varak this is Nyapal, Gwek's new apprentice. These are Zyaliep and Kwoth, the Sister's parents. And this is Nyaliep, the Sister's *'single'* Aunt."

Cormac had stressed the word *'single'* and Varak had taken notice.

Nyaliep stood up and looked across the room at Varak, "Now there is a man", she commented excitedly, but quietly, as she looked Varak up and down.

"Sister! I know what you're thinking", Zyaliep replied.

"Sister! He is so tall. He is strong. He is so beautiful", Nyaliep replied, her eyes growing wider.

Candy chimed in, "That is Varakhan Utana. He is the man who can build anything!", sweetening the pot just a little.

Zeealas cottoned on to what Cormac and Candy had started, and added loudly, "Aunty. Varak speaks kiswahili", knowing that her aunt was almost fluent in that language.

Varak's sharp ears heard that remark.

"He speaks kiswahili?", Nyaliep queried, replying to herself, "My kiswahili is very good."

Zeealas nodded in confirmation.

Candy stood up and gently took Nyaliep by the arm, leading her over to Varak, "Nyaliep. Let me introduce you two. Varak this is Nyaliep. Nyaliep this is Varak. Perhaps Varak, you'd be so kind as to show Nyaliep around the academy?"

Varak took one look at Nyaliep, she was very much to his liking and he replied in kiswahili, "Ingekuwa furaha yangu", then he held out his arm.

Nyaliep smiled and took Varak's arm, then they both left the dormitory's common room for her tour of the academy.

"What did Varak say?", asked Roseanne.

"He said, *'It would be my pleasure'* in kiswahili", Zyaliep translated.

Selene looked at Cormac and Candy, "You two. You just can't help yourselves, can you?"

"Well, we are incorrigible. You did say that yourself Selene", Candy replied smiling.

Marcus snickered and Charlene gave him a glaring look.

"Marcus. Will you please not encourage them", Selene scolded lightly.

Zyaliep, knowing her Sister, was more understanding and sighed, "Today. Tomorrow. Nyaliep would have seen him soon enough. It was always going to happen."

Forkbraid entered the dormitory and introduced himself to the new comers before taking a seat. He noticed that Gwek's apprentice, although her eyes were cloudy and unseeing, that the child could still in fact see. That in itself indicated a very high potential.

Forkbraid half jokingly said to Selene, "I bring news from the front."

Selene half jokingly replied, "What be the news from the front?"

"I've had word from Governor Anderson. His people will have the four hundred or so Trojans that volunteered to stay behind, relocated within days", he informed her.

"That is good news", Selene replied, adding, "From what I gather from Gwek, they'll settle down nicely as new Martian colonists."

"I believe they will. The Governor did ask about what we wanted to do with all the scrap metal and lumber the Trojans left behind. I asked him to deliver it all to the Elysium Colony for recycling", Forkbraid replied.

"The site must be a right mess, with all those destroyed weapons systems", Selene pondered.

"There is also the one hundred and thirty plus cannon and a ton of other assorted medieval weapons to consider", Forkbraid further informed, "I've asked the Governor to have the lot delivered to the Elysium Colony as well."

"Those Trojans were busy little beavers weren't they", Selene replied.

"Yes they were. Very busy little beavers. Very busy!", Forkbraid agreed.

"Anyway. We need to discuss the bride price, Jim has to pay for Zuawalo and Zeealas", Selene informed Forkbraid.

"Oh yes. Zyaliep. What happens to the bride price?", Forkbraid enquired.

"It is usually distributed amongst the sons, so they can pay for their future brides", Zyaliep explained, "Kwoth and I have no sons. So it will stay with Zuawalo and Zeealas. That is to be, our decision."

"Is that why you still have your bride price Zyaliep?", Selene asked.

"Yes. I have no Brothers, so my Father had no sons to distribute it too. So he decided I should keep it", Zyaliep confirmed, adding, "So I kept it for a rainy day."

"Is now the right time to pay the bride price?", Forkbraid enquired.

"Anytime between now and the ceremony is a good time", Zyaliep explained.

"Okay then. Jim take a seat", Forkbraid instructed as he reached into his impossible pocket.

Jim took a seat and watched as Forkbraid's impossible pocked appeared inside his cloak, from out of nowhere. Forkbraid rummaged around for a short time, then pulled out a large leather pouch and placed it on the table in front of Agent Murphy. He then reached back into the impossible pocket a second time and again after a short while, pulled out a second leather pouch of exactly the same size. This too was placed on the table in front of Agent Murphy. Both pouches were large and looked quite heavy.

Zyaliep had also watched the impossible pocket miraculously appear and then disappear, remarked, "You must be the Great Wizard who executed Leroy McGuvan."

Selene replied for Forkbraid, "He is, but here, male or female, a Witch is a Witch. We don't usually use the term Wizard."

"Is this man Witch single?", Zyaliep enquired.

"No Zyaliep. Forkbraid is my man Witch", Selene replied.

"That is good. Nyaliep does not like to share. There is no guarantee that she will keep this man Varak", Zyaliep replied.

Agent Murphy opened up the first bag and looked inside, he then did the same with the second. Both contained golden credits, in equal number.

"This is too much FB, way too much!", a shocked Agent Murphy told him.

"Nonsense Jim", Forkbraid replied, "Now you can pay the bride price."

"How much is in here?", Agent Murphy asked.

"Each pouch contains a little over three times what was in Zyaliep's own pouch. I was thinking it would be enough", Forkbraid informed him.

"Thank you FB. Thank you", Agent Murphy replied, then to Zyaliep he asked, "Is it enough?"

"It is more than enough Jim", Zyaliep replied, "Your friends are very generous."

Agent Murphy picked up the heavy leather pouches and passed them both across the table to Zyaliep.

"Zuawalo! Zeealas! Your husband has paid your bride price", Zyaliep informed her daughters, "Take these to your room and keep it safe."

Agent Murphy heard Zyaliep use the word *'husband'* and repeated it in query, "Husband?"

"Yes Jim. You are now Zuawalo's and Zeealas's husband. You are our son in law", Zyaliep replied, motioning to her husband Kwoth with her hand, "This is official. The ceremony tomorrow is just a formality."

Kwoth nodded in agreement, "It will also be a celebration and a feast."

Charlene heard the word, *'feast'* mentioned and quickly motioned to Marcus with the simple thought, *"Feast!"*

Marcus was quick to reply, "Feast! Got it. I'm on it people", as he stood up and walked out the door tapping keystrokes on his grip. There was going to be a feast.

Then the embarrassing questions started.

"Jim. Why my daughters share only the one room?", Zyaliep asked.

This was unexpected, Jim was somewhat taken aback, he slowly replied, "Your daughters", then he stopped and started over, "My wives, chose their own sleeping arrangements."

"Zuawalo! Zeealas! Is this true?", Zyaliep asked, then without waiting for an answer, "You will wear your husband out! You should have one room each and your husband, one night, one wife. One night, two wives is not a good thing!"

Zuawalo protested, "Mother. Our bed is big enough for three!"

Zeealas added, "Mother. Jim shows no signs of wearing out!"

Agent Murphy went bright red. The others in the room pretty much tried to look anywhere else they could. Cormac and Candy, greatly amused, giggled amongst themselves.

Selene remarked, "Well, perhaps that's a discussion for another time. Like, when there's a lot less people around."

The gathering broke up shortly afterwards and those not billeted to the dormitory went about their daily business.

The next morning around eight am, the door on the dormitory opened. In walked Nyaliep, barefoot and carrying her shoes in her right hand. Everyone in the dormitory was in the kitchen eating their breakfast. Zyaliep got up and walked into the common room.

"Sister! Look at what time this is", Zyaliep scolded.

Nyaliep replied, "Sister. I might keep this one. This Varak, he is a lot of fun."

"Gnarr! You will not keep him! You will throw him back, just like all the others!", Zyaliep snapped back.

"No. No. This Varak. He is very different. I like this one", Nyaliep protested.

"So you said with the last one. And the one before that. Always you say, '*I think I keep this one*'. Sister, you never do", Zyaliep frowned, commenting with teary eyes, "I want you to be happy Sister. How are you going to be happy, when you do not know what you want?"

"Hmm. Maybe this Varak will make me happy Sister", Nyaliep replied, hoping herself that it would be true this time.

"Nyaliep. Get yourself cleaned up. We have to prepare my Daughters for their wedding. There is too much to do and little time", Zyaliep instructed, "Selene will be here soon to help us get ready."

The wedding had been hastily scheduled for twelve noon, with the reception scheduled for one pm. If it wasn't for the use of androids, things would never have been ready in time. The wedding itself was fairly typical of a christian wedding, with the groom and the brides each saying their vows. Zyaliep had made alterations to the standard christian vows, in order to take into account the cultural differences of her people.

In the end the wedding went as planned with the groom, Jim Murphy wearing a tailored tuxedo and the brides, Zuawalo and Zeealas wearing identical ornate white wedding dresses. Forkbraid and Selene stood in for Jim's Parents, with Marcus being the best man and Charlene the maid of honour. Roseanne became the brides maid. After the wedding ceremony was over, everyone headed off to the main assembly hall for the reception.

There were a lot of people present in the main assembly hall. It appeared nearly the whole academy was present for the occasion. Agent Murphy sat at the centre of the main table with his brides, as there were two of them, sitting on either side of him. Zuawalo on his right and Zeealas on his left. On Zuawalo's right sat her Mother, Zyaliep and next to her sat Forkbraid, then

Charlene and Roseanne.   On Zeealas's left sat her Father, Kwoth and next to him sat Selene, then Marcus. The arrangement was not quite typical for a wedding reception, as there were two brides and the grooms parents were millions of miles away at the L5 colonies.

All of the other tables had been set up in broad arcs in front of the main table, several layers deep, but leaving the immediate space in front of the main table empty for dancing. Cormac and his wife Candy, Gwek and his new apprentice Nyapal, the Swann family and Varak and his new friend Nyaliep had been seated at the middle table in the first arc.

Candy and Cormac had smiled to each other and silently sent, telepathic messages to each other about, *"A new couple to marry off"*, incorrigible romantics both.

All the other friends of the wedding party sat at the tables on either side. All of the other tables were filled to capacity.

The five course meal was served. Starting off with simple appetisers for the first course. The second course was leek and potato soup, which was followed by a greek style salad for the third course. The forth, the main course, was a mix of either fish, quail, chicken, guinea pig or duck with vegetables, chips and gravy. Vegetarian options were of course available.

Zeealas, had of course requested slork, the meat of the slig. A choice that was available, yet no one else requested it, with the exception of Zeealas's Aunt Nyaliep.

Zuawalo had remarked at the time it was served, "Zeealas. A slig is not a pig, slork is not pork!"

This was followed by the fifth and final course which was desert. The remainder of the night was filled with dancing and trivolity, which lasted until the wee, small hours of the morning.

This day, Zuawalo's and Zeealas's wedding day, had been a good day.

Good times were being had by all.

23. Bad Times

A meeting had been arranged at the High Prince's palace by the High Prince himself. All of the Horridian Brothers were present, having travelled to Ganymede Prime from their respective colonial realms. The Horridian Sisters, being Princesses of the Trojan Asteroid Colonies were millions of mile away and were not available, although they did have their representatives present. Several Generals were present as well. The Prophet and Matthew were seated patiently waiting for the meeting to begin. After the Princes and the High Prince had arrived and taken their seats, the meeting kicked off.

"Gentlemen. It appears that our Mars campaign has been a complete failure!", the High Prince began, informing all present, "The Aft Trojan Armed Forces have left Mars and are currently flying back to their Colonies in complete and total defeat", he then nodded to General Tarzan.

"Our last communique from the Aft Trojan Fleet tells us the following", General Tarzan began, before giving them a summary of the details, "Within the very first twenty four hours, the enemy was able to totally eliminate all of their weapons systems, right down to their pulse pistols. From that point forward, the enemy harassed and strafed their encampment on a regular basis, eliminating any chance of recovering and formulating a new attack plan. The General in charge, General Verne, began summarily executing his Captains and was subsequently removed from power. The remaining Captains made the unanimous decision to leave and return home."

"General Sir", Matthew caught the General's attention and asked, "Do we know what weapon, the enemy used to eliminated the Trojan Armed Force's weapons systems?"

"No Matthew. We do not", General Tarzan replied.

"So they took out every weapons system our troops had, right down to their pulse pistols and we have absolutely no idea how they did that?", Matthew queried.

"That is the case Matthew. We currently don't know how it was done", the General admitted.

"Just like how they took down our first strike, our missiles", Matthew remarked.

"That is correct. In both cases, we are at a complete loss as to how our enemy did these things", General Tarzan again freely admitted.

"What's your thinking Matthew?", asked the High Prince.

"Your Majesty. When we fled Mars, our enemies did not have any means to do these things. We would not be here if they had. Yet they have done it now, twice", Matthew answered, then speculating, "Either this new ability, this technology, has been imported since then or they've developed it in situ."

"We have been watching the space lanes like hawks Your Majesty. Nothing, nothing at all, has come from the Earth or L5 since the Spartan left Mars orbit. Not even Interplanetary Liners. L5 cancelled all of those, when they detected our inbound missiles", General Tarzan informed them, repeating known and accepted information.

"Then General, that leaves two options, in situ development or delivery from somewhere this side of Mars orbit", Matthew quickly replied.

"This side of Mars orbit?", General Snide scoffed, "Unlikely! We watch the space lanes between the outer satellites almost as much as we watch those between the inner planets!"

General Tarzan scoffed as well and nodded in agreement.

"Almost as much?", Matthew queried, then not waiting for an answer, Matthew remarked, "Space lanes."

"Space lanes?", the High Prince repeated questioningly.

"Yes Your Majesty. Space lanes", Matthew replied, explaining, "Think of the Jovian System. Every major colony, the Primes, control the space lanes in their orbital zone. If you want to travel across the orbital zones or to the Trojan colonies and beyond, where do go to first?"

The High Prince quickly replied, "You would come here, to Ganymede Prime!"

"Yes Your Majesty", Matthew replied, further explaining, "Ganymede Prime is the central hub, controlling the space lanes for the whole of Jupiter's orbital zone. Just as Titan Prime is the central hub for the Saturnian System and so on and so on."

"Matthew, you might want to get to your point", the Prophet advised.

"I'm just about to my Lord", Matthew replied, then continued, "The inner solar system is just like the Jovian system, just a lot bigger. Venus Central controls the space lanes in Venus's orbital zone. Mars Central, in High Martian orbit controls the space lanes in Mars's orbital zone. The generally excepted space lanes in the inner Solar system, use the Earth and L5 specifically, as their central hub. The usual practice is, to go from Venus or Mars, back to the Earth and L5, then travel out from L5 to the asteroid belt and the outer solar system. Those are the accepted space lanes."

"But Matthew, we travelled directly from Mars to Ceres and then to Jupiter. We didn't go back to the Earth and L5 first", the Prophet reminded him.

General Tarzan stepped in, "I think I understand what Matthew is saying. We may be surveilling the standard *'accepted'* space lanes. We only knew that you two were heading our way, because L5 issued a system wide arrest warrant for the Prophet. So we put surveillance in place specifically for your ship, the Delilah."

"And that is my point exactly General", Matthew confirmed.

"So our surveillance of the space lanes is exactly that, just the generally accepted space lanes?", the High Prince questioned.

"Your Majesty. The inner solar system is a big place. It is difficult, if not impossible to watch every possible transit route", the General replied, "Matthew definitely has a point."

Matthew followed up with, "General. If we assume that no new technology has transferred to Mars from outside of Mars obit, then that leaves in situ development."

The Prophet followed up Matthew's comment with, "Gentlemen, we are all forgetting something here. We are talking about demons. These new weapons, these new technologies, could very well be something conjured by our enemy's use of the Dark Arts!"

"Dark Arts! New Technologies!", the High Prince spat out, "Gentlemen! I am far more concerned with our missile strike and followup occupation of the the Earth and L5. How will this effect our plans Gentlemen?"

General Tarzan replied, "Your Majesty. Without knowing how our Mars campaign was thwarted, it becomes very difficult to predict what will happen with our Earth and L5 campaigns."

General Snide added, "You Majesty. We are attacking the Earth and L5 with nearly two hundred and twenty times as many missiles. Ten missiles is one thing. Twenty two hundred is another matter entirely. I seriously cannot foresee, how the Earth or L5 could possibly stop that many missiles."

General Tarzan nodded in agreement, "And let us not forget Your Majesty. The Leading Trojan Armed Forces, comprise ten times the number of troops and weapons systems. These are not landing on the Earth. They are intended to occupy L5, so that we will command the high ground. Whatever the demons did on Mars, cannot be done at L5. Perhaps on the Earth maybe, but not at L5", he was adamant about that.

Matthew then threw in the remark, "Your Majesty, Your Highness's, Generals. I have concerns about those missiles. If we lose those, the occupation of L5 will fail!", he was equally adamant.

"Twenty two hundred missiles Matthew. Each with ten, two megaton, independently targeting re-entrant warheads", General Snide replied, adding, "I think we have that covered Matthew."

"With all due respect General Snide", Matthew began, then remarking,"Without knowing what took out our Martian missile strike, we have no idea if our Earth and L5 missile strikes will succeed. Please excuse the phrase Gentlemen, but I believe, we may be pissing into the wind and no one wants the blow back from that."

The Prophet was quick to reply, "Matthew! You've overstepped your bounds!"

"My apologies my Lord", Matthew replied, informing everyone, "However, it had to be said. I fully recommend that Prince Wulfric build up and prepare the Jovian outer defences accordingly. As the threat will be entirely external, I further recommend that Prince Valdamar assist in that process. We should be fully prepared for failure, even if that failure never eventuates. Prepare for the worst, hope and pray for the best. That is my mindset at present my Lord."

Prince Leopold then spoke up, "My Brothers, I have to agree with Matthew. We cannot leave our defences hanging in the wind. I second Matthew's recommendations."

The High Princes sat quietly for a moment, all eyes in the room were on him.

"Matthew. I appreciate your forthrightness. I don't often hear people speak before me with such candour", the High Prince replied, then turning to his Brother, Prince Wulfric of Callisto, "Increase our outer defences as recommended", he then turned to his Brother, Prince Valdamar of Europa,

"Provide all the necessary assistance to aid your Brother in this endeavour."

Both Princes, Wulfric and Valdamar agreed in unison, "Your will be done Your Majesty!"

"There was another matter I wanted to bring up Gentlemen", the High Prince told everyone, then to the Prophet he stated, "Your man, McGuvan is still alive!"

"Your Majesty?", the Prophet replied questioningly, "To the best of our knowledge, Leroy McGuvan died fighting the rear guard action. The very rear guard action that allowed Matthew and I to escape from Mars. If not for Leroy McGuvan, we would not be here Gentlemen."

"Our last communique from the Aft Trojan Armed Forces, tells us that Leroy McGuvan is alive and well", the High Prince informed them, "He apparently survived the battle of New Tortuga, was then captured and executed post battle. McGuvan was tossed into the Hebes Sea, to drown in its cold, deep, dark waters or so we are told. He was saved from certain death by a local Martian fisher woman."

"Your Majesty. This is the first I'm hearing of this", the Prophet replied.

"It does get better my dear Prophet. Apparently, Leroy McGuvan has swapped sides. At least, that is what our current information tells us", the High Princes informed the Prophet.

"Swapped sides?", the Prophet queried, adding"Your Majesty. I've known Leroy McGuvan for most of his life. Since he was a small boy. Swapping sides? That is very hard to believe Sir. Can we be sure of the accuracy of this information?"

General Snide stepped in, "Leroy McGuvan told the Trojans that the demon's lair was school for Martian boarding students. Specifically for seven to twenty one year old children."

"Technically that would be true", the Prophet admitted, "However it is also, a so called Psychic Academy. So those boarding students would be taught the Dark Arts at the very least. Of course any of them that showed true talent, would in all likelihood, be offered up for Demon possession."

"Yes, but Leroy McGuvan would know this, wouldn't he?", General Snide asked bluntly, then he remarked, "He even went so far as to tell the Trojans, that the demons don't even exist and that they are all inside your head, Prophet!"

"We don't really know the circumstances of Leroy McGuvan's survival General", Matthew chimed in, "Only what Leroy himself has told the Trojans."

The Prophet then remarked, "It is highly likely that Leroy has been in our enemy's custody for a long period of time. He may have even been brain washed or perhaps even possessed."

"Perhaps", General Snide replied, adding, "He was accompanied by two local woman, the communique described them as, tall dark women."

"Probably Witches!", the Prophet answered straight away, replying emphatically, "They were more than likely his handlers! There are no local people in the Elysium region!"

"Yes, but whatever the case, we can not let this information out", the High Prince told everyone, adding, "Leroy McGuvan is considered by the people to be a hero and a martyr. If the populace finds out that he has flipped sides, well, we simply cannot have that happen can we."

The High Prince then reminded his Brothers, "We control the narrative my Brothers. We cannot allow anything to interfere with that, can we?"

Prince Wulfric replied, "Your Majesty, my Brothers, we will need to have our people watching the news feeds constantly", he looked around at his Siblings.

"Yes", Prince Valdamar agreed, "We mustn't have anything untoward pop up in the new feeds my Brothers."

"Agreed", Prince Leopold stated simply, nodding his head.

"What about this General Verne?", the High Prince enquired.

General Snide replied, "Your Majesty. I've had the General's file pulled. I don't think any of us here have met the man. He was a hard core military man. Highly decorated. General Verne was instrumental in putting down the Aft Trojan rebellion of twenty three fifty six."

"Aft Trojan rebellion?", the Prophet queried, "I don't think I've ever heard of that."

"Nor I", Matthew added.

General Snide replied, "Six years ago, there was a small rebellion against

Princess Luisa's rule. It was quite short lived. General Verne put down the rebellion mercilessly."

"Neither of you have heard of it?", Prince Leopold questioned.

"Your Highness. No. This is the first we're hearing of it now", the Prophet replied.

Matthew replied "You Highness. I doubt anyone at L5 has heard of it either."

"Extraordinary. We were under the impression that the rebellion was organised from L5", Prince Leopold informed them, adding, "Here in the Jovian System, it's often called the L5 plot."

General Snide continued, "Your Majesty. If I may", then after the High Prince nodded, "It appears that General Verne attempted to summarily execute one of his Captains. He only failed due to his pulse pistol malfunctioning. At that stage, none of their weapons systems were working. Not even their pulse weapons. Later the General executed two of his other Captains, using a sabre. The remaining Captains unanimously agreed that none of these actions were justified. They believed that the General had gone insane, so they removed General Verne from power."

"Define removed from power? General", the High Prince ordered.

"Your Majesty. The remaining Captains had General Verne executed", General Snide replied.

"Was General Verne favoured by our Sister, the Princess in anyway?", the High Prince asked.

"It appears that he was Your Majesty", General Snide informed him.

"Brothers, our Sister, Luisa may be somewhat, shall we say, upset by this news", the High Prince remarked, "I'll contact Luisa myself later. It is possible that she, may act out."

The High Prince turned to his Sister's representative, "Callthrope. Make sure my Sister Luisa understands. Princess Luisa is not to undertake any action that will destabilise her realm. Is that clearly understood?"

"Your Majesty. I will do my best to ensure that Princess Luisa understands", representative Callthrope replied, adding, "Your will be done."

"Your Majesty", Prince Valdamar caught his Brother's attention, "I should point out Brother, that had we used my original plan, the Martian campaign would not have failed."

Prince Wulfric turned to Prince Valdamar and laughed, "Your plan was unnecessary. Totally and completely superfluous."

The High Prince raised his hand to silence his Brothers before they could begin arguing, as they were sometimes prone to do.

The Prophet asked, "Your Majesty. We are not familiar with Prince Valdamar's plan."

"You wouldn't be. It was never implemented", the High Prince replied, while motioning to General Tarzan to elaborate further.

General Tarzan nodded to the High Prince and informed the Prophet and Matthew, "Prince Valdamar's plan was a strategy that was considered in response to the Aft Trojan rebellion. We had reliable information that L5 was behind the rebellion and that they were aided and abetted by certain Belter Colonies. The plan in simplest terms was to launch a military campaign to capture, occupy and annex Ceres, Vesta, Pallas, Hygiea and Juno."

Matthew interjected, "The five largest Belter Colonies?", questioning.

"Yes Matthew. The big five. Had we captured and annexed those five colonies, we would have effectively controlled the entire Asteroid Belt. That would have given us five positions from which we could launch military campaigns on the inner solar system at a later date.", General Tarzan concluded.

"But that didn't happen General?", Matthew replied questioningly.

"No it did not", the General replied, adding, "It would have taken many valuable resources, but more importantly, time. To consolidate control over those newly annexed colonies would have taken more than five years, minimum. It would have alienated us from the other Belter Colonies as well. We decided upon the current course of action instead. Which you are aware of."

"More importantly Gentlemen", Prince Wulfric chimed in, "It was considered superfluous. Had our Martian campaign succeeded, we would have had defacto control over everything between Martian orbit and Jove's orbit. Every Belter Colony would have had no choice but to fall into line to be annexed. We could have had the lot!"

"Our Martian Campaign has failed Brother", Prince Valdamar reminded him.

The High Prince raised his hand again to silence his Brothers once more, "It is done my Brothers. There is no point arguing about it."

There was silence in the room, then Prince Leopold broke the silence, "I need to understand something", he remarked.

Prince Leopold was youngest of the Horridian Siblings. His older Brothers thought him to be quite slow. Perhaps that was why, he was High Prince Heinrich's favourite. Prince Leopold was anything but slow however, he was actually highly intelligent. Prince Leopold was simply quiet by nature and very methodical, always dotting the i's and crossing the t's. When he had things fully formulated in his mind, only then did he implement them.

High Prince Heinrich smiled at his youngest Brother, "Yes Leopold", he answered.

Prince Leopold continued, "Our enemies had the ability to take out our missile salvo en-route. Clearly they did that. Clearly they could have used that same technology to take out the Aft Trojan Armed Forces, the Trojan occupation forces, en-route. Why didn't they do that?"

No one answered. It was true. Why didn't they take out the occupation forces en-route. No one had an answer for him.

High Prince Heinrich finally responded after long moments of silence, "Little Brother. We do not know why."

"That's my problem Heinrich. I need to know", Prince Leopold replied, adding, "Why did our enemies wait until the Trojan occupation forces landed? It makes absolutely no sense. They could have destroyed them all en-route, millions of miles from Mars!"

Again there was silence. No one knew the answer.

Prince Leopold continued, "Even after the Trojan Armed Forces landed. Our enemies, only destroyed their weapons systems and denied them any ability to make any further weapons. They left their drop ships completely untouched. Why? Again it makes absolutely no sense!"

There was an even longer pause, before Prince Leopold answered his own questions with, "Unless our enemy was trying to avoid casualties."

Prince Wulfric laughed, then replied, "Avoid casualties Leo. Those demon bastards killed over a thousand Trojans in the landing zone."

"Yes my Brother, they did", Prince Leopold replied, further adding, "Mostly specialists, who were billeted with or closely by the very weapons systems they were responsible for. Unavoidable collateral damage!"

Prince Wulfric fell silent. He had no reply. Leopold often had that effect.

Matthew stepped into the silence, "Your Highness. Are you suggesting that our enemies left the drop ships untouched, to give the Trojans the option to leave peacefully?"

Prince Leopold stated very boldly, "I'm not suggesting anything Matthew. I am merely pointing out, that is exactly what our enemies have done! Nearly every infantry man and over a thousand specialists are flying home as we speak. In the end, they all left peacefully!"

"I've read the reports Leo", High Prince Heinrich replied to his Brother, "Given their circumstances. I don't believe, that the Trojan occupation forces could have done anything else."

"Heinrich. My Brother. That is entirely my point", Prince Leopold replied, adding, "Our enemies, left the Trojans only that one option. Just that one!"

The Prophet replied, "Your Highness. Our enemies are demons. Any 'mercy' they show, is false, it's nothing more than an attempt to manipulates us."

"Perhaps Prophet", Prince Leopold replied, adding, "Yet, I do find it strange that those demons should do this thing. Why would demons show mercy at all?"

The High Prince finished their meeting with, "I cannot know the motivations of demons Gentlemen. What I do know is this", he rattled off a list,

"Our missile strike was somehow thwarted.

Our occupation forces have somehow been routed.

The martyr of New Tortuga is not only alive, he has flipped sides.

A decorated General has gone insane and been executed by his own men.

We now have far more questions than we have answers.

Our Martian campaign has turned into what General Snide described to me only yesterday, as a complete and total cluster fuck!

This certainly does not bode well for us here in the Jovian System.

Gentlemen, we may be in for some very, very bad times!"

24. Worse Times!

Forkbraid looked out from Selene's apartment balcony at the dark night sky. The night sky was clear and the stars twinkled brightly. The unblinking planets were clearly visible. There was no light pollution to affect the view and the milky way was clearly visible in all its splendour. Far off in the distance there was a small, unblinking dot, slightly blueish of colour. That was the Earth.

Forkbraid could just barely see the Moon with his naked eye and he moved to a nearby telescope on the balcony for a better view. It was not a big telescope, but more than sufficient in power to separate out the Earth and its Moon more clearly. Increasing the magnifications, Forkbraid could just make out the many smaller lights of L5, but even with the telescope, just barely. Forkbraid sighed.

"Wow!", Selene exclaimed as she walked through the balcony doorway, "I felt that sigh from more than fifteen feet away."

Forkbraid sighed once more, then replied, "I need to return home Selene."

"Home? This is our home Forkbraid", Selene corrected.

"Back to the Earth and L5 is what I meant Selene", Forkbraid clarified, adding, "Captain Carmichael is going to need my help."

"So you intend to place yourself in harms way once again I take it", Selene replied worryingly.

"Harms way. No. Not so much", Forkbraid replied, explaining, "Using the Solstice, we easily took down ten missiles. If we do the same thing for the Earth and L5, we could take down ten, even twenty times that number. Maybe even more."

"That may be true, but we are a long way from the Earth Forkbraid", Selene replied, then querying, "How long will it take you to get to the Earth?"

Forkbraid thought about it, then replied, "With the micro-fusion thrusters on full, perhaps two weeks or so. The Solstice is easily as fast as the Delilah. Not that I want to do that to a ship, that hasn't been fully run in yet."

"Okay. So what's the ETA on those missile?", Selene asked.

"There's our problem. Those missiles are already in acceleration mode", Forkbraid informed her, "We need to be in front of them and we don't have enough time. All of this messing about with those damned Trojans cost us too much valuable time. So we have about two weeks to be ready."

"Then it's a moot point. You simply can't get there on time", Selene noted.

Forkbraid thought long and hard about that, then replied, "Perhaps we can."

"What are you thinking Forkbraid?", Selene asked.

"The Solstice has multiple methods of motility", Forkbraid informed her, "The micro-fusion thrusters are just one method."

"So what other *methods of motility* are we talking about?", Selene asked.

"The Solstice has a levity disk in the mid section of the saucer and each nacelle is a hamel thruster. These in theory, used in conjunction with the micro-fusion thrusters, should cut the travel time down considerably", Forkbraid informed her.

"Levity disk? Hamel thrusters? In theory?", Selene questioned, "I take it, that none of this has even been tested?"

"No, not yet", Forkbraid admitted, "But it does look like we're going to have to test them very soon. Maybe as early as tomorrow in fact."

It was now Selene's time to sigh, "Anything else you haven't told me about?"

"There is a bit of tech on the Solstice that could be very useful. It was also meant to be used with the levity disk and hamel thrusters", Forkbraid admitted.

"And this bit of tech? What does it do?", Selene enquired.

"It's a sensor array that's designed to locate, track and analyse gravitational frame dragging events and magnetic anomalies", Forkbraid explained.

"Gravitational frame dragging events and magnetic anomalies?", Selene questioned.

"Folcrom Tafazah's idea", Forkbraid freely admitted, "Rotating gravitational wells create frame dragging effects. Tafazah believed that those effects, when embedded in and subject to magnetic fields would cause anomalies that could be used like", he stumbled for the correct words, "like a rail line between two points in spacetime."

"Mars has no global magnetic field Forkbraid", Selene replied.

"Yes, but the Earth does, the outer Planets do and so does the Sun", Forkbraid replied, adding, "The greater the mass, the deeper the gravitational well and the stronger the magnetic field, the greater the effects and the more pronounced the magnetic anomalies."

"And I bet, none of this is tested either has it?", Selene asked incredulously.

"Of course not. It's all new, bright and shiny", Forkbraid admitted once more while smiling, "but if it works! We'll have 'rail lines', fast tracks between one point in spacetime and another. Fast interplanetary and even interstellar travel."

"If it works Forkbraid. If it works", Selene chide him.

"I guess we'll find out tomorrow", Forkbraid responded, informing Selene further, "I'll organise a meeting at the air field for tomorrow morning."

The following morning, everyone had gathered at the airfield, southeast of the academy. The Solstice had been taxied out onto the tarmac. Leroy had never seen the Solstice before and neither had the Pod Sister's Parents or their Aunt.

"Oh my!", Leroy exclaimed, "You guys built that thing?"

"That is a big ship!", the Pod Sister's Father, Kwoth remarked.

"Yes Leroy. We built this", Varak replied.

"More correctly, Varak built this", Forkbraid corrected.

A smiling Nyaliep who was holding Varak's left arm, squeezed it lightly and quietly asked, "You built that ship?"

"Yes Nyaliep. I built that ship", Varak confirmed. Nyaliep was seriously impressed.

"Okay", Forkbraid began, then informing the gathering, "We will be flying to the Earth and L5 later today. We need to help Captain Carmichael and the combined Earth Defence Forces and L5 Colonial Fleet destroy those inbound cold fusion missiles. Charlene and Roseanne have designed uniforms for us and have had them tailored for each crew member. These have been delivered to your cabins. So we will even look the part", he then paused for a moment the hear any comments.

Catherine Swann was the first to speak up, "How long will you be gone for?", thinking more in terms of her husband Peter.

"We can't be certain", Forkbraid admitted, informing everyone, "We can't be sure how long this mission will take. First, we need to take out as many missiles as we can. After that, we have to help deal with the Leading Trojan Armed Forces. It could be a month, perhaps longer. I'm hoping less."

"Peter. You can't go. I forbid it!", Catherine told Peter in no uncertain terms.

Peter Swann pushed back, "Is there a choice Cath? We have to do this. This ship, the Solstice can take down more of those missiles than anything that the Earth and L5 have. We can decimate that missile swarm twice over, even before the Earth and L5 can engage it. I am the Ship's science officer. I literally control the ships computers. I have to do this!"

"And what about us?", Catherine asked.

"We are doing this for you Cath. Think about it. If we don't defeat these attacks, we won't ever be safe", Peter replied, stating, "We are doing do this to keep everyone safe, including our family."

"Peter's right Catherine", Selene told her, "They have to do this to keep everyone safe."

Catherine Swann knew they were right, still that didn't stop tears flowing freely from her eyes.

"It's okay mother", Miranda told her, as she took her mother's hand, "Forkbraid will keep them all safe."

"Remember everyone. Those missiles are no threat to us", Forkbraid assure them, "Even the Trojan Armed Forces are no threat to us. Once those missiles are destroyed, the Trojan Armed Forces will have no purpose. They'll be facing off against both the Earth Defence Forces and the Colonial Fleet combined. They will fold like a house of cards."

"Jim. You are going?", asked Zuawalo. Both the Pod Sisters were holding his arms.

"Of course I am. I have to", Agent Murphy replied, "I'm the Ship's tactical officer. I have to go."

"And Leroy McGuvan has to go as well", Forkbraid told everyone, "His redemption may just come in very useful."

Leroy agreed, "Yes. I can see how I may be useful in some fashion, at some point."

"Leroy is my responsibility", Zuawalo replied, "If Leroy goes. I must as well!"

"If Zuawalo goes", Zeealas replied, "I must go also!"

"You can not go!", Zyaliep told her daughters.

Kwoth squeezed Zyaliep's hand, "How can we stop them? You know our daughters. We say no. They will sneak on board anyway."

Zyaliep frowned and let out a low growl, "Gnarr! Jim! You keep my daughters safe! You keep your wives safe! You must do this thing!"

"I haven't agreed to them coming Mother Zyaliep", Agent Murphy replied.

Zuawalo whispered in his ear quite loudly, "You just try and stop us Jim!"

Agent Murphy looked at Zuawalo, then at Zeealas, then back to Zyaliep, "Correction Mother Zyaliep. I will keep your daughters, my wives very safe."

Zyaliep nodded in reply.

"And you Varak!", Nyaliep queried while squeezing his arm, "You must go also?"

"Of course Nyaliep", Varak replied, adding, "The ship cannot fly without its engineer."

"Nyaliep. I know you two have only just met. And I know that you would prefer Varak to stay here with you, but Varak is needed. Varak is an integral part of this ship. He is the Ship's engineer. Without Varak, we cannot go", Forkbraid informed her.

Nyaliep nodded.

Agent Murphy asked, "FB. Do we have a couple of uniforms for my wives?"

Forkbraid replied, "I anticipated this Jim. Your cabin has been expanded to suit three people. Your uniforms are already in your cabin's lockers. Zuawalo and Zeealas are to be your security team. They will spend their time on board learning about the ship and its tactical systems. Charlene, Marcus, Varak has expanded your cabin as well. It made no sense you two having separate cabins, when you only use the one. Varak has also increased the sound proofing for privacy purposes."

Charlene blushed at that last remark.

Zuawalo looked at her ferret Zigg, then walked over to Miranda, "Would you like to look after my Zigg for me Miranda? Please?"

Miranda took Zigg's lead, "I'd love to look after Zigg for you Zuawalo" and she gave Zuawalo a huge hug.

"Can I be Varak's assistant?", Nyaliep requested.

Forkbraid thought for a few moments, then replied, "We hadn't thought of that Nyaliep", he turned to Varak, "I'll leave that decision up to you Varak."

"It is okay with me FB", Varak replied, but then noted, "Although there is only one other large cabin on board the ship."

Forkbraid sighed, "The Captain's cabin."

"Yes FB. The Captain's cabin", Varak confirmed.

"So be it", Forkbraid replied, adding, "You and Nyaliep can have my cabin. I'll use yours Varak. We can make more appropriate cabin changes when we get back. Varak, you will need to train your new assistant. Everything you know about this ship, your assistant needs to know was well."

"I will have an Android tailor some new uniforms for my new engineering assistant", Varak replied while looking into Nyaliep's deep, dark eyes.

Nyaliep smiled broadly and squeezed Varak's left arm even tighter.

Cormac and Candy sent each other mental notes, *"Candy, we might see another wedding when they return."*

"It's looking like more wedding bells Cormac", Candy replied, *"How wonderful!"*

Selene rolled her eyes at the pair, *"Incorrigible!"*, was the simple message she sent them both.

The crew members of the Solstice, now numbering nine plus Leroy, boarded the ship. Before attending the bridge, the crew members checked out their new uniforms. Forkbraid and Varak of course had to swap cabins first. They did so more quickly using a pair of Androids.

During the process of moving, Forkbraid asked Varak, "Have you given the ship access to the new systems Varak?"

"Oh yes. I gave the ship access to those systems and their schematics last night. By now she should have a fairly good grasp of them", Varak replied.

"Good. Once we get into orbit, we'll be testing them out", Forkbraid informed Varak.

"How did you know the Pod Sisters would be coming with us FB?", Varak asked.

"We are taking Leroy with us, that meant Zuawalo would insist on coming along and as the two Sisters are so close, that meant Zeealas was coming along as well", Forkbraid explained, "I pretty much expected this would happen."

"So they came for Leroy, but not for Jim?", Varak queried.

"Zuawalo saved Leroy's life, that somehow makes her responsible for him and of course Zeealas follows along", Forkbraid answered, adding, "Jim, is just their Husband."

"That is very confusing for me. I will have to learn more about their culture to understand Nyaliep", Varak confided in low tones.

"You do that Varak. Their culture is quite complicated", Forkbraid advised.

Charlene and Marcus were the first to enter the Ship's bridge, their uniforms consisted of pants and a top, both a dark navy blue in colour. There was also a double breasted jacket, again dark blue in colour, although a slightly deeper shade of blue, than the pants and top. They were tailored specifically to fit each crew member and them both perfectly

"I hope the others like our choice", Charlene remarked, "Roseanne and I agonised over these for days. Our only brief from Selene was, don't make them look like pirates."

"Well it's all very blue", Marcus replied, then joking, "Maybe pirate uniforms wouldn't have been so bad."

Charlene gave Marcus a light slap, "I am not amused. Anyway, blue symbolises trust, responsibility, dedication and bravery", she informed him.

The other crew members stepped onto the bridge and once they were present Marcus informed them, "If you are not happy with your uniforms.

Remember, my wife helped design them. So be nice. Be very, very nice!"

Charlene gave Marcus an awkward look, "Really! That was completely unnecessary", she whispered, again she was not amused.

Forkbraid remarked, "The uniforms are fine. Clean, sharp and consistent. Maybe a few minor changes here and there, but otherwise excellent. If everyone can go to their stations."

"Where do we sit?", asked Nyaliep.

"Each station has a secondary console. You may take seats at the secondary consoles for now", Forkbraid replied, adding, "However, the main engineering consoles are back in the engineering department. The security department is next door to engineering as well. Varak will show you to your stations before we launch. For now please locate a seat."

Once everyone had located a seat, Forkbraid began, "Once we are in orbit, we will be testing out some new equipment. Two new methods of motility, that should significantly shorten our travel times and a new sensor array."

Marcuse queried, "Methods of motility Captain?"

"A levity disk and our two hamel thrusters", Forkbraid replied, adding, "You may have noticed the nacelles under the Ship's wings. They are our hamel thrusters. The new sensor array is designed to locate, track and analyse gravitational frame dragging events and the formation of associated magnetic field anomalies. I'm hoping that we can uses such anomalies to further, significantly shorten our travel times. You will find you now have access to the relevant manuals. These are required reading. Varak, please show the non bridge crew members to their stations. Make sure they study the Ship's manuals, they have a hell of a lot of catching up to do."

"Captain. Technically, I'm not a member of the crew", Leroy remarked.

"Yes Leroy. Which is why you don't have a uniform", Forkbraid replied, adding, "I'm sure Varak can find something to keep you occupied while you're onboard and maybe even have some suitable clothing tailored for you."

Varak nodded, "Absolutely Captain."

As soon as Varak had notified the bridge that they were ready for lift off, Forkbraid gave Marcus, the Ship's Helm Officer, orders for both take off and low equatorial orbital insertion. Marcus quickly went through his check list for take off and low equatorial orbital insertion and the Solstice was soon on her way. The small crowd gathered on the tarmac, watched and waved as the Solstice disappeared into the clouds and beyond. Very quickly the Solstice attained a high Martian equatorial orbit.

Once in orbit, the crew of the Solstice found themselves again in awe of the view of Mars. Although they had seen the view before, it was not yet such a regular occurrence that they could simply take it for granted. Even back in engineering, Varak had the same view on the main engineering screen as well, so that the new crew members could view it.

"Marcus. Keep us on our current heading", Forkbraid commanded, then to Peter Swann, the Ship's Science Officer, "Peter. Activate the new sensor array, let's start scanning for gravitational frame dragging events."

"Aye Captain", Peter Swann replied, then asked, "Do we have a name for this sensor array?"

"Not yet Peter. We'll come up with something later", Forkbraid replied.

"Captain. We are picking up frame dragging effects and the Ship's Computer is analysing them. Are we looking for anything in particular?", Peter asked.

"We are looking for magnetic field anomalies tied to frame dragging events to be precise Peter", Forkbraid informed him.

"Captain. Technically, Mars does not have a global magnetic field. What Mars does have, is localised magnetic regions within the Martian crust. These anomalous regions are exceedingly week and provide week, patchy magnetic fields", Peter explained.

"Understood Peter. What we are looking for is unlikely to be generated from Mars. At least, not Mar is its current state. We are looking for anomalies caused externally, from other planetary magnetic fields", Forkbraid replied.

"Other planetary magnetic fields? Like Jupiter, Saturn and the Earth?", Peter queried.

"That is the theory, yes Peter", Forkbraid confirmed.

It was at that point that the Ship's Computer responded, "Anomalous event detected. Anomalous event detected."

"Computer. Examine anomalous event, followup with provision of information", Peter Swann instructed.

"Complying", the Ship's Computer responded in its sweet sounding feminine voice, then after a few minutes, "The anomalous event is a magnetic anomaly within a frame dragging effect region."

"Computer. What is the source of the magnetic anomaly?", Peter asked.

"An external source tracing back to Jupiter's magnetic field", the Computer replied.

Forkbraid turned to Peter and clapped his hands together, "That's what I'm talking about."

Peter Swann checked over the data, the Ship's Computer was analysing and mumbled loudly, "An external planetary magnetic field, causing an anomaly from a distance, on a localised frame dragging event region", his voice was full of wonder.

"Exactly what we're looking for Peter", Forkbraid confirmed, then asked, "Is this anomaly useful? More importantly, is this anomaly traversable?"

Peter ran his eyes over the data once again, "I'm inclined to say no Captain, but I'll ask the Computer to double check."

"Computer. Is this anomaly traversable? If it is, where does it go?", Peter asked.

The Computer responded, "Point of origin is Jupiter's magnetic field, two point five million kilometres from the planet Jupiter. Traversal is ill-advised. This magnetic anomaly forms a slip stream that is unidirectional."

Peter was quiet for a short moment, "Slip stream scanner would be a good name for the new scanning array Captain", he paused then added, "I agree with the Computer's analysis. To give you an analogy, think of a mouse trying swim up the s-bend of a flushing toilet."

"Thank-you for that wonderful analogy Peter. I am more than happy to call the new sensor array, our slip steam scanner. Make it so", Forkbraid replied, adding, "So this anomaly is only useful from Jupiter's side. From our side it would be virtually impossible."

"Yeah. I would agree with that assessment Captain", Peter Swann confirmed.

"Share your data with Varak, Peter", Forkbraid ordered, "These *'slipstreams'* will only be useful if they're bi-directional and I suspect that can only happen if both ends have a magnetic field. The task is, firstly, how to give Mars a magnetic field and secondly, how to trigger these slipstreams as needed. You guys can work those problems."

"Aye Captain. We'll get on it straight away", Peter Swann replied.

"Marcus. Lay in an intercept course for that missile swarm heading to the Earth and L5. I want to pass through the swarm and take down as many missile as we can on the first pass. And Marcus, we'll be using our micro-fusion thrusters in conjunction with our levity disk and hamel thrusters. Once we're through the missile swarm, we're heading straight for L5", Forkbraid commanded.

Aye Captain. Laying in the new course now. Levity disk and hamel thruster are online and will be engaged", Marcus replied.

The course plotted, Marcus then issued a command to the computer, "Computer. Proceed along intercept course as calculated. Fusion thrusters on full, utilising both levity disk and hamel thrusters."

The Computer responded with, "Complying."

The Solstice quickly broke orbit and began its journey to intercept the missile swam bound for the Earth and L5.

Forkbraid asked the computer, "Computer. What is the estimated time to intercept."

The computer responded with, "Seventy two hours", in its sweet feminine voice.

"Three days?", Forkbraid questioned, "Computer. I was under the impression, that with the micro-fusion thrusters on their own, it would take at least two weeks. Please confirm the time to interception."

The computer responded with, "Correct. Time to interception with micro-fusion thrusters alone would be almost thirteen days. Incorporating the levity disk and hamel thrusters, decreases that time down to seventy two hours", again in its sweet feminine voice.

"Extraordinary!", Forkbraid exclaimed, then to the Ship's Tactical Officer, Agent Murphy he ordered, "Jim, we're going to need a firing solution for that missile swarm. We need to take down as many missiles as we can in one pass and we can't use our rail guns."

"No rail guns Captain?", Agent Murphy queried.

"The regions around the Earth and L5 are too busy, too populated. We can't take the risk", Forkbraid explained.

Agent Murphy nodded in understanding, "Aye Captain. I'll have a tactical solution ready in time, one that does not include the rail guns."

The communicator buzzed in the Prophets apartment at Ganymede Prime. General Tarzan was on the line. Matthew, the Prophet's pilot and right hand man, was quick to join him.

"General. It's a pleasure to hear from you", the Prophet greeted.

"It's a pleasure to see you both as well", the General greeted them both, then continued, "I have some disturbing news gentlemen."

"How so General?", the Prophet queried.

"Our surveillance team assigned to watching Mars, detected something highly unusual", the General replied.

"Highly unusual?", Matthew queried.

"Yes. They detected a ship performing a long burn with an inward trajectory", the General informed them both.

"A ship travelling from Mars back to the Earth", Matthew noted, remarking, "That does not sound terribly unusual General."

"This ship was unusual for two reasons gentlemen", the General replied, informing them both, "It had a configuration we have never seen before. It also disappeared off our long range scopes so fast, we couldn't even determine its exact trajectory or speed. It was fast gentlemen, very fast!"

Matthew and the Prophet looked gobsmacked.

Finally the Prophet stated, "If it's flying between Mars and the Earth, you should be able to track it General."

"As I said, it was off of our scopes so fast, our people couldn't keep track of it gentlemen", the General replied, adding, "We have no idea what it was, but we think, we now know what happened to our missile strike aimed at Mars."

"You think it's going after our missile strike against the Earth and L5?", Matthew queried.

"It's a long way from Mars to the Earth. As fast as this thing was, we don't think it can possibly intercept our missile strike in time to stop them. Our people are suggesting, it's more likely to be going after our Trojan Armed Forces. If they intercept our occupation forces, there will be no occupation of

L5", the General informed them both.

"No occupation forces means we won't control the high ground", Matthew replied.

The Prophet remarked, "It is only the one ship and our missile strike should leave the Earth and L5 completely devastated."

"Yes. Yes", the General agreed, "The Bothers have decided to prepare the Jovian fleet just in case. If anything happens to the Trojan Armed Forces, we may be sending in the fleet."

"General. This could get very messy, very quickly", Matthew told him bluntly.

"You're not wrong lad, you're not wrong", the General admitted, "Our fait accompli could become a bloody hard slog!"

The Prophet looked at Matthew, he was right all along, this was getting far more complicated than the Horridian Brothers and all their Generals had envisioned. The cost of war was on the increase and the balance sheet was looking to be stained blood red.

The Solstice was four hours out from the interception point and the crew had gathered in the Captain's conference room.

"Well Jim, what's our targeting solution?", Forkbraid asked.

Agent Murphy put the latest scans on the screen for everyone to see, "Captain. I've arranged with Marcus to adjust our course, to take the Solstice through this section of the missile swarm."

Agent Murphy shone his pointer to mark out their projected course on the screen, "This particular course, provides us the best opportunity to take down as many missiles as possible. The Ship's Computer has calculated that this is the course required for us to have maximum effect. At the velocity we are travelling at, we can only make one single attack run."

"It's looking good so far Jim", Forkbraid replied, then asked, "How many missiles can we take down? Do we have an estimate?"

"The Ship's Computer estimates somewhere between two hundred and twenty and two hundred and sixty", Agent Murphy replied.

"So we are looking at least a ten percent kill rate", Forkbraid noted.

"Yes. That is the Computer's prediction", Agent Murphy confirmed.

Peter Swann stepped in, "Captain. I have discussed this with the Ship's Computer at length. The Computer has agreed that this task is necessary. The Computer understands that these missiles contain no life forms and that they are in-fact targeting humans. The Ship's Computer completely agrees with this course of action."

"Well that is good to know Peter. So our Ship's Computer won't interfere?", Forkbraid replied.

"Our Ship's Computer will do everything possibly to ensure our success Captain", Peter Swann confirmed, informing him further, "When we go up against the Trojan Armed Forces however, that will be a different matter. Human life will be involved. When we go after the Trojans, we will need to use our tactical operations mode."

"Understood Peter, understood", Forkbraid replied, then to Agent Murphy, "Jim, which weapons systems are you going to use?"

"Captain. We'll be using all of our weapons systems, except for the electromagnetic rail guns. A miss with the rail guns would leave projectiles flying around cis-lunar space and we can't have that. Cis-lunar space is way too busy to take that kind of risk.", Agent Murphy replied.

Forkbraid nodded in agreement.

Agent Murphy continued, "As we approach the missile swarm we'll hit them with our hyper resonant disrupters and rapid fire pulse plasma machine cannons. As we enter the swarm, we'll open up the phased laser arrays and quad pulse plasma cannons. While we are passing through the swarm, all of the above mentioned weapons systems will be in use. Finally as we begin exiting the swarm, we'll launch several salvos of torpedoes."

"That's a lot of fire power Jim", Forkbraid noted.

"Yes Captain, it is. It will be necessary for the Hornet's nest to be auto targeting and firing at will. It's the most efficient method", Agent Murphy explained.

Marcus enquired, "You mentioned several salvos of torpedoes Jim?"

"Six to eight salvos I expect", Agent Murphy replied.

"Do we even have that many torpedoes in stock?", Marcus asked.

Varak answered, "The Ship is capable of manufacturing torpedoes as needed. I also have our model 295 Androids helping out as well. We should have enough for eight salvos, perhaps more."

"Sounds like we have a plan people", Forkbraid stated, "I'll require all bridge crew members at their stations and at the ready at least one hour before the intercept."

Everyone replied, "Aye Captain" and the meeting broke up.

"Is it always like this?", a frowning Nyaliep asked.

"We are at War Nyaliep", Varak replied, adding, "This is the way of War."

"Aunty Nyaliep. This is not a cruise ship", Zuawalo remarked, adding, "We are going to save many lives today. Many, many lives!"

"Yes Aunty. Many lives are all relying on us", Zeealas seconded.

"When I was on Mars, my world seemed so small", Nyaliep told them, "Now I find it is so big and I am only a tiny little part of it. I feel so small, like a little mouse."

The Pod Sisters both hugged their Aunty and Zuawalo noted, "Your world was always big Aunty, you have simply opened your eyes much, much wider."

At interception minus one hour Agent Murphy was already at his tactical console. He had invited Zuawalo and Zeealas to sit beside him at the secondary tactical console. With only the one seat, they had to share it. Agent Murphy took note, to have Varak correct that situation.

Peter Swann was already at his station and making sure there would be no *three laws safe Betty* issues. Varak sat at the secondary science console, which could double as an engineering console, when the appropriate configuration overlay was applied. Varak wanted to ensure that all of the Ship's systems performed to specification.

Nyaliep and Leroy sat in the engineering compartment surrounded by a handful of busy Androids. Varak had them learning the Ship's systems and reading manuals for nearly three days. While much of it was over Nyaliep's head, Leroy on the other hand, did already have significant engineering knowledge and could be useful.

Marcus and Charlene sat at the helm and communications consoles. They held hands across the small gap between their work stations. Zuawalo and Zeealas had noticed this and giggled amongst themselves. Agent Murphy admonished them lightly and quietly asked them to be a little bit more professional. Zeealas replied by quietly pointing to Marcus and Charlene.

Agent Murphy had replied by saying, "I know."

Agent Murphy went through his command sequence preparations.

"Tactical! Hyper Resonant Disrupters online. Check!"

"Rapid Fire Pulse Plasma Machine Cannons online. Check!"

"Phased Laser Arrays online. Check!"

"Quad Pulse Plasma Cannons online. Check!"

"Torpedo Launch systems online. Check!"

"Torpedo Carousel and Loading systems online. Check!"

"Long Range Sensors online. Check!"

"Short Range Sensors online. Check!"

"Ultra Sensors online. Check!"

"Targeting Array online. Check!"

"Targeting Missile Nose Cone Fairings. Check!"

"Sequencing. On target zone approach, utilise Hyper Resonant Disrupters and Rapid Fire Pulse Plasma Machine Cannons. Check!"

"On passage through target zone, utilise Hyper Resonant Disrupters, Rapid Fire Pulse Plasma Machine Cannons, Phased Laser Arrays and Quad Pulse Plasma Cannons. Check!"

"On exiting target zone, utilise Torpedo Launch systems for Multiple Torpedo Salvos. Check!"

"Enabling Auto Targeting online. Check!"

"Enabling Firing at Will online. Check!"

Agent Murphy then issued the command, "Tactical. Lock in the command sequence in readiness for tactical operation as Missile Mission One."

The Hornet's nest went through the sequence of instructions and responded with, "Complying", the Hornet's nest's voice again sound quite masculine.

"Captain. The Hornet's nest is primed and ready for Missile Mission One", Agent Murphy informed him.

"And Marcus. How are the course corrections going? Primed and ready?",

Forkbraid enquired.

"Aye Captain. Primed and ready", Marcus confirmed.

Time moved swiftly and the appointed intercept point approached.

"Marcus. Begin your course adjustments", Forkbraid commanded.

"Aye Captain", Marcus at the helm replied, before commanding, "Computer. Perform course adjustments as primed. Show course progress on screen in separate window."

The Computer responded with, "Complying", in its usual feminine tones.

"Jim. Time for the fire works", Forkbraid commanded.

"Aye Captain", Agent Murphy responded, before commanding, "Computer. Activate shield grid at maximum. Activate passive and active cloaking. Tactical. Perform tactical operation Missile Mission One as listed. Auto targeting and firing at will."

The Computer responded with, "Complying."

The Hornet's nest went through the sequence of instructions, ticking them off one by one and responded with, "Complying", in its usual masculine tones.

The result was almost immediate as the hyper resonant disrupters and pulse plasma machine cannons blazed away with red disrupter beams and purple pulses of plasma. Ahead of the Solstice, cold fusion missiles with their multiple war heads popped off like popcorn in multiple explosions of brilliant blue light. As they approached closer, the bursts of blue light were visible on all sides, left, right, up, down and straight ahead.

Entering the trailing edge of the missile swarm, the Solstice's phased laser arrays and quad pulse cannons joined the fray with brilliant blue beams of light and even more purple pulses of plasma. Missiles on all sides exploded into multiple bursts of brilliant blue light.

The Ship's Computer automatically adjusted the main screen to dampen the effects of the exploding warheads. The Solstice's inertial dampers struggled hard against the shock-waves and the whole ship shuddered slightly. On screen the course progress was displayed in a smaller window at the top left. It not only showed the course progress, but also kept a kill count of missiles being destroyed.

After what seemed like an eternity, the Solstice approached the leading edge of the missile swarm. The torpedo launch systems kicked into actions as salvo after salvo of torpedoes were launched. Yet more missiles exploded into multiple bursts of brilliant blue light. By the time they had cleared the missile swarm, eight torpedo salvos had been launched.

"Damage report", Forkbraid commanded.

After a few seconds a smiling Varak replied, "Captain. No damage to report. Our shields worked as expected. All systems have functioned as expected. All is well."

"Varak. This ship is bloody impressive. Good work man", Forkbraid commended him.

"Peter. What's the kill count", Forkbraid asked.

"It's on the upper side of our estimates Captain. Two hundred and fifty three missiles destroyed", Peter Swann replied.

"Jim. Excellent work", Forkbraid commended him.

Agent Murphy nodded in acknowledgement.

"Marcus. Adjust our course to rendezvous with the Colonial Cruiser Spartan at L5", Forkbraid commanded.

"Aye Captain. Laying in the course now", Marcus replied.

"Charlene. Send an encrypted message to Captain Carmichael. Give him a heads up, we are heading his way. Let him know we've knocked out a few missile for him", Forkbraid commanded.

"Aye Captain. Compiling the message as we speak", Charlene at the comms console replied.

"Captain Sir. We're detecting multiple explosions in space", one of the Spartan's bridge Lieutenants informed.

"Multiple explosions in space? I'll need more information than that Lieutenant", Captain Carmichael replied.

"It's the inbound missile swarm Captain. We're detecting multiple individual bursts. A great number of them", the Lieutenant replied.

"A great number?", Captain Carmichael queried.

"Captain. It looks like more than two hundred of those missiles have detonated Sir", the Lieutenant replied, then after looking hard into the screen and his data, "Sir. I'd say that at least ten percent of those missile have been destroyed."

"I want exact numbers Lieutenant", Captain Carmichael ordered, thinking to himself, *"What the bloody hell is going on here?"*

"Aye Captain. I'll have exact figures for you shortly", the Lieutenant replied.

Another lieutenant, the Spartan's Communications Officer reported, "Captain Sir. We're receiving a message."

"Put it on my screen Lieutenant", Captain Carmichael ordered.

Captain Carmichael silently read the message that appeared on his screen, *"Captain Carmichael. Lord Folcrom Forkbraid, Captain of the Spaceship Solstice is underway to rendezvous with your fleet at L5. We took the liberty of eliminating two hundred and fifty three cold fusion missiles during transit from Mars. Over and out."*

At which point, the first Lieutenant informed him, "Captain Sir. Two hundred and fifty three missiles have disappeared from our scans."

An unexpected turn of events, Captain Carmichael was perplexed, *"Lord Folcrom Forkbraid, Captain of the Solstice? What the fuck!"*

Another meeting had been arranged at the High Prince's palace by the High Prince. All of the Horridian Brother's were present as were several of their Generals. The Prophet and Matthew had also been called into the meeting. The representatives of his Sister's had not been called into the meeting this time. Something was afoot that the High Prince wanted kept from them.

"Gentlemen. As you all know, an unusual event was detected in Mars orbit", the High Prince began, then after a short pause continued, "Specifically, a ship that performed a long burn that should have placed it on an Earth bound trajectory. A ship so fast that our people could not track it. General Snide, please continue."

"By all means Your Majesty", General Snide replied, then divulged, "We thought that the *'unknown'* ship was going after our occupation forces. We were wrong gentlemen, very wrong. That ship was much, much faster than we thought. It made a bee line straight to our missile swarm. It traversed the distance from Mars to our missile swarm in three days gentlemen!"

"Three days! That's impossible!", Prince Wulfric exclaimed.

"Brother!", the High Prince shouted, "The data has been checked and double checked."

"Your Highness's. The impossible, is now possible. That ship traversed the distance to our missiles in three days", General Snide confirmed.

"General Snide. What was the result?", Matthew asked, cutting to the chase.

General Snide replied, "They took out over two hundred and fifty missiles in a single pass."

"No! No! I simply cannot believe that! That is impossible!", Prince Wulfric protested.

"Your Highness. It has happened. Our people have confirmed it", General Snide replied.

"Wulfric. I have seen the surveillance myself. It has happened", the High Prince also confirmed.

"My Brother. Your Majesty. What do we do now?", Prince Wulfric enquired.

Matthew interjected and asked, "Gentlemen. How are the missiles triggered?"

General Tarzan answered, "Most of the missiles have specific targets, cities on the Earth. As they have multiple independently targeting warheads, each missile can target multiple cities in fact. The missiles targeting L5 also have specific colonial targets. What are you thinking Matthew?"

"Gentlemen. It's extremely likely, that they're going to go after the missiles again. They'll try to take down as many as they can en-route. This new ship is a real threat to our missile strike", Matthew told everyone.

"And what is your suggestion Matthew?", General Tarzan asked.

"You need to reprogram some of those missile to defend the rest. Is that possible?", Matthew asked them.

"I'm no expert Matthew, but I expect it should be", General Tarzan responded.

"Excellent General", Matthew replied, then looked at the High Prince,

"Your Majesty. Most of those missiles are targeting the Earth. I recommend that some of those Earth bound missiles, the ones in the lead, be reprogrammed. They need to defend the rest of the swarm by attacking any ship that approaches them."

The High Prince was silent for a long moment considering what Matthew had recommended, then he ordered, "General Tarzan. Have Matthew's recommendation implemented."

"I'll attend to it straight away Your Majesty", General Tarzan replied.

The meeting broke up shortly afterwards and the Prophet and Matthew left the palace to return to their apartments.

"General Tarzan. What do you think of this Matthew?", the High Prince asked.

"Your Majesty. It is my understanding that he was trained by the L5 Military as a pilot", the General informed the High Prince.

"Perhaps General, this Matthew should be inducted into our armed services and given a brevet rank", the High Prince recommended.

"Your Majesty. I will look into it", the General replied.

It was almost two days after the Jovian missile swarm had been attacked and Captain Carmichael sat in the Captain's chair on the bridge of the Colonial Cruiser Spartan. His eyes were focused on the screen in front of him. A ship was approaching his position, the Spaceship Solstice. The ship had a disk and sled style of construction, but beyond that, was unlike any ship configuration he had ever seen. The Captain noted as the Solstice approached, it was bristling with weapons modules. The Solstice came to a halt one hundred yards in front of the Spartan.

The Communications Officer reported, "A request for visual and audio comms is coming in Sir."

"Put it on the main screen Lieutenant", the Captain ordered.

Forkbraid appeared on the screen, sitting in his Captain's chair, "Good to see you again Captain Carmichael", he greeted.

"It's good to see you again Forkbraid", Captain Carmichael replied, adding, "I must thank you for taking out those missiles. It was not something that we were expecting."

"Well Captain. We were on our way here and thought we could be of service", Forkbraid replied.

"That you were Forkbraid. That you were. Might I ask, where you managed to obtain such an advanced ship?", Captain Carmichael asked.

"I had Varak, our engineer, start work on it before you left Mars orbit and returned to L5", Forkbraid informed the Captain, "It took quite a while, but now she's ready for action."

"Ready for action?", Captain Carmichael questioned.

"Yes Captain. Please come aboard so we can discuss how we can help destroy more of those missiles", Forkbraid replied with an invitation.

"Will do Forkbraid. I'll be over in a shuttle within an hour", Captain Carmichael agreed, "Over and out."

Forty minutes later a Gull Wing Skimmer docked at the Solstice's main docking portal. Captain Carmichael and one of his Lieutenants, a Lieutenant Hans Blixen, stepped through the portal.

"Captain Carmichael", Agent Murphy greeted him, then turning to the Lieutenant, he pointed, "Lieutenant Blixen, Deimos right?"

"Agent Murphy", the Captain acknowledged.

"Yes Agent Murphy", the Lieutenant replied.

"I never forget a face", Agent Murphy noted, "General, Lieutenant, if you'll both follow me."

A few short minutes and they were in the Captain Forkbraid's conference room.

Forkbraid greeted Captain Carmichael and introduced his crew, "Captain", he nodded, then continued, this is my crew, "Agent Murphy, my Tactical Officer, Peter Swann, my Science Officer, Marcus Greyhelm, my Helm and Navigation Officer, Charlene Fewkes, my Communications Officer and Varak, my Engineering Officer. Varak is the man who built this ship, The Solstice. Over here we have Nyaliep, our Engineering Assistant, Zuawalo and Zeealas Pod, our Security Team and Leroy McGuvan. Crew, this is Captain Bartholomew Carmichael, Captain of the Colonial Heavy Cruiser Spartan and his Lieutenant Adjutant Hans Blixen. Gentlemen, please take your seats."

Captain Carmichael was familiar with some of the Solstice's crew members, however many of the faces were new to him. One name in particular stood out, Leroy McGuvan. The Captain and the Lieutenant took their seats.

The Captain pointed to McGuvan, "This is man is a wanted terrorist. I had heard he was dead."

"Yes Captain. Leroy McGuvan was a terrorist and I personally executed him for his crimes", Forkbraid freely admitted.

"Then how is it, he is here and still alive?", the Captain enquired, all the while Lieutenant Blixen was keying in notes into the Grip attached to his left arm.

Forkbraid pointed to Zuawalo, "Leroy was fortunate. He was lucky to be saved by Zuawalo."

"Well. He is still a wanted terrorist. I expect him to be handed over to the authorities at L5", the Captain strongly recommended.

"No Captain", Forkbraid responded quite bluntly.

"No? I don't believe you have a choice in this matter", Captain Carmichael remarked.

"I have my reasons Captain. Firstly, this is not the same man as the one who was the terrorist. A colleague of mine has demolished Leroy. He is now a completely new man. Secondly, I have already tried, convicted and executed him, so I believe double jeopardy comes into play. You cannot try and convict a man of the same crimes more than once", was Forkbraid's formal response.

Lieutenant Blixen leaned over to the Captain and spoke in his ear, the Captain replied, "That's up to the authorities at L5 to decide. Until then, I'll leave McGuvan in your custody. He's all yours."

"So Forkbraid, how do you propose to help us with these attacks?", Captain Carmichael asked.

"Captain, on our way here, we passed through that swarm and took out more than ten percent of those missiles. We plan to do exactly the same thing again", Forkbraid informed the Captain.

Captain Carmichael nodded, "That would be extremely helpful. You may be a bit late though. Our *'front foot'* is already on the move and will be engaging those missile tomorrow."

"Tomorrow?", Forkbraid questioned, "How many ships?"

"There will be seventy five ships of various smaller classes. Fifty of ours and twenty five from the Earth Defence Forces. I wanted to send more, many more, but the authorities at L5 wanted to keep the bulk of the fleet on the *'back foot'* so to speak", General Carmichael replied.

Forkbraid rubbed his brow and shook his head, he then replied, "Captain, you'll need twice that number. It's a bloody good thing we came here."

"Tell me about it", Captain Carmichael replied, "L5 wants us to have the fleet in place to protect the colonies. They don't understand, that we need to hit them en-route, before they launch their warheads. At that point, the targets multiply by ten. Damned politicians!"

"Okay. Here's what we'll do Captain. After your *'front foot'* offence engages those missiles, we'll follow up with a second punch. We'll try to take out as many missiles as we did on our way here", Forkbraid informed the Captain, adding, "After passing through the swarm, we'll circle back and rejoin your fleet here at L5 once more, to help out with your *'back foot'* defence."

"Jim, prepare a firing solution for tomorrow. We're following L5's *'front foot'* into the fray", Forkbraid commanded, adding, "Marcus, work with Jim on suitable course. Once we pass though the swarm, I want to swing back here to L5."

"Aye Captain. I already have a firing solution in the can", Agent Murphy replied.

"Aye Captain. I'll prepare an appropriate course", Marcus replied.

"Thank you gentlemen. We really appreciate this, we really do", Captain Carmichael responded.

The meeting broke up and Agent Murphy showed Captain Carmichael and Lieutenant Blixen back to their Gull Wing Skimmer.

The next day, the Solstice was flying en-route to intercept the missile swarm once more, this time head on. Captain Carmichael watched the screen showing long range scans of the missile swarm with apprehension. Forkbraid and his bridge crew watched the approaching missile swarm on their screen. Both Captain Carmichael and Captain Forkbraid could see the L5's *'front foot'* offensive fleet approaching the missile swarm.

Captain Carmichael could see the Solstice following up behind L5's fleet, still a long way back, but catching up fast, he thought to himself, *"Damn! That ship is fast!"*

And the Solstice was fast. With micro-fusion thrusters on full and both levity disk and hamel thrusters activated, the Solstice cut through space quicker than any other ship in human existence.

L5's front foot offence began and the fleet of seventy five ships engaged the missile swarm. At first they were being quite successful, but then the unthinkable happened. One by one, the cold fusion missiles in than van, launched their warheads. Ten each, independently targeting, each with a two megaton yield.

Multiple bursts and brilliant blue light appeared on the Spartan's bridge view screen. Captain Carmichael watched as the first missiles exploded, with their multiple war heads popping off like popcorn. His apprehension began to lift. Then shortly afterwards, when Captain Carmichael noticed the explosions changing in colour from brilliant blues, to include streaks of orange, yellow and red, his heart dropped and his apprehension began to increase dramatically. The cold fusions missiles were being destroyed yes, but so were his ships.

On the approach to the missile swarm, Forkbraid also watched the Solstice's bridge view screen. He too saw the first missiles popping of like popcorn in brilliant, blue bursts of light. He too saw the colours changing to include oranges, yellows and reds. He too came to the same conclusion as Captain Carmichael. L5's front foot offensive fleet was being hammered!

"Peter", Forkbraid caught Peter Swann's attention and pointed at the screen, "What's your take?"

"Those are ships being destroyed Captain", Peter Swann replied.

"Yes, but why?", Forkbraid asked, adding, "We didn't encounter anything like that."

"Captain. We approached the swarm from the rear, not head on", Peter began to speculate.

"We hit that smaller swarm en-route to Mars head on Peter", Forkbraid reminded him.

"That we did Captain", Peter replied, speculating further, "Us having hit two missile swarms so successfully, the Jovian's have probably responded by reprogramming their main missile swarm to defend itself Captain. I expect that some of the missiles in the lead are now primed to launch warheads against any approaching ships."

Forkbraid thought about that for a brief second, "Your hypothesis seems likely Peter", then to agent Murphy, "Jim, activate the shield grid on maximum. Activate both passive and active cloaking systems."

"Aye Captain", Agent Murphy replied, "Computer. Activate shield grid on maximum. Active passive cloaking. Activate active cloaking. Place fusion thruster into stealth mode."

The Ship's Computer responded with, "Complying."

"Captain, we are fully shielded and cloaked", Agent Murphy confirmed.

Back on the bridge of the Spartan, Captain Carmichael was watching the screen as the Solstice vanished from their long range scans without a trace.

"What in God's name?", Captain Carmichael thought to himself.

"Marcus. Adjust our current course. After we exit the missile swarm, take us through that debris field", Forkbraid ordered, then to Peter Swann, "Peter. I want a complete analysis and identification of the debris. Captain Carmichael will need a complete damage and loss report."

Both Marcus and Perter replied, "Aye Captain" and made the appropriate arrangements.

"Jim. Start your firing solution preparations", Forkbraid ordered.

"Aye Captain", Agent Murphy replied, then to the Hornet's nest, "Tactical. Retrieve Missile Mission One. Hold in preparation and relabel as Missile Mission Two."

Varak who was sitting at the secondary science console, smiled. He'd been a clever little monkey once more, "Captain. I have made some modifications to the electromagnetic rail gun rounds."

"How so Varak?", Forkbraid enquired.

"Captain. The penetrating explosive rounds will now be able to self destruct", Varak replied, adding, "If they miss their target, fifteen minutes later, they will explode and self destruct."

"Oh, that is nice work Varak. We can use that. Thanking you", Forkbraid replied, turning to Agent Murphy, "Jim. Can you incorporate the rail guns into your firing solution."

"Captain. It's a bit short notice, but yeah, I think I can do that", Agent

Murphy agreed.

Agent Murphy adjusted his checklist and inserted, "Electromagnetic Rail Guns online. Check!" and "Loading Electromagnetic Rail Carousel with penetrating, explosive rounds. Check!", right before the *'Hyper Resonant Disrupters online. Check!'*.

Agent Murphy then adjusted the sequencing and prior to the *'On target zone approach'*, he inserted, "Prior to target zone approach, utilise Electromagnetic Rail Guns", knowing that the Hornet's nest would calculate in advance when the usage was appropriate.

Agent Murphy then issued the command, "Tactical. Lock in the adjusted command sequence in readiness for tactical operation as Missile Mission Two."

The Hornet's nest went through the sequence of instructions and responded with, "Complying."

"Captain. The Hornet's nest is primed and ready for Missile Mission Two", Agent Murphy informed him.

As the Solstice approached the missile swarm head on, Forkbraid gave the simple command, "Jim. It is time!"

"Aye Captain", Agent Murphy responded, before commanding, "Computer. Double check shield grid is activated at maximum. Double check passive and active cloaking are both activated. Keep micro-fusion thrusters in stealth mode. Tactical. Perform tactical operation Missile Mission Two as listed. Auto targeting and firing at will."

The Computer and the Hornet's nest both replied, "Complying."

Almost immediately the electromagnetic rail guns swung into action. The Hornet's nest chose its targets in a logical sequence, positioning the electromagnet rail guns as necessary to fire upon their designated targets. Bright orange tracer rounds could be seen streaking towards their targets. Shortly thereafter there were multiple explosions of brilliant blue light, again missiles popping off like popcorn.

As they approached the leading edge of the swarm, the electromagnetic rails guns cut out and the   Hornet's nest activated the hyper resonant disrupters and pulse plasma machine cannons. Red disrupter beams and purple pulses of plasma entered the missile swarm and hit their targets. Missiles and warheads popped off like popcorn once more. At first in front of them and then shortly after, all around them.

Once they were in the swarm proper, the Hornet's nest activated the phased laser arrays and quad pulse cannons. Brilliant blue beams of light and even more purple pulses of plasma joined the light show. Missiles on all sides exploded into multiple bursts of brilliant blue light.

Again the inertial dampers struggled hard against the shock-waves and the whole ship shuddered. Eventually the Solstice approached the trailing edge of the missile swarm. The Hornet's nest activated the torpedo launch systems and salvo after salvo of torpedoes were issued forth. Yet more missiles exploded into multiple bursts of brilliant blue light.

Then it was over and the Solstice continued onward towards the debris field left behind by the missile swarms previous encounter with the combined L5 and Earth Defence Force fleet.

Forkbraid requested a damage report and Varak replied that they had come through unscathed. The Solstice's shields had held just as before, but more importantly, none of the missiles had detected the ship during their attack run. The Ship's cloaking system had worked perfectly.

"Peter. Do we have a kill count?", Forkbraid asked.

Peter Swann checked the Computer, "Two hundred and seventy five Captain."

"That's even better than the first run", Forkbraid remarked.

"Peter. Scan the fleet. How many ships survived the encounter? Can you discern if any were damaged? Then scan the debris field. Ascertain which ships were lost and locate any survivors?", Forkbraid ordered.

A short while later Peter adjusted the main screen. It displayed the remaining Ships in the fleet, which were still performing their course correction burns.

"Captain. I'm counting forty two intact ships", Peter informed Forkbraid, "As their fleet started out with seventy five, that indicates thirty three ships were destroyed by the missile swarm."

"Captain Carmichael will not be pleased with that news", Forkbraid remarked, then querying further, "The debris scans?"

"I'm just checking the scans now Captain", Peter replied, then frowning,

"No survivors. I guess that's to be expected. A ship gets slapped with a two megaton warhead, no one survives that. I can at least identify the lost ships."

"A sad day indeed. Peter, put together a report, then hand over your report and the associated data to Charlene", Forkbraid instructed.

Forkbraid turned to Charlene, "Charlene. After you receive Peter's report and data, send it straight to Captain Carmichael on the Spartan at L5"

"Aye Captain", Peter and Charlene both replied.

"Marcus. Adjust course to rendezvous with the Spartan at L5", Forkbraid commanded.

"Aye Captain", Marcus replied and they began their journey back to L5.

The Solstice was fast, very fast, quickly overtaking the surviving ships of the L5 fleet on the return leg of their latest mission. The Ship's Captains, still smarting at the destruction over thirty ships in their fleet, watched in awe as the Solstice flew past them.

When the Solstice approached the Colonial Fleet stationed just outside of L5, even Captain Carmichael was surprised. Firstly, because they'd dropped off their long range scans, but secondly, he had underestimated the Solstice's speed. When the Solstice came to a halt one hundred yards in front of the Spartan, Captain Carmichael was quick to hail them.

Captain Carmichael appeared on the screen, "How is that ship of yours so damned fast?", he asked without even greeting them.

Forkbraid replied flippantly, "We have a device that negates the Ship's mass. That enables our ship to reach extremely high velocities."

"Forkbraid. We could certainly use that technology here in the Colonial Fleet", Captain Carmichael informed him.

"True Captain, but that would be very dangerous wouldn't it. Imagine being able to fly around the solar system at these kinds of speeds and the amount of havoc and devastation that could be wrought, if this technology fell into the wrong hands", Forkbraid replied, then stating, "This is not a technology that can be released. The risks far out way the gains. At least for now."

Captain Carmichael shook his head, "We could certainly use it, but I figure you're right. There are some out there, who would abuse it."

"Perhaps, when time permits, Varak could provide you with some advanced shielding technologies that could be of use", Forkbraid replied, holding out a carrot to keep Captain Carmichael on side.

"Perhaps. Yes, that would be useful", Captain Carmichael agreed, then changing tack, "We received your data Forkbraid. My God! Thirty three ships! Nearly all of them from L5. Our ships were in the van. We're still tallying the deaths. Each of those ships had forty to seventy five crew aboard, so we're looking at a death toll of well over a thousand souls."

Forkbraid was silent for a short moment before asking, "How many missiles are left Captain?"

The Captain turned to his Lieutenant, who analysed the data on the long range scanners, he replied, "Captain. There are eight hundred and twenty seven missile left Sir."

Peter Swann did the math in his head, "Captains. The fleet took down eight hundred and thirty five missiles, leaving us with roughly thirty seven percent left."

"Thank you Peter", Forkbraid replied, then back to the Captain, "We still have a huge problem to deal with Captain."

"Can we count on your ship and your crew to help us defend L5?", Captain Carmichael asked, adding, "We need all this ships we can get."

Forkbraid replied, "Yes Captain. My ship and my crew will be joining your defence of L5."

"Thank you Forkbraid", Captain Carmichael replied, "Your ship and your crew are greatly appreciated. This must be the worst of times, but I fear there are worse times to come!"

25. Never Again!

Yet another meeting had been arranged at the High Prince's palace by the High Prince. The Prophet and Matthew arrived early and waited patiently in their seats. They didn't have to wait very long. First the Generals arrived, followed by the Princes, then finally the High Prince. Everyone stood as the Princes and High Prince arrived and took his seat.

"Be seated gentlemen", the High Prince requested.

Everyone took their seats.

"General Snide. Bring everyone up to speed", the High Prince commanded.

"Your Majesty. The enemy sent a fleet from L5 to intercept our missiles gentlemen", General Snide informed everyone, then waited for any questions.

Matthew was quick off the mark and asked, "What was the result?"

"We lost a lot of missiles", General Snide replied, but then he informed the others, "But it cost them a lot as well. It cost them dearly in fact. Spectrographic analysis of the explosions, indicates a lot of carbon, nitrogen, oxygen, titanium, aluminium, iron and other assorted elements. Our experts tell me, that our enemies at L5 lost a lot of ships."

"That they lost a lot ships, is a good thing", the Prophet noted.

"Yes my Lord, but how many missiles are left?" Matthew queried.

"Eight hundred and seventy seven to be precise", General Snide informed everyone.

Matthew looked at the Prophet with his best *'What did I say'* look.

The Prophet caught the look and thought to himself, *'Matthew was right. He's always right!'*

General Snide noted the silence in the room and added, "Let us not forget gentlemen, each missile has ten warheads. So this is far from over. We are still very much in this fight!"

General Tarzan had been reading through the reports, he replied, "It appears there were two waves of attacks on our missiles General. The first wave was the L5 fleet, followed by a second wave shortly thereafter. A second punch!"

General Snide admitted, "Yes. There were two waves of attacks. One after the other."

"This report says, the second wave was not detected by our missiles", General Tarzan noted, "General Snide. That, is a serious concern."

General Snide replied, "Our experts believe that the second attack wave was performed by the unknown Martian ship."

This was too much for Prince Wulfric, "So this mysterious fucking Martian ship is not only fast, it's also undetectable!", it was not a question.

The High Prince raised his right hand to silence his Brother, he then looked to General Snide.

General Snide admitted, "This new Martian ship appears to be capable of evading detection."

There was a long silence in the conference room.

General Snide broke the silence by changing the topic, "Matthew. I've been looking at your file."

Matthew looked at General Snide thinking, *"Where is this going?"*

The General continued, "Your skill set is very impressive. You have also been quite helpful with your recommendations as well. More importantly, you have had military training. I have discussed this at length with His Majesty, the High Prince and we both agree. We would like to invite you to join the Jovian Armed Forces. We are offering you, the brevet rank of Captain."

This was unexpected and caught Matthew completely off guard, "General, Your Majesty. This is quite a surprise. I don't know what to say. Would it be okay if I thought about for a couple of days?"

The High Prince replied, "Yes Matthew. That would be fine. We do need good men in our armed services though, so please, do not take too long to make your decision."

"Understood Your Majesty", Matthew replied.

The meeting then broke up and as The Prophet and Matthew were leaving the conference room, "Matthew, you should accept the post. It could be very useful to us."

The Jovian missile swarm was getting closer, too close for comfort. Forkbraid had asked Agent Murphy to prepare another firing solution and this was in the process of being compiled.

"Charlene. Get Captain Carmichael on the line please", Forkbraid requested.

"Aye Captain", Charlene replied and soon Captain Carmichael's visage appeared on the screen.

"Forkbraid. What can I do for you?", the Captain greeted.

"Just the opposite Captain. We're going to do something for you", Forkbraid replied.

"Okay. What's the plan?", Captain Carmichael asked.

"There are still too many missiles Captain", Forkbraid began, then continued, "We need to knock out as many as possible before they can deploy their warheads. So to that end, we're going to make another run through the swarm."

"That will be very helpful Forkbraid, very helpful indeed", Captain Carmichael acknowledged.

"Captain. I would advise, that after we make our run through the swarm, that your *'front foot'* fleet follows up and runs through the swarm as well", Forkbraid advised.

"The Captains won't be happy to do that all. We lost thirty three ships the last time. Quite a lot of lives were lost", the Captain remarked.

"Understood Captain. The missiles can't detect our ship, so for us the risk is quite low", Forkbraid admitted, "However, this time around, your fleet will know the missiles are capable of targeting them and they can take the necessary evasive action."

"I'll put the plan to the Captains and ask for volunteers", Captain Carmichael replied, "These are all good men. They will understand how important this is. It is, a necessary action."

"We'll be heading out in four hours. If you can get your fleet on their way in two, we'll overtake them and together we can give the swarm another one-two punch", Forkbraid informed the Captain.

"Then I'd better get the ball rolling", Captain Carmichael agreed.

"Once we're through the swarm, we'll swing around and come back to L5 to help you with your back foot defence", Forkbraid informed the Captain, adding, "It is going to be a long day."

"That it will be Forkbraid. That it will be", the Captain agreed before signing off.

Four hours later and true to his word the Solstice flew out to meet the missile swarm once more. Ahead of them were forty two ships of the Colonial Fleet and the Earth Defence Forces. Every Captain had volunteered for this new mission. The Solstice overtook the fleet and prepared for their second, one-two punch at the swarm, this time with the Solstice in the van.

"Marcus. Adjust our course to maximise our strike and ensure we circle back to L5", Forkbraid instructed.

"Aye Captain", Marcus replied, "Making it so."

"Jim. Prepare your firing solution", Forkbraid ordered.

"Aye Captain", Agent Murphy replied, then began preparations, "Tactical. Load Missile Mission Two. Designate as Mission Missile Three and hold in preparation."

The Hornet's nest went through the sequence of instructions and responded with, "Complying."

"Captain. The Hornet's nest is primed and ready for Missile Mission Three", Agent Murphy informed him.

The Solstice approached the missile swarm head on once again and Forkbraid instructed, "Jim. It's time!"

"Aye Captain", Agent Murphy responded, before commanding, "Computer. Activate shield grid at maximum. Activate both passive and active cloaking. Place micro-fusion thrusters in stealth mode. Tactical. Perform tactical operation Missile Mission Three as listed. Auto targeting and firing at will."

The Computer and the Hornet's nest both replied with, "Complying", their mix of both feminine and masculine voices.

The Hornet's nest activated the electromagnetic rail guns. Bright orange tracer rounds could be seen streaking towards their targets and then the brilliant blue lights of exploding missiles began. As they approached the leading edge of the swarm, the electromagnetic rails guns cut out, however before the next weapons systems could activate, the missile swarm changed its trajectory. Ninety percent of the missiles altered their trajectory and changed their course towards the Earth. The remaining missiles adjusted their course slightly, making a bee line straight for L5.

The Hornet's nest activated the hyper resonant disrupters and pulse plasma machine cannons. Red disrupter beams and purple pulses of plasma began hitting their targets. Again, there were more flashes of brilliant blue light.

Then they were in the swarm proper and the Hornet's nest activated the phased laser arrays and quad pulse cannons. Even more brilliant blue beams of light and even more purple pulses of plasma started striking their targets. Missiles on all sides exploded into multiple bursts of brilliant blue light. Some of the explosions were closer than the crew would like. The inertial dampers struggled hard to against the shock-waves as the whole ship shuddered, somewhat violently.

The Solstice approached the trailing edge of the missile swarm and the Hornet's nest activated the torpedo launch systems, salvo after salvo of torpedoes were issued forth. More missiles exploded into multiple bursts of brilliant blue light. Then as quickly as it began, it was all over and once more the Solstice came through the action unscathed. The Solstice's began following its course back to L5.

"Peter. What was our kill count?", Forkbraid asked.

"Much lower than the first two runs Captain", Peter Swann replied, adding, "Only one hundred and sixty. We missed a lot of our targets."

"Most of our targets changed course and moved well out of range", Agent Murphy explained.

"Charlene. Put the fleet on the screen. Window in window" Forkbraid instructed.

"Aye Captain", Charlene replied and a window popped up on the screen showing the fleet as it appeared in the Ship's scanners.

The fleet was approaching the swarm, however now the swarm had broken into two smaller swarms and their appeared to be some confusion amongst the fleet as to what to do. The ships of the fleet broke formation, as around half the ships altered course to follow the bulk of the swarm that was headed for the Earth. While others adjusted their course to tackle the missiles headed for L5.

Forkbraid noticed, the divide amongst the ships appeared to be based on allegiances. The Earth Force ships were chasing the Earth bound missiles. The L5 Colonial Fleet ships were chasing the L5 bound missiles. Each was intent on looking after their own and as the Earth Force ships were originally the lesser component of this small fleet, the bulk of the missiles were being chased down by a slightly lesser force. Forkbraid shook his head. Even now, under such threat, they could not effectively work together.

"Is this a divide and conquer strategy by the Jovians?", Marcus asked.

Agent Murphy replied, "I doubt it. Jupiter is a long way from here. So there is no real time communications happening."

Peter Swann added, "Jim is correct. The missile swarm appears to have hit their designated separation point. This was probably planned from the outset."

Forkbraid queried, "So the bulk of the missiles were heading for the Earth."

"Yes Captain", Peter Swann confirmed, "It looks like around ninety percent."

Charlene expanded the window, so that it now showed both fleet components and the now two, missile swarms, "Captain. I thought this might be more useful."

"Thank you Charlene", Forkbraid replied.

Then the unthinkable happened. Nose cone fairings separated from the missiles and fell away.

Peter Swann noted, "Captain. That does not bode well at all."

Shortly thereafter, there was the tell tale sign of thrusters igniting as the missiles launched their warheads. Now there were well over seven thousand independently targeting warheads en-rout to the Earth and L5.

"Sweet Mother of God!", Varak exclaimed.

"Charlene. Send a message to all forty two of those ships. The priority is those warheads. Take them down! Keep sending the message until each and every ship acknowledges they've received it", Forkbraid commanded.

"Aye Captain", Charlene replied and then sent the message to the ships over and over, each time following up with a request for acknowledgement. It didn't take long for all forty two ships to acknowledge its receipt.

"Captain. All of the ships have acknowledged", Charlene informed Forkbraid.

"Good. The next message is to the Spartan, Captain Carmichael. Let him know that the missiles have deployed their warheads. He has over seven hundred warheads inbound to L5. I want Captain Carmichael to acknowledge receipt of the message personally", Forkbraid ordered.

"Aye Captain", Charlene replied and sent the new message. The message was received and Captain Carmichael acknowledged its receipt just as quickly.

"Message number three Charlene", Forkbraid began, "Send word to the Earth Defence Forces. Let them know that the missiles have deployed their warheads and that they have nearly six and half thousand warheads heading their way. I need them to acknowledge receipt of this message. Not from some low level functionary either. I need to know that an upper level officer has received it."

"Aye Captain", Charlene replied and began sending the message.

"Marcus. Get us back to L5 as quickly as you can", Forkbraid ordered, "I promised Captain Carmichael that we'd help out with this mess and I intend to keep that promise", Forkbraid ordered.

"Aye Captain. Adjusting course for L5 now", Marcus replied.

"Jim. How good are you at that tactical station?", then before Agent Murphy could answer, "We need to take down those warheads before they can target anything and there could be civilian ships or even colonies in the way."

"Captain. It's best we get to L5 before those warheads", Agent Murphy advised Forkbraid, "I can instruct the Hornet's nest to take out the warheads at will, when it's safe to do so. If we get into L5 proper though, I'd prefer to control the tactical station and firing control manually."

Forkbraid nodded in understanding, "Prepare the Hornet's nest Jim."

"Captain", Charlene at the communications console called out, "Earth Defence Forces have acknowledged our message. A General Arch Stanton, asked me to pass on his personal thanks for the heads up."

"Thank you Charlene. Ship wide comms please", Forkbraid instructed.

"Aye Captain. Ship wide comms on line", Charlene replied.

"Crew of the Solstice. The missiles have deployed their warheads. We are currently heading back to L5 to help with their defence. All crew members are to remain at their stations. Repeat, remain at your stations", Forkbraid informed everyone aboard the Solstice.

"Varak. I need you back in engineering", Forkbraid commanded.

"Understood Captain", Varak replied and left for his main engineering station.

Agent Murphy went quietly through his command sequence preparations.

"Tactical! Phased Laser Arrays online. Check!"

"Quad Pulse Plasma Cannons online. Check!"

"Long Range Sensors online. Check!"

"Short Range Sensors online. Check!"

"Ultra Sensors online. Check!"

"Targeting Array online. Check!"

"Targeting Cold Fusion Warheads when safe to do so. Check!"

"Sequencing. On passage through warhead target zone, utilise Phased Laser Arrays and Quad Pulse Plasma Cannons. Check!"

Agent Murphy then commanded, "Tactical. Lock in the command sequence in readiness for tactical operation as Warhead Mission One."

Agent Murphy informed Forkbraid, "Captain. Tactical operation is in the can and ready."

"Thank you Jim", Forkbraid replied.

"Marcus. Adjust our course. I want this ship to be in between those warheads and the L5 fleet. Put us in a spiral in front of those warheads. With a bit of luck, only a handful of warheads will get through", Forkbraid instructed.

"Aye Captain", Marcus replied, then queried, "What about the warheads heading to the Earth?"

Forkbraid sighed, then replied, "The colonies of L5 are far more fragile. A single hit and thousands, perhaps scores of thousands will die. Whatever the Earth's *never again* policy is, it had better be bloody good, because we can't be in two places at the same time."

Marcus nodded, "Understood Captain."

Peter Swann stepped in "It is a moot point anyway Captain."

"How so Peter", Forkbraid enquired.

"Captain, our current course takes us back to the Colonial Fleet at L5. To put the ship ahead of the warheads bound for L5 is a very minor course adjustment. The warheads bound for the Earth however, is an entirely different matter. A major course correction would be required and we would be late to the party anyway. The Solstice is fast, but she's not that fast", Peter informed Forkbraid.

"A moot point then Peter", Forkbraid repeated.

"Yes Captain. I've done the math. The only real option, is the one you've already chosen", Peter Swann confirmed.

As the Solstice approached the warheads heading for the L5 colonies, Peter who had been watching the long range sensors noted, "Captain. You'll want to see this."

"Put it on screen. Window in window., "Forkbraid instructed.

An image of the Earth appeared on the screen in a window on the left hand side. The Earth appeared smallish, but it wasn't the Earth that was the interesting point. A huge number of small lights appeared to be heading away from the Earth in the direction of the inbound warheads.

"Those are interceptor missiles Captain", Peter Swann informed him, then explaining further, "Earth Defence Forces appear to have had thousands of interceptor missiles at the ready."

"Do they have enough Peter?", Forkbraid enquired.

"No Captain. I expect they'll fall short, by maybe a couple of thousand", Peter Swann replied.

"So much for their *never again* policy", Forkbraid remarked.

"We can't count them out yet Captain", Peter Swann noted as he highlighted the Earth with a pointer and expanded the image.

"What is that?", a perplexed Forkbraid asked

"Captain. That, I'm thinking is their *'never again'* policy", Peter Swann replied.

"Not the missiles then?", Forkbraid enquired.

"No. Although the missiles could well be part of it", Peter Swann responded, explaining, "What we're looking at on the screen are orbital battle platforms. At least that is what our scanners are indicating."

"Orbital battle platforms?", Agent Murphy questioned.

"Yes. Orbital battle platforms. It looks like Earth Defence Forces have recently launched them. They are sitting well above the Earth in extreme high orbit", Peter Swann responded, adding, "There are a lot of them. A hell of lot. Between the interceptor missiles and those orbital battle platforms, I think they may just have this covered. Maybe? "

"Well then, that's a load off of our minds. Take it off the screen Peter", Forkbraid instructed.

"Captain. You don't want to watch?", Peter asked.

"The Earth Defence Forces either have this or they don't. Whatever the case, we can't be distracted from our task", Forkbraid responded.

"Aye Captain. Understood", Peter acknowledged.

The Solstice was close to the swarm of warheads inbound to the L5 Colonies and would soon be passing across the front the swarm.

"Marcus we need to maximise our time in front of that swarm to give Jim his best shot at taking down those warheads. I don't expect they'll target us, but be ready for evasive action at a moments notice, just in case", Forkbraid instructed.

"Aye Captain", Marcus replied.

"Jim. We want to avoid becoming collateral damage, so no cloaking on this run. Ensure our shield grid is on maximum though", Forkbraid instructed.

"Aye Captain", Agent Murphy replied.

"Charlene. Please let Captain Carmichael know, that we are entering the fray. Tell him anything that gets past us, is in his ball park", Forkbraid instructed.

"Aye Captain." Charlene replied.

As the Solstice slipped in front of the missile swam, Agent Murphy commanded, "Computer. Activate shield grid at maximum. Tactical. Perform tactical operation Warhead Mission One as listed. Auto targeting and firing at will."

The Computer and the Hornet's nest both replied, "Complying."

Immediately the Hornet's nest began targeting and firing at the nearest warheads. Brilliant blue beams of light and purple pulses of plasma shot forth and stuck their targets. Warheads began to explode in brilliant blue balls of light.

The swarm of warheads was large and Marcus adjusted the Ship's course into a spiral as previously instructed, so as to linger as long as possible, in front of the swarm. The Hornet's nest continued firing at will, taking out warhead after warhead. It was not nearly enough, there were warheads getting through.

"Captain. There's a message coming through from the Solstice Sir", the Communications Officer informed Captain Carmichael.

"Put it on my screen Lieutenant", Captain Carmichael replied.

Captain Carmichael quickly read the message on his screen, he then turned to the bridge's main screen and watched as brilliant blue explosions began to pop off in the distance."

"Lieutenant. Notify the fleet. The Solstice has entered the fray. Anything that gets past the Solstice is our responsibility. Destroy all incoming warheads! Nothing gets past us! Make that clear. Nothing gets past us!", Captain Carmichael ordered.

"Aye Captain. Message being sent now Sir", the Lieutenant replied.

"Lieutenant. All pilots to their Wisps. Launch our interceptors", Captain Carmichael ordered.

"Aye Captain", the Lieutenant replied.

With those orders, the Colonial Fleet and the Cruiser Spartan entered the fray and began intercepting any warheads that managed to elude the Solstice. There was a lot of them.

Lieutenant Blixen was manning the Spartan's surveillance station on the bridge and noted something interesting in the long range scans.

"Captain Sir. You'd better take a look at this", Lieutenant Blixen informed the Captain.

"Well, what are you waiting for Blixen? Put it on screen. View in view, top left corner", Captain Carmichael ordered.

Lieutenant Blixen did as ordered and began to narrate, "Captain. You can see the Earth in background. The major swarm of warheads is en-route, nearly six and a half thousand strong, that is clearly visible. In between, getting right close to those warheads, you can see the Earth's response."

Lieutenant Blixen then focused the window on the warhead swarm and the Earth's missiles.

"Interceptor missiles?", Captain Carmichael queried.

"Thousands of missiles Captain", Lieutenant Blixen corrected, adding, "And there's more."

Lieutenant Blixen popped up a second window below the first, with a clearer view of the Earth.

All around the Earth at the extremes of high Earth orbit, were small glints of light. Hundreds and hundreds of them.

"Orbital battle platforms in extreme stationary high orbit", Captain Carmichael remarked, adding, "Now we know what they're *never again* policy is."

As Captain Carmichael and Lieutenant Blixen watched, the Earth bound warhead swarm met the Earth Defence Force's interceptor missile response and bursts of brilliant blue light began appearing in the bridge screen's top left window. Burst after burst after burst. Too many to count.

"Off screen Blixen", the Captain ordered, "Let's focus on our task."

By the time the Solstice had reached the limit of its spiralling course and thus the outer limits of the warhead's swarm, the battle for L5 was well and truly underway. Many of the warheads had been destroyed, however many had also gotten through. These were now being destroyed by L5's Colonial Fleet, their back foot defence, but all was not well. Forkbraid ordered Marcus to alter the Solstice's course to help chase down the warheads.

"Captain! Warheads are getting past!", Lieutenant Blixen urgently informed Captain Carmichael.

"Lieutenant! Alert the interceptors. Chase down those warheads. We have to get every last one!", the Captain ordered the Communications Officer.

"Aye Captain", the Comms Lieutenant replied.

"How many ships do we have at our rear Blixen?", Captain Carmichael asked.

"More than a few Captain", Lieutenant Blixen replied.

"Get them intercepting those warheads now Blixen", Captain Carmichael ordered.

"Aye Captain", Lieutenant Blixen acknowledged.

Lieutenant Blixen looked to the Communications Officer, "Make it so Lieutenant."

"On it now Sir", the Comms Lieutenant replied.

"Captain. It looks like those warheads have begun final targeting", Lieutenant Blixen advised, "We may not get them all!"

"We have to Lieutenant. We have to. To miss even one of those warheads would be a disaster", Captain Carmichael responded.

"We're being hailed by one of our Corvette Captains Sir. The Pegasus", the Communications Officer informed him.

"Put it on screen Lieutenant", Captain Carmichael instructed.

"On screen now Captain", the Communications Officer replied.

"Captain Carmichael", the face on the screen began, "We are out of missiles and still have one warhead left in our zone to intercept. It's targeting a toroidal colony. One of the larger ones. We're going to take it down with our ship!"

"Is there no other way Captain?", a shocked Captain Carmichael asked.

"No Sir. It is the only way!", the Captain of the Corvette Pegasus replied, his face showing a combination of both fear and resolve.

"Gods speed Captain", Captain Carmichael replied.

The Corvette's Captain saluted and Captain Carmichael returned the salute.

The Corvette Pegasus continued on its course, placing itself between the warhead and the colony. The Pegasus was then it was struck amidships, on the starboard side. There was a huge explosion of brilliant blue light, mixed with streaks of orange, yellows and reds. The communications window on the Spartan bridge's main screen dropped out.

"Sweet Mother of God! We're reduced to throwing ourselves at those fucking things", Captain Carmichael swore, "How many crew were on the Pegasus Blixen."

"Assuming a full compliment Captain. One hundred and fifty Sir", Lieutenant Blixen replied.

"And that colony?", Captain Carmichael asked.

"Toroidal colony Semipalatinsk has a population of just over twenty five thousand Sir", Lieutenant Blixen informed the Captain.

"One hundred and fifty brave souls just saved twenty five thousand", Captain Carmichael remarked, then ordered, "Blixen. Note the actions of the Captain and Crew of the Pegasus for posthumous accommodation."

"Aye Captain", Lieutenant Blixen replied.

Lieutenant Blixen informed Captain Carmichael, "Captain. The Solstice is still in action Sir. They're helping us take down the remaining warheads."

"Thank God for that Ship Lieutenant. It may not be a big ship, buts it's certainly powerful. The Solstice has taken out more missiles and warheads than our entire fleet. Note that down as well Blixen", Captain Carmichael instructed.

"Captain Sir. One warhead appears to have gotten through the net Sir!", Lieutenant Blixen shouted out loudly.

"Get our interceptors on it. Who's closest Blixen?", Captain Carmichael instructed and enquired.

Lieutenant Blixen was slow to respond, "There's no one Sir! We can't stop this rogue!"

"Plot its course and put it on screen", Captain Carmichael ordered, then asked, "What's that damned thing targeting?"

Lieutenant Blixen looked directly at the Captain as the warhead and its target came up in a window on the screen, "Captain. It's going to hit, Nova Hollandia colony Sir."

Captain Carmichael stared at the screen, "Holy fucking crap!", he swore.

Nova Hollandia was an O'Neil type colony consisting of connected ,twin counter rotating cylinders, each with north and south end caps, docking rings, heat radiators, reflective mirrors and everything else you'd expect for a colony of that type.

"Population Blixen?", Captain Carmichael asked, still staring at the screen and understanding they could do nothing, nothing at all to save the colony.

Lieutenant Blixen's reply was slow and mournful, "Captain. Nova Hollandia is a big colony Sir. It has a population of well over a quarter of a million people."

And then the warhead struck. It struck the eastern cylinder of Nova Hollandia, right in its southern end cap. A burst of brilliant blue light suddenly burst into view on the screen, it was heavily polluted with massive streaks of orange, yellows and reds. The ball of light expanded greatly and then ever so slowly died down, fading away, taking very long minutes to do so.

All the colonies of L5 had been placed on the highest alert, so in theory, their inhabitants had gone to their colony's shelters. Air tight compartments designed to keep their populations safe in case of a major hull breach or an extreme colony failure. However, no one had prepared the colonies for this kind of damage.

As the explosion petered out, the damage became clearly visible. Nova Hollandia's eastern cylinder's southern end cap had a massive, gaping hole in it. The hole was easily bigger than a third the size of the end cap and it extended deep into the main cylinder body. Both structures were now completely open to the vacuum of space and devoid of life supporting air.

The massive hole was surrounded by jagged, twisted, melted metal that had been the end cap and cylinder's structure. Chunks of debris of various sizes floated freely in space. Some of them on collision courses with the Nova Hollandia's nearby western cylinder.

The entire southern end cap and southern end of the eastern cylinder had been completely irradiated with deadly ionising radiation. Many of the connecting guy wires and some of the transport tubes had broken away and were now floating loose in space. The entire eastern cylinder was no longer aligned to the Sun and that was a major, major problem.

The Communications Officer remarked, "How could anyone survive that? There must be fifty thousand dead. Probably more", he had tears welling up in his eyes.

There was no time to consider the dead, "Lieutenant. Pull yourself together man. There'll be four times that number dead if we don't act now!", Captain Carmichael ordered.

"Aye Captain", the Lieutenant responded, wiping his eyes, his voice was still somewhat grief stricken.

"Lieutenant. Contact Nova Hollandia's western cylinder, who ever is in charge", Captain Carmichael ordered, "Tell them they have to cut all the remaining guy wires and connections to their eastern cylinder. Every connection has to be severed. Every last one. It's imperative that they do this and they do it now. This has to be done quickly. Very quickly. Make them understand!"

"Aye Captain. I'm contacting them now Sir. I'll make them understand", the communications Lieutenant acknowledged.

Shortly after the Communications Officer contacted the Nova Hollandia colony, the guy wires and other connections between the two cylinders began to be released and disconnected on the western cylinder side. It was happening so quickly, that one could see the urgency in the matter.   One by one the guy wires were disconnected. One by one the connecting transport tubes were blown away. It would not be long before Nova Hollandia's western cylinder was set completely free from its severely damaged eastern cylinder.

Then what Captain Carmichael had anticipated, began to happen. Nova Hollandia's eastern cylinder's automatic attitude control thrusters began firing. Normally these would work in unison with those on the western cylinder. However, with all of the damage to the eastern cylinder and now being disconnected from the western cylinder, they were acting alone and completely out of control. It had been absolutely necessary to separate Nova Hollandia's colony cylinders from each other.

The eastern cylinder was way off station and the automatic attitude control thrusters began firing repeatedly in their attempt to correct the situation. This began a repeating cycle, a positive feed back loop. With all of the structural damage to the eastern cylinder's southern end cap and the actual cylinder itself, the response was the further buckling and twisting of that cylinder.

This increased damage put the Nova Hollandia's eastern cylinder further off station and the automatic attitude control thrusters, increased their firing in order to attempt a correction. The eastern cylinder responded by buckling and twisting even further, exaggerating the feed back loop even further. The eastern cylinders rotational rate began increasing at the same rate as the increased automatic attitude control thruster firing. The more the thrusters fired, the faster the eastern cylinder spun and the positive feed back loop grew even stronger.

On board the Spartan, Captain Carmichael and his crew could do nothing but watch. It was the same for the engineers on Nova Hollandia's western cylinder. Disconnected from the eastern cylinder, they were now relatively safe, only having to watch out for debris collisions and fixing the issues arising from those. With regards Nova Hollandia's eastern cylinder however, there was absolutely nothing they could do.

"She's going to concertina, collapse in on herself Captain", Lieutenant Blixen remarked.

"Yes Lieutenant", Captain Carmichael replied, "That is what I was afraid of."

"Captain Sir. If we can't shut those attitude control thrusters down, that cylinder will literally tear itself apart", Lieutenant Blixen observed.

"Don't you think I know that Blixen?", Captain Carmichael replied, pointing at the screen, "Look at that fucking damage. The whole southern end cap is a radioactive dead zone. There is no one alive at the controls over there."

"Captain. The Solstice is hailing us Sir", the Communications Officer interjected.

"On screen Lieutenant", Captain Carmichael ordered.

"Aye Captain", the Communications Officer replied and a new window popped up on the screen.

"Forkbraid", Captain Carmichael greeted.

"Captain", Forkbraid greeted in reply, then informing the Captain, "Our Ship's scans tell us, all the L5 bound warheads are destroyed."

"Yes. Thank you Forkbraid, I was aware of that", Captain Carmichael replied, adding, "We do have another, more pressing issue to deal with at the present moment."

"We can see that Captain. My Science Officer has informed me that Nova Hollandia's eastern cylinder is going to rip itself to pieces", Forkbraid noted, then asked, "Is there anything we can do to help?"

"Unlikely, unless you can shut down that cylinder's attitude control thrusters", Captain Carmichael informed Forkbraid.

"How do we access the cylinder's attitude control Captain?", Forkbraid asked.

"You can't Forkbraid", Captain Carmichael replied, informing Forkbraid, "Those thruster are controlled from the attitude control centre. That's in the southern end cap."

Forkbraid had the same images on the screen and the same data as well, "Oh, I see", he replied.   Forkbraid could see the massive hole in the southern end cap, extending deep into the main eastern cylinder and the radiation readings displayed on the screen indicated an extremely high degree of lethality. It was a complete dead zone.

"Are there no controls we can use in the northern end cap?", Forkbraid asked.

"Your from the Earth Forkbraid, so you wouldn't know", Captain Carmichael replied, "The northern end caps in O'Neil type colonies are for governance, politics, commerce, business etc. The southern end caps are the engine rooms. That's where all the engineering and control systems are found. So, no, there's no controls in the northern end cap. Nothing we can use anyway."

"Okay. Can the attitude control thrusters be controlled from the western cylinder?", Forkbraid enquired.

"I wish that was the case Forkbraid", Captain Carmichael replied, "In a paired colony like this one, each cylinder controls its own thrusters. They work in unison yes, but at the end of the day, they are separate systems. The western cylinder has no control over those thrusters."

By now the main cylindrical section of the eastern cylinder had collapsed and compressed to less than half its normal length. If the collapse continued, the entire northern end cap would also be lost as well.

Peter Swann interjected, "Captain. I have an idea."

Forkbraid replied straight away, "Spill it Peter!"

"There are still people alive over there Captain. Attitude control thrusters are not hard wired. Those thrusters are wirelessly controlled with encrypted data instruction streams", Peter informed Forkbraid, further illuminating, "If we give the Ship's Computer the task of shutting those attitude control thrusters down, being three laws safe and with further loss of life being imminent, I'm certain the ship will find a way to do so."

"That's actually a good idea Peter. Make it so", Forkbraid instructed.

"Computer. Scan Nova Hollandia's eastern cylinder's access control thrusters. Access their command stream inputs. Break their encryption coding and shut them down. Lives are at stake! This task is imperative! Reporting required.", Peter Swann instructed the Ship's Computer.

The Ship's Computer replied in its pleasant feminine voice, "Complying" and began scanning the cylinder's attitude control thrusters.

"What's happening Forkbraid? What's your plan?", Captain Carmichael enquired.

"My Science Officer, Peter Swann, has instructed our Ship's Computer to hack into those attitude control thrusters and shut them down", Forkbraid replied.

"Can it do that?", Captain Carmichael queried, knowing his own ship's computer could not.

"We are about to find out Captain", Forkbraid replied, informing him further, "Our Ship's Computer is a three laws safe, advanced positronic matrix and there are still survivors on that cylinder. If there is a solution, it will find it."

"I hope that Computer of yours is quick. We don't have a lot of time", Captain Carmichael noted.

By now the main cylindrical section of the eastern cylinder had collapsed and compressed to less than a third of its normal length.

The Solstice's Ship's Computer reported, "Compliance. Encryption broken. Command shutdown sequences are being issued. Attitude control thrusters are shutting down."

As they all watch the screens and the images of Nova Hollandia's eastern cylinder, one by one, the attitude control thrusters shut down. The cylinder was still spinning quite rapidly, but it had stopped collapsing in on itself and compressing. There were sighs of relief on both ships.

"Captain. I recommend getting emergency services over there right away", Forkbraid advised.

Captain Carmichael turned to his Communications Officer, "Get on it Lieutenant."

The Communications Officer replied, "Aye Captain."

Peter Swann enquired of their Ship's Computer, "Computer. Calculate a death toll estimate."

The Ship's Computer replied, "Complying" and then after a few short moments, "The death toll is estimated to be higher than sixty thousand lives lost."

Both Captain Carmichael and Captain Forkbraid sat back in their chairs.

Captain Carmichael sighed, "At least sixty thousand, plus the crew of the Pegasus."

Forkbraid corrected him, "Plus the crews of the other two ships that took direct hits Captain."

"Other two ships?", Captain Carmichael queried.

"Yes. They flew straight in between the warheads and their targets. No word, nothing. They just flew in and took the hit. Bloody brave men!", Forkbraid informed the Captain.

"Bloody brave men indeed", Captain Carmichael agreed.

Peter Swann had been keeping an eye on the warheads inbound to the Earth and later that day, he drew Forkbraid's attention to the latest developments.

"Captain. You'll want to see this", Peter informed Forkbraid.

A window opened up on the bridge's main screen. It displayed an image of the Earth, its high orbital zone, complete with a multitude of battle platforms and in the distance the remaining warheads still inbound to the Earth.

"Peter. Share this data feed with the Spartan. Include both long rang scan and ultra scan data."

"Aye Captain", Peter Swann replied.

"Captain. Captain Carmichael of the Spartan is on the line", Charlene informed Forkbraid.

"Put him on screen Charlene."

Captain Carmichael appeared on the screen, "Forkbraid", he greeted, then, "It looks like we're going to see how the Earth's *never again* policy pans out."

"Captain", Forkbraid greeted then replied, "Let's hope it's not a disaster."

"Yes. We've had enough of those for one day", Captain Carmichael agreed.

As they watched their screens, the Earth Defence Force's orbital battle platforms rearranged their configuration, changing their orbits to provide maximum defensive coverage in the direction of the remaining warhead swarm. By the time the warheads reached the Earth, the orbital battle platforms were in place and ready for action. One by one the orbital battle platforms opened fire from the extremes of high Earth orbit at the approaching warheads. One by one, warheads began exploding in brilliant bursts of blue light.

Peter Swann remarked, "Captain. It looks like fifteen hundred or more warheads got past the Earth's missile defences."

"That's a lot Peter. Can the Earth survive this?", Forkbraid queried.

"Without knowing the specifications of their battle platforms, I really can't say", Peter replied.

Captain Carmichael, who was still on screen snapped, "Can you speculate man? Give us some idea of what to expect?"

Forkbraid reminded him, "Captain. We are not a military crew!"

"Of course. My apologies. Speculation at this point would be useful Mr Swann", Captain Carmichael replied.

"My take Captain. It's touch and go. Some of those warheads may get through", Peter replied, informing further, "You have to remember. None of us knew the Earth Defence Force's even had those orbital battle platforms until they were launched. And the sheer number of warheads that the Horridians launched was unprecedented. I'm also hoping that those warhead explosions are generating significant electromagnetic pulses."

"Why so Peter", Forkbraid asked.

"Hopefully to damage the guidance systems on any warheads they might just get through", Peter explained.

"All of our modern electronics are hardened against EMPs Peter. Why would Jovian electronics be any different?", Forkbraid noted and asked.

"During the outer satellite insurrection, it was the inner solar system, the Earth in particular that was on the receiving end. That's the reason our electronics are all hardened against EMPs. That may not be the case with the Jovian system", Peter explained, adding, "They may be hardened enough for Jupiter's radiation belts, but not enough for EMPs."

As they continued watching, more and more warheads exploded and then they noticed something different. An explosion of brilliant blue light occurred far closer to the Earth. It was so close that it was difficult to discern whether it was the Earth that had been hit or a lucky near miss.

"Computer. Analysis of close Earth explosion. Divulge details of explosion", Peter asked the Ship's Computer.

The Ship's Computer replied, "Complying", then after a few short moments, "Upper atmospheric air burst with a two megaton yield. Ultra scans indicate surface to air warhead interception."

As they were digesting that information, there were several more explosions of brilliant blue light. Warheads were getting past the orbital battle platforms in greater numbers.

The Ship's Computer continued the analysis without being requested, "Nine further upper atmospheric air bursts, each with a two megaton yields. All surface to air warhead interceptions."

Peter Swann informed Forkbraid and Captain Carmichael, "Captains. I hate to say I'm right, but this is beginning to look a bit *'touch and go'*. Those warheads are getting awfully close."

Straight after Peter spoke, there was another series of bursts of blue light even closer to the Earth's surface and the Ship's Computer reported, "Warhead strike in far Northern Atlantic Ocean, between Iceland and Norway. Two megaton yield. Warhead strike in Northern Europe, Northern reaches of Gulf of Bothnia, Oulu, Finland. Two megaton yield. Population at risk, four hundred thousand human beings. Warhead strike in Northern Europe, White Sea, Arkangelsk, Russia. Two megaton yield. Population at risk, five hundred thousand human beings."

Everyone was shocked by the Computer's reports, Agent Murphy noted, "Those are not big cities. I can't believe there's a tactical advantage in targeting them."

Peter Swann replied, "Those warheads were probably off course. Their proper targets were probably further south in Europe."

"And that means their electronics were not hardened against EMPs", Agent Murphy noted.

"A logical conclusion, but without actually capturing a warhead and analysing its circuitry, we could not know for certain", Peter replied.

It didn't end there. There were more explosions that also appeared to be on the surface of the Earth itself.

The Ship's Computer responded once more, "Warhead strike in far Mid Northern Atlantic Ocean, eight hundred miles east of Washington, USA. Two megaton yield. Warhead strike in far Mid Northern Atlantic Ocean, eight hundred miles west of Lisbon, Portugal. Two megaton yield. Warhead strike in Western Europe, Lisbon, Portugal. Two megaton yield. Population at risk, nine hundred thousand human beings. Warhead strike in Western Europe, Palma de Mallory, Spain. Two megaton yield. Population at risk, eight hundred thousand human beings."

Shocked faces continued to watch their screens and as they watched the remaining warheads were quickly destroyed. Mostly in space by the Earth Defence Force's orbital battle platforms. Only a few more reached the Earth's upper atmosphere and were destroyed long before they could reach the surface.

The Ship's Computer announced, "All warheads destroyed. Four Earth cities destroyed. Precise casualties unknown at present, however, casualties including deaths could reach two point six million human beings. We will monitor the Earth's emergency services and disaster relief communications for more accurate information."

"Well that was an unmitigated disaster", Captain Carmichael remarked.

"No necessarily Captain", Forkbraid replied, explaining, "Considering that the Horridians launched two thousand two hundred missiles, containing twenty two thousand cold fusion warheads. For the Earth to have only four destroyed cities is actually a miracle. It should have been a far, far worse."

"Thinking of it that way Captain, the Earth's policy of *'never again'*, could be considered a huge success.", Agent Murphy added.

"Whether their policy of *'never again'* was a success or a failure, I'll leave that up to history to decide. That is not my call", Captain Carmichael replied, then added, "One thing I can tell you though, with four dead cities on the Earth and a destroyed colony up here in L5, there will be plenty of people baying for blood in both camps. The Horridians have got to pay for this!"

"And pay they shall Captain. I just hope that the calmer minds prevail", Forkbraid replied.

26. Baying for Blood

"Captain. I have a Tanya on the line, secretary Tanya? President Banyan's secretary?", Charlene informed Forkbraid questioningly.

"Put her on the screen Charlene, but also get Captain Carmichael on the line as well", Forkbraid replied, "He will want to be in on this call as well I expect."

"Aye Captain", Charlene replied and only a few seconds later a window appeared on the screen and President Banyan's secretary came into view.

"It's nice to see you again Tanya", Forkbraid greeted the President's secretary.

"It's nice to see you again as well Forkbraid", Tanya replied, then straight to the point, "President Banyan would like to speak with you."

"By all means, please put the President on screen", Forkbraid responded, adding, "Does the President mind if Captain Carmichael joins us?"

Tanya looked over to her left and then replied, "The President is more than happy for Captain Carmichael to join in. Putting President Banyon on the line now."

"Mr President. It's good to see you again. It has been quite a while", Forkbraid greeted when President Banyan's face appeared on the screen.

"Yes Forkbraid, it has been quite a while and it's good to see you as well. I just wish times were somewhat less troubling", the President of Colonial Central Command Colony and thus the President of the whole of L5 replied.

Another window popped up on the screen and Captain Carmichael greeted them, "Mr President, Forkbraid. Good to see you both "

Forkbraid and President Banyon both returned the greeting.

"You always seem to be two steps ahead of everyone Forkbraid", President Banyan remarked, then informing both Captain Carmichael and Forkbraid, "With the battle for L5 over and the loss of so many innocent lives, we are going to be holding a commemoration ceremony for the victims. For both the victims here at L5 and those victims on the Earth."

"A commemoration ceremony?", Forkbraid queried, adding, "It does seem a bit too soon to me Mr President."

"Yes perhaps, but we do need a good distraction at the moment. There are many folk up here literally baying for blood. The people want revenge and a commemoration ceremony might help to simmer that down just a little bit. Trust me, distractions work", President Banyon explained.

"I see Mr President, but why would you need to be calling me?", Forkbraid asked.

"During the ceremony we will be awarding medals. Everyone involved in L5's defence will receive a medal in thanks for their service. Commemorating the Battle of L5, but there are also those who paid the ultimate price to save the people of L5", President Banyon explained.

"Yes. Those thirty three ships that were destroyed during the missile interception", Forkbraid noted in response.

"And those three Corvettes that flew in front of those warheads, trading their lives to save the lives of innocent colonists", Captain Carmichael added.

"Yes exactly gentlemen", President Banyon replied, he then turned to his secretary, "Tanya. What were the names of those Corvettes?"

"They were the Pegasus, the Griffin and the Chimera, each with one hundred and fifty crew", Tanya replied.

"Thank you Tanya. Make sure they're well noted down. I want to especially mention those three ships. Deliberately flying in front of a warhead to save innocent lives is especially noteworthy", the President commented.

President Banyon then turned back to the screen, "We will be handing out both medals of honour and gallantry, posthumously to the families of each of the crew members, who gave their lives for L5. It is the very least we can do to recognise their sacrifice."

"Agreed Mr President. That is the very least you should do", Forkbraid replied, adding, "Along with compensation to those families, for their loss."

"Yes. Yes. We are working on a suitable compensation package as well", the President replied, then added, "But that is not why I've called you Forkbraid. I've called to invite you and your crew to the commemoration ceremony."

Forkbraid was slow to answer, so President Banyon added, "You and your crew are heroes!"

Forkbraid looked gobsmacked, "Heroes?", he queried.

Captain Carmichael threw in, "Forkbraid. You and your crew are responsible for the destruction of well over thirty percent of those inbound missiles. Not to mention all the warheads that your ship took down. What else are you, if not heroes?"

"I'd never thought about it that way. We were just helping out", Forkbraid responded.

"My God man", President Banyon replied, "Had you not helped out, we would have lost a hell of a lot more lives. Maybe double or even triple. There's no telling how many more cities on the Earth, that might have been destroyed as well."

Forkbraid was eerily quiet. He had never thought about it that way. They were just helping out.

"Forkbraid, we'll need to know the names of your crew", President Banyon remarked, explaining, "For the medals I'll be presenting to you all. Medals of honour and gallantry."

"Charlene. Send the President's secretary, Tanya, a list of our crew", Forkbraid instructed.

"Aye Captain", Charlene replied, then sent off a list of the Solstice's crew, "Captain Folcrom Forkbraid. Officers. Tactical: James Murphy. Engineering: Varakhan Utana. Helm and Navigation: Marcus Greyhelm. Communications: Charlene Fewkes. Science: Peter Swann. Security: Zuawalo Pod and Zeealas Pod. Engineering Assistant: Nyaliep Pod. Special Consultant: Leroy McGuvan."

"We won't be able to attend the ceremony Mr President. Our task up here is not yet complete. There is one little bit of unfinished business that we need to attend to", Forkbraid informed President Banyon.

"Unfinished business did you say?", the President queried.

"Mr President. There's the little matter of one hundred thousand Trojan occupation troops heading your way and their heavy weapons transports", Forkbraid reminded the President.

"I was thinking that the Earth's Defence Forces and our own Colonial Fleet, combine forces and fly out to obliterate them. It does seem fair after all, considering what they've done", President Banyon replied.

"Except of course Mr President, "The Trojans haven't actually done anything. Not yet anyway."

"What do you mean? We can all see the results for ourselves", President Banyon responded.

"What's been done thus far, was done by the Horridians!", Forkbraid responded forcefully, "The Trojans colonies are occupied territory Mr President. They have been since the end of the outer satellite insurrection. You'll probably find most of those troops don't want to be here. They'd rather be back home in their asteroid colonies, with their families."

"You don't seem to understand Forkbraid. People are baying for blood. Not just here in L5, but down there on the Earth as well. Earth Gov is livid! Everybody wants revenge! We have to respond!", President Banyon was adamant.

"And respond we shall, but not in the way you're thinking. That would be like throwing petrol on a naked flame. It would be incendiary! Nothing good will come of it!", Forkbraid pushed back even more forcefully.

"What do you suggest then? We give them a free pass?", President Banyon questioned.

"Actually Mr President. That is exactly what I want to do", Forkbraid replied.

At that point the President's secretary, Tanya, caught President Banyon's attention, "Yes Tanya", the President enquired.

"The Solstice's crew Mr President. There's an anomaly. Look at the last crew member's name", the President's secretary, Tanya replied.

"Leroy McGuvan?", President Banyon questioned, then stated, "He is a wanted terrorist!"

"Yes Mr President. Leroy McGuvan was a wanted terrorist", Forkbraid replied.

"Was? He still is!", President Banyon responded.

"Well. There will be a problem with double jeopardy in that case. Double jeopardy is still a thing here in L5, I do believe", Forkbraid replied.

"Well yes, but I don't see how that's relevant in this case", President Banyon stated.

"I personally tried, convicted and executed Leroy McGuvan on Mars Mr

President", Forkbraid informed him.

"He appears to be alive and well and working on your ship", President Banyon noted.

"Yes. After I executed him, a local fisher woman saved his life", Forkbraid replied, then stated, "Irrespective of his survival, he cannot be tried for the same crimes twice. Double jeopardy!"

President Banyon turned to his secretary, "Is Forkbraid right Tanya?"

"Mr President. I'm no expert, but I believe that Forkbraid has a very valid point", Tanya replied.

"There is another matter Mr President", Forkbraid remarked, then informed, "After Leroy McGuvan had been saved and recovered from his ordeal, he was demolished."

"Demolished?", President Banyon enquired.

"Yes, demolished. It's psychic procedure that fundamentally changes a person.", Forkbraid informed the President, adding, "Our Leroy McGuvan is no longer the same man as the terrorist."

President Banyon turned to his secretary once more, "Tanya. Have you heard of this demolishing? Is that a thing?"

"Give me a second or two Mr President", Tanya replied as she searched the colonies databases, then after a couple of minutes, "Yes Mr President. It is an Earth psychic procedure. Demolishing a person is used to completely alter a persons fundamental personality at the deepest levels. At the end of the process, they are a completely new person and are incapable of committing any further crimes. It is used on the worst of the worst criminals on the Earth."

"Thank you Tanya", President Banyon replied, then turning back to Forkbraid, "We'll have to leave Leroy McGuvan in your custody for the moment Forkbraid."

"Now, about those Trojans. You want to give them a free pass?", President Banyon circled back.

"Yes Mr President and Leroy McGuvan will be crucial to that process", Forkbraid informed him.

"How so?", President Banyon asked, adding, "You'll need to explain that one to me."

"Leroy McGuvan was crucial in getting the Trojans to peacefully leave Mars", Forkbraid replied, further informing the President, "To the Trojans and the Jovians for that matter, Leroy is considered a hero and a martyr. When they hear that he not only survived the Battle of New Tortuga, but has also flipped sides and tells them his story. I believe it will have a profound affect on the Trojans."

"And then what? They'll just leave and go home", President Banyon asked. He had a rather incredulous look on his face.

"Mr President. It worked on Mars. I believe it will work here as well", Forkbraid told him boldly, "And further more, what choice do they have?", he didn't wait for an answer, "They either leave or they will be obliterated. Those are their only two options!"

"I don't know Forkbraid. A colony in ruins and more than sixty thousand dead and that's just up here. Down there on the Earth, they have four ruined cities and two point six million dead or close enough to it", President Banyon replied, "And you want me to just let them slide on by? As I've already said, everybody is baying for blood!"

"So you keep saying Mr President. So you keep saying", Forkbraid replied and decided to engage his psychic abilities subtly, "Two wrongs don't make it right Mr President. There are one hundred and twenty five thousand Trojans in the occupation forces on their way here. Do you want the blood of one hundred and twenty five thousand Trojans on your hands! That blood will never, never wash off!"

The subtle lilt in Forkbraid's voice had its effect, "No of course not! I don't want that!", the President snapped back, "No one wants that kind of blood on their hands! What do you propose we do about them?"

"You let us deal with the Trojans. Myself and Captain Carmichael that is. If we can get them to leave peacefully, then that's a wonderful thing", Forkbraid replied, but then added, "If not, if they stay the course. Then in that case the Earth Defence Forces and the Colonial Fleet can have them. We cannot save men, who don't want to be saved."

"That sounds fair Forkbraid. I'll let you and Captain Carmichael have your chance. If you can turn those Trojans around, so be it", President Banyon decided.

"Captain Carmichael. You'll assist Forkbraid in this task", President Banyon instructed.

"Yes Mr President", Captain Carmichael replied.

"Forkbraid. We'll hold the medal ceremony for your crew in absentia", President Banyon stated.

"Captain. After the Trojan action is completed. Hold a medal ceremony aboard the Spartan for the crew of the Solstice. Have it filmed for distribution over the news feeds at a later date", President Banyon ordered.

"Yes Mr President", Captain Carmichael replied, not clarifying what, at a later date meant.

"Now, something else I've noted here on your crew list Forkbraid", President Banyon commented, adding, "Special Agent James Murphy is your Tactical Officer. How'd that happen?"

"He is the best man for the job Mr President", Forkbraid quickly replied, adding, "Jim is also the New Flinders Psychic Academy's and the Elysium Colony's Head of Security."

"A man of many hats it seems", President Banyon remarked, then replied, "I was kind of hoping James would be coming back to L5 at some point in time. He has been one of our best Agents."

Agent Murphy stood up from his station and moved closer to Forkbraid, so he could be seen by President Banyon on the screen.

"Mr President", he greeted, then informed, "Unfortunately, I won't be returning to L5, not to live anyway. I have recently sent through my letter of resignation. Perhaps that information hasn't filtered through to your office yet."

"Ah. There you are James. No, that information has not come across my desk as yet. So, there's no chance of luring you back to L5 then? A better salary offer perhaps? We can negotiate something better, far more to your liking maybe?", President Banyon queried.

Agent Murphy chuckled, "No Mr President, although the offer is very much appreciated."

Usually a person who keeps to himself, Jim informed President Banyon,

"A lot has happened since I was left for Mars Mr President. I've very recently married two local Martian girls and I now have a couple of children on the way. So I need to consider my new family on Mars and make a new life there, for them."

"Ah family. Yes well, family should always come first. You are quite correct there Mr Murphy", President Banyon replied, "Two wives did you say?"

"Yes Mr President. It is funny how things turn out", Agent Murphy replied, further noting, "It all happened so quickly and unexpectedly, it even caught me by surprise."

"Well Mr Murphy. Good luck to you", President Banyon replied, further remarking, "If you and your family ever decide to emigrate back here to L5, you will all be welcome here of course."

"Thank you Sir", Agent Murphy replied and soon there after the call ended.

It was now official, Special Agent James Murphy of Colonial Central Command at L5, was now the Security and Tactical Officer James Murphy of Mars.

The very next day, a warship from the Earth approached the Solstice. The bridge crew had watched as the Earth ship approached and were not overly surprised when it hailed them.

"The Earth ship is hailing us Captain", Charlene informed Forkbraid.

"Put them on screen Charlene", Forkbraid replied.

A man appeared on the screen before them. They were not aware of who he was, but from his insignia, they could see he was a five star General.

"General Stanton here. Where is your Ship's Captain?", the General demanded.

"You are talking to him General", Forkbraid replied.

"Good. Good. I'm here to take possession of your ship", the General informed Forkbraid.

"Possession of my ship?", Forkbraid queried, then replied, "The hell you are."

"You don't have a choice Captain", the General replied, informing Forkbraid further, "Earth Gov has authorised me to take your ship into custody. We are commandeering your ship!"

"Really. First of all, this ship is a private vessel and secondly, Earth Gov does not have any jurisdiction over my ship. So General, you can bugger off and go annoy someone else", Forkbraid replied, basically telling General Stanton where to go.

"Did you not hear me? You have no say in this matter", the General replied.

"General. My crew risked their lives to take down well over a third of that Jovian missile swarm, that was heading towards the Earth. Your Earth Gov should be bloody well thankful", Forkbraid reminded the General.

"Earth Gov is thankful Captain. We are all very thankful Captain", the General admitted.

"Really General. They certainly have a strange way of showing it!", Forkbraid threw back.

"You don't understand Captain", the General replied, explaining, "Your ship has superior technology. Technology that we are going to need in our fight against the Jovians. Earth Gov doesn't think it's appropriate for a ship, with your Ship's capabilities, to be in private hands."

"Firstly General, my ship does not have any superior technology", Forkbraid lied convincingly, "And secondly, Earth Gov has no jurisdiction over Mars or for that matter my ship. You can politely tell Earth Gov to go bugger off."

"No superior technology?", the General questioned, "If that is the case, why is your ship so damned fast?"

Forkbraid thought quickly to himself, *"Hide the lie within the truth"*, then he replied simply, "Micro fusion thrusters General."

"Micro fusion thrusters?", the General questioned.

"When I commissioned the building of this ship, I specified that it must be the fastest ship in the solar system", Forkbraid admitted, "I figured that I would need that, with the Horridians arking up and causing all kinds of trouble."

"And that is one of the reasons Earth Gov wants your ship", the General admitted.

"General. When my engineer designed this Ship's thrusters, he simply took the original thruster designs for a much larger ship and made a handful of very clever tweaks, some enhancements and modifications. That's why, our ship is so fast", Forkbraid informed the General.

"Again that's why we want your ship", the General again told Forkbraid.

"We want your ship! Now there's the truth of the matter! Earth Defence Forces want the Solstice, not Earth Gov. This is the General's decision!", Forkbraid thought to himself, before replying with a question, "If you take standard fusion thrusters, then modify them to be extremely efficient and then scale them down in size to suit a ship of the Solstice's size, all the while maintaining their original power outputs, what do you get?"

General Stanton thought for a moment, you could almost hear the wheels turning in his head, then he replied, "Micro fusion thrusters."

"Exactly General", Forkbraid replied, adding, "It takes an Interplanetary Liner, a little over three weeks to get from the Earth to Mars. The Colonial Cruiser Spartan, can cover that same distance in around two and half weeks if the Captain pushes his ship. The Solstice can cover that very same distance in around a week."

Forkbraid did not specify if that week was seven days long or fives days long and he just left that part completely ambiguous.

"So you're telling me, it's all just a thrust to mass ratio sort of thing?", the General answered, as if he understood what Forkbraid had told him.

"That pretty much sums it up General", Forkbraid again lied convincingly, "Smaller fusion thrusters, with the same power output as the original specifications and mounted to a much, much smaller ship. The end result is exactly what you've observed."

"We will still need your ship Captain", General Stanton reiterated.

"Well you can't have my ship General!", Forkbraid told him in no uncertain terms, then he made him an offer, "How about, I ask my engineer to send you a report on what design changes he made to develop my Ship's micro fusion thrusters? Will that suffice?"

"Yes, yes. That would definitely save us some time", General Stanton agreed, "However, we will still need your ship!"

"Save us some time? It would negate their need to reverse engineer the micro fusion thrusters. That's all he means", Forkbraid thought to himself, then asked, "You'll have the thruster designs. Why do you still need my ship?"

"Your weapons technology. We are going to need that as well", General Stanton admitted.

"Again General. Our weapons systems are nothing new. You have exactly the same weapons technology available to you, that we have. Where do you think our designs came from?", Forkbraid replied, this time it was the absolute truth.

"If that is the case, how did you take down all those missiles?", the General asked.

Forkbraid avoided the question and steered the General down another path, "General. I'm going to list our weapons systems. You tell me yea or nay, as to whether you have the same technology."

"Okay", General Stanton replied.

"Phased laser arrays?", Forkbraid began the list.

"Yes. We have those", the General replied.

"Okay. How about hyper resonant disrupters?", Forkbraid questioned.

"Ah yeah. We have those as well", the General admitted.

"Good. Good. What about pulse plasma cannons?", Forkbraid asked.

"Yes. Of course we have those", the General replied.

"Okay. I expect you also have electromagnetic rail guns", Forkbraid questioned.

"Yes. Or course we have those as well", the General remarked, he was becoming impatient.

"One final one General. You do have torpedoes and torpedo tubes, yes?", Forkbraid asked.

"Of course we do. Where is this going? Are you telling me that's all you have?", the General demanded.

Forkbraid lied convincingly once more, "Yes General. That's all the weapons systems we have", conveniently leaving our any mention of the Ship's defensive and cloaking systems or its use of a quantum singularity for its energy storage.

"If that is the case Captain, then how the hell was your ship so effective against those missiles?", General Stanton asked.

"General. How do your tactical officers control their weapons systems?", Forkbraid asked the General in reply.

"They use the standard ships computer systems of course", the General replied.

"Exactly General. Your tactical officers have to do a lot of the work themselves. Sure they can use the Ship's computers and the Ship's sensors to pick out targets and line them up. Ducks in a row sort of a thing, but your tactical officers have to actually do the work and then take the shots", Forkbraid replied.

"Of course they do. That's the case with any ship. Your tactical officer would be no different", General Stanton noted.

"And that is where you are completely wrong General", Forkbraid replied.

"Wrong? In what way?", the General asked.

"The Solstice doesn't have a standard ships computer. How could we? Those are military computer and control systems. We don't have access to those", Forkbraid replied.

"Then what the blazes does your ship use?", General Stanton asked.

Forkbraid replied with a half truth, completely leaving out the Hornet's nest, "My ship, the Solstice, its main computer, is a three laws safe positronic matrix."

General Stanton was gob smacked, "No way!", he replied.

"Yes way General", Forkbraid replied, "My Ship's main computer is an Android brain. That is why my ship is able to use its weapons systems so effectively. The ship does most of the work!"

It was again a half truth, but Forkbraid had no choice. He could not let the General know that his ship was not entirely three laws safe.

"But Captain", General Stanton protested, "That would mean your ship is only useful against unmanned targets. Missiles, drones and the like. Against a real fleet, with manned ships involved, it would be complete bloody useless."

"And there you have it General", Forkbraid replied, "So. Do you still want my ship?"

General Stanton rubbed his chin, "Not if the damnable thing can't fire on live targets I don't. It's an absurdity. It's completely useless to me. What would

I do with a three laws safe warship?"

"My point exactly General", Forkbraid lied again convincingly, he had however achieved the result he wanted. The General no longer wanted his ship.

"Now we've gotten past that little problem General", Forkbraid began, "Let me introduce myself, "I am Captain Forkbraid, Captain of the Spaceship Solstice. I'm also Lord Folcrom Forkbraid and I use to run the Psi-corp remote viewing teams."

For once the General concentrated more fully on Forkbraid's face. Forkbraid altered his appearance ever so slightly with a glamour and ever so slightly took on the visage of a viper.

General Stanton suddenly realised who he had been talking to, worse of all, who he been making demands of. Lord Folcrom Forkbraid, the most powerful Wizard on the Earth.

"Holy fuck!", were the two words that escaped the General's mouth.

Forkbraid sighed, "It's okay General. I'm not going to do anything horrible to you."

"You're not?", a far more contrite General Stanton replied.

"No General", Forkbraid replied, reassuring him, "I'm not that petty. I can have a heated discussion with someone and not lash out at them."

"That is good to know Captain Forkbraid", the General replied, informing him further, "Because we need to discuss this another issue."

"And that would be?", Forkbraid queried.

"As you probably know, Earth Gov is baying for blood", the General noted.

"Yes. Yes General. I am hearing that phrase a lot lately", Forkbraid replied with a sigh.

"Earth Gov wants us to team up with the Colonial Fleet and wipe out the Trojan Armed Forces, that are headed our way", General Stanton admitted.

"General. I'm going to tell you exactly what I told President Banyon", Forkbraid replied, adding, "The Trojans haven't actually done anything yet. I fully intend to convince them to go back to where they came from."

"I don't know Captain", the General replied, adding, "Four cities destroyed! We haven't even finished tallying the dead. It could actually reach beyond two and a half million. The people of the Earth want revenge!"

"You think I don't know that General?", Forkbraid responded, adding, "You can't put out a fire by throwing petrol on it!"

"I know that Captain. You know that Captain", General Stanton agreed, "But, you try telling those damned politicians that. They are hell bent on revenge!"

"Here's the deal General", Forkbraid began, then informed him, "The Colonial Cruiser Spartan is going to accompany my ship, on an intercept course of the Trojan Armed Forces. We will attempt to convince them go home. If we succeed, they'll all head home. Job done! If any of their fleet, come this way and threaten the Earth or L5, then they're fair game."

"Okay Captain. That actually sounds quite fair", the General agreed, "Any Trojans that come this way. We'll obliterate them."

"Agreed General", Forkbraid agreed with him, but then he warned, "Those Trojans that decide to return home, will be under my protection!"

General Stanton rubbed his chin once more, then agreed, "As you wish Captain. As you wish."

After General Stanton signed off, Charlene turned around and looked at Forkbraid.

"Yes Charlene. I told the General a few porky pies. I needed him to completely reject our ship and it worked", Forkbraid replied to her look.

"It's not that Captain. It's just how easily you manipulated him", Charlene told him, "You didn't even need to use your gifts."

"No. I didn't. I figured if I could convince the General that our ship was useless to him, that he'd change his mind about wanting it", Forkbraid replied, adding, "This was all him, this was not Earth Gov. The General, was the one who wanted our ship."

Charlene nodded in understanding.

"Charlene. Please request Varak's presence on the bridge", Forkbraid commanded.

"Aye Captain", Charlene replied, then over the intercom, "Varak, your presence is required on the bridge."

A few minutes later Varak appeared on the bridge with Nyaliep in close step behind him.

"I hope you don't mind Captain. I have Nyaliep shadowing me, so that she can learn what daily checks and balances I do aboard the ship", Varak informed him.

"Good idea Varak", Forkbraid agreed, "I've just be talking to a General Stanton."

Varak replied straight away, querying, "An Earth General?"

"Yes Varak", Forkbraid replied, then asked, "How'd you know it was an Earth General?"

"There are no Generals up here in L5 Captain", Varak replied, adding, "That is an Earth thing."

Forkbraid turned to Jim Murphy questioningly, "Jim?"

"The highest rank in the L5 Colonial Fleet is Captain", Jim replied.

"How does that work Jim?", Forkbraid queried.

"Ostensibly all the Colonial Fleets Captains are equals, except the Fleet Captain, Captain Carmichael, who is the first among equals", Jim explained, adding, "You have to remember, L5 is supposed to be, in theory, an egalitarian society."

"So there's no hierarchy?", Forkbraid questioned.

"Officially not, but in practice, of course there is", Jim answered, "The Captain of a Corvette, is lower than the Captain of a Frigate, who is lower than the Captain of a Destroyer. At the top you have the Heavy Cruiser Captains, like Captain Carmichael."

"So the command hierarchy is based on the class of ship a Captain commands?", Forkbraid asked for clarification.

"Yes Captain. That's what it boils down to. The bigger your ship, the higher up you are in the command hierarchy", Jim confirmed, adding, "And within each class of ship, it's the length of the Captain's tenure. Time served so to speak."

Forkbraid nodded in understanding.

"FB, when you were introduced as the Captain of the Solstice, that would have given Captain Carmichael pause for thought", Jim noted, "The Solstice is an unknown class of ship, so where would you fit in, in their hierarchy?"

"Oh. I see Jim", Forkbraid replied.

"You resolved that yourself when you reminded him, that this is a civilian ship", Jim noted.

"Thank you Jim. I had no idea", Forkbraid replied.

"You wouldn't. It is a Colonial Fleet peculiarity", Jim Murphy replied.

"And the Earth?", Forkbraid enquired.

"Well you already know", Jim replied, adding, "The Earth is more traditional and has typical Naval rankings. You know, with ensigns, lieutenants, commanders, rear admirals, vice admirals, admirals and fleet admirals. A rather complicated and antiquated system in my opinion."

Forkbraid nodded again in understanding.

Forkbraid turned back to Varak, "I have made a deal with General Stanton. We need to give him some fusion thruster design changes."

"What kind of changes?", Varak queried.

"Changes to make his fusion thrusters more efficient, somewhat smaller in size, but somehow keeping their thruster output as high as the original designs", Forkbraid informed him.

"Captain. You want me to give him, micro fusion thruster technology?", Varak questioned.

"Hell no Varak! That's the very last thing I want to do. We just have to give him a little something to keep him happy. That's all we need, just enough to keep the man happy", Forkbraid clarified.

Varak rubbed his face, he was thoughtful for a few moments, "I think I can come up with something Captain", he replied nodding.

"Excellent Varak. When you have, put it all together in a special report for General Stanton and hand it over to Charlene for transmission", Forkbraid ordered.

"Aye Captain", Varak replied.

"Charlene. After sending Varak's report to General Stanton, send a copy of it to Captain Carmichael as well. Let's keep them both happy and more importantly at the same level technologically", Forkbraid instructed.

"Aye Captain", Charlene replied.

27. Reality Check

With the missile attack on L5 and the Earth over, the Jovian High Prince called another meeting of his Brothers and his Generals. The Prophet and his pilot Matthew had been requested as was usually the case. An analysis of their surveillance data had been carried out and this also needed to fit into their deliberations.

The Prophet arrived at the meeting on his own. His pilot Matthew had accepted his new commission with the Jovian Armed Forces and had been helping them with their analysis of the surveillance data. When the Prophet arrived at the meeting, he was the last one to arrive. High Prince Heinrich greeted him and requested he take his seat.

The High Prince started the meeting with, "For those of you who haven't yet heard. The Prophet's pilot Matthew, has accepted his commission with the Jovian Defence Forces. Matthew now holds the brevet rank of Captain. Welcome Captain Matthew Murphy."

The High Prince started clapping and all the others in the room, all joined in.

"Thank you Your Majesty", Matthew replied

After the clapping stopped, the High Prince requested, "Captain Murphy. If you would please let everyone know the results of our surveillance analysis."

Matthew stood up and began, "I have been working closely with a team of analysts reviewing the surveillance logs", Matthew informed everyone.

He continued, "These surveillance logs are from our inner surveillance station three, which is just inside the main asteroid belt. This station was at the time of our missile strike's final approach to the Earth and L5, our closest surveillance station at that time."

"The first attack on our missiles came from the rear, as the mystery Martian ship approached in transit from Mar to the cis-lunar space", Matthew informed the room, adding, "What could be ascertained, is that the destruction of our missiles began as the ship approached the missiles swarm. That destruction then continued as the ship flew through our missile swarm. The ship itself was extremely fast and could not be detected by our optical scans."

Prince Wulfric interjected loudly, "How? How the hell does a ship not show up on our optical scans?", he demanded.

The High Prince held up his right hand to silence and calm his Brother.

"Your Highness. We are still working on that and we have some theories, which I will divulge later. Please allow me to continue", Matthew replied.

A not so happy Prince Wulfric nodded for him to continue.

"During the second attack on our missiles, there were two strikes in quick succession. A one two punch, so to speak. The first was by a small fleet of Earth and L5 Colonial ships. Our missiles detected the fleet and actually managed to destroy over thirty ships", Matthew informed everyone.

He then added. "However, quickly after that, the mystery Martian ship appears to have struck. The pattern was very similar to its first attack. Our missiles are destroyed on approach and as the ship passes through the swarm. Again, the ship is not detected by our optical scans, nor by our missiles. It passed through our missile swarm unscathed."

Matthew looked around the room, in case anyone had any questions. He made sure to look at Prince Wulfric, however Prince Wulfric simply nodded to Matthew to continue.

"The third strike against our missiles was very similar to the second, except it appears that the mystery ship hit first this time. Exactly the same as before. Same result. We could not detect the ship and neither could our missiles", Matthew remarked.

He then noted, "It was at this point that our missile swarm split into two groups for their final approach to the Earth and L5. After that, our missiles then of course launched their warheads. The combined Earth and L5 fleet then split up into two groups to chase down our warheads."

Prince Valdamar stepped in, "My Brother Wulfric, is being extremely patient at present, however I must admit, I am getting a little impatient myself and would like to hear these *'theories'* of yours."

"Your Highness. I am getting to them. Please, just a couple more minutes", Matthew replied.

"The next time we see the mysterious Martian ship is in L5's defence against our warheads", Matthew began, he then brought a slide up onto the rooms video screen, "And there is our mysterious Martian ship!", he pointed at the highlighted image on the screen before sitting down.

The images was small, it was somewhat darkish, but it was also fairly clear. Barely visible at the rear of the ship, one could even make out the exhaust plumes from the micro fusion thrusters.

Prince Wulfric was perplexed and remarked, "I've never seen a ship like that before", then asked, "What the hell class of ship is that?"

"We don't know Your Highness", Matthew replied, stating, "It has to be something new. Something very, very new."

"Why the hell are we able to see it now?", Prince Valdamar asked.

Matthew replied, "Your Highness. The ship was flying in a spiral pattern as the warheads flew past it. I expect they did this, in order to maximise their time on targets. In this image, it is being illuminated by warhead detonations, both in front and behind the ship. That might be the only reason we are able to see it at all."

"Just how big is that thing? It doesn't look very big at all", Prince Wulfric asked.

"It is much bigger than a patrol ship and yet at the same time, much smaller than a Corvette", Matthew informed him, adding, "I'd say it's about the same size as a large space yacht."

"What? Like your Delilah?", Prince Wulfric queried in disbelief.

"Your Highness. We can't tell exactly, but I suspect it is somewhat larger than the Delilah", Matthew replied, noting, "Which is my Lord's ship, not mine Your Highness."

"So your theories?", Prince Valdamar asked.

"Yes. Yes. Let's hear them", Prince Wulfric seconded.

"Our analysts came up with the following and I do tend to agree with them, at present", Matthew began and then continued, "The ship itself has a midnight black hull. A black hull against the black of space and our optical scans are unlikely to see that ship at all. The only reason we see it now in that image, is because of the illumination from the warhead detonations around it."

Matthew looked around the room once more, waiting for any questions before continuing, "Its fusion thrusters appear to be rather small. Much smaller than anything I'm aware of. During its previous attack runs, it may have been coasting. At least that is what our analysts believe. I am not so sure. It is possible, that it can run its thrusters in some kind of stealth mode, which is again unheard of. We do need more information to clarify to truth of the matter."

"Coasting? Stealth mode? How can we tell which?", Wulfric enquired.

"Your Highness. We can't. At least, not with the information we currently have", Matthew admitted to him, having already stated clearly that they needed more information.

Prince Valdamar stepped in, "Those fusion thrusters look awfully bloody small. I'm not aware of anything like that. Even on your Delilah, the photon thrusters take up more than half of the ship."

"Yes Your Highness. That is very true", Matthew agreed, "Even compared to the Delilah's thrusters, which are considered small photon thrusters by the way. Those fusion thrusters are very small and yet that ship, is much faster than the Delilah."

High Prince Heinrich summed up, "So that's what we know. It's extremely fast. It's hull is likely mid night black in colour and it has fusion thrusters that are very small, extremely powerful and possibly able to run in a stealth mode. So that's what we have, yes?"

"Yes Your Majesty. Sadly, that does sum it up. We do need more information", Matthew agreed.

"Thank you Captain Murphy", the High Prince replied using Matthew's new title.

"General Snide. Would you like to cover our missile attack on the Earth and L5?", High Prince Heinrich asked.

"Yes Your Majesty", General Snide answered.

"We have only partial success in our missile attack on the Earth and L5", the General remarked.

The General then put a short video on the screen, "What you are looking at here, is more surveillance from inner surveillance station three. You can see a lot of our warheads detonating. The Colonial Fleet managed to put up an incredible defence. Now you can see here, how our warheads took down at least three Corvettes and if you watch very, very closely."

He paused for a few long moments until a large flash appeared on the screen, "Bingo! That is an L5 colony being ripped apart by a two megaton warhead!"

The whole room watched the after effects of the warhead strike on the L5 colony. It was absolutely devastating. Everyone was clapping and applauding.

The High Prince raised his right hand to quieten the room.

"Unfortunately, that was the only L5 colony that was struck", the General admitted, informing the room further, "Based on the damage we see in the optical scans, at least a quarter of those colonists have died. This unfortunately will not be enough damage to sow the fear, confusion and doubt we were hoping for. We were hoping for far more devastation than we achieved!"

Prince Wulfric asked, "What of the Earth?"

"I was just about to get to that Your Highness", the General replied.

The General put on another video, "Here you can see that most of our warheads were intercepted by Earth's defensive missiles."

The screen portrayed warheads detonating by the scores, still a very good distance from the Earth. It quickly became obvious that most of the warheads had been intercept long before they reached the Earth. Thousands of warheads in fact. The video continued to play and then after several more minutes of showing brilliant blue detonations, it stopped. General Snide then replaced that video with another.

"This gentlemen, is much, much closer to the Earth. These are the warheads that evaded the Earth's first missile defences. Our analysts believe, there were around fifteen hundred warheads that got through", the General informed the room, "You can now see the Earth's second ring of defences. It appears the Earth has a great number of orbital defence platforms. These were not there earlier, so they were obviously launched very recently."

They watched the video for many long minutes as warhead after warhead detonated in brilliant blue bursts, almost to many to count.

Then finally General Snide noted, "There! You see! Right there!", he pointed to the screen, "Warheads! They got through their defences and struck the Earth!"

Every one in the room stood up to get a closer look. General Snide replayed that section and they all watched it once more.

"How many General? How many warheads got through?", Prince Wulfric enquired.

General Snide answered, "It's very difficult to say Your Highness. At the distance our scans were taken from. Our estimates are somewhere between six and twelve."

"Somewhere between six and twelve!", Prince Wulfric screamed, he was livid, "We attacked them with twenty two hundred missiles! You know, that's like twenty two thousand warheads! And what, we've one damaged L5 Colony and the Earth gets hit with six to twelve warheads! Is that all we have to show for it?", he questioned.

Prince Wulfric was on his feet and pacing up and down the room, he turned to Matthew, "Captain Murphy! You were bloody well right! Thank God you advised us to build up our defences!"

The High Prince stood up, "Brother!", he shouted, then in a lower tone, "Wulfric. Will you calm down and take your seat." Everyone else had sat back down.

Prince Wulfric replied, "Brother! Those bastards are going to come here. All we've done is piss them off. They'll be baying for blood. Our blood! They are coming here!"

Prince Wulfric was frantic.

High Prince Heinrich walked over to his Brother Wulfric and placed his hands on Wulfric's shoulders, "Brother. Calm down!", he said softly and then he leant in and touched his forehead to his Brother's forehead gently for a moment, before stepping back.

"Wulfric. Will you please sit down?", the High Prince requested in gentle tones once more.

Wulfric walked to his seat and sat down.

"Your Majesty", Prince Valdamar spoke up, "Brother. If we had gone with my original plan, we would not be in this situation. We would instead have control of the Belter Colonies!"

The High Prince looked at Prince Valdamar, "Really! Really Brother! That's all you have to say, 'I told you so'. Unless you have something more constructive to say, then maybe you should just, say nothing at all!"

Prince Valdamar looked away sheepishly as he replied, "I am sorry Heinrich."

Matthew stepped in, "This is not the time to panic Your Highness's. Now is the time to start working the problem."

"You are correct Captain", High Prince Heinrich agreed, "We need to start working the problem", he then looked around the room for any suggestions.

The Prophet spoke up, "Whatever Matthew advised the last time. Building up our outer defences. Whatever has been done to date, it won't be enough. Whatever was planned, double it, triple it!"

"Yes my Lord", Matthew agreed, "That is a good starting point. If they get out this far, we can't let them inside our outer defences."

"Agreed Captain", the High Prince agreed, then to his Brothers, "Wulfric, Valdamar, Make it so? Make our outer defences into an impenetrable barrier. Leopold. Provide what ever assistance you can to your Brothers", he commanded.

"Yes Your Majesty", All three Horridian Brothers answered.

"More ideas people?", the High Prince requested.

"Missile defences", Matthew tossed in, "If they start heading our way. We need to hit them en-route. They can't breach our outer defences, if they can't get here."

"Good, good!", High Prince Heinrich agreed once more, then to his, "Brothers. Keep building our strategic missiles by all means, however, now I'm adding tactical missiles to your list. We need them and we need them fast."

"We have tactical missiles already in stock Brother", Prince Wulfric noted.

"Your Highness. It won't be enough", Matthew replied, "Whatever we now have, assume we'll need a lot more."

"Yes, but exactly how many Captain?", Prince Wulfric enquired.

"Your Majesty", Matthew addressed the High Prince, "If your Brothers can provide me with data, on what they currently have and the capacity of their manufacturing systems. I can put together a team to work out what to prioritise on. What we'll need and the likely timeline that we'll need it."

"That is a good idea Captain", High Prince Heinrich agreed, "Brothers makes it so!", he ordered.

"Aren't we forgetting something Brothers?", Prince Leopold interjected softly.

Prince Valdamar caught on quickly, "Our occupation forces!"

"Yes. Yes. Our occupation forces! The Trojans!", Prince Wulfric noted as well.

General Snide stepped in, "We could have our occupation forces hit anything that flies in cis-lunar space. If we can't control the high ground, we can at least cause a great deal of havoc."

"Yes. Yes", Prince Valdamar agreed, adding, "Let's fuck them all right up!"

Matthew stepped in quickly to bring them all to reality, "Our occupation forces consist of two hundred troop transports containing one hundred thousand troops. They were expecting to arrive at a beaten and demoralised L5 with little means to defend itself. That is not the current situation."

"Yes Captain", Prince Valdamar agreed, "However, you are forgetting the two hundred weapons transports. They each contain ten heavy weapons stowage bays."

"Yes Your Highness, but what is in those stowage bays?", Matthew enquired.

"Brother Wulfric. What did we put in those stowage bays?", Prince Valdamar asked.

"It's better to think in terms of weapons transports Brother", Prince Wulfric replied noting, "Each transport is carrying four small patrol ships, four small gun ships and four interceptors. We did managed to fit two interceptors per stowage bay."

Matthew quickly did the math in his head, "So all up eight hundred of each. Those patrol ships won't last long. Not against the Colonial Fleet. The gun ships and interceptors will put up a good fight. In the end though, they are no match for a combined forces of the Earth and the Colonial Fleet. We'll only be slowing them down, with what is ostensibly just a suicide mission. And the Trojan troops, they'll be next to useless, absolutely useless."

"They will buy us some time Captain", the High Prince noted, "Valuable time for us to prepare our defences. We also have to remember, they are only Trojans after all."

Matthew found the last statement quite distasteful, but said nothing.

"General Snide. Order our Trojan occupation forces to engage the Earth Defence Forces and the Colonial Fleet. They are to destroy everything in their path. Tell them to make us proud!"

"Yes Your Majesty", General Snide responded.

It was not long after that, that the meeting broke up.

As Matthew and the prophet were leaving, the High Prince remarked, "It's a good thing we have you onboard Captain Murphy."

"I'm happy to help Your Majesty", Matthew replied, "It's a shame my cousin James isn't here to lend a hand. He's a bit of tactical genius. A very clever man my cousin."

"I take it he's back at L5 then Captain", the High Prince enquired.

"Yes. He is Your Majesty", Matthew confirmed, "I doubt that he'd help us though. He works for the L5 security on Colonial Central as a Special Agent. My cousin and I, have never really seen eye to eye on anything. It is a real shame."

"Oh I see Captain. In that case it's probably better that you're here and he is all the way back there", the High Prince suggested.

"Agreed Your Majesty. Agreed", Matthew replied.

The Prophet and Matthew then headed back to their apartments.

The Prophet queried, "Matthew. How is it you're always right?"

"My Lord. There are times when I wish I wasn't", Matthew replied, "And today is just one of those times."

"You have a cousin that works as a Special Agent for the L5 security?", the Prophet questioned.

"Yes my Lord. He's quite high up in their Security Department. He even advises the President on all security matters", Matthew confirmed.

"You've never mentioned him before Matthew", the Prophet remarked.

"It wasn't important before my Lord", Matthew informed him, "But now, that's all changed. My cousin James is likely advising our enemies. He is effectively now my nemesis."

"And they will be coming here?", the Prophet questioned.

Matthew stood back and looked squarely at the Prophet, then replied, "It is precisely as Prince Wulfric put it my Lord. Earth Gov and the Gov of L5 for that matter, are going to be baying for blood. I have no doubts about that. Revenge is all they'll see. Mark my words. They are definitely coming our way my Lord. Definitely!"

28. Calmer Minds

It was a wonderful day in the northern end cap of Io Prime, but then, weren't they always. The Prime colonies of the Jovian system were big yes, but in the smaller confines of their end caps, the weather was largely controlled. The days were generally warm and delightful, with rain being programmed for the late evening and wee small hours of the morning. Only in the southern end cap were things a little different. In that end cap, a somewhat cooler, more brisk climate had been chosen, allowing for snow.

The colonial pattern in the Solar System was similar for all cylindrical colonies and the Jovian System was no different. The northern end caps were all about commerce, business and politics. The southern end caps however, were the engines rooms, all technology and control systems. In the north they manage the people, in the south they manage everything else was often said. The northern end caps faced towards the sun, the southern end caps faced the darkness of deep space.

Lakshmi and Pavarti lay on a colourful picnic rug, looking up across the northern end cap, at the penthouse apartment where they lived. It seemed quite small across the intervening distance. Neither of them seemed in the least disturbed by the buildings literally hanging above their heads, nor the even more disturbing scene of buildings jutting out sideways to their left of right around the northern end cap.

The sun, actually a hemispherical redirection mirror, shone brightly or more correctly concentrated and distributed the sun's rays optimally. The two sisters giggled to themselves as they talked about the latest school yard gossip.

Miriam, Rani and Princess Giselle sat on another picnic rug nearby preparing food. Young Prince Ulrick lay in his bouncer, being looked after by his nanny. The men folk, Abram, Rajsheev and Prince Leopold were sitting on soft grass by one of the many lakes in the Palace grounds. Abram had just finished casting his line and placing his fishing rod in its rod holder. He was the only one who seemed to have any interest in fishing today. Rajsheev being Hindu that made sense, however Prince Leopold was being unusually quiet.

"You're not saying much Leo?", Abram who had become accustomed to addressing the Prince informally enquired, before asking, "The meetings at Ganymede Prime didn't go well I take it."

A sombre Prince Leopold replied simply, "No. They certainly did not."

Abram was about to ask if the Prince wanted to talk about it, but before he could Prince Leopold continued, "My Brother Heinrich, the High Prince. His war is not going according to his plans."

Abram and Rajsheev had figured out something was wrong, but only now were they finding out what it was.

Prince Leopold continued, "Some years back, My Brother, Prince Valdamar put forward a plan to conquer the five largest of the Belter Colonies. You know, Ceres, Vesta, Pallas, Hygiea and Juno. It was a simple plan and in my estimations, probably would have worked. Heinrich though, he's so damned ambitious. Instead of doing the simple thing, Valdamar's plan, He and Wulfric concocted this grandiose plan to conquer the entire inner solar system."

"And that is now going badly?", Rajsheev, who didn't know if he should even ask, enquired.

"Oh Rajsheev. That is an understatement", Prince Leopold replied, informing them, "With Valdamar's plan, no one in the inner solar system would have batted an eyelid. Who would have cared about the Belters? Only the other Belters and they're no match for the Jovian Realm. Heinrich's and Wulfric's plan however? All they have done is poke a sleeping Dragon with a very, very pointy stick!"

"That really does sound bad Leo", Abram agreed.

"It is. Heinrich chose a high stakes gambit. Slap the Earth and L5 with twenty two thousand warheads, delivered by twenty two hundred missiles. Hit Mars as part of the attack plan for good measure as well", Prince Leopold informed them, "Sounds simple enough doesn't it. Leave the Earth completely devastated, with L5 in total disarray. All ripe for the picking. My Brothers did not consider the Earth's response."

"What happened Leo?", Rajsheev asked.

"Here's what my Brothers wanted. They wanted Mars occupied as a habitable Jovian world. The Earth completely devastated and unable to defend itself, totally at our mercy. L5 completely occupied, giving the Jovian Realm the high ground in cis-lunar space", Prince Leopold explained, adding, "That would have given them control of the entire inner solar system or at least they thought it would."

"And so what did they achieve?", Abram enquired.

"Mars came through completely unscathed. At L5, they lost maybe thirty to forty ships and one twin cylindrical colony was damaged", the Prince informed them, "And the Earth? Maybe, just maybe, six to twelve warheads got through their defences."

"Six to twelve out of over twenty thousand?" Abram questioned, asking further, "You did say twenty two thousand didn't you?"

"Yes", Prince Leopold confirmed, "My Brothers had not considered that the Earth and L5 might just have the ability to defend themselves. Maybe they just thought that the sheer size of the attack would overwhelm their defences. I don't know. I'm pretty sure though, that after the last war, the Earth and L5 were not just going to sit on their hands and do nothing."

"I would have thought that was obvious", Abram remarked, explaining, "The Earth and L5 are technological power houses. After the last war, I would have expected very formidable defences."

"Yes and yet, my Brothers failed to take that in account", Prince Leopold replied, adding, "And now, the bill is coming due. We've been scanning the news feeds from the Earth and L5. That one crippled colony in L5. That one colony alone is over sixty thousand dead. Then there's the Earth. Oh my God! We're hearing about four cities wiped out and a death toll approaching two point five million. They don't even have their bodies! Most of them have been vaporised. They count the dead by locating the living. If people can't be located, then they must be dead! It is truly horrifying!"

Abram understood what was worrying Prince Leopold, "The Earth and L5 will join forces. They'll be sending a huge fleet here. They're going to come here! They're going to make us pay!"

"Yes Abram. Did I not say the my Brothers have simply poked a sleeping Dragon with a very pointy stick?", Prince Leopold reiterated.

"You did Leo. You certainly did", Abram responded, "And the Earth and L5 governments will blame you along with your Brothers."

"Yes they will", the Prince replied, "I will be tarred with the same brush. No doubt about that."

"So you did try to stop this, didn't you Leo?", Rajsheev asked.

"Of course I did Rajsheev. Many times", Prince Leopold told them, "I've told my Brothers many, many times, the Jovian Realm has all the resources we need. Conquering others is not necessary."

"And your Brothers. They did not listen?", Rajsheev queried.

"Of course they didn't", the Prince answered, adding, "The voice of reason is seldom heard and ofttimes ignored."

Princess Giselle, who had walked over to bring the trio a plate of sandwiches, heard their conversation and chimed in with, "It doesn't help, that they think my Leo is slow."

Prince Leopold smiled, he understood exactly what his wife meant.

"He's not you know. Slow that is", Giselle continued, "His Siblings think he's slow because he's quiet and doesn't often speak his mind. My Leopold is actually smarter than all of them put together. If his Brothers had followed his advise, we wouldn't be in this mess."

Giselle sat down on the grass and Prince Leopold took her hand in his and patted it.

"You know where Hubert is right now don't you?", Giselle asked Abram and Rajsheev.

"No", they both replied.

"Hubert is looking into how the Ionian Realm can aid in bolstering the Jovian Realm's outer defences", Giselle informed them, adding, "It's an edict from the High Prince."

"Even though the Ionian Realm is not involved in the Military?", Rajsheev asked.

"We may not be involved in the Military, but they do need our resources", Giselle replied, "So we have to supply Callisto Prime with what ever we can."

At that point the float on Abram's fishing line disappeared under the waters of the lake. The bells on his fishing rod went off. Abram removed the bells and clipped them to his fishing jacket. He carefully reeled in the fish, a medium sized rainbow trout. After removing the hook from the corner of the fish's mouth, Abram carefully placed the fish back into the water and released it.

"Somehow, I don't feel like fishing anymore", Abram stated in a sad, mournful tone.

All of the others felt the same way.

Varak was busy in the engineering department, familiarising Nyaliep with more of the Ship's systems when Forkbraid walked through the door.

"Captain", Varak and Nyaliep greeted.

"Varak, Nyaliep", Forkbraid replied, "Everything going okay?", he enquired.

"Everything is good Captain. My assistant, Nyaliep, is learning at more than an adequate pace", Varak informed Forkbraid.

Nyaliep remarked, "Captain. My work is more about managing these systems. That is not so hard. It allows my Varak to concentrate on more important matters."

Forkbraid caught the phrase, *'my Varak'* and thought to himself, *"Nyaliep has chosen Varak! Another wedding when we get back to Mars. Candy and Cormac will be stoked"*, before replying, "That's great Nyaliep. Although don't shy away from the more complex work. You might enjoy it."

"Yes Captain", Nyaliep replied smiling

"Varak. There are a few things to discuss", Forkbraid stated.

"Yes Captain?", Varak asked.

"I did agree to give Captain Carmichael some advanced shielding technologies Varak", Forkbraid admitted.

"That does sound dangerous Captain. If every one has this technology, it could easily be misused", Varak expressed his concerns.

"Yes Varak. I do agree", Forkbraid replied, "However, I did actually agree to give Captain Carmichael something."

"Yes I see, quite the conundrum", Varak replied, remarking, "Perhaps, promise less in the future Captain."

"Noted Varak, you're absolutely right of course. For the moment though, put together some enhancements to their existing technology", Forkbraid suggested, "Nothing approaching anywhere near what the Solstice has, but something far better than they currently have."

"Ah Captain, I see. You want me to find that fine line between what they have, what they need and what we have", Varak understood.

"Yes Varak. Give them better than what they have, to give them an edge against the Jovians, but keep them well short of what we have", Forkbraid confirmed, "That should suffice."

"I will make it so Captain", Varak agreed.

Forkbraid tossed in as an afterthought, "Varak. What do you think about giving Captain Carmichael, passive cloaking technology?"

"Captain. Passive cloaking is simply re-skinning our ship with an appropriate camouflage colouration for every possible situation", Varak replied, "I see no problem with giving that technology to Captain Carmichael."

"Excellent Varak", ForkBraid replied, adding, "Give Captain Carmichael passive cloaking technology, but limit its usage for space only. Do not give him the full chameleon."

"The ability to turn their ships dark", Varak mused, "Black ships, on the black background of space. That should suffice nicely. I'll make it so Captain."

"Excellent Varak, put together some detailed reports and ask Charlene to send them to Captain Carmichael", Forkbraid replied, commenting, "If they're smart cookies, they'll work out how to extend that technology further, but that will take them time and then, they will have earned it."

Varak nodded in agreement.

"Have you made any headway with detection and triggering of slipstreams?", Forkbraid asked.

"Actually I have Captain. I believe the process will be much easier from the Earth than it was from Mars", Varak replied.

"Due to the Earth having a strong magnetic field?", Forkbraid queried.

"Precisely Captain", Varak answered, informing him further, "We should be able to detect frame dragging events and associated magnetic field anomalies much more readily. The Earth's gravity is stronger, its magnetic field is stronger. Detection should be far easier."

"If we find a slip stream, will it be usable?", Forkbraid asked.

"If we find one and if it's stable enough, then yes", Varak replied, remarking, "If the slip stream connects to Mars. We'll be upstream. To use Peter's toilet flushing analogy, we'd be going with the flow, not against it."

"I'd rather not use Peter's toilet flushing analogies Varak, but it's good to know we can possibly use a slip stream to get back to Mars", Forkbraid noted.

"Captain. From my analysis of our existing data, the usefulness of slipstreams is tied to magnetic fields. Having a magnetic field at both ends, lends itself to bi-directional traversal. Having a magnetic field only at one end however, lends itself to unidirectional traversal from the side that has the magnetic field", Varak explained.

"So from Mars, Venus or Mercury, without a significant magnetic field, we can't use a slip steam?", Forkbraid asked for clarification.

"Not quite Captain", Varak replied, informing him, "Mercury should not be a problem. It has a weak, but significant magnetic field. For Mars and Venus, I may even have a solution."

"A solution?", Forkbraid queried.

"Yes. A technological solution. However, I will need to work on it, in my lab on Mars. It is not something I can cobble together here in space. It requires a large, complicated technological device", Varak replied.

"My Varak is a very clever Man", Nyaliep commented smiling and beaming with pride.

Varak smiled in response to Nyaliep's comment.

"That he is Nyaliep, that he is", Forkbraid agreed.

"What about triggering slipstreams Varak?", Forkbraid queried.

Varak smiled once more, "I believe I can *'pulse'* a frame dragging event, to induce a magnetic field anomaly, a slip stream."

"Wow! Now that would be extremely useful Varak", Forkbraid replied, now smiling as well.

"It gets even better Captain", Varak replied, remarking, "I may even be able to direct, where the slip stream opens up at the other end. Which planet the slip stream will connect to."

For once Forkbraid was gobsmacked. Varak was close to being able to create usable slipstreams.

Nyaliep stepped in once more, "Did I not say, my Varak is a very, very clever Man", the pride was beaming off her smiling face once more.

Later that day Captain Carmichael and his Lieutenant Adjutant Hans Blixen came aboard the Solstice for a meeting with Captain Forkbraid and his crew. Jim Murphy, the Solstice's tactical officer greeted them at the docking portal and led them to the Captain's conference room.

"Captain. Lieutenant. Good to see you both again", Forkbraid greeted as the Captain and his Lieutenant entered the room, "Please take a seat."

"It's good to see you all as well Captain", Captain Carmichael replied before taking his seat.

Lieutenant Hans Blixen simply nodded and took his seat.

"Firstly Captain Forkbraid, I must thank you for those two reports", Captain Carmichael began, adding, "It has our engineers pulling their hair out. Simple tweaks to increase shield efficiency. Enhancements that no one had even thought of. Passive cloaking? Turning a ship dark in order to hide it. Now that one, was like a slap in their faces."

Captain Carmichael burst out laughing.

"Captain. You have Varak to thank for those reports. He is our engineer. Those reports are all his work", Forkbraid explained, "By the way, you don't need to call me Captain. This is, as I've mentioned before, a civilian ship."

"Well Forkbraid, your engineer Varak", Captain Carmichael nodded to Varak, "has certainly set the cat amongst the pigeons. Our engineers are wondering how the hell such obviously useful tweaks and enhancements were so completely overlooked."

Forkbraid nodded to Varak, indicating Varak should answer the Captain's question.

"What is obvious to one, is not necessarily obvious to another Captain. It is only when one points it out, that others notice it", Varak replied, explaining, "We humans have a whole history of over looking the obvious. History is full of such examples."

"Really Varak? Do you have many others?", Captain Carmichael asked.

Varak replied, "There are too many to list. I could spend many years just collating them all."

"Really?", a dumb founded Captain Carmichael answered.

Nyaliep commented, "My Varak is the best engineer. He is so very clever!", as she squeezed Varak's arm tightly. Nyaliep was completely enthralled by Varakhan Utana.

Captain Carmichael over looked the unprofessional crew behaviour, this was a civilian ship after all, "Yes Ma'am, I fully agree with you", then turning back to Varak, "Why passive cloaking? Why not simply paint the entire ship black?"

"A ship that is painted black and is black all the time, would be a navigational hazard", Varak replied, "Ships need to be visible for navigation and visual identification purposes. Cloaking is required only for very specific circumstances. Warfare for instance."

"Yes of course Varak", Captain Carmichael agreed, "Well, I certainly must thank you."

"I am simply doing my part in these uncertain times Captain", Varak responded.

"Well let's get down to brass tacks shall we. Those Trojans", Captain Carmichael suggested.

"Yes of course, but first", Forkbraid agreed, asking, "There was an earlier report we sent to General Stanton. I made sure you got a copy as well. What did your engineers make of that one?"

"Oh yes, that report", the Captain answered, "My engineers have been seriously studying that one as well. Varak's work I take it?"

"Oh yes. Definitely Varak's work Captain", Forkbraid replied.

"You know Forkbraid. I can push the Spartan and cover the Mars run in two and half weeks", Captain Carmichael informed Forkbraid, with already known information, then the Captain added, "With Varak's tweaks, his enhancements, the Spartan can cover that very same run, in a shade over two weeks."

Nyaliep asked Varak, "Is that good?"

The Captain answered for Varak, "Nyaliep, your Varak has given us the ability to increase my ships thruster efficiency by up to twenty percent. That is phenomenal!"

"Oh! That is good", Nyaliep remarked, smiling and squeezing Varak's arm once more.

"Have all of the enhancements been installed?", Forkbraid enquired.

"Most of them have Forkbraid", the Captain informed him, "But not quite all of them."

"Well then, are you ready to test out those that you have installed?", Forkbraid asked.

"Absolutely. What did you have in mind?", the Captain queried.

"Well it's back to those Trojans isn't it", Forkbraid reminded the Captain, informing him, "I've had Marcus prepare an intercept course", then he turned to Marcus and gave him the nod.

"Captain Carmichael", Marcus began, "Here we have an interception course plotted", he passed the data tablet to Lieutenant Blixen to upload the information.

"The idea is for both the Spartan and the Solstice to run a course that loops us out and behind the Trojans", Marcus explained, "That way we can approach their fleet from the rear."

"That is actually a good idea", Captain Carmichael commented, adding, "Most ships, if they have weapons, they are generally forward facing. Although, I do notice that the Solstice seems to be an exception to that rule."

"Well yes Captain, hence the rear approach", Marcus replied adding, "We'll come up behind them and then begin our *'negotiations'*, so to speak with our weapons systems locked on."

"Lieutenant Blixen", the Captain turned to his Lieutenant Adjutant, "Can we match that course?"

The Lieutenant tapped away at his grip's virtual key board, "With the new enhancements we have installed, yes Captain. It should not be a problem."

"Excellent. It sounds like we have a plan", the Captain agreed and clapped his hands together.

29. Calmer Minds Prevail

The Solstice and the Spartan flew along their intercept course and as planned approached the Trojan fleet from the rear. As with the Aft Trojan Fleet that had been dispatched to Mars, the Fore Trojan Fleet also flew in formation. As there were ten times the number of transports, the formation was somewhat different.

A large cone of two hundred troop transport ships were at the rear. Far out in front of the troop transports, was another cone of two hundred weapons transport ships. The weapons transports were the same as those in the Aft Trojan Fleet. They were of a known design with forward facing scanning arrays and forward facing defensive weaponry. It was highly unlikely the Trojan Fleet even knew that the Solstice and the Spartan were there.

Forkbraid had requested both Varak and Leroy be on the bridge during the negotiations. Varak in case any engineering issues cropped up. Leroy for his unique abilities, his redemption.

"Captain. I have Captain Carmichael on the line", Charlene informed Forkbraid.

"Put the Captain on screen Charlene", Forkbraid replied.

Captain Carmichael appeared on the screen, "Well Forkbraid, the Trojans are in front of us. How did you want to begin these negotiations?"

"Well Captain, first we need to isolate their command ship. We need to negotiate with their Fleet Commander", Forkbraid replied.

"That's actually the easy part Forkbraid", Captain Carmichael replied, informing him, "Their command ship, is the lead ship in the troop transport formation."

"How can you be sure Captain?", Forkbraid questioned.

"Two formations. Unarmed troop transports at the rear. Armed weapons transports out front. If I was their commander, that's precisely where I'd be. Right in the middle of it all", Captain Carmichael explained.

"Good Captain. I now know who to talk to and where he is", Forkbraid replied as he stood up and walked towards Leroy McGuvan.

"Leroy. On your feet man. I'm going to jaunt us, over to their command ship and we'll get that redemption of yours doing its job", Forkbraid informed him.

Without thinking, Jim stood up from his station, quickly walked over to Forkbraid and grabbed him by the right wrist, holding on firmly.

Jim Murphy looked directly into Forkbraid's eyes and thought at him as strongly as he could, mentally screaming, *"NO Forkbraid! Are you out of your mind? We are travelling at high speed, matching the Trojan Fleet's course and you have no idea what their command Ship's bridge interior even looks like. You're both likely to end up in space or worse, stuck in that Ship's bulkheads."*

The strength of Jim's thoughts caught Forkbraid completely by surprise. Jim was not a psychic!

"How Jim?", Forkbraid enquired.

"Selene!", Jim answered, "Selene told me, that if you were considering doing something so ridiculously foolish, to grab you physically by the arm, look you directly in the eyes and scream at you with my thoughts. Selene said that should catch your attention."

"Selene! That figures. You can let go now Jim", Forkbraid replied, "Leroy. Take your seat. We won't be jaunting anywhere today."

"Is everything okay over there?", Captain Carmichael enquired.

"Yes Captain", Forkbraid answered, "My tactical officer, Jim, was just reminding me that jaunting under the circumstances would be dangerous in the extreme. We'll just have to find some other method to employ Leroy's particular talents."

"That's a good first officer you have there Forkbraid", Captain Carmichael commented.

"Jim? First officer?", Forkbraid questioned himself.

Varak caught Forkbraid's attention, "Captain. Every human has an aura, an energy field. If I get the Ship's computer to scan Leroy and use that information to create an expanded energy field around the ship, that might just work. We could in theory, expand that energy field to cover a great deal of the Trojan Fleet. We will need to be well ahead of their command ship though."

"Okay. We can try that then Varak. I knew there was a reason for you to be on the bridge today", Forkbraid replied, then to Captain Carmichael, "Captain. We're going to cloak and position ourselves in front of their command ship. When we're in position, we'll let you know."

As Captain Carmichael watched, the Solstice disappeared from the Spartan's scanners, even more disturbing, the Solstice disappeared from view as well.

After a few long minutes Forkbraid signalled Captain Carmichael to hail the Trojan command ship. Forkbraid requested Charlene hail the Trojan command ship as well.

"General Sir", Captain Sharky, the Trojan Fleet Captain caught General Trask's attention, "We're being hailed by two ships."

"Two ships", the General enquired, "Ours?"

"I don't think they're ours General", Captain Sharky replied, "I think these are Colonial ships."

"Then where the bloody hell are they?", General Trask asked.

The Captain replied, "There's nothing on our scanners. They must be behind us General."

"Put them on screen", the General commanded.

Captain Sharky nodded to his communications officer.

A window popped up on command Ship's screen with Captain Carmichael's face within it. Another window popped up on the same screen with Forkbraid's face within it.

"Gentlemen", Captain Carmichael greeted, "I am Captain Carmichael, Captain of the Colonial Heavy Cruiser Spartan. My colleague is Captain Forkbraid, Captain of the Solstice."

"I take it your ships are behind us, sneaking up on our rear", General Trask replied disapprovingly.

Forkbraid replied, "Not quite. The Spartan is behind you, my ship however, is in front of you."

Forkbraid nodded to Jim to switch off the cloaking.

"What the fuck!", General Trask let out as the Solstice suddenly appeared in front of them. The Solstice was a smallish ship, like a large space yacht, but she was also quite heavily armed, bristling with weapons pods.

Captain Carmichael, noting the General's insignia, told him, "General. You need to alter your fleet's course."

"And why should we do that?", General Trask asked.

"Your current course will take you straight to the combined Earth and Colonial Fleets", Captain Carmichael informed him, adding further, "The Jovian missile attack was a complete failure. You and your fleet are flying to your deaths."

Now the General understood why their orders had been changed, "We have orders to engage your fleet Captain", the General replied.

Forkbraid quietly retrieved information from out of the General's mind, "You have Patrol ships, Gun ships and Interceptors. Eight hundred of each. Your fleet will not last long against what's waiting for you. Especially your Troop Transports", he advised.

"Captain Forkbraid is right General. His ship alone took down more than a third of your missile swarm", Captain Carmichael informed the General, "What awaits you at L5 is certain death."

"I can't just turn the fleet around", the General replied.

"We know that", Forkbraid responded, "Just change your course and fly past the far side of the moon, outside of L2 and go home. That's your only safe course. If you keep on your current course and enter cis-lunar space, your entire fleet will be obliterated."

"Yes General. Any course, other than the one just given to you, will be most unpleasant. Your fleet will be destroyed", Captain Carmichael confirmed.

Forkbraid nodded to Varak who activated the extended energy field that was based upon Leroy's aura. The huge energy field quickly expanded to encompass most of the Trojan fleet. Leroy stood up and approached Forkbraid.

"Your entire mission was a lie from the start General", Forkbraid informed him, "Perhaps Leroy McGuvan might be able to explain it to you better than I."

The General stared at the screen. So did Captain Sharky and his bridge crew. Before them stood the Hero of New Tortuga, the Martyr himself. Leroy began to tell them his story. Varak transmitted everything, visual and audio, over open channels that anyone in the Trojan Fleet could pick up on.

Leroy told them how he had been manipulated by the Prophet his entire life. He explained to them his story about the Battle of New Tortuga and how he had survived. Then he told them, what he had told the Aft Trojans on Mars before them. He told them the truth as openly as he could, there were no Christian persecutions on the Earth or L5, there were no demons on Mars, the Earth or L5 either. More importantly, all the reported deaths had been caused by the Prophet and his terrorists. Everything that the Trojans had been told had been a complete and total lie.

The General and the command Ship's bridge crew heard the message. Across the fleet many Trojans had picked up the broadcast as well. Many had even recorded it. The extended energy field covered most of the Trojan Fleet, but not all of it. There were some ships in the lead and outer formation of the Trojan Weapons transports, where the field did not quite reach. Did it work? Could Leroy's redemption be transmitted by an energy field?

"I know General. The truth is hard to swallow when it flies in the face of everything you've been told all your life", Forkbraid told him, "Especially so when your society has been subjected to a constant stream of propaganda."

"How can we trust you?", the General questioned.

That was a actually good sign, the General had not denied the truth of the matter, he simply wanted to know about trust. Could he trust Captain Carmichael and Captain Forkbraid.

Forkbraid had the answer ready, he nodded to Peter Swann, who directed their long range scanner and ultra scanner data feeds over to the Trojan command ship.

The Trojans communications officer put the scans on the bridge's screens, "Captain. General. Those are long range scans of L5 and cis-lunar space."

The General looked at the screen. Clearly there were two large formations of spaceships visible. One close to L5, the Colonial Fleet. The other midway between the Earth and L5, the Earth Defence Force Fleet. Any one of those fleets would have been bad enough, but both of these fleets were combining, merging into one.

"Oh my God!", the General exclaimed, "We're heading into a death trap!"

"What's at L2?", the General asked.

"L2 is used for scientific, astronomical research and surveillance", Forkbraid replied, "To the best of my knowledge, there's nothing military there at all."

Captain Carmichael stepped in, "I can confirm that neither the Earth, nor L5 station military equipment at L2. It's just research and surveillance stations. If you want, you can adjust your course further out, to keep your fleet at a safer distance."

"Why are you helping us Captain?", General Trask asked.

Forkbraid replied as honestly as possible, "You're not responsible for the missile attack on the Earth and L5 General. That was the work of the Horridian Dynasty. The Trojan Asteroid Colonies are occupied territories. Your people, the Trojans, deserve to be free!"

The General ordered Captain Sharky, "Captain. Plot an immediate course change. One that takes our fleet past the far side of the Earth's moon, well outside of L2. Send word to the fleet. We are going home!"

The General turned back to the screen, "Thank you gentlemen for the heads up. It is greatly appreciated and we will remember it. We are now going home!"

"General. My ship and the Spartan will escort your fleet past the Earth/Moon system. When we consider your fleet safe, we'll break away", Forkbraid informed him.

"That won't be necessary Captain", the General responded.

"Necessary or not General, I've already informed both the Earth and L5 governments, that we will be doing so", Forkbraid informed him, "They have been told that you are under my protection."

"Pardon my saying so Captain. I can understand a Colonial Cruiser, like the Spartan, but your ship Captain Forkbraid?", the General questioned.

Captain Carmichael stepped in, "General, I did mention earlier. Captain Forkbraid's ship, the Solstice, destroyed a third of that Jovian missile swarm en-route. It took down a shit-ton of warheads to boot. Now I don't want to denigrate my own ship, but seriously, sometimes I think that the Solstice could give the Spartan a run for it money."

"Noted Captain Carmichael, noted. My apologies Captain Forkbraid. I meant no disrespect", the General replied.

"It's all good General. I took no offence. If you need anything from us, just let us know", Forkbraid responded. The communications window from the Trojan command ship dropped out.

"Well the cats out of the bag now isn't it Captain", Forkbraid noted.

"I'd say so. They got a good look at your ship, its armaments, its ability to cloak. They even know its name. Yeah, I'd say the cats well and truly out of the bag", Captain Carmichael agreed.

Peter Swann interjected, "Captain. The Trojan fleet is changing course. It appears that they have taken your advice", he informed Forkbraid, then noted, "But not all of them. The Trojan Weapons Transports in the outer regions of their formation and a few in the van, they're staying the course."

"Thank you Peter", Forkbraid replied, then to Captain Carmichael, "Captain. It looks like some of the Trojans weren't convinced. Our extended energy field didn't reach as far as we'd have liked."

"I'll take care of it for you Forkbraid", Captain Carmichael replied.

"Nothing harsh I hope?", Forkbraid queried.

"No. Not at all. I'll just communicate with them and remind them of what's waiting for them", Captain Carmichael explained, "Maybe I can make them see sense. Maybe I can't."

"Thank you Captain", Forkbraid replied and the on screen window dropped out.

Forkbraid turned to his Tactical Officer, "I hate to do this to you Jim. You're already wearing way too many hats as it is. What with Head of Elysium Security, Head of New Flinders Psychic Academy Security and the Solstice's Tactical and Security Officer. It seems way too much to ask you be my First Officer as well."

Jim thought about it for a moment, then, "Sure, why not? It's just one more hat to wear. Maybe I can get Charlene and Roseanne to design me a *'multi-hat'*?"

Charlene turned around at that comment, "Yeah. No. I would not even know what a multi hat looks like. So no!"

"Okay then, it's official. Jim Murphy, you are the Solstice's First Officer",

Forkbraid stated for the record, then jokingly asked, "Charlene. Could you look into multi hat designs please?"

Charlene rolled her eyes, "Seriously Captain?"

"Of course not Charlene. It was a joke", Forkbraid informed her.

"Peter. How many of those Trojan Transports are still heading towards L5?", asked Forkbraid.

Peter Swann checked the scans, "At least two dozen Captain. Likely more", he replied.

"Charlene. Please send the following message to General Stanton", Forkbraid instructed, "General Stanton. Two dozen plus Trojan Weapons Transports are inbound to L5. Each transport is armed and contains four Patrol ships, four Gun ships and four Interceptors. They are heading your way. Deal with them as you see fit. We cannot save those who are hell bent on their own self destruction. May the Gods have mercy upon their souls. Captain Forkbraid."

A minute later Charlene replied, "Message sent Captain."

"General Stanton Sir. We have a message from Captain Forkbraid", his Communications Officer noted.

"Put in on my screen Lieutenant", the General replied.

General Stanton read through the message, "Lieutenant. Reply to the message. Thanks for the heads up. We will deal with any Trojans that come our way."

General Stanton then turned to the Ship's Captain, "We have two dozen armed bogeys heading our way. Warn the fleet. Each bogey has four Patrol ships, four Gun ships and four Interceptors. Prepare the fleet to intercept the Trojans. Our orders are simple. Locate and destroy the enemy!"

The Solstice and the Spartan were now passing by the far side of the Moon, well beyond Lagrangian point L2, keeping between the retreating Trojan Fleet and the L2 scientific and surveillance stations.

"Captain. I'm just receiving a relayed message from the Earth Defence Fleet", Charlene noted.

"What does it say Charlene?", Forkbraid asked.

"Captain. It's from General Stanton. They have destroyed the renegade Trojan Weapons Transports and their ships. Not all of them though. They apparently captured a handful of each class of ship and destroyed the rest", Charlene read Forkbraid the gist of the message.

"That does make sense. The good General will be wanting to tear those ships apart and reverse engineer everything he can. General Stanton will definitely want to know the current state of Jovian technology", Forkbraid assessed.

The bulk of the Trojan Fleet were safely on their way home. It was unlikely they could be easily intercepted on their current course back to the leading Trojan Asteroid fields. Captain Carmichael and his Lieutenant Adjutant Hans Blixen, had come aboard the Solstice once again. This time to hold a medal ceremony for the Solstice's Captain and Crew. Three medals were being awarded per crew member. The Battle of L5 medal, the Medal of Honour and Medal of Gallantry.

Captain Carmichael called Leroy McGuvan aside.

"Leroy. I'm pinning on your medals now", he informed Leroy, explaining, "As you can imagine, if we televise you receiving medals over the news feed, people might not understand. That is considering your past activities of course."

"I fully understand Captain", Leroy replied.

Captain Carmichael pinned the three medals to the left breast of Leroy's uniform jacket, performed a quick salute and then moved on.

"Okay, if you can all line up in some semblance of rank, lowest to highest, we can begin the ceremony", Captain Carmichael requested, then to Lieutenant Blixen, "If you can record the proceedings Lieutenant", he ordered.

"Aye Captain", Lieutenant Blixen replied as he quickly transformed his 'grip' into audio/visual recording mode.

The Solstice's crew all lined up from left to right in order of perceived rank. They all looked very professional in their uniforms. Navy blue trousers and shirts, with a royal blue double breasted blazers on top. Lieutenant Blixen began recording the line up of the crew straight away.

"Citizens of L5 and the Earth. I am Captain Bartholomew Carmichael, the Captain of the Colonial Heavy Cruiser Spartan and the Captain of the Colonial Fleet. Assembled before me are the Captain and crew of the Martian Spaceship Solstice", Captain Carmichael stated before the camera.

Captain Carmichael approached Nyaliep, "Engineering Assistant Nyaliep Pod", he then pinned the three medals upon her jacket's left breast, saluting her after doing so.

The Captain then moved on to the Pod Sisters, "Security Officer Zeealas Pod", he proceeded to pin on Zeealas's three medals and then saluted her.

"Security Officer Zuawalo Pod", the Captain continued. He pinned on Zuawalo's three medals, saluted her and moved on. This was the general pattern.

The Captain continued, "Communications Officer Charlene Fewkes", then pinned on her three medals, saluted her and moved on.

"Helm and Navigation Officer Marcus Greyhelm", the Captain continued. He then pinned on Marcus's three medals, saluted him and moved on.

"Science Officer Peter Swann", Captain Carmichael continued. Peter then received his three medals, the Captain saluted him and moved on.

"Engineering Officer Varakhan Utana", the Captain continued, then pinned on Varak's three medals, saluted him and moved on.

"First Officer, Tactical and Chief Security Officer James Murphy", Captain Carmichael stated. He then pinned Jim's three medals onto his blazer, saluted him and then moved on.

"Captain Folcrom Forkbraid, Captain of the Martian Spaceship Solstice", the Captain continued, he then pinned on Forkbraid's thee medals, saluted him and then turned to face his Lieutenant Adjutant.

"Citizens of L5 and the Earth. I give you the Captain and Crew of the Martian Spaceship Solstice. Heroes of the Battle of L5, who single handedly destroyed over thirty percent of the inbound Jovian missiles", Captain Carmichael stated clearly as he motioned his hand in front of the Solstice's crew, then began clapping.

Shortly thereafter Lieutenant Blixen shut off the recording.

"All good Blixen?", the Captain asked.

"All good Captain. It's a take", Lieutenant Blixen replied.

Captain Carmichael told everyone, "Thank you ladies and gentlemen."

"Forkbraid, I do prefer to keep these things short and sweet. This video should hit the news feeds tomorrow", Captain Carmichael informed Forkbraid.

"It is a bit of a worry Captain", Forkbraid began, explaining, "The Trojans already have had a good look at the Solstice, so that cat's already out of the bag as you know. The Horridians will have that information very soon. After the news feeds tomorrow, they'll also know the names of the Captain, the Crew members and that the Solstice is a Martian ship."

"Yes. I can see your concerns there Forkbraid. It could draw some unwanted attention your way", Captain Carmichael replied, commenting, "President Banyan has asked us to film this little ceremony, but he didn't mention exactly when to have it aired on the news feeds. He did say at some time in the future. I do seem to remember that."

"Blixen, when we get back to the Spartan, misfile that video. Misfile it well.", the Captain ordered, "We'll miraculously find it again, after this war is over", he continued with a broad smile.

Lieutenant Blixen smiled and replied, "Aye Captain."

"Does that work for you Forkbraid?", Captain Carmichael asked.

"It does indeed Captain", Forkbraid replied.

"Good then. We'll get back to the Spartan. Lieutenant Blixen has to find a good filing place for that video", Captain Carmichael replied, adding, "And we do need to get back to the fleet at L5."

Forkbraid shook the Captain's hand and First Officer James Murphy showed them back to the main docking portal.

On the way to the docking portal, Jim asked Captain Carmichael, "How many Trojans do you think we saved Captain?"

"It's difficult to say Jim. We figure that whole Trojan fleet had around a hundred and twenty five thousand personnel or thereabouts. The twenty five ships that General Stanton dealt with had around twenty five hundred personnel, so what's that tell you?"

Jim did a quick calculation in his head, "I'd say Captain, that around ninety eight percent of the Trojans survived. That's not too bad. Perhaps the Trojan leadership should be giving us all medals?"

"Don't hold you breath Jim. Their leadership is the Horridian Dynasty."

You'll get no thanks from them", Captain Carmichael replied, adding, "Those Trojans are so damned lucky that calmer minds prevailed in the end."

Shortly thereafter, Captain Carmichael and Lieutenant Adjutant Blixen were back onboard the Colonial Cruiser Spartan, which then peeled away from the Solstice on its journey back to the Colonial Fleet at L5.

First Officer James Murphy returned to his station on the Solstice's bridge and sat down.

Forkbraid nodded to him and then turned to Marcus, "Marcus, put us on a course for an equatorial low Earth orbit."

"Aye Captain", Marcus replied and the Solstice was on its way to the Earth.

30. Homeward Bound

High Prince Heinrich called for another meeting with regards their attacks on the inner solar system. All requested parties had arrived and taken their seats. One was noticeably absent.

The High Prince began the meeting, "My younger Brother, Prince Leopold is absent today and won't be attending today's meeting."

The Prophet enquired, "Is Prince Leopold okay?"

"Yes. Yes. It's nothing serious. He's just a little sensitive to today's subject matter and decided to stay at Io Prime. Today's subject matter would definitely upset him", the High Prince explained, then handed over to General Snide, "General. If you'd please."

General Snide began, "We have been intercepting the Earth and L5 news feeds. Some very interesting information has come to light. None of this has been released locally. It is important that we keep this information on a *'needs to know'* basis."

"Okay General. Spill it!", an impatient Prince Wulfric ordered.

The General looked at the Prince before continuing, "It has been confirmed, our missile strike on L5 did damage a rather larger twin cylinder colony. Nova Hollandia to be precise. It's south east end cap and southern eastern cylinder were destroyed. The number of lives lost is tallied at over sixty five thousand."

Both Princes Wulfric and Valdamar let out soft cries of, "Yes!"

General Snide continued, "With regards the Earth, seven warheads got through their defences. Three detonated in the Atlantic Ocean. Four detonated above the following cities. Oulu, Finland. Arkangelsk, Russia. Lisbon, Portugal and Palma de Mallory, Spain. They haven't finished counting the victims yet, but the number is above two point five million lives lost at present."

Both Princes Wulfric and Valdamar let loose cries of , "Yes! Yes!" once more, followed by pumping of fists in the air and multiple cries of, "Whoot, whoot!"

The whooting continued until the High Prince raised his right hand to bring the room to silence.

Matthew felt appalled by the Prince's disgusting attitude to the loss of so many lives. No wonder Prince Leopold didn't want to attend. A better Prince than Wulfric and Valdamar in his estimation.

General Snide continued, "We cannot know what the Primary targets of those warheads were, however one thing for certain is, they were off course and did not strike their intended targets."

Matthew quickly asked, "So those cities, were not actually targeted?"

"No Captain", General Snide admitted, "They were not even on the target list."

That appeared to put a dampener on Princes Wulfric and Valdamar.

"As I noted at the beginning. This information is not for general release and must remain amongst us. This is information that is only dispersed on a *'need to know'* basis gentlemen", General Snide reminded everyone, before nodding to General Tarzan.

General Tarzan stood up as General Snide sat down.

"We do have some very, very interesting information coming back from the Trojan occupation forces", General Tarzan informed everyone.

Prince Wulfric spat out, "I would have thought they'd all be dead by now!"

"Apparently not Your Highness", General Tarzan replied, adding, "The Trojan Fleet General, a General Trask, has reported the following. Two ships approached their fleet from the rear. One of them was the Spartan, an L5 colonial heavy cruiser. The other was a ship was called the *'Solstice'*, which was of an *'unknown'* class and configuration. We have multiple images taken of this ship. Not only by the bridge crew of the transport ships, but also by crew members taking their own pictures."

General Tarzan placed the best of those images, taken from nearly every angle, onto the conference room's screen, stating confidently, "There is our mystery Martian ship!"

The cat was well and truly unbagged.

"What the fuck class of ship is that?", Prince Wulfric asked.

Prince Valdamar apparently wanted to appear smarter than his Brother and replied, "Some kind of disk and sled style of ship", which was of course obvious to everyone in the room.

Matthew stood up and walked over to the screen, scrutinising the pictures carefully, before stating, "I can't say what class of ship this is, but it is very, very new. I've never seen a design like it. I'd call it the first of its class, the Solstice Class Gunship."

"Gunship?", the Prophet enquired.

"My Lord. I can easily discern three dozen weapons modules on that ship", Matthew replied, then commenting, "If that is not a gunship, then what the hell is?"

"Thirty six weapons modules?", Prince Wulfric queried rhetorically, "We don't have anything that small, with that kind of fire power."

"No Your Highness", General Tarzan replied, confirming a second time, "No we don't."

General Tarzan then continued with the information, "Other things to consider. This ship is not painted black. You'll notice it's painted a typical fleet grey in colour. Yet this ship materialised out of nowhere, directly in front of the lead troop transport. General Trask's ship. This ship is capable of cloaking or at the very least, making itself dark and unseen."

Gasps of shock sprung up around the room and Prince Valdamar queried, "Cloaking?"

"We don't know how they did it Your Highness, but somehow they just magically appeared in front of General Trask's ship, without being detected", General Tarzan replied, before adding, "There's more. Look at this image."

The General was pointing out an image of the Solstice's stern, "Clearly I can see four fusion thruster nozzles. And yes, I can see that these fusion thrusters are indeed capable of running in some kind of stealth mode."

More gasps of shock erupted from around the room.

"We will need to study these images. We hope to get clues to their technology out of them", General Tarzan informed the room, "But there is something else I'd like to point out. If those are the nozzles of their fusion thrusters, then what the hell are those nacelles for?"

Matthew was still on his feet to one side, still studying the images on the screen. He rubbed his face with his right hand.

"One under each wing. A secondary method of motility perhaps?", Matthew queried to himself, before further querying, "This could very well be, the most advanced ship in the solar system?"

"Yes Captain. That was my thought as well", General Tarzan replied, adding, "We certainly don't have anything that can match it and what we see here, may not be all that she's got either. She may have other teeth we can't see in these images."

Matthew nodded in agreement.

Prince Valdamar commented, "Yes. They have an advanced ship. So what, they only have the one of them. What's one ship? We have a whole fleet!"

Matthew replied, "That one ship appears to have taken down over thirty percent of our missile swarm. On its own! Never overlook one ship Your Highness."

Prince Wulfric chimed in with "Good advice Captain. We will need to keep an eye out for that one. Now what happened to our Trojan Fleet?"

General Tarzan answered, "The Captains of the Spartan and the Solstice informed General Trask, that the Earth Defence Force and the L5 Colonial Fleet were waiting in ambush for them."

The General continued after a quick pause, "General Trask checked their long range scans and confirmed that they were indeed heading directly into a death trap. It would have been certain death for the whole fleet, so he ordered a course change to avoid it."

"A course change?", Prince Wulfric enquired.

"Yes. A course change. One that avoided the trap and cis-lunar space all together for that matter. Both the Spartan and the Solstice escorted them away from the Earth and L5. So our Trojan Fleet is now on its way home. Although twenty five weapons transports did stay on their original course and were destroyed by the Earth's Defence Force Fleet.", the General informed everyone.

"Why would the Captains of the Spartan and the Solstice give General Trask a heads up?", the Prophet asked, adding, "That makes absolutely no sense at all."

"We do not know their motivations good Prophet", General Tarzan admitted.

"So the Trojans are heading back to the Leading Trojan Colonies?", Matthew enquired.

"Not exactly Captain", General Tarzan answered, "Not all of the Trojans are from the Leading Trojan Colonies. Many of those troops, specialists and ships are from the Trailing Trojans. There are even a few ships from here, more than a few in fact. It is a combined fleet."

Matthew put two and two together, "So the fleet will be splitting up on its way. The trailing Trojans, then the Jovian System, then finally the Leading Trojans?"

"Yes Captain. That's exactly what they'll do", General Tarzan replied.

"Captain. What is it you're thinking?", High Prince Heinrich enquired.

"Your Majesty. Just a thought, but how well do you trust these Trojans?", Matthew asked.

"They're Trojans! I trust them as far as I can kick them", the High Prince replied.

"Yes Your Majesty. I think we should keep that in mind", Matthew advised.

General Snide stood up once more as General Tarzan returned to his seat, "There is more gentlemen", he stated as he put up some more surveillance pictures.

"These images have been captured by the long range optics at our inner surveillance stations three and four", Captain Snide informed the room, "You can clearly see the Earth Defence and Colonial Fleets in separate staging regions just outside of L5."

The General paused to allow everyone in the room to get a good look at the pictures before continuing, "What we can see here is a bit of a mix. You can see some of their older ships being upgraded and modernised", pointing to the images as he commented.

"Over here, you can see their more modern ships. These appear to be being retrofitted. We can't sure, but it does appear to be some kind of new technology. It is difficult to tell at this range", the General remarked.

As the General Continued, Matthew was once again on his feet and studying the images, "Over here is another section of their staging area, theses are new ships being outfitted. When I say new ships, yes brand new, straight off the manufacturing line."

"They are building up their forces General", Matthew remarked, adding,

"I can't be sure, but it is quite possible these ships being retrofitted. Maybe receiving newly acquired Martian technology."

Gasps of shock travelled around the conference room.

"Your Majesty", Matthew began, "To me this indicates two things. One, we have time. It will take the Earth and L5 time to build up their forces. Modernising, retrofitting and building new ships takes time. That in turn buys us time. The time we need to build up our own forces and we will need all of that time, as much as we can get", he remarked before pausing.

"And the second thing Captain", the High Prince enquired.

"Your Majesty. When those two fleets arrive in Jovian territory, they will be formidable!", Matthew replied, then to the Generals, "I expect we'll start seeing the Earth and L5 Military placing recruitment adverts in their news feeds. Keep an eye out for them. They can tell us a hell of a lot."

The meeting broke up shortly thereafter.

"General. I'm picking something up on our defence scanners", Lieutenant Armstrong noted.

"What have you got Armstrong?", Genera Zammit questioned.

That is a hard to say General", the Lieutenant replied, "Its pulse identification beacon is either offline or they don't have one Sir."

"Precise location?", the General queried.

"Outside of our defence platforms, but approaching rapidly General", the Lieutenant replied.

"Hail them Lieutenant. Urgently! Find out what they're up to", General Zammit ordered, noting, "If they get too much closer without a beacon. Our defence platforms will assume, that they are an enemy combatant and they will be destroyed."

"Hailing them now General", Lieutenant Armstrong replied.

Charlene Fewkes noted, "Captain. We're being hailed by the Earth Defence Grid."

"Hmm. What do they want?", Forkbraid asked.

"They want to know who we are and what we're up to. Apparently were heading into their Defence Grid and without a pulse identification beacon, it will respond to us as enemy combatants", Charlene noted.

"Nice! They've given us a heads up. I was expecting that", Forkbraid replied, "However, I don't want to discuss this with them. Let's go dark instead."

"Jim. Activate our defence grid and our passive and active cloaking", Forkbraid ordered.

"Aye Captain", Jim replied, "Defence grid, passive and active cloaking are online and active."

"General Zammit Sir", the Lieutenant called out.

"Yes Lieutenant?", General Zammit answered.

"General Sir. That bogeys gone dark. It's no longer on our scanners", Lieutenant Armstrong informed the General, puzzlement showing in his voice.

"Keep scanning for them Lieutenant", General Zammit replied, adding, "We have the most powerful defence scanners available. They can't possibly hide from us!"

"Yes Sir", the Lieutenant replied.

The General turned to his communications officer, Lieutenant Sutter, "Get the Earth Defence Forces on the line. Inform them, we had a bogey on our screens without a pulse identity beacon. Tell them it's gone dark. Tell them, I want them to send out interceptors to track that bogey down."

"Captain. We're through the Earth's defence grid", Marcus noted, "It appears they can't detect us either. We'll be in low equatorial orbit in a few minutes."

A few minutes later the Earth loomed large on the Ship's view screen. A beautiful site to behold. Most of the bridge crew members, having been born on the Earth found the site truly spectacular. Jim Murphy and Peter Swann had only ever seen the Earth from L5, from which the planet looked much smaller. Even for them however, it was still an impressive sight.

"Low equatorial orbit achieved Captain", Marcus noted.

"Excellent! Thank you Marcus", Forkbraid acknowledged, "Peter. If you could kindly scan for frame dragging events. We're interested in those events that have magnetic anomalies and those anomalies that form slipstreams to

Mars."

"Aye Captain", Peter responded, "Scanning for slipstreams now."

"Varak. Get an in depth analysis of these slipstreams", Forkbraid ordered Varak who was sitting beside Peter at the secondary science console, "I want to know if you can truly trigger these things."

Peter Swann noted, "We are detecting slipstreams Captain. Not that many Mars bound ones though. I would not even call these close to being useful."

"Define useful Peter?", Forkbraid asked

"Useful would be, having access to slipstreams at short notice and not having to hunt them down Captain", Peter replied.

"Varak. How is your analysis gong?", Forkbraid asked.

"It is going very well Captain", Varak replied, noting, "You can guarantee that Peter is running his own analysis as well."

"You're also running an analysis Peter?", Forkbraid questioned.

"Yes Captain. Two independent analysis by two separate people. It will save running a second or backup analysis later. Especially if we both come to the same conclusions", Peter explained.

"Good idea Peter. Have at it", Forkbraid agreed.

After several long minutes Varak looked up from his console, "Captain. I have analysed three separate Mars bound slipstreams. The results are promising. Very promising."

Peter looked up from his console, "Captain. Three different slipstreams, however I chose Venus bound slipstreams. These look like very promising results as well."

Peter and Varak compared their results, then after several more minutes, Peter commented, "It's just as you suspected Varak."

"Just as Varak suspected?", Forkbraid enquired.

Varak smiled a huge beaming smile, then replied, "If we fire our plasma pulse cannons into a slipstream without a plasma charge, utilising only the electro-magnetic pulse, it will shutdown the slipstream anomaly."

"That is pretty cool Varak, but it's not exactly what I had in mind", Forkbraid commented.

"Ah yes Captain. Let me allay your concerns", Varak replied, still with the huge beaming smile on his face, "If we fire our plasma pulse cannons into a frame dragging event. One that does not have an anomaly, it will be the opposite result. We have to fire it without a plasma charge of course, utilising only the electro-magnetic pulse. It will create a navigable slipstream."

"Now that's what I'm talking about Varak!", Forkbraid replied in excitement.

Peter Swann stepped in, "Varak and I will need to perform a few tasks first Captain."

"And those tasks will be?", Forkbraid enquired.

"First, we have to to tie the slipstream scanner into the targeting array, so that we can fire the electro-magnetic pulse from the pulse cannons into frame dragging events. We only need to fire the one pulse and we have to ensure it fires without a plasma charge.", Peter explained.

Varak stepped in, "That will give Jim another option for his tactical console. The ability to fire off electro-magnetic pulses. Not just pulsed plasma charges."

"That should be very handy", Jim remarked, "For disabling enemy ships", he explained.

"Yes Jim exactly", Peter began, adding "Our second task is to make this available to helm and navigation as well. If we do this correctly, Marcus will be able set a course from say, the Earth to Mars using a slipstream and Bob's your uncle. We end up at Mars very, very quickly", using an old Earth English expression.

"Guys. Just how quickly?", Forkbraid queried.

Varak looked at Peter. Peter then looked back at Varak. Then together they both replied, "We do not know Captain."

Many interceptors were in the skies above the Earth covering low Earth orbit. They were looking for the Solstice or more correctly, the unknown bogey, but to no avail, they could not detect her.

More than once Marcus had to adjust course so as to keep a good distance between the Solstice and the searchers. In the end he requested the Ship's computer, with its three laws safe positronic brain, to do so automatically, based upon the same techniques he'd been using.

It took both Peter and Varak a good twenty four hours to complete the changes, hooking the slipstream scanners into the targeting array and the helm/navigation systems. And that was with Leroy and Nyaliep assisting them. The last six hours of that time were spent on testing the changes and running simulations. Finally the task was completed. All simulations were good.

The very next morning, with the Solstice still in low Earth equatorial orbit, the bridge crew members and Varak gathered on the bridge. Leroy, Nyaliep and the Pod Sisters took to their stations and prepared themselves for morning's main event. Which was to be, assuming all things checked out okay, the traversal of Mars bound slipstream from the Earth. Exciting, but scary was the common theme.

"Varak. Have you and Peter detected a suitable frame dragging event", Forkbraid enquired.

"Yes Captain", Varak replied, then asked, "Marcus, give me control of the helm."

"All yours Varak", Marcus replied.

Varak took control of the helm and navigation, steering the Solstice to a full stop, with a frame dragging event taking place two hundreds metres away.

Varak triggered the plasma pulse cannons to fire once without a plasma charge. The electro-magnetic pulse pushed forwards towards the frame dragging event. Immediately upon contacting the frame dragging event, it reacted and a slipstream anomaly was generated.

Peter quickly analysed the result, "Shit!"

"A problem Peter?", Forkbraid queried.

"Not if you want to go to Uranus", Peter replied, then to Varak, "I think you need to adjust the resonant frequency."

"Yes, yes. I see my mistake", Varak replied, "It was a simple decimal error."

Peter Swann rolled his eyes and rubbed his sweating forehead.

Varak triggered the plasma pulse cannons to fire a second electro-magnetic pulse towards the frame dragging event. Immediately upon contacting the frame dragging event, the slipstream anomaly collapsed and vanished. Varak adjusted the frequency for the next pulse. It was an educated guess.

"I'm trying again, with a new frequency", Varak informed everyone, "It is a bit like trial and error. Once we have a slipstream to Mars working, the Ship's computer should be able to extrapolate the data and calculate slipstreams for the other planets."

Varak triggered the plasma pulse cannons to fire a third electro-magnetic pulse towards the frame dragging event. Immediately upon contacting the frame dragging event, it reacted and a created a new slipstream. Varak turned and looked to Peter Swann.

Peter looked back to Varak, "Nailed it in three my man. Nailed it in three. Mars is on the far side."

Peter and Varak high fived each other.

Varak spoke to the Ship's computer, "Computer. Is this slipstream navigable? Is it safe?"

The Ship's computer replied in its sweet feminine voice, "The Slipstream is navigable. The Slipstream is safe. The planet Mars is accessible via this slipstream."

"Marcus. I'm handing the helm back to you", Varak advised, "If we attempt to use this slipstream, aim for the middle of the anomaly."

Marcus looked around to Forkbraid, who ordered, "Check we have our shield grid up and then proceed Marcus."

"Aye Captain", Marcus replied, then explicitly to the Ship's computer, "Computer. Check that the shield grid is active, then proceed into the slipstream at optimal point of optimal entry and at optimal speed."

The Ship's computer replied "Compliance" and the Solstice began moving forward.

As the Solstice approach close to the slipstream, the Ship's computer automatically showed the gravitational field lines overlaid on the screen. The slipstream itself was invisible. It was only visible on their screen, due to the overlaying field lines. They approached what appeared to be a rotating funnel, leading into a tunnel like structure. The Solstice shuddered violently as she lurched over the lip of the slipstream's funnel towards the tunnel within it.

Varak commented, "Captain. I may need to adjust our inertial dampeners before our next run."

Forkbraid replied, "Agreed!", as they entered the slipstream's tunnel with violent shuddering.

The sides of the slipstream tunnel showed definite spatial distortions and the crew of the Solstice began to feel somewhat nauseous. Leroy watched as the Pod Sisters both externalised their mornings breakfast. Leroy considered that to be a natural thing to happen, considering their current predicament and the fact that both Pod Sisters were pregnant.

Then when Leroy watched as the Pod Sister's Aunt Nyaliep threw up her breakfast as well, he wondered to himself, *"was this a woman thing or was he going to throw up as well?"*

Zuawalo caught a glimmer of Nyaliep vomiting and caught Zeealas's attention. Zeealas look at her Aunt and then looked back to Zuawalo.

"Aunty Nyaliep must be pregnant", Zeealas speculated.

"Yes. Aunty Nyaliep must have chosen Varak", Zuawalo agreed, as that was the way in their village. If a woman chooses a man, pregnancy would quickly follow.

Back in the Ship's bridge, the inside of the slipstream tunnel was filled with strange swirling distorted lights and colours. The visual effects of the experience were both psychedelic and surreal.

Turbulence was noted in the slipstream tunnel and Varak was making mental notes, to make major changes to the inertial damper systems, to interactively scan and adjust for the intense gravimetric distortions.

The crew members ears began to pop as if the air pressure in the Solstice was fluctuating wildly. Temperature variations were noted as well and some crew members felt hot, whilst others felt cold.   Varak was having a hard time keeping his mental notes in place, *"How much of this will I actually remember when I came out the other side"*, he thought to himself.

Even time itself seemed out of joint. Were they inside the slipstream's tunnel? Were they still inside the slipstream's entry funnel? Had they already passed through the exit funnel on the other side? It was extremely difficult to say and they were all heavily disoriented.

Then they exited the tunnel and entered the spiralling exit funnel. The Solstice shuddered violently and lurched from side to side, as she traversed the short, spiralling exit funnel. To the crew members of the Solstice inside the exit funnel, it felt like they were being excreted through some kind of sphincter. Then the Solstice shuddered again violently, as she lurched over the lip of the exit funnel and came out into normal space once more.

Everyone was still feeling nauseated. The Pod Sisters and their Aunt Nyaliep were literally sitting in their own vomit. Everyone was feeling just a little off to say the least.

"What the fuck was that!", Jim Murphy shouted.

Forkbraid asked the Ship's computer, "Computer. What was our traversal time? That is to say, the time spent in the slipstream?"

The Ship's computer replied, "There are two traversal times and they are both different, due to differing frames of reference. Would you like to hear both?"

"Yes. Yes Computer. Tell me both", Forkbraid replied.

The Ship's computer replied, "Complying. External frame of reference, time differential, T-Exit minus T-Entry equals three seconds. Internal slipstream frame of reference, time differential, T-Exit minus T-Entry equals two minutes and ten seconds. These are a slipstream constant."

Forkbraid shook his head in an attempt to clear it, "Varak translate please?"

Varak interpreted the computer's reply for Forkbraid, "An observer outside of the ship in normal space, would have observed three seconds pass while we transited the slipstream. We being in the Ship and in the slipstream however, observed two minutes and ten seconds. It is all relative. It appears that all slipstream wormholes are the same length and these times are are constants."

"Constant? How does that work out Varak?", Forkbraid queried.

"When you bend space time to the extent that a slipstream forms, the connecting wormhole has the same parameters, irrespective of the distance between the two points in space time. The result, it take two minutes and ten seconds of slipstream travel to go anywhere", Varak explained.

"Right Varak. Got it", Forkbraid replied, even though it made no sense to him, then he asked, "Now what's with the nausea and all the turbulence?"

"We will need to create reactive inertial stabilisation modules to handle slipstream traversal", Varak replied, adding, "Our current inertial dampers were never designed for slipstreams."

"By we Captain, I believe that means, Varak and I", Perter Swann added.

"Yes. I will need Peter's help with that task. It is, most complicated", Varak agreed.

"So next time we won't all feel like shit afterwards?", Forkbraid asked.

"Yes Captain. That is precisely what we are aiming for", Varak replied.

As the crew members looked up at the bridge's screen, the view that had once shown the Earth was now showing the planet Mars.

"Marcus, are you feeling up to the task of taking use home?", Forkbraid enquired.

"Yes Captain", Marcus replied, "Quite frankly, I think Charlene and I, can't wait to be on solid ground once more."

"Agreed Marcus. I'm feeling a bit that way myself", Forkbraid replied, then over the Ship's intercom, "All crew members, when we disembark the ship, please remain in uniform and wear your medals. I'd like our families to be proud of all that we have achieved."

The intercom buzzed from back in engineering, "Captain. Leroy here."

"Yes Leroy", Forkbraid acknowledged.

"You might want to give the girls thirty minutes or so to change and cleanup before disembarking", Leroy informed Forkbraid, explaining, "That slipstream was a bit rough on them. The poor darlings are covered in their own vomit."

Forkbraid lowered his forehead into his right hand and replied, "Yes Leroy. By all means. The girls can take as long as they require", then he turned to Jim and exclaimed, "What the fuck!"

Jim looked back and simply nodded. It was like that for everyone on board the Solstice.

31. More Good Times

Marcus landed the Solstice at the airfield south east of the New Flinders Psychic Academy. While Marcus landed the Ship, Charlene helped the Pod women change and cleanup. Varak, Peter and Leroy helped clean up the mess left behind in the Engineering department. The Solstice landed quite quickly and sat on the tarmac, while the families and friends waited outside for the crew to disembark. They waited for many long minutes on the tarmac before the exit ramp descended.

The first crew members to exit the Solstice were the Pod Sisters and their Aunt Nyaliep. The Sister's parents, Zyaliep and Kwoth were not present, they had already returned to their village on the other side of Mars sometime ago.

Roseanne, Miranda, Candy and Cormac were there to greet them along with Gwek and Nyapal. Zigg the ferret caught sight of Zuawalo and quickly ran up and jumped into Zuawalo's open arms.

"My Zigg. I missed you my little pole cat", Zuawalo cried out, holding her pet tightly, then to Miranda, "Thank you so much for looking after my Zigg."

The Pod Sisters then hugged their friends Roseanne and Miranda, before greeting Gwek and his apprentice Nyapal.

Leroy McGuvan, Peter Swann and Varak descended the exit ramp next. Leroy had no one to meet him, but he was use to that. Considering his past, it was somewhat understandable.

Peter was of course met by his wife Catherine, his son Chiron and daughter Miranda. The family hugged their father as if he had been gone for years.

"Medals?", Catherine noted, "You have medals? You look so sharp in that uniform", she stated before holding him tightly and kissing him for many long moments.

Varak joined up with Nyaliep and began talking with the others gathered on the airfield.

Charlene and Marcus came out of the Solstice next, followed lastly by Jim and Forkbraid. Everyone converged upon Charlene and Marcus, while Jim made a bee line straight for his wives.

Forkbraid found himself falling into Selene's arms and they kissed long and passionately.

Selene called the Solstice's crew to line up on the tarmac, wanting to get some memorable photographs of the crew. Especially as they were all in uniform and wearing medals.

After the photos were taken Selene remarked loudly, "Wow! You guys look great in your uniforms", then asked, "Don't they look great people?"

Everyone gathered for the home coming agreed with Selene, who then asked, "Now what's the story with these medals?"

Forkbraid stepped forward and informed her, "We've been declared Heroes of the Battle for L5, by President Banyon. We each received three medals, one for participation in the battle and medals of honour and gallantry."

"My husband's a hero. Why have we not heard about this?", Catherine Swann asked.

Forkbraid informed her, "That information hasn't been released to the public yet."

Catherine then asked, "How are you back so soon?"

"Yes, I'd like to know that as well. The last we heard, you were still at L5", Selene commented.

"Well we actually have Varak and Peter to thank for that", Forkbraid informed them, adding, "They developed a method of using slipstream *'wormholes'* to get from the Earth to Mars."

Catherine was both stunned and proud of her husband's part in that development, "Really! Wow! Peter, that's brilliant."

Peter Swann replied to his wife, "Yes, but it wasn't all my work. Varak's work was just as crucial as mine."

Nyaliep added, as she liked to do, "My Varak is ever so clever", then further added, "He can make anything! Anything!"

"Slipstream worm holes?", Selene queried and asked, "How quick are they?"

Forkbraid replied, "That depends. If you're an external observer however, it's about three seconds. If your on board the ship, the Earth to Mars trip is around two minutes and ten seconds. That time is also a constant. It actually takes two minutes and ten seconds to go anywhere!"

"That sounds very confusing", Selene admitted.

"It is Selene", Forkbraid confirmed, "That two minutes and ten seconds also feels a lot longer. It feels as though time slows down even more. Not to mention the side effects."

"Side effects?", Roseanne questioned.

Leroy answered, "That short trip had us all completely disoriented, nauseated and three Pod ladies all vomited uncontrollably."

"Yes. It was quite rough. Like a wild roll-a-coaster ride", Varak admitted, "We hope to have the inertial dampening system upgraded to cope with those issues next time."

"Oh my", Selene was somewhat shocked, "Is everyone okay?"

"Yes Selene. We are now", Forkbraid informed her, "That's why we took so long to disembark. There was quite a bit of cleanup to do."

"I can imagine", Selene replied, suggesting, "We should get back to the academy. You guys really need to rest and as your all heroes of L5, I guess you've earned it."

On the way back, Candy noticed two things. One, the Pod Sisters were starting to show. Not so unusual considering they were both pregnant. Two, the Pod Sister's Aunt Nyaliep had a very unique way of cradling her stomach. The sort of thing that a pregnant woman might do.

"Cormac. Notice Nyaliep?", Candy thought to her husband.

"Oh yes. I'm almost as quick as you are Candy", Cormac replied, adding, *"Another wedding perhaps do you think?"*

"It certainly looks like it Cormac, but I don't think Varak knows yet", Candy replied.

Roseanne sat patiently in the Pod Sister's dormitory common room, waiting for them to finish talking to their parents. Roseanne was hoping to hear all about how the crew of the Solstice saved the Earth and L5 from certain doom and destruction. Jim sat patiently in the common room as well. It was quite a while before the Sisters and their Aunt Nyaliep had finished talking to the Pod Sister's parents. It was all in the Nuer language and no one knew what the discussion was about.

"It is done", Zuawalo informed Jim, who had no idea what Zuawalo was talking about.

Roseanne looked at Nyaliep, her face was beaming with a broad smile, yet at the same time showed signs of deep apprehension.

"What has been done?", Roseanne asked Zuawalo.

"Nyaliep is pregnant. Nyaliep has chosen Varak", Zuawalo informed them both.

Zeealas chimed in with, "Nyaliep is going to marry Varak."

Roseanne look to Jim, then back to Zuawalo, "Does Varak know this?"

"Not yet. We tell him when Mother arrives", Zuawalo replied.

"Shouldn't Varak know? Shouldn't you discuss this with Varak first?", Roseanne questioned.

"That is not our way Roseanne", Nyaliep replied, "They chosen man finds out when the Mother of the bride tells him."

"As our grandmother is no longer with us, our Mother is now responsible", Zeealas explained.

Jim nodded in understanding, remembering that this is pretty much what happened to him, "Sounds like a bit of déjà vu to me, only this time Varak is on the receiving end."

"Are you unhappy with us, your wives?", Zuawalo queried.

"No. Not at all", Jim replied, "I didn't say anything like that."

Zeealas put her arm around Jim, squeezed his cheek with her fingers, "No you did not. You are so sweet my Jim."

"Ahem", Zuawalo cleared her throat to get Zeealas's and Jim's attention, "He is my Jim too Zeealas. Jim. You must go to our village and bring Mother and Father here."

"I won't be able to pick them up personally, but I can arrange for your parents to be brought here", Jim replied.

"That is good", Zuawalo agreed, "Now you must go and make the arrangements quickly. Our Aunty Nyaliep is worried that Varak will run away."

Zeealas stepped in with, "That sometimes happens in our village. The man will run away."

"We can't have that, can we? I'll make the arrangements straight away", Jim replied, thinking to himself, *"Running away was an option?"* and quickly left the dormitory for the communications centre, thinking, *"FB, I could do with your about now. Help!"*

When Jim arrived at the psychic academy's main communications centre, Forkbraid was already waiting for him, just outside in the hallway.

"How? I haven't called you yet?", Jim asked.

"I heard you requesting my help. Strangely enough it was a telepathic request. Which boggles the mind, because Jim, you are not a telepath", Forkbraid replied.

"Yeah right, How the hell did that happen?", Jim asked.

"Hmm", Forkbraid thought about it for a moment, then "Back on the Solstice, just before we contacted the Trojan command ship. You grabbed me by the wrist and screamed your thoughts into my mind. I wasn't telepathic, but it did get my attention."

"And how does that connect here?", Jim queried.

"That's the operative word Jim, *'connect'*, you created a connection or more correctly, triggered me to create a connection", Forkbraid explained, " and now that connection remains active."

"Okay. So how do we cut that connection?", Jim asked.

"We don't. If you ignore it and don't use it, it will atrophy over time and vanish. It will just take a little bit of time", Forkbraid advised.

"Oh crap", Jim let slip, then "FB, I need you to get up to speed. Just lift whatever you need straight out of my head."

"Okay Jim. I'll be quick", Forkbraid replied.

After a few short seconds Forkbraid commented, "Okay. I think I've got it. Nyaliep has chosen Varak. Varak doesn't know yet. You want to discuss defending Mars with Governor Anderson and to use the Governor's pilot to bring your wive's parents here to the academy. Two bird, one stone!"

"Yep, that's it in a nutshell", Jim confirmed, as they entered the communications centre.

The communications officer put through the call when requested and very soon Governor Anderson's face appeared on the screen.

"It's good to see you both. Now what can I do for you two?", the Governor asked.

Jim replied, getting straight to business, "We need to discuss Mar's defences Governor."

"Okay Agent Murphy. What did you have in mind?", the Governor enquired.

"We'd like you to request, that the Earth Defence Forces and L5 Colonial Fleet, send us six heavy cruisers each, for the Martian defences Governor", Jim replied, adding, "It's no longer Agent Murphy by the way. I'm now Head of Security James Murphy or if you prefer, simply Jim."

"Okay Jim", Governor Anderson replied, adding, "I doubt very much that we'll get six heavy cruisers from either the Earth Defence Forces or the L5 Colonial Fleet."

"We don't expect to Governor", Jim replied, "Start off with six heavy cruisers each, then negotiate from there. Get whatever you can out them."

"Okay. Now I get it", the Governor understood, adding, "What's the bare minimum we require to defend this planet?"

"Sadly Governor, the bare minimum we need is six heavy cruisers each, so a total of twelve heavy cruisers all up, but we're not going to get that and we know it", Jim admitted, further adding, "Maybe, just maybe, we can get three heavy cruisers each from them."

"And if they balk at three each?", Governor Anderson queried.

Jim shook his head, "Governor, I'm hoping for three heavy cruisers each, so six all up. If they balk at that, the absolute, absolute bare minimum is one heavy cruiser and two destroyers, each! No less than that. And they also have to be modern, I don't want them dumping ships fit for the scrap yard on us."

Governor Anderson scribbled down some notes on his notepad.

"And Governor", Forkbraid chimed in, "You might want to remind them. If not for us, the Earth would be burning and L5 would be occupied by the Trojan Armed Forces."

"That is a very good point", the Governor replied, adding, "I'll leave that argument for last. What about your ship Forkbraid? It seems quite formidable."

"Yes it is Governor, but I believe the best defence is a good offence", Forkbraid informed him, adding, "I can't be defending Mars, if I'm taking the fight to their doorstep."

"Okay. I see. That is a very good point as well", the Governor replied, "I'll see that I can do."

"And Governor. One small request?", Jim tossed in.

"Yes Jim", Governor Anderson asked.

"Do you remember Zuawalo and Zeealas?", Jim asked.

"Yes of course. Delightful Girls", the Governor replied.

"I need to get their parents transported from their village, south of New Tortuga to Elysium. Their names are Zyaliep and Kwoth Pod", Jim requested.

"We know the location of their village already. It should be no problem at all. I'll make the necessary arrangements", Governor Anderson replied while writing down some more notes.

Varak and Peter were working in Varak's construction hanger on a new and very important project. Varak had worked on the designs, while aboard the Solstice during their trip to the Earth and L5. With Nyaliep learning and performing many of the routine checks and balances on the ship, Varak was freed up to do the more esoteric design work that he enjoyed. In expectation of their return to Mars, Varak encrypted and transmitted the final designs to the computer work station in his construction hanger. He had then tasked his hyper dynamic 303 Androids with the job of implementing those designs.

Jim Murphy and his wive's Zuawalo and Zeealas walked into the construction hanger, closely followed by Nyaliep and Roseanne. Of course you couldn't keep the Farmers, Cormac and Candy away and they were not far behind. Jim had also requested that Selene and Forkbraid be present as well. Not far behind them all, was the Pod Sister's parents, Zyaliep and Kwoth. Everyone had big smiles on their faces.

Varak greeted them, "Ah. It is good to see you all. What can I do for you all?"

Nyaliep walked up to Varak and took him in her arms, she whispered in his ear, "I love you."

Varak was very tall, even taller than the Pod women, he looked down at Nyaliep affectionately and whispered back, "And I love you too my Nyaliep."

"That is very good", Nyaliep replied and then stepped back.

Zyaliep walked over to Varak and looked him up and down, "Your Varak is very tall Nyaliep. He is a very strong man,very handsome. He seems to be a very good choice."

Varak had not been present when Zyaliep confronted Jim, the Pod Sister's choice and had no idea what was going on. He was somewhat confused.

"Nyaliep. This is your choice? This Varak? This man?", Zyaliep asked her sister.

"Yes my Sister. Varak is my choice", Nyaliep confirmed.

"Then it is final. No more choosing Nyaliep", Zyaliep declared, then to her husband, "Kwoth, this man is to be our new Brother in law."

Varak was taken aback, he did not know the ways of Nyaliep's people, "What the?"

Jim walked over to Varak, put his hand on Varak's shoulder and told him quietly, "Trust me. It's best to go along with it. It is their way."

Varak did not understand, "Their way? What is going on here?"

Nyaliep now had tears welling up in her eyes, *"Was Varak going to run away?"*, she thought.

Zyaliep looked Varak straight in the eyes, "My Sister, Nyaliep is with child. Your child. Will you live up to your responsibilities? Will you marry my Sister and take care of your child?"

Varak looked at Nyaliep and quietly mouthed the words, "You are with child?", to her.

With tears in her eyes, Nyaliep nodded and softly replied, "Yes. Your child?"

Now tears welled up in Varak's eyes as he took Nyaliep in his strong arms and held her tightly.

"Now I am not so sure", Zyaliep commented, "Now this big, strong man, he cries like baby!"

Zeealas took her Mother's hand, remarking, "Nyaliep has chosen Varak. That is all that matters."

Everyone congratulated Varak and Nyaliep on their betrothal. Zyaliep was looking around at all the construction equipment in the hanger and at the newest project that Varak and Peter had been working on.

"I think this Varak of yours Nyaliep. I think he can pay your bride price", Zyaliep remarked.

Varak heard the remark and queried, "Bride price?"

Jim stepped in, informing him, "It's okay Varak. We can sort out the bride price out later. You can pay in cattle, golden credits, but definitely not sligs."

Varak rubbed his head, "Who do I pay the bride price to?"

"You pay it to Zyaliep, who will then hand it to Nyaliep", Jim explained.

Zyaliep stepped in, "Once you have paid the bride price, you are married. Then we have a ceremony and celebrate with a big feast."

Jim then told Varak, "Welcome to the club bro. Oh and you're lucky by the way. Mother Zyaliep called me a short, pale ghost. At least she called you, tall, strong and handsome."

Varak looked at Jim and laughed, "I am tall, strong and handsome!"

"Varak", Forkbraid, who had been inspecting Varak's latest project, called out.

Varak walked over to Forkbraid and the whole group followed him. He was the man of the moment, so to speak.

"What is the this Varak?", Forkbraid enquired.

"Yes. I'm more than a little curious myself Varak", Selene added.

"This is the ultimate technological solution to the problem of planetary magnetic fields", Varak informed everyone, adding, "The one I mentioned when we were in cis-lunar space."

Varak began explaining from the beginning, "You know. Many centuries ago, all of the atomic and nuclear waste was collected up. Everyone was told it would be dumped into the Sun. It was not. It was all carefully lowered down the throat of Olympus Mons here on Mars."

Selene stepped in, "Varak, we know that story. Once it was all collected at the deepest chamber under Olympus Mons, it was compressed to make it go critical."

"Yes and indeed it did go critical", Varak confirmed, informing everyone further, "All of that radioactive waste melted down. It reached phenomenal temperatures and began to sink through the Martian crust. It was hoped that in time, it would sink through the Martian mantle as well and eventually reach the Martian core."

It was Roseanne's time to step in, "Varak, we do know all this. I learnt it in school recently."

Zeealas then chimed in, "We do not these things."

Zuawalo then remarked, "These are new things to us. Let Varak continue. It is his story."

Varak continued, "It was hoped that all of that radioactive waste, centuries of it, all collected and melting down into the Martian core would kick start the Martian core into rotation. The theory was, that it would cause Mars to generate a new magnetic field. One that would protect Mars from solar radiation and cosmic rays."

"It would also in theory protect the newly terraformed Martian atmosphere from solar stripping", Jim added in, further noting, "The whole process was expected to take many centuries and they were never sure if the amount of radioactive waste was even enough."

"Yes Jim. That is the case", Varak confirmed, adding, "So we do not know if it will work and if it does work, we do not know how long it will take. Maybe the Martian core starts rotating tomorrow, maybe it will start rotating in a thousand years. Maybe it will never start rotating. We do not know."

"So circling back to this new project?", Selene enquired.

"Ah yes", Varak agreed, adding, "The old plan is too slow and might not even work. So Peter and I came up with this new plan."

"It is a five Tesla dipole", Peter informed everyone.

"A five Tesla dipole?", Roseanne queried.

"It is a big artificial magnet, capable of generating a huge five Tesla magnetic field", Varak replied, explaining, "If we place this device, in the Sun, Mars Lagrangian point one, about one million kilometres from Mars in the direction of the Sun, it will sit there in a stable orbit. When activated, it will create a five Tesla magnetic field."

"How does putting a five Tesla magnetic field at Mar's L1 protect Mars?", Roseanne asked.

"Ah Roseanne", Varak began, "The Solar Wind deforms the dipole's magnetic field, dragging it outward from the Sun to cover the whole of Mars. Mars will sit within the tail of the dipole's magnetic field and this will protect Mars from the solar wind and the cosmic rays."

Having caught on, it was now Forkbraid's time to chime in, "In addition Mars is a Planet, a gravitational mass and it will be rotating within the tail of the dipole's magnetic field."

"Exactly!", Varak pointed to Forkbraid, confirming his statement, "Mars rotates and this causes frame dragging events to occur in its gravity well. By creating this dipole, those frame dragging events will now occur within a magnetic field", then he summed up very simply, "We can create slipstreams from Mars, to anywhere in the solar system."

"By the Gods Varak, you are a genius", Forkbraid commended.

"Did I not say it. My Varak is very, very clever!", Nyaliep stated, beaming with pride.

"Nyaliep my love. It is not only me. Peter did a lot of work on this", a humble Varak replied.

Peter stepped in, "It isn't quite that simple. The magnetic field will be oriented to match Mar's rotational axis. However, Mars will sit in the magnetic field's tail. The magnetic field will not be centred on Mar's core. So there will be an offset to work with of about a million kilometres."

"We will figure it out", Varak replied confidently.

"Varak. What's the lower limit of mass? At what point does a planet, moon or asteroid for that matter, become too small?", Jim questioned.

"Yes Jim. That's a good question. Would this technique work with Venus, Mercury or even Ceres? We need to know the lower limits of mass", Forkbraid also questioned.

Varak and Peter both looked at each other, thinking about that question of lower limits.

Peter commented, "With Mercury it should in theory work, but Mercury's rotation is very slow. One day on Mercury is fifty nine Earth days. Mercury also has a weak magnetic field of its own. I believe it would work, but we would need to experiment in the Sun, Mercurian L1 point to know for sure."

"Yes Peter is right", Varak agreed, adding, "Even with Venus, it is close to the Earth mass, but its rotation is very slow. One day on Venus is Two hundred and forty three Earth days long. We would need to experiment in the Sun, Venusian L1 point as well. Unless we can speed up Venus's rotation, then it would definitely work."

"Okay, so after all the Horridian issues are dealt with, we'll have some experiments to perform", Forkbraid noted, "When will you guys have a handle on the lower planetary mass limits?"

Varak was thoughtful for a moment, "It would not make sense to use this technology for moons. Especially gas giant moons. They already have a parent planets with their own magnetic fields. It would be useful perhaps, for dwarf planets perhaps like Ceres or even those dwarf planets in the Kuiper Belt like Pluto and Eris. "

Jim noted, "If that's true, it could revolutionise transport right across the entire solar system."

"Yes", Varak agreed, "But will have to wait until after the war. These are very uncertain times."

"Something to note Varak", Peter began, "Even for the moons of gas giants, I can definitely still find a few a uses."

"Yes of course", Varak replied, "Protecting the moons and colonies from radiation fields. The dipoles could form a protective magnetic bubble around them. It would be very useful in Jupiter's case. Jupiter's radiation can be extreme. You wouldn't want to rely on it though. In case of failure."

"Definitely. A backup system or two would be necessary", Peter Agreed.

"So how soon can this device be implemented?", Selene asked.

"Perhaps in a few days. I've had the 303s working on it while we were in cis-lunar space", Varak informed her.

32. News Feeds

Later that day, with everyone relaxing at home in the psychic academy a new advert appeared across the news feeds.

Two women in uniform appeared on the screen. One woman, on the left wore the uniform of the Earth Defence Forces. The other woman, on the right wore the uniform of the L5 Colonial Fleet. Both appeared to have the rank of Lieutenant.

"Do you have qualifications?", the Earth Lieutenant asked in a sweet, almost melodious tone.

"or other highly sort after skills?", the L5 Lieutenant continued, her tone equally sweet and melodious.

Then both together, the pronounced, "If you do, then the Earth Defence Forces and the L5 Colonial Fleet need you!"

"We need Doctors", the Earth Lieutenant noted.

"We need Engineers", the L5 Lieutenant noted.

"We need Pilots", the Earth Lieutenant noted.

"We need Nurses", the L5 Lieutenant noted.

"and we need many, many more professionals", the pair remarked together.

"Extremely generous sign up bonuses are available. Sign up today", they both continued.

"You don't have qualifications?", the Earth Lieutenant questioned.

"or any useful skills?", the L5 Lieutenant questioned.

"That's no problem", they both replied to their own questions, "Let the Earth Defence Forces and the L5 Colonial Fleet, pay for your new training and qualifications."

"That's right. We'll give you on the job training and we will pick up the tab?", both Lieutenants continued in their sweet melodious tones.

"You will, at the end of your service and demobilisation, have solar system wide, fully recognised qualifications", they both continued.

"Very generous sign up bonuses are available. Sign up today", they continued.

"Let us take the fight to those horrible Horridians and give them their Just Rewards!", the two Lieutenants stated strongly in unison.

"That's right. Let's give those horrible Horridians the spanking they deserve!", the two Lieutenants both stated in unison.

"And remember", they both stated, before the Earth Lieutenant continued, "Service in the Earth Defence Forces guarantees Earth Citizenship and a house in the suburbs, in the city of your choice", before the L5 Lieutenant took over, "Service in the L5 Colonial Fleet guarantees L5 Citizenship and a furnished apartment in the colony of your choice."

They both continued in unison, "Join the Earth Defence Forces or the L5 Colonial Fleet. You choose which and we'll take it from there."

Then they both finished with, "Sign up today. Very generous sign up bonuses are available."

This was followed up with a male voice providing caveats, "All recruits must be over eighteen years of age. All qualified professional recruits must provide proof of qualifications and/or skills. All recruits wanting to learn a new profession and/or new skills, will be tested for the required aptitude necessary to attain those skills. While we endeavour to provide our recruits with a safe working environment and value all of our personnel, during a time of war your safety cannot always be guaranteed."

"Well then", Forkbraid remarked, "It's official. We are now at War!"

"Really Forkbraid?", Selene replied, "I would have thought the missile attack would have been a vary big indication."

"Ah yes Selene, but it's not really official until the recruitment adverts start appearing in the news feeds", Forkbraid replied, "Now it's official."

"Here's a question for you Forkbraid. Since you're such a smart arse", Selene replied, "Why aren't there two separate adverts? Hmm? One for the Earth Defence Forces and another separate advert for the Colonial Fleet?"

"A good question and I do prefer the term, anal intelligence", Forkbraid replied, speculating, "Perhaps they want to show solidarity? The Horridians will see these adverts. Having the Earth and L5 combined, both lined up against them, that could have some profound psychological effects."

"And there you go Forkbraid, you have an answer for everything", Selene replied.

The following day, Zyaliep was presented with Nyaliep's bride price. It was a hefty bag of golden credits. Forkbraid had help Varak out, just as he had with Jim. Nyaliep tucked the bride price away safely in her room. She was ecstatic, the wedding ceremony was scheduled for the next day and so was the feast. It wasn't so complicated as with the Girl's wedding as there was only one bride after all. Jim Murphy stepped in as Varak's best man and the wedding ceremony and reception proceeded without a hitch. It was yet another great and eventful day on Mars and good times were had by who were present.

The following day after the wedding, a video message arrived from Captain Carmichael aboard the Colonial Cruiser Spartan. Obviously an important message, Forkbraid, Selene, Jim, Marcus and Charlene gathered at the communications centre to watch it.

Captain Carmichael appeared on the screen, "By now you've probably seen the recruitment adverts on the news feeds. The Governments of the Earth and L5 have decided to work on this Horridian War issue together. You know, show a united front sort of thing. Truth be known, it turns out L5 had just a little bit of leverage."

The Captain Continued, "L5's population is somewhat smaller than the Earth's and recruiting would probably fall short of necessary requirements. The Earth on the other hand has the opposite problem, probably more recruits than they could possibly deal with. That's where you guys came into this. You gave General Stanton and myself, those fusion drive enhancements and refinements, but you only gave me the defence shield enhancements and the passive cloaking technology."

There was a slight pause before he continued, "Our President Banyon decided to use that extra technology like a carrot. You know, we share that extra technology with the Earth Defence Forces and they send us a good supply of recruits from the Earth. It worked a treat I must say. Combining the adverts into one was genius as well. Guaranteeing citizenship and providing free housing for the recruits at the end of the conflict was another very clever idea. Let's hope the politicians all live up to their promises."

"The bulk of both of our fleets are now in their staging areas. We are building and outfitting quite a few new ships, kind of hand over fist. We are kind of good at that at L5. Our older ships are all being upgraded and our modern ships are all being retrofitted with the technology you guys have provided us. Those damnable Horridians aren't going to know what hit them", the Captain informed them all.

"Your Governor Anderson of Chryce. He's created quite a stir for all of us. Demanding that both the Earth Gov and L5 Gov send six heavy cruisers each to Mars to help defend your Planet. It is palpable how ungrateful these damnable politicians are. You guys took out a third of those missile and a shit ton of those warheads, you gave us these incredible technology innovations and these muppets are are all upset, because Anderson wants a few cruises", Captain Carmichael informed them, adding, "Seriously, they are an embarrassment. I do apologise for their ludicrous behaviour."

"Well, I appreciate all that you've done, even if those political numbnuts don't. So I've gone into bat for you guys. You won't be receiving those twelve heavy cruisers, however you will receive three heavy cruisers and six destroyers. I'm also going to see if I can send you a few frigates as well. Possibly six if I can, we'll see. I know it's not what you guys wanted, but it will have to do for now", the Captain explained.

"We've got a problem with your medal ceremony video. My Lieutenant Adjutant Blixen misfiled that video really, really well. Unfortunately President Banyon remembered it and made some enquiries. I told him, I'd put my best men on the task of locating it and then I assigned a pair of incompetent knuckleheads to that task. You know, the kind of personnel that you assign to jobs where they can do absolutely no harm. Unfortunately it turned out that one of those knuckleheads was actually a malingering, miscreant. Turns out he was a very clever one as well. He not only found that video, I've been informed that he has sold it to one of the news services. I've put the man on charges and he will be dishonourably discharged. None the less, the damage is done and I sincerely apologise for that", the Captain informed them.

"Now here's something I'd like to know. How the bloody hell did you get to Mars so quickly?", Captain Carmichael queried, "One day you were here in cis-lunar space and as far as I can tell, the next day you're on Mars. Maybe it's best that I don't know. So don't tell me. Over and out."

The screen went blank.

"Wow!", Jim exclaimed, "We don't get those twelve heavy cruisers, but we get at least nine, maybe as many as fifteen other ships. That's more than I'd hoped for. Quite a fleet in fact."

"Yeah well, we've scratched his back more than a few times and now he's remembering that. Captain Carmichael is a good man", Forkbraid replied.

"What is it about this medal ceremony?", Selene asked.

"We're all in it. The crew of the Solstice that is", Forkbraid replied, adding, "The Horridians are going to know all of our names. I was hoping to avoid that. They already know way too much about our ship already. There's no telling what they'll do if they know the names of the crew as well."

Five days later towards the early evening, Roseanne came to Selene's apartment with a very concerned look on her face. Selene had been sitting comfortably on her couch reading a book.

"Okay Roseanne, what's on your mind?", Selene, who was Roseanne's mentor for both her majikal and her professional training.

"It's kind of personal and I'm not sure I should be discussing it with anyone", Roseanne replied.

"If it's affecting you the way it is, maybe you should. I mean, seriously Roseanne, I can easily sense your discomfort. There is no hiding it, at least not in a psychic academy", Selene explained.

"It's Zuawalo and Zeealas. They are my friends and I love them dearly, but they can be a bit strange. Maybe it's a cultural thing, maybe it's just me", Roseanne vented.

Selene closed her book and put it down on the coffee table, then indicated to Roseanne that she should take a seat, "Okay. Let's talk", she told her.

"You know how the women from their village choose their partners?", Roseanne began.

"Yes Roseanne, I know", Selene replied, noting, "They choose the man and in their culture the man is expected to go along with the woman's choice. It's their way."

"It's not as simple as that Selene. It's somewhat muddier", Roseanne commented.

"Muddier? You might need to elaborate on that just a tad", Selene responded,

"The woman does make her choice, but then she seduces the man and if she decides to keep him as her life partner, she allows herself to fall pregnant", Roseanne divulged, "Isn't that entrapment?"

"Oh! Yes, it could be construed that way", Selene replied thinking to herself, *"This could get just a little delicate"*, then continued, "You have to remember Roseanne. It's their particular culture and they all agree to this method of choosing their life partners. So we really shouldn't judge them."

Roseanne bit her lip and then remarked, "There's more."

"More?", Selene queried.

"Zuawalo and Zeealas both know I'm an orphan", Roseanne noted.

"Yes Roseanne, but here, please don't feel like you're an orphan", Selene reassured her, "Here, you are kind of like my own daughter."

Roseanne smiled, "That's is good to know and it is very reassuring, but that's not what I meant."

"Okay then, what did you mean?", Selene enquired.

"The Girls know I'm an orphan and they kind of want to adopt me", Roseanne explained.

"Oh okay, like another Sister? That actually sounds quite nice", Selene queried.

"Kind of", Roseanne replied, before dropping the bombshell, "The Girls have asked me to become their Sister Wife!"

"A what?", Selene questioned, not knowing what Roseanne meant.

"A Sister Wife", Roseanne repeated, before explaining, "In their culture a woman can chose a married man. It's up to the existing wives as to whether or not she gets her wish. They either except her or they do not. Then the husband goes along with their decision."

"Yes, yes Roseanne, I already know that", Selene replied, now more than a little concerned herself, "but I'm not sure what you mean?"

"It cuts both ways Selene", Roseanne informed her, "If a wife likes another woman, she can offer the woman her husband as a choice and if the woman agrees, she becomes a Sister Wife."

"Oh. Oh. I had no idea. That is kind of different", Selene responded.

"It's gets even crazier", Roseanne informed Selene.

"It does?", Selene responded, the concern was beginning to show on her face.

"Zuawalo and Zeealas have not only asked me to be their Sister Wife, they have said that we could all play together", Roseanne told her.

"Play together?", Selene questioned, not really sure that she wanted to know the answer.

"As in play with Jim, Zuawalo and Zeealas in their bed room", Roseanne replied, dropping another bombshell, "Selene, the Girls are bi-sexual!"

"Shit!", Selene exclaimed, "That was the last thing I expected you to say. Are you sure about that? They are Sisters after all."

"Absolutely", Roseanne replied, "I don't think it's taboo thing in their culture."

"I don't know Roseanne. I seem to remember, that when Zyaliep found out that they all shared the same bedroom. She said something like, *'one night, one wife. One night two wives is not a good thing'* or something similar", Selene remembered, then speculating, "Then again maybe she personally just doesn't approve of that kind of behaviour?"

"Selene I don't know what to tell them", Roseanne explained, adding, "I don't want to hurt their feelings or anything. That's the very last thing I want to do. This could even be my fault?"

"What do you mean Roseanne?", Selene asked.

"I remember hearing that the Girls could have been low level threes, if they'd been discovered at the right age", Roseanne commented.

"Yes. That is possible, but how does that have any bearing on this?", Selene questioned.

Roseanne bit her lower lip and admitted, "I've been training them."

"Oh, okay. Well they're far too old for that, so that won't work Roseanne", Selene replied.

"Well it kind of did", Roseanne confessed.

"Really! That is really unusual. In what way?", a curious Selene asked.

"I can be anywhere in the academy grounds, even as far away as the airfield and if the Girls think about me, I can pick up their thoughts", Roseanne explained, adding, "If I think back to them, they can pick up my thoughts as well."

"That is really unusual Roseanne. Can they do this with anyone else?", Selene queried.

"No. It seems to be only between us", Roseanne informed her, adding, "but it affects them as well. They have a bond, a connection that's become more than sisters, now they're more like twins."

"Oh. Okay. I think I understand", Selene replied, explaining, "You've triggered a low level, three way psychic bond. That may have increased their desire to be around you Roseanne."

"So it is all my fault?", Roseanne asked.

"No not necessarily. I wouldn't say it was anyone's fault. You three have simply grown very close to each other, through your mutual shared experiences", Selene informed her.

Roseanne become silent, in deep thought, so Selene took the conversion in a different direction.

"Roseanne. How do you feel about all this? About becoming a Sister Wife?", Selene asked.

"Well, it's not what I want. I mean, I love them both dearly, but I don't want to sleep with Jim and I'm certainly not interested in sleeping with the Girls either", Roseanne replied, adding with a small chuckle, "It is kind of flattering though isn't it? That they both think of me as, Sister Wife material."

"Then the answer is simple Roseanne. You need to explain to the Girls and you need to explain it to them delicately. Very delicately", Selene advised, "Our ways, are not their ways."

Roseanne smiled and reached over to give Selene a big hug, "Thank you Selene."

"No problem Roseanne, I'm always happy to help. So, you're all good now?", Selene responded.

"I think so. I'll tell them, that I love them dearly as Sisters, but not as Sister Wives. That's not our way", Roseanne replied, adding, "If I get cold feet, I'll come back and ask for more advise."

At that point Forkbraid stepped into Selene's apartment.

"Off you go now Roseanne", Selene instructed, adding, "And let me know how things turn out."

Roseanne then left the apartment.

"How much of that did you pick up on?", Selene asked Forkbraid.

"Way, way too much Selene. That was just too weird. I stayed out there in the hallway as long as I thought necessary", Forkbraid replied.

"Okay then, we don't need to discuss it any further", Selene replied noting, "It is a very delicate matter for the Girls to sort out. Kind of bizarre as well. I think it's best we don't interfere in it."

"Agreed", Forkbraid replied, commenting, "I can't imaging what Jim thinks of all this."

"I'd bet he doesn't even know", Selene suggested, "Remember, in their society the men are the very last know. They only find out after all the decisions are finalised."

"So how'd you go with that magnetic dipole?", Selene asked.

"It's up in L1 as we speak. Took us most the day", Forkbraid informed her.

"That thing was huge. How'd you get it up there?", Selene asked.

"Varak thought of everything. He had it moved out onto the tarmac and we flew over it in the Solstice, lowered down onto it and simply picked it up", Forkbraid explained, elaborating further, "Varak had the foresight to design it so that the Solstice's landing geared docked into the dipole."

"And the Solstice had no trouble taking off with that stuck underneath it?", Selene asked.

"The Solstice didn't seem to be affected. We took off, not a shudder, not a shake", Forkbraid informed her, adding, "The biggest problem we had, was getting the dipole started. It took us six attempts. You'll laugh when I tell you what was wrong with it."

"So what was it?", Selene curiously asked.

"There was a spanner in the works!", Forkbraid chuckled.

Selene laughed, "You're joking!", then "You are joking, aren't you?"

"Nope. Varak left a spanner in the last section he'd worked on. He was so embarrassed", Forkbraid replied.

"I bet he was", Selene replied.

"I figure it's all the stress he's been under lately. You know, with all the work he's been doing, then finding out Nyaliep is pregnant and getting married. It all adds up", Forkbraid speculated.

"Well that would do it", Selene agreed.

"So you got the dipole running?", Selene enquired.

"Sure did. Didn't you guys notice. Mars now has a protective magnetic field. We're currently sitting in the middle of its tail", Forkbraid informed her.

"Honestly. I can't say that I even noticed. I doubt anyone did", Selene admitted.

"Perhaps that's to be expected. Varak and Peter do know their stuff", Forkbraid remarked.

Later that same evening a notification popped up on Selene's video wall. Selene had told the apartment's computer to monitor the news feed for any medal ceremonies involving the Solstice or anything to do with Mars. The computer was to record the news feed and notify the occupants. Now the notification had popped up.

Selene turned on the video wall and watched the medal award ceremony. The nine members of the crew of the Solstice all stood lined up in their nice, new uniforms. Selene noted that Charlene and Roseanne had done a wonderful job designing the uniforms and the tailoring to match each of the crew was perfect.

One by one, Captain Carmichael handed the crew members three medals each. Selene noted that Leroy McGuvan wasn't included, but remembered Forkbraid had mentioned that to her earlier and she understood why. The medal award ceremony was fairly short, but it was just the sort of fluff piece that L5's President Banyon would like. Having watched the recording, Selene went to find Forkbraid, thinking he would like to see it as well

Selene made her way to her meditation room where Forkbraid often spent hours in deep samadhi, the deepest state of meditation.

"Forkbraid, I've got a recording of the medal awarding ceremony if you'd like to see it", Selene called out as she approached the room.

That there was no reply was not unusual, in deep meditation, he often did not respond. Upon entering the meditation room however, Selene found the Forkbraid was not present.

Selene thought to herself, *"Where the hell has he disappeared to? He's always here at this time of the evening."*

Selene then left the meditation room to look around the rest of her apartment and could not find him anywhere she thought, *"Maybe he left the apartment and I didn't notice?"*

As Selene walked past her meditation room once more, Forkbraid walked out of the door.

"What? Where have you been?", Selene asked him.

"I've been meditating. Why?", Forkbraid replied.

"I was just in there", Selene replied, pointing to the meditation room, "And didn't see you at all."

"Oh. I was in there. Only I was astral projecting and then I jaunted", Forkbraid informed her.

"Where did you jaunt to?", Selene enquired.

"You won't believe it Selene", Forkbraid responded, explaining, "I jaunted to Tafazah's Tower."

"Tafazah's Tower?", Selene queried, further asking, "The Tafazah's Tower, in the hills east of Melbourne back on the Earth?"

"The very same one. I blinked into its Ariel Chamber. I'm lucky it was after hours, so the museum was closed, otherwise I might have caused quite a stir", Forkbraid informed her.

"You jaunted from here on Mars to the Earth and back again?", Selene asked for clarification, the information hadn't quite sunk in.

"Yes Selene. I jaunted to the Earth and back again. I've only just now, blinked back in", Forkbraid confirmed.

"That's incredible Forkbraid. You've been wanting to master that kind of skill for months", Selene replied, then remembered why she was looking for him, "I have a copy of the medal award ceremony on the video wall. Did you want to see it?"

"Absolutely. I'll grab a bottle of wine and a couple of glasses", Forkbraid replied, adding, "We can watch the news feeds afterwards to see if anything else is happening."

Then they both sat down to watch the medal award ceremony, with glasses of Cormac's Martian sweet cherry red wine in hand.

33. Elysium

Captain Matthew Murphy was presenting some of his handy work to the Horridian Princes, a few of their Generals and his Master, the Prophet.

"As you can see from this video, we now have the identities of every crew member of the Martian spaceship, the Solstice", Matthew commented after showing everyone the medal ceremony.

Matthew then continued, "I've taken one of the earlier frames, showing them lined up, before they were awarded their medals and I've created this."

An image appeared on the screen, it showed the crew of the Solstice, all nicely lined up in their nice new uniforms. Above the crew was a caption, big and bold, WANTED FOR PIRACY. Beneath the crew was another caption, almost as big and bold, THE CREW OF THE MARTIAN PIRATE SHIP SOLSTICE and beneath that was a set of co-ordinate in Martian latitude and longitude.

"So far so good Captain, what else have you got", General Snide queried.

Matthew smiled and pressed a few keystrokes, "Gentlemen. Please enjoy the show."

A square frame appeared around Nyaliep's picture and then the frame expanded to fill the screen. A caption above Nyaliep, big and bold, read out WANTED FOR PIRACY. Below her picture was another caption, again big and bold, ENGINEERING ASSISTANT NYALIEP POD and below her name, REWARD ONE MILLION JOVIAN CREDITS. Nyaliep's reward poster hung on the screen for almost ten seconds before shrinking back to the main image.

Another square frame appeared, this time around Zeealas's picture and then the frame expanded to fill the screen. A caption above Zeealas, big and bold, read out WANTED FOR PIRACY. Below her picture was another caption, again big and bold, SECURITY OFFICER ZEEALAS POD and below her name, REWARD ONE MILLION JOVIAN CREDITS. Zeealas's reward poster hung on the screen for almost ten seconds before shrinking back to the main image.

The pattern continued. Now Zuawalo's picture was selected and then the frame expanded to fill the screen. The same WANTED FOR PIRACY caption appeared above Zuawalo. Below her picture was the caption, SECURITY OFFICER ZUAWALO POD and below her name, REWARD ONE MILLION JOVIAN CREDITS. Zuawalo's reward poster hung on the screen for almost ten seconds before shrinking back to the main image.

Charlene's face expanded next, she too was WANTED FOR PIRACY and under her picture, her details, COMMUNICATIONS OFFICER CHARLENE FEWKES and beneath that, REWARD ONE MILLION JOVIAN CREDITS.

The procession continued with Marcus. He too was WANTED FOR PIRACY. Under his picture appeared his details, HELM AND NAVIGATION OFFICER MARCUS GREYHELM and beneath that, REWARD ONE MILLION JOVIAN CREDITS.

Peter Swann was next. As with the others, WANTED FOR PIRACY. Under his picture, SCIENCE OFFICER PETER SWANN and again beneath that, REWARD ONE MILLION JOVIAN CREDITS.

Not to be left out of the list, Peter's colleague Varak follow next. Yet again WANTED FOR PIRACY. Beneath his picture, ENGINEERING OFFICER VARAKHAN UTANA and beneath that, REWARD ONE MILLION JOVIAN CREDITS. The Solstice's were valuable commodities.

When Jim Murphy popped up on the screen, Matthew paused. He too was a WANTED FOR PIRACY and his details also appeared, FIRST OFFICER, TACTICAL AND CHIEF SECURITY OFFICER JAMES MURPHY. However under his details was, REWARD TWO MILLION JOVIAN CREDITS.

Matthew turned to High Prince Heinrich, "Your Majesty. I know that we decided earlier to set the crew rewards at one million credits each. With cousin James however, he's kind of special .We can get a lot of information out of him. The secrets his brain holds will be very, very useful to us. So I took the liberty of doubling his reward."

The High Prince looked at the reward poster for James Murphy and replied, "Valuable information you say? Captain Murphy. Make it five million credits."

"Your will be done Your Majesty", Matthew replied as he pressed a few key strokes.

The reward for James Murphy changed and now read, REWARD FIVE MILLION JOVIAN CREDITS. The High Prince nodded in agreement.

After Jim's reward poster faded from the screen, Forkbraid's images appeared. Just like the others, he too was WANTED FOR PIRACY. His details appeared, CAPTAIN FOLCROM FORKBRAID, CAPTAIN OF

THE MARTIAN PIRATE SHIP SOLSTICE and beneath, REWARD TEN MILLION JOVIAN CREDITS. Slowly his reward poster faded away and the main collective poster reappeared.

The room erupted with applause and woots.

Matthew slowly raised his right hand to quieten the room stating, "But there's more gentlemen."

Matthew pressed a few more keystrokes and another images expanded onto the screen. It was Leroy McGuvan. He was not a wanted pirate. Above his picture appeared the caption, WANTED FOR HIGH TREASON AGAINST THE JOVIAN REALM. Directly below his picture was the caption, TRAITOR LEROY MCGUVAN and beneath that, REWARD TEN MILLION JOVIAN CREDITS.

When Leroy McGuvan's reward poster faded from the screen, the collective crew reward poster reappeared side by side with Leroy McGuvan's reward poster on its right. The overall caption, WANTED FOR THE UNPROVOKED AND UNJUSTIFIABLE MASS HOMICIDE OF ONE HUNDRED AND TWENTY THOUSAND TROJAN TROOPS, was bold as brass and highlighted underneath the combined wanted poster.

The room erupted with applause and woots one again.

This time High Prince Heinrich raised his right hand to quieten the room, "Captain Murphy. I don't remember discussing that caption with you", he commented.

"Yes Your Majesty I added it in ", Matthew admitted, explaining to the High Prince, "We control the narrative Your Majesty. The Jovian and Trojan public only see what we allow them to see."

"So you want to put a spin on this?", the High Prince asked.

"Yes Your Majesty. The public have not been told about the medal award ceremony. They haven't been told that the Trojan Army is on its way home. We can spin this any which way we like", Matthew informed the High Prince.

"Okay then Captain, how do we spin it?", High Prince Heinrich enquired.

"Your Majesty", Matthew began, "We inform our people the following. We tell them that when we learnt that the combined Earth fleet and L5 fleet were waiting in ambush, that your being so concerned for the Trojan's safety, you immediately ordered them straight home. After the Trojan fleet accepted the order, we found out it had been ambushed and destroyed by Martian Pirates. It is important we inform the public, that our last communication with the fleet was at the time of the fleets destruction. That should generate enough hate amongst the Trojan and Belter colonies for our purposes. Being that they are both asteroidal based colonies, they do share a close affinity for each other after all."

"Okay Captain. What happens when the Trojan fleet actually returns home? That will become a problem, won't it?", the High Prince asked.

"Well your Majesty. It took many months for the Trojan fleet to reach the Earth. It will take just as many months for them to return home", Matthew explained, adding, "During those many months, the bounty hunters will be highly motivated. When the fleet finally does comes home, we'll just spin things a slightly different way."

"How so Captain?", the High Prince asked.

"You Majesty. We know the Earth Defence Fleet destroyed twenty five of our Trojan ships that actually followed your orders", Matthew replied, explaining, "We release to the public, that after we lost communications with the Trojan fleet, we were sure certain that it had been destroyed. Then upon learning that the fleet survived. We found out that those twenty five ships had been destroyed in a very brave rear guard action, that saved the main body of the Trojan fleet. We then pin the destruction of those twenty five ships on the Martian Pirates. That's twenty five hundred Trojans. The crew of the Solstice is going to cop it in the neck either way."

"You're brilliant Captain", the High Prince commended, "That ship and her crew will have every bounty hunter from here to Mars hunting for them."

"Yes Your Majesty", Matthew agreed, adding, "It will give them a motivation well beyond any reward money. Revenge can be highly motivating."

"Captain. How soon can you have that uploaded to the news feed?", the High Prince asked.

"One click of a button Your Majesty and up it goes", Matthew replied, adding, "Then it will less than a day to spread to every news feed across the solar system, starting with the closest"

"Then click that button Captain", the High Prince commanded, "Let's give that crew hell!"

Matthew click the send button and the wanted reward video was sent into the news services.

It was dark now in the Elysium plateau where the New Flinders Psychic Academy was located. Selene almost choked on her red cherry wine when she saw the latest item come up on the news feeds. Up came a wanted reward video from the Jovian Realm. It looked like a parody of the medal awards ceremony, that they had watched only a few hours earlier.

"Forkbraid", Selene called out, "You'll want to see this. It's breaking news and it appears to be on every feed", adding, "You aren't going to like it."

Forkbraid entered the room once more and watched the Jovian wanted reward video. He was stunned into silence as he watched and remained silent after it finished, only to see it repeat again.

"Forkbraid. You did save those Trojans didn't you?", Selene asked him.

"Absolutely. We saved a good ninety eight percent of their fleet", Forkbraid informed her, adding, "The only ships we couldn't save, were the ones that made a suicide run against the Earth Defence Force fleet and we were not even involved in that action at all."

Forkbraid recorded the entire Jovian wanted reward video, then replayed it back so he could study it further. After watching it several times, he paused it on the very first frame.

"It's bad enough to be called Pirates and that bullshit about mass homicide is absolutely atrocious", Forkbraid stated, "but what gets my goat is that."

Selene looked at the screen, "That they've named your ship, as being the Martian Pirate Ship Solstice?"

"Well yes there is that. They've named our ship, named our crew and even told the entire solar system, that it's from Mars, but have a look underneath, at the bottom", Forkbraid informed Selene.

"Those number Forkbraid?", Selene queried.

"Yes Selene, those numbers", Forkbraid replied, informing her, "Those are the latitude and longitude of your New Flinders Psychic Academy."

"Oh. That's not good", Selene's response was a complete understatement.

"No Selene. That is not good! Every bounty hunter in the solar system will see this video and they'll know our precise location. Those damnable Horridian bastards have not only endangered the people I love, they've endangered everyone here at this academy", Forkbraid noted, his face becoming more and more enraged by the second.

Forkbraid's visage altered ever so slightly, becoming somewhat darker and more viperous.

Then he thought to himself caustically, *"When I get my hands on High Prince Heinrich von Horridian and his Brothers, I will gut them like the disgusting, evil sligs that they are! I will rip out their intestines and flay them while they are still alive. Then I will adorn the Solstice's bulkheads with their bloodied hides!"*

The intensity of Forkbraid's enraged thoughts caught Selene completely by surprise.

Shocked, Selene grabbed Forkbraid by the wrist, stared into his eyes and screamed into his mind, "Forkbraid! No!"

Forkbraid snapped out of his enragement, the dark and viperous look on his face quickly fading away, he reached out to Selene and took her into his arms, "I'm sorry Selene. I promise you. I won't do that!"

Selene replied, "Forkbraid. What are we going to do?"

Selene and Forkbraid held each tightly for long moments, before Forkbraid gently broke away.

Forkbraid sent a copy of the Jovian wanted video recording to Jim and flagged it as urgent.

Forkbraid didn't have to wait long, Jim Murphy appeared on the screen in a dressing robe.

"FB? What the fuck was that?", Jim asked.

"That Jim is some very disturbing shite being distributed across the solar system by the Horridian Dynasty", Forkbraid replied.

"Yeah, but Piracy, mass homicide, high treason!", Jim exclaimed, "It's all a bit over the top don't you think?"

"Of course it is Jim. Obviously we've really pissed them off", Forkbraid agreed.

Selene stepped in, "Jim. What are we going to do?"

Jim sat in thought for a few moments, then replied, "Selene, FB, we work the problem."

Jim started thinking aloud, "We are definitely going to have bounty hunters heading our way. That video was designed to rile them up. Mainly the Trojans and the Belters. That's actually a good thing. They're far enough out, that it will take them a lot of time to get here. And we'll likely see them coming. We'll need to watch out for any unusual Mars bound ship transits."

Jim continued his train of thought, "Huh, that video didn't specify dead of alive. That means they want us alive! They'll need us for information. Probably our ships technology as well. They may even want to parade us around for propaganda purposes."

"Okay, so we have time to prepare", Selene replied.

"Yes Selene. Tomorrow I'll contact Governor Anderson and discuss this him. He will have seen that video himself by then. Hell, most of Mars will have", Jim replied, adding, "I'll get Governor Anderson to keep and eye out for bounty hunters. I'll get him to coordinate the other Governors to do the same. The Governors can also refute these baseless allegations as well. I can also guarantee that President Banyon at L5 will."

"Okay that's a start Jim", Forkbraid responded.

"Yeah FB. I'll contact Lieutenant Roberts as well and get him to surveil the space lanes and space in general. If bounty hunters are heading our way, I want to see them coming", Jim informed them.

"Okay Jim. So we'll have the main colonies covered and the approaches", Forkbraid replied, "Make sure you step up our security. Not just here, but down in the Elysium colony as well."

"I'll take care of that personally. It is my job after all", Jim assured them both, "The immediate problem will be any bounty hunters that are already here. We'll need to keep an eye out for them."

Selene chimed in, "Maybe it's time we started setting up our Wyvern covens?"

"Yes. Yes Selene", Forkbraid agreed, "If we can get enough Wyvern covens setup, any bounty hunters on Mars will have nowhere to hide."

"Good then, I'll take the Wyvern covens off the back burner and we'll start working on a new setup plan", Selene agreed.

"I'll need to go through your personnel records with you Selene", Forkbraid informed her, "We will need to select suitable candidates for the Wyvern covens."

"Let's hope we can find enough psychics to fill those roles", Selene commented.

"I recommend starting off with six Wyverns, each with four members", Forkbraid suggested, adding, "We can build them up further as time permits."

"Then Forkbraid, you'll be the first Serpent Council member and its head", Selene decided, adding with a wry smile, "Oh Viperous one."

"That's it then, We'll all work the problem", Chief Security Officer Murphy concluded.

War had come!
The peace has been shattered!
Millions are already dead!
What now the cost of War!